Omnibus of New T

Ramsey Campbell was bo...
since (now with his wife Je...
along in the Inland Reven...
rather more in Liverpool l...
he took the risk of becomi...
support. Other people who...
August Derleth, his Englis...
Bob Lowndes, Carol Smith ... .es. Lovecraft, M. R. James,
Leiber, Bloch, Aickman, Nabokov, Graham Greene, Alain Resnais,
Hitchcock, all sorts of horror films he sneaked into the Essoldo
London Road to see at the age of fifteen, and above all *The Princess
and the Goblin*. His novels include *The Doll who ate his Mother* (of
which Bernice Williams Foley wrote: 'Thank goodness, this distasteful
manhunt is fiction'), *The Face must Die*, *The Parasite*, *The Nameless*,
Incarnate and *Obsession*. His short stories are collected in *Demons by
Daylight*, *The Height of the Scream*, *Dark Companions* and *Cold Print*,
and he has edited *Superhorror* and *New Tales of Cthulhu Mythos*. One
of these days he means to write a history of horror fiction. He reviews
films and horror fiction (at least, for those few publishers who send
out review copies) for BBC Radio Merseyside, and is president of the
British Fantasy Society. He has been given the World Fantasy Award
twice for best short story, and also holds two British Fantasy Awards,
for best short story and for best novel.

MAGGIE
&
FRANK

Omnibus of New Terrors

edited by Ramsey Campbell

Pan Original
Pan Books London and Sydney

First published 1980 in two volumes as
New Terrors one and *New Terrors two* by
Pan Books Ltd
This edition published 1985 by Pan Books Ltd,
Cavaye Place, London SW10 9PG
9 8 7 6 5 4 3 2
This collection © Ramsey Campbell, 1980, 1985
Individual copyright notices are given on pages 9 and 10
ISBN 0 330 28854 7
Printed and bound in Great Britain by
Cox & Wyman Ltd, Reading

for Cherry and Henry
with memories of grassy Wales

for Sue and Neil
with Scotch and Black Russians

Contents

Acknowledgements

Robert Aickman for *The Stains* © Robert Aickman 1980;
Steve Rasnic Tem for *City Fishing* © Steve Rasnic Tem 1980;
Lisa Tuttle for *Sun City* © Lisa Tuttle 1980; Manly Wade
Wellman for *Yare* © Manly Wade Wellman 1980; Tanith Lee
for *A Room with a Vie* © Tanith Lee 1980; Daphne Castell
and her agent Virginia Kidd for *Diminishing Landscape with
Indistinct Figures* © Daphne Castell 1980; Marc Laidlaw for
Tissue © Marc Laidlaw 1980; Peter Valentine Timlett and his
agent Carole Blake for *Without Rhyme or Reason* © Peter
Valentine Timlett 1980; Bob Shaw and his agent Leslie Flood
for *Love Me Tender* © Bob Shaw 1980; Gene Wolfe and his
agent Virginia Kidd for *Kevin Malone* © Gene Wolfe 1980;
Joan Aiken for *Time To Laugh* © Joan Aiken Enterprises Ltd
1980; Kit Reed and her agent A. P. Watt Ltd for *Chicken
Soup* © Kit Reed 1980; James Wade for *The Pursuer* ©
James Wade 1980; Graham Masterton for *Bridal Suite* ©
Graham Masterton 1980; Dennis Etchison and Mark Johnson
for *The Spot* © Dennis Etchison and Mark Johnson 1980;
Cherry Wilder and her agent Virginia Kidd for *The
Gingerbread House* © Cherry Wilder 1980; Russell Kirk and
his agent Kirby McCauley for *Watchers at the Strait Gate* ©
Russell Kirk 1980; Karl Edward Wagner for *·220 Swift* © Karl
Edward Wagner 1980; Errol Undercliffe and Montgomery
Comfort for *The Fit* © Ramsey Campbell 1980; Christopher
Priest and his agent A. P. Watt Ltd for *The Miraculous Cairn*
© Christopher Priest 1980; John Brunner and his agent Leslie
Flood for *The Man Whose Eyes Beheld the Glory* © John
Brunner 1980; Robert Bloch for *The Rubber Room* © Robert
Bloch 1980; Giles Gordon and his agent Elaine Greene Ltd
for *Drama in Five Acts* © Giles Gordon 1980; Jack Sullivan
for *The Initiation* © Jack Sullivan 1980; John Burke and his
agent David Higham Associates for *Lucille Would Have
Known* © John Burke 1980; Rosalind Ashe and her agent
Carol Smith for *Teething Troubles* © Rosalind Ashe 1980;

Introduction

Nick Webb, then the fiction editor of Pan Books, proposed this book to me at the end of the 1978 British Fantasy Convention. Birmingham at Sunday lunchtime is a desert of concrete and dead restaurants; where better to discuss a book of contemporary terrors? Back at the hotel the conventioneers were being instructed in Tolkien, but we were champing hamburgers and imagining a book that would display today's masters of terror, both famous and potentially famous. Here, not without a struggle (Karl Wagner and Russell Kirk almost succumbed to the British postal troubles of mid-1979), is the result.

Why do people still read tales of terror? This is probably the hardest question in the field. 'Still' usually means either that the psychologists have exorcized our terrors or that 'reality' (nuclear and post-nuclear warfare, terrorism, and so on) is so disturbing that it makes the tale of terror redundant. I believe this book is an answer in itself, but my own response would be: some of the stories (Aickman's visions, Kirk's moral allegories) deal with states of being which are necessarily inexplicable, while the more openly horrific stories deal with fears and obsessions (which have certainly not been cleared away by science – indeed, science has created some of them) in a form sufficiently metaphorical to make them bearable to confront. Of course they include our own fascination with horror. Writers in this field expose the dark side of the imagination and at the same time keep the imagination alive. I believe this has never been so important as now.

If you read the tales in order you will soon discover that there are no taboos left in this field. From the early sixties the boundaries of what one could say in print widened spectacularly; perhaps they are still widening. But the tale of terror, even more than science fiction, clung to its taboos as long as it could. There may be several reasons for this: fans of the genre are conservative in their tastes and like to be sure they won't be too disturbed (at the lowest level, readers – I wouldn't call them fans – like their sadism so long as they aren't forced to confront its nature); the tale of terror has tended to deal with taboo subjects metaphorically (for example, all vampire stories, incest and inbreeding in Lovecraft and Poe's 'House of Usher', venereal disease in 'The White Powder', child sexuality in *The Exorcist*, which implies that it must be the work of the devil); the tale of terror deals obsessively with death, the greatest and perhaps the last of all taboos, and may have had no room to take on others. Still, now the taboos are down, and far from falling to bits, the genre is expanding. The terrors are clearer, but they are hardly explained away. On the whole the tale of terror probes deeper than it used to.

And now the book must speak for itself. On behalf of the stories I ask only that you read each one without interruption. Writing fiction is, among other things, about how it feels to be alone in a room with a pen and paper or with a typewriter; reading it, especially reading this kind of fiction, ought to be about how it feels to be alone with the story. Here are thirty-eight writers to lead you into the dark of their imagination and yours.

Ramsey Campbell
Liverpool, England
January 1985

Robert Aickman

The stains

With the death of Robert Aickman in 1981, the ghost story lost one of its greatest talents. I believe there is no author in the field more worth rereading. In his essay in Gahan Wilson's anthology The First World Fantasy Awards *(which also contains the tale that gained him the award, 'Pages from a Young Girl's Journal'), he writes: 'I do not regard my work as fantasy at all, except, perhaps, for commercial purposes. I try to depict the world as I see it; sometimes artistically exaggerating no doubt (*artistically *is here a descriptive not a qualitative term), and occasionally exaggerating for purposes of parable, as in my story 'Growing Boys'. I believe in what the Germans term Ehrfurcht: reverence for things one cannot understand.' (The essay is well worth reading entire.)*

His books include The Late Breakfasters *(now back in print),* Dark Entries, Powers of Darkness, Sub Rosa, Cold Hand in Mine, Tales of Love and Death, Intrusions *and* Night Voices. *He edited the first eight volumes of the* Fontana Book of Great Ghost Stories, *with splendid introductions. There is a great deal more to him for which I have no room here, but some of it can be found in the first volume of his autobiography, which was published as* The Attempted Rescue. *It is about time someone published the second.*

Robert Aickman's combination of the supernatural (for want of a better term) and the erotic is unique, and a perfect start for this book.

After Elizabeth ultimately died, it was inevitable that many people should come forward with counsel, and doubtless equally inevitable that the counsel be so totally diverse.

There were two broad and opposed schools.

The first considered that Stephen should 'treasure the memory' (though it was not always put like that) for an indefinite period, which, it was implied, might conveniently last him out to the end of his own life. These people attached great importance to Stephen 'not rushing anything'. The second school urged that Stephen marry again as soon as he possibly could. They said that, above all, he must not just fall into apathy and let his life slide. They said he was a man made for marriage and all it meant.

Of course, both parties were absolutely right in every way. Stephen could see that perfectly well.

It made little difference. Planning, he considered, would be absurd in any case. Until further notice, the matter would have to be left to fate. The trouble was, of course, that fate's possible options were narrowing and dissolving almost weekly, as they had already been doing throughout Elizabeth's lengthy illness. For example (the obvious and most pressing example): how many women would want to marry Stephen now? A number, perhaps; but not a number that he would want to marry. Not after Elizabeth. That in particular.

They told him he should take a holiday, and he took one. They told him he should see his doctor, and he saw him. The man who had looked after Elizabeth had wanted to emigrate, had generously held back while Elizabeth had remained alive, and had then shot off at once. The new man was half-Sudanese, and Stephen found him difficult to communicate with, at least upon a first encounter, at least on immediate topics.

In the end, Stephen applied for and obtained a spell of compassionate leave, and went, as he usually did, to stay with his elder brother, Harewood, in the north. Harewood was in orders: the Reverend Harewood Hooper BD, MA. Their father and grandfather had been in orders too, and had been incumbents of that same small church in that same small parish for thirty-nine years and forty-two years respectively. So far, Harewood had served for only twenty-three years. The patron of the living, a private individual, conscientious and very long lived, was relieved to be able to rely upon a succession of such dedicated men. Unfortunately, Harewood's own son, his one child, had dropped out, and was now believed to have disappeared into Nepal. Harewood himself cared more for rock growths than for controversies about South Africa or for other such fashionable church preoccupations. He had published

2

two important books on lichens. People often came to see him on the subject. He was modestly famous.

He fostered lichens on the flagstones leading up to the rectory front door; on the splendidly living stone walls, here grey stone, there yellow; even in the seldom used larders and pantries; assuredly on the roof, which, happily, was of stone slabs also.

As always when he visited his brother, Stephen found that he was spending much of his time out of doors; mainly, being the man he was, in long, solitary walks across the heathered uplands. This had nothing to do with Harewood's speciality. Harewood suffered badly from bronchitis and catarrh, and nowadays went out as little as possible. The domestic lichens, once introduced, required little attention – only observation.

Rather it was on account of Harewood's wife, Harriet, that Stephen roamed; a lady in whose company Stephen had never been at ease. She had always seemed to him a restless woman; jumpy and puzzling; the very reverse of all that had seemed best about Elizabeth. A doubtful asset, Stephen would have thought, in a diminishing rural parish; but Stephen himself, in a quiet and unobtruding way, had long been something of a sceptic. Be that as it might, he always found that Harriet seemed to be baiting and fussing him, not least when her husband was present; even, unforgivably, when Elizabeth, down in London, had been battling through her last dreadful years. On every visit, therefore, Stephen wandered about for long hours in the open, even when ice was in the air and snow on the tenuous tracks.

But Stephen did not see it as a particular hardship. Elizabeth, who might have done – though, for his sake, she could have been depended upon to conceal the fact – had seldom come on these visits at any time. She had never been a country girl, though fond of the sea. Stephen positively liked wandering unaccompanied on the moors, though he had little detailed knowledge of their flora and fauna, or even of their archaeology, largely industrial and fragmentary. By now he was familiar with most of the moorland routes from the rectory and the village; and, as commonly happens, there was one that he preferred to all the others, and nowadays found himself taking almost without having to make a decision. Sometimes even, asleep in his London flat that until just now had been *their* London flat, he found himself actually dreaming of that

3

particular soaring trail, though he would have found it difficult to define what properties of beauty or poetry or convenience it had of which the other tracks had less. According to the map, it led to a spot named Burton's Clough.

There was a vague valley or extended hollow more or less in the place which the map indicated, but to Stephen it seemed every time too indefinite to be marked out for record. Every time he wondered whether this was indeed the place; whether there was not some more decisive declivity that he had never discovered. Or possibly the name derived from some event in local history. It was the upwards walk to the place that appealed to Stephen, and, to an only slightly lesser extent, the first part of the slow descent homewards, supposing that the rectory could in any sense be called home: never the easily attainable but inconclusive supposed goal, the Clough. Of course there was always R. L. Stevenson's travelling hopefully to be inwardly quoted; and on most occasions hitherto Stephen had inwardly quoted it.

Never had there been any human being at, near, or visible from the terrain around Burton's Clough, let alone in the presumptive clough itself. There was no apparent reason why there should be. Stephen seldom met anyone at all on the moors. Only organizations go any distance afoot nowadays, and this was not an approved didactic district. All the work of agriculture is for a period being done by machines. Most of the cottages are peopled by transients. Everyone is supposed to have a car.

But that morning, Stephen's first in the field since his bereavement six weeks before, there *was* someone, and down at the bottom of the shallow clough itself. The person was dressed so as to be almost lost in the hues of autumn, plainly neither tripper nor trifler. The person was engaged in some task.

Stephen was in no state for company, but that very condition, and a certain particular reluctance that morning to return to the rectory before he had to, led him to advance further, not descending into the clough but skirting along the ridge to the west of it, where, indeed, his track continued.

If he had been in the Alps, his shadow might have fallen in the early autumn sun across the figure below, but in the circumstances that idea would have been fanciful, because, at the moment, the sun was no more than a misty bag of gleams in a confused sky. None the less, as Stephen's figure passed, comparatively high above, the figure below glanced up at him.

4

Stephen could see that it was the figure of a girl. She was wearing a fawn shirt and pale green trousers, but the nature of her activity remained uncertain.

Stephen glanced away, then glanced back.

She seemed still to be looking up at him, and suddenly he waved to her, though it was not altogether the kind of thing he normally did. She waved back at him. Stephen even fancied she smiled at him. It seemed quite likely. She resumed her task.

He waited for an instant, but she looked up no more. He continued on his way more slowly, and feeling more alive, even if only for moments. For those moments, it had been as if he still belonged to the human race, to the mass of mankind.

Only once or twice previously had he continued beyond the top of Burton's Clough, and never for any great distance. On the map (it had been his father's map), the track wavered on across a vast area of nothing very much, merely contour lines and occasional habitations with odd, possibly evocative, names: habitations which, as Stephen knew from experience, regularly proved, when approached, to be littered ruins or not to be detectable at all. He would not necessarily have been averse from the twelve or fourteen miles solitary walk involved, at least while Elizabeth had been secure and alive, and at home in London; but conditions at the rectory had never permitted so long an absence. Harriet often made clear that she expected her guests to be present punctually at all meals and punctually at such other particular turning points of a particular day as the day itself might define.

On the present occasion, and at the slow pace into which he had subsided, Stephen knew that he should turn back within the next ten to fifteen minutes; but he half-understood that what he was really doing was calculating the best time for a second possible communication with the girl he had seen in the clough. If he reappeared too soon, he might be thought, at such a spot, to be pestering, even menacing; if too late, the girl might be gone. In any case, there was an obvious limit to the time he could give to such approach as might be possible.

As the whole matter crystallized within him, he turned on the instant. There was a stone beside the track at the point where he did it; perhaps aforetime a milepost, at the least a waymark. Its location seemed to justify his action. He noticed that it too was patched with lichen. When staying with Harewood, he always noticed; and more and more at other times too.

5

One might almost have thought that the girl had been waiting for him. She was standing at much the same spot, and looking upwards abstractedly. Stephen saw that beside her on the ground was a grey receptacle. He had not noticed it before, because its vague colour sank into the landscape, as did the girl herself, costumed as she was. The receptacle seemed to be half-filled with grey contents of some kind.

As soon as he came into her line of sight, and sometime before he stood immediately above her, the girl spoke.

'Are you lost? Are you looking for someone?'

She must have had a remarkably clear voice, because her words came floating up to Stephen like bubbles in water.

He continued along the ridge towards her while she watched him. Only when he was directly above her did he trust his own words to reach her.

'No. I'm really just filling in time. Thank you very much.'

'If you go on to the top, there's a spring.'

'I should think you have to have it pointed out to you. With all this heather.'

She looked down for a moment, then up again. 'Do you live here?'

'No. I'm staying with my brother. He's the rector. Perhaps you go to his church?'

She shook her head. 'No. We don't go to any church.'

That could not be followed up, Stephen felt, at his present distance and altitude. 'What are you doing?' he asked.

'Collecting stones for my father.'

'What does he do with them?'

'He wants the mosses and lichens.'

'Then,' cried Stephen, 'you *must* know my brother. Or your father must know him. My brother is one of the great authorities on lichens.' This unexpected link seemed to open a door; and, at least for a second, to open it surprisingly wide.

Stephen found himself bustling down the rough but not particularly steep slope towards her.

'My father's not an *authority*,' said the girl, gazing seriously at the descending figure. 'He's not an authority on anything.'

'Oh, you misunderstand,' said Stephen. 'My brother is only an amateur too. I didn't mean he was a professor or anything like that. Still, I think your father must have heard of him.'

'I don't think so,' said the girl. 'I'm almost sure not.'

Stephen had nearly reached the bottom of the shallow vale.

6

It was completely out of the wind down there, and surprisingly torrid.

'Let me see,' he said, looking into the girl's basket, before he looked at the girl.

She lifted the basket off the ground. Her hand and forearm were brown.

'Some of the specimens are very small,' he said, smiling. It was essential to keep the conversation going, and it was initially more difficult now that he was alone with her in the valley, and close to her.

'It's been a bad year,' she said. 'Some days I've found almost nothing. Nothing that could be taken home.'

'All the same, the basket must be heavy. Please put it down.' He saw that it was reinforced with stout metal strips, mostly rusty.

'Take a piece for yourself, if you like,' said the girl. She spoke as if they were portions of iced cake, or home-made coconut fudge.

Stephen gazed full at the girl. She had a sensitive face with grey-green eyes and short reddish hair – no, auburn. The *démodé* word came to Stephen on the instant. Both her shirt and her trousers were worn and faded: familiar, Stephen felt. She was wearing serious shoes, but little cared for. She was a part of nature.

'I'll take this piece,' Stephen said. 'It's conglomerate.'

'Is it?' said the girl. Stephen was surprised that after so much ingathering, she did not know a fact so elementary.

'I might take this piece too, and show the stuff on it to my brother.'

'Help yourself,' said the girl. 'But don't take them all.'

Feeling had been building up in Stephen while he had been walking solitarily on the ridge above. For so long he had been isolated, insulated, incarcerated. Elizabeth had been everything to him, and no one could ever be like her, but 'attractive' was not a word that he had used to himself about her, not for a long time; not attractive as this girl was attractive. Elizabeth had been a part of him, perhaps the greater part of him; but not mysterious, not fascinating.

'Well, I don't know,' said Stephen. 'How far do you have to carry that burden?'

'The basket isn't full yet. I must go on searching for a bit.'

'I am sorry to say I can't offer to help. I have to go back.'

7

All the same, Stephen had reached a decision.

The girl simply nodded. She had not yet picked up the basket again.

'Where do you live?'

'Quite near.'

That seemed to Stephen to be almost impossible, but it was not the main point.

Stephen felt like a schoolboy; though not like himself as a schoolboy. 'If I were to be here after lunch tomorrow, say at half past two, would you show me the spring? The spring you were talking about.'

'Of course,' she said. 'If you like.'

Stephen could not manage the response so obviously needed, gently confident; if possible, even gently witty. For a moment, in fact, he could say nothing. Then – 'Look,' he said. He brought an envelope out of his pocket and in pencil on the back of it he wrote: 'Tomorrow. Here. 2.30 p.m. To visit the spring.'

He said, 'It's too big,' and tore one end off the envelope, aware that the remaining section bore his name, and that the envelope had been addressed to him care of his brother. As a matter of fact, it had contained the final communication from the undertaking firm. He wished they had omitted his equivocal and rather ridiculous OBE.

He held the envelope out. She took it and inserted it, without a word, into a pocket of her shirt, buttoning down the flap. Stephen's heart beat at the gesture.

He was not exactly sure what to make of the situation or whether the appointment was to be depended upon. But at such moments in life, one is often sure of neither thing, nor of anything much else.

He looked at her. 'What's your name?' he asked, as casually as he could.

'Nell,' she answered.

He had not quite expected that, but then he had not particularly expected anything else either.

'I look forward to our walk, Nell,' he said. He could not help adding, 'I look forward to it very much.'

She nodded and smiled.

He fancied that they had really looked at one another for a moment.

'I must go on searching,' she said.

She picked up the heavy basket, seemingly without particular effort, and walked away from him, up the valley.

Insanely, he wondered about *her* lunch. Surely she must have some? She seemed so exceptionally healthy and strong.

His own meal was all scarlet runners, but he had lost his appetite in any case, something that had never previously happened since the funeral, as he had noticed with surprise on several occasions.

Luncheon was called lunch, but the evening meal was none the less called supper, perhaps from humility. At supper that evening, Harriet referred forcefully to Stephen's earlier abstemiousness.

'I trust you're not sickening, Stephen. It would be a bad moment. Dr Gopalachari's on holiday. Perhaps I ought to warn you.'

'Dr Who?'

'No, not Dr Who. Dr Gopalachari. He's a West Bengali. We are lucky to have him.'

Stephen's brother, Harewood, coughed forlornly.

For luncheon the next day, Stephen had even less appetite, even though it was mashed turnip, cooked, or at least served, with mixed peppers. Harriet loved all things oriental.

On an almost empty stomach, he hastened up the long but not steep ascent. He had not known he could still walk so fast uphill, but for some reason the knowledge did not make him particularly happy, as doubtless it should have done.

The girl, dressed as on the day before, was seated upon a low rock at the spot from which he had first spoken to her. It was not yet twenty past. He had discerned her seated shape from afar, but she had proved to be sitting with her back to the ascending track and to him. On the whole, he was glad that she had not been watching his exertions, inevitably comical, albeit triumphant.

She did not even look up until he actually stood before her. Of course this time she had no basket.

'Oh, hullo,' she said.

He stood looking at her. 'We're both punctual.'

She nodded. He was panting quite strenuously, and glad to gain a little time.

He spoke. 'Did you find many more suitable stones?'

She shook her head, then rose to her feet.

He found it difficult not to stretch out his arms and draw her to him.

'Why is this called Burton's Clough, I wonder? It seems altogether too wide and shallow for a clough.'

'I didn't know it was,' said the girl.

'The map says it is. At least I think this is the place. Shall we go? Lead me to the magic spring.'

She smiled at him. 'Why do you call it *that*?'

'I'm sure it *is* magic. It must be.'

'It's just clear water,' said the girl, 'and very, very deep.'

Happily, the track was still wide enough for them to walk side by side, though Stephen realized that, further on, where he had not been, this might cease to be the case.

'How long are you staying here?' asked the girl.

'Perhaps for another fortnight. It depends.'

'Are you married?'

'I *was* married, Nell, but my wife unfortunately died.' It seemed unnecessary to put any date to it, and calculated only to cause stress.

'I'm sorry,' said the girl.

'She was a wonderful woman and a very good wife.'

To that the girl said nothing. What could she say?

'I am taking a period of leave from the civil service,' Stephen volunteered. 'Nothing very glamorous.'

'What's the civil service?' asked the girl.

'You ought to know *that*,' said Stephen in mock reproof: more or less mock. After all, she was not a child, or not exactly. All the same, he produced a childlike explanation. 'The civil service is what looks after the country. The country would hardly carry on without us. Not nowadays. Nothing would run properly.'

'Really not?'

'No. Not run *properly*.' With her it was practicable to be lightly profane.

'Father says that all politicians are evil. I don't know anything about it.'

'Civil servants are not politicians, Nell. But perhaps this is not the best moment to go into it all.' He said that partly because he suspected she had no wish to learn.

There was a pause.

'Do you like walking?' she asked.

'Very much. I could easily walk all day. Would you come with me?'

'I *do* walk all day, or most of it. Of course I have to sleep at night. I lie in front of the fire.'

'But it's too warm for a fire at this time of year.' He said it to keep the conversation going, but, in fact, he was far from certain. He himself was not particularly warm at that very moment. He had no doubt cooled off after speeding up the ascent, but the two of them were, none the less, walking reasonably fast, and still he felt chilly, perhaps perilously so.

'Father always likes a fire,' said the girl. 'He's a cold mortal.'

They had reached the decayed milestone or waymark at which Stephen had turned on the previous day. The girl had stopped and was fingering the lichens with which it was spattered. She knelt against the stone with her left arm round the back of it.

'Can you put a name to them?' asked Stephen.

'Yes, to some of them.'

'I am sure your father has one of my brother's books on his shelf.'

'I don't think so,' said the girl. 'We have no shelves. Father can't read.'

She straightened up and glanced at Stephen.

'Oh, but surely—'

For example, and among other things, the girl herself was perfectly well spoken. As a matter of fact, hers was a noticeably beautiful voice. Stephen had noticed it, and even thrilled to it, when first he had heard it, floating up from the bottom of the so-called clough. He had thrilled to it ever since, despite the curious things the girl sometimes said.

They resumed their way.

'Father has no eyes,' said the girl.

'That is terrible,' said Stephen. 'I hadn't realized.'

The girl said nothing.

Stephen felt his first real qualm, as distinct from mere habitual self-doubt. 'Am I taking you away from him? Should you go back to him?'

'I'm never with him by day,' said the girl. 'He finds his way about.'

'I know that does happen,' said Stephen guardedly. 'All the same—'

'Father doesn't need a civil service to run him,' said the girl. The way she spoke convinced Stephen that she had known all along what the civil service was and did. He had from the first supposed that to be so. Everyone knew.

'You said your dead wife was a wonderful woman,' said the girl.

'Yes, she was.'

'My father is a wonderful man.'

'Yes,' said Stephen. 'I am only sorry about his affliction.'

'It's not an affliction,' said the girl.

Stephen did not know what to say to that. The last thing to be desired was an argument of any kind whatever, other perhaps than a fun argument.

'Father doesn't need to get things out of books,' said the girl.

'There are certainly other ways of learning,' said Stephen. 'I expect that was one of the things you yourself learned at school.'

He suspected she would say she had never been to school. His had been a half-fishing remark.

But all she replied was, 'Yes'.

Stephen looked around him for a moment. Already, he had gone considerably further along the track than ever before. 'It really is beautiful up here.' It seemed a complete wilderness. The track had wound among the wide folds of the hill, so that nothing but wilderness was visible in any direction.

'I should like to live here,' said Stephen. 'I should like it *now*.' He knew that he partly meant 'now that Elizabeth was dead'.

'There are empty houses everywhere,' said the girl. 'You can just move into one. It's what Father and I did, and now it's our home.'

Stephen supposed that that at least explained something. It possibly elucidated one of the earliest of her odd remarks.

'I'll help you to find one, if you like,' said the girl. 'Father says that none of them have been lived in for hundreds of years. I know where all the best ones are.'

'I'll have to think about that,' said Stephen. 'I have my job, you must remember.' He wanted her to be rude about his job.

But she only said, 'We'll look now, if you like.'

'Tomorrow, perhaps. We're looking for the spring now.'

'Are you tired?' asked the girl, with apparently genuine concern, and presumably forgetting altogether what he had told her about his longing to walk all day.

'Not at all tired,' said Stephen, smiling at her.

'Then why were you looking at your watch?'

'A bad habit picked up in the civil service. We all do it.'

He had observed long before that she had no watch on her lovely brown forearm, no bracelet; only the marks of thorn

12

scratches and the incisions of sharp stones. The light golden bloom on her arms filled him with delight and with desire.

In fact, he had omitted to time their progression, though he timed most things, so that the habit had wrecked his natural faculty. Perhaps another twenty or thirty minutes passed, while they continued to walk side by side, the track having as yet shown no particular sign of narrowing, so that one might think it still led somewhere, and that people still went there. As they advanced, they said little more of consequence for the moment; or so it seemed to Stephen. He surmised that there was now what is termed an understanding between them, even though in a sense he himself understood very little. It was more a phase for pleasant nothings, he deemed, always supposing that he could evolve a sufficient supply of them, than for meaningful questions and reasonable responses.

Suddenly, the track seemed not to narrow, but to stop, even to vanish. Hereunto it had been surprisingly well trodden. Now he could see nothing but knee-high heather.

'The spring's over there,' said the girl in a matter of fact way, and pointing. Such simple and natural gestures are often the most beautiful.

'How right I was in saying that I could never find it alone!' remarked Stephen.

He could not see why the main track should not lead to the spring – if there really was a spring. Why else should the track be beaten to this spot? The mystery was akin to the Burton's Clough mystery. The uplands had been settled under other conditions than ours. Stephen, on his perambulations, had always felt that, everywhere.

But the girl was standing among the heather a few yards away, and Stephen saw that there was a curious serpentine rabbit run that he had failed to notice – except that rabbits do not run like serpents. There were several fair-sized birds flying overhead in silence. Stephen fancied they were kites.

He wriggled his way down the rabbit path, with little dignity.

There was the most beautiful small pool imaginable: clear, deep, lustrous, gently heaving at its centre, or near its centre. It stood in a small clearing.

All the rivers in Britain might be taken as rising here, and thus flowing until the first moment of their pollution.

Stephen became aware that now the sun really *was* shining. He had not noticed before. The girl stood on the far side of the pool in her faded shirt and trousers, smiling seraphically. The

13

pool pleased her, so that suddenly everything pleased her.

'Have you kept the note I gave you?' asked Stephen.

She put her hand lightly on her breast pocket, and therefore on her breast.

'I'm glad,' said Stephen.

If the pool had not been between them, he would have seized her, whatever the consequences.

'Just clear water,' said the girl.

The sun brought out new colours in her hair. The shape of her head was absolutely perfect.

'The track,' said Stephen, 'seems to be quite well used. Is this where the people come?'

'No,' said the girl. 'They come to and from the places where they live.'

'I thought you said all the houses were empty.'

'What I said was there are many empty houses.'

'That *is* what you said. I'm sorry. But the track seems to come to an end. What do the people do then?'

'They find their way,' said the girl. 'Stop worrying about them.'

The water was still between them. Stephen was no longer in doubt that there was indeed something else between them. Really there was. The pool was intermittently throwing up tiny golden waves in the pure breeze, then losing them again.

'We haven't seen anybody,' said Stephen. 'I never do see anyone.'

The girl looked puzzled.

Stephen realized that the way he had put it, the statement that he never saw anyone, might have been tactless. 'When I go for my long walks alone,' he added.

'Not only then,' said the girl.

Stephen's heart turned over slightly.

'Possibly,' he said. 'I daresay you are very right.'

The kites were still flapping like torn pieces of charred pasteboard in the high air, though in the lower part of it.

'You haven't even looked to the bottom of the pool yet,' said the girl.

'I suppose not.' Stephen fell on his knees, as the girl had done at the milestone or waymark, and gazed downwards through the pellucid near-nothingness beneath the shifting golden rods. There were a few polished stones round the sides, but little else that he could see, and nothing that seemed of significance. How should there be, of course? Unless the girl

14

had put it there, as Stephen realized might have been possible.

Stephen looked up. 'It's a splendid pool,' he said.

But now his eye caught something else; something other than the girl and the pool. On the edge of the rising ground behind the girl stood a small stone house. It was something else that Stephen had not previously noticed. Indeed, he had been reasonably sure that there had been nothing and no one, not so much as a hint of mankind, not for a quite long way, a quite long time.

'Is that where one of the people lives?' he asked, and in his turn pointed. 'Or perhaps more than one?'

'It's empty,' said the girl.

'Should we go and look?'

'If you like,' said the girl. Stephen quite saw that his expressed response to the glorious little spring had been inadequate. He had lost the trick of feeling, years and years ago.

'It's a splendid pool,' he said again, a little self-consciously.

Despite what the girl had said, Stephen had thought that to reach the house above them, they would have to scramble through the high heather. But he realized at once that there was a path, which was one further thing he had not previously noticed.

The girl went before, weaving backwards and forwards up the hillside. Following her, with his thoughts more free to wander, as the exertion made talking difficult, Stephen suddenly apprehended that the need to return for Harriet's tea-time had for a season passed completely from his mind.

Apprehending it now, he did not even look at his watch. Apart from anything else, the struggle upwards was too intense for even the smallest distraction or secondary effort. The best thing might be for his watch simply to stop.

They were at the summit, with a wider horizon, but still Stephen could see no other structure than the one before him, though this time he gazed around with a certain care. From here, the pool below them seemed to catch the full sun all over its surface. It gleamed among the heathered rocks like a vast luminous sea anemone among weeds.

Stephen could see at once that the house appeared basically habitable. He had expected jagged holes in the walls, broken panes in the windows, less than half a roof, ubiquitous litter.

The door simply stood open, but it was a door, not a mere gap; a door in faded green, like the girl's trousers. Inside, the floorboards were present and there was even a certain amount

15

of simple furniture, though, as an estate agent would at once have pointed out with apologies, no curtains and no carpets.

'Nell. Somebody lives here already,' Stephen said sharply, before they had even gone upstairs.

'Already?' queried the girl.

Stephen made the necessary correction. 'Someone lives here.'

'No,' said the girl. 'No one. Not for centuries.'

Of course that was particularly absurd and childish. Much of this furniture, Stephen thought, was of the kind offered by the furnishing department of a good Co-op. Stephen had sometimes come upon such articles on visits paid in the course of his work. He had to admit, however, that he had little idea when such houses as this actually were built at these odd spots on the moors. Possibly as long ago as in the seventeenth century? Possibly only sixty or eighty years ago? Possibly—?

They went upstairs. There were two very low rooms, hardly as much as half lighted from one small and dirty window in each. One room was totally unfurnished. The sole content of the other was a double bed which absorbed much of the cubic capacity available. It was a quite handsome country object, with a carved head and foot. It even offered a seemingly intact mattress, badly in need of a wash.

'Someone *must* be living here,' said Stephen. 'At least sometimes. Perhaps the owners come here for the weekend. Or perhaps they're just moving in.'

As soon as he spoke, it occurred to him that the evidence was equally consistent with their moving out, but he did not continue.

'Lots of the houses are like this,' said the girl. 'No one lives in them.'

Stephen wondered vaguely whether the clear air or some factor of that kind might preserve things as if they were still in use. It was a familiar enough notion, though, in his case, somewhat unspecific. It would be simpler to disbelieve the girl, who was young and without experience, though perfectly eager, at least when others were eager. They returned downstairs.

'Shall we see some more houses?' asked the girl.

'I don't think I have the time.'

'You said you had a fortnight. I know what a fortnight is.'

'Yes.' He simply could not tell her that he had to report for Harriet's astringent teatime; nor, even now, was that in the forefront of his mind. The truth was that whereas hitherto he had been trying to paddle in deep waters, he was now floundering in them.

The girl had a suggestion. 'Why not live *here* for a fortnight?'

'I am committed to staying with my brother. He's not very fit. I should worry about him if I broke my word.' He realized that he was speaking to her in a more adult way than before. It had really begun with her speaking similarly to him.

'Does your worrying about him do him any good?'

'Not much, I'm afraid.'

'Does your worrying about everything do *you* any good?'

'None whatever, Nell. None at all.'

He turned aside and looked out of the window; the parlour window might not be too grand a term, for all its need of cleaning.

He addressed her firmly. 'Would you give me a hand with all the things that need to be done? Even for a tenancy of a fortnight?'

'If you like.'

'We should have to do a lot of shopping.'

The girl, standing behind him, remained silent. It was an unusual non-response.

'I should have to cook on a primus stove,' said Stephen. 'I wonder if we can buy one? I used to be quite good with them.' Rapture was beginning.

The girl said nothing.

'We might need new locks on the doors.'

The girl spoke. 'There is only one door.'

'So there is,' said Stephen. 'In towns, houses have two, a front door and a back door. When trouble comes in at one, you can do a bolt through the other.'

'People don't need a lock,' said the girl. 'Why should they?'

He turned away from the filthy window and gazed straight at her. 'Suppose I was to fall in love with you?' he said.

'Then you would not have to go back after a fortnight.'

It could hardly have been a straighter reply.

He put one arm round her shoulders, one hand on her breast, so that the note he had written her lay between them. He remembered that the first letter written to a woman is always a love letter. 'Would you promise to visit me every day?'

'I might be unable to do that.'

'I don't want to seem unkind, but you did say that your father could manage.'

17

'If he discovers, he will keep me at home and send my sister out instead. He has powers. He's very frightening.'

Stephen relaxed his hold a little. He had been all along well aware how sadly impracticable was the entire idea.

For example: he could hardly even drive up to this place with supplies; even had his car not been in the course of an opportune overhaul in London, a very complete overhaul after all this anxious time. And that was only one thing; one among very many.

'Well, what's the answer?' Stephen said, smiling at her in the wrong way, longing for her in a very different way.

'I can't come and go the whole time,' said the girl.

'I see,' said Stephen.

He who had missed so many opportunities, always for excellent reasons, and for one excellent reason in particular, clearly saw that this might be his last opportunity, and almost certainly was.

'How should we live?' he asked. 'I mean how should we eat and manage?'

'As the birds do,' said the girl.

Stephen did not inquire of her how she came to know Shakespeare, as people put it. He might ask her that later. In the meantime, he could see that the flat, floating birds he had taken to be kites, were indeed drifting past the dirty window, and round and round the house, as it seemed. Of course his questions had been mere routine in any case. He could well have killed himself if she had made a merely routine response.

'Let's see,' he said. He gently took her hand. He kissed her softly on the lips. He returned with her upstairs.

It would perhaps have been more suitable if he had been leading the party, but that might be a trifle. Even the damp discolouration of the mattress might be a trifle. Harriet's tea-time could not, in truth, be forced from the mind, but it was provisionally overruled. One learned the trick in the course of one's work, or one would break altogether.

There were of course only the bed and the mattress; no sheets or blankets; no Spanish or Kashmiri rugs; no entangling silkiness, no singing save that of the moor. Elizabeth had never wished to make love like that. She had liked to turn on the record player, almost always Brahms or Schumann (the Rhenish Symphony was her particular favourite), and to ascend slowly into a deep fully made bed. But the matter had

18

not seriously arisen for years. Stephen had often wondered why not.

Nell was lying on her front. Seemingly expectant and resistant at the same time, she clung like a clam. Her body was as brown as a pale chestnut, but it was a strong and well-made body. Her short hair was wavy rather than curly. Stephen was ravished by the line of it on her strong neck. He was ravished by her relaxed shoulder blade. He was ravished by her perfect waist and thighs. He was ravished by her youth and youthful smell.

'Please turn over,' he said, after tugging at her intermittently, and not very effectively.

Fortunately, he was not too displeased by his own appearance. The hair on his body was bleaching and fading, but otherwise he could, quite sincerely, see little difference from when he had been twenty-four, and had married Elizabeth. He knew, however, that at these times sincerity is not enough; nor objectivity either. When are they?

'Please,' he said softly in Nell's ear. Her ears were a slightly unusual shape, and the most beautiful he had ever beheld, or beheld so intently.

He put his hand lightly on her neck. 'Please,' he said.

She wriggled over in a single swift movement, like a light stab from an invisible knife. He saw that her eyes were neither closed nor open, neither looking at him, nor looking at anything but him.

On the skin between her right shoulder and her right breast was a curious, brownish, greyish, bluish, irregular mark or patch, which had been hidden by her shirt, though Stephen could not quite see how. It was more demanding of attention than it might have been, partly because of its position, and partly, where Stephen was concerned, because of something vaguely else. In any case, it would mean that the poor girl could not reposefully wear a low-cut dress, should the need arise. Though it was by no means a birthmark in the usual sense, Nell had probably been lying on her front through chagrin about it. Upon Stephen, however, the effect was to make him love her more deeply; perhaps love her for the first time. He did not want her or her body to be quite perfect. In a real person, it would be almost vulgar. At this point, Harriet and Harriet's teatime came more prominently into view for a few seconds.

Nell might say something about the mark sooner or later. He would never take an initiative.

19

At the moment, she said nothing at all. He simply could not make out whether she was watching him or not. Her mouth was long and generous; but had not her whole proceeding been generous in a marvellous degree? He could not even make out whether she was taut or relaxed. No small mystery was Nell after years and years of a perfect, but always slow-moving, relationship with Elizabeth!

He kissed her intimately. When she made no particular response, not even a grunt, he began to caress her, more or less as he had caressed his wife. He took care not to touch the peculiar blemish, or even to enter its area. There was no need to do so. It occurred to Stephen that the mark might be the consequence of an injury; and so might in due course disappear, or largely so. In the end that happened even to many of the strangest human markings. One day, as the nannies used to say.

Suddenly she made a wild plunge at him that took away his breath. The surprise was directly physical, but moral also. He had found it a little difficult to assess Nell's likely age, and inquiry was out of the question; but he had supposed it probable that she was a virgin, and had quite deliberately resolved to accept the implication. Or so he had believed of himself.

Now she was behaving as a maenad.

As an oread, rather; Stephen thought at a later hour. For surely these moors were mountains, often above the thousand-foot contour; boundless uplands peopled solely by unwedded nymphs and their monstrous progenitors? Stephen had received a proper education at a proper place: in Stephen's first days, one had not made the grade, Stephen's grade, otherwise. Stephen's parents had undertaken sacrifices so immense that no one had fully recovered from them.

The last vestige of initiative had passed from Stephen like a limb. And yet, he fancied, it was not because Nell was what Elizabeth would have called unfeminine, but merely because she was young, and perhaps because she lived without contamination, merging into the aspect and mutability of remote places. So, at least, he could only suppose.

Soon he ceased to suppose anything. He knew bliss unequalled, unprecedented, assuredly unimagined. Moreover, the wonder lasted for longer than he would have conceived of as possible. That particularly struck him.

Nell's flawed body was celestial. Nell herself was more wonderful than the dream of death. Nell could not possibly exist.

*

He was fondling her and feeling a trifle cold; much as Elizabeth would have felt. Not that it mattered in the very least. Nell was no maenad or oread. She was a half-frightened child, sweetly soft, responsive to his every thought, sometimes before he had fully given birth to it. She was a waif, a foundling. And it was he who had found her. And only yesterday.

'Tell me about your sister,' said Stephen. He realized that it was growing dark as well as chilly.

'She's not like *me*. You wouldn't like her.'

Stephen knew that ordinary, normal girls always responded much like that.

He smiled at Nell. 'But what *is* she like?'

'She's made quite differently. You wouldn't care for her.'

'Has she a name?'

'Of a sort.'

'What do you and your father call her?'

'We call her different things at different times. You're cold.'

So she was human, after all, Stephen thought.

She herself had very little to put on. Two fairly light garments, a pair of stout socks, her solid shoes.

They went downstairs.

'Would you care to borrow my sweater?' asked Stephen. 'Until tomorrow?'

She made no reply, but simply stared at him through the dusk in the downstairs room, the living place, the parlour, the *salon*.

'Take it,' said Stephen. It was a heavy garment. Elizabeth had spent nearly four months knitting it continuously, while slowly recovering from her very first disintegration. It was in thick complex stitches and meant to last for ever. When staying with Harewood, Stephen wore it constantly.

Nell took the sweater but did not put it on. She was still staring at him. At such a moment her grey-green eyes were almost luminous.

'We'll meet again tomorrow,' said Stephen firmly. 'We'll settle down here tomorrow. I must say something to my brother and sister-in-law, and I don't care what happens after that. Not now. At least I *do* care. I care very much. As you well know.'

'It's risky,' she said.

'Yes,' he replied, because it was necessary to evade all discussion. 'Yes, but it can't be helped. You come as early as you can, and I'll arrive with some provisions for us. We really need

21

some blankets too, and some candles. I'll see if I can borrow a Land-Rover from one of the farms.' He trusted that his confidence and his firm, practical actions would override all doubts.

'I may be stopped,' she said. 'My father can't read books but he can read minds. He does it all the time.'

'You must run away from him,' said Stephen firmly. 'We'll stay here for a little, and then you can come back to London with me.'

She made no comment on that, but simply repeated, 'My father can read *my* mind. I only have to be in the same room with him. He's frightening.'

Her attitude to her father seemed to have changed considerably. It was the experience of love, Stephen supposed; first love.

'Obviously, you must try to be in a *different* room as much as possible. It's only for one more night. We've known each other now for two days.'

'There's only one room.'

Stephen had known that such would be her rejoinder.

He well knew also that his behaviour might seem unromantic and even cold-hearted. But the compulsion upon him could not be plainer: if he did not return to the rectory tonight, Harriet, weakly aided by Harewood, would have the police after him; dogs would be scurrying across the moors, as if after Hercules, and perhaps searchlights sweeping also. Nothing could more fatally upset any hope of a quiet and enduring compact with such a one as Nell. He was bound for a rough scene with Harriet and Harewood as it was. It being now long past teatime, he would be lucky if Harriet had not taken action before he could reappear. Speed was vital and, furthermore, little of the situation could be explained with any candour to Nell. First, she would simply not understand what he said (even though within her range she was shrewd enough, often shrewder than he). Second, in so far as she did understand, she would panic and vanish. And he had no means of tracking her down at all. She was as shy about her abode as about the mark on her body; though doubtless with as little reason, or so Stephen hoped. He recognized that parting from her at all might be as unwise as it would be painful, but it was the lesser peril. He could not take her to London tonight, or to anywhere, because there was no accessible transport. Not nowadays. He could not take her to the rectory, where Harriet might make Harewood lay an anathema upon her. They could not stay in the moorland house without food or warmth.

'I'll walk with you to the top of the clough,' he said.

She shook her head. 'It's not there I live.'

'Where then?' he asked at once.

'Not that way at all.'

'Will you get there?'

She nodded: in exactly what spirit it was hard to say.

He refrained from inquiring how she would explain the absence of specimens for her father. Two or three stones dragged from the walls of the house they were in, might serve the purpose in any case, he thought: outside and inside were almost equally mossed, lichened, adorned, encumbered.

'Goodnight, Nell. We'll meet tomorrow morning. Here.' He really had to go. Harriet was made anxious by the slightest irregularity, and when she became anxious, she became frenzied. His present irregularity was by no means slight already; assuredly not slight by Harriet's standards.

To his great relief, Nell nodded again. She had still not put on his sweater.

'In a few days' time, we'll go to London. We'll be together always.' He could hardly believe his own ears listening to his own voice saying such things. After all this time! After Elizabeth! After so much inner peace and convinced adoration and asking for nothing more! After the fearful illness!

They parted with kisses but with little drama. Nell sped off into what the map depicted as virtual void.

'All the same,' Stephen reflected, 'I must look at the map again. I'll try to borrow Harewood's dividers.'

He pushed back through the heather, rejoicing in his sense of direction, among so many other things to rejoice about, and began lumbering down the track homewards. The light was now so poor that he walked faster and faster; faster even than he had ascended. In the end, he was running uncontrollably.

Therefore, his heart was already pounding when he discovered that the rectory was in confusion; though, at the rectory, even confusion had a slightly wan quality.

During the afternoon, Harriet had had a seizure of some kind, and during the evening had been taken off in a public ambulance.

'What time did it happen?' asked Stephen. He knew from

23

all too much experience that it was the kind of thing that people did ask.

'I don't really know, Stephen,' replied Harewood. 'I was in my specimens room reading the *Journal*, and I fear that a considerable time may have passed before I came upon her. I was too distressed to look at my watch even then. Besides, between ourselves, my watch loses rather badly.'

Though Stephen tried to help in some way, the improvised evening meal was upsetting. Harriet had planned rissoles sautéd in ghee, but neither of the men really knew how to cook with ghee. The home-made Congress Pudding was nothing less than nauseous. Very probably, some decisive final touches had been omitted.

'You see how it is, young Stephen,' said Harewood, after they had munched miserably but briefly. 'The prognosis cannot be described as hopeful. I may have to give up the living.'

'You can't possibly do that, Harewood, whatever happens. There is Father's memory to think about. I'm sure I should think about him more often myself.' Stephen's thoughts were, in fact, upon quite specially different topics.

'I don't wish to go, I assure you, Stephen. I've been very happy here.'

The statement surprised Stephen, but was of course thoroughly welcome and appropriate.

'There is always prayer, Harewood.'

'Yes, Stephen, indeed. I may well have been remiss. That might explain much.'

They had been unable to discover where Harriet hid the coffee, so sat for moments in reverent and reflective silence, one on either side of the bleak table: a gift from the nearest branch of the Free India League.

Stephen embarked upon a tentative *démarche*. 'I need hardly say that I don't want to leave you in the lurch.'

'It speaks for itself that there can be no question of that.'

Stephen drew in a quantity of air. 'To put it absolutely plainly. I feel that for a spell you would be better off at this time without me around to clutter up the place and make endless demands.'

For a second time within hours, Stephen recognized quite clearly that his line of procedure could well be seen as cold-blooded; but, for a second time, he was acting under extreme compulsion – compulsion more extreme than he had expected ever again to encounter, at least on the hither side of the Styx.

'I should never deem you to be doing that, young Stephen. Blood is at all times, even the most embarrassing times, thicker than water. It was Cardinal Newman, by the way, who first said that; a prelate of a different soteriology.'

Stephen simply did not believe it, but he said nothing. Harewood often came forward with such assertions, but they were almost invariably erroneous. Stephen sometimes doubted whether Harewood could be completely relied upon even in the context of his private speciality, the lichens.

'I think I had better leave tomorrow morning and so reduce the load for a span. I am sure Doreen will appreciate it.' Doreen was the intermittent help; a little brash, where in former days no doubt she would have been a little simple. Stephen had always supposed that brashness might make it more possible to serve Harriet. Doreen had been deserted, childless, by her young husband; but there had been a proper divorce. Harewood was supposed to be taking a keen interest in Doreen, who was no longer in her absolutely first youth.

'You will be rather more dependent upon Doreen for a time,' added Stephen.

'I suppose that may well be,' said Harewood. Stephen fancied that his brother almost smiled. He quite saw that he might have thought so because of the ideas in his own mind, at which he himself was smiling continuously.

'You must do whatever you think best for all concerned, Stephen,' said Harewood. 'Including, of course, your sister-in-law, dear Harriet.'

'I think I should go now and perhaps come back a little later.'

'As you will, Stephen. I have always recognized that you have a mind trained both academically and by your work. I am a much less coordinated spirit. Oh yes, I know it well. I should rely very much upon your judgement in almost any serious matter.'

Circumstanced as at the moment he was, Stephen almost blushed.

But Harewood made things all right by adding, 'Except perhaps in certain matters of the spirit which, in the nature of things, lie quite particularly between my Maker and myself alone.'

'Oh, naturally,' said Stephen.

'Otherwise,' continued Harewood, 'and now that Harriet is unavailable – for a very short time only, we must hope – it is upon you, Stephen, that I propose to rely foremost, in many pressing concerns of this world.'

Beyond doubt, Harewood now was not all but smiling. He was smiling nearly at full strength. He explained this immediately.

'My catarrh seems very much better,' he said. 'I might consider setting forth in splendour one of these days. Seeking specimens, I mean.'

Stephen plunged upon impulse.

'It may seem a bit odd in the circumstances, but I should be glad to have the use of a Land-Rover. There's a building up on the moors I should like to look at again before I go, and it's too far to walk in the time. There's a perfectly good track to quite near it. Is there anyone you know of in the parish who would lend me such a thing? Just for an hour or two, of course.'

Harewood responded at once. 'You might try Tom Jarrold. I regret to say that he's usually too drunk to drive. Indeed, one could never guarantee that his vehicle will even leave the ground.'

Possibly it was not exactly the right reference, but what an excellent and informed parish priest Harewood was suddenly proving to be!

Harewood had reopened the latest number of the *Journal*, which he had been sitting on in the chair all the time. His perusal had of course been interrupted by the afternoon's events.

'Don't feel called upon to stop talking,' said Harewood. 'I can read and listen at the same time perfectly well.'

Stephen reflected that the attempt had not often been made when Harriet had been in the room.

'I don't think there's anything more to say at the moment. We seem to have settled everything that *can* be settled.'

'I shall be depending upon you in many different matters, remember,' said Harewood, but without looking up from the speckled diagrams.

As soon as Stephen turned on the hanging light in his bedroom, he noticed the new patch on the wallpaper; if only because it was immediately above his bed. The wallpaper had always been lowering anyway. He was the more certain that the particular patch was new because, naturally, he made his own bed each morning, which involved daily confrontation with that particular surface. Of course there had always been the other such patches among the marks on the walls.

Still, the new arrival was undoubtedly among the reasons why Stephen slept very little that night, even though, in his own estimation, he needed sleep so badly. There again, however, few do sleep in the first phase of what is felt to be a reciprocated relationship: equally fulfilling and perilous, always deceptive, and always somewhere known to be. The mixed ingredients of the last two days churned within Stephen, as in Harriet's battered cook-pot; one rising as another fell. He was treating Harewood as he himself would not wish to be treated; and who could tell what had really led to Harriet's collapse?

In the end, bliss drove out bewilderment, and seemed the one thing sure, as perhaps it was.

Later still, when daylight was all too visible through the frail curtains, Stephen half dreamed that he was lying inert on some surface he could not define and that Nell was administering water to him from a chalice. But the chalice, doubtless a consecrated object to begin with, and certainly of fairest silver from the Spanish mines, was blotched and blemished. Stephen wanted to turn away, to close his eyes properly, to expostulate, but could do none of these things. As Nell gently kissed his brow, he awoke fully with a compelling thirst. He had heard of people waking thirsty in the night, but to himself he could not remember it ever before happening. He had never lived like that.

There was no water in the room, because the house was just sufficiently advanced to make visitors go to the bathroom. Stephen walked quietly down the passage, then hesitated. He recollected that nowadays the bathroom door opened with an appalling wrench and scream.

It would be very wrong indeed to take the risk of waking poor Harewood, in his new isolation. Stephen crept on down the stairs towards the scullery, and there *was* Harewood, sleeping like the dead, not in the least sprawling, but, on the contrary, touchingly compressed and compact in the worn chair. For a moment, he looked like a schoolboy, though of course in that curtained light.

Harewood was murmuring contentedly. 'Turn over. No, right over. You can trust me'; then, almost ecstatically, almost like a juvenile, 'It's beautiful. Oh, it's beautiful.'

Stephen stole away to the back quarters, where both the luncheon and the supper washing-up, even the washing-up after tea, all awaited the touch of a vanished hand.

The cold tap jerked and jarred as it always did, but when Stephen went back, Harewood was slumbering still. His self-converse was now so ideal that it had fallen into incoherence. The cheap figure on the mantel of Shiva or somebody, which Stephen had always detested, sneered animatedly.

But there Nell really was; really, really was.

In his soul, Stephen was astonished. Things do not go like that in real life, least of all in the dreaded demesne of the heart.

However, they unloaded the Land-Rover together, as if everything were perfectly real; toiling up the heather paths with heavy loads, Nell always ahead, always as strong as he: which was really rather necessary.

'I must take the Rover back. Come with me.'

He had not for a moment supposed that she would, but she did, and with no demur.

'It's rough going,' he said. But she merely put her brown hand on his thigh, as she sat and bumped beside him.

They were a pair now.

'It won't take a moment while I settle with the man.'

He was determined that it should not. It must be undesirable that the two of them be seen together in the village. Probably it was undesirable that he himself, even alone, be seen there before a long time had passed. He might perhaps steal back one distant day like Enoch Arden, and take Harewood completely by surprise, both of them now bearded, shaggily or skimpily. What by then would have become of Nell?

They walked upwards hand in hand. Every now and then he said something amorous or amusing to her, but not very often because, as he had foreseen, the words did not come to him readily. He was bound to become more fluent as his heart re-opened. She was now speaking more often than he was: not merely more shrewd, but more explicit.

'I'm as close to you as that,' she said, pointing with her free hand to a patch of rocky ground with something growing on it – growing quite profusely, almost exuberantly. She had spoken in reply to one of his questions.

He returned the squeeze of the hand he was holding.

'We'll be like the holly and the ivy,' she volunteered later, 'and then we'll be like the pebble and the shard.'

He thought that both comparisons were, like Harewood's comparisons, somewhat inexact, but, in her case, all the more adorable by reason of it. He kissed her.

At first he could not see their house, though, as they neared it, his eyes seemed to wander round the entire horizon: limited in range, however, by the fact that they were mounting quite steeply. But Nell led the way through the rabbit and snake paths, first to the spring, then upwards once more; and there, needless to say, the house was. Earlier that afternoon, they had already toiled up and down several times with the baggage. The earlier occupants had been sturdy folk; men and women alike; aboriginals.

It was somewhere near the spring that Nell, this time, made her possibly crucial declaration.

'I've run away,' she said, as if previously she had been afraid to speak the words. 'Take care of me.'

They entered.

When they had been lugging in the food and the blankets and the cressets and the pans, he had of policy refrained from even glancing at the walls of the house; but what could it matter now? For the glorious and overwhelming moment at least? And, judging by recent experience, the moment might even prove a noticeably long moment. Time might again stand still. Time sometimes did if one had not expected it.

Therefore, from as soon as they entered, he stared round at intervals quite brazenly, though not when Nell was looking at him, as for so much of the time she was now doing.

The upshot was anti-climax: here was not the stark, familiar bedroom in the rectory, and Stephen realized that he had not yet acquired points, or areas, of reference and comparison. He was at liberty to deem that they might never be needed.

Nell was ordering things, arranging things, even beginning to prepare things: all as if she had been a *diplomée* of a domestic college; as if she had been blessed with a dedicated mamma or aunt. After all, thought Stephen, as he watched her and intercepted her, her appearance is largely that of an ordinary modern girl.

He loved her.

He turned his back upon her earlier curious intimations. She had run away from it all; and had even stated as much, unasked and unprompted. Henceforth, an ordinary modern girl was what for him she should firmly be; though loyaller, tenderer, stronger than any other.

When, in the end, languishingly they went upstairs, this time they wrapt themselves in lovely new blankets, but Stephen was in no doubt at all that still there was only the one mark on her.

Conceivably, even, it was a slightly smaller mark.

He would no longer detect, no longer speculate, no longer be anxious, no longer imagine. No more mortal marks and corruptions. For example, he would quite possibly never sleep in that room at the rectory again.

Thus, for a week, he counted the good things only, as does a sundial. They were many and the silken sequence of them seemed to extend over a lifetime. He recollected the Christian Science teaching that evil is a mere illusion. He clung to the thesis that time is no absolute.

Nell had the knack of supplementing the food he had purchased with fauna and flora that she brought back from the moor. While, at a vague hour of the morning, he lay long among the blankets, simultaneously awake and asleep, she went forth, and never did she return empty-handed, seldom, indeed, other than laden. He was at last learning not from talk but from experience, even though from someone else's experience, how long it really was possible to live without shops, without bureaucratically and commercially modified products, without even watered cash. All that was needed was to be alone in the right place with the right person.

He even saw it as possible that the two of them might remain in the house indefinitely: were it not that his 'disappearance' would inevitably be 'reported' by someone, doubtless first by Arthur Thread in the office, so that his early exposure was inevitable. That, after all, was a main purpose of science: to make things of all kinds happen sooner than they otherwise would.

Each morning, after Nell had returned from her sorties and had set things in the house to rights, she descended naked to the spring and sank beneath its waters. She liked Stephen to linger at the rim watching her, and to him it seemed that she disappeared in the pool altogether, vanished from sight, and clear though the water was, the clearest, Stephen surmised, that he had ever lighted upon. Beyond doubt, therefore, the little pool really was peculiarly deep, as Nell had always said: it would be difficult to distinguish between the natural movements of its ever-gleaming surface, and movements that might emanate from a submerged naiad. It gave Stephen special pleasure that they drank exclusively from the pool in which Nell splashed about, but, partly for that reason, he confined his own lustrations to dabblings from the edge, like a tripper.

Stephen learned by experience, a new experience, the difference between drinking natural water and drinking safeguarded water, as from a sanitized public convenience. When she emerged from the pool, Nell each day shook her short hair like one glad to be alive, and each day her hair seemed to be dry in no time.

One morning, she washed her shirt and trousers in the pool, having no replacements as far as Stephen could see. The garments took longer to dry than she did, and Nell remained unclothed for most of the day, even though there were clouds in the sky. Clouds made little difference anyway, nor quite steady rain, nor drifting mountain mist. The last named merely fortified the peace and happiness.

'Where did you get those clothes?' asked Stephen, even though as a rule he no longer asked anything.

'I found them. They're nice.'

He said nothing for a moment.

'*Aren't* they nice?' she inquired anxiously.

'Everything to do with you and in and about and around you is nice in every possible way. You are perfect. Everything concerned with you is perfect.'

She smiled gratefully and went back, still unclothed, to the house, where she was stewing up everything together in one of the new pots. The pot had already leaked, and it had been she who had mended the leak, with a preparation she had hammered and kneaded while Stephen had merely looked on in delighted receptivity, wanting her as she worked.

He had a number of books in his bag, reasonably well chosen, because he had supposed that on most evenings at the rectory he would be retiring early; but now he had no wish to read anything. He conjectured that he would care little if the capacity to read somehow faded from him. He even went so far as to think that, given only a quite short time, it might possibly do so.

At moments, they wandered together about the moor; he, as like as not, with his hand on her breast, on that breast pocket of hers which contained his original and only letter to her, and which she had carefully taken out and given to him when washing the garment, and later carefully replaced. Than these perambulations few excursions could be more uplifting, but Stephen was wary all the same, knowing that if they were to meet anyone, however blameless, the spell might break, and paradise end.

31

Deep happiness can but be slighted by third parties, whosoever, without exception, they be. No one is so pure as to constitute an exception.

And every night the moon shone through the small windows and fell across their bed and their bodies in wide streaks, oddly angled.

'You are like a long, sweet parsnip,' Stephen said. 'Succulent but really rather tough.'

'I know nothing at all,' she replied. 'I only know you.'

The mark below her shoulder stood out darkly, but, God be praised, in isolation. What did the rapidly deteriorating state of the walls and appurtenances matter by comparison with that?

But in due course, the moon, upon which the seeding and growth of plants and of the affections largely depend, had entered its dangerous third quarter.

Stephen had decided that the thing he had to do was take Nell back quickly and quietly to London, and return as soon as possible with his reinvigorated car, approaching as near as he could, in order to collect their possessions in the house. The machine would go there, after all, if he drove it with proper vigour; though it might be as well to do it at a carefully chosen hour, in order to evade Harewood, Doreen, and the general life of the village.

He saw no reason simply to abandon all his purchases and, besides, he felt obscurely certain that it was unlucky to do so, though he had been unable to recall the precise belief. Finally, it would seem likely that some of the varied accessories in the house might be useful in Stephen's new life with Nell. One still had to be practical at times, just as one had to be firm at times.

Nell listened to what he had to say, and then said she would do whatever he wanted. The weather was entirely fair for the moment.

When the purchased food had finally run out, and they were supposedly dependent altogether upon what Nell could bring in off the moor, they departed from the house, though not, truthfully, for that reason. They left everything behind them and walked down at dusk past Burton's Clough to the village. Stephen knew the time of the last bus which connected with a train to London. It was something he knew wherever he was. In a general way, he had of course always liked the train journey and disliked the bus journey.

It was hard to imagine what Nell would make of such experiences, and of those inevitably to come. Though she always said she knew nothing, she seemed surprised by nothing either. Always she brought back to Stephen the theories that there were two kinds of knowledge; sometimes of the same things.

All the others in the bus were old age pensioners. They had been visiting younger people and were now returning. They sat alone, each as far from each as space allowed. In the end, Stephen counted them. There seemed to be eight, though it was hard to be sure in the bad light, and with several pensioners already slumped forward.

There were at least two kinds of bad light also; the beautiful dim light of the house on the moor, and the depressing light in a nationalized bus. Stephen recalled Ellen Terry's detestation of all electric light. And of course there were ominous marks on the dirty ceiling of the bus and on such of the side panels as Stephen could see, including that on the far side of Nell, who sat beside him, with her head on his shoulder, more like an ordinary modern girl than ever. Where could she have learned that when one was travelling on a slow, ill-lighted bus with the man one loved, one put one's head on his shoulder?

But it was far more that she had somewhere, somehow learned. The slightest physical contact with her induced in Stephen a third dichotomy: the reasonable, rather cautious person his whole life and career surely proved him to be, was displaced by an all but criminal visionary. Everything turned upon such capacity as he might have left to change the nature of time.

The conductor crept down the dingy passage and sibilated in Stephen's ear. 'We've got to stop here. Driver must go home. Got a sick kid. There'll be a reserve bus in twenty minutes. All right?'

The conductor didn't bother to explain to the pensioners. They would hardly have understood. For them, the experience itself would be ample. A few minutes later, everyone was outside in the dark, though no one risked a roll call. The lights in the bus had been finally snuffed out, and the crew were making off, aclank with the accoutrements of their tenure, spanners, and irregular metal boxes, and enamelled mugs.

Even now, Nell seemed unsurprised and unindignant. She, at least, appeared to acknowledge that all things have an end, and to be acting on that intimation. As usual, Stephen persuaded her to don his heavy sweater.

*

It was very late indeed, before they were home; though Stephen could hardly use the word now that not only was Elizabeth gone, but also there was somewhere else, luminously better – or, at least, so decisively different – and, of course, a new person too.

Fortunately, the train had been very late, owing to signal trouble, so that they had caught it and been spared a whole dark night of it at the station, as in a story. Stephen and Nell had sat together in the buffet, until they had been ejected, and the striplighting quelled. Nell had never faltered. She had not commented even when the train, deprived of what railwaymen call its 'path', had fumbled its way to London, shunting backwards nearly as often as running forwards. In the long, almost empty, excursion-type coach had been what Stephen could by now almost complacently regard as the usual smears and blotches.

'Darling, aren't you cold?' He had other, earlier sweaters to lend.

She shook her head quite vigorously.

After that, it had been easy for Stephen to close his eyes almost all the way. The other passenger had appeared to be a fireman in uniform, though of course without helmet. It was hard to believe that he would suddenly rise and rob them, especially as he was so silently slumbering. Perhaps he was all the time a hospital porter or a special messenger or an archangel.

On the Benares table which filled the hall of the flat (a wedding present from Harewood and poor Harriet, who, having been engaged in their teens, had married long ahead of Stephen and Elizabeth), was a parcel, weighty but neat.

'Forgive me,' said Stephen. 'I never can live with unopened parcels or letters.'

He snapped the plastic string in a second and tore through the glyptal wrapping. It was a burly tome entitled *Lichen, Moss, and Wrack. Usage and Abusage in Peace and War. A Military and Medical Abstract.* Scientific works so often have more title than imaginative works.

Stephen flung the book back on the table. It fell with a heavy clang.

'Meant for my brother. It's always happening. People don't seem to know there's a difference between us.'

He gazed at her. He wanted to see nothing else.

She looked unbelievably strange in her faded trousers and

the sweater Elizabeth had made. Elizabeth would have seen a ghost and fainted. Elizabeth really did tend to faint in the sudden presence of the occult.

'We are not going to take it to him. It'll have to be posted. I'll get the Department to do it tomorrow.'

He paused. She smiled at him, late though it was.

Late or early? What difference did it make? It was not what mattered.

'I told you that I should have to go to the Department tomorrow. There's a lot to explain.'

She nodded. 'And then we'll go back?' She had been anxious about that ever since they had started. He had not known what to expect.

'Yes. After a few days.'

Whatever he intended in the first place, he had never made it clear to her where they would be living in the longer run. This was partly because he did not know himself. The flat, without Elizabeth, really was rather horrible. Stephen had not forgotten Elizabeth for a moment. How could he have done? Nor could Stephen wonder that Nell did not wish to live in the flat. The flat was disfigured and puny.

Nell still smiled with her usual seeming understanding. He had feared that by now she would demur at his reference to a few days, and had therefore proclaimed it purposefully.

He smiled back at her. 'I'll buy you a dress.'

She seemed a trifle alarmed.

'It's time you owned one.'

'I don't own anything.'

'Yes, you do. You own me. Let's go to bed, shall we?'

But she spoke. 'What's this?'

As so often happens, Nell had picked up and taken an interest in the thing he would least have wished.

It was a large, lumpy shopping bag from a craft room in Burnham-on-Sea, where Elizabeth and he had spent an unwise week in their early days. What the Orient was to Harriet, the seaside had been to Elizabeth. Sisters-in-law often show affinities. The shopping bag had continued in regular use ever since, and not only for shopping, until Elizabeth had been no longer mobile.

'It's a bag made of natural fibres,' said Stephen. 'It belonged to my late wife.'

'It smells. It reminds me.'

'Many things here remind *me*,' said Stephen. 'But a new

35

page has been turned.' He kept forgetting that Nell was un-accustomed to book metaphors.

She appeared to be holding the bag out to him. Though not altogether knowing why, he took it from her. He then regretted doing so.

It was not so much the smell of the bag. He was entirely accustomed to that. It was that, in his absence, the bag had become sodden with dark growths, outside and inside. It had changed character completely.

Certainly the bag had been perfectly strong and serviceable when last he had been in contact with it; though for the moment he could not recollect when that had been. He had made little use of the bag when not under Elizabeth's direction.

He let the fetid mass fall on top of the book on the brass table.

'Let's forget everything,' he said. 'We still have a few hours.'

'Where do I go?' she asked, smiling prettily.

'Not in there,' he cried, as she put her hand on one of the doors. He very well knew that he must seem far too excitable. He took a pull on himself. 'Try *this* room.'

When Elizabeth had become ill, the double bed had been moved into the spare room. It had been years since Stephen had slept in that bed, though, once again, he could not in the least recall how many years. The first step towards mastering time is always to make time meaningless.

It was naturally wonderful to be at long last in a fully equipped deep double bed with Nell. She had shown no expectation of being invited to borrow one of Elizabeth's expensive nightdresses. Nell was a primitive still, and it was life or death to keep her so. He had never cared much for flowing, gracious bedwear in any case; nor had the wonder that was Elizabeth seemed to him to need such embellishments.

But he could not pretend, as he lay in Nell's strong arms and she in his, that the condition of the spare room was in the least reassuring. Before he had quickly turned off the small bedside light, the new marks on the walls had seemed like huge inhuman faces; and the effect was all the more alarming in that these walls had been painted, inevitably long ago, by Elizabeth in person, and had even been her particular domestic display piece. The stained overall she had worn for the task, still hung in the cupboard next door, lest the need arise again.

It was always the trouble. So long as one was far from the

place once called home, one could successfully cast secondary matters from the mind, or at least from the hurting part of it; but from the moment of return, in fact from some little while before that, one simply had to recognize that, for most of one's life, secondary matters were just about all there were. Stephen had learned ages ago that secondary matters were always the menace.

Desperation, therefore, possibly made its contribution to the mutual passion that charged the few hours available to them.

Within a week, the walls might be darkened all over; and what could the development after *that* conceivably be?

Stephen strongly suspected that the mossiness, the malady, would become more conspicuously three-dimensional at any moment. Only as a first move, of course.

He managed to close his mind against all secondary considerations and to give love its fullest licence yet.

Thread was in the office before Stephen, even though Stephen had risen most mortifyingly early, and almost sleepless. It was a commonplace that the higher one ascended in the service, the earlier one had to rise, in order to ascend higher still. The lamas never slept at all.

'Feeling better?' Thread could ask such questions with unique irony.

'Much better, thank you.'

'You still look a bit peaky.' Thread was keeping his finger at the place he had reached in the particular file.

'I had a tiresome journey back. I've slept very little.'

'It's always the trouble. Morag and I make sure of a few days to settle in before we return to full schedule.'

'Elizabeth and I used to do that also. It's a bit different now.'

Thread looked Stephen straight in the eyes, or very nearly.

'Let me advise, for what my advice is worth. I recommend you to lose yourself in your work for the next two or three years at the least. Lose yourself completely. Forget everything else. In my opinion, it's always the best thing at these times. Probably the only thing.'

'Work doesn't mean to me what it did.'

'Take yourself in hand, and it soon will again. After all, very real responsibilities do rest in this room. We both understand that quite well. We've reached that sort of level, Stephen. What we do nowadays, *matters*. If you keep that in mind at all times, and I do mean at *all* times, the thought will see you through. I know what I'm talking about.'

37

Thread's eyes were now looking steadily at his finger, lest it had made some move on its own.

'Yes,' said Stephen, 'but you're talking about yourself, you know.'

Stephen was very well aware that the sudden death some years before of Arthur Thread's mother had not deflected Thread for a day from the tasks appointed. Even the funeral had taken place during the weekend; for which Thread had departed on the Friday evening with several major files in his briefcase, as usual. As for Thread's wife, Morag, she was a senior civil servant too, though of course in a very different department. The pair took very little leave in any case, and hardly any of it together. Their two girls were at an expensive boarding school on the far side of France, almost in Switzerland.

'I speak from my own experience,' corrected Thread.

'It appears to me,' said Stephen, 'that I have reached the male climacteric. It must be what's happening to me.'

'I advise you to think again,' said Thread. 'There's no such thing. Anyway you're too young for when it's supposed to be. It's not till you're sixty-three; within two years of retirement.'

Thread could keep his finger in position no longer, lest his arm fall off. 'If you'll forgive me, I'm rather in the middle of something. Put yourself absolutely at ease. I'll be very pleased to have another talk later.'

'What's that mark?' asked Stephen, pointing to the wall above Thread's rather narrow headpiece. So often the trouble seemed to begin above the head. 'Was it there before?'

'I'm sure I don't know. Never forget the whole place is going to be completely done over next year. Now do let me concentrate for a bit.'

As the time for luncheon drew near, another man, Mark Tremble, peeped in.

'Glad to see you back, Stephen. I really am.'

'Thank you, Mark. I wish I could more sincerely say I was glad to *be* back.'

'Who could be? Come and swim?'

Stephen had regularly done it with Mark Tremble and a shifting group of others; usually at lunchtime on several days a week. It had been one of twenty devices for lightening momentarily the weight of Elizabeth's desperation. The bath was in the basement of the building. Soon the bath was to be extended and standardized, and made available at times to additional grades.

'Very well.'

Stephen had at one time proposed to tear back; to be with Nell for a few moments; perhaps to buy that dress: but during the long morning he had decided against all of it.

His real task was to put down his foot with the establishment; to secure such modified pension as he was entitled to; to concentrate, as Thread always concentrated; to depart.

He had not so far said a word about it to anyone in the place.

The two seniors changed in the sketchy cubicles, and emerged almost at the same moment in swimming trunks. There seemed to be no one else in or around the pool that day, though the ebbing and flowing of table tennis were audible through the partition.

'I say, Stephen. What's that thing on your back?'

Stephen stopped dead on the wet tiled floor. 'What thing?'

'It's a bit peculiar. I'm sure it wasn't there before. Before you went away. I'm extremely sorry to mention it.'

'What's it look like?' asked Stephen. 'Can you describe it?'

'The best I can do is that it looks rather like the sort of thing you occasionally see on trees. I think it may simply be something stuck on to you. Would you like me to give it a tug?'

'I think not,' said Stephen. 'I am sorry it upsets you. I'll go back and dress. I think it would be better.'

'Yes,' said Mark Tremble. 'It does upset me. It's best to admit it. Either it's something that will just come off with a good rub, or you'd better see a doctor, Stephen.'

'I'll see what I can do,' said Stephen.

'I don't feel so much like a swim, after all,' said Mark Tremble. 'I'll dress too and then we'll both have a drink. I feel we could both do with one.'

'I'm very sorry about it,' said Stephen. 'I apologize.'

'What have *you* been doing all day?' asked Stephen, as soon as he was back and had changed out of the garments currently normal in the civil service, casual and characterless. 'I hope you've been happy.'

'I found this on the roof.' Nell was holding it in both her hands; which were still very brown. It was a huge lump: mineral, vegetable, who could tell? Or conceivably a proportion of each.

'Your father would be interested.'

Nell recoiled. 'Don't talk like that. It's unlucky.' Indeed, she had nearly dropped the dense mass.

It had been an idiotic response on Stephen's part; mainly the consequence of his not knowing what else to say. He was aware that it was perfectly possible to attain the roof of the building by way of the iron fire ladder, to which, by law, access had to be open to tenants at all hours.

'I could do with a drink,' said Stephen, though he had been drinking virtually the whole afternoon, without Thread even noticing, or without sparing time to acknowledge that he had noticed. Moira, the coloured girl from the typing area, had simply winked her big left eye at Stephen. 'I've had a difficult day.'

'Oh!' Nell's cry was so sincere and eloquent that it was as if he had been mangled in a traffic accident.

'*How* difficult?' she asked.

'It's just that it's been difficult for me to make the arrangements to get away, to leave the place.'

'But we *are* going?' He knew it was what she was thinking about.

'Yes, we are going. I promised.'

He provided Nell with a token drink also. At first she had seemed to be completely new to liquor. Stephen had always found life black without it, but his need for it had become more habitual during Elizabeth's illness. He trusted that Nell and he would, with use, wont, and time, evolve a mutual equilibrium.

At the moment, he recognized that he was all but tight, though he fancied that at such times he made little external manifestation. Certainly Nell would detect nothing; if only because presumably she lacked data. Until now, he had never really been in the sitting room of the flat since his return. Here, the new tendrils on the walls and ceiling struck him as resembling a Portuguese man of war's equipment; the coloured, insensate creature that can sting a swimmer to death at thirty feet distance, and had done so more than once when Elizabeth and he, being extravagant, had stayed at Cannes for a couple of weeks. It had been there that Elizabeth had told him finally she could never have a child. Really that was what they were doing there, though he had not realized it. The man of war business, the two victims, had seemed to have an absurd part in their little drama. No one in the hotel had talked of anything else.

'Let's go to bed *now*,' said Stephen to Nell. 'We can get up again later to eat.'

She put her right hand in his left hand.

Her acquiescence, quiet and beautiful, made him feel compunctious.

'Or are you hungry?' he asked. 'Shall we have something to eat first? I wasn't thinking.'

She shook her head. 'I've been foraging.'

She seemed to know so many quite literary words. He gave no time to wondering where exactly the forage could have taken place. It would be unprofitable. Whatever Nell had brought in would be wholesomer, inestimably better in every way, than food from any shop.

As soon as she was naked, he tried, in the electric light, to scrutinize her. There still seemed to be only the one mark on her body, truly a quite small mark by the standards of the moment, though he could not fully convince himself that it really was contracting.

However, the examination was difficult: he could not let Nell realize what exactly he was doing; the light was not very powerful, because latterly Elizabeth had disliked a strong light anywhere, and he had felt unable to argue; most of all, he had to prevent Nell seeing whatever Mark Tremble had seen on his own person, had himself all the time to lie facing Nell or flat on his back. In any case, he wondered always how much Nell saw that he saw; how much, whatever her utterances and evidences, she analysed of the things that he analysed.

The heavy curtains, chosen and hung by Elizabeth, had, it seemed, remained drawn all day; and by now the simplest thing was for Stephen to switch off what light there was.

Nell, he had thought during the last ten days or ten aeons, was at her very best when the darkness was total.

He knew that heavy drinking was said to increase desire and to diminish performance; and he also knew that it was high time in his life for him to begin worrying about such things. He had even so hinted to Arthur Thread; albeit mainly to startle Thread, and to foretoken his, Stephen's, new life course; even though any such intimation to Thread would be virtually useless. There can be very few to whom most of one's uttered remarks can count for very much.

None the less, Nell and Stephen omitted that evening to arise later; even though Stephen had fully and sincerely intended it.

The next morning, very early the next morning, Nell vouch-safed to Stephen an unusual but wonderful breakfast – if one could apply so blurred a noun to so far-fetched a repast.

Stephen piled into his civil service raiment, systematically non-committal. He was taking particular trouble not to see his own bare back in any looking glass. Fortunately, there was no such thing in the dim bathroom.

'Goodbye, my Nell. Before the weekend we shall be free.'

He supposed that she knew what a weekend was. By now, it could hardly be clearer that she knew almost everything that mattered in the least.

But, during that one night, the whole flat seemed to have become dark green, dark grey, plain black: patched every-where, instead of only locally, as when they had arrived. Stephen felt that the walls, floors, and ceilings were beginning to advance towards one another. The knick-knacks were de-materializing most speedily. When life once begins to move, it can scarcely be prevented from setting its own pace. The very idea of intervention becomes ridiculous.

What was Nell making of these swift and strange occur-rences? All Stephen was sure of was that it would be unwise to take too much for granted. He must hew his way out; if neces-sary, with a bloody axe, as the man in the play put it.

Stephen kissed Nell ecstatically. She was smiling as he shut the door. She might smile, off and on, all day, he thought; smile as she foraged.

By that evening, he had drawn a curtain, thick enough even for Elizabeth to have selected, between his homebound self and the events of the daylight.

There was no technical obstacle to his retirement, and never had been. It was mainly the size of his pension that was affec-ted; and in his new life he seemed able to thrive on very little. A hundred costly substitutes for direct experience could be rejected. An intense reality, as new as it was old, was burning down on him like clear sunlight or heavenly fire or poetry.

It was only to be expected that his colleagues should shrink back a little. None the less, Stephen had been disconcerted by how far some of them had gone. They would have been very much less concerned, he fancied, had he been an acknowledged defector, about to stand trial. Such cases were now all in the day's work: there were routines to be complied with, though not too strictly. Stephen realized that his appearance was probably against him. He was not sure what he looked like from hour to hour, and he was taking no steps to find out.

Still, the only remark that was passed, came from Toby Strand, who regularly passed remarks.

'Good God, Stephen, you're looking like death warmed up. I should go home to the wife. You don't want to pass out in this place.'

Stephen looked at him.

'Oh God, I forgot. Accept my apology.'

'That's perfectly all right, Toby,' said Stephen. 'And as for the other business, you'll be interested to learn that I've decided to retire.'

'Roll on the day for one and all,' said Toby Strand, ever the *vox populi*.

Mercifully, Stephen's car had been restored to a measure of health, so that the discreet bodywork gleamed slightly in the evening lustre as he drove into the rented parking space.

'Nell, we can leave at cockcrow!'

'I forgot about buying you that dress.'

He was standing in his bath gown, looking at her in the wide bed. The whole flat was narrowing and blackening, and at that early hour the electric light was even weaker than usual.

'I shan't need a dress.'

'You must want a change sometime.'

'No. I want nothing to change.'

He gazed at her. As so often, he had no commensurate words.

'We'll stop somewhere on the way,' he said.

They packed the rehabilitated car with essentials for the simple life; with things to eat and drink on the journey and after arrival. Stephen, though proposing to buy Nell a dress, because one never knew what need might arise, was resolved against dragging her into a roadside foodplace. He took all he could, including, surreptitiously, some sad souvenirs of Elizabeth, but he recognized plainly enough that there was almost everything remaining to be done with the flat, and that he would have to return one day to do it, whether or not Nell came with him. In the meantime, it was difficult to surmount what was happening to the flat, or to him. Only Nell was sweet, calm, and changeless in her simple clothes. If only the nature of time were entirely different!

'You'll be terribly cold.'

She seemed never to say it first, never to think of it.

He covered her with sweaters and rugs. He thought of offering her a pair of his own warm trousers, but they would be so hopelessly too wide and long.

Islington was a misty marsh, as they flitted through; Holloway pink as a desert flamingo. The scholarly prison building was wrapped in fire. Finsbury Park was crystal as a steppe; Manor House deserted as old age.

When, swift as thoughts of love, they reached Grantham, they turned aside to buy Nell's dress. She chose a rough-textured white one, with the square neck outlined in black, and would accept nothing else, nothing else at all. She even refused to try on the dress and she refused to wear it out of the shop. Stephen concurred, not without a certain relief, and carried the dress to the car in a plastic bag. The car was so congested that a problem arose.

'I'll sit on it,' said Nell.

Thus the day went by as in a dream: though there are few such dreams in one lifetime. Stephen, for sure, had never known a journey so rapt, even though he could seldom desist from staring and squinting for uncovenanted blemishes upon and around the bright coachwork. Stephen recognized that, like everyone else, he had spent his life without living; even though he had had Elizabeth for much of the time to help him through, as she alone was able.

Northwards, they ran into a horse fair. The horses were everywhere, and, among them, burlesques of men bawling raucously, and a few excited girls.

'Oh!' cried Nell.

'Shall we stop?'

'No,' said Nell. 'Not stop.'

She was plainly upset.

'Few fairs like that one are left,' said Stephen, as he sat intimately, eternally beside her. 'The motors have been their knell.'

'Knell,' said Nell.

Always it was impossible to judge how much she knew.

'Nell,' said Stephen affectionately. But it was at about that moment he first saw a dark, juicy crack in the polished metalwork of the bonnet.

'Nell,' said Stephen again; and clasped her hand, always brown, always warm, always living and loving. The huge geometrical trucks were everywhere, and it was an uncircumspect

44

move for Stephen to make. But it was once more too misty for the authorities to see very much, to take evidence that could be sworn to.

The mist was more like fog as they wound through Harewood's depopulated community. Harewood really should marry Doreen as soon as it becomes possible, thought Stephen, and make a completely new start in life, perhaps have a much better type of youngster, possibly and properly for the cloth.

Stephen was struck with horror to recollect that he had forgotten all about the costly book which had been almost certainly intended for Harewood, and which Harewood would be among the very few fully to appreciate and rejoice in. The book had not really been noticeable at first light in the eroding flat, but his lapse perturbed Stephen greatly.

'A fungus and an alga living in a mutually beneficial relationship,' he said under his breath.

'What's that?' asked Nell.

'It's the fundamental description of a lichen. You should know that.'

'Don't talk about it.'

He saw that she shuddered; she who never even quaked from the cold.

'It's unlucky,' she said.

'I'm sorry, Nell. I was thinking of the book we left behind, and the words slipped out.'

'We're better without the book.'

'It wasn't really our book.'

'We did right in leaving it.'

He realized that it had been the second time when, without thinking, he had seemed ungracious about the big step she had taken for him: the second time at least.

Therefore, he simply answered, 'I expect so.'

He remained uneasy. He had taken due care not to drive past the crumbling rectory, but nothing could prevent the non-delivery of Harewood's expensive book being an odious default, a matter of only a few hundred yards. To confirm the guilt, a middle-aged solitary woman at the end of the settlement suddenly pressed both hands to her eyes, as if to prevent herself from seeing the passing car, even in the poor light.

The ascending track was rougher and rockier than on any of Stephen's previous transits. It was only to be expected, Stephen realized. Moreover, to mist was now added dusk. At the putative Burton's Clough, he had to take care not to drive over the edge of the declivity; and thereafter he concentrated upon not colliding with the overgrown stony waymark. Shapeless creatures were beginning to emerge which may no longer appear by daylight even in so relatively remote a region. Caution was compelled upon every count.

Thus it was full night when somehow they reached the spot where the track seemed simply to end – with no good reason supplied, as Stephen had always thought. Elizabeth would have been seriously upset if somehow she had seen at such a spot the familiar car in which she had taken so many unforgettable outings, even when a virtual invalid. She might have concluded that at long last she had reached the final bourne.

The moon, still in its third quarter, managed to glimmer, like a fragrance, through the mist; but there could be no visible stars. Stephen switched on his flash, an item of official supply.

'We don't need it,' said Nell. 'Please not.'

Nell was uncaring of cold, of storm, of fog, of fatigue. Her inner strength was superb, and Stephen loved it. But her indifference to such darkness as this reminded Stephen of her father, that wonderful entity, whom it was so unlucky ever to mention, probably even to think of. None the less, Stephen turned back the switch. He had noticed before that he was doing everything she said.

As best he could, he helped her to unload the car, and followed her along the narrow paths through the damp heather. Naturally, he could not see a trace of the house, and he suddenly realized that, though they struggled in silence, he could not even hear the gently heaving spring. They were making a pile at the spot where the house must be; and Nell never put a foot wrong in finding the pile a second, third, and even fourth time. Much of the trip was steep, and Stephen was quite winded once more by his fourth climb in almost no moonlight at all, only the faint smell of moonlight; but when, that time, he followed Nell over the tangled brow, the mist fell away for a moment, as mist on mountains intermittently does, and at last Stephen could see the house quite clearly.

He looked at Nell standing there, pale and mysterious as the moonlight began to fade once more.

'Have you still got my letter?'

She put her hand on her breast pocket.

'Of course I have.'

They re-entered the house, for which no key was ever deemed necessary. It might be just as well, for none was available.

Stephen realized at once that what they were doing was moving into the house pretty finally; not, as he had so recently proposed, preparing to move out of it in a short time. It was clear that once Nell truly and finally entered one's life, one had simply to accept the consequences. Stephen could perceive well enough that Nell was at every point moved by forces in comparison with which he was moved by inauthentic fads. Acquiescence was the only possibility. The admixture in Nell of ignorance and wisdom, sometimes even surface sophistication, was continuously fascinating. In any case, she had left familiar surroundings and completely changed her way of life for him. He must do the same for her without end; and he wished it.

The moonlight was now insufficient to show the state of the walls or the curiously assorted furnishings or the few personal traps he had omitted to bear to London. Stephen had worn gloves to drive and had not removed them to lug. He wore them still.

None the less, when he said, 'Shall we have a light now?' he spoke with some reluctance.

"Now,' said Nell. 'We're at home now.'

He fired up some of the rough cressets he had managed to lay hands on when he had borrowed the sottish Jarrold's Land-Rover.

Nell threw herself against him. She kissed him again and again.

As she did so, Stephen resolved to look at nothing more. To look was not necessarily to see. He even thought he apprehended a new vein of truth in what Nell had said on that second day, still only a very short time ago, about her father.

Nell went upstairs and changed into the dress he had bought her. She had done it without a hint, and he took for granted that she had done it entirely to give pleasure. In aspect, she was no longer a part of nature, merging into it, an oread. Not surprisingly, the dress did not fit very well, but on Nell it looked like a peplos. She was a sybil. Stephen was scarcely surprised. There was no need for him to see anything other than Nell's white and black robe, intuitively selected, prophetically insisted upon; quite divine, as ordinary normal girls used to say.

When he dashed off his gloves in order to caress her, he regarded only her eyes and her raiment; but later there was eating to be done, and it is difficult, in very primitive lighting, to eat without at moments noticing one's hands. These particular hands seemed at such moments to be decorated with horrid subfusc smears, quite new. Under the circumstances, they might well have come from inside Stephen's driving gloves; warm perhaps, but, like most modern products, of no precise or very wholesome origin. If ineradicable, the marks were appalling; not to be examined for a single second.

When Nell took off her new dress, Stephen saw at once (how else but at once?) that her own small single mark had vanished. She was as totally honied as harvest home, and as luscious, and as rich.

Stephen resolved that in the morning, if there was one, he would throw away all the souvenirs of Elizabeth he had brought with him. They could be scattered on the moor as ashes in a memorial garden, but better far. The eyes that were watching from behind the marks on the walls and ceilings and utensils glinted back at him, one and all. The formless left hands were his to shake.

In the nature of things, love was nonpareil that night; and there was music too. Nell's inner being, when one knew her, when one really knew her, was as matchless as her unsullied body. Goodness is the most powerful aphrodisiac there is, though few have the opportunity of learning. Stephen had learned long before from the example of Elizabeth, and now he was learning again.

Time finally lost all power.

The music became endlessly more intimate.

'God!' cried Stephen suddenly. 'That's Schumann!' He had all but leapt in the air. Ridiculously.

'Where?' asked Nell. Stephen realized that he was virtually sitting on her. He dragged himself up and was standing on the floor.

'That music. It's Schumann.'

'I hear no music.'

'I don't suppose you do.'

Stephen spoke drily and unkindly, as he too often did, but he knew that everything was dissolving.

For example, he could see on the dark wall the large portrait of Elizabeth by a pupil of Philip de Laszlo which had hung in their conjugal bedroom. The simulacrum was faint and ghostly, like the music, but he could see it clearly enough for present purposes, dimly self-illuminated.

He had taken that picture down with his own hands, years and years ago; and the reason had been, as he now instantly

48

recalled, that the light paintwork had speedily become blotched and suffused. They had naturally supposed it to be something wrong with the pigments, and had spoken between themselves of vegetable dyes and the superiorities of Giotto and Mantegna. Stephen had hidden the festering canvas in the communal basement storeroom, and had forgotten about it immediately. Now he could see it perfectly well, not over the bed, but in front of it, as always.

'Come back,' said Nell. 'Come back to me.'

The music, which once, beyond doubt, had been the music of love, was dying away. In its place, was a persistent snuffling sound, as if the house from outside, or the room from inside, was being cased by a wolf.

'What's that noise? That noise of an animal?'

'Come back to me,' said Nell. 'Come back, Stephen.' Perhaps she was quite consciously dramatizing a trifle.

He had gone to the window, but of course could see nothing save the misleading huge shapes of the flapping birds.

He went back to the bed and stretched out both his hands to Nell. He was very cold.

Though there was almost no light, Nell grasped his two hands and drew him down to her.

'You see and hear so many things, Stephen,' she said.

As she spoke, he had, for moments, a vision of a different kind.

Very lucidly, he saw Nell and himself living together, but, as it might be, in idealized form, vaguely, intensely. He knew that it was an ideal of which she was wonderfully capable, perhaps because she was still so young. All that was required of him was some kind of trust.

Held by her strong hands and arms, he leaned over her and faltered.

'But whatever animal is that?' he demanded.

She released his hands and curled up like a child in distress. She had begun to sob.

'Oh, Nell,' he cried. He fell on her and tried to reach her. Her muscles were as iron, and he made no impression at all.

In any case, he could not stop attending to the snuffling, if that was the proper word for it. He thought it was louder now. The noise seemed quite to fill the small, low, dark, remote room; to leave no space for renewed love, however desperate the need, however urgent the case.

Suddenly, Stephen knew. A moment of insight had come to him, an instinctual happening.

49

He divined that outside or inside the little house was Nell's father.

It was one reason why Nell was twisted in misery and terror. Her father had his own ways of getting to the truth of things. She had said so.

Stephen sat down on the bed and put his hand on her shoulder. Though he was shivering dreadfully, he had become almost calm. The process of illumination was suggesting to him the simple truth that, for Nell too, the past must be ever present. And for her it was, in common terms, the terms after which he himself was so continuously half-aspiring, a past most absurdly recent. How could he tell what experiences were hers, parallel to, but never meeting, his own?

It would be no good even making the obvious suggestion that they should dwell far away. She could never willingly leave the moor, even if it should prove the death of her; no more than he had been able all those years to leave the flat, the job, the life, all of which he had hated, and been kept alive in only by Elizabeth.

'What's the best thing to do, Nell?' Stephen inquired of her. 'Tell me and we'll do it exactly. Tell me. I think I'm going to dress while you do so. And then perhaps you'd better dress too.'

After all, he began to think, there was little that Nell had ever said about her father or her sister which many girls might not have said when having in mind to break away. He would not have wanted a girl who had no independent judgement of her own family.

The processes of insight and illumination were serving him well, and the phantom portrait seemed to have dissipated completely. The snuffling and snorting continued. It was menacing and unfamiliar, but conceivably it was caused merely by a common or uncommon but essentially manageable creature of the moors. Stephen wished he had brought his revolver (another official issue), even though he had had no experience in discharging it. He could not think how he had omitted it. Then he recollected the horrible furred-up flat, and shuddered anew, within his warm clothes.

For the first time it occurred to him that poor Elizabeth might be trying, from wherever she was, to warn him. Who could tell that Harriet had not made a miraculous recovery (she was, after all, in touch with many different faiths); and was not now ready once more to accept him for a spell into the life at the rectory?

Nell was being very silent.

Stephen went back to the bed.

'Nell.'

He saw that she was not in the bed at all, but standing by the door.

'Nell.'

'Hush,' she said. 'We must hide.'

'Where do we do that?'

'I shall show you.' He could see that she was back in her shirt and trousers; a part of the natural scene once more. Her white dress glinted on the boards of the floor.

To Stephen her proposal seemed anomalous. If it really was her father outside, he could penetrate everywhere, and according to her own statement. If it was a lesser adversary, combat might be better than concealment.

Nell and Stephen went downstairs in the ever more noisy darkness, and Nell, seemingly without effort, lifted a stone slab in the kitchen floor. Stephen could not quite make out how she had done it. Even to find the right slab, under those conditions, was a feat.

'All the houses have a place like this,' Nell explained.

'Why?' inquired Stephen. Surely Nell's father was an exceptional phenomenon? Certainly the supposed motion of him was akin to no other motion Stephen had ever heard.

'To keep their treasure,' said Nell.

'You are my treasure,' said Stephen.

'You are mine,' responded Nell.

There were even a few hewn steps, or so they felt to him. Duly it was more a coffer than a room, Stephen apprehended; but in no time Nell had the stone roof down on them, almost with a flick of the elbow, weighty though the roof must have been.

Now the darkness was total; something distinctly different from the merely conventional darkness above. All the same, Stephen of all people could not be unaware that the stone sides and stone floor and stone ceiling of the apartment were lined with moss and lichen. No doubt he had developed sixth and seventh senses in that arena, but the odour could well have sufficed of itself.

'How do we breathe?'

'There is a sort of pipe. That's where the danger lies.'

'You mean it might have become blocked up?'

'No.'

He did not care next to suggest that it might now be blocked deliberately. He had already made too many tactless suggestions of that kind.

She saved him the trouble of suggesting anything. She spoke in the lowest possible voice.

'He might come through.'

It was the first time she had admitted, even by implication, who it was: outside or inside – or both. Stephen fully realized that. It was difficult for him not to give way to the shakes once more, but he clung to the vague possibilities he had tried to sort out upstairs.

'I should hardly think so,' he said. 'But how long do you suggest we wait?'

'It will be better when it's day. He has to eat so often.'

It would be utterly impossible for Stephen to inquire any further; not at the moment. He might succeed in finding his way to the bottom of it all later. He was already beginning to feel cramped, and the smell of the fungi and the algae were metaphorically choking him and the moss realistically tickling him; but he put his arm round Nell in the blackness, and could even feel his letter safe against her soft breast.

She snuggled back at him; as far as circumstances permitted. He had only a vague idea of how big or small their retreat really was.

Nell spoke again in that same lowest possible voice. She could communicate, even in the most pitchy of blackness, while hardly making a sound.

'He's directly above us. He's poised.'

Stephen mustered up from his school days a grotesque recollection of some opera: the final scene. The Carl Rosa had done it: that one scene only; after the film in a cinema near Marble Arch. Elizabeth had thought the basic operatic convention too far-fetched to be taken seriously; except perhaps for Mozart, who could always be taken seriously.

'I love you,' said Stephen. No doubt the chap in the opera had said something to the like effect, but had taken more time over it.

Time: that was always the decisive factor. But time had been mastered at last.

'I love *you*,' said Nell, snuggling ever closer; manifesting her feeling in every way she could.

*

Curiously enough, it was at the verge of the small, lustrous pool that Stephen's body was ultimately found.

A poor old man, apparently resistent to full employment and even to the full security that goes with it, found the corpse, though, after all those days or weeks, the creatures and forces of the air and of the moor had done their worst to it, or their best. There was no ordinary skin anywhere. Many people in these busy times would not even have reported the find.

There were still, however, folk who believed, or at least had been told that the pool was bottomless; and even at the inquest a theory was developed that Stephen had been wandering about on the moor and had died of sudden shock upon realizing at what brink he stood. The coroner, who was a doctor of medicine, soon disposed of that hypothesis.

None the less, the actual verdict had to be open; which satisfied nobody. In these times, people expect clear answers; whether right or wrong.

Harewood, almost his pristine self by then, inquired into the possibility of a memorial service in London, which he was perfectly prepared to come up and conduct. After all, Stephen was an OBE already, and could reasonably hope for more.

The view taken was that Stephen had been missing for so long, so entirely out of the official eye, that the proper moment for the idea was regrettably, but irreversibly, past.

The funeral took place, therefore, in Harewood's own church, where the father and the grandfather of both the deceased and the officiant had shepherded so long with their own quiet distinction. People saw that no other solution had ever really been thinkable.

Doreen had by now duly become indispensible to the rector; in the mysterious absence of Stephen, to whom the rector had specifically allotted that function. At the funeral, she was the only person in full black. Not even the solitary young man from the Ministry emulated her there. It had not been thought appropriate to place Stephen's OBE on the coffin, but during the service the rector noticed a scrap of lichen thereon which was different entirely, he thought, from any of the species on the walls, rafters, and floors of the church. Performing his office, Harewood could not at once put a name to the specimen. The stuff that already lined the open grave was even more peculiar; and Harewood was more than a little relieved when the whole affair was finally over, the last tributes paid, and he free

53

to stumble back to Doreen's marmite toast, and lilac peignoir. The newest number of the *Journal* had come in only just before, but Harewood did not so much as open it that evening.

As Stephen's will had been rendered ineffective by Elizabeth's decease, Harewood, as next of kin, had to play a part, whether he felt competent or not, in winding everything up. Fortunately, Doreen had been taking typing lessons, and had bought a second-hand machine with her own money.

The flat was found to be in the most shocking state, almost indescribable. It was as if there had been no visitors for years; which, as Harewood at once pointed out, had almost certainly been more or less the case, since the onset of Elizabeth's malady, an epoch ago.

A single, very unusual book about Harewood's own speciality was found. It had been published in a limited edition: a minute one, and at a price so high that Harewood himself had not been among the subscribers.

'Poor fellow!' said Harewood. 'I never knew that he was really interested. One can make such mistakes.'

The valuable book had of course to be disposed of for the benefit of the estate.

Stephen's car was so far gone that it could be sold only for scrap; but, in the event, it never was sold at all, because no one could be bothered to drag it away. If one knows where to look, one can see the bits of it still.

Steve Rasnic
City fishing

*Steve Rasnic appeared in my mail one day with four stories,
two poems, and a letter telling me about* Umbral, *the quarterly
of speculative poetry which he edits. Since then he has married
and changed his name to Steve Rasnic Tem, and earned himself
a considerable reputation as a writer of horror fiction, mostly
quiet and enigmatic. This was his first professionally published
story.*

After weeks of talking about it, Jimmy's father finally decided
to take his son fishing. Jimmy's friend Bill, and Bill's father
who was Jimmy's dad's best friend, also were to go. Their
mothers didn't approve.

Jimmy wasn't sure he approved either, actually. He had
somewhat looked forward to the event, thought that he should
go, but as the actual moment of departure approached he knew
fishing was the last thing he wanted to do. It seemed to be
important to his father, however, so he would go just to please
him.

'Now look what we have here, Jimmy.' Jimmy's father was
tall and dark-haired, and the deep resonance in his voice made
his every word seem like a command. He gestured towards a
display of tools, utensils, and weaponry. 'Hunting knife, pistol,
wire, gunpowder, hooks and sinkers, poles, small animal trap,
steel trap, fish knife, stiletto, .22 rifle, shotgun, derringer. You
have to have all this if you're going to get along in the wild.
Remember that, son.'

Jimmy nodded his head with hesitation.

Bill had run up beside him. 'See what I got!'

Jimmy had noted out of the corner of his eye a dark shape
in Bill's left hand. As he turned to greet his friend he saw that
it was a large, dead crow, its neck spotted with red.

'Dad caught it, then I wrung its neck while we had the feet
tied together. I thought I'd bring it along.'

55

Jimmy nodded his head.

There were loud screams and shouting coming from the house. Jimmy could hear his mother weeping, his father cursing. He walked up to the front steps and watched through the screened door.

He could make out Bill's father, his father, his own mother, and a young red-headed woman back in the shadows who must have been Bill's mother.

'You can't take them!' he could hear his mother sob.

Then there was a struggle as his dad and Bill's dad started forcing the women into the bedroom. Bill's mother was especially squirmy, and Bill's father was slapping her hard across the face to make her stop. His own mother was a bit quieter, especially after Bill's mother got hurt, but she still cried.

His father locked the door. 'We'll let you out, maybe after we get back.' He chuckled and looked at Bill's father. 'Women!'

It all seemed very peculiar.

As Jimmy's father pulled the battered old station wagon out of the driveway he began singing. He looked back over his shoulder at Jimmy and winked. Jimmy figured that singing was all part of fishing since first Bill's father, then Bill, joined in. Jimmy couldn't follow the words.

'Make a real man out of him, I think,' his father said to Bill's father. Bill's father chuckled.

They didn't seem to be getting any further out of the city. In fact, they seemed to be driving into the downtown section, if anything. Jimmy had never been downtown.

'Are you sure this is the right way to the stream, dad?'

Jimmy's father turned and glared at him. Jimmy lowered his head. Bill was gazing out the window and humming.

They passed several old ladies driving cars with packages and shopping bags filling the back seats. His father snickered.

They passed young girls on bicycles, their dresses fluttering in the wind. They passed several strolling couples, and a man with a baby carriage.

Jimmy's father laughed out loud and punched Bill's father on the shoulder. Then they were both laughing, tears in their eyes. Jimmy just stared at them.

The shopping malls were getting smaller, the houses darker and shabby.

Jimmy's father turned to him and said forcefully, almost angrily, 'You're going to make me proud today, Jimmy.'

56

Bill was beginning to get fidgety as he looked out of the window. Every once in a while he would gaze at the back of his father's head, then at the buildings along the street, then back out the rear window. He began scratching his arms in agitation.

Jimmy gazed out of his own window. The pavement was gettting worse – dirtier, and full of potholes. The buildings were getting taller, and older, the further they drove. Jimmy had always thought that only new buildings were tall.

They passed a dark figure, clothed in rags, crumpled on the sidewalk.

Jimmy's father chuckled to himself.

They had left the house at noon. Jimmy had just eaten the lunch of soup and crackers his mother had prepared, so he knew it had been noon.

The sky was getting dark.

Jimmy put his left cheek against the car window and tilted his head back so that he could see above the car. Tall smoke stacks rising out of the dark roofs of the buildings across the street blew night-black clouds into the sky. The smoke stacks were taller than anything he'd ever seen.

Jimmy felt a lurch as the car started down the steep hill. He had been in San Francisco once, and there were lots of hills that steep. He couldn't remember anything like that in their city, but then, he had never been downtown.

Bill was jerking his head back and forth nervously, his eyes very white.

The buildings seemed to get taller and taller, older and older. Some had tall columns out front, or wide wrap-around porches. Many had great iron or wooden doors. There didn't seem to be any people on the streets.

It suddenly occurred to Jimmy that the buildings shouldn't be getting taller as they went downhill. The bottoms of these buildings were lower than the ones further up the hill, behind them, so their rooftops should be lower too. That was the way it had been in San Francisco. But looking out the back window Jimmy could see that the roofs got further away, taller still as they descended the hill. The buildings were reaching into the sky.

Dark figures scurried from the mouth of an alley as they passed. Jimmy couldn't tell what they looked like; it seemed to be almost night time out.

Jimmy's father and Bill's father were perched on the edge of their seats, apparently searching every building corner. His father was humming.

Bill began to cry softly, his feet shuffling over the rumpled carcass of the crow.

The street seemed to get steeper and steeper. Occasionally they would hit a flat place in the road, the car would make a loud banging noise, bounce, then seemingly leap several feet into the air. The car was going faster.

His father laughed out loud and honked the horn once.

It was completely black outside, so black Jimmy could hardly see. The two fathers were singing softly again. The car was picking up speed with every clank, bounce, and leap. Bill was crying and moaning. Jimmy couldn't even see the sky any more, the buildings were so tall. And so old! Bricks were falling into the street even as they passed. Stone fronts were sagging, the foundations obscured by piles of powdered rock. Beams were obviously split and cracked, some hanging down like broken bones. Windowpanes were shattered, curtains torn, casements grimed. Jimmy couldn't understand how the buildings held themselves up, especially when they were so tall. Miles high, it seemed.

If he hadn't been taught better, he would have thought they hung down from the sky on wires. How else could they stand?

He was bouncing wildly up and down in the seat, periodically bumping into Bill, who was crying more loudly than ever. The car was like a train, a plane, a rocket.

A loud clank, then something rattled off to his left. He turned and saw that a hubcap had fallen off and was lying in the street behind them. Shadows moved in a side doorway.

The car was groaning. Bill's wails were even more high-pitched.

'Daddy . . . daddy, Bill's afraid!'

His father stared at the windshield. The car dropped another hubcap.

'Daddy, the hubcaps!'

His father remained motionless, his hands tightly gripping the wheel. A brick fell and bounced off the car. A piece of timber cracked the windshield.

The car squealed, roared, dropped further and further into the heart of the city. It seemed as if they had been going downhill for miles.

58

It suddenly occurred to Jimmy they hadn't passed a cross street in some time.

'Daddy . . . please!'

The car hit a flat section of pavement. The car body clanked loudly, the engine died, and the car rolled a few feet before stopping. They faced an old building with wide doors.

Jimmy looked around. They were in a small court, faced on all sides by the ancient buildings which soared upwards, completely filling the sky. It was so dark he couldn't see their upper storeys.

He looked behind them. The steep road rose like a grey ribbon, dwindling into nothingness at the top. It was the only road into the court.

Everything was quiet. Bill stared silently at his father. The dead crow was at his feet, trampled almost flat by Bill's agitated feet. The floorboard was filled with feathers, pieces of skin, bone and blood.

There were shapes in the darkness between buildings.

Jimmy's father turned to his friend. 'Bottom. We made it.' He began rummaging in his knapsack.

He was handing Jimmy the rifle, smiling, laughing, saying, 'That's my boy!' and 'Today's the day!' when the dark and tattered figures began closing in on the car.

Lisa Tuttle
Sun city

Lisa Tuttle was born in 1952. She received a BA in English from Syracuse University in 1973, and the John W. Campbell Award for the best new science fiction writer of the year (in conjunction with Spider Robinson) in 1974. By now she is equally well-known for her tales of terror, including the novels Familiar Spirit *and* Gabriel. *In a recent anthology for which horror writers were invited to choose their favourite story in the field, William F. Nolan chose the tale you are about to read.*

It was three a.m., the dead, silent middle of the night. Except for the humming of the soft-drink machine in one corner, and the irregular, rumbling cough of the ice machine hidden in an alcove just beyond it, the lobby was quiet. There weren't likely to be any more check-ins until after dawn – all the weary cross-country drivers would be settled elsewhere by now, or grimly determined to push on without a rest.

Clerking the 11 p.m. to 7 a.m. shift was a dull, lonely job, but usually Nora Theale didn't mind it. She preferred working at night, and the solitude didn't bother her. But tonight, for the third night in a row, she was jumpy. It was an irrational nervousness, and it annoyed Nora that she couldn't pin it down. There was always the possibility of robbery, of course, but the Posada del Norte hadn't been hit in the year she had worked there, and Nora didn't think the motel made a very enticing target.

Seeking a cause for her unease, Nora often glanced around the empty lobby and through the glass doors at the parking lot and the highway beyond. She never saw anything out of place – except a shadow which might have been cast by someone moving swiftly through the bluish light of the parking lot. But

61

it was gone in an instant, and she couldn't be sure she had seen it.

Nora picked up the evening paper and tried to concentrate. She read about plans to build a huge fence along the border, to keep illegal aliens out. It was an idea she liked – the constant flow back and forth between Mexico and the United States was one of the things she hated most about El Paso – but she didn't imagine it would work. After a few more minutes of scanning state and national news, Nora tossed the paper into the garbage can. She didn't want to read about El Paso; El Paso bored and depressed and disturbed her. She couldn't wait to leave it.

Casting another uneasy glance around the unchanged lobby, Nora leaned over to the file cabinet and pulled open the drawer where she kept her books. She picked out a mystery by Josephine Tey and settled down to it, determined to win over her nerves.

She read, undisturbed except for a few twinges of unease, until six a.m. when she had to let the man with the newspapers in and make the first wake-up call. The day clerk arrived a few minutes after seven, and that meant it was time for Nora to leave. She gathered her things together into a shoulderbag. She had a lot with her because she had spent the past two days in one of the motel's free rooms rather than go home. But the rooms were all booked up for that night, so she had to clear out. Since her husband had moved out, Nora hadn't felt like spending much time in the apartment that was now hers alone. She meant to move, but since she didn't want to stay in El Paso, it seemed more sensible simply to let the lease run out rather than go to the expense and trouble of finding another temporary home. She meant to leave El Paso just as soon as she got a little money together and decided on a place to go.

She didn't like the apartment, but it was large and cheap. Larry had picked it out because it was close to his office, and he liked to ride his bicycle to work. It wasn't anywhere near the motel where Nora worked, but Nora didn't care. She had her car.

She parked it now in the space behind the small, one-storey apartment complex. It was a hideous place; Nora winced every time she came home to it. It was made of an ugly pink fake-adobe, and had a red-tiled roof. There were some diseased-looking cactuses planted along the concrete walkway, but no grass or trees: water was scarce.

The stench of something long-dead and richly rotting struck

Nora as she opened the door to her apartment. She stepped back immediately, gagging. Her heart raced; she felt, oddly, afraid. But she recovered in a moment – it was just a smell, after all, and in her apartment. She had to do something about it. Breathing through her mouth, she stepped forward again.

The kitchen was clean, the garbage pail empty, and the refrigerator nearly bare. She found nothing there, or in the bedroom or bathroom, that seemed to be the cause of the odour. In the bedroom, she cautiously breathed in through her nose to test the air. It was clean. She walked slowly back to the living room, but there was nothing there, either. The whiff of foulness had gone as if it had never been.

Nora shrugged, and locked the door. It might have been something outside. If she smelled it again, she'd talk to the landlord about it.

There was nothing in the kitchen she could bear the thought of eating, so, after she had showered and changed, Nora walked down to the Seven-Eleven, three blocks away, and bought a few essentials: milk, eggs, bread, Dr Pepper and a package of sugared doughnuts.

The sun was already blazing and the dry wind abraded her skin. It would be another hot, dry, windy day – a day like every other day in El Paso. Nora was glad she slept through most of them. She thought about North Carolina, where she had gone to college, reflecting wistfully that up there the leaves would be starting to turn now. As she walked back to her apartment with the bag of groceries in her arms, Nora thought about moving east to North Carolina.

The telephone was ringing as Nora walked in.

'I've been trying to get in touch with you for the past three days!'

It was her husband, Larry.

'I've been out a lot.' She began to peel the cellophane wrapping off the doughnuts.

'Do tell. Look, Nora, I've got some papers for you to sign.'

'Aw, and I thought maybe you'd called to say happy anniversary.'

He was silent. One side of Nora's mouth twitched upwards: she'd scored.

Then he sighed. 'What do you want, Nora? Am I supposed to think that today means something to you? That you still care? That you want me back?'

'God forbid.'

'Then cut the crap, all right? So we didn't make it to our third wedding anniversary – all right, so *legally* we're still married – but what's the big deal?'

'I was joking, Larry. You never could recognize a joke.'

'I didn't call to fight with you, Nora. Or to joke. I'd just like you to sign these papers so we can get this whole thing over with. You won't even have to show up in court.'

Nora bit into a doughnut and brushed off the spray of sugar that powdered her shirt.

'Nora? When should I bring the papers by?'

She set the half-eaten doughnut down on the counter and reflected. 'Um, come this evening, if you want. Not too early, or I'll still be asleep. Say . . . seven-thirty?'

'Seven-thirty.'

'That won't cut into your dinner plans with what's-her-name?'

'Seven-thirty will be fine, Nora. I'll see you then. Just be there.' And he hung up before she could get in another dig.

Nora grimaced, then shrugged as she hung up. She finished the doughnut, feeling depressed. Despite herself, she'd started thinking about Larry again, and their marriage which had seemed to go bad before it had properly started. She thought about their brief honeymoon. She remembered Mexico.

It had been Larry's idea to drive down to Mexico – Nora had always thought of Mexico as a poor and dirty place, filled with undesirables who were always sneaking into the United States. But Larry had wanted to go, and Nora had wanted to make Larry happy.

It was their *luna de miel*, moon of honey, Larry said, and the Spanish words sounded almost sweet to her, coming from his mouth. Even Mexico, in his company, had seemed freshly promising, especially after they escaped the dusty borderlands and reached the ocean.

One afternoon they had parked on an empty beach and made love. Larry had fallen asleep, and Nora had left him to walk up the beach and explore.

She walked along in a daze of happiness, her body tingling, climbing over rocks and searching for shells to bring back to her husband. She didn't realize how far she had travelled until she was shocked out of her pleasant haze by a sharp cry, whether human or animal she could not be certain. She heard some indistinct words, then, tossed to her by the wind.

Nora was frightened. She didn't want to know what the

sounds meant or where they came from. She wanted to get back to Larry and forget that she had heard anything. She turned around immediately, and began to weave her way back among the white boulders. But she must have mistaken her way, for as she clambered back over a rock she was certain she had just climbed, she saw them below her, posed like some sacrificial tableau.

At the centre was a girl, spread out on a low, flat rock. The victim. Crouching over her, doing something, was a young man. Another young man stared at them greedily. Nora gazed at the girl's face, which was contorted in pain. She heard her whimper. It was only then that she realized, with a cold flash of dread, what she was seeing. The girl was being raped.

Nora was frozen with fear and indecision, and then the girl opened her eyes, and gazed straight up at Nora. Her brown eyes were eloquent with agony. Was there a glimmer of hope there at the sight of Nora? Nora couldn't be sure. She stared into those eyes for what seemed like a very long time, trying desperately to think of what to do. She wanted to help this girl, to chase away the men. But there were *two* men, and she, Nora, had no particular strengths. They would probably be pleased to have two victims. And at any time one of them might look up and see her watching.

Trying to make no noise, Nora slipped backwards off the rock. The scene vanished from her sight; the pleading brown eyes could no longer accuse her. Nora began to run as best she could over the uneven ground. She hoped she was running in the right direction, and that she would soon come upon Larry. Larry would help her – she would tell him what she had seen, and he would know what to do. He might be able to frighten away the men, or, speaking Spanish, he could at least tell the police what she had seen. She would be safe with Larry.

The minutes passed and Nora still, blindly, ran. She couldn't see their car, and knew the horrifying possibility that she was running in the wrong direction – but she didn't dare go back. A cramp in her side and ragged pains when she drew breath forced her to walk: she felt the moment when she might have been of some help, when she could have reached Larry in time, drain inexorably away. She never knew how long she had walked and run before she finally caught sight of their car, but, even allowing for her panic, Nora judged it had been at the very least a half an hour. She felt as if she had been running desperately all day. And she was too late. Much too late. By now, they would have finished with the girl. They might have killed her, they might have let her go. In either case, Nora and Larry would be too late to help her.

'There you are! Where'd you go? I was worried,' Larry said, slipping off the hood of the car and coming to embrace her. He sounded not worried but lazily contented.

It was too late. She did not tell him, after all, what she had witnessed. She never told him.

Nora became deathly ill that night in a clean, American-style hotel near Acapulco. Two days later, still shaking and unable to keep anything in her stomach, Nora flew back to her mother and the family doctor in Dallas, leaving Larry to drive back by himself.

It was the stench that woke her. Nora lurched out of sleep, sitting up on the bed, gagging and clutching the sheet to her mouth, trying not to breath in the smell. It was the smell of something dead.

Groggy with sleep, she needed another moment to realize something much more frightening than the smell: there was someone else in the room.

A tall figure stood, motionless, not far from the foot of her bed. The immediate fear Nora felt at the sight was quickly pushed out of the way by a coldly rational, self-preserving consciousness. In the dim light Nora could not tell much about the intruder except that that he was oddly dressed in some sort of cloak, and that his features were masked by some sort of head mask. The most important thing she noticed was that he did not block her path to the door, and if she moved quickly

. . .

Nora bolted, running through the apartment like a rabbit, and bursting out through the front door into the courtyard.

It was late afternoon, the sun low in the sky but not yet gone. One of her neighbours, a Mexican, was grilling hamburgers on a little *hibachi*. He stared at her sudden appearance, then grinned. Nora realized she was wearing only an old t-shirt of Larry's and a pair of brightly coloured bikini pants, and she scowled at the man.

'Somebody broke into my apartment,' she said sharply, cutting into his grin.

'Want to use our phone? Call the police?'

Nora thought of Larry and felt a sudden fierce hatred of him: he had left her to this, abandoned her to the mercy of burglars, potential rapists, and the leers of this Mexican.

'No, thanks,' she said, her tone still harsh. 'But I think he's still inside. Do you think you could . . .'

'You want me to see if he still there? Sure, sure, I'll check. You don't have to worry.' He sprang forward. Nora hated his eagerness to help, but she needed him right now.

There was no one in her apartment. The back door was still locked, and the screens on all the windows were undisturbed.

Nora didn't ask her neighbour to check behind every piece of furniture after he had looked into the closets: she was feeling the loathing she always felt for hysterical, over-emotional reactions. Only this time the loathing was directed at herself.

Although one part of her persisted in believing she had seen an intruder, reason told her she had been mistaken. She had been tricked by a nightmare into running for help like a terrified child.

She was rude to the man who had helped her, dismissing him as sharply as if he were an erring servant. She didn't want to see the smug, masculine concern on his face; didn't want him around knowing he must be chuckling inwardly at a typical hysterical female.

Nora intended to forget about it, as she had forgotten other embarrassing incidents, other disturbing dreams, but she was not allowed.

She had a hard time falling asleep the next day. Children were playing in the parking lot, and her doze was broken time and again by their shouts, meaningless fragments of talk, and the clamour of a bicycle bell.

When, at last, she did sleep in the afternoon, it was to dream that she and Larry were having one of their interminable, pointless, low-voiced arguments. She woke from the frustrating dream with the impression that someone had come into the room and, certain it was Larry and ready to resume the argument in real life, she opened her eyes.

Before she could speak his name, the stench struck her like a blow – that too familiar, dead smell – and she saw the tall, weirdly draped figure again.

Nora sat up quickly, trying not to breathe in, and the effort made her dizzy. The figure did not move. There was more light in the room this time, and she could see him clearly.

The strange cloak ended in blackened tatters that hung over his hands and feet, and the hood had ragged holes torn for eyes and mouth – with a rush of horror, Nora realized what she was seeing. The figure was dressed in a human skin. The gutted shell of some other human being flapped grotesquely against his own.

Nora's mouth dropped open, and she breathed in the smell of the rotting skin, and, for one horrible moment, she feared she was about to vomit, that she would be immobilized, sick and at the monster's mercy.

Fear tightened her throat and gut, and she managed to stumble out of the room and down the hall.

She didn't go outside. She remembered, as she reached the front door, that she had seen that figure before. That it was only a nightmarish hallucination. Only a dream. She could scarcely accept it, but she knew it was true. Only a dream. Her fingers clutched the cool metal doorknob, but she did not turn it. She leaned against the door, feeling her stomach muscles contract spasmodically, aware of the weakness in her legs and the bitter taste in her mouth.

She tried to think of something calming, but could not chase the visions from her mind: knives, blood, putrefaction. What someone who had been skinned must look like. And what was he, beneath that rotten skin? What could that ghastly disguise hide?

When at last she bullied and cajoled herself into returning to the bedroom, the thing, of course, was gone. Not even the cadaverine smell remained.

Nightmare or hallucination, whatever it was, it came again on the third day. She was ready for it – had lain rigidly awake for hours in the sunlit room knowing he would come – but the stench and the sight were scarcely any easier to endure the third time. No matter how much she told herself she was dreaming, no matter how hard she tried to believe that what she saw (and smelled?) was mere hallucination, Nora had not the cold-bloodedness to remain on her bed until it vanished.

Once again she ran from the room in fear, hating herself for such irrational behaviour. And, again, the thing had gone when she calmed herself and returned to look.

On the fourth day Nora stayed at the motel.

If someone else had suggested escaping a nightmare by sleeping somewhere else, Nora would have been scornful. But she justified her action to herself: this dream was different. There was the smell, for one thing. Perhaps there was some real source to the smell, and it was triggering the nightmare. In that case, a change of air should cure her.

The room she moved into when she got off work that morning was like all the other rooms in the Posada del Norte. It was clean and uninspired, the decor hovering between the merely bland and the aggressively ugly. The carpet was a stubby, mottled gold; the bedspread and chair cushions were dark orange. The walls were covered in white, textured vinyl with a mural painted above the bed. The murals differed from room to room – in this room, it was a picture of a stepped Aztec pyramid, rendered in shades of orange and brown.

Nora turned on the air conditioning, and a blast of air came out in a frozen rush. She took a few toilet articles into the bathroom, but left everything else packed in the overnight bag which she had dropped on to a chair. She had no desire to 'settle in' or to intrude herself on the bland anonymity of the room.

She turned on the television and lay back on the bed to observe the meaningless interactions of the guests on a morning talk show. She had nothing better to do. After the network show was a talk show of the local variety, with a plain, overly made-up hostess who smiled, blinked and nodded a lot. Her guests were a red-faced, middle-aged man who talked about the problems caused by illegal aliens; and a woman who discussed the ancient beauties of Mexico. Nora turned off the set halfway through her slide show featuring pyramids and other monuments in Mexico.

The television silent, she heard the sound of people moving in next door. There seemed to be a lot of them, and they were noisy. A radio clicked on, bringing in music and commercials from Mexico. There was a lot of laughter from the room, and Nora caught an occasional Spanish-sounding word.

Nora swore, not softly. Why couldn't they party on their own side of the border? And who ever carried on in such a way at ten o'clock in the morning? But she hesitated to pound on the wall: that would only draw attention to herself, and she didn't imagine it would deter them.

Instead, to shield herself, she turned on the television set again. It was game-show time, and the sounds of hysteria, clanging bells and idiotic laughter filled the room. Nora sighed, turned the volume down a bit, and pulled off her clothes. Then she climbed under the blankets and gazed blankly at the flickering images.

She was tired, but too keyed-up to sleep. Her mind kept circling until she deliberately thought about what was bothering her: the man in the skin. What did it mean? Why was it haunting her?

It seemed more a hallucination than an ordinary dream, and that made Nora doubly uneasy. It was too *real*. When she saw, and smelled, the nightmarish figure, she could never quite convince herself she was only dreaming.

And what did the hideous figure itself mean? It must have come crawling out of her subconscious for some reason, thought Nora. But she didn't really think she had just made it up herself – the idea of a man draped in another's skin stirred some deep memory. Somewhere, long before, she had read about, or seen a picture of, a figure who wore the stripped-off skin of another. Was it something from Mexico? Some ancient, pre-Columbian god?

Yet whenever she strained to recall it, the memory moved perversely away.

And why did the dream figure haunt her now? Because she was alone? But that was absurd. Nora shifted uncomfortably in bed. She had no regrets about the separation or the impending divorce; she was glad Larry was gone. They should have had the sense to call it quits years before. She didn't want him back under any circumstances.

And yet – Larry was gone, and old two-skins was haunting her.

Finally, worn out by the useless excavations of her memory, Nora turned off the television and went to sleep.

She woke feeling sick. She didn't need to turn her head or open her eyes to know, but she did. And, of course, he was in the room. He would come to her wherever she fled. The stench came from the rotting skin he wore, not from a neighbour's garbage or something dead between the walls. He didn't look like something hallucinated – he seemed perfectly substantial standing there beside the television set and in front of the draperies.

Staring at him, Nora willed herself to wake up. She willed him to melt and vanish. Nothing happened. She saw the dark gleam of his eyes through ragged eye holes, and she was suddenly more frightened than she had ever been in her life.

She closed her eyes. The blood pounding in her ears was the sound of fear. She would not be able to hear him if he moved closer. Unable to bear the thought of what he might be doing, unseen by her, Nora opened her eyes. He was still there. He did not seem to have moved.

She had to get out, Nora thought. She had to give him the chance to vanish – he always had, before. But she was naked – she couldn't go out as she was, and all her clothes were on the chair beside the window, much too close to him. In a moment, Nora knew, she might start screaming. Already she was shaking – she had to do *something*.

On fear-weakened legs, Nora climbed out of bed and stumbled towards the bathroom. She slammed the door shut behind her, hearing the comforting snick of the lock as she pressed the button in.

Then she stood with palms pressed on the Formica surface surrounding the basin, head hanging down, breathing shallowly in and out, waiting for the fear to leave her. When she had calmed herself, she raised her head and looked in the mirror.

There she was, the same old Nora. Lost her husband, driven out of her apartment by nerves, surrounded by the grey and white sterility of a hotel bathroom. There was no reason for her to be here – not in this building, not in El Paso, not in Texas, not in this *life*. But here she was, going on as if it all had some purpose. And for no better reason than that she didn't know what else to do – she had no notion of how to start over.

Nora caught a glimpse of motion in the mirror, and then the clear reflection of the one who had come for her: the lumpish head with the mask of another's face stretched crudely over his own. She looked calmly into the mirror, right into the reflections of his eyes. They were brown, she realized, very much like a pair of eyes she remembered from Mexico.

Feeling a kind of relief because there was no longer anywhere else to run, Nora turned away from the mirror to face him, to see this man in his dead skin for the first time in a fully lighted room. 'She sent you to me,' Nora said, and realized she was no longer afraid.

The skin was horrible – a streaky grey with ragged, black edges. But what of the man underneath? She had seen his eyes. Suddenly, as she gazed steadily at the figure, his name came into her mind, as clearly as if he had written it on the mirror for her: Xipe, the Flayed One. She had been right in thinking him some ancient Mexican god, Nora thought. But she knew nothing else about him, nor did she need to know. He was not a dream to be interpreted – he was here, now.

She saw that he carried a curved knife; watched without fear

71

as he tore seams in the skin he wore, and it fell away, a discarded husk.

Revealed without the disfiguring, concealing outer skin, Xipe was a dark young man with a pure, handsome face. Not a Mexican, Nora thought, but an Indian, of noble and ancient blood. He smiled at her. Nora smiled back, realizing now that there had never been any reason to fear him.

He offered her the knife. So easy, his dark eyes promised her. No fear, no question in their brown depths. Shed the old skin, the old life, as I have done, and be reborn.

When she hesitated, he reached out with his empty hand and traced a line along her skin. The touch of his hand seared like ice. Her skin was too tight. Xipe, smooth, clean and new, watched her, offering the ritual blade.

At last she took the knife and made the first incision.

Manly Wade Wellman

Yare

*Manly Wade Wellman was born in Angola in 1903, but now is
thoroughly identified with North Carolina, where he lives with
his equally charming and hospitable wife Frances (who used to
contribute to* Weird Tales, *and who has now returned to
writing).*

*Manly is a large gentlemanly Southerner who drinks
tumblers of Jack Daniels and smokes horrid cigars. He has
written under many pseudonyms, listed (along with much more
essential information) in* Who's Who in Horror and Fantasy
Fiction. *His books include* Who Fears the Devil? *about the
occult fighter John (who now also figures in novels),* Lonely
Vigils, The Beyonders, The Old Gods Waken, After Dark,
Sherlock Holmes' War of the Worlds *(written in collaboration
with his son Wade, and unpublishable in Britain) and the huge
collection* Worse Things Waiting. *This last won the World
Fantasy Award, as well it might, and in 1978 he was given the
North Carolina Award for Literature. August Derleth called
his stories of John 'sui generis and at the same time authentic
American folklore'. This is true also of 'Yare'.*

They were four in the last grey of evening, by the windblown
coals of the fire with utensils propped ready. Trees tufted this
slope below Black Ham Mountain, with grassy stretches between. Young Hal Stryker felt privileged to be there. He let
the others study his flowing sandy hair and his patched jeans.

'This here is Hal Stryker, the feller I said I'd fetch,' Poke
Jendel introduced him when they arrived. 'Hal, shake hands
with Seth Worley and with this here beardy one. He's Reed
Lufbrugh, he makes a good distill of blockade and looks to me
he fetched on some in a jug. Seth and Reed, Hal's a lowlander
who wants to see how we do things up here in the mountains.'

'Such as this fox hunt,' amplified Stryker. 'I've heard about

73

how you hunt foxes, but it's better to see a thing done than hear about it.'

'Truer word was nair spoke,' approved Seth Worley, lean as a hunting knife and as ready looking with his black hair and ploughshare jaw. Jendel was the smallest man there, but hard-knit, shrewd about his horsey face, with broad hands that were wise with guns, tools and especially with a banjo. Lufbrugh was the oldest, with thinning grey hair, a bush of beard, moustaches that curled like buffalo horns. They sat on square chunks of rock, rough-clad, good-humoured. All had brought guns but Stryker. These were laid carefully, within quick reach of hands.

Tied to nearby roots strained half a dozen dogs. All but one were brown-blotched hounds. The exception was of a Scandinavian breed, heavy furred, with ears that stood up expectantly.

'Them dogs is ready to go,' declared Worley, 'and I aim to hark at them a-running something down tonight.'

He arranged the joints of two chickens in a skillet above the coals. Poke Jendel stirred meal and water and salt into another skillet for pone. Lufbrugh unstoppered his jug. Each drank in turn, with the jug draped on a forearm. 'Good,' Stryker praised the sharp tang of the liquor.

'Better'n the government whisky,' said Lufbrugh. 'Pure as spring water. Naught touched it but the wood of the keg and the copper of the still and the clay of the jug.'

Stryker studied the rock on which he sat. 'It looks as if a house was built here once.'

'Long years back,' nodded Jendel above the pone. 'Feller they called Yare lived here. His house is gone and so's he. I don't recollect him, he was before my time.'

'What kind of name is Yare?' wondered Stryker.

'Just only a nickname, I reckon,' said Jendel. 'I don't know his true name. Folks just called him Yare.'

'I was a young chap when Yare was a-using round here-abouts,' contributed Lufbrugh, the jug in his lap. 'He come from somewheres outland, he allowed he loved the animals and hated the hunters.'

'How did that suit the people?' asked Stryker, who was no enthusiastic huntsman himself.

'They fussed with him and he fussed with them,' replied Lufbrugh. 'He had powers from somewhere, I heard say. Could fetch down a rain by a-singing a certain song, could kill a crop in the field if so happen he didn't like the feller who'd planted it.'

74

'My old daddy done told me about him,' elaborated Jendel above his cooking. 'If you killed a deer, he'd set his big old handprint in blood on to your door, and the blood wouldn't dry, would drip and drip for days.'

'I've heard that same thing,' said Worley, shaking dark powder into the chicken gravy. 'This ain't no poison spell, boys, just some instant coffee. It goes good thattaway.'

'Well, but you say this Yare is dead,' said Stryker.

'So folks say,' said Lufbrugh. 'Me, I ain't nair yet heard tell where his grave might could have been dug.'

Jendel took knife and fork and cautiously turned the cake of pone in his skillet. 'Near about time to set them dogs on,' he said.

'I'll do that,' volunteered Worley, rising and unsnapping the leashes from the collars. He walked a few steps with the dogs, until they bunched and sniffed the ground attentively. Then they sprang away, noses to earth. They ran towards where, about the distant hunch of Black Ham Mountain, rose a pale melon of a moon. The men watched them.

'We're near about ready to eat,' said Jendel at length. He cut wedges of pone and slid them on to paper plates. Worley forked on juicy pieces of chicken. Lufbrugh passed out iron knives and forks. Stryker bit into his chicken. It was as savoury as Worley had promised. Away in the dimness, a dog bayed tremulously, musically.

'That there's Tromp,' Jendel informed them. 'I'd know him amongst a thousand.'

'Don't you follow them?' Stryker suggested.

'Nair a step, son,' said Lufbrugh, spooning gravy on his pone. 'Not this here bunch of smart dogs. We sit and hark at them a-singing, and directly they fetch what they're after back to us here, close to where it wants to hole up.'

'I hear tell the lowlands hunters ride after a fox with red coats on,' said Jendel. 'A sight of trouble to do that.'

Another dog's voice pealed like a bell.

'That's my Giff,' Worley told them. 'When he talks up thataway, the trail's hot. They're a good piece off from here already.'

'And they'll fetch him back,' predicted Lufbrugh, gnawing at a drumstick.

Stryker ate pone and gravy. 'What you said about that man Yare is interesting,' he prompted.

'I know you, Hal,' grinned Jendel. 'You enjoy to hear about hants and witches and all like that.'

75

'You say he lived here. Right where we are now.'

'His house got burnt off these here very stones,' said Lufbrugh.

'Why?' asked Stryker.

'Folks didn't much like Yare.'

They watched Stryker, and he smiled. As Jendel had said, he liked this sort of story, here in this sort of place, at this time of the night, with the dogs baying at a distance.

'Why didn't they like him?' he asked, because they waited for him to ask it.

'Well, he fussed with folks about hunting,' said Lufbrugh between mouthfuls. 'He loved animals another sight better'n folks – wild animals, that is. Yare didn't value cows or chickens or hogs, said they was tame, deserved to die. Folks figured he stole such things at night and ate them up. But he hated deer killing, coon killing, even fish catching.'

'Did he have any family?' asked Stryker. 'A wife?'

'Nair girl would have looked at him,' said Lufbrugh. 'Hairy, the way he was.'

'How hairy was that?'

'All over,' replied Lufbrugh. 'Not just a beard like mine. His face was all hair, even the nose, the one-two times I seen him. And his arms, his hands, a-sticking out of his old clothes, they was hairy, too, like on a bear or a wildcat. Dark hair, no shine to it. Pure down ugly to look at.' Lufbrugh bit into the drumstick. 'Better off dead, if he is dead.'

'He'd have to be better'n a hundred by now,' said Jendel.

'My old granddaddy lived past a hundred,' Worley said. 'Walked a couple miles, a-gathering walnuts, the morning of the day he died.'

'And Yare was long and tall,' resumed Lufbrugh. 'Must have been near seven foot. With long arms, they like to drag on the ground.'

Stryker was silent, trying to visualize such a figure. Jendel ate chicken and pone.

'Like what I say, I wasn't round here when he was,' he said. 'But a heap of folks said Yare wasn't true human blood, he'd been born of some kind of devil blood.'

'He looked devilish enough,' endorsed Lufbrugh. 'And cut up devilish enough. Scared folks, maybe even killed a couple of fellers—'

'I've heard tell that a couple of hunter nair come home from time to time,' nodded Worley. 'Nobody found their bodies.'

'Nobody found Yare's body,' said Lufbrugh.

Remotely, the dogs lifted their voices together, like a choir.

'They're sure enough on to something,' said Jendel. 'They're a-trying now to catch up on it.'

They finished eating, to the remote music. Jendel threw scraps into the fire, which crackled hungrily. Lufbrugh passed the jug again. The moon soared well above Black Ham Mountain.

'Now, hark at them dogs,' said Worley.

The chorus lifted, far off to one side, as though the pack were following a trail along the slope. Joy was in the voices, and deadly intent.

'They reckon they're a-getting close,' decided Worley. 'Soon's they can see what they're after, they'll purely get a move on.'

The clarion voices rang together, then all died out but one.

'Tromp,' Jendel identified it. 'He must be a-leading the way just now.'

Those cries grew fainter.

'They're a-heading away after it, but they'll fetch it, sure enough, back here,' said Lufbrugh confidently. 'Somebody want another whet out of this here jug?'

It went the rounds.

'Now,' said Stryker, 'what about the question of whether this Yare is dead or not?'

'Oh, hell,' said Worley, wiping his mouth, 'you know how some folks are, a-talking. They'll tell you that their corn dies down with a blight, or their dogs go mad and have to be shot, and they figure Yare's got something to do with it. Or they see something at the window, and get pestered about that.'

'I've heard such stuff as that,' chimed in Jendel. 'How if he comes up and looks in at your window, somebody in your family dies.'

'Do you hold with that, Poke?' inquired Lufbrugh.

'Nair said I did, but I know folks that does.'

Worley drank again. 'All right,' he addressed Stryker. 'Weuns been a-telling you tales. It's your turn now. Tell us some of these here things Poke says you seen and done.'

'Do that thing, Hal,' encouraged Jendel.

Stryker did so, somewhat hesitantly. He told of how he had managed to destroy an evil spirit that haunted an ancient stage house on a half-forgotten road, and of how he had managed to get into a remote cabin literally besieged by evil, cunning trees, and then had managed to get out again. As he spoke, he watched his companions. They acted as though they were weighing every word he spoke.

'Shoo,' said Jendel at last. 'You done done more such things than air one of us has, Hal. And the doing of it must have sure enough done something for you.'

Remotely, the dogs bayed on their resolute quest.

'What do you mean by that?' Stryker demanded.

'You been up against hants and all like that. You whupped them. That means, you've found out how.'

'I don't see that I have,' said Stryker, mystified.

'Like when you're in a war,' offered Lufbrugh. 'They train you, they give you a gun, call you a soldier. Only you ain't no such thing, no soldier, till you been in where the shooting is and seen the monkey show, so to speak it.'

The dogs sang to them again, far away there somewhere. They sounded more excited, less light-hearted.

'Hark at them,' spoke up Worley. 'They might could have caught a glimp of what they want to catch up with.'

A series of half-screaming yelps.

'Old Tromp, a-telling the others he'll lead,' Jendel said approvingly.

'Son,' said Lufbrugh to Stryker, his voice weighty, 'what you tell us gives me the thought you're what we've been a-needing here in the Black Ham neighbourhood.'

'Me?' Stryker half cried out.

'You done been a-studying these things,' said Lufbrugh. 'You can figure what to do in some cases.'

The fire flickered there among them, lighting the faces that looked at Stryker. Jendel put wood on the blaze. It fought briefly with the fuel, then sent up tongues of flame, yellow as butter. The dogs sang to them again, they sounded nearer by now.

'What does all this have to do with fox hunting?' Stryker asked.

'Fox hunting?' said Lufbrugh after him.

'Who said aught about foxes?' inquired Worley.

'Why—' Stryker stammered. 'Why, I came out here with Poke because you were going to hunt a fox.'

'I nair said pea turkey to you about foxes,' said Poke solemnly. 'Back yonder at my place, I said we were a-bringing out our dogs here tonight, and did you relish to come along.'

'Are you having some kind of fun with me?' challenged Stryker, half angrily.

'No, Hal.' Jendel's voice was patient. 'I might could have fooled you up a tad, but we're dead serious about this. On account of them strange things you narrated to us. We'd had the word on you about them before now.'

'Them witches and hants and them,' added Worley. 'And you a-being able to do something about them if they come a-pestering you.'

Stryker stared at them, from one solemn face to another. 'Well,' he said slowly, 'I've had some unusual experiences. I didn't think you'd believe them.'

'We believe,' said Lufbrugh. 'We come out here to believe. Look, son,' and his beard jutted emphatically, 'that's why we had Poke to fetch you out with us tonight.'

'I don't get it,' groaned Stryker, fidgeting on his rock.

'Ain't it a natural fact that if a man's had them experiences you say you had,' said Jendel, 'been up against such things and made out to handle them some way – he's got a power, ain't he?'

'What Poke means,' said Worley from his own rock, 'he can do away with such things.'

'That's the old supposition,' admitted Stryker, feeling a chill in his stomach.

'Then look, Hal,' urged Jendel. 'Hark at me good. It ain't no fox that we come out here tonight to have the dogs run.'

'In God's name, what is it then?'

'Shoo,' said Jendel, 'we been a-talking about that. It's Yare we fetched them out after.'

The dogs bayed, and the sound of baying was stronger, it was nearer. Stryker jumped to his feet.

'If this is a joke—' he began.

'If it was a joke, it'd be a plumb foolish one,' said Jendel. 'It ain't nair joke, Hal. We mean the last mumbling word of it.'

They sat on those rocks that once had held up a house, sat like a panel of judges passing sentence on him. The moonlight picked out their faces.

'We come out here to track up on Yare, once for all,' said Jendel. 'To stop what he does hereabouts. And you're the one is a-going to stop it for us.'

'You're all out of your heads!' cried Stryker.

'If that's a fact,' said Lufbrugh, 'you'll have you the chance to find out directly. Because they're a-running Yare in here to us, like a fox to his hole.'

The voices of the pack rose louder, louder, building a crescendo.

'They can see him now,' said Worley expertly. 'They're a-running him fast.'

'And he wants to hole up right where we are,' said Jendel. 'Where he used to live. Hal, I said it's up to you.'

'Up to you, son,' said Lufbrugh, as though he pronounced a benediction.

The excited clamour of the chase grew louder. Across open ground towards them came something, swift as a shadow.

It was big and black, Stryker saw as he faced towards it. A bear, or a midnight bull, would be that size. The dogs thronged after it, leaping to close in.

The others had risen, their rifles in their hands. Stryker, weaponless, snatched a pole from the stack of firewood. It was perhaps four feet long, sharpened to a rough point. It might help in a fight. A fight – his blood stirred at the thought.

He stepped away from the fire. The ground seemed to quake under him. Whatever the something was, it had come near enough to see. It came swiftly at a crouch, huddled and huge. Its long forelimbs swept like shaggy wings, close to the ground. Suddenly it rose erect in front of him.

It loomed like a rearing horse. It plunged uncouthly against the night sky, those great shaggy arms outflung. Stars winked around it. He wondered why nobody fired, and it occurred to him that shots might not hurt it. It closed in.

Rakelike paws swooped at him. The moonlight touched what must be a face higher up, dark and tufted except for pale crumbs of eyes, so close set that they almost merged. Jagged picket rows of teeth.

Then the dogs were upon its bushy flanks. It screamed deafeningly and floundered back from Stryker, its paws slapping right and left. He caught a pale shimmer through the fur on one arm, a glint as of ivory. A dog yelped in agony as it flew through the air like a blown leaf. The grotesque hugeness shook itself free from the pack and clumped towards Stryker again.

A wave of foul stench smote his nostrils, so overwhelming that he tottered as at a blow. The shaggy shape rose against the sky. The coat of hair rippled. He had another glimpse of streaky pallor, like a row of naked ribs. Desperately he swung the pole with both hands. The blow rang where it struck, as though on

80

a dulled gong. The creature did not even flinch under the impact. It clawed for him. His shirt ripped and he threw himself backwards and fell head over heels. As he rolled over and came up on one knee, it towered above him again. It hunched great shoulders, bannered with black hair. It stunk so strongly that Stryker's eyes swam. The talons scooped for him.

He whirled the pointed pole in his hands, sharp end forward. He jabbed frantically, and the murky bulk dodged away. The dogs snarled and yelped and danced all around.

'Yare!' he cried its name at it. And it knew its name, it heaved its shoulders and snarled back at him.

Who was Yare, what had Yare become? This floundering, looming entity, wing-armed, talon-fingered, was grown out of Yare who had loved the wild, had hated tame mankind. It wanted to fight, it must be fought, this dark blotch in the dancing glow of the moon.

Somehow he got the pole in position. Again he jabbed, trying without real hope to keep the murky bulk away. He saw the shaggy face open up, with teeth like a monstrous skull. It slammed itself at him.

His pointed pole struck into something, as into earth. Above his head rang a deafening scream of startled pain. The stench welled around him like a foul torrent.

The ramming force of his thrust had brought him to his feet again. He surged forward with the pole. The giant shadow almost enveloped him. Then, abruptly, it gave back. With all his summoned strength he drove the pole in and in.

It had floundered down, it sprawled and thrashed there. A paw raked upward at him. He felt the sting of talons on his cheek. Leaning all his weight on the pole, he felt it strike into something other than what he had transfixed. Into earth, pinning the shape there like a gigantic insect upon a card. His mind churned within him and he staggered away and slammed to the grass. He dreamed horribly of something.

His senses returned to him furtively, as though they were not quite sure that they should come back. Voices chattered. Then he felt hands upon him. He blinked his eyes, and he could see. Jendel was on one side of him, helping him to his feet. Worley came up on the other, an arm around him.

'He sure enough gouged you,' Jendel babbled. 'Looks like as if a knife come on your cheek. Let me have that there jug, Reed.'

Lufbrugh passed it to Jendel, who sloshed it at Stryker's

face. The liquor stung sharply, and helped clear his head. He touched his face timidly. It was wet with blood, with the whisky.

'None of you got into the fight,' Stryker said.

'None of us could have done aught,' Lufbrugh replied. 'It was up to you.'

'Got a clean handkerchief?' Worley asked, his hands at Stryker's pockets. 'Here you are, hold it there. It'll staunch up the blood.'

Stryker wadded the handkerchief against the wound. 'What happened?'

'What happened?' Lufbrugh echoed him. 'You done what we fetched you here to do. You finished Yare off.'

Stryker looked at Jendel for some sort of enlightenment.

'Yonder he lies.' Jendel pointed. 'When you got up against him with just a stick, we wondered ourselves if things hadn't gone against us. But you stuck right through where he was biggest. Spiked him to the ground. No, Hal, don't go over yonder.'

'He's dead,' said Worley.

'Dead all the way through,' amplified Lufbrugh. 'All the way back along them years. He stinks rotten.'

Stryker gazed. The great shadowy form lay motionless in the soft moonlight. Around it capered the dogs, weaving a pattern. They did not venture too near.

'He appears like to be just bones inside his skin,' said Lufbrugh. 'Not even them dogs want air part of him.'

'He done slapped my Giff clean out of this life,' mumbled Worley miserably. 'Crushed him like a duck egg.'

'That there's too bad, Seth,' Lufbrugh comforted him. 'I knowed you valued that there dog a right much. Thought the world of him. Too bad it happened.'

All of them walked away from the patterned rocks, the motionless fallen bulk of what had been something called Yare.

'You know, fellers,' said Lufbrugh, 'that there pole that Hal Stryker took into the fight with him? It was an ash pole.'

'Ash pole,' Stryker echoed him tonelessly.

'Sure thing. Ash. I've talked to old Injun fellers round here, they used to allow ash was something you could use to fight evil spirits with. It must have done its part just now.'

Stryker mopped his bloody, sweaty face. Wearily he walked along with the others. The dogs followed them, all but the one that lay limply apart from that larger dead mass.

'What shall we do with the body?' Stryker asked all three of them at once.

'Hell,' said Jendel, 'we won't do aught with it.'

'We'll just leave it where it is,' seconded Lufbrugh.

Already they were a considerable distance from where those things had happened. They quickened their feet. They headed towards where a tiny point of radiance made a token of a cabin in the night.

Tanith Lee
A room with a vie

Tanith Lee is prolific and mysterious. She was born in north London in 1947 and began writing at the age of nine. She has been a library assistant, a clerk, a shop assistant, an art student for a year. 'In 1976 I was able to jettison these interruptions and become a full-time writer. I am interested in classical music, painting, reading, cinema, all of which influence my writing. In fact, I am influenced by everything which I see and which happens to me.' She writes fantasy and science fiction for children, young adults and the full-grown, both in prose and for radio and television. Her work ranges from the lyrical to the subversive (Red as Blood, Sabella). *Somehow she finds time to grace quite a few conventions, and to win awards at them. Her imagination seems indefatigable.*

Here is a tale in a setting far from the vivid fantasy worlds of The Storm Land *and* Volkhavaar – *a contemporary tale which follows through its implications with a nightmare logic.*

'This is it, then.'

'Oh, yes.'

'As you can see, it's in quite nice condition.'

'Yes it is.'

'Clothes there, on the bed. Cutlery in the box. Basin. Cooker. The meter's the same as the one you had last year. And you saw the bathroom across the corridor.'

'Yes. Thank you. It's all fine.'

'Well, as I said. I was sorry we couldn't let you have your other room. But you didn't give us much notice. And right now, August, and such good weather, we're booked right up.'

'I understand. It was kind of you to find me this room. I was lucky, wasn't I? The very last one.'

'It's usually the last to go, this one.'

'How odd. It's got such a lovely view of the sea and the bay.'

'Well, I didn't mean there was anything wrong with the room.'

'Of course not.'

'Mr Tinker always used to have this room. Every year, four months, June to September.'

'Oh, yes.'

'It was quite a shock last year, when his daughter rang to cancel. He died, just the night before he meant to take the train to come down. Heart attack. What a shame.'

'Yes, it was.'

'Well, I'll leave you to get settled in. You know where we are if you want anything.'

'Thank you very much, Mrs Rice.'

Mr Tinker, she thought, leaning on the closed door. *Tinker.* Like a dog, with one black ear. Here, Tinker! Don't be silly, she thought. It's just nerves. Arrival nerves. By-the-sea nerves. By-yourself nerves.

Caroline crossed to the window. She stared out at the esplanade where the brightly coloured summer people were walking about in the late afternoon sun. Beyond, the bay opened its arms to the sea. The little boats in the harbour lay stranded by an outgoing tide. The water was cornflower blue.

If David had been here, she would have told him that his eyes were exactly as blue as that sea, which wasn't at all the case. How many lies there had been between them. Even lies about eye colour. But she wasn't going to think of David. She had come here alone, as she had come here last season, to sketch, to paint, to meditate.

It was a pity, about not being able to have the other room. It had been larger, and the bathroom had been 'contained' rather than shared and across the hall. But then she hadn't been going to take the holiday flat this year. She had been trying to patch things up with David. Until finally, all the patching had come undone, and she'd grasped at this remembered place in a panic – I must get *away.*

Caroline turned her back to the window. She glanced about. Yes. Of course it was quite all right. If anything, the view was better because the flat was higher up. As for the actual room, it was like all the rooms. Chintz curtains, cream walls, brown rugs and jolly cushions. And Mr Tinker had taken good care of it. There was only one cigarette burn in the table. And probably that wasn't Mr Tinker at all. Somehow, she couldn't imagine Mr Tinker doing a thing like that. It must be the result of the other tenants, those people who had accepted the room as their last choice.

Well now. Make up the bed, and then go out for a meal. No, she was too tired for that. She'd get sandwiches from the little café downstairs, perhaps some wine from the off-licence. It would be a chance to swallow some sea air. Those first breaths that always made her giddy and unsure, like too much oxygen.

She made the bed up carefully, as if for two. When she moved it away from the wall to negotiate the sheets, she saw something scratched in the cream plaster.

'Oh, Mr Tinker, you naughty dog,' she said aloud, and then felt foolish.

Anyway, Mr Tinker wouldn't do such a thing. Scratch with a penknife, or even some of Mrs Rice's loaned cutlery. Black ink had been smeared into the scratches. Caroline peered down into the gloom behind the bed. *A room with a view*, the scratching said. Well, almost. Whoever it was had forgotten to put in the ultimate double-'u': *A room with a vie*. Either illiterate or careless. Or smitten with guilt nine-tenths through.

She pushed the bed back again. She'd better tell the Rices sometime. God forbid they should suppose she was the vandal.

She was asleep, when she heard the room breathing. She woke gradually, as if to a familiar and reassuring sound. Then, as gradually, a confused fear stole upon her. Presently she located the breathing sound as the noise of her own blood rhythm in her ears. Then, with another shock of relief, as the sea. But, in the end, it was not the sea either. It was the room, breathing.

A kind of itching void of pure terror sent her plunging upwards from the bed. She scrabbled at the switch and the bedside light flared on. Blinded and gasping, she heard the sound seep away.

Out at sea, a ship mooed plaintively. She looked at the window and began to detect stars over the water, and the pink lamps glowing along the esplanade. The world was normal.

Too much wine after too much train travel. Nightmare.

She lay down. Though her eyes watered, she left the light on.

'I'm afraid so, Mrs Rice. Someone's scratched and inked it on the wall. A nostalgia freak: *A room with a view*.'

'Funny,' said Mrs Rice. She was a homely woman with jet black gipsy hair that didn't seem to fit. 'Of course, there's been two or three had that room. No one for very long. Disgusting. Still, the damage is done.'

Caroline walked along the bay. The beach that spread from the south side was packed with holidaymakers. Everyone was paired, as if they meant to be ready for the ark. Some had a great luggage of children as well. The gulls and the children screamed.

Caroline sat drawing and the children raced screaming by. People stopped to ask her questions about the drawing. Some stared a long while over her shoulder. Some gave advice on perspective and subject matter. The glare of sun on the blue water hurt her eyes.

She put the sketchbook away. After lunch she'd go further along, to Jaynes Bay, which she recollected had been very quiet last year. This year, it wasn't.

After about four o'clock, gangs of local youth began to gather on the esplanade and the beach. Their hair was greased and their legs were like storks' legs in tight trousers. They whistled. They spoke in an impenetrable mumble which often flowered into four-letter words uttered in contrastingly clear diction.

There had been no gangs last year. The sun sank.

Caroline was still tired. She went along the esplanade to her block, up the steps to her room.

When she unlocked the door and stood on the threshold, for a moment—

What?

It was as if the pre-twilight amber that came into the room was slowly pulsing, throbbing. As if the walls, the floor, the ceiling were—

She switched on the overhead lamp.

'Mr Tinker,' she said firmly, 'I'm not putting up with this.'

'Pardon?' said a voice behind her.

Caroline's heart expanded with a sharp thud like a grenade exploding in her side. She spun around, and there stood a girl in jeans and a smock. Her hand was on the door of the shared bathroom. It was the previously unseen neighbour from down the hall.

'I'm sorry,' said Caroline. 'I must have been talking to myself.'

The girl looked blank and unhelpful.

'I'm Mrs Lacey,' she said. She did not look lacy. Nor married. She looked about fourteen. 'You've got number eight, then. How is it?'

Bloody nerve, Caroline thought.

'It's fine.'

'They've had three in before you,' said fourteen-year-old Mrs Lacey.

'All together?'

'Pardon? No. I meant three separate tenants. Nobody would stay. All kinds of trouble with that Mrs Rice. Nobody would, though.'

'Why ever not?' Caroline snapped.

'Too noisy or something. Or a smell. I can't remember.'

Caroline stood in her doorway, her back to the room.

Fourteen-year-old Mrs Lacey opened the bathroom door.

'At least we haven't clashed in the mornings,' Caroline said.

'Oh, *we're* always up early on holiday,' said young Mrs Lacey pointedly. Somewhere down the hall, a child began to bang and quack like an insane automatic duck. A man's voice bawled: 'Hurry up that piss, Brenda, will you?'

Brenda Lacey darted into the bathroom and the bolt was shot.

Caroline entered her room. She slammed the door. She turned on the room, watching it.

There *was* a smell. It was very slight. A strange, faintly buttery smell. Not really unpleasant. Probably from the café below. She pushed up the window and breathed the sea.

As she leaned on the sill, breathing, she felt the room start breathing too.

She was six years old, and Auntie Sara was taking her to the park. Auntie Sara was very loving. Her fat warm arms were always reaching out to hold, to compress, to pinion against her fat warm bosom. Being hugged by Auntie Sara induced in six-year-old Caroline a sense of claustrophobia and primitive fright. Yet somehow she was aware that she had to be gentle with Auntie Sara and not wound her feelings. Auntie Sara couldn't have a little girl. So she had to share Caroline with Mummy.

And now they were in the park.

'There's Jenny,' said Caroline. But of course Auntie Sara wouldn't want to let Caroline go to play with Jennifer. So Caroline pretended that Auntie Sara *would* let her go, and she ran very fast over the green grass towards Jenny. Then her foot caught in something. When she began to fall, for a moment it was exhilarating, like flying. But she hit the ground, stunning, bruising. She knew better than to cry, for in another moment Auntie Sara had reached her. 'It doesn't hurt,' said Caroline. But Auntie Sara took no notice. She crushed Caroline to her. Caroline was smothered on her breast, and the great round arms bound her like hot, faintly dairy-scented bolsters.

Caroline started to struggle. She pummelled, kicked and shrieked.

It was dark, and she had not fallen in the grass after all. She was in bed in the room, and it was the room she was fighting. It was the room which was holding her close, squeezing her, hugging her. It was the room which that faint cholesterol smell of fresh milk and butter. It was the room which was stroking and whispering.

But of course it couldn't be the damn room.

Caroline lay back exhausted, and the toils of her dream receded. Another nightmare. Switch on the light. Yes, that was it. Switch on the light and have a drink from the small traveller's bottle of gin she'd put ready in case she couldn't sleep.

'Christ.' She shielded her eyes from the light.

Distantly, she heard a child crying – the offspring probably of young Mrs unlacy Lacey along the hall. 'God, I must have yelled,' Caroline said aloud. Yelled and been heard. The unlacy Laceys were no doubt discussing her this very minute. The mad lazy slut in number eight.

The gin burned sweetly, going down.

This was stupid. The light – no, she'd have to leave the light on again.

Caroline looked at the walls. She could see them, very, very softly lifting, softly sinking. Don't be a fool. The smell was just discernible. It made her queasy. Too rich – yet, a human smell, a certain sort of human smell. Bovine, she concluded, exactly like poor childless Sara.

It was hot, even with the window open.

She drank halfway down the bottle and didn't care any more.

'Mr Tinker? Why ever are you interested in him?'

Mrs Rice looked disapproving.

'I'm sorry. I'm not being ghoulish. It's just – well, it seemed such a shame, his dying like that. I suppose I've been brooding.'

'Don't want to do that. You need company. Is your husband coming down at all, this year?'

'David? No, he can't get away right now.'

'Pity.'

'Yes. But about Mr Tinker—'

'All right,' said Mrs Rice. 'I don't see why I shouldn't tell you. He was a retired man. Don't know what line of work he'd been in, but not very well paid, I imagine. His wife was dead. He lived with his married daughter, and really I don't think it suited him, but there was no alternative. Then, four months of the year, he'd come here and take number eight. Done it for years. Used to get his meals out. Must have been quite expensive. But I think the daughter and her husband paid for everything, you know, to get a bit of time on their own. But he loved this place, Mr Tinker did. He used to say to me: "Here I am home again, Mrs Rice." The room with his daughter, I had the impression he didn't think of that as home at all. But number eight. Well, he'd put his ornaments and books and pieces round. My George even put a couple of nails in for him to hang a picture or two. Why not? And number eight got quite cosy. It really *was* Mr Tinker's room in the end. My George said that's why other tenants'd fight shy. They could feel it waiting for Mr Tinker to come back. But that's a lot of nonsense, and I can see I shouldn't have said it.'

'No. I think your husband was absolutely right. Poor old room. It's going to be disappointed.'

'Well, my George, you know, he's a bit of an idiot. The night – the night we heard, he got properly upset, my George. He went up to number eight, and opened the door and told it. I said to him, you'll want me to hang black curtains in there next.'

Beyond the fence, the headland dropped away in dry grass and the feverish flowers of late summer to a blue sea ribbed with white. North spread the curved claw of Jaynes Bay and the grey vertical of the lighthouse. But the sketch pad and pencil case sat on the seat beside Caroline.

She had attempted nothing. Even the novel lay closed. The first page hadn't seemed to make sense. She kept reading the words 'home' and 'Tinker' between the lines.

She understood she was afraid to return to the room. She had walked along the headlands, telling herself that all the room had wrong with it was sadness, a bereavement. That it wasn't waiting. That it wasn't alive. And anyway, even sadness didn't happen to rooms. If it did, it would have to get over that. Get used to being just a holiday flat again, a space which people filled for a few weeks, observed indifferently, cared nothing about, and then went away from.

Which was all absurd because none of it was true.

Except, that she wasn't the only one to believe—

She wondered if David would have registered anything in the room. Should she ring him and confide in him? Ask advice? No. For God's sake, that was why she was imagining herself into this state, wasn't it? So she could create a contact with him again. No. David was out and out David would stay.

It was five o'clock. She packed her block and pencils into her bag and walked quickly along the grass verge above the fence.

She could walk into Kingscliff at this rate, and get a meal.

She wondered who the scared punster had been, the one who knew French. She'd got the joke by now. A room with a vie: a room with a *life*.

She reached Kingscliff and had a pleasantly unhealthy meal, with a pagoda of white ice cream and glacé cherries to follow. In the dusk the town was raucous and cheerful. Raspberry and yellow neons splashed and spat and the motorbike gangs seemed suitable, almost friendly *in situ*. Caroline strolled by the whelk stalls and across the car park, through an odour of frying doughnuts, chips and fierce fish. She went to a cinema and watched a very bad and very pointless film with a sense of superiority and tolerance. When the film was over, she sat alone in a pub and drank vodka. Nobody accosted her or tried to pick her up. She was glad at first, but after the fourth vodka, rather sorry. She had to run to catch the last bus back. It was not until she stood on the esplanade, the bus vanishing, the pink lamps droning solemnly and the black water far below, that a real and undeniable terror came and twisted her stomach.

The café was still open, and she might have gone in there, but some of the greasy stork-legs she had seen previously were clustered about the counter. She was tight, and visualized sweeping amongst them, ignoring their adolescent nastiness. But presently she turned aside and into the block of holiday flats.

She dragged up the steps sluggishly. By the time she reached her door, her hands were trembling. She dropped her key and stifled a squeal as the short-time automatic hall light went out.

Pressing the light button, she thought: Supposing it doesn't come on?

But the light did come on. She picked up her key, unlocked the door and went determinedly inside the room, shutting the door behind her.

She experienced it instantly. It was like a vast, indrawn, sucking gasp.

'No,' Caroline said to the room. Her hand fumbled the switch and the room was lit.

Her heart was beating so very fast. That was, of course, what made the room also seem to pulse, as if its heart were also swiftly and greedily beating.

'Listen,' Caroline said. 'Oh God, talking to a *room*. But I have to, don't I? Listen, you've got to stop this. Leave me alone!' she shouted at the room.

The room seemed to grow still.

She thought of the Laceys, and giggled.

She crossed to the window and opened it. The air was cool. Stars gleamed above the bay. She pulled the curtains to, and undressed. She washed, and brushed her teeth at the basin. She poured herself a gin.

She felt the room, all about her. Like an inheld breath, impossibly prolonged. She ignored that. She spoke to the room quietly.

'Naughty Mr Tinker, to tinker with you, like this. Have to call you Sara now, shan't I? Like a great big womb. That's what she really wanted, you see. To squeeze me right through herself, pop me into her womb. I'd offer you a gin, but where the hell would you put it?'

Caroline shivered.

'No. This is truly silly.'

She walked over to the cutlery box beside the baby cooker. She put in her hand and pulled out the vegetable knife. It had quite a vicious edge. George Rice had them frequently sharpened.

'See this,' Caroline said to the room. 'Just watch yourself.'

When she lay down, the darkness whirled, carouselling her asleep.

In the womb, it was warm and dark, a warm blood dark. Rhythms came and went, came and went, placid and unending as the tides of the sea. The heart organ pumped with a soft deep noise like a muffled drum.

How comfortable and safe it was. But when am I to be born? Caroline wondered. Never, the womb told her, lapping her, cushioning her.

Caroline kicked out. She floated. She tried to seize hold of something, but the blood-warm cocoon was not to be seized.

'Let me go,' said Caroline. 'Auntie Sara, I'm all right. Let me go. I want to – please—'

Her eyes were wide and she was sitting up in her holiday bed. She put out her hand spontaneously towards the light and touched the knife she had left beside it. The room breathed, regularly, deeply. Caroline moved her hand away from the light switch, and saw in the darkness.

'This is ridiculous,' she said aloud.

The room breathed. She glanced at the window – she had left the curtains drawn over, and so could not focus on the esplanade beyond, or the bay: the outer world. The walls throbbed. She could *see* them. She was being calm now, and analytical, letting her eyes adjust, concentrating. The mammalian milky smell was heavy. Not precisely offensive, but naturally rather horrible, under these circumstances.

Very carefully, Caroline, still in darkness, slipped her feet out of the covers and stood up.

'All right,' she said. 'All right then.'

She turned to the wall behind the bed. She reached across and laid her hand on it—

The *wall*. The wall was – *skin*. It was flesh. Live, pulsing, hot, moist—

It was—

The wall swelled under her touch. It adhered to her hand eagerly. The whole room writhed a little, surging towards her. It wanted – she knew it wanted – to clutch her to its breast.

Caroline ripped her hand from the flesh wall. Its rhythms were faster, and the cowlike smell much stronger. Caroline whimpered. She was flung backwards and her fingers closed on the vegetable knife and she raised it.

Even as the knife plunged forwards, she knew it would skid or rebound from the plaster, probably slicing her. She knew all that, but could not help it. And then the knife thumped in, up to the handle. It was like stabbing into – into meat.

She jerked the knife away and free, and scalding fluid ran down her arm. I've cut myself after all. That's blood. But she felt nothing. And the room—

The room was screaming. She couldn't hear it, but the

scream was all around her, hurting her ears. She had to stop the screaming. She thrust again with the knife. The blade was slippery. The impact was the same. Boneless meat. And the heated fluid, this time, splashed all over her. In the thick un-light, it looked black. She dabbed frantically at her arm, which had no wound. But in the wall—

She stabbed again. She ran to another wall and stabbed and hacked at it.

I'm dreaming, she thought. Christ, why can't I wake up?

The screaming was growing dim, losing power.

'Stop it!' she cried. The blade was so sticky now she had to use both hands to drive it home. There was something on the floor, spreading, that she slid on in her bare feet. She struck the wall with her fist, then with the knife. 'Oh, Christ, please die,' she said.

Like a butchered animal, the room shuddered, collapsed back upon itself, became silent and immobile.

Caroline sat in a chair. She was going to be sick, but then the sickness faded. I'm sitting here in a pool of blood.

She laughed and tears started to run from her eyes, which was the last thing she remembered.

When she woke it was very quiet. The tide must be far out, for even the sea did not sound. A crack of light came between the curtains.

What am I doing in this chair?

Caroline shifted, her mind blank and at peace.

Then she felt the utter emptiness that was in the room with her. The dreadful emptiness, occasioned only by the presence of the dead.

She froze. She stared at the crack of light. Then down.

'Oh no,' said Caroline. She raised her hands.

She wore black mittens. Her fingers were stuck together.

Now her gaze was racing over the room, not meaning to, trying to escape, but instead alighting on the black punctures, the streaks, the stripes along the wall, now on the black stains, the black splotches. Her own body was dappled, grotesquely mottled with black. She had one white toe left to her, on her right foot.

Woodenly, she managed to get up. She staggered to the cur-tains and hauled them open and turned back in the full flood of early sunlight, and saw everything over again. The gashes in the wall looked as if they had been accomplished with a drill or a pick. Flaked plaster was mingled with the – with the – blood. Except that it wasn't blood. Blood wasn't black.

Caroline turned away suddenly. She looked through the window, along the esplanade, pale and laved with morning. She looked at the bright sea, with the two or three fishing boats scattered on it, and the blueness beginning to flush sky and water. When she looked at these things, it was hard to believe in the room.

Perhaps most murderers were methodical in the aftermath. Perhaps they had to be.

She filled the basin again and again, washing herself, arms, body, feet. Even her hair had to be washed. The black had no particular texture. In the basin it diluted. It appeared like a superior kind of Parker fountain-pen ink.

She dressed herself in jeans and shirt, filled the largest saucepan with hot water and washing-up liquid. She began to scour the walls.

Soon her arms ached, and she was sweating the cold sweat of nervous debility. The black came off easily, but strange tangles of discoloration remained behind in the paint. Above, the holes did not ooze, they merely gaped. Inside each of them was chipped plaster and brick – not bone, muscle or tissue. There was no feel of flesh anywhere.

Caroline murmured to herself. 'When I've finished.' It was quite matter-of-fact to say that, as if she were engaged in a normality. 'When I've finished, I'll go and get some coffee downstairs. I won't tell Mrs Rice about the holes. No, not yet. How can I explain them? I couldn't have caused that sort of hole with a knife. There's the floor to do yet. And I'd better wash the rugs. I'll do them in the bath when the ghastly Laceys go out at nine o'clock. When I've finished, I'll get some coffee. And I think I'll ring David. I really think I'll have to. When I finish.'

She thought about ringing David. She couldn't guess what he'd say. What could *she* say, come to that? Her back ached now, and she felt sick, but she kept on with her work. Presently she heard energetic intimations of the Laceys visiting the bathroom, and the duck-child quacking happily.

She caught herself wondering why blood hadn't run when the nails were hammered in the walls for Mr Tinker's pictures. But that was before the room really came to life, maybe. Or maybe the room had taken it in the spirit of beautification, like having one's ears pierced for gold earrings. Certainly the knife scratches had bled.

Caroline put down the cloth and went over to the basin and was sick.

Perhaps I'm pregnant, she thought, and all this is a hallucination of my fecundity.

David, I am pregnant, and I stabbed a room to death.

David.

David?

It was a boiling hot day, one of the last-fling days of the summer. Everything was blanched by the heat, apart from the apex of the blue sky and the core of the green-blue sea. Caroline wore a white dress. A quarter before each hour, she told herself she would ring David on the hour: ten o'clock, eleven, twelve. Then she would 'forget'. At one o'clock she rang him, and he was at lunch as she had known he would be, really.

Caroline went on the pier. She put money into little machines which whizzed and clattered. She ate a sandwich in a café. She walked along the sands, holding her shoes by the straps.

At half past four she felt compelled to return.

She had to speak to Mrs Rice, about the holes in the walls.

And then again, perhaps she should go up to number eight first. It seemed possible that the dead room would somehow have righted itself. And then, too, there were the washed rugs drying over the bath that the unlaceys might come in and see. Caroline examined why she was so flippant and so cheerful. It was, of course, because she was afraid.

She went into the block, and abruptly she was trembling. As she climbed the steps, her legs melted horribly, and she wished she could crawl, pulling herself by her fingers.

As she came up to the landing, she beheld Mr Lacey in the corridor. At least, she assumed it was Mr Lacey. He was overweight and tanned a peachy gold by the sun. He stood, glowering at her, blocking the way to her door. He's going to complain about the noise, she thought. She tried to smile, but no smile would oblige.

'I'm Mr Lacey,' he announced. 'You met the wife the other day.'

He sounded nervous rather than belligerent. When Caroline didn't speak, he went on, 'My Brenda, you see. She noticed this funny smell from number eight. When you come along to the bathroom, you catch it. She was wondering if you'd left some meat out, forgotten it.'

'No,' said Caroline.

'Well, I reckoned you ought to be told,' said Mr Lacey.

'Yes, thank you.'

'I mean, don't take this the wrong way, but we've got a kid. You can't be too careful.'

'No. You can't.'

'Well, then.' He swung himself aside and moved a short way down the corridor towards the Lacey flat. Caroline went to her door. She knew he was watching her with his two shining Lacey piggy eyes. She turned and stared at him, her heart striking her side in huge bruising blows, until he grunted and went off.

Caroline stood before the door. She couldn't smell anything. No, there was nothing, nothing at all.

The stink came in a wave, out of nowhere. It smote her and she nearly reeled. It was foul, indescribably foul. And then it was gone.

Delicately, treading soft, Caroline stepped away from the door. She tiptoed to the head of the stairs. Then she ran.

But like someone drawn to the scene of an accident, she couldn't entirely vacate the area. She sat on the esplanade, watching.

The day went out over the town, and the dusk seeped from the sea. In the dusk, a police car came and drew up outside the block. Later, another.

It got dark. The lamps, the neons and the stars glittered, and Caroline shuddered in her thin frock.

The stork-legs had gathered at the café. They pointed and jeered at the police cars. At the garden pavilion, a band was playing. Far out on the ocean, a great tanker passed, garlanded with lights.

At nine o'clock, Caroline found she had risen and was walking across the esplanade to the holiday block. She walked right through the crowd of stork-legs. 'Got the time?' one of them yelled, but she paid no heed, didn't even flinch.

She went up the steps, and on the first flight she met two very young policemen.

'You can't come up here, miss.'

'But I'm staying here,' she said. Her mild voice, so reasonable, interested her. She missed what he asked next.

'I said, what number, miss.'

'Number eight.'

'Oh. Right. You'd better come up with me, then. You hang on here, Brian.'

They climbed together, like old friends.

'What's the matter?' she questioned him, perversely.

'I'm not quite sure, miss.'

They reached the landing.

All the way up from the landing below, the stench had been intensifying, solidifying. It was unique. Without ever having smelled such an odour before, instinctively and at once you knew it was the perfume of rottenness. Of decay and death.

Mrs Rice stood in the corridor, her black hair in curlers, and she was absentmindedly crying. Another woman with a handkerchief to her nose, patted Mrs Rice's shoulder. Behind a shut door, a child also cried, vehemently. Another noise came from the bathroom; someone vomiting.

Caroline's door was wide open. A further two policemen were on the threshold. They seemed to have no idea of how to proceed. One was wiping his hands with a cloth, over and over.

Caroline gazed past them, into the room.

Putrescent lumps were coming away from the walls. The ceiling dribbled and dripped. Yet one moment only was it like the flesh of a corpse. Next moment, it was plaster, paint and crumbling brick. And then again, like flesh. And then again—

'Christ,' one of the policemen said. He faced about at his audience. He too was young. He stared at Caroline randomly. 'What are we supposed to do?'

Caroline breathed in the noxious air. She managed to smile at last, kindly, inquiringly, trying to help.

'Bury it?'

99

Daphne Castell

Diminishing landscape with indistinct figures

*The late Daphne Castell didn't answer my letter which asked
what she had been up to since the last time I used one of her
stories, and it is quite possible that she was too busy to respond.
When I wrote about her in* Superhorror *I noted that she taught
ESN children, evening classes on effective speaking and
English for the profoundly deaf, played percussion in a band,
sang contralto in a choir, broadcast on the BBC, lived in
Oxford with three eccentric children and five evil cats, and was
interested in all manner of things. Her work has appeared in*
Fantasy and Science Fiction, New Worlds, Amazing, Science
Fantasy, *various anthologies and a host of journals. She
dreamed most of her plots, and this may be the most dreamlike
of her tales, and the most subtly disturbing.*

At the top of the hill, I stopped for a moment, before coasting
down the last great sweep of road.

My friend's estate lay under the sunset, basking submissively
in its medieval colours. In this lonely bay, a niche in the curved
heights of hills, I looked down over little trailing plumes of
blue smoke from a dozen roofs, no more. They invited comment, and then companionship. Not entirely distinct from the
small clouds which skirted hillsides, or from the ground-cling-
ing mists which masked marshes or snared thickets, they were
still strong with the scent of humanness; and the mist and the
clouds were the persuasive voices of wild places.

The thin trembling sticks of saplings blemished the new
brown ploughland, as young as the baby crows that squawked
in nests, high in the elms but still a hundred feet below me.
There were very small blue and yellow flowers in a bracket of
earth mounted on the stone wall round my solitary bay, and
something lacewinged and skinny was hatching out from a

101

chrysalis at my elbow. Spring was at its beginnings, and so many things were young and small and new that they had more power to spread and overtake than you would have thought possible. You looked at an elm tree and saw its significant rough power, not the brown heart-rot that ate away its strength in age and disease. The ploughed earth ran at your feet, a simple and elementary statement of all foundations, but everywhere runnelled and channelled with fine feathery green, the new-planted stuff that disdained and conquered its sources.

The coming of evening quietened even the light wind that had done no more than move the old tufts of last year's seed pods, and I felt frost coming quietly with the night, and shivered, and got into my car.

The visit was so ill-arranged, really almost inexplicable. I had known him, but not seen him, for many years, I had read with interest of his work, I was on holiday in these regions, and a little bored.

We talked on the phone, and he had referred vaguely to what he was doing now, and said that he was taking a break. I might come and stay with him for a few days perhaps? I would be very welcome. But don't decide in too much of a hurry. There was really nothing to do there. 'It's all being done, anyway,' he said, laughing faintly over the telephone. 'It takes care of itself, my research.'

The idea of research that you started, and that then proceeded happily and perhaps inevitably of its own accord, pleased and attracted me. He was always such a gentle, apologetic person. He seemed to approach the processes that he set in motion with polite caution, as if he hoped not to offend them by influencing them at all. This was understandable – after all, for much of his life he was in close contact with the mentally disturbed, and with their investigators and protectors and interpreters. It was sometimes difficult to know which of these people was the most easily roused. Certainly I have seen a specialist near to frothing at the mouth, at a suggestion that some of his patients were not nearly fit to be loosed upon society; and I have seen a nurse actually strike heavily a new trainee who had been impatient with some old man, lugging him about like a sack.

My friend hovered about these distinctive little worlds, never really resting in any of them, observing and using, and sensibly not involving himself too far or too deeply, like so many men.

Like his name, he remained aloft and distant – I have forgotten to say that he was called Peregrine, Peregrine Ogden. He wasn't married, and his friends did not use his first name – I don't know why, except perhaps that in friendship, as in knowledge and observation, he did not settle closely, or cling, only touched in passing, and remained near but apart. It is not easy to call a man by his Christian name when his attention is partly elsewhere.

My own name is John Bates – my acquaintances, and my one or two friends call me 'Jack', and the laboratory assistants and technicians call me 'Batesy', behind my back. I am not in the least like my friend Ogden, but we used to get on very well indeed, in a quiet way, though I cannot truthfully say I have ever understood him. However, he tells me that he doesn't understand me, or at least cannot appreciate the way in which the mind functions in a man of my type, which comes to almost the same thing.

I drove slowly and peaceably as usual, conscious now that I was slightly nonplussed about how I was going to meet him, and what we were going to say to each other. I contemplated with dismay the idea that we might say everything we had to say in the first hour or two, and then not really be able to speak to each other for the rest of the few days I was to remain there. As the lancets of trees striped past my window in the late sun, I was wishing I had not decided to come; only commonsense told me that this had happened so often on other visits to other places, and that I would no doubt enjoy myself very much, when the initial embarrassments and insistence upon courtesies had been overcome. And there would be other people there, I assumed. It was a very large place; and the dead relative had left him a good deal of money with it.

I wondered what his research was exactly – he had plenty of room for it, as I could see. I drove through a barely noticeable metal gate and along a weedy stretch of gravel path. Then there was another entry – this time a pair of high old stone pillars with some sort of mythical bird on each, and no gate. The bird, I thought, was a phoenix open-mouthed with envy and ecstasy, poised and just about to arise in renewed life, balanced on one toe and a crude stone ball that might have represented a new world.

The pillars extended and dwindled rapidly down into an ancient wall on each side of the drive. The round tops of the walls were mossy, sage-green and orange with lichen, and under them stones had crumbled out like pieces of rotten cheese, leaving holes bordered by lips and teeth of more rotting stone. In the park beyond the fences that followed the disappearance of these walls, deer ambled in sparse, anxious herds, taking off with huge fretful leaps as my car came level with them.

I fancied that their hides looked pitted and motheaten, with lack of care, like the wall, but they did not stay still long enough for me to be sure. Perhaps Ogden's relative had not left him so much money that he could afford to keep the estate going smoothly.

But when I reached the house itself, it was apparent that a good deal had been spent on retaining its massive dignified charm. Smoothly reticent about its age, it contained a number of styles, none of them recent, all of them harmoniously blending. The colour of the walls was indescribable – dull cream with apricot shadows moving imperceptibly into grey stone shaded with moss and stencilled with small creepers, with here and there an unobtrusive patch of old mellow brick, lined with thick dark timber. Even a small modern shed, which obviously housed an electric generator, sheltered itself apologetically in shrubs, and appeared to have attempted to reduce its new wood as quickly as possible to a shade congenial to the more aristocratic tones that neighboured it.

Perhaps the only discordant note was struck by the statue of a man that stood some way off amongst the trees. It was extraordinarily modern – it wore clothes; and, in fact, I might have been able to mistake it for a more than ordinarily motionless human being, except for the pitted grey stone texture of the face, and the arms and legs, which were not covered. I thought that Ogden's relative must have been unusually eccentric, to cover his statues with simulacra of clothing; and then I wondered whether Ogden himself had changed, or extended his personality to encompass a new oddity.

The small patches of vivid orange lichen that had grown on the old wall along the driveway grew on the statue too, and on the roof of the house I was looking at, and above some of the windows. I have always liked the colours of lichens and mosses, and this particular orange was a charming flare of contrast.

There seemed to be absolutely no one around, but it was obvious that I was approaching the house by the back quarters, and therefore I presumably had quite a long way to go before I found living company, apart from the deer.

I could not imagine how guests had approached in their

coaches, in times gone by, invited to some wedding festivity or to celebrate Christmas with Ogden's ancestors. There must be a broader sweep of drive, perhaps with an entry on to some old coach road, now closed and gone, turned into farmland, perhaps.

I had stopped the car at first sight of the house, preserved and almost new-looking in its well-cared-for serenity, and now I drove on, through two more sets of stone entries and several arched gateways, presumably once leading to mews and kennels, since the drive gave way first to paved stone, and then to cobbles.

Once more I stopped the car, anxious not to miss any entry to the part of the house in which Ogden lived. From the passage in which I was now, several other large passages led off. They all appeared to be covered in, and some had walls all along them, but some were open to the weather in many places, and it seemed possible to run in and out of one side of a passage, into another, and so to another. I could almost have driven the car in and out of each aperture, like a horse in a bending race, at a gymkhana. I got out to explore one passage. There was absolutely nothing in it, except for a few large doors, locked and barred. At the end, in the open air, stood a large iron trolley. To this day I have no idea whether it was ever used, or for what purpose. There was so much about the house I never discovered.

At the end of another passage, I thought I could just see the figure of a woman, her head bent to one side as if she were listening. However, when I moved towards her, she disappeared round the corner of the passage, and although I stepped outside as quickly as I could, she was not visible outside the passage, along the wall. It was as if she had stepped sideways into some other dimension. I did not see her again, and I have no idea who she was, though I think, from what I learnt later, that she must have been a patient.

All the passages were empty, and all the doors in them were closed, and even when they looked as if they might easily be unbarred, they led only to the outside – perhaps at some former time there had been other outbuildings attached to them.

I thought it better to drive on, though I seemed to be taking a long time, by this route, to get to the house proper. My arrival, at last, was quite unexpected. I turned through one more pair of high gates, masking everything before me from sight, and found myself facing a lower, smaller portion of the house, more informal and cottage-like, apart from a high central part, rather like a flat-roofed water tower.

Round the circular gravel patch in which the drive ended were several cars, and a number of people were moving quickly in and out of the building. It was such an odd sensation to have been driving through and past apparently uninhabited buildings for so long, and now to find this busy corner of human beings, that for a moment I was almost uneasy. It was so stupid, for obviously the whole of the house was too big to be lived in, and Ogden and his friends, or staff, or whoever the cars belonged to, would not waste any time in wandering through the unusable part of it. They would come straight here. At the same time, looking back on the areas I had left, I could see that they were sometimes used by somebody for something. A group of heads had gathered in one of the more distant windows, obviously to watch the activities near the water tower buildings. I could see a hand waving from the window, and one of the people near me responded cheerfully, with a wave of his own.

I could see Ogden now, and he hadn't changed. He was apparently deep in conversation with a friend or employee, and he was wearing a white coat. From time to time he looked absently round him, as if he were expecting some event. And so he was, of course – he was awaiting my arrival, but he hadn't yet noticed the car. As I edged it gently forward, it shuddered a little, as it does occasionally when I drive it too slowly. As I brought it to a halt, I noticed a slow puff of some kind of vapour or smoke coming from an upper window of the tower. Even above the engine I heard a sharp thumping blast of sound, and then there was another puff, this time of a different colour, a sort of dim pink. It could have been flame-lit smoke, or a crowd of very tiny fragments of something.

Ogden saw the car and started forward, his face open with welcome. He looked really pleased to see me. Most of the people with him had hurried into the building. I got out of the car, and he exclaimed, and shook my hand, and patted me on the shoulder, and made all the proper remarks about how long the time had been, and how little the changes.

'An unsuccessful experiment?' I asked, gesturing at the smoking window. At once, the expression on his face changed peevishly.

'Oh, a great disappointment, really, my dear Bates, you remember how *wrong* things can go. And we were really rather looking forward to seeing the results of this. We didn't expect quite such a disaster, though I suppose one must be prepared for anything, and it was just on the cards that a similar sad thing might happen.'

I was rather struck by the tone of mourning in which he referred to a sad thing happening. Ogden had always been dedicated, of course, but experiments can always be set up again. Nothing is unrepeatable. I said something of the sort, as I was getting my bag out of the car, and Ogden sighed.

'This one would only be repeatable by sweet chance, I'm afraid, my friend. Some experiments, as you know, demand the cooperation of human beings, and the human element is always unpredictable. Tell me, what do you think of the place?' He said this with childlike eagerness.

'Marvellous!' I said. 'But so huge I was almost afraid to venture in. How on earth do you look after it all?'

He looked round him thoughtfully, and I heard from him a deep sigh as if of pleasure and refreshment. Certainly the trees and the sweep of grass and the old distant building were a fulfilment in themselves.

'I think, you know, I really think the place looks after itself. Or at least, the parts of it sometimes seem self-sufficient. There are plenty of – er – plenty of people scattered about in it. They all do their own work, where it's necessary, Bates, where it's necessary. And where it isn't—' he shaded his eyes with his hand, and looked beyond me and into long distances, apparently lost in the intricacies of his own musings.

'Where it isn't—?' I prompted him, remembering the uncared-for wall.

'Oh—' he waved a dismissive hand '—well, where it isn't, things are probably self-renewing, like trees or other living things, or perhaps they simply fade and crumble and decay, and that, too, in its own way is very picturesque and satisfactory.'

He called over a pleasant, round-faced man in a green jacket, who picked up my bag and beamed at me.

'Charley Tent,' introduced Ogden. 'Part nurse, part orderly, part guardian, entirely whole, kind, helpful human. Not a dissident notion in him, no maladjustment anywhere.' It seemed to me rather a dubiously detailed compliment, but Charley Tent obviously liked it.

'Not many we can say that of here, Mr Ogden,' he grinned,

107

but Ogden, for a moment, looked distinctly put out.

'That's not fair, Charley – they're all settling in their various ways – well, most of them.' His eyes strayed unhappily towards the window in the tower-like building.

'That's all right, Mr Ogden, only my little way, you know that,' said Charley, not at all disturbed. 'Very nice to meet you, sir. I do hope you'll find it both interesting and peaceful here. Our work, Mr Ogden's, that is to say, but we're all with him in it, absolutely heart and soul, our work, sir, couldn't possibly be more fascinating or more worthwhile. I hope you'll stay to see that for yourself.

'And the place, sir, well, you can see that already – we're very fortunate indeed, that Mr Ogden should have needed us to help him here, don't you think that already, sir?' He looked anxiously at me, almost as if he were wagging a non-existent tail, and I thought him a simple and warming personality – a bit gushing, true, but very much at one with his own way of life.

Ogden introduced me to half a dozen more of his staff, or friends, or colleagues – it's still difficult for me to know what to call them. There was Margaret, a still, kindly person, thick-set and reassuring in a tweed suit, a specialist of some kind, I didn't catch what.

There was a tall slender foreign girl, Magdalen Anima, of all unlikely things a most expert anaesthetist, so Ogden assured me, shy but smiling. I wondered if there were more than a trace of self-consciousness about him, as he introduced her. She was certainly very lovely and poised, as darkly beautiful and well-groomed as a model.

There was Henry, Bruggins, or Druggins, whose surname I never did learn properly – perhaps I wasn't paying sufficient attention after Magdalen. Henry was a doctor, and so were two or three more of them – a man called Sayers, with a perpetual tic, and sandy, greying hair, Stein, very silent, short, fat, dark – Macdonald, whom I remembered vaguely from a convention in London, a gawky young man with an irritating laugh. There were two or three nurses, too, and a scattering of the psychiatric arts.

Ogden produced two of them with great pride, from the crowd, like a magician with a rabbit from a hat, and I wondered again why they were all gathered on the ground in front of the building. But perhaps they had anticipated the technical trouble that led to the explosion or whatever it had been.

'Dr Aimy,' said Ogden almost formally, 'and his colleague, Dr Briars, both of them extremely interested in our work here, and really responsible in the main for our successes. If I hadn't persuaded them to leave their Geneva and their Toronto clinics respectively – well, the place wouldn't be here, it wouldn't be working, and now I'm wasting your time, because we're all going in to have food in a moment, and when Charley has taken your bag up, you'll be meeting all these quite splendid people properly and talking to them as you would wish.'

Aimy and Briars, plump, fair men, remarkably alike, smiled at me with sleepy sympathy, and continued a subdued conversation, after just the little break necessary to say something polite. One of them – Aimy, I fancy – patted Charley on the shoulder affectionately, as if he hadn't seen him for a while. Indeed, as I followed Charley through the gently dispersing nuclei of people, most of them seemed to have some greeting or smile for him, and one or two shouted anxious questions, to which he replied reassuringly.

We went in under the tower, turned right, and found ourselves in yet another of the long bare passages, punctuated with barred doors.

'Will the car be all right there?' I asked.

Charley turned, with a smile and a nod, and shifted my bag to his other hand. 'I'll move it for you – soon as I've seen them serving dinner, I'll go and see that it's put away in one of the garages.'

'That's kind of you,' I said, 'but don't miss your food for me. Oh, and let me know where the garage is, won't you? I'd hate to come to the day of my departure, bags packed and everything, and then find I'd mislaid my car.'

Charley answered quite seriously: 'Well, I'll tell you what, sir, you wouldn't be the first. Of course, if you consider what we've got here—' but then his voice died away and he seemed to be communing contentedly with himself, as he went before me, down the long bare windswept passage.

We trod through a couple of completely empty rooms, through a short, dark annexe of some kind, and up a flight of carpetless stairs.

'The Vera Locke wing, this is,' explained Charley. 'Come here with all her money, she did, not a friend or relative to leave it to, and she give it all to Mr Ogden. "Peregrine," she says – I can hear her hoarse old voice now, "People think I'm as mad as a hatter, and they're not far wrong" – but of course she had a lot of sane moments, sir, they all do – "but," she says to him "I'm giving you all my money now, because I've known you for years, and I know you'll either do me some good, or you'll do someone else some good. And if you can't do anything else man, and I'm pushing up the daisies, for heaven's sake use it to put some central heating into this benighted dump." That's what she said, sir, and we're going to have that done. Only we haven't got round to it. We've got a lift in, though, which was another thing she fancied. I'll show you, in case you want it – but it's a bit further over, round the other side of the building, away from most of the offices, but near the gardens, the herb gardens that is and the knot garden. Here's your room, sir. I brought you the quickest way, though you mightn't think it.'

The room was extraordinarily pleasant and comfortable, very low, with long, low, white-painted windows, and natural-coloured wooden walls and floor. There were large hand-made rugs on the floor, and a brilliant patchwork quilt on the enormous bed. There were several large cupboards, not with doors but with bright, woven hangings, and a number of mirrors, as if whoever had planned the room fancied that people might enjoy watching themselves from all angles. The windows were open, and I could smell the old-fashioned scent of clove-pinks.

'This is delightful,' I said. 'Mrs Locke – Miss Locke? – must be pleased, in her moments of clarity, with what her money has done?' I looked inquiringly at Charley, and he obliged me with an evasive reply. 'Well, she's still here, yes, but in a sense, she doesn't know much of what goes on about her. Poor lady! Yes, it's a nice room, isn't it? Mr Ogden, he always says that people, and where and how they fit in are the most important things he knows, never mind what they've done in the past, or how wrong the human race has been. Mr Ogden says we must concentrate on getting even a small part of it right, in the mind, you know, not so much the body, and if we get the mind comfortable and suited in itself, whatever that happens to be for it, then we shall be doing as we ought to.'

'And what do you think about the body, Charley?'

He looked sorrowfully at me. 'I wish I knew – when I looks about and sees what some of them can do to themselves, just for want of understanding, and sheer common care and affection and attention – I was thinking of things like drink and drugs, you understand, sir, but mostly of little things like not feeding themselves properly, because they was in a depression, or always knocking the same place, partly out of awkwardness,

110

but partly because they've picked that spot out deliberately, to kind of pay themselves back for something – they couldn't tell you what, and I can't, though Mr Ogden might know. And then there's those that'll really tear themselves, not all the time, only perhaps when they see or hear one thing, or when there's something particular they've got on their plate, or perhaps on some days of the week – we get a lot of what they call the autistic ones, here. He has mostly those, and some with schizoid tendencies.'

Charley brought the words out smoothly enough, and with a lack of self-consciousness that told me how long he must have been helping Peregrine Ogden with his work.

Observation and treatment of mental diseases is not something I know much about, but I knew how well Peregrine had succeeded in many of the cases he undertook – though who can ever say how much of a cure is due to the work of the psychiatrist, and how much to the efforts of a patient? When the mind is not quite submerged enough for it to have lost all desire to return to dry land, it will sometimes, somehow, reach out from what seems a wild waste of uncontrollable waters, and cling to the most unlikely spar of rescue, and somehow bring itself ashore. It hadn't happened, evidently, to Vera Locke.

Charley laid my bags beside the bed, and quietly straightened rugs, pulled curtains across, for it was nearly dark now. He showed me how to find light switches, and politely guided me out of the room towards the lift.

'Nice and new, it is, all clean pink paint.' And it was, a smooth curving expanse of pillars and panelling and decoration, with a small moving box that slid up and down so silently you couldn't hear it from outside the panels. As I stepped into it, something nagged at my attention. I stopped and leaned back to look sideways – I had been right. Something about the pillars at the side, and the decorations above reminded me of a woman's limbs – curving, rounded cylinders, stretching up, as if she lifted her arms straight above her hair, from the bend of her waist, above her hips. The head must be turned sideways, because the flow of the decoration was so much like spread curls, running along the top of the lift. Charley's thick fist, laid negligently just above the waist, somehow enhanced the impression.

'This is really a most unexpected place, in many ways,' I said.

'Ah. Depends on what we expect, don't it, sir? Precon-
ceived notions, what they say. I wish I knew what some of
those poor folk expect, I really do.' It was spoken with affec-
tionate, but disquieting passion. 'Still,' communed Charley to
himself, 'Mr Ogden knows most of it, and we watches. We
takes hints, and does a bit of guiding, whenever it seems, like,
necessary. It'd surprise you how many find themselves here,
what've been pretty well lost for good, it seems like, in other
places.'

'I'm sure,' I said inadequately. Charley's passionate concern
for the misplaced mind in a world of solidly domiciled minds
shamed me deeply. It was not that I did not feel the same concern; it was more that I had never taken it upon myself to be
its champion, its protagonist against the invisible hydra monster, mist-world of delusion. I suppose that basically, in my
core of being, I like a world of construction. I have always
supposed that you could never mix construction and delusion.
How wrong I was!

We went downstairs in the lift, and round a number of turns
in the everlasting long high passages. At one stage I was not in
the least surprised to find myself under the cone of a medieval
dovecote, or pigeon house. It was a little like the Colosseum,
with its tiers of roosting perches, but no windows, of course.

'Hello, Marion.' Charley opened a door, and peeped in,
smiling. It was most extraordinary – I tried to follow him in,
but you could hardly enter the place for the crowded, happy
noise of children bustling about the place, swinging on each
other's hands and playing, falling over unsteady feet, half-
singing as they went. You really could not find room, for the
place was full, or seemed full, to capacity. Yet there was only a
pretty, middle-aged, rather haggard woman, very skinny,
crouched in a corner. She had the deepest, most welcoming
smile. I have felt the same sensation once in a house where a
very successful party had been held, just after the last of the
guests had left.

'Going well, is it, dear? Mr Ogden's ever so pleased, I know,'
said Charley tenderly. She nodded and smiled that beautiful,
enveloping smile, full of secret and undirected happiness, but
her eyes were turned upon other corners of the room, and I
am quite certain she saw neither of us, though she obviously
heard Charley.

I seemed to be fending off small humanity at large, as we

staggered out, but really I was most unclear about what had actually happened.

'Marion'll be going soon, I should think – as clear as ever I saw. You could feel it yourself, couldn't you? Now wasn't that lovely, don't you think?' Charley guided me skilfully by the elbow round another of the interminable bends.

I didn't know what to say. 'You mean you think she'll be fit to leave?' I asked. 'It seemed to me—'

Charley interrupted reproachfully. 'Oh, she wouldn't want to say leave – not *leave*, that is. Not that any of us'd want to – though there's a lot who've got good other places to go to. No, no, I meant her treatment was obviously coming along so successful – nearly there, she is. I wish I'd be able to find something as good.'

I wanted to pursue the topic of Marion's fitness or unfitness for real life – she had looked to me so totally remote from human communion, but this was a new and fascinating side track.

'Do you mean you had treatment of this sort, or something like it once?'

'Oh, yes, but with me it didn't really take – or perhaps you could say it wasn't needed. I was too near to normal you see. I came back before Mr Ogden could properly get to me.' It seemed an odd way of putting it. Charley threw back his head and laughed, a clear chuckle of enjoyment, full of kindness and indulgence. 'I was very near what they called a mass murderer, you see. I couldn't see my way to bringing up a family in this nuclear world we've got now. So I shot my wife and the kiddie, and I went out with the rifle. That's where I'm a bit unclear, but I must have been near enough insane then, because I wanted to go and shoot a whole lot of innocent people who might have had different ideas about living in the nuclear society. Just as well the police caught up with me then, and of course, when Mr Ogden asked to have me, partway through treatment – silly, isn't it, I still keep fancying what he might have made of me if only I'd been that bit further off. But I had to come back – oh, I'd had fancies, grant you, but then they were based on something very near and real.'

I don't deny that this revelation came as a shock to me; but there was something about the atmosphere of the whole place, which cushioned the shock, as it were. And, in fact, my attention had already been caught by clean white doors opening off to the right, through which I fancied I could see perhaps familiar instruments and equipment, and smell well-known odours. There would have to be laboratories in a place like this, of course. It has always seemed to me that a well-kept, well-equipped laboratory, preferably without other research workers, but with perhaps one unobtrusive assistant, must be the nearest thing to perfection that the limits of our unsatisfactory sciences can show. I had begun insensibly to edge towards the white doors, each with its little oval window, shining like a tender jewel.

Charley's arm drew me firmly onwards, as he observed: 'I expect Mr Ogden'll want to show you over them himself, personal. Then there's the computer, too. We had another patient left us another legacy to pay for that – mind, I don't want to give the idea a lot of them die. Most of them is a great success. It's rare we has one die, but some of 'em prefer to give us something before they go on to the next stage.'

At the very point of my muttering: 'Computer! Good gracious, his own computer,' Charley threw open a large, ornately panelled door with a flourish, and I was in the dining room. It was a pleasantly luxurious place, with good thick carpeting, small tables, none holding more than six people, concealed lighting, and, I was pleased to see, waitress service at the tables. The walls were elegantly dressed with pale-green Regency striped paper, and the carved wooden pairs of wall candlesticks that adorned them at intervals were beautifully designed. A view of the lawns and some of the trees was framed in the heavy brown velvet curtains.

Charley left me with a slight mutter, and went forward rather quickly to shut a pair of doors that lay just open beyond them.

I could catch only a glimpse of a much more disordered series of tables, and figures either motionless or moving very quickly. One pair appeared to be waltzing, and were leaning back from each other at an extreme angle that reminded me oddly of something I had seen.

'Patients' dining room,' said Charley apologetically, and then, with perhaps slight reproach, to Peregrine Ogden, who was waving at me from a window table: 'The new guest, Mr Ogden – the guest, I should say, anyway, and the doors were open again, sir.'

'Doesn't matter, doesn't matter,' Peregrine tapped a fork on the table, and one of the stout, kind-eyed women came over to bring me a menu. The two doctors, Aimy and Briars, Magdalen

Anima, and the taciturn but amiable Henry Bruggins or Druggins, shared the table. Charley disappeared towards a table in the darkest corner of the dining room. Apparently all staff here ate together. Even the waitresses, when they had ascertained (from Charley, of course) that no one else was to come, sat down together at a larger table along one side of the room, and had their own meal.

'I suppose not all your patients will eat,' I remarked, for want of something better to say. Ogden put down his fork and looked at me with an air of pleased surprise.

'There, now,' he nodded at Aimy. 'I knew it. I knew that keen analytical mind of yours would begin to enjoy itself as soon as you got here.' Aimy smiled back at me, and said, 'Yes, yes, indeed!', in what sounded like a rather complimentary tone of voice. I wondered what my research colleagues, and the rather objectionable technicians who call me 'Batesy' behind my back would have felt about the respect of those around me now. Surprised, I am almost certain.

'Now just what made you draw that conclusion, in particular, I am wondering?' asked Briars, lighting a cigarette. I do object to people who smoke between courses. But I suppose all of us need some dummy, some crutch, to support us against too much contact with rude reality.

'Oh, the patient Charley called Marion,' I explained. 'I could see that she was quite removed from the normal commerce of the everyday world – or at last, I hope I am allowed to say that. I'm speaking as someone with no knowledge whatsoever, of course.'

'But that's good, that's very good,' said Magdalen Anima, with a shake of her pretty hair, 'for one so new to the place to see and feel that. It's wonderful for Marion, isn't it?'

Fortunately, some soup was brought for me. I ate it, without knowing quite what reply to make.

In the meantime Ogden was continuing to congratulate himself on the inspiration that had led him to invite me. I was surprised to hear how much he remembered about me.

'You'll like it here, you in particular,' he was saying. 'The peace, the tolerance. We have to have tolerance, of course.'

'An essential,' smiled Aimy. 'But then tolerance should be an essential to all human creatures who do not consider that, being founded from the animal, they have a duty at times to make obeisance to it.'

'And the laboratories, you'll be welcome to go there, use

115

them, browse if you want to,' Ogden was saying to me, 'help if you want, don't if you don't want. Small staff, well-trained, decent people with nice manners and a genuine interest in research.' I had almost forgotten that such people existed. 'Some of our work comes fairly near your own field, you see,' continued Ogden. 'One can't always tell just what part chemistry will take in the troubles of our people.

'The child with galactosaemia, phenylketonuria, born into a scheme of nourishment foreign to its own body, but undoubtedly born of human parents. Of course, that could be true of so many more – how are we to know? In our own way, Dr Aimy and Dr Briars and I try to find out – but it is a small way, as I have said. Charley, perhaps, does even more, for he is in everyone's world at once, and feels empathy with whatever strange place it may seem to be.'

'And yet he once could not tolerate his own world,' I could not resist remarking. Ogden looked at me with troubled concentration. 'Ah, he told you. Yes, he would do. He's taken a great liking to you. We could all see that. I think he'd want you to stay.' He laughed a little, and so did Magdalen.

'You see,' said Briars, leaning forward, 'we all of us believe here that there is some way for these people out of the intolerable impasse in which they find themselves. The mind cannot discover an existing remedy – so it makes one. Or perhaps these minds are already born knowing of states of existence which are not yet here. So they look for them. To people existing in what they would call a normal state, these people are mad.'

'Charley wasn't mad, of course,' said Ogden. 'He would have taken a great deal more stress without actually going beyond the irrecoverable point.'

'And what a real treat it is for all of us now to know that we share these experiences with a man like Charley!' This enthusiasm came, quite uncharacteristically it seemed to me, from Henry Bruggins/Druggins? 'A fully rounded man, a persona *per se*, a fellow who has accepted and remembered and come to terms with all he has executed.'

It seemed to me that Charley had executed his family – I could not quite believe it possible to come to terms with that. But, of course, it was not my field. In the peace of one's laboratory, one deals with absolute quantities, named substances, infinite but determinable variables. There are as many possible results as one cares to take the trouble to find. But one must use only known facts, naturally, to explore the unknown.

'Which reminds me,' said Ogden, thoughtfully prodding at the holes in a clogged salt cellar with an unused fork, 'has anyone been to see Lawrence today?'

Aimy clapped his hands in almost childlike glee: 'But, my very dear colleague, you have missed a genuine experience – the most splendid thing! In fact, I would go almost as far as saying that he is one of this institution's greatest successes – better than dear Vera, and such a great comfort after that unfortunate affair with the Twist boy.'

The atmosphere round the table turned sad and stilted. Ogden looked stiffly at me, and said: 'But tell me about Lawrence. I noticed he hadn't had meals for some time.'

'It is virtually impossible to approach him, for some yards round,' said Aimy merrily, 'and then when he walks, you know, on his accustomed paths, his repetitive tread, there are turns at which you really cannot see him. And the colours – the colours he produces are quite beyond imagination. I wish I could compare them to anything. You must simply see for yourselves. I believe he has begun to assimilate red a little – you remember the red business – the screams at the buses, the pillar boxes. No, I am sure I could distinguish a little red today – he has somehow internalized that.' Everyone laughed at this, and I looked at Ogden, perplexed, I may as well confess.

'Highly autistic type of patient,' said Ogden, in an aside. Not that that explained anything.

I tried to look as if I was participating, but, as usually happens, it was not a successful attempt.

Magdalen, obviously a most intuitive person – almost a telepath, one would say, only I do not believe in that sort of thing – felt it her duty to assist me.

'There is much we can do – much our dear and talented Peregrine can do – to help such lost minds find a more congenial track. At last, perhaps, in fact, nowadays in most cases, they find and retrieve the route for which they originally looked. Then they take it, of course.'

'Take it?'

'Adjust themselves into their new settings,' explained Ogden. 'The things, or the directions, or the modes of behaviour, or the people they need are within their reach suddenly. It is as if they have been looking with their eyes closed, or in total dark-

117

ness, as if something living underwater was looking for something living above water.'

'Or in a vacuum, sir,' Charley had come over, apparently having finished his meal, and was leaning rather familiarly behind Ogden, with his hands on the back of his chair. 'Just as well not too many of our customers want the almost impossible, wouldn't you say, Mr Ogden?'

In spite of his gay smile, Ogden looked at him reproachfully. Obviously Charley had touched upon a sore spot. 'That wasn't too good, Charley. Really not too good. Now would you say that was anyone's fault? Anyone's at all? And who could have got nearer to it than us? Eh? I suppose it counts for something that poor Mr Anstruther's last days were such utterly happy ones? He was quite convinced of it himself, and that usually helps so much.' But it seemed that no one could be annoyed with Charley for long, and Ogden's tones ended up in indulgence, though Charley looked perhaps a little crestfallen.

'Well, you know how it is with me, Mr Ogden – plain jealous, and I don't have to tell anyone that. They all know it here, and it's plain to see. Here I am cured, and never another chance, and I see all this going on around me – oh well, who am I to complain? There can't be many men have a happier life than meself. I think I was upset too, in a way, over Mr Anstruther – I mean, I knew within meself that it was impossible, but it didn't seem so, and everyone else seemed so sure.'

'Everyone has a failure,' said Briars heavily. 'Life would be too full of miracles to be good for us, otherwise. A proper balance of failures is essential to nature.'

'Are you talking about the – ah – the explosion?' It seemed unmannerly curiosity, but I felt I had to know. The pink confetti-like stuff – I would really rather not be sure, but it seemed necessary at least to ask. If they refused to give details, that would, in its way, be equally satisfactory.

'Dear, dear, yes. I suppose that was all it seemed,' said Ogden unhappily, and the others were silent.

We seemed to have ended our meal. Peregrine Ogden asked me to come and have coffee with him, in his study, but excused himself first for ten minutes. He had a patient to talk to.

Charley went off by himself, whistling, with a friendly nod back to me. I had the curious feeling that if I had shown any anxiety, he would have trotted back, and kept me company, even to standing guard outside my room, while I slept. But, on the contrary, I had begun to feel as if this were a place I had been looking for for a great while, without ever being able to formulate to myself any very exact image of what I hoped to find.

I looked out through the full warm curtains at the dimly moving expanses of grass, blotted now and then by slabs of furry-backed stones, fenced and patched by hastening ranks of trees, and beyond that a colourless blur of sky, reddening now a little at the death of the sun, still with blue curls of smoke scrolled upon it.

If I must look at a landscape – and frankly, I am not an outdoors man – this is how I prefer to see it.

As I left the room, with Magdalen talking quietly at my side, I suddenly remembered the waltzing figures in the other room, and knew that they had reminded me of the beautifully carved pairs of candlesticks on the walls.

Magdalen said that she would show me the way to Ogden's study, and on the way we passed the door of the room which held Marion. For some reason, I felt impelled to look inside. However, I could not open the door fully – it was as if something was pressing against it from within. This was odd, because although the sounds and movements of children were as strong as ever, from the tiny glimpse I could gain of Marion's corner, she was no longer there.

Magdalen, too, peered over my shoulder, and uttered one of those soft, caressing murmurs which one associates with people who disturb young birds in a nest, or puppies or kittens nursing.

'Ah, dear Marion; I must go and tell Peregrine,' she whispered. '*How* pleased he will be – so soon, though we all expected it.'

And still the empty room, and the great pressures and sounds and movements, which gradually thrust the door shut, against my shoulder.

'Would you like—' Magdalen hesitated for a moment. 'You see, I should talk to Peregrine about this – technically, it is one of our major achievements. It may perhaps be dull for you and, of course, there are things he might wish to say to me about it that—' she hesitated again, but very gracefully.

'Oh, I can understand that quite easily,' I said immediately, 'a case history – that will need some discussion, I suppose. You won't need me there for a while. You must keep that coffee warm for me, though.'

'In the meantime, perhaps, you would like to look through our laboratories – Charley said you were interested, and

Peregrine told us something of your work, naturally. They are through here—' She began leading me towards the doors Charley had pulled me gently away from, before the meal.

'A passion of mine, a well-kept laboratory, properly equipped, waiting for work and its occupant,' I said, with pleasure.

'Oh, everyone here has a passion,' replied Magdalen lightly. 'Some more important than others. Yours, I would think, could only be a most important one. Your opinions will be most valuable to us.'

'Tell me, how do you help – if you won't think me rude?'

Magdalen shrugged expressively. 'There are so many ways of helping these people – drugs, the injections of the right chemicals, an operation, perhaps, to fit them for the right sphere. Even a humble anaesthetist – ' she curtseyed swiftly ' – is a necessary appendage. In some cases, I am called upon to keep certain patients under just the right amount of anaesthetic for really quite long periods. That can work marvels – perhaps you know?'

No, I hadn't known. 'So everyone has their own passion, and some their great and unattainable peculiarities. Even you?'

Magdalen laughed. 'Oh, this is the last place in which to say that there is such a thing as true normality. Everyone is a little mad, yes? What is that saying your people have about the method in madness? All one has to do is to find a little method, and then direct, in any of a number of ways. Don't be too sure of yourself, my friend – perhaps only poor Charley is one who has truly and unalterably graduated. But then he should have never been here, in the first place. Everyone is very kind to him, though, and he is so good, such a help, so full of intuitions and love.'

We walked slowly down the passages between the white-topped benches. The instruments, the burners, the beakers – great cupboards, full of glassware, gleaming through transparent doors – it all looked as though it had hardly been used. Where there were not windows, there were mirrors – a most pleasing prospect. The mirrors seemed to extend the laboratory serenely and infinitely. I saw a continuous motion of my own image, in many directions, and everywhere the tools of my trade, not smoke-blackened or acid-burned or dye-stained, as in the workshops I was used to, but pristine and virgin, worthy of the best uses.

The coffee would wait, and Magdalen had to have her chat with Ogden. There were journals on the shelves, whose numbers I hadn't yet looked into, though I had always promised myself—

'Well, this is certainly my weakness.' I sighed. 'Someone will have to come and fetch me, you know, Magdalen, or I shall be lost for ever in the immensities of my own researches. The whole place, the people, the atmosphere – there's something that almost demands one's attention and affection – perhaps devotion. You feel it, of course, more than I do, as a member of the staff.'

'Someone will come and help you,' said Magdalen practically. 'You'll need an assistant, even though I know you will find something to do without our aid. Yes, I am fortunate, as you say. In my world, where I was born, we have no such places as Peregrine has made. It was by pure chance that I found my way from my own world to this – and there, I think, no one would have recognized me.'

She was laughing, as she let herself out. A joke, of course, no wonder her clear amusement lingered in the air, after the doors had closed, and left me wrapped in the quietness of the laboratory. A strange joke – but the memory of it began to leave me as I looked around at the shelves, the containers, the inviting benches.

There was so much I could do here. And I had plenty of time – it was not as if I had to hurry. There is always plenty of time when great changes or great improvements are to be made, to things or to people or to life itself.

A cupboard to hand so obviously stood a little ajar, suggesting clean white overalls. As I eased my shoulders into one, I found myself hoping that perhaps Charley had had laboratory experience. It might perhaps be Charley whom they sent to help me.

Marc Laidlaw

Tissue

*Marc Laidlaw was born in 1960, and I wish I could have
written as well as that when I was eighteen, or have been half
as energetic and professional. Many a writer trying for his first
solo professional sale would have given up after the first
rejection, yet when I rejected two stories (fine, but not right
for this book) he bounced back with 'Tissue'. I couldn't resist
that ending, but I wanted revisions elsewhere, which he sent
almost by return of post. Although he is a student at the
University of Oregon he manages to write scripts and to sell
stories to* Omni, Year's Best Science Fiction, The Future at
War *and, I'm sure by the time this sees print, others. He has
also written novels (*The Mistress of Shadows, The Minions of
L'Thoa) *which will have reached a friendly editor by now, I
hope.*

*At the age of seventeen he played 'Son' in an educational
film about divorce. His father was played by Hal Landon
Junior, who is one of the more unnerving characters in*
Eraserhead, *the most nightmarish film ever made. A good start
for a writer of nightmares like this one.*

'Here,' Daniel said, handing Paula the photograph. 'Take a
look at this, then tell me you *still* want to meet my father.'

Paula hefted it in one hand; it was framed in dark wood,
covered with a heavy rectangle of glass. A fringe of dust clung
to the glass's edges, under the frame, blurring the borders of
the photograph into a spidery haze.

'What is it? *Who* is it?'

'Us. My family.'

'But there's only . . .'

Paula's words faded away as she stared at the photograph,
trying to understand. Squinting her eyes, polishing the glass —
nothing seemed to resolve it. It was merely a simple figure, a

123

person, but as blotched and mottled as an old wall, with sharply ragged edges that unsettled Paula: she couldn't focus, it was like looking through a prism. There was a disturbing disparity within it, too; abrupt internal changes of tone and texture.

'Your *family*?' she repeated.

Daniel nodded, looking straight ahead at the road as he drove. The shadows were lengthening, the gloom descending. Through the endless stand of trees along the roadside, fields and hills were visible.

'It's a composite,' he said. 'You know, like a collage.' He glanced down at the photograph and pointed at the figure's left hand. 'That's my hand. The right one's my mother's.'

'*What?*'

'And the chin, there, is my sister's. That's my brother's . . . forehead, I think, yeah – and that's his nose, too. The clothes, I – I'm not sure.'

'And the eyes?'

'My father's.'

'Daniel, what is this? I mean, why?'

His hands tightened on the steering wheel. Paula found herself staring at his left hand. The one from the picture.

'Daniel, why?'

He shook his head. 'My father's a madman, that's why. No reason for it, he's just . . . Well, yeah, to *him* there's a reason. This, to him, shows us as a group – close-knit. "One optimally functioning individual organism," he used to say.'

Paula looked at the picture with apparent distaste, then slid it back into the briefcase from which Daniel had taken it.

'It's grotesque,' she said, rubbing dust from her hands.

'He sent that to me three years ago, when I had just moved away from home. Made it out of old photographs, begging me to come back. God, he must have worked on that thing for weeks – the joints are almost invisible.'

He fell silent, perhaps watching the road for their turn-off, perhaps just thinking. After a while he sighed, shook his head.

'I don't know,' he said. 'I don't know why I'm doing this – why I'm giving in and going back after all this time.'

Paula moved closer and put her hand on his arm. 'He's human – he's alone. Your mother just died. You didn't even go to the funeral, Daniel – I think this is the least you can do. It's only for a few days.'

Daniel looked resentfully thoughtful. 'Maybe that's the problem. Maybe that started the whole thing.'

124

'What?'

'Loneliness. He must be awfully lonely, though, to have come up with his obsessions. He used to play with a jigsaw puzzle, Paula, made entirely out of a shattered pane of glass. For hours. And then that . . . thing.' He gestured towards the briefcase, but Paula knew he meant what was in it.

'You'll survive,' she said.

'Yeah. To survive. That's the whole thing.'

There was another silence as he considered this.

'Funny,' he said presently. 'That's exactly what my father was always saying.'

The shadows had swallowed the old farmhouse by the time they found it, trapped in ancient trees at the end of a rough dirt road. The sun was gone, only a pale wash of orange light marking the direction in which it had sunk. Paula looked for a sign of light or life around the weathered building, but found only flooding blackness, shining where it was a window, splintered and peeling where it was the front door.

Daniel stopped the car and stretched back in his seat, yawning. 'I feel like I've been driving for a month.'

'You look it, too,' said Paula. 'I offered to drive . . .'

He shrugged. 'I'll get to sleep early tonight,' he said, pushing open the door. They got out of the car, into the quiet grey evening.

'Is anyone home?' Paula asked as Daniel came around the car.

'With my luck, yes. Come on.'

They walked through a fringe of dead grass, then carefully up the rotten steps. Daniel paused at the top, stepping back on the step beneath him. It creaked and thumped. Creaked and thumped. Daniel smiled nostalgically. Paula reminded herself that he had grown up in this house, out here in the middle of nowhere, far from the city and the campus where she had met him, where they were now living together. Daniel never spoke of his childhood or family, for reasons Paula was unsure of. He seemed bothered by his past, and perhaps somewhat afraid of it.

Across the porch, the door was a panel of emptiness, suddenly creaking as it opened. Paula tried to look through the widening gap; she jerked back as something pale came into view.

'Dad?'

125

The voice that replied was as worn and weathered as the house: 'Daniel, son, you've come. I knew you would.' The dim pale head bobbed and nodded in the darkness, coarse grey hair stirring. Something white fluttered into view, lower in the frame of darkness: a hand. Daniel's father was coming out.

'Um, I'm sorry I didn't make the funeral, dad. I was really busy with school and my job . . . uh . . .'

And here he came, swimming through the gloom, both white hands coming forward like fish, grasping Daniel. Paula saw the hunched dark figure of the old man only dimly; her eyes were fastened on those hands. They clutched, grabbed, prodded Daniel, exploring as if hungry. It was vaguely revolting. Daniel stood motionless; he had determined to be firm with his father, now he was faltering.

'Dad . . .'

Daniel pushed away one flabby hand but it was clever; it twisted, writhed, locked around his own. Paula gasped. The sluggish white fingers intertwined with Daniel's. He looked up at her, aghast, silently crying for help.

'Uh, hello,' Paula blurted, stepping towards them.

The hands jerked, stopped. The old man came around.

'Who are you? Daniel, who is this?'

'Dad, this is Paula, I told you about her. We're living together.'

Paula started to extend her hand. She remembered what might meet it, and drew away. 'Hello.'

'Living together?' Daniel's father said, watching him. 'Not married?'

'Uh, no, dad. Not yet, anyway.'

'Good . . . good. Good. It would weaken the bond, *break* the bond between us.' He did not even look at Paula again. His hands returned to Daniel, though not so frantically this time. They guided him forward into the house. Paula followed, shutting the door behind her, waiting for her eyes to adjust to the dark. When her vision had cleared, she could see Daniel and his father vaguely limned against a distant doorway; there was light beyond.

When she caught up, they were seating themselves on an antique sofa. It had been poorly kept; springs and padding spilled through in places. The room around them had been equally neglected; darkness lay upon it like soot. A single dull lamp glowed beside the sofa.

126

Daniel caught Paula's eye when she entered, warning her away from them. She sat in a nearby chair. Daniel was shrugging away the proddings of his father, fighting off the creeping fingers. But they kept coming, peering around the long shadows, then hurrying across Daniel while he sat at last unmoving, silent.

'We . . . we were terribly sorry to hear about your wife,' said Paula. The sound of her words muffled the rustling noises.

'Hm?' The old man sat up, leaving Daniel for a moment. His eyes were sharp, intense. 'Yes, it's bad . . . bad. She and I, we were – *close*, towards the end. Locked. Like this.' He clasped his two puffy hands together before his face, staring at them.

Daniel took this opportunity to move to a chair beside Paula, where his father could not follow. The old man hunched after him, hands straining, but didn't rise.

'Daniel, come back here. Sit beside me.'

'Uh, I think I'd better stay right here, dad.'

'Ah.' The old man hissed like a serpent. 'Stubborn. You were always stubborn – all of you. Your sister, your brother, they both resisted. Look what happened to them.'

Daniel looked nervously away from the old man's black stare. 'Don't talk about Louise like that, dad. It's all over now. And it had nothing to do with stubbornness.'

'Nothing? She ran away, Daniel, as you all did. She could not function, Daniel, she could not maintain herself. No more than the liver, the heart, the lungs, can function outside of the body. No more than the individual cells can function outside of the tissue that maintains them; even as this tissue is dependent on the organ it contributes to; as this organ in turn is dependent on all other organs to keep the whole intact.'

Paula had gone rigid in her chair, watching the old man speak. Suddenly that hanging black gaze turned to her.

'You,' he said. 'Do you know how an organism survives?'

'Pardon me?' she said weakly.

'It survives because its components work together, each one specialized towards its specific contribution to the organism. Specialization, yes. Louise was specialized; she did not survive.'

Daniel sighed, rubbing his forehead. 'Dad, it wasn't specialization. It was drugs. She made some mistakes.'

'And your brother?'

'What about him? He's doing fine. He has his own business now, he seems to be happy.'

'But he deserted us! He threatened the existence of us all. Your sister deteriorated. Your mother crumbled. And then you . . .'

'What about me?'

The old man shrugged. 'You returned. We still have a chance.'

Paula, through all this, said nothing. But she was thinking: *My God. My God.*

'I'm going to be going home, dad. I'm not staying very long.'

The old man snapped, 'What?'

'I told you that in my letter. I'm only staying for a day or two.'

'But you can't go back! You – you can't! Otherwise I have no chance – not alone. Nor you either, Daniel.'

'Look, dad—'

'Together we can survive, perhaps recover. And . . . and maybe your brother will return.'

'He's raising a family.'

'Ah, see?' He raised one pallid finger. 'He has learned!'

'Maybe we'd better not stay at all,' said Daniel, rising. His features had gone hard, faced with all this. Easier to run than worry about it.

'No!' This was a bleat, a plea, escaping from the old man as if he had been punctured. His expression, too, was wounded. 'Daniel, you can't . . .'

Paula rose and touched Daniel gently on the arm until he turned to her. Thank God he hadn't pulled away from *her* touch.

'Daniel,' she said, 'it's really getting late. I don't think you should do any more driving tonight.'

Daniel searched her expression, saw only concern. He nodded.

'We'll stay the night then, dad. But we're leaving in the morning.'

The old man started forward, then sank back in apparent despair. His breath was loud and laboured, wheezing; his hands crouched upon his knees, waiting for Daniel to stray near.

'You can't leave me, Daniel. I need you to survive, I *need* you!' His eyes glimmered, turning to Paula. '*You* know, don't you? That's why you're taking him from me . . . to strengthen yourself. Well you'll never have him. He's mine. Only mine.'

The words slid into Paula like a blade of ice, malevolent in their cold precision. She felt weak.

128

'I—' she began. 'Honestly, it's nothing like that. I don't want Daniel that way.'

The worm-white head rotated. 'Then you are a fool.'

'Paula,' Daniel repeated, 'maybe we'd better leave right now.'

'Haven't you heard what I've said? You mustn't leave!' Again, pain had replaced malicious insanity on the old man's pale features. Paula felt sorry for him.

'Daniel,' she said, 'just the night. It's really too late to leave.'

Daniel looked once at the poised hands of his father. Then he sighed, tensely, and nodded. 'But I don't want to hear any more of this, dad. One more word of it and we're going for sure.'

He turned back to Paula. 'Come on, I'll show you to your room. Hopefully there's something to eat around here.'

They started to leave, stepping towards another dark doorway.

'Daniel.' The voice was cold again, chilling. They stopped and looked back at the old man.

'You forget,' he said, eyes narrowing, face hardening. 'I'm stronger than you. I always was. You cannot resist the organism.'

Paula felt Daniel's muscles tighten beneath her hand.

'Good night, dad,' he said. They walked out.

Much later, in the darkened hallway upstairs, Daniel apologized again.

'He's gotten worse, Paula – worse than I had ever expected.' Daniel was nervous, his expression intensely bothered.

'It's all right, Daniel, really. Things happen to people as they get old.'

Daniel pulled her closer to him. It was cold in the draughty darkness, only the feeble grey moonlight trickling in through the window at the end of the hall. But the embrace was not warming; Daniel seemed to be protecting himself with Paula.

'It's as if he wants to swallow me – the way he keeps touching and grabbing. So . . . so *greedy!* I wouldn't have come back if I thought he'd be this way.'

'What did he used to be like?' Paula asked.

She looked up at Daniel, but he wasn't looking at her. His eyes were fixed on the door to his father's room, where a narrow fringe of light spread into the hall from under the door. His gaze seemed clouded, distant; he was remembering something. Something unpleasant.

'What is it, Daniel?'

He shook his head, slightly disgusted. It was the look he always got when she asked him about his childhood. She could feel his heart pounding against her breasts.

'*Daniel*, please, what's *wrong*?'

'I – I never told you. I never thought I'd tell anyone . . .'

She began to urge him on, but he continued without prompting.

'When I was a kid, I came out here one night – I'd had a nightmare, I think. It was late. I thought I heard noises in my parents' room; the light was coming out just like it is now. I knocked, but no one answered, so I opened the door – just a little, you know? – and started to go in.

'They were – they – just lying there, my mother and my father, wrapped around each other, and the light was so bright I wasn't sure that – that it was my mother there –

'I thought it was my *sister*, Paula!'

Paula caught her breath, then instantly relaxed. Daniel had been young – he'd seen his parents having sex. Such experiences often led to traumas, delusions. She could imagine it lurking in his mind all these years, breaking free now. Daniel was trembling.

'I yelled,' he continued. 'I remember yelling. But . . . *they didn't even move*. They just lay there until I ran away.'

He paused. Then, 'It wasn't my sister, of course. It *couldn't* have been, I can't believe it. She and my mother had the same colour of hair, and that was all I could see; the light was so bright, they were so close together . . . not moving. But I thought, for just a moment, that he . . .' Daniel looked towards the door and shuddered again.

'Daniel, do you want me to stay with you tonight?'

'What? Oh, no, that's all right.' He forced a laugh. 'Might be a little too hard on my dad. Maybe later, when he's asleep, you can sneak over . . .'

She yawned uncontrollably. 'Maybe. If I can stay awake.'

They kissed and said goodnight. Daniel parted with obvious reluctance, then went through the door into his room, closing it softly behind him. Paula looked down the hall, where light still spilled from beneath his father's door. Thank God she was on the other side of Daniel; he was between her and that old man. Daniel's story was ridiculous, of course: a childhood hallucination, magnified by the years. Things like that . . . incest . . . just didn't happen.

130

She slipped into her own room, and was somewhat dismayed to find that the lock didn't work. It needed a key that was nowhere to be found. Just another inconvenience among many. She was surprised, actually, that this place even had electricity. The room itself was dusty and suffocating, but she supposed she could stand it for one night.

In a minute she was in bed, trying to warm herself, the small table lamp shut off. When the sounds of her settling in had faded, the darkness swarmed around her uncomfortably, creaking and breathing in the manner of such old houses. She tried to ignore it, suddenly glad that they had stayed the night. Another nap in the car and she would have gone mad. At least she had been able to shower here. The old man was bearable when she didn't have to confront him directly.

Presently she drifted off, breathing with the house, her thoughts muffled by its thick atmosphere. But her sleep was restless, uncertain.

Paula was never positive she had slept at all when she realized that she was wide awake again. The stillness was incredible. The house was holding its breath. She sat up, certain that something had jarred her from sleep. A noise.

There. Perhaps from Daniel's room, perhaps from the hall. Perhaps trailing from the hall *into* Daniel's room . . .

Suddenly Paula was certain she'd heard a door shut. And – footsteps? But where were they going? Where had they been?

Those sounds were clear in the swollen darkness. But after a moment came less certain ones – rising and falling, always soft, as deceptive as the rush of blood in her ears. She was hearing things. No. Paula shook her head. She did *not* imagine things. Straining her ears, the sounds resolved themselves.

Voices. From Daniel's room.

They stopped.

Paula waited; heard nothing. A slight dragging sound that might have been the night passing through her mind. A dull footstep. And then, quite distinctly, three words, in the old man's voice:

'I need you!'

And creaking.

Paula was out of bed in an instant, hurrying quietly across the floor. She didn't trust that old man, not for a minute, not alone with Daniel. She found the door, jerked on the knob—

It was locked.

Paula remembered the sound that had awakened her; it re-

131

turned very clearly now that she could place it. It had clicked, metallically. A lock engaging.

She pounded once on the door. Again, louder, tugging at the knob.

And still not a sound from the other room.

'Daniel, *Daniel!*' Paula began to sob, wishing that there would be another sound, Daniel's voice.

The door. Quieting, she returned her attention to it. The lock didn't seem terribly strong, it was old. For a minute she considered throwing herself against the door, but it opened the wrong way. Chanting Daniel's name, she wrenched at the knob, pulling it back with all her strength. It seemed to give a little. Paula glanced back into the room, hoping for something useful. Her hand mirror glimmered on the table, reflecting moonlight. It was heavy, had a sturdy handle.

In a moment she was cracking the doorframe with it, chipping away the splintered wood, ripping and tearing. There was a grinding, and she yanked on the doorknob and the door crashed open, stunning her. She stood for just a second, considering the darkened hall beyond, then moved forward, into it, the mirror dropping from her fingers.

No sound from Daniel's room. None at all. Not through all her screaming and pounding and thundering . . . nothing.

'Daniel?' she called softly. She stopped outside his door, listening. Everything was grey and dim, shrouded in shadows. 'Daniel?'

Before she could reason with herself, she had turned the knob, had found it unlocked, had opened the door and entered.

Entered.

'Daniel?'

On the bed, something grey, tangled in blankets, two shapes. God help her, she was going forward, approaching the bed.

'Please, Daniel, are you all right?' The words came as a whimper.

She was at the bedside, eyes squinted with fear, so that all she could see was the two of them, vaguely, Daniel and his father pressed close together as if . . . as if kissing, or making love, his father on top.

Down in the gloom, a huge spider, almost filling the bed.

Her eyes closed.

'Daniel—'

Her hand went forward, to touch. Gingerly.

'Please—'

132

And there, on top, was the back of the old man's head, his hair coarse around her fingers. She moved her hand down, consciously, forcing it to touch his ear, and pass around it, still down. Over a rough cheek, withered skin. Skin that abruptly smoothed; skin that continued, unbroken . . .

Unbroken . . .

Straight to another cheek, another ear, and the back of Daniel's head.

Peter Valentine Timlett

Without rhyme or reason

Peter Valentine Timlett was born in London in 1933. He has two daughters 'who are quite the most magnificent thing that has ever happened to me'. He has worked as a jazz musician and in the distribution department of Howard & Wyndham; for several years he was a practising ritual magician, until he became frustrated by the aims of the occult group of which he was a member. His Seedbearers *trilogy is based on his occult experiences. His later work includes an Arthurian trilogy and a novel based on the witchcraft trial of Father Urbain Grandier,* Nor All Thy Tears *– none of which prepares us for the following.*

It was a large house, far bigger than she had expected. Must be five or six bedrooms at least. Not all that old, late Victorian probably, and the gardens were superb. It was set well back off a very minor road about a mile outside the village with not another house in sight, and as a consequence it was beautifully quiet and peaceful. She could be very happy here indeed.

She rang the bell and waited. After a couple of minutes she rang again. There must be someone at home, surely. Her appointment was for three o'clock, and she was punctual almost to the second.

'Yes?' said a sharp voice behind her.

She spun round, startled. 'Oh, I'm sorry. I didn't hear you come up.' The woman was in her late forties, tall and slimly built, with clear grey eyes that studied her firmly, almost fiercely. 'I am Miss Templeton – Deborah Templeton. The agency sent me. Are you Mrs Bates?'

The woman nodded. 'You are punctual. I like that.' The grey eyes swept her from head to foot. 'You are also very pretty. I told the agency that you had to be pretty. I like to be surrounded by beautiful things, including people. You are not

135

beautiful but you are very pretty. It's the dress, I think, and the hairstyle. Pretty but not beautiful.'

Miss Templeton's hand strayed involuntarily to her hair. 'I usually wear it down,' she said.

'Yes, you should. With your hair down, a decent eyeshadow, green I think, and a daring evening gown you could look quite stunning.'

The girl smiled. 'It's been a long time since I dressed like that. There has been no occasion.' Mrs Bates was no advertisement for her own philosophy. She wore patched and faded jeans, muddy at the knees, and a shapeless smock-like top that did little for her figure, and her hair was pushed up under an old hat that looked as though it might have begun life a decade earlier as a chic jockey-cap in a Chelsea boutique. But she had that classical facial bone structure that most women envy, giving her face that precious ageless look. Given the right clothes this woman could also look quite stunning, despite her age.

Mrs Bates was aware of her appraisal. 'One should dress to please oneself, not others,' she said firmly. 'When I am in the garden I dress like a gardener. In the evenings I dress like a woman, even when I'm alone.' She turned and walked away. 'Come into the house,' she said over her shoulder.

Miss Templeton followed her round the side of the house and into a sun-lounge through a pair of French windows. A curious woman, this Mrs Bates. The agency had been right to describe her as somewhat eccentric. But the room was beautiful. Each piece of furniture, as far as she could tell, was a genuine antique, and the woman waved her to a Victorian chaise-longue that alone would be worth a fortune by her own standards.

'As I am in my gardening clothes I will remain standing,' said Mrs Bates. 'I am a wealthy woman, Miss Templeton. The contents of this house are worth far more than the house itself, and for that reason alone I have to be careful whom I invite to live with me.'

'I understand.'

'And there is also the question of compatible personalities.' Again those grey eyes scanned her from head to toe. 'I imagine that the agency told you that I am an eccentric.'

'They said that you were a strongly individualistic person,' said Miss Templeton carefully.

'And so I am. This is my house and thus I have the right to determine how it shall be run.'

'Of course.'

'I am a fanatical gardener, Miss Templeton. Summer or winter I spend most of my time in the garden. I do not want a companion, let's be clear about that. I want someone to look after the house, leaving me free to tend the garden. Anything to do with the house, anything at all, will be your province.'

'So I understand. The agency gave me a list of all the duties and conditions and I find them very acceptable.'

'Good. As to meals, I see to myself during the week. You will be required to cook only one meal a week, on Saturday evening, for which I trust you will join me. I am a fanatic about the garden but not about the house. Providing it is kept reasonably clean and tidy you may come and go as you please. If you like walking you will find the countryside around here quite delightful. I am not a sociable woman, Miss Templeton. I can be quite charming when I put my mind to it but basically I prefer my own company. During the week, when you are not actually engaged upon work in the house, I would be grateful if you would remain in your rooms, but I would welcome your company on the Saturday evening.'

The girl nodded. 'You want the house to run smoothly without you being bothered about it, and I am to stay out of your way except on Saturdays.'

The woman smiled. 'Exactly. All this may sound a bit odd to you but I find that it suits me very well and I need someone who can fit in with that pattern, someone who is also quite happy with their own company most of the time. Your letter said that you are twenty-eight, an only child, and that your parents are dead. Any other attachments?'

'No, none, not even a romance.'

'I see. Sorry to ask these rather personal questions but the reasons are obvious. However, I think it is only fair that I reciprocate. So, Miss Templeton, I can tell you that I am forty-eight and do not give a damn who knows it. Like yourself, my parents also died when I was young, and like yourself, I am also an only child. Because of that I was already fairly wealthy in my own right even before I married, and my husband had money as well. We were married for ten years before he ran off with a younger woman.'

'Oh, I am sorry.'

'To be candid so was I. It was a good marriage, or so I thought, even though there were no children.'

'Why did he leave?'

For a brief moment a look of bleak hatred crossed her eyes. 'Let us say that the girl in question used her physical assets to good effect. So I, too, am quite alone with no attachments whatever. Did the agency tell you the salary?'

'Yes, the money is fine.'

'Good.' Again those grey eyes surveyed her critically. 'Well, Miss Templeton, I think we will get on very well indeed. I'll leave you for a few minutes to think about it. By all means have a look round the house. Your rooms are the first two on the right at the top of the stairs. There is a bedroom with your own bathroom attached, and a small sitting room with a connecting door. I'm sure you will be comfortable. When you are ready you'll find me in the garden,' and she turned and walked out on to the patio.

Deborah Templeton continued to sit there in the sun-lounge for a few moments. What a curious woman, she thought, and what an extraordinary interview. It was the sort of interview that a man might have conducted, not a woman. For a brief moment the thought crossed her mind that Mrs Bates might have unusual tastes, hence the reason perhaps why her husband had left her for a more normal woman and hence the reason perhaps why she was so insistent that her employee be young and attractive, but she dismissed the idea almost as soon as it arose. The woman might be odd but that oddness certainly didn't stem from Sappho.

She rose and walked through the house. She had not exactly come from penurious circumstances herself, but she had never lived in such luxurious surroundings as this. The kitchen was enormous and fitted with just about every labour-saving device on the market, and the main lounge was a superb room of elegance and grace. She walked up the main staircase and directly she entered what was to be her bedroom she knew that she simply had to have this position, for there was the most gorgeous four-poster bed curtained in woven tapestry of gold and red like something out of a fairy tale. It was silly, she knew, to let such a trivial thing as a bed clinch the decision, but it had always been a fantasy of hers to sleep in a four-poster.

She looked at herself in the tall cheval mirror and pulled a wry smile. Pretty but not beautiful. An accurate but deflating description. There had been a time, oh so many years ago now, when she had been stunningly attractive, in the days when she had deliberately dressed for that effect, but the image that stared back at her from the mirror was suburbanly 'mumsy' and hardly likely to stir the male libido.

She walked over to the window and stared down into the garden to where Mrs Bates was busy weeding the flowerbeds. The woman was certainly an autocrat, but if it was true that she would not see her for most of the time then that was no real problem. And yet there was still something odd about the whole thing. It was all too good to be true. Or perhaps the oddness was more to do with Mrs Bates herself than the position she was offering. Anyway, she would be a fool to turn it down.

The name on the list of duties that the agency had given her was Mary Elizabeth Bates, followed by an indecipherable signature. The name, Mary, was really quite apposite. 'Mary, Mary, quite contrary,' she murmured, 'how does your garden grow?' and the answer was that it grew very well, though Mary Bates herself was certainly contrary, contrary indeed.

The girl left the room and went downstairs into the garden. 'I think I will be very happy here,' she said simply.

The woman smiled. 'When I read your letter and saw your photograph I was already half certain, but when I saw you standing at the door I knew that you were going to be the one. When can you come?'

'Would Monday be too soon?'

Mrs Bates held out her hand. 'Monday will be fine. I'll see you then.'

Deborah had said Monday just to give herself the weekend should she wish to change her mind, but by Saturday lunch time she had given the landlady of her bedsit a week's rent in lieu of notice and was already packed and eager to go. Saturday evening and all day Sunday stretched to a seeming eternity but at last the Monday came and the taxi delivered her to her new home by noon.

Mrs Bates, still in the same old pair of jeans, welcomed her kindly but not effusively. 'You know where your rooms are. Use today to get settled in. Cook yourself a meal when you feel like it. I'll talk to you more fully, and go over the house accounts with you, tomorrow,' and she turned and went back into the garden. Deborah smiled wryly and lugged her suitcases up to her rooms, and by two o'clock she was unpacked and ready to explore the house.

Her mother had always said that you could know almost

everything there was to know about a woman's environment, temperament, and character by the contents of her kitchen cupboards, her wardrobe, and her laundry bin. The kitchen harboured no surprises, in view of the evidence of wealth in the rest of the house. The tins and jars and bottles in the cupboards revealed a highly expensive epicurean taste that promised a future of delightful cuisine, though no doubt it would prove a disaster to any calorie-controlled diet, and the wine rack contained a dozen or more bottles, mostly German hocks, though in amongst the array of white wine there were two bottles of Nuit St George. Mrs Bates obviously dined well.

The girl did not dare go into her employer's bedroom to see her wardrobe, but she did make a quick examination of the contents of the laundry bin and there met with a surprise that almost bordered on shock. There were two suspender belts, one of black and purple and one of black and scarlet, and five pairs of the scantiest briefs that she had ever seen, again in scarlet, black, and purple, and all of them lacy and highly revealing. And in addition there were two bras, one black and one red, so brief that they simply had to be quarter-bras that would make the point quite clear on any normally endowed woman. It was puzzling. These were the underclothes of a young Soho showgirl, not those of a forty-eight year old rural semi-recluse. Mrs Bates was proving to be something of an intriguing mystery.

At four o'clock it began to rain and Deborah rushed to her sitting room window to see what Mrs Bates would do. The woman hurried into the conservatory and emerged a few minutes later dressed in wellington boots, oilskin trousers, and a waterproof anorak with the hood pulled up over her head, and calmly went back to work. She really did look quite ridiculous bent over the flowerbeds with the rain drumming on her back. Being late June the weather was still quite warm despite the rain, and if you are suitably waterproofed then there was no logical reason why you should not work in the rain, and yet it seemed ludicrous. People didn't tend their gardens in the pouring rain. It simply wasn't *done*. And how on earth could you equate that comical and eccentric figure down there in the rain with the sort of woman that wore lurid and provocative underclothes? It was delightfully mysterious.

Deborah did not see Mrs Bates that evening, but on the following morning she found a note in the kitchen asking her to come into the library after breakfast to go over the house accounts. Well at last Deborah would see Mrs Bates in something other than jeans, but when she entered the library the result was oddly disappointing. She was dressed in pale blue slacks and a white high-necked blouse. The outfit was simple, tasteful, and hardly in keeping with the erotic contents of the laundry bin. And Mrs Bates proved to have a good brain, neat, precise, and logical. The house accounts were all neatly annotated and filed in alphabetical order in a proper filing cabinet in the library, and within half an hour the familiarization talk was over and Mrs Bates changed back into her jeans and returned to the garden.

In accordance with her instructions Deborah Templeton kept out of her employer's way for the rest of that Tuesday and all day Wednesday, though Mrs Bates in the garden was constantly in her view from the house. And it was this constant view of her employer that revealed yet another oddity. It was true that Mary Bates gave her attention to all parts of the garden, but again and again she returned to that same flowerbed where Deborah had first seen her. If she moved to another part of the garden it would only be a matter of minutes, ten at the most, before she returned to what was obviously her favourite spot.

The flowerbed was a low mound some twenty feet long and six feet wide, and it would have been called a rockery but for the fact that it had no rocks. Deborah Templeton was no gardener and could scarce put a name to any particular plant in that blaze of colour except for the tulips and the aubretia, and indeed to her untutored eye some of them seemed very unusual and thus probably quite rare, but it was certainly a beautiful bed and obviously thrived on the loving care that Mrs Bates lavished upon it. 'With silver bells and cockleshells,' she murmured as she saw Mrs Bates move back to her favourite spot for the umpteenth time.

On Thursday she went shopping in the village and there discovered yet another oddity, one that was rather disquieting. 'Well, I will say this for Mrs Bates,' said the butcher, an enormous man with fat red cheeks, 'she certainly knows how to pick 'em!'

'How do you mean?'

Fortunately the shop was empty, otherwise the man might not have been so forward and thus the oddity would have remained hidden a little longer. 'Well, you're a very attractive young lady, Miss Templeton, if I may say so, but then all of Mrs Bates' girls have been good lookers.'

From the later viewpoint of hindsight Deborah decided that it was at that precise moment that the first warning bell began to sound inside her. 'All of them?' she said. 'Why, how many have there been?'

The butcher pursed his lips. 'You're the seventh, I think.'

She signed the bill and was just about to leave when on impulse she said: 'Do you remember their names?'

'Of course,' he said, and rattled off six names, 'and you're the best looking one so far,' he added gallantly.

Once outside the shop she wrote the names in her pocket diary before she forgot them and then began the mile walk home, but before she left the village she placed a call from the public telephone box. It was not a call that she would have cared to make from the house.

The agency was polite and apologetic but not very forthcoming. Yes, she was indeed the seventh. Yes, the six names were correct. No, they had not told her about her predecessors because of Mrs Bates' instructions to that effect. As far as they understood, all the girls had quickly grown bored with the job, having little to do, and had left. No, they had not seen any of the girls after they had left. In each case they had not known that the girl had left until Mrs Bates had contacted the agency for a replacement. No, they did not think it particularly unusual.

Deborah did not see Mrs Bates to speak to that Thursday, nor the Friday. It was not until the Saturday morning that her employer sought her out. 'I do trust that you have not forgotten that today is Saturday.'

'No, of course not. Dinner will be at eight.'

At seven o'clock, with everything prepared and going nicely, Deborah went up to dress. She took a quick shower and then combed her hair down long and full. She then tried on her only full-length evening gown. She had not worn it for several years and it still fitted surprisingly well. She had not put on as much weight as she had feared. The gown was black with a simple flowing line. It was a cross-over halter-neck that left half her breasts exposed and all her midriff to below the navel. Not content with that the dress was slashed up the front to mid-thigh and fitted so tightly around her hips and bottom that any underclothing at all, even the merest wisp, always spoiled the line of it, and she wondered how on earth she had ever had the courage to wear it. She looked at herself critically in the cheval mirror and shook her head. It was a great dress, and she would love to wear it just to disprove that 'pretty but not beautiful' tag, but it really wasn't very suitable for this present occasion. Reluctantly she stripped and folded it away, put on underclothes and a simple calf-length cocktail dress that did not reveal anything, and left the room to go downstairs.

As she was closing her bedroom door she saw her employer going down the stairs, and the sight almost made her gasp. Her own black evening gown would have been declared modest by comparison to the creation that Mrs Bates was wearing. It was a pure white gown cut in a Grecian style of a material so fine that she trailed wisps of it behind her as she moved, and it was quite staggering how little of Mrs Bates it covered. The contrast to the wellington-booted figure in the garden was so startling that it was scarcely believable that it was the same woman.

Without even thinking about it Deborah went back into her bedroom, stripped off her cocktail dress and her underclothes, put on her evening gown, and went downstairs to serve dinner.

Neither gown was mentioned during dinner, indeed little was said at all. Mrs Bates made an appreciative comment about the prawn cocktail, was quite complimentary in respect to the Tournedos Rossini, and said that she found the lemon sorbet to be delicious. It was only when they withdrew to the main lounge for coffee that the first mention was made. 'An excellent meal, my dear,' said Mrs Bates, 'and I completely withdraw my earlier remark about being merely pretty. You look quite stunning. I doubt that any man could keep his hands off you.'

The girl smiled. 'With you in the room I doubt that he would even see me.'

Mrs Bates looked down at herself. 'Yes, men are quite stupidly physical. With a dress like this, or one like yours, a man's every instinct prompts him to reach out and remove what little there is. All female virtues are as nothing compared to the power of a revealing gown, as I know to my cost.'

Deborah sipped her coffee. 'The girl who took your husband?' she said softly.

The woman smiled grimly. 'We entertained a lot in those days, mostly business acquaintances of my husband's, and people from his office. I did not dress then as you see me now. I used to dress elegantly and tastefully, but never revealingly. An old-fashioned attitude, perhaps, in these days of blatant sexuality, but we all have our own particular tastes and standards.'

143

'And the girl?'

'A personal assistant to one of my husband's directors. She came to one of our dinner parties dressed in a gown almost exactly like this one and made it perfectly obvious to my husband that he need only snap his fingers for her to remove it altogether.' Mrs Bates put her coffee cup on a side table and leant back in the armchair. 'Two weeks later he left me and went off with her.'

'I'm sorry,' said the girl quietly.

The woman was silent for a moment. 'He would have come back to me, you know, when the novelty had worn off, and I would have taken him. It was a good marriage. Men are so vulnerable to a really determined and blatant advance from an attractive woman. Few of them can resist. It is almost part of their nature, you might say.'

'What happened?'

'Three weeks after he left they were both killed in a car crash in southern France, and I hope she rots in hell for all time. And it was all so unnecessary. A discreet affair would have been far better. It would have satisfied the sexual attraction and preserved the marriage.'

The girl did not comment. Her sympathy was instinctively with the husband. An autocratic woman such as Mrs Bates would not be easy to live with from any aspect, sexual or otherwise. There was probably more than one reason why he had left her.

'And all because of a revealing evening gown,' said Mrs Bates bitterly. 'That girl had worked at that office for two years and I *know* that there had been nothing between them prior to that dinner party. It was the gown that did it.'

Deborah sipped at her coffee again. Possible, but not likely. If it had only been a question of sex then a discreet affair would indeed have satisfied the situation. There had to be more to it than that. The way this woman kept harping on that one particular aspect seemed to suggest that Mrs Bates felt very inadequate and inferior in that area.

'And so I went out and bought this gown, and some other clothing,' said Mrs Bates. 'And do you know why?'

Deborah shook her head. She didn't like the way this was going. The woman really did have a most peculiar expression in her eyes.

Mrs Bates stood up abruptly. 'Then I will show you. Come with me,' and she took the girl's hand and led her to the other

144

end of the lounge to where a large mirror hung on the wall. 'That's why,' she said, pointing to the two reflections. 'Having come off second best on one notable occasion I wanted to see how I would compare if I were similarly dressed.'

The girl felt her spine begin to tingle. Not fear exactly, but that instinctive nervous apprehension that the sane sometimes feel in the company of the insane. By God, how long had this woman brooded on her misfortune to have produced this sort of crazy reaction? This obviously explained the long string of attractive girls. Mrs Bates was measuring herself against them, one after the other. And then what? If the measurement was in the older woman's favour then presumably that was an end of the matter, honour having been satisfied. But what if the comparison was unfavourable?

Deborah looked at the two reflections. Mary Bates really was an attractive woman. Her body was trim and taut, and her figure was still quite superb, even without a bra, and in that wisp of a gown she looked like a high priestess of a pagan cult, sensual, uninhibited, and devastatingly provocative. Few women her age could even begin to compare. But she was forty-eight years of age, and she looked it. Nothing could hide that difference in age between the two women reflected in that mirror, and ironically the two provocative gowns served only to reveal that difference more clearly. Deborah was not vain about her own looks, but she knew that if a choice had to be made at that precise moment then most men would choose herself. Mrs Bates simply did not compare.

The girl smiled nervously. 'There's no comparison,' she said lightly. 'If there were any men around I wouldn't stand a chance.' In the mirror she saw the woman's eyes narrow to an expression of cold hatred.

'Nonsense, my dear,' said Mrs Bates smoothly. 'You are far more attractive than I. If the whole situation occurred again my husband would undoubtedly go off with you.'

Deborah released her hand and walked away back to the coffee table. 'You underestimate yourself, Mrs Bates.' She picked up her shawl. 'I'm not attractive to men and never have been, no matter what I wear. Why do you think I live on my own? It's not by choice, I assure you.' She began to move towards the door. Oh God, she simply had to escape from this stupid insanity. 'Anyway, it's getting late, and the wine has given me a headache. If you'll excuse me I think I'll go to bed.'

The look of hatred had vanished from the woman's eyes. 'By

all means,' she said coldly. 'Thank you for a lovely dinner, and a most entertaining evening.'

The girl could not get to her room fast enough. Once inside the bedroom she leant back against the door and closed her eyes. Her hands were trembling, and sweat had broken out over her whole body. What a weird scene! No wonder the others had left in so much of a hurry. First thing tomorrow she would see if she could get her old bedsit back again. She was not going to stay in this house with that crazy woman a minute longer than absolutely necessary. She stripped off her gown, towelled herself dry, put on her nightdress, and lay down on the bed, but her mind was in too much of a turmoil for sleep.

It was about half past eleven when she heard Mrs Bates come up the stairs and go to her own bedroom, but an hour later Deborah was still fretfully awake. She went to the open window and stared down into the garden. It looked even more beautiful by moonlight, and the silver bells really did look silver. It was a warm night, and oppressively close. Perhaps a walk round the garden would calm her down.

Silently she opened the bedroom door and stood there listening, but all was quiet. That wretched woman must be fast asleep by now, dreaming whatever weird images would rise in such a neurotic as Mrs Bates. She slipped on her dressing gown over her nightdress and went downstairs and out into the garden.

It was a lovely night, and for the first time during that entire evening she was able to breathe more easily. It was in many ways a dreadful shame that she had to leave. On the surface it was an ideal job in ideal surroundings, but even from the beginning it had seemed too good to be true, and so it had proved. She sighed and meandered across the lawn. Such a beautiful garden, but such a weird gardener. Even here in the garden the behaviour of her employer had been decidedly odd, coming back again and again to this particular spot. Deborah looked down at the long low mound of Mrs Bates' favourite flower-bed. 'Mary, Mary, quite contrary,' she murmured, 'how does your garden grow? With silver bells and cockleshells, and pretty maids all in a row.'

And it was then, at that precise moment, that the earlier warning bells, the odd behaviour of Mrs Bates, and the fact of the missing girls, all came together in an explosion of realization in her mind. So sudden was the revelation, and so terrifying, that for a full minute she could not move at all even though every instinct in her screamed out for her to get away, and her

146

whole body trembled with wave after wave of piercing coldness. Then slowly she began to back away. Oh dear God, it cannot be, surely!

'Admiring the flowers in the moonlight?' said a voice behind her.

Deborah spun round and there, just a few feet away, was Mrs Bates looking pale and ghostly in a flowing white dressing gown. This second shock, coming so close on the first, came near to causing a fatal heart attack, quite literally. The girl gave a piercing shriek of terror and fled in panic towards the house, bursting in through the French windows and flying up the stairs to her bedroom.

There was no key to the bedroom door, and no straight-backed chair to prop under the door handle. Frantically she dragged the dressing table across the carpet and rammed it against the door, and only just in time.

'What on earth is the matter, girl!' Mrs Bates called out from the corridor, rattling the handle and pushing against the door. 'Let me in. You frightened the life out of me, shrieking like that. What on earth is the matter? Let me in!'

Deborah said nothing. She picked up a pair of scissors and backed away to the middle of the room. Mrs Bates had shoved the door open a couple of inches but could move it no more, and Deborah saw her pale hand come snaking round the edge to identify the obstruction.

'This is ridiculous!' the woman shouted. 'Remove that thing and open this door!'

'Get out! Get out!' the girl shrieked.

The hand disappeared and then there was silence. Fifteen seconds passed, half a minute, and still there was no sound from the corridor.

'You forgot the connecting door,' said a calm voice behind her, and a hand descended on her shoulder.

Again that shriek of hysterical terror rang out. Deborah spun round and stabbed blindly with her scissors, again and again. She stabbed the woman's eyes, and her face, and her shoulders, and fell with her to the floor, and kept on stabbing again and again, at her arms, at her breast, and again and again and again at what was left of her face, and then she sprang clear, flung away the scissors, raced through the connecting door, through the sitting room and out into the corridor, and stumbled hysterically down the stairs to the telephone.

The police arrived twenty minutes later; an inspector, a

147

sergeant, two male constables, and a policewoman. Little sense had been made of the hysterical babble on the telephone and they had come prepared for almost anything, though hardly for what they actually found. The girl was covered in blood from head to foot, and at first they assumed that she had been attacked and savagely beaten, but as her story began bubbling out they began to realize that here was something far more grim. 'They're out there, I tell you, buried in the flowerbed, murdered by that crazy woman upstairs!' she finished. 'And I was to be next! If you don't believe me, go and look!' and she burst into great racking sobs.

Leaving the constables downstairs with the girl, the Inspector and the sergeant went up to the bedroom. They came out two minutes later and leant against the wall, fighting down the nausea. 'You knew Mrs Bates quite well,' said the inspector at last. 'Is that her?'

The sergeant wiped his brow. 'How the hell can I say! It doesn't even look human!'

Presently the two men came down the stairs and walked over to the open french windows. 'There should be a spade or a fork out there somewhere,' said the inspector. 'Take the two lads. Just dig enough to verify the story. The rest can wait.'

Thirty minutes later the sergeant returned and the two men exchanged a whispered conversation, and then the inspector came over to Deborah. 'Now let's take this again from the beginning.'

'What more do you want!' said the girl hysterically. 'You've seen what's upstairs and you've seen what's in the garden! For God's sake get me out of this place.'

'I've seen you, and certainly I've seen what's upstairs,' said the inspector grimly. 'It's the rest of the story I don't understand.'

The girl sprang to her feet. 'Good God, there are six dead girls buried in the flowerbed! I've told you why and how! What else is there to understand!'

The inspector shook his head. 'There is no one buried in the flowerbed, Miss Templeton,' he said quietly, 'no one at all. Now let's start right from the beginning – and take it very, very slowly.'

Bob Shaw

Love me tender

Bob Shaw was born in 1931 and educated in Belfast. He worked in structural engineering and aircraft design, then in 1958 he became a journalist. After three years on a daily newspaper he began to specialize in industrial public relations, but in 1975 he became a full-time author. In 1973 he and his wife Sadie and three children moved to Stan Laurel's birthplace in the English Lakes. All of which, apart from Stan Laurel, is an awfully po-faced introduction to this large shy man who can drink everyone else into a state so euphoric that they will laugh at his horrid jokes about koalas and Brighton Pier and a great deal else. He has been guest of honour at conventions in Sweden, USA, England, Scotland, Italy and Belgium, and is to be found at most British sf conventions. You can locate him by the groans at the end of the joke.

Among his novels are The Shadow of Heaven, Vertigo, *and* Invisible Mountains. *He also has several collections of short stories to his name.*

It's a funny thing – I can think all right, but I can't think about the future. Tomorrow doesn't seem to exist for me any more. There's only today, and this drowsy, dreamy acceptance.

Most of the time it's cool here in the shack, the mosquito screens are holding together fairly well, and the bed is a whole lot better than some of the flea pits I've been in lately.

And she waits on me hand and foot. Couldn't be more attentive. Brings me food and drink – all I can stomach – and cleans me up afterwards. Even when I wake up during the night I can see her standing at the door of the room, always watching, always waiting.

But what's she waiting for? That's what I ask myself every so often, and when I do . . .

149

The swamp buggy had started off life as an ordinary Volkswagen, a beetle convertible, but somebody had extended the axles and fitted pudgy aircraft tyres which spread the vehicle's weight sufficiently to keep it from sinking in mud. Snow chains had been wrapped around the tyres to provide traction. The buggy was noisy, ungainly and uncomfortable, but it was able to negotiate the narrow tracks that ran through the Everglades, and Joe Massick felt it had been well worth the trouble he had taken to steal it.

He sat upright at the wheel, glancing over his shoulder every now and again as though expecting to see a police helicopter swooping down in pursuit, but the sky remained a featureless grey void. The air was hot and so saturated with water that it reminded him of the atmosphere inside the old-fashioned steam laundry where he had once worked as a boy. He did his best to ignore the sweat which rolled down his slab-like body, concentrating his attention on maintaining a north-westerly course in the general direction of Fort Myers.

His best chance of avoiding capture lay in making a quick crossing of the Florida peninsula without being seen, but it was beginning to dawn on him that the journey was not one to be undertaken lightly. The sloughs and swamps of the northern Everglades made up one of the last truly wild regions of the country, and as a confirmed town-dweller he felt threatened by every aspect of the flat and prehistoric landscape through which he was travelling. For the past thirty minutes he had been encountering stands of lifeless trees draped with Spanish moss, and now the intervals between the trees were growing so brief that he appeared to be entering a dead forest which provided a habitat for countless varieties of birds, insects and reptiles. The sound of the buggy's engine was almost drowned by the protests of the colonies of birds it disturbed, and on all sides there was a furtive agitation of other life forms, a sense of resentment, of being scrutinized and assessed by primeval eyes.

It was a feeling which Massick disliked intensely, prompting him to seek reassurance from the buggy's fuel gauge. The position of the needle showed that he still had three-quarters of a tank – more than enough, even allowing for forced detours, to take him to the far side of Big Cypress. He nodded, relaxing slightly into the burlap-covered seat, and had driven for perhaps another minute when a disturbing thought lodged itself like a pebble in the forefront of his mind.

According to the fuel gauge the tank had been three-quarters full when he first set out in the buggy almost an hour earlier. An optimist might have concluded that the vehicle's modest engine was using practically no gasoline, but Massick was beyond such naïvety. He tapped the gauge with his knuckles and saw that the needle was immovable, locked in place.

Doesn't prove a thing, he thought, vainly trying to sell himself the idea. *For all I know, the tank was filled right up.*

A mile further along the track, as he had known in his heart it was bound to do, the engine cut without even a preliminary cough. Massick turned the steering wheel and brought the buggy to rest in a thicket of saw grass and huge ferns. He sat for a moment with his head bowed, whispering the same swear word over and over again until it came to him that he was wasting precious time. The girl back in West Palm Beach might have died – he had been forced to hit her pretty hard to keep her quiet – but if she was still alive she would have given his description to the police and they would have connected him with the one in Orlando and the other one up in Fernandino. In any case, there was no time for sitting around feeling sorry for himself.

Massick picked up the plastic shopping bag which contained all his belongings, stepped down from the buggy, squelched his way back on to the trail and began walking. The surface was better for walking on than he had expected – probably owing its existence to the oil prospecting that had been carried out in the area some years earlier – but it soon became apparent that he was not cut out for trekking across swamps. He had been desperately tired to start off with, and before he had taken a dozen paces his clothes were sopping with perspiration, binding themselves to his well-larded body, maliciously hampering every movement. The air was so humid that he felt himself to be drinking with his lungs.

Now that he was proceeding without the roar of an engine and the clatter of chains, the swamp seemed ominously quiet and again he had the impression of being watched. The profusion of tree trunks and the curtains of hanging moss made it difficult to see far in any direction, and for all he knew he could have been accompanied by a stealthy army whose members were waiting until he collapsed with exhaustion before closing in. Childish though the fantasy was, he was unable to dismiss it completely from his mind and occasionally as he walked he fingered the massy solidity of the .38 pistol in his bag. The sky sagged close overhead, heavy with rain.

Two hours later he crossed one of the innumerable small concrete bridges which carried the track over dark streams and found that it forked in two directions, both of them uninviting to an equal degree. The sun had been invisible all along, and now that dusk was falling Massick's rudimentary trail sense was totally unable to ·cope with the task of identifying the branch which lay closest to the north-westerly course he wanted. He paused, breathing heavily, and looked around him in the tree-pillared gloom, suddenly understanding why in local Indian legend the big swamp was regarded as the home of ancestral spirits. It was easy to see the ghosts of dead men standing in slim canoes, drifting in silence through the endless colonnades and caverns.

The realization that he was going to have to spend the night in such surroundings jerked Massick out of his indecision. He chose the right-hand path and moved along it at an increased pace, looking out for a hillock of any description upon which he would have a reasonable chance of remaining dry while he slept. It was only when he recalled that snakes also had a preference for high ground, especially in the wet season, that he admitted to himself the seriousness of his situation. He had no real idea how far he was from the townships of the west coast, and even if he did succeed in making his way through Big Cypress on foot he was going to emerge looking conspicuously bearded and filthy – the sort of figure that any cop would want to interrogate on sight.

The thought of being caught and put back in prison after less than a month of freedom caused Massick to give an involuntary moan. He reached into the plastic bag, took out the bottle of rum he had acquired at the same time as the swamp buggy and drank the few ounces of neat liquor it contained. The rum was warm and had an aftertaste of burnt brown sugar which made him wish he had a full fifth for solace during the approaching night. He hurled the bottle away, heard it come down with a splash and on the instant a cicada began to chirp nearby as though he had startled it into life. Within seconds a hundred others had taken up the chorus, walling him in with sound, advertising his presence for the benefit of any creature – human or inhuman – which might be lurking in the encompassing darkness. Startled, prey to fears he was unable to acknowledge, he quickened his pace even though each passing minute made the track more difficult to see. He was beginning to contemplate retracing his steps to the last concrete bridge when a yellow glow sprang into existence some distance ahead and slightly to his left.

Convinced for the moment that he had seen the headlights of an approaching vehicle, Massick snatched his pistol out of the bag, then realized there were no mechanical sounds such as another swamp buggy would have made. Keeping the gun at the ready, he went forward until he reached a barely discernible side track which branched off to the left and seemed to lead straight towards the glimmer of light. All the indications were that, against the odds, he had found some kind of habitation in the heart of the swamp.

The pang of pleasure and relief Massick experienced was not quite enough to obliterate his natural wariness. The only reason he could envisage for people living in the waterlogged wilderness was that they were wardens for one of the area's wildlife sanctuaries – and, for him, walking into an official establishment which had radio equipment could be as disastrous as calling in at a police station. He threaded his way along the path, trying not to make any sound as he negotiated successive barriers of dark vegetation, and after several minutes reached a hummock upon which was perched a wooden shanty. The wan radiance which seeped from the windows and the screen door was swallowed up by the surrounding blackness, but there was enough refraction to show that the building had been constructed from second-hand timbers – which pretty well ruled out the possibility of it being an outpost of authority. Emboldened by what he had found thus far, Massick crossed a cleared area to the nearest window and cautiously looked through it.

The room beyond the smeared glass was lit by oil lanterns hanging from hooks in the ceiling. Much of the floor space was taken up with stacks of cardboard boxes, and in the centre of the room was a rough wooden table at which sat a small stoop-shouldered man of about sixty. He had cropped grey hair, a sprinkling of silver stubble around his chin, and tiny crumpled ears which gave the impression of being clenched like fists. He was dressed in well-worn slacks and a faded green beach shirt. On the table before him was a bottle of whisky and several glass jars containing what looked like small twists of coloured paper. He was preoccupied with removing the coloured objects from the jars and carefully placing them in individual plastic boxes, pausing now and then to swig whisky straight from the bottle.

The room had two interior doors, one of them leading into a

primitive kitchen. The other door was closed, but Massick guessed it led into a bedroom. He remained at the window long enough to assure himself that the occupant of the shanty was alone, then slipped the pistol into his side pocket, walked quietly to the screen door and tapped on it. The mosquito mesh made a noise like distant thunder. A few seconds later the small man appeared with a flashlight which he shone on Massick's face.

'Who's out there?' he growled. 'Whaddaya want?'

'I got stranded,' Massick explained, enduring the searching brilliance. 'I need shelter for the night.'

The man shook his head. 'I got no spare room. Go away.'

Massick opened the door and went inside, crowding the other man back. 'I don't need much room, and I'll pay you twenty dollars for the night.'

'What's the idea? What makes you think you can just walk in here?'

For a reply Massick used a trick he had perfected over a period of years. He smiled broadly and at the same time hardened his gaze and projected a silent message with all the conviction he could muster: *If you cross me up I'll tear your head right off your body.* The little man suddenly looked uncertain and backed further into the room.

'I got to be paid in advance,' he said, trying to retain some advantage.

'Fair enough. I tell you what I'll do, Pop. I could use a few drinks to make up some of the sweat I lost, so here's an extra ten for a share in that bottle. How's that?' Massick took his billfold from his pocket, counted out thirty dollars and handed them over.

'Okay, I guess.' The man took the money and, looking mollified, tucked it into his shirt pocket. 'The whole bottle didn't cost ten.'

'Consider it a reward for your hospitality to a weary traveller,' Massick said jovially, smiling again. He was prepared to be generous while armed with the knowledge that when he left he would be taking the money back, along with any other cash and valuables his host happened to have around. 'What's your name, Pop?'

'Ed. Ed Cromer.'

'Nice to meet you, Ed.' Massick went on into the room he had surveyed from the outside and picked up the whisky bottle from the table, observing as he did so that the small coloured objects his host had been packaging were dead butterflies and moths. 'Is this some kind of a hobby you've got here?'

'Business,' Cromer replied, squaring his thin shoulders importantly. 'Profession.'

'Is that a fact? Is there much demand for bugs?'

'Me and my partner supply lepidopterists – them's collectors – all over the state. All over the country.'

'Your partner?' Massick slid his hand into the pocket containing the pistol and glanced towards the closed door of the bedroom. 'Is he in there?'

'No!' The expression of pride vanished from Cromer's face and his eyes shuttled anxiously for a moment. 'That's my private room in there. There's nobody allowed in there bar me.'

Massick noted the reaction with mild interest. 'There's no need to get up tight, Ed. It was just when you mentioned your partner . . .'

'He runs the store up in Tampa. Only comes down one day a month to pick up the new catch.'

'He'll be here soon, will he?'

'Not for a couple of weeks. Say, mister, what's the third degree for? I mean, I could ask you who you are and where you're from and what you're doin' wanderin' around Big Cypress in the dark.'

'That's right,' Massick said comfortably. 'You could ask.'

He cleared some magazines from a wicker chair and sat down near the window, suddenly realizing how close he was to total exhaustion. His intention had been to press on towards the west coast in the morning, but unless Cromer had a swamp buggy parked out of sight nearby it might be best to wait until the partner arrived with transportation. It would be difficult to find a safer place to lie low and rest for a couple of weeks. Turning the matter over in his mind, he took off his sweat-stained jacket and draped it over the back of the chair, then settled back to drink whisky.

There followed fifteen minutes of almost total silence during which Cromer, who had returned to his meticulous sorting and mounting of butterflies, glanced expectantly at Massick each time he raised the bottle to his lips. At length, realizing there was going to be no taking of turns, he took a fresh bottle of Canadian Club from a cupboard in the corner and began drinking independently. After his initial querulousness he showed no sign of resenting his unexpected guest, but Massick noticed he was drinking somewhat faster than before and becoming less precise in his movements. Massick watched contentedly, enjoying his ability to cause apprehension in others simply by being near them, as Cromer fitted a jeweller's magnifier over his right eye and began examining a small heap of blue-winged insects one by one, using his flashlight to supplement the room's uncertain illumination.

'What are you doing now, Pop?' he said indulgently. 'Is it all that hard to tell the boys from the girls?'

'Checkin' for look-alikes,' Cromer mumbled. 'Mimics, they're called. You don't know nothin' about mimics, do you?'

'Can't say I do.'

Cromer sniffed to show his contempt. 'Didn't think you would somehow. Even them so-called experts up in Jacksonville with their fancy college degrees don't know nothin' about mimics. *Nobody* knows more about mimics than I do, and one of these days . . .' He broke off, his narrow face taut with sudden belligerence, and took a long drink of whisky.

'You're going to show them a thing or two, are you, Professor?' Massick prompted. 'Make them all sit up and take notice?'

Cromer glanced at the bedroom door, then selected two pale blue butterflies from the table and held them out on the palm of his hand. 'Whaddaya say about them? Same or different?'

Massick eyed the closed door thoughtfully before turning his attention to the insects. 'They look the same to me.'

'Want to bet on it?'

'I'm not a gambling man.'

'Just as well – you'da lost your money,' Cromer said triumphantly. 'This one on the left has a kinda blue glaze all over his wings and the birds leave him alone because he don't taste good. This other feller does taste good to birds, so he fools them by copyin' the same blue, but he does it by mixin' in blue bits and white bits on his wings. Of course, you need one of them microscopes to see it proper. I'm goin' to get me one of them microscopes real soon.'

'Very interesting,' Massick said, abstracted, noticing for the first time that the door to the room he had presumed to be a bedroom was secured by a farmhouse-type latch and that the latch was held down by a twist of wire. Was it possible, he wondered, that Cromer had something valuable hidden away? It was difficult to imagine what the shabby recluse might have, but it was a well-known fact that elderly people who lived in conditions of abject poverty often had large sums of money

156

tucked into mattresses and under floorboards. In any case, there would be no harm in investigating the matter while he was actually on the premises. Deciding that no immediate action was required, he continued sipping whisky and pretending to listen to Cromer's rambling discourse on entomology.

The little man appeared to have an extensive though informal knowledge of his subject which he dispensed in an anecdotal folksy style, with frequent references to Seminole legends, but his words were becoming so slurred that it was almost impossible to follow his meaning at times. The practice of mimicry among insects, fish and animals seemed to fascinate him and he kept returning to it obsessively, drinking all the while, his face and clamped-down ears growing progressively redder as the level in his bottle went down.

'You ought to go easy on that stuff,' Massick told him with some amusement. 'I don't want to put you to bed.'

'I can handle it.' Cromer stood up, swaying even though he was holding the edge of the table, and gazed at Massick with solemn blue eyes. 'I gotta consult the head of the family.'

He lurched to the outer door and disappeared through it into the night, already fumbling with his trouser zip. Massick waited a few seconds, stood up and was surprised to discover that he too was unsteady on his feet. He had forgotten that exhaustion and hunger would enhance the effects of the liquor he had consumed. Blinking to clear his vision, he crossed the room to the locked door, pulled the wire away from the latch and dropped it on the floor. He opened the door, took one step into the room beyond and froze in mid-stride, his jaw sagging in surprise.

There was a young woman lying on the narrow bed, her body covered by a single sheet.

At the sound of Massick's entrance she raised herself on one elbow – a strangely languid movement, as though she was weakened by illness – and he saw that she had smooth, swarthy skin and black hair. His impression that she was an Indian was strengthened by the fact that she had three dots tattooed in a triangle on her forehead, although he had never seen that particular marking before. She stared at him in silence for a moment, showing no signs of alarm, and began to smile. Her teeth were white, forming a flawless crescent.

'I'm sorry,' Massick said. 'I didn't know . . .' He backed out of the room, pulling the door closed, trying to understand why the sight of the woman had been so disconcerting. Was it the

157

sheer unexpectedness of her presence in Cromer's bedroom? Was it that the circumstances suggested she was being held captive? Massick picked up his bottle, gulped some whisky and was wiping his mouth with the back of his hand when the answer to his questions stole quietly into his mind. She had looked at him – and had smiled.

He could not remember a single occasion in the twenty-odd years of his adult life on which a woman had set eyes on him for the first time and had reacted by smiling. As a youth he had spent hours before the mirror trying to decide what it was about his appearance that made all the girls in his age group avoid his eyes and refuse point blank to date him. There had been a two-year period in which he had done his best to conform to the same image as the sexually successful young men in the neighbourhood – trying to put a twinkle into the slate pellets that were his eyes, trying to smile when every muscle in his face wanted to scowl, trying to crack jokes, to be lean-hipped, to be a good dancer – but the net result had been that the girls had shunned him more assiduously than before. After that he had simply begun taking them, whether they liked it or not. And none of them had liked it.

Over the years Massick had grown accustomed to the arrangement, so much so that he found real stimulation in the sudden look of mingled terror and disgust on a woman's face as she realized what was going to happen to her. Underneath it all, however, imprisoned far down in buried layers of his mind-body complex, there still lived a boyish Joe Massick who yearned for another kind of encounter, one in which there was gentleness in place of force, gladness in place of revulsion, in which soft arms welcomed as the world flowed out and away until there was nothing to see anywhere except eyes that shone with a special warm lustre and lips that smiled . . .

'That's better,' Cromer said, coming in through the screen door. He went straight to his chair at the table, executed a lateral shuffle which showed he was quite drunk, and sat down before the assortment of insects and plastic boxes.

Massick returned to his own seat and gazed at Cromer with speculative eyes. Was it possible that the little man, in spite of his scrawny and dried-up appearance, had a taste for hot-blooded Indian girls? The notion inspired Massick with a sharp pang of jealousy. He had seen enough of the girl's body to know that she was strong-breasted, lush, ripe – and that she would be totally wasted on a miserable old stick like Cromer. If anybody was to bed down with her that night it ought to be Joe Massick, because he was the one who had been going through hell and needed relief from the tensions that racked his body, he was the one who had the size and strength to give the chick what she deserved, and because he was in that kind of a mood. Besides, she had smiled at him . . .

'The Calusas was the ones who knew this swamp,' Cromer was muttering, staring down at a moth in its tiny crystal coffin. 'They were here long before the Seminoles ever even *seen* the place, and they knew all about it, that's for sure . . . knew when the nymphs was turnin' into imagos . . . knew when it was time to pull up stakes and move on.'

'You're a wily old bird, aren't you?' Massick said. 'You've got this place stocked up with everything you need.'

'Hear them cicadas out there?' Cromer, apparently unaware that Massick had spoken, nodded towards the black rectangle of the door. 'Seventeen years they live under the ground, gettin' ready to come up and breed. It stands to reason there must be other critturs that takes longer – maybe thirty years, maybe fifty, maybe even a . . .'

'I'm a bit disappointed in you, Ed. I just didn't think you were the selfish type.'

'Selfish?' Cromer, looking puzzled and hurt, attempted to focus his gaze on Massick. 'What's this selfish?'

'You didn't introduce me to your friend.'

'Friend? I got no . . .' Cromer's flushed, narrow face stiffened with consternation as he turned to look at the bedroom door. He threw himself forward on to his hands and knees, picked up the piece of wire Massick had discarded, and wrapped it around the latch, snorting with urgency as his clumsiness protracted an operation that should have been instantaneous.

Massick watched the performance with good humour. 'Do you generally keep your lady friends locked up?'

'She . . . She's sick.' Cromer got to his feet, breathing audibly, his eyes nervous and pleading. 'Best left alone in there.'

'She didn't look all that sick to me. What's her name?'

'Don't know her name. She wandered in here a couple of days ago. I'm lookin' after her, that's all.'

Massick shook his head and grinned. 'I don't believe you, Ed. I think you're a horny old goat and you're keeping that young piece in there for your own amusement. Shame on you!'

'You don't know what you're talkin' about. I tell you she's sick, and I'm looking after her.'

Massick stood up, bottle in hand. 'In that case we'll give her a drink – best medicine there is.'

'No!' Cromer darted forward, grabbing for Massick's arm. 'Listen, if you want to know the . . .'

Massick swung at him more out of irritation than malice, intending merely to sweep the little man out of his way, but Cromer seemed to fall on to his fist, magnifying the effect of the blow. The force of the impact returning along his forearm told Massick he had done some serious damage, and he stepped back. Cromer went down into a collision with the table, his eyes reduced to blind white crescents, and dropped to the floor with a slapping thud which could have been produced by a side of bacon. The sound alone was as good as a death certificate to Massick.

'You stupid old bastard,' he whispered accusingly. He stared down at the body, adjusting to the new situation, then knelt and retrieved his money from Cromer's shirt pocket. A search of the dead man's personal effects yielded only a cheap wristwatch and eleven extra dollars in single bills. Massick put the watch and money away in his pocket. He took a firm grip on Cromer's collar, dragged the body to the screen door and out into the raucous darkness of the swamp. The chorus of insect calls seemed to grow louder as he moved away from the shanty, again creating the impression of an all-pervading sentience. In spite of the stifling heat Massick felt a crawling coldness between his shoulderblades. Suddenly appreciating the futility of trying to dispose of the body before daylight, he released his burden and groped his way back towards the sallow glimmers of the hurricane lamps.

Once inside the building, he bolted the outer door and went around the main room twitching curtains into place across the windows. As soon as he felt safe from the pressures of the watchful blackness he picked up the whisky bottle and drank from it until his throat closed against the rawness of the liquor. Somewhat restored by the alcohol, he allowed his thoughts to return to the bedroom door and there was a stirring of warmth low down in his belly as he remembered what lay beyond.

It's cosier this way, he thought. *Three always was a crowd.*

He put the bottle aside, went to the door and removed the wire from the latch. The door swung open easily, allowing a swath of light to fall across the bed, revealing that the black-haired girl was still lying down, apparently undisturbed by any commotion she may have heard. As before, she raised herself on one elbow to look up at him. Massick stood in the doorway and scanned her face, waiting for the change of expression to which he was so accustomed, the clouding of the eyes with fear and loathing, but – exactly as before – the girl began to smile. He bared his own teeth in a manufactured response, scarcely able to believe his luck.

'What's your name, honey?' he said, moving closer to the bed.

She went on smiling at him, her gaze locked into his, and there was nothing anywhere in her face to show that she had heard the question.

'Don't you have a name?' Massick persisted, a new idea beginning to form at the back of his mind. *Never had a deaf-mute before!*

The girl reacted by sitting up a little further, a movement which allowed the sheet to slip down from her breasts. They were the most perfectly formed that Massick had ever seen – rounded, almost pneumatic in their fullness, with upright nipples – and his mouth went dry as he advanced to the side of the bed and knelt down. The girl's dark eyes remained fixed on his, bold and yet tender, as he put out his hand and with his fingertips gently traced a line from the three dots on her forehead, down her cheek and neck and on to the smooth curvature of her breast. His hand lingered there briefly and was moving on towards the languorous upthrust of her hip – taking the edge of the sheet with it – when she made a small, inarticulate sound of protest and caught his wrist.

Thwarted and tantalized, Massick gripped the sheet with the intention of ripping it away from the lower part of her body, then he saw that the girl was still smiling. She let go of his wrists, raised her hands to his chest and began to undo his shirt, fumbling in her eagerness.

'You raunchy little so-and-so,' Massick said in a gratified whisper. He got to his feet, tearing at his clothing and in a few seconds was standing naked beside the bed. The girl relaxed on to her pillow, waiting for him. He lowered his thick torso on to the bed beside her and brought his mouth down on hers. She returned his kiss in a curiously inexpert manner which served only to heighten his pleasure. Giving way to his impatience, he propped himself up on one elbow and used his free hand to throw back the sheet, his eyes hungering for the promised magical concourse of hip and belly and thigh unique to woman.

The ovipositor projecting from the she-creature's groin was

a tapering, horny spike. Transparent eggs were already flowing from the aperture at its tip, bubbling and winking, sliming its sides, adding to the jellied mass of spawn which had gathered on her distended abdomen:

Massick had time for a single whimper of despair, then the she-creature was on him, bearing down with an inhuman strength which was scarcely necessary. The first probing stab from the ovipositor had hurt for only an instant, then ancient and merciful chemistries had taken over, obliterating all pain, inducing a flaccid paralysis which gripped his entire frame. He lay perfectly still, hushed and bemused, as his lover worked on him, stabbing again and again, skilfully avoiding vital organs, filling his body cavities with the eggs which would soon produce a thousand hungry larvae.

It's a pity she had to change. I liked her better the other way – before those dots on her forehead changed into watchful black beads, before her eyes developed the facets and began to drift to the side of her head, before those magnificent breasts began reshaping themselves into a central pair of legs.

But she's kind to me, and that counts for a lot. Waits on me hand and foot, like an attentive lover. Even when I wake up during the night I can see her standing at the door of the room, always watching, always waiting.

But what's she waiting for? That's what I ask myself every so often, and when I do . . .

Gene Wolfe
Kevin Malone

Gene Wolfe was born in Brooklyn in 1931 and sent me a biographical essay as engrossing as his stories. 'Here it is,' he wrote at the top. 'Good luck.' I'm tempted to run it complete, but this book is already longer than it was supposed to be. Soon he was in Poeria, where little Rosemary Dietch lived next door, but by the late thirties he was established in Houston, where he attended Edgar Allan Poe elementary school (read 'Masque of the Red Death' in fifth grade, learned 'The Raven' in sixth, enviably – I had to make do with Jane Austen and Matthew Arnold). Five blocks away from home was the Richmond Pharmacy, where he read Famous Fantastic Mysteries *behind the candy case. High school led by a devious route to the National Guard, whence he landed at Texas A & M ('an all-male land-grant university specializing in animal husbandry and engineering – only Dickens could have done justice to A & M as I knew it, and he would not have been believed'). He married Rosemary Dietch five months after taking a job in engineering development. After sixteen years he joined the staff of Plant Engineering. The Wolfe children are Roy II, Madeleine, Therese and Matthew.*

Soon after the marriage he began to write 'in the hope of making enough money to buy furniture'. Since then he has published more than eighty stories. The Death of Doctor Island (*not to be confused with* The Island of Doctor Death *or the* Doctor of Death Island) *won a Nebula Award for best novella, his contemporary novel* Peace *won the Chicago Foundation for Literature Award. Other novels include* The Fifth Head of Cerberus *and the tetralogy beginning with* The Shadow of the Torturer, *which have received a remarkable number of awards. His approach to the tale of terror is as subtle as any of his work, as you will see.*

Marcella and I were married in April. I lost my position with Ketterly, Bruce & Drake in June, and by August we were desperate. We kept the apartment – I think we both felt that if we lowered our standards there would be no chance to raise them again – but the rent tore at our small savings. All during July I had tried to get a job at another brokerage firm, and by August I was calling fraternity brothers I had not seen since graduation, and expressing an entire willingness to work in whatever businesses their fathers owned. One of them, I think, must have mailed us the advertisement.

> Attractive young couple, well educated and well connected, will receive free housing, generous living allowance for minimal services.

There was a telephone number, which I omit for reasons that will become clear.

I showed the clipping to Marcella, who was lying with her cocktail shaker on the chaise-longue. She said, 'Why not,' and I dialled the number.

The telephone buzzed in my ear, paused, and buzzed again. I allowed myself to go limp in my chair. It seemed absurd to call at all; for the advertisement to have reached us that day, it must have appeared no later than yesterday morning. If the position were worth having—

'The Pines.'

I pulled myself together. 'You placed a classified ad. For an attractive couple, well educated and the rest of it.'

'I did not, sir. However, I believe my master did. I am Priest, the butler.'

I looked at Marcella, but her eyes were closed. 'Do you know, Priest, if the opening has been filled?'

'I think not, sir. May I ask your age?'

I told him. At his request, I also told him Marcella's (she was two years younger than I), and gave him the names of the schools we had attended, described our appearance, and mentioned that my grandfather had been a governor of Virginia, and that Marcella's uncle had been ambassador to France. I did not tell him that my father had shot himself rather than face bankruptcy, or that Marcella's family had disowned her – but I suspect he guessed well enough what our situation was.

'You will forgive me, sir, for asking so many questions. We are almost a half day's drive, and I would not wish you to be disappointed.'

I told him that I appreciated that, and we set a date – Tuesday of the next week – on which Marcella and I were to come out for an interview with 'the master'. Priest had hung up before I realized that I had failed to learn his employer's name.

During the teens and twenties some very wealthy people had designed estates in imitation of the palaces of the Italian Renaissance. The Pines was one of them, and better preserved than most – the fountain in the courtyard still played, the marbles were clean and unyellowed, and if no red-robed cardinal descended the steps to a carriage blazoned with the Borgia arms, one felt that he had only just gone. No doubt the place had originally been called *La Capana* or *Il Eremitaggio*.

A serious-looking man in dark livery opened the door for us. For a moment he stared at us across the threshold. 'Very well . . .' he said.

'I beg your pardon?'

'I said that you are looking very well.' He nodded to each of us in turn, and stood aside. 'Sir. Madame. I am Priest.'

'Will your master be able to see us?'

For a moment some exiled expression – it might have been amusement – seemed to tug at his solemn face. 'The music room, perhaps, sir?'

I said I was sure that would be satisfactory, and followed him. The music room held a Steinway, a harp, and a dozen or so comfortable chairs; it overlooked a rose garden in which old remontant varieties were beginning that second season that is more opulent though less generous than the first. A kneeling gardener was weeding one of the beds.

'This is a wonderful house,' Marcella said. 'I really didn't think there was anything like it left. I told him you'd have a john collins – all right? You were looking at the roses.'

'Perhaps we ought to get the job first.'

'I can't call him back now, and if we don't get it, at least we'll have had the drinks.'

I nodded to that. In five minutes they arrived, and we drank them and smoked cigarettes we found in a humidor – English cigarettes of strong Turkish tobacco. A maid came, and said that Mr Priest would be much obliged if we would let him know when we would dine. I told her that we would eat whenever it was convenient, and she dropped a little curtsy and withdrew.

'At least,' Marcella commented, 'he's making us comfortable while we wait.'

*

Dinner was lamb in aspic, and a salade, with a maid – another maid – and footman to serve while Priest stood by to see that it was done properly. We ate at either side of a small table on a terrace overlooking another garden, where antique statues faded to white glimmerings as the sun set.

Priest came forward to light the candles. 'Will you require me after dinner, sir?'

'Will your employer require us; that's the question.'

'Bateman can show you to your room, sir, when you are ready to retire. Julia will see to madame.'

I looked at the footman, who was carrying in fruit on a tray.

'No, sir. That is Carter. Bateman is your man.'

'And Julia,' Marcella put in, 'is my maid, I suppose?'

'Precisely.' Priest gave an almost inaudible cough. 'Perhaps, sir – and madame – you might find this useful.' He drew a photograph from an inner pocket and handed it to me.

It was a black and white snapshot, somewhat dogeared. Two dozen people, most of them in livery of one kind or another, stood in brilliant sunshine on the steps at the front of the house, men behind women. There were names in India ink across the bottom of the picture: James Sutton, Edna DeBuck, Lloyd Bateman . . .

'Our staff, sir.'

I said, 'Thank you, Priest. No, you needn't stay tonight.'

The next morning Bateman shaved me in bed. He did it very well, using a straight razor and scented soap applied with a brush. I had heard of such things – I think my grandfather's valet may have shaved him like that before the First World War – but I had never guessed that anyone kept up the tradition. Bateman did, and I found I enjoyed it. When he had dressed me, he asked if I would breakfast in my room.

'I doubt it,' I said. 'Do you know my wife's plans?'

'I think it likely she will be on the South Terrace, sir. Julia said something to that effect as I was bringing in your water.'

'I'll join her then.'

'Of course, sir.' He hesitated.

'I don't think I'll require a guide, but you might tell my wife I'll be with her in ten minutes or so.'

Bateman repeated his, 'Of course, sir,' and went out. The truth was that I wanted to assure myself that everything I had carried in the pockets of my old suit – car keys, wallet, and so

166

on – had been transferred to the new one he had laid out for me; and I did not want to insult him, if I could prevent it, by doing it in front of him.

Everything was where it should be, and I had a clean handkerchief in place of my own only slightly soiled one. I pulled it out to look at (Irish linen) and a flutter of green came with it – two bills, both fifties.

Over eggs Benedict I complimented Marcella on her new dress, and asked if she had noticed where it had been made.

'Rowe's. It's a little shop on Fifth Avenue.'

'You know it, then. Nothing unusual?'

She answered, 'No, nothing unusual,' more quickly than she should have, and I knew that there had been money in her new clothes too, and that she did not intend to tell me about it.

'We'll be going home after this. I wonder if they'll want me to give this jacket back.'

'Going home?' She did not look up from her plate. 'Why? And who are "they"?'

'Whoever owns this house.'

'Yesterday you called him *he*. You said Priest talked about *the master*, so that seemed logical enough. Today you're afraid to deal with even presumptive masculinity.'

I said nothing.

'You think he spent the night in my room – they separated us, and you thought that was why, and you just waited there – was it under a sheet? – for me to scream or something. And I didn't.'

'I was hoping you had, and I hadn't heard you.'

'Nothing happened, dammit! I went to bed and went to sleep; but as for going home, you're out of your mind. Can't you see we've got the job? Whoever he is – wherever he is – he likes us. We're going to stay here and live like human beings, at least for a while.'

And so we did. That day we stayed on from hour to hour. After that, from day to day; and at last from week to week. I felt like Klipspringer, the man who was Jay Gatsby's guest for so long that he had no other home – except that Klipspringer, presumably, saw Gatsby from time to time, and no doubt made agreeable conversation, and perhaps even played the piano for him. Our Gatsby was absent. I do not mean that we avoided him, or that he avoided us; there were no rooms we were forbidden to enter, and no times when the servants seemed eager that we should play golf or swim or go riding. Before the good weather ended, we had two couples up for a weekend; and when Bette Windgassen asked if Marcella had inherited the place, and then if we were renting it, Marcella said, 'Oh, do you like it?' in such a way that they left, I think, convinced that it was ours, or as good as ours.

And so it was. We went away when we chose, which was seldom, and returned when we chose, quickly. We ate on the various terraces and balconies, and in the big, formal dining room, and in our own bedrooms. We rode the horses, and drove the Mercedes and the cranky, appealing old Jaguar as though they were our own. We did everything, in fact, except buy the groceries and pay the taxes and the servants; but someone else was doing that; and every morning I found one hundred dollars in the pockets of my clean clothes. If summer had lasted for ever, perhaps I would still be there.

The poplars lost their leaves in one October week; at the end of it I fell asleep listening to the hum of the pump that emptied the swimming pool. When the rain came, Marcella turned sour and drank too much. One evening I made the mistake of putting my arm about her shoulders as we sat before the fire in the trophy room.

'Get your filthy hands off me,' she said. 'I don't belong to you.'

'Priest, look here. He hasn't said an intelligent word to me all day or done a decent thing, and now he wants to paw me all night.'

Priest pretended, of course, that he had not heard her.

'Look over here! Damn it, you're a human being, aren't you?'

He did not ignore that. 'Yes, madame, I am a human being.'

'I'll say you are. You're more a man than he is. This is your place, and you're keeping us for pets – is it me you want? Or him? You sent us the ad, didn't you. He thinks you go into my room at night, or he says he does. Maybe you really come to his – is that it?'

Priest did not answer. I said, 'For God's sake, Marcella.'

'Even if you're old, Priest, I think you're too much of a man for that.' She stood up, tottering on her long legs and holding on to the stonework of the fireplace. 'If you want me, take me.

If this house is yours, you can have me. We'll send him to Vegas – or throw him on the dump.'

In a much softer tone than he usually used, Priest said, 'I don't want either of you, madame.'

I stood up then, and caught him by the shoulders. I had been drinking too, though only half or a quarter as much as Marcella; but I think it was more than that – it was the accumulated frustration of all the days since Jim Bruce told me I was finished. I outweighed Priest by at least forty pounds, and I was twenty years younger. I said: 'I want to know.'

'Release me, sir, please.'

'I want to know who it is; I want to know now. Do you see that fire? Tell me, Priest, or I swear I'll throw you in it.'

His face tightened at that. 'Yes,' he whispered, and I let go of his shoulders. 'It was not the lady, sir. It was you. I want that understood this time.'

'What the hell are you talking about?'

'I'm not doing this because of what she said.'

'You aren't the master, are you? For God's sake tell the truth.'

'I have always told the truth, sir. No, I am not the master. Do you remember the picture I gave you?'

I nodded.

'You discarded it. I took the liberty, sir, of rescuing it from the wastecan in your bedroom. I have it here.' He reached into his coat and pulled it out, just as he had on the first day, and handed it to me.

'It's one of these? One of the servants?'

Priest nodded and pointed with an impeccably manicured forefinger to the figure at the extreme right of the second row. The name beneath it was *Kevin Malone*.

'Him?'

Silently, Priest nodded again.

I had examined the picture on the night he had given it to me, but I had never paid special attention to that particular half-inch-high image. The person it represented might have been a gardener, a man of middle age, short and perhaps stocky. A soft, sweat-stained hat cast a shadow on his face.

'I want to see him.' I looked towards Marcella, still leaning against the stonework of the mantel. 'We want to see him.'

'Are you certain, sir?'

'Damn you, get him!'

Priest remained where he was, staring at me; I was so furious that I think I might have seized him as I had threatened and pushed him into the fire.

Then the french windows opened, and there came a gust of wind. For an instant I think I expected a ghost, or some turbulent elemental spirit. I felt that pricking at the neck that comes when one reads Poe alone at night.

The man I had seen in the picture stepped into the room. He was a small and very ordinary man in worn khaki, but he left the windows wide behind him, so that the night entered with him, and remained in the room for as long as we talked.

'You own this house,' I said. 'You're Kevin Malone.'

He shook his head. 'I am Kevin Malone – this house owns me.'

Marcella was standing straighter now, drunk, yet still at that stage of drunkenness in which she was conscious of her condition and could compensate for it. 'It owns me too,' she said, and walking almost normally she crossed the room to the baronial chair Malone had chosen, and managed to sit down at his feet.

'My father was the man-of-all-work here. My mother was the parlour maid. I grew up here, washing the cars and raking leaves out of the fountains. Do you follow me? Where did you grow up?'

I shrugged. 'Various places. Richmond, New York, three years in Paris. Until I was sent off to school we lived in hotels, mostly.'

'You see, then. You can understand.' Malone smiled for a moment. 'You're still recreating the life you had as a child, or trying to. Isn't that right? None of us can be happy any other way, and few of us even want to try.'

'Thomas Wolfe said you can't go home again,' I ventured.

'That's right, you can't go home. There's one place where we can never go – haven't you thought of that? We can dive to the bottom of the sea and some day NASA will fly us to the stars, and I have known men to plunge into the past – or the future – and drown. But there's one place where we can't go. We can't go where we are already. We can't go home, because our minds, and our hearts, and our immortal souls are already there.'

Not knowing what to say, I nodded, and that seemed to satisfy him. Priest looked as calm as ever, but he made no move to shut the windows, and I sensed that he was somehow afraid.

'I was put into an orphanage when I was twelve, but I never forgot The Pines. I used to tell the other kids about it, and it got bigger and better every year; but I knew what I said could never equal the reality.'

He shifted in his seat, and the slight movement of his legs sent Marcella sprawling, passed out. She retained a certain grace still; I have always understood that it is the reward of studying ballet as a child.

Malone continued to talk. 'They'll tell you it's no longer possible for a poor boy with a second rate education to make a fortune. Well, it takes luck; but I had it. It also takes the willingness to risk it all. I had that too, because I knew that for me anything under a fortune was nothing. I had to be able to buy this place – to come back and buy The Pines, and staff it and maintain it. That's what I wanted, and nothing less would make any difference.'

'You're to be congratulated,' I said. 'But why . . .'

He laughed. It was a deep laugh, but there was no humour in it. 'Why don't I wear a tie and eat my supper at the end of the big table? I tried it. I tried it for nearly a year, and every night I dreamed of home. That wasn't home, you see, wasn't The Pines. Home is three rooms above the stables. I live there now. I live at home, as a man should.'

'It seems to me that it would have been a great deal simpler for you to have applied for the job you fill now.'

Malone shook his head impatiently. 'That wouldn't have done it at all. I had to have control. That's something I learned in business – to have control. Another owner would have wanted to change things, and maybe he would even have sold out to a subdivider. No. Besides, when I was a boy this estate belonged to a fashionable young couple. Suppose a man of my age had bought it? Or a young woman, some whore.' His mouth tightened, then relaxed. 'You and your wife were ideal. Now I'll have to get somebody else, that's all. You can stay the night, if you like. I'll have you driven into the city tomorrow morning.'

I ventured, 'You needed us as stage properties, then. I'd be willing to stay on those terms.'

Malone shook his head again. 'That's out of the question. I don't need props, I need actors. In business I've put on little shows for the competition, if you know what I mean, and sometimes even for my own people. And I've learned that the only actors who can really do justice to their parts are the ones who don't know what they are.'

'Really—' I began.

He cut me off with a look, and for a few seconds we stared at one another. Something terrible lived behind those eyes.

Frightened despite all reason could tell me, I said, 'I understand,' and stood up. There seemed to be nothing else to do. 'I'm glad, at least, that you don't hate us. With your childhood it would be quite natural if you did. Will you explain things to Marcella in the morning? She'll throw herself at you, no matter what I say.'

He nodded absently.

'May I ask one question more? I wondered why you had to leave and go into the orphanage. Did your parents die or lose their places?'

Malone said, 'Didn't you tell him, Priest? It's the local legend. I thought everyone knew.'

The butler cleared his throat. 'The elder Mr Malone – he was the stableman here, sir, though it was before my time. He murdered Betty Malone, who was one of the maids. Or at least he was thought to have, sir. They never found the body, and it's possible he was accused falsely.'

'Buried her on the estate,' Malone said. 'They found bloody rags and the hammer, and he hanged himself in the stable.'

'I'm sorry . . . I didn't mean to pry.'

The wind whipped the drapes like wine-red flags. They knocked over a vase and Priest winced, but Malone did not seem to notice. 'She was twenty years younger and a tramp,' he said. 'Those things happen.'

I said, 'Yes, I know they do,' and went up to bed.

I do not know where Marcella slept. Perhaps there on the carpet, perhaps in the room that had been hers, perhaps even in Malone's servants' flat over the stables. I breakfasted alone on the terrace, then – without Bateman's assistance – packed my bags.

I saw her only once more. She was wearing a black silk dress; there were circles under her eyes and her head must have been throbbing, but her hand was steady. As I walked out of the house, she was going over the Sévres with a peacock-feather duster. We did not speak.

I have sometimes wondered if I were wholly wrong in

anticipating a ghost when the french windows opened. How did Malone know the time had come for him to appear?

Of course I have looked up the newspaper reports of the murder. All the old papers are on microfilm at the library, and I have a great deal of time.

There is no mention of a child. In fact, I get the impression that the identical surnames of the murderer and his victim were coincidental. *Malone* is a common enough one, and there were a good many Irish servants then.

Sometimes I wonder if it is possible for a man – even a rich man – to be possessed, and not to know it.

Joan Aiken
Time to laugh

*Joan Aiken is the daughter of Conrad Aiken, author of at
least two minor classics of the macabre (*Mr Arcularis *and*
Silent Snow, Secret Snow*). Her mother educated her at home
until she was twelve, when she went to a small progressive
boarding school in Oxford. She worked for the BBC and the
United Nations, and was features editor for* Argosy *for five
years before, in the early sixties, she began to write full time.
By now she has written about fifty books, three of which won
the Guardian Award for children's literature; one (*The Wolves
of Willoughby Chase*) also won the Lewis Carroll Award,
while* Nightfall *was honoured by the Mystery Writers of
America. She is married to the American painter Julius
Goldstein.*

*Does she also get an award for the greatest number of title
changes? In America,* Trouble with Product X *became* Beware
of the Bouquet; Hate Begins at Home *became* Dark Interval;
The Ribs of Death *turned into* The Crystal Crow; The Butterfly
Picnic *ended up as* A Cluster of Separate Sparks, *and yet some
of us would be content to invent just one title as striking. Here
is more of her originality.*

When Matt climbed in at the open window of The Croft, it had
been raining steadily for three days – August rain, flattening
the bronze-green plains of wheat, making dim green jungles of
the little woods round Wentby, turning the motorway which
cut across the small town's southern tip into a greasy nightmare on which traffic skidded and piled into crunching heaps;
all the county police were desperately busy trying to clear up
one disaster after another.

If there had been a river at Wentby, Matt might have gone
fishing instead, on that Saturday afternoon . . . but the town's
full name was Wentby Waterless, the nearest brook was twenty

miles away, the rain lay about in scummy pools on the clay, or sank into the lighter soil and vanished. And if the police had not been so manifestly engaged and distracted by the motorway chaos, it might never have occurred to Matt that now would be the perfect time to explore The Croft; after all, by the end of three days' rain, what else was there to do? It had been ten years since the Regent Cinema closed its doors for the last time and went into liquidation.

A grammar-school duffelcoat would be too conspicuous and recognizable; Matt wore his black plastic jacket, although it was not particularly rainproof. But it was at least some protection against the brambles which barred his way.

He had long ago worked out an entry into The Croft grounds, having noticed that they ended in a little triangle of land which bit into the corner of a builder's yard where his father had once briefly worked; Matt had a keen visual memory, never forgot anything he had once observed and, after a single visit two years ago to tell his father that Mum had been taken off to hospital, was able to pick his way without hesitation through cement mixers, stacks of two-by-two, and concrete slabs, to the exact corner, the wattle palings and tangle of elderberry bushes. Kelly never troubled to lock his yard, and, in any case, on a Saturday afternoon, no one was about; all snug at home, watching telly.

He bored his way through the wet greenery and, as he had reckoned, came to the weed-smothered terrace at the foot of a flight of steps; overgrown shoots of rambler rose half blocked them, but it was just possible to battle upwards, and at the top he was rewarded by a dusky, triangular vista of lawn stretching away on the left towards the house, on the right towards untended vegetable gardens. Amazingly – in the very middle of Wentby – there were rabbits feeding on the lawn, who scattered at his appearance. And between him and the house two aged, enormous apple trees towered, massive against the murky sky, loaded down with fruit. He had seen them in the aerial photograph of the town, recently exhibited on a school noticeboard; that was what had given him the notion of exploring The Croft; you could find out a few things at school if you kept your eyes open and used your wits. And he had heard of The Croft before that, of course, but it was nowhere to be seen from any of the town streets: a big house, built in the mid nineteenth century on an inaccessible plot of land, bought subsequently, after World War Two, by a rich retired actress and her company director husband, Lieutenant-Colonel and Mrs Jordan. They were hardly ever seen; never came out, or went anywhere; Matt had a vague idea that one of them – maybe both? – had died. There was a general belief that the house was haunted; also full of treasures; also defended by any number of burglar alarms inside the building, gongs that would start clanging, bells that would ring up at the police station, not to mention mantraps, spring guns, and savage alsatians outside in the grounds.

However the alsatians did not seem to be in evidence – if they had been, surely the rabbits would not have been feeding so peacefully? So, beginning to disbelieve these tales, Matt picked his way, quietly but with some confidence, over the sodden tussocky grass to the apple trees. The fruit, to his chagrin, was far from ripe. Also they were wretched little apples, codlins possibly, lumpy and misshapen, not worth the bother of scrumping. Even the birds appeared to have neglected them; numbers of undersized windfalls lay rotting already on the ground. Angrily, Matt flung a couple against the wall of the house, taking some satisfaction from the squashy thump with which they spattered the stone.

The house had not been built of local brick like the rest of Wentby, but from massive chunks of sombre, liver-coloured rock, imported, no doubt at great expense, from farther north; the effect was powerful and ugly; dark as blood, many-gabled and frowning, the building kept guard over its tangled grounds. It seemed deserted; all the windows were lightless, even on such a pouring wet afternoon; and, prowling round to the front of the house, over a carriage sweep pocked with grass and weeds, Matt found that the front doorstep had a thin skin of moss over it, as if no foot had trodden there for months. Perhaps the back—? but that was some distance away, and behind a screen of trellis work and yellow-flecked ornamental laurels. Working on towards it, Matt came to a stop, badly startled at the sight of a half-open window, which, until he reached it, had been concealed from him by a great sagging swatch of untrimmed winter jasmine, whose tiny dark-green leaves were almost black with wet. The coffin-shaped oblong of the open window was black too; Matt stared at it, hypnotized, for almost five minutes, unable to decide whether to go in or not.

Was there somebody inside, there, in the dark? Or had the house been burgled, maybe weeks ago, and the burglar had left the window like that, not troubling to conceal evidence of his entry, because nobody ever came to the place? Or? – unnerving thought – was there a burglar inside now, at this minute?

Revolving all these different possibilities, Matt found that he had been moving slowly nearer and nearer to the wall with the window in it; the window was about six feet above ground, but so thickly sleeved around with creeper that climbing in would present no problem at all. The creeper seemed untouched; showed no sign of damage.

Almost without realizing that he had come to a decision, Matt found himself digging toes into the wet mass and pulling himself up – showers of drops flew into his face – until he was able to lean across the windowsill, bracing his elbows against the inner edge of the frame. As might have been expected, the sill inside was swimming with rainwater, the paint starting to crack; evidently the window had been open for hours, maybe days.

Matt stared into the dusky interior, waiting for his eyes to adjust to the dimness. At first, all he could see was vague masses of furniture. Slowly these began to resolve into recognizable forms: tapestried chairs with high backs and bulbous curving legs, side tables covered in ornaments, a standard lamp with an elaborate pleated shade, dripping tassels, a huge china pot, a flower-patterned carpet, a black shaggy hearthrug, a gold-framed portrait over the mantel. The hearth was fireless, the chair beside it empty, the room sunk in silence. Listening with all his concentration, Matt could hear no sound from anywhere about the house. Encouraged, he swung a knee over the sill, ducked his head and shoulders under the sash, and levered himself in; then, with instinctive caution, he slid the sash down behind him, so that, in the unlikely event of another intruder visiting the garden, the way indoors would not be so enticingly visible.

Matt did not intend to close the window completely, but the sash cord had perished and the heavy frame, once in motion, shot right down before he could stop it; somewhat to his consternation, a little catch clicked across; evidently it was a burglar-proof lock, for he was unable to pull it open again; there was a keyhole in the catch, and he guessed that it could not now be opened again without the key.

Swearing under his breath, Matt turned to survey the room. How would it ever be possible to find the right key in this cluttered, dusky place? It might be in a bowl of odds and ends on the mantelpiece – or in a desk drawer – or hanging on a nail – or in a box – no casual intruder could hope to come across it. Nor – he turned back to inspect the window again – could he hope to smash his way out. The windowpanes were too small, the bars too thick. Still, there would be other ways of leaving the house, perhaps he could simply unlock an outside door. He decided that before exploring any farther he had better establish his means of exit, and so took a couple of steps towards a doorway that he could now see on his right. This led through to a large chilly dining room where a cobwebbed chandelier hung over a massive mahogany dining table, corralled by eight chairs, and reflecting ghostly grey light from a window beyond. The dining room window, to Matt's relief, was a casement; easy enough to break out of that, he thought, his spirits rising; but perhaps there would be no need, perhaps the burglar catch was not fastened; and he was about to cross the dining room and examine it closely when the sound of silvery laughter behind him nearly shocked him out of his wits.

'Aha! Aha! Ha-ha-ha-ha-ha-ha!' trilled the mocking voice, not six feet away. Matt spun round, his heart almost bursting out through his rib cage. He would have been ready to swear there wasn't a soul in the house. Was it a spook? Were the stories true, after all?

The room he had first entered still seemed empty, but the laughter had certainly come from that direction, and as he stood in the doorway, staring frantically about him, he heard it again, a long mocking trill, repeated in exactly the same cadence.

'Jeeez!' whispered Matt.

And then, as he honestly thought he was on the point of fainting from fright, the explanation was supplied: at exactly the same point from which the laughter had come, a clock began to chime in a thin silvery note obviously intended to match the laughter: *ting, tong, ting, tong.* Four o'clock.

'Jeez,' breathed Matt again. 'What do you know about that? A laughing clock!'

He moved over to inspect the clock. It was a large, elaborate affair, stood on a kind of bureau with brass handles, under a glass dome. The structure of the clock, outworks, whatever you call it, was all gilded and ornamented with gold cherubs who were falling about laughing, throwing their fat little heads back, or doubled up with amusement.

'Very funny,' muttered Matt sourly. 'Almost had me dead of heart failure, you can laugh!'

Over the clock, he now saw, a big tapestry hung on the wall, which echoed the theme of laughter: girls in frilly tunics this time, and a fat old guy sitting on a barrel squashing grapes into his mouth while he hugged a girl to him with the other arm, all of them, too, splitting themselves over some joke, probably a rude one to judge from the old chap's appearance.

Matt wished very much that the clock would strike again, but presumably it would not do that till five o'clock – unless it chimed the quarters; he had better case the rest of the house in the meantime, and reckon to be back in this room by five. Would it be possible to pinch the clock? he wondered. But it looked dauntingly heavy – and probably its mechanism was complicated and delicate, might go wrong if shifted; how could he ever hope to carry it through all those bushes and over the paling fence? And then there would be the problem of explaining its appearance in his father's council flat; he could hardly say that he had found it lying on a rubbish dump. Still he longed to possess it – think what the other guys in the gang would say when they heard it! Maybe he could keep it in Kip Butterworth's house – old Kip, lucky fellow, had a room of his own and such a lot of electronic junk all over it that one clock more or less would never be noticed.

But first he would bring Kip here, at a time just before the clock was due to strike, and let *him* have the fright of his life . . .

Sniggering to himself at this agreeable thought, Matt turned back towards the dining room, intending to carry out his original plan of unfastening one of the casement windows, when for the second time he was stopped dead by terror.

A voice behind him said, 'Since you are here, you may as well wind the clock.' And added drily, 'Saturday is its day for winding, so it is just as well you came.'

This time the voice was unmistakably human; trembling like a leaf, Matt was obliged to admit to himself that there was no chance of its being some kind of electronic device – or even a spook – it was an old woman's voice, harsh, dry, a little shaky, but resonant; only, where the devil *was* she?

Then he saw that what he had taken for wall beyond the fireplace was, in fact, one of those dangling bamboo curtains, and beyond it – another bad moment for Matt – was this motionless figure sitting on a chair, watching him; had been watching him – must have – all the time, ever since he had

180

climbed in, for the part of the room beyond the curtain was just a kind of alcove, a big bay window really, leading nowhere. She must have been there all the time . . .

'Go on,' she repeated, watching Matt steadily from out of her black triangles of eyes, 'wind the clock.'

He found his voice and said hoarsely, 'Where's the key, then?'

'In the round bowl on the left side.'

His heart leapt; perhaps the window key would be there too. But it was not; there was only one key: a long heavy brass shaft with a cross-piece at one end and a lot of fluting at the other.

'Lift the dome off; carefully,' she said. 'You'll find two key-holes in the face. Wind them both. One's for the clock, the other for the chime.'

And, as he lifted off the dome and began winding, she added thoughtfully, 'My husband made that clock for me, on my thirtieth birthday. It's a recording of my own voice – the laugh. Uncommon, isn't it? He was an electrical engineer, you see. Clocks were his hobby. All kinds of unusual ones he invented – there was a Shakespeare clock, and a barking dog, and one that sang hymns – my voice again. I had a beautiful singing voice in those days – and my laugh was famous of course. ' "Miss Langdale's crystalline laugh", the critics used to call it . . . My husband was making a skull clock just before he died. There's the skull.'

There it was, to be sure, a real skull, perched on top of the big china jar to the right of the clock.

Vaguely now, Matt remembered reports of her husband's death; wasn't there something a bit odd about it? Found dead of heart failure in the underpass below the motorway, at least a mile from his house; what had he been *doing* there, in the middle of the night? Why walk through the underpass, which was not intended for pedestrians anyway?

'He was going to get me some cigarettes when he died,' she went on, and Matt jumped; had she read his thought? How could she know so uncannily what was going through his head?

'I've given up smoking since then,' she went on. 'Had to, really . . . They won't deliver, you see. Some things you can get delivered, so I make do with what I can get. I don't like people coming to the house too often, because they scare the birds. I'm a great bird person, you know—'

Unless she has a servant, then, she's alone in the house, Matt thought, as she talked on, in her sharp, dry old voice. He began to feel less terrified – perhaps he could just scare her into letting him leave. Perhaps, anyway, she was mad?

'Are you going to phone the police?' he asked boldly. 'I wasn't going to pinch anything, you know – just came in to have a look-see.'

'My dear boy, I don't care *why* you came in. As you *are* here, you might as well make yourself useful. Go into the dining room, will you, and bring back some of those bottles.'

The rain had abated, just a little, and the dining room was some degrees lighter when he walked through it. All along the window wall Matt was amazed to see wooden wine racks filled with bottles and half-bottles of champagne. There must be hundreds. There were also, in two large log baskets beside the empty grate, dozens of empties. An armchair was drawn close to an electric bar fire, not switched on; a half-empty glass and bottle stood on a silver tray on the floor beside the armchair.

'Bring a glass too,' Mrs Jordan called.

And when he returned with the glass, the tray, and several bottles under his arm, she said,

'Now, open one of them. You know how to, I hope?'

He had seen it done on television; he managed it without difficulty.

'Ought to be chilled, of course,' she remarked, receiving the glass from him. One of her hands lay limply on the arm of her chair – she hitched it up from time to time with the other hand when it slipped off; and, now that he came near to her for the first time, he noticed that she smelt very bad; a strange, fetid smell of dry unwashed old age and something worse. He began to suspect that perhaps she was *unable* to move from her chair. Curiously enough, instead of this making him fear her less, it made him fear her more. Although she seemed a skinny, frail old creature, her face was quite full in shape, pale and puffy like underdone pastry. It must have been a handsome one long ago – like a wicked fairy pretending to be a princess in a fairy-tale illustration; now she just looked spiteful and secretive, grinning down at her glass of bubbly. Her hair, the colour of old dry straw, was done very fancy, piled up on top of her head. Perhaps it was a wig.

'Get a glass for yourself, if you want,' she said. 'There are some more in the dining-room cupboard.'

He half thought of zipping out through the dining-room window while he was in there; but still, he was curious to try the fizz, and there didn't seem to be any hurry, really; it was pretty plain the old girl wasn't going anywhere, couldn't be any actual danger to him, although she did rather give him the 'gooeys'. Also he did want to hear that chime again.

As he was taking a glass out from the shimmering ranks in the cupboard, a marvellous thought struck him: why not bring all the gang here for a banquet? Look at those hundreds and hundreds of bottles of champagne – what a waste, not to make use of them! Plainly *she* was never going to get through them all – not in the state she was in. Maybe he could find some tinned stuff in the house too – but anyway, they could bring their own grub with them, hamburgers and crisps or stuff from the Chinese Takeaway; if the old girl was actually paralysed in her chair, she couldn't stop them; in fact it would add to the fun, the excitement, having her there. They could fetch her in from the next room, drink her health in her own bubbly; better not leave it too long, though, didn't seem likely she could last more than a few days.

Candles, he thought, we'd have to bring candles; and at that point her voice cut into his thoughts, calling,

'Bring the two candles that are standing on the cupboard.'

He started violently – but it was only a coincidence, after all; picked up the candles in their tall cut-glass sticks and carried them next door with a tumbler for himself.

'Matches on the mantel,' she said.

The matches were in a fancy enamel box. He lit the candles and put them on the little table beside her. Now he could see more plainly that there was something extremely queer about her: her face was all drawn down one side, and half of it didn't seem to work very well.

'Electricity cut off,' she said. 'Forgot to pay bill.'

Her left hand was still working all right, and she had swallowed down two glasses in quick succession, refilling them herself each time from the opened bottle at her elbow. 'Fill your glass,' she said, slurring the words a little.

He was very thirsty – kippers and baked beans they always had for Saturday midday dinner, and the fright had dried up his mouth too. Like Mrs Jordan he tossed down two glasses one after the other. They fizzed a bit – otherwise didn't have much taste.

'Better open another bottle,' she said. 'One doesn't go anywhere between two. Fetch in a few more while you're up, why don't you.'

183

She's planning, he thought to himself; knows she can't move from that chair, so she wants to be stocked up for when I've gone. He wondered if in fact there was a phone in the house. Ought he to ring for doctor, police, ambulance? But then he would have to account for his presence. And then he and the gang would never get to have their banquet; the windows would be boarded up for sure, she'd be carted off to the Royal West Midland geriatric ward, like Auntie Glad after her stroke.

'There isn't a phone in the house,' said Mrs Jordan calmly. 'I had it taken out after Jock died; the bell disturbed the birds. That's right, put them all down by my chair, where I can reach them.'

He opened another bottle, filled both their glasses, then went back to the other room for a third load.

'You like the clock, don't you,' she said, as he paused by it, coming back.

'Yeah. It's uncommon.'

'It'll strike the quarter in a minute,' she said, and soon it did – a low, rather malicious chuckle, just a brief spurt of sound. It made the hair prickle on the back of Matt's neck, but he thought again – Just wait till the rest of the gang hear that! A real spooky sound.

'I don't want you making off with it, though,' she said. 'No, no, that would never do. I like to sit here and listen to it.'

'I wasn't going to take it!'

'No, well, that's as maybe.' Her triangular black eyes in their hollows laughed down at him – he was squatting on the carpet near her chair, easing out a particularly obstinate cork. 'I'm not taking any chances. Eight days – that clock goes for eight days. Did you wind the chime too?'

'Yeah, yeah,' he said impatiently, tipping more straw-coloured fizz into their glasses. Through the pale liquid in the tumbler he still seemed to see her eyes staring at him shrewdly.

'Put your glass down a moment,' she said. 'On the floor – that will do. Now, just look here a moment.' She was holding up her skinny forefinger. Past it he could see those two dark triangles. 'That's right. Now – watch my finger – you are very tired, aren't you? You are going to lie down on the floor and go to sleep. You will sleep – very comfortably – for ten minutes. When you wake, you will walk over to that door and lock it. The key is in the lock. Then you will take out the key and push it under the door with one of the knitting needles that are lying on the small table by the door. Ahhh! You are so sleepy.'

She yawned, deeply. Matt was yawning too. His head flopped sideways on to the carpet and he lay motionless, deep asleep.

While he slept it was very quiet in the room. The house was too secluded in its own grounds among the builders' yards for any sound from the town to reach it; only faintly from far away came the throb of the motorway. Mrs Jordan sat impassively listening to it. She did not sleep; she had done enough sleeping and soon would sleep even deeper. She sat listening, and thinking about her husband; sometimes the lopsided smile crooked down one corner of her mouth.

After ten minutes the sleeping boy woke up. Drowsily he staggered to his feet, walked over to the door, locked it, removed the key and, with a long wooden knitting needle, thrust it far underneath and out across the polished dining-room floor.

Returning to the old lady he stared at her in a vaguely bewildered manner, rubbing one hand up over his forehead.

'My head aches,' he said in a grumbling tone.

'You need a drink. Open another bottle,' she said. 'Listen: the clock is going to strike the half-hour.'

On the other side of the room the clock gave its silvery chuckle.

Kit Reed
Chicken soup

*Kit Reed lives in Connecticut, and there isn't much more I can
say about her. Her science fiction novels are* Magic Time *and*
Armed Camps, *but she also writes novels outside that field (for
example,* The Ballad of T. Rantula). *Her play* The Bathyscape
*was produced on American public radio. I get the impression
that she likes her work to speak for her, and so it does, not least
in the collections* Mr Da V., The Killer Mice, *and* Attack of
the Giant Baby. *So does this.*

When he was little Harry loved being sick. He would stay in
bed with his books and toys spread out on the blankets and
wait for his mother to bring him things. She would come in
with orange juice and aspirin at midmorning; at lunchtime he
always brought him chicken soup with Floating Island for
dessert, and when he had eaten she would straighten the pillow
and smooth his covers and settle him for his nap. As long as he
was sick he could stay in this nest of his own devising, safe
from schoolmates' teasing and teachers who might lose their
tempers, and falling down and getting hurt. He could wake up
and read or drowse in front of the television, perfectly content.
Some time late in the afternoon, when his throat was scratchy
and boredom was threatening his contentment, he would start
watching the bedroom door. The shadows would be long by
that time and Harry restless and perhaps faintly threatened
by longer shadows that lurked outside his safe little room:
the first intimations of anxiety, accident and risk. Finally he
would hear her step on the stair, the clink of ice in their best
glass pitcher, and she would come in with cookies and lemonade. He would gulp the first glass all at once and then, while
she poured him another, he would feel his own forehead in
hopes it would be hot enough to entitle him to another day. He

187

would say: I think my head is hot. What do you think? She would touch his forehead in loving complicity. Then the two of them would sit there together, Harry and Mommy, happy as happy in the snug world they had made.

Harry's father had left his widow well fixed, which meant Mommy didn't have to have a job, so she had all the time in the world to make the house pretty and cook beautiful meals for Harry and do everything he needed even when he wasn't sick. She would wake him early so they could sit down to a good hot breakfast together, pancakes with sausage and orange juice, after which they would read to each other out of the paper until it was time for Harry to go. They always talked over the day when he came home from school and then, being a good mother, she would say, Don't you want to play with a little friend? She always made cookies when his friends came over, rolling out the dough and cutting it in neat circles with the rim of a wine glass dusted with sugar. She sat in the front row at every violin and flute recital, and when Harry had trouble with a teacher, any kind of trouble at all, she would go up to the grammar school and have it out with him. Harry's bed was made for him and his lunches carefully wrapped and, although nobody would find out until they reached middle school and took communal showers, Harry's mother ironed his underwear. In return Harry emptied the garbage and made the phone calls and did most of the things the man of the house would have done, if he had been there.

Like all happy couples they had their fights, which lasted only an hour or two and cleared the air nicely. Usually they ended with one of them apologizing and the other saying, with admirable largess, I forgive you. In fact the only bad patch they had came in the spring of the year Harry was twelve, when Charles appeared with a bottle of wine and an old college yearbook in which he and Harry's father were featured. Naturally Mommy invited him to dinner and Harry was shocked to come out of the kitchen with the bottle opener just in time to hear his mother saying, 'You don't know what a relief it is to have an adult to talk to for a change.'

Didn't Harry get asthma that night, and wasn't he home sick for the rest of the week? He did not spend his usual happy sick time because his mother seemed distracted almost to the point of being neglectful, and he was absolutely astonished at lemonade time that Friday. There were two sets of footsteps on the stairs.

188

Mommy came in first. 'Oh Harry, I have a surprise for you.'

'I'm too sick.'

She managed to keep the smile in her voice. 'It's Charles. He's brought you a present.'

'I don't want it.' He flopped on his stomach and put the pillows over his head.

'Oh Harry.'

'Let me handle this.' There was Charles's voice in his bedroom, his bedroom, that had always been sacrosanct. Harry wanted to rage and drive him out, he might even brain him with a bookend, but that would involve showing himself, and as long as he stayed under the pillows there was the chance Charles would give up and go away.

There was something wriggling on his bed.

'Help. What's that?'

'It's a puppy.'

'Go away.'

'Charles has brought you a lovely puppy.'

'A puppy?'

There it was. He was so busy playing with it that he only half-heard when Mommy said the puppy's name was Ralph and Ralph was going to keep him company while she and Charles went out for a little while. Wait, Harry said, or tried to, but the puppy was warm under his hands and he couldn't keep his mind on what he was saying. It had already wet the blanket, and Harry was riveted by the experience. The wet was soaking right through the blanket and the sheet and into Harry's pyjama leg, and by the time he had responded to the horror and the wonder of it, Mommy had already kissed him and she and Charles were gone.

For the first hour or two he and the puppy were happy together, but just as he began to take it into his confidence, convincing himself that it was company enough, the puppy flopped on its side and slept like a stone, leaving Harry alone in the room, jabbering to the gathering shadows. He clutched the covers under his chin and kept on talking, but the empty house was terrifying in its silence, so that Harry too fell silent, certain that both he and the house were listening.

She took for ever to come home. When she did come in she was voluble and glowing, absently noting that she had forgotten to leave him anything for supper, passing it off with a halfhearted apology and a long recital of everything Charles had said and thought. She approached the bed with the air of a

189

jeweller unveiling his finest creation and proffered a piece of Black Forest cake she had wrapped carefully right there in the restaurant and brought halfway across town cradled in her lap.

Harry did the only logical thing under the circumstances. He started wheezing. The puppy woke and blundered across the blanket to butt him with its head. He picked it up, murmuring to it between wheezes.

'Harry, Harry, what's the matter?'

He said, to the puppy, 'I told you I was sick.'

'Harry, please!' She proffered cough medicine and he spurned it; she held out the inhaler and he knocked it away.

He said, not to her, but to the puppy, 'Mommy left me alone when I was sick.'

'Harry, please.'

'Right, puppy?'

'Oh Harry, please take your medicine.'

'It's you and me, puppy. You and me.'

Harry and the puppy were thick as thieves for the next couple of days. They refused to read the paper with his mother when she came in with breakfast and they wouldn't touch anything on any of her trays. Instead they bided their time and sneaked down to raid the kitchen when she was asleep. They talked only to each other, refusing all her advances, brooking no excuses and no apologies.

On the third day she cracked. She came to Harry's room empty-handed and weeping. 'All right, what do you want me to do?'

He answered in a flash. 'Never leave me alone when I'm sick.'

'Is that all?'

'I don't like that guy.'

'Charles?'

'I don't like him.'

Her face was a study: whatever she felt for Charles in a tug-of-war with the ancient, visceral pull. After a pause she said, 'I don't like him either.'

Harry smiled. 'Mommy, I'm hungry.'

'I'll bring you a nice bowl of chicken soup.'

That was the end of Charles.

After that Harry and his mother were closer than ever. If it cost her anything to say goodbye to romance she was gallant about it and kept her feelings well hidden. There was Harry to think about. She was the one who argued with his teachers

190

over that last quarter of a point and prepped him for tests and sent the coach packing when he suggested that, with his build, Harry was a natural for basketball; and if Harry seemed at all reluctant to give up the team trips, boys and girls together on a dark and crowded bus, his mother pointed out that it would be the worst possible thing for his asthma. It was his mother who badgered the dean of admissions until Harry was enrolled in the college of his choice, located three convenient blocks from their house. They were both astonished when, at the end of the first term, the dean suggested that he take a year off because he needed to mature. Harry and his mother talked about it privately and concluded that, for whatever reasons, the administration objected to the presence of a middle-aged woman, however attractive, at the college hangout and in various seminars and waiting with Harry on the bench outside the dean's office until it was his turn to go in.

'Who needs college?' she said.

Harry thought, but did not say: Hey, wait.

'After all,' she was saying. 'We both know you're going to be an artist.'

Harry was not so sure. His mother had enrolled him in the class because she had always wanted art lessons and so she assumed he would want them too, and Harry dutifully went to the Institute on Tuesday to do still lifes of fruit of the season with the same old clay wine bottle, in pencil, charcoal, pastels and acrylics. His colours all ran together and the shapes were hideous, but his mother admired them all the same.

'Oh Harry,' she would say, promiscuous in her approval, 'that's just beautiful.'

'That's what you always say.' It irritated him because it meant nothing, so that he was both flattered and fascinated when the cute girl from the next class came in just as he was finishing a depressing oil of that same old wine bottle, with dead leaves and acorns this time, and said, in hushed tones:

'Gee, that really stinks.'

'Do you really think so?'

'Sorry, I just . . .'

'You're the first person who's ever told the truth. What's your name?'

'Marianne.'

Harry fell in love with her.

It was around this time that his mother began to get on his nerves. If he lingered after class to talk to Marianne or buy her a cup of coffee, his mother would spring out the front door before he put his key in the lock. She would be a one-woman pageant of anxiety: Where have you been? What kept you? I thought you'd been hit by a taxi or run over by a truck, oh Harry, don't frighten me like that again. He would say, Aw, Ma, but she would already be saying: The least you could do is call when you're going to be late. She managed to be in the hall every time he used the phone, and when he began to go out with Marianne she could not keep herself from asking where he was going, how long he would be; it didn't matter whether he came home at ten or twelve or two or four a.m., she would be rattling in the kitchen, her voice would take on the high hum of hysteria: I couldn't sleep.

He should have known better than to bring Marianne home to meet her. She didn't do much; she didn't say much, but she brought in his puppy, which was no longer a puppy but instead was ageing, balding, with broken, rotting teeth. When Harry squatted to pet the dog his mother looked at Marianne over his head. 'That's the only thing Harry has ever loved. Can't sleep without him.'

Marianne looked at her in shock. 'What?'

'Right next to him on the pillow, too. Head to head. I tried to get him to put that thing in the cellar, but all I have to do is mention it and Harry starts to wheeze.'

'Harry wheezes?'

'Oh all the time,' his mother said cheerfully, opening the front door for her.

When she was gone, Harry turned on his mother in a rage, but she managed to stop him in his tracks. 'I only do these things because I love you. Think of what I have given up for you.' She was wheezing herself, as she confronted him with their whole past history in her face.

'Oh Mother. I—'

'I don't like Marianne.'

All their years together accumulated and piled into him like the cars of a fast express. 'I don't like her either,' he said.

At the same time he knew he could not stand the force of his mother's love, wanted to leave her because he was suffocating; did not know how. He didn't know whether he would ever find another girl who loved him but, if he did, he was going to handle it differently.

His first vain thought was to marry his mother off, but she would not even accept a date. 'You might need me,' she said, in spite of all his protests that he was grown now, would do fine without her. 'I wouldn't do that to you.'

It was implied that he wouldn't do that to her, either. but he would in a flash. if he could only figure out how. It was around this time that he started going into the library in the evenings, and it was natural that he should find himself attracted to one of the librarians. She liked him too, and they had a nice thing going there in the stacks, late-night sandwiches and hurried kisses. But one night Harry heard a distinct rustling in the next aisle, and when he came around the end of Q-S and into T-Z he found his mother crouching, just as the girl he had been fondling saw her and began to scream . . .

When he stamped into the house that night she greeted him with a big smile and an apple pie.

'Mother, how could you?'

'Look, Harry, I baked this for you. Your favourite.'

'How could you do a thing like that?'

'Why Harry, you know I would do anything for you.'

'But you . . . damn . . . ruined . . .' He was frothing, raging and inarticulate. He looked into that face suffused by blind mother love and in his fury took desperate measures to dramatize his anger and frustration. 'You . . .' He snatched the pie from her, ignoring her craven smile. 'Have . . .' He raised it above his head, overriding her hurried 'It's-your-favourite', and screamed: 'Got to stop.' He took the fruit of her loving labour and dashed it to the floor.

There.

He was exhausted, quivering and triumphant. He had made her understand. She had to understand.

When the red film cleared and he could see again she was on her hands and knees in front of him, scraping bits of pie off the rug as if nothing could make her happier. 'Oh Harry,' she said, imperturbable in her love, 'you know I would do anything for you.'

A less determined son would have given up at that point, sinking into the morass of mother love, but two things happened to Harry around that time, each peculiarly liberating. First his puppy died. Then they began life classes at the Institute and Harry, who up to that point had seen only selected fragments of his mother, saw his first woman nude.

Her name was Coral and he fell in love with her. They began to stay after class, Harry pretending to keep sketching, Coral pretending to pose, until the night their hands met as he pretended to adjust her drape, and Coral murmured into his ear and Harry took her home. He may have been aware of rustling in the bushes outside the studio, or of somebody following as they went up the drive to Coral's bungalow; he may have sensed a determined, feral presence under Coral's bedroom window, but he tried to push back the awareness, to begin what Coral appeared to be so ready to begin. He would have, too, kissing her as he took off his shirt, but as he clasped her to him Coral went rigid and began to scream. He turned quickly to see what had frightened her and although he caught only a glimpse of the face in the window it was enough.

'Harry, what is it?'

He lied. 'Only a prowler. I think it's gone.' He knew it wasn't.

'Then kiss me.'

'I can't.' He just couldn't.

'Please.'

'I can't – yet. There's something I have to take care of.'

'Don't go.'

'I have to.'

'When will you come back?'

'As soon as I can. It may not be until tomorrow.'

'Tomorrow, then.' Gradually, she let go. 'Tomorrow or never, Harry. I don't wait.'

'I promise.' He was buttoning his shirt. 'But right now there's something I have to do.'

She was waiting for him at the end of the driveway, proffering something. He didn't know how she had got there because he had taken the car; he had the idea she might have run the whole way because she was breathing hard and her clothes were matted with brambles; her stockings were torn and muddy at the knees. Her face was a confusing mixture of love and apprehension, and as he came towards her she shrank.

'I thought you might need your sweater.'

He looked at her without speaking.

'I only do these things because I love you.'

He opened the car door.

'Harry, you know I'd do anything for you.'

He still did not speak.

'It you're mad at me, go ahead and get good and mad at me. You know I'll forgive you, no matter what you do.'

'Get in.'

She made one more stab. 'It's raining, Harry. I thought you might be cold.'

Later, when they made the turn away from their house and up the road into the foothills, she said, 'Harry, where are we going? Where are you taking me?'

His response was dredged from millennia of parent–child dialogues. He leaned forward, taking the car into rocky, forbidding country, up an increasingly sharp grade. He said, 'We'll see.'

Maybe he only planned to frighten her, but at that last terrible moment she said, blindly, 'I'll always be there when you need me.'

He got rid of her by pushing her into Dumbman's Gorge. She got right out of the car when he told her to – she would have done anything to keep on his right side – and when he pushed her she looked back over her shoulder with an inexorable motherly smile. There were dozens of jagged tree stumps and sharp projecting rocks and she seemed to ricochet off every single one of them going down but, in spite of that and perhaps because of the purity of the air and the enormous distance she had to tumble, he thought he heard her calling to him over her shoulder, I forgive you – the words trailing behind her in a dying fall.

He didn't know whether it was guilt or the simple result of going all the way to the peak above Dumbman's Gorge and standing out there arguing in such rotten weather, but he was sick by the next evening, either flu or pneumonia, and there was no going to Coral's house that evening to take his reward. He telephoned her instead and she came to him, looking hurried and distracted and shying off when he began to cough and sneeze.

'I really want to, Harry, but right now you're too contagious.'

'But Coral.' He could hardly breathe.

'As soon as you get better.' She closed the bedroom door behind her.

When he tried to get up to plead with her he found he was too weak to stand. 'But Coral,' he said feebly from his bed.

'I'll lock the front door behind me,' she said, her voice rising behind her as she descended the stairs. 'Do you want some chicken soup?'

His voice was thin but he managed to say, 'Anything but that.'

He heard the thump as she closed the front door.

Despairing, he fell into a fevered sleep.

It may have been partly the depression of illness, the frustration of having his triumph with Coral postponed, it may have been partly delirium and partly the newly perceived flickering just beyond the circle of his vision: the gathering shadows of mortality. It may only have been a sound that woke him. All Harry knew was that he woke suddenly around midnight, gasping for breath and sitting bolt upright, swaying in the dark. He was paralysed, trembling in the fearful certainty that something ominous was approaching, coming slowly from a long way off. When he found that his trunk could not support itself and his legs would no longer move he sank back into the pillows, bloating with dread.

There had been a sound: something on the walk, sliding heavily and falling against the front door.

I came as soon as I could.

'What?' Why couldn't he sit up?

He did not know how much time passed but, whatever it was, it was in the house now. It seemed to be dragging itself through the downstairs hall. Was that it in the kitchen? In his terror and delirium he may have blacked out. He came to, returning from nowhere, thought he might have been hallucinating, tried to slow his heart. Then he heard it again. It was on the stairs leading to his room, mounting tortuously.

You're sick.

'My God.' He tried to move.

The sound was in the hall outside his room now, parts of whatever it was were thumping or sliding wetly against his bedroom door in a travesty of a knock. In another second it would start to fumble with the knob. He cried out in terrible foreknowledge: 'Who's there?'

Harry, it's Mother.

196

James Wade

The pursuer

*The late James Wade was born in 1930 in Illinois, but lived for
years in Korea, where he worked as a journalist and translator.
The death of his wife in 1973 (the circumstances of which were
incorporated into his friend Fritz Leiber's novel* Our Lady of
Darkness *to prevent that novel from becoming uncomfortably
autobiographical) stopped him, alas, from writing fiction after
that year. His stories are collected as* Such Things May Be, *but
he was best known as a composer: his operas include* A Wicked
Voice, *based on Vernon Lee's ghost story, and* The Martyred,
highly praised by the conductor Fritz Mahler.

In Such Things May Be *he described horror fiction as,
'further and subtler variations on ever more familiar, and
archaic, themes. I think this tells us more about his attitude to
his work than about the field. The best macabre fiction is
timeless; 'The Pursuer' was written in 1951 and rejected by*
Weird Tales *and* Magazine of Fantasy, *both of which folded
soon after. Urban horror fiction is more plentiful now, but this
story has not been left behind by the field.*

He has been following me for longer than I dare to remember.
And it scares me to think how long he may have been following
me before I noticed him.

He follows me when I go to work in the morning, and when
I come home at night. He follows me when I am alone, and
when I date a girl or go out with friends – although I've almost
stopped doing those things because it's no fun to be with people
while he's around.

I can't say to my friends, or to the police or anyone, 'That
man there – he's following me! He's been following me for
months!' They'd think I was crazy. And if I tried to point him
out to them another time, somewhere else far away from the

197

first place, to prove it, why – he just wouldn't be there. I'm sure of that.

I think I know now what he wants.

I remember when I first noticed him – noticed that he was following me, that is. I was down in the Loop on a Saturday night, just messing around, planning to take in a few of the cheaper bars and lounges. Saturday night is a pretty big night in Chicago.

I was getting some cigarettes in a drug store, and when I turned around he was there standing right next to me: small and seedy-looking, in a long brown overcoat and a brown hat pulled low. His face was long and leathery, with a thin nose and wide, wet lips. He didn't seem to be looking at me or at anything in particular.

I recognized him as the little guy I'd seen around my neighbourhood a lot, in stores and on the street. I didn't know who he was, and I'd never talked to him, but I started to open my mouth and say something in a conversational way about running into him down here. Then I looked closer at his face and for some reason I didn't say anything. I just edged past him and left the store. He followed.

Every bar. Every lounge. Every joint.

As I fled from him, one spot to another, I kept remembering other unlikely times and places I'd seen him in the last few days, and longer ago than that, it seemed to me. Maybe I imagined a few of them, but there were plenty I could be pretty sure about.

And I began to get scared. I didn't know what he wanted; I thought he might be planning to rob me or kill me (why, I didn't know; I had little enough). I couldn't face him, I couldn't look at him.

He would come into a place like he always does, just a little after me – very quiet, very unnoticeable – and stay just a medium distance away from me. Nothing suspicious. And he wouldn't leave just when I did, he was too clever for that; but soon after I left a spot, I'd know that he was coming on behind me.

I have never heard him speak.

The last place I went to that night, I must have been pretty shook up. I couldn't take my eyes away from the door, but I couldn't stand to keep looking at it, either. The barkeep, a big bald-headed guy, leaned forward and squinted at me through the foggy neon light.

' 'S matter, buddy, you expecting somebody?'

I got up and went out.

It took a lot of courage to go through that door; I was deadly afraid of meeting him coming in.

I didn't, and I didn't see him on the street, either, but right away I knew he was behind me.

I was pretty drunk by that time, with all the doubles I had knocked back in the bars I'd visited, and it was like some crazy nightmare, staggering along Randolph Street under all the glaring neon signs, with the loudspeakers blaring music from inside the lounges, and the crowds pushing in every direction. I felt sick, and scared enough almost to cry. People looked at me, but I guess they thought I was just drunk. Naturally, no one ever noticed him.

After a while I threw up in an alley, and then I felt a little calmer and headed for home. I knew he was on the street car with me, and I knew he got off at my stop. I went down the street as fast as I could, hardly able to tell my rooming house from all the others just like it.

At last I found it and staggered upstairs, groped open my door, and threw the bolt behind me. I went to the window and looked down, peering intently through the darkness towards the splashes of light from the street lamps, but I didn't see him below on the street; it was dark and quiet and empty. (I never do see him down there, in fact; but somehow he's always after me as soon as I come out.)

I went over to the mirror and stood there, as if for company. If only I'd had some family, or anyone that cared enough to believe such a crazy story! But there was no one.

I was very scared; at that time I believed he wanted to hurt me. I know better now.

I went over and lay down on the bed, trembling. After a while I fell asleep, and slept all the next day.

When I went out that evening, he was standing on the corner.

That's how it's been ever since: day or night, anywhere, everywhere, I can always spot him if I dare look. I've tried every way to dodge or elude him, even made a sort of grim game out of it, but nothing is any good.

All this time I couldn't think of anything to do about him.

I knew that I couldn't prove a thing, that there was no way to get any witnesses without making people think I was crazy. I knew that even if I took a train or plane and went a thousand miles, he'd be there, if he wanted to be, as soon as I was there or sooner, and it would start all over.

After a while I began almost to get used to it. I became convinced he wouldn't try to hurt me; he'd had too many chances to do that already. The only thing I could think of to do was to keep working, to act as if nothing was the matter, and to ignore him. Maybe some day he wouldn't be there.

I started staying in, not seeing anyone, pretending to be sick if friends called. Gradually they stopped calling. I tried to read magazines all the time I was off work.

Lately I find that I can't stand that any more. I can't sit in my room and do nothing, and not know where he is. As bad as it is, it's better to know that he's walking behind me, or standing at the end of the bar, or waiting on the corner outside – better than imagining all sorts of things.

So I walk.

I walk in all kinds of weather, in all kinds of places. I walk at any time of the day or night. I walk for hours and if I get tired I get on a street car or a bus, and when I get off I walk some more.

I walk along shabby streets of lined-up flats and brownstones, where the prostitutes stand under the street lights after dark and writhe their bodies when you pass by. I walk in the park during afternoon rains, when no one is there but us and the thunder. I walk on the lake-front breakwater at midnight, while the cold wind sends waves slithering inland to shatter into nets of spray.

I walk in suburban neighbourhoods; the sun bakes the brick and concrete, cars are parked in neat rows under shade trees. I walk in the snow and slush along Skid Row, where legless beggars and awful cripples and drunks and degenerates sprawl on the sidewalks. I walk through market day on Maxwell Street, with all the million-and-one things in stalls and booths, with the spicy food smells and the crazy sales *spiels* and the jabbering crowds of every kind of people on earth.

I walk by the university campuses, and the churches, and the blocks and blocks of stores and bars, stores and bars. And I know that whenever I look behind, I'll be able to see his small shuffling form, that brown hat and overcoat, that long expressionless face – never looking at me, but knowing I'm there.

And I know what he wants.

He wants me, some night on a dark street (or in the neon glow outside a tavern, or in a park at noon, or by a church while they're holding services inside and you can hear the hymn singing) – he wants me to turn around and wait for him. No – he wants me to walk back and come up to him.

He wants more than that. He doesn't expect me to ask what he's doing, why he's following me. The time is long past for that. He wants me – he is inviting me to come up to him in blind rage and attack him; to try to kill him in any way I'm able.

And that I must not do. I don't know why, but the thought of doing that – as satisfying as it should be after all I've been through – makes me run cold with a sweat of horror beyond any revulsion I felt for him up to now.

I must not, I dare not approach him. Above all, I must not touch him, or try to injure him in any way. I can't imagine what would happen if I did, but it would be very awful.

I must continue not to pay him any heed at all.

And yet I know, if he keeps on following me, some time, somewhere, I'll not be able to help myself; I will turn back on him with insane fury and try to kill him. And then . . .

Graham Masterton

Bridal suite

*Graham Masterton was born in 1947, and sends me a
mysterious paragraph about himself. He and his wife and
three children divide their time between Epsom Downs in
England and Key West in Florida. He is a skilled underwater
swimmer and a collector of rare umbrellas. Eh? Maybe living
in Philip Marlowe territory does things to a man.*

His novels include The Manitou *(filmed by the late William
Girdler),* The Sphinx, The Djinn, *and* Charnel House. *He
specializes in visiting myths from the past on the present. If
'Bridal suite' is in some ways more traditional, nevertheless
until recently it could hardly have been published.*

They arrived in Sherman, Connecticut, on a cold fall day when
the leaves were crisp and whispery, and the whole world seemed
to have crumbled into rust. They parked their rented Cordoba
outside the front steps of the house, and climbed out. Peter
opened the trunk and hefted out their cases, still new, with
price tags from Macy's in White Plains, while Jenny stood in
her sheepskin coat and smiled and shivered. It was a Saturday,
mid-afternoon, and they had just been married.

The house stood amongst the shedding trees, white weather-
boarded and silent. It was a huge old colonial, 1820 or there-
abouts, with black-paint railings, an old coach lamp over the
door, and a flagged stone porch. All around it stretched silent
leafless woods and rocky outcroppings. There was an abandoned tennis court, with a sagging net and rusted posts. A
decaying roller, overgrown with grass, stood where some gardener had left it, at some unremembered moment, years and
years ago.

There was utter silence. Until you stand still in Sherman,
Connecticut, on a crisp fall day, you don't know what silence
is. Then suddenly a light wind, and a scurry of dead leaves.

They walked up to the front door, Peter carrying the suitcases. He looked around for a bell, but there was none.

Jenny said: 'Knock?'

Peter grinned. 'With that thing?'

On the black-painted door was a grotesque corroded brass knocker, made in the shape of some kind of howling creature, with horns and teeth and a feral snarl. Peter took hold of it tentatively and gave three hollow raps. They echoed inside the house, across unseen hallways and silent landings. Peter and Jenny waited, smiling at each other reassuringly. They had booked, after all. There was no question but they had booked.

There was no reply.

Jenny said: 'Maybe you ought to knock louder. Let me try.'

Peter banged louder. The echoes were flat, unanswered. They waited two, three minutes more. Peter, looking at Jenny, said: 'I love you. Do you know that?'

Jenny stood on tippy-toes and kissed him. 'I love you, too. I love you more than a barrelful of monkeys.'

The leaves rustled around their feet and still nobody came to the door. Jenny walked across the front garden to the living-room window and peered in, shading her eyes with her hand. She was a small girl, only five-two, with long fair hair and a thin oval face. Peter thought she looked like one of Botticelli's muses, one of those divine creatures who floated two inches off the ground, wrapped in diaphanous drapery, plucking at a harp. She was, in fact, a *sweet* girl. Sweet-looking, sweet-natured, but with a slight sharpness about her that made all that sweetness palatable. He had met her on an Eastern Airlines flight from Miami to La Guardia. He had been vacationing, she had been visiting her retired father. They had fallen in love, in three months of beautiful days that had been just like one of those movies, all out-of-focus swimming scenes and picnics in the grass and running in slow motion across General Motors Plaza while pigeons flurried around them and passing pedestrians turned and stared.

He was an editor for Manhattan Cable TV. Tall, spare, given to wearing hand-knitted tops wih floppy sleeves. He smoked Parliament, liked Santana and lived in the village amidst a thousand LPs, with a grey cat that liked to rip up his rugs, plants and wind chimes. He loved Doonesbury and never knew how close it got to what he was himself.

Some friends had given them a polythene bag of grass and a pecan pie from the Yum-Yum Bakery for a wedding present.

Her father, dear and white-haired, had given them three thousand dollars and a water-bed.

'This is crazy,' said Peter. 'Did we book a week at this place or did we book a week at this place?'

'It looks deserted,' called Jenny, from the tennis court.

'It looks more than deserted,' complained Peter. 'It looks run down into the ground. *Cordon bleu* dining, they said in *Connecticut*. Comfortable beds and all facilities. It looks more like Frankenstein's castle.'

Jenny, out of sight, suddenly called: 'There's someone here. On the back terrace.'

Peter left the cases and followed her around the side of the house. In the flaking trees, black-and-white wood warblers flurried and sang. He walked around by the tattered tennis-court nets, and there was Jenny, standing by a deck chair. In the chair, asleep, was a grey-haired woman, covered by a blanket of dark green plaid. On the grass beside her was a copy of the New Milford newspaper, stirred by the breeze.

Peter bent over the woman. She had a bony, well-defined face, and in her youth she must have been pretty. Her mouth was slightly parted as she slept, and Peter could see her eyeballs moving under her eyelids. She must have been dreaming of something.

He shook her slightly, and said: 'Mrs Gaylord?'

Jenny said: 'Do you think she's all right?'

'Oh, she's fine,' he told her. 'She must have been reading and just dozed off. Mrs Gaylord?'

The woman opened her eyes. She stared at Peter for a moment with an expression that he couldn't understand, an expression that looked curiously like suspicion, but then, abruptly, she sat up and washed her face with her hands, and said: 'Oh, dear! My goodness! I think I must have dropped off for a while.'

'It looks that way,' said Peter.

She folded back her blanket, and stood up. She was taller than Jenny, but not very tall, and under a grey plain dress she was as thin as a clothes horse. Standing near her, Peter detected the scent of violets, but it was a strangely closeted smell, as if the violets had long since died.

'You must be Mr and Mrs Delgordo,' she said.

'That's right. We just arrived. We knocked, but there was no reply. I hope you don't mind us waking you up like this.'

'Not at all,' said Mrs Gaylord. 'You must think that I'm

awful . . . not being here to greet you. And you just married, too. Congratulations. You look very happy with each other.'

'We are,' smiled Jenny.

'Well, you'd better come along inside. Do you have many bags? My handyman is over at New Milford this afternoon, buying some glass fuses. I'm afraid we're a little chaotic at this time of year. We don't have many guests after Rosh Hashanah.'

She led the way towards the house. Peter glanced at Jenny and shrugged, but Jenny could only pull a face. They followed Mrs Gaylord's bony back across the untidy lawn and in through the door of a sun room, where a faded billiard table mouldered, and yellowed framed photographs of smiling young men hung next to yachting trophies and varsity pennants. They passed through a set of smeary french doors to the living room, dark and musty and vast, with two old screened fireplaces, and a galleried staircase. Everywhere around there was wood panelling, inlaid flooring and dusty drapes. It looked more like a neglected private house than a 'cordon bleu weekend retreat for sophisticated couples'.

'Is there . . . anybody else here?' asked Peter. 'I mean, any other guests?'

'Oh, no,' smiled Mrs Gaylord. 'You're quite alone. We are very lonely at this time of year.'

'Could you show us our room? I can always carry the bags up myself. We've had a pretty hard day, what with one thing and another.'

'Of course,' Mrs Gaylord told him. 'I remember my own wedding day. I couldn't wait to come out here and have Frederick all to myself.'

'You spent your wedding night here too?' asked Jenny.

'Oh, yes. In the same room where you will be spending yours. I call it the bridal suite.'

Jenny said: 'Is Frederick – I mean, is Mr Gaylord—?'

'Passed over,' said Mrs Gaylord. Her eyes were bright with memory.

'I'm sorry to hear that,' said Jenny. 'But I guess you have your family now. Your sons.'

'Yes,' smiled Mrs Gaylord. 'They're all fine boys.'

Peter took his luggage from the front doorstep and Mrs Gaylord led them up the staircase to the second-floor landing. They passed gloomy bathrooms with iron claw-footed tubs and amber windows. They passed bedrooms with unslept-in beds and drawn blinds. They passed a sewing room, with a silent pedal sewing machine of black enamel and inlaid mother-of-pearl. The house was faintly chilly, and the floorboards creaked under their feet as they walked towards the bridal suite.

The room where they were going to stay was high-ceilinged and vast. It had a view of the front of the house, with its driveway and drifts of leaves, and also to the back, across the woods. There was a heavy carved-oak closet, and the bed itself was a high four-poster with twisting spiral posts and heavy brocade drapes. Jenny sat on it, and patted it, and said: 'It's kind of hard, isn't it?'

Mrs Gaylord looked away. She seemed to be thinking about something else. She said: 'You'll find it's most comfortable when you're used to it.'

Peter set down the cases. 'What time do you serve dinner this evening?' he asked her.

Mrs Gaylord didn't answer him directly, but spoke instead to Jenny. 'What time would you like it?' she asked.

Jenny glanced at Peter. 'Around eight would be fine,' she said.

'Very well. I'll make it at eight,' said Mrs Gaylord. 'Make yourself at home in the meanwhile. And if there's anything you want, don't hesitate to call me. I'm always around someplace, even if I am asleep at times.'

She gave Jenny a wistful smile and then, without another word, she left the room, closing the door quietly behind her. Peter and Jenny waited for a moment in silence until they heard her footsteps retreating down the hall. Then Jenny flowed into Peter's arms, and they kissed. It was a kiss that meant a lot of things: like, I love you, and thank you, and no matter what everyone said, we did it, we got married at last, and I'm glad.

He unbuttoned her plain wool going-away dress. He slipped it from her shoulder and kissed her neck. She ruffled his hair with her fingers and whispered: 'I always imagined it would be like this.'

He said: 'Mmh.'

Her dress fell around her ankles. Underneath, she wore a pink gauzy bra through which the darkness of her nipples showed and small gauzy panties. He slipped his hand under the bra and rolled her nipples between his fingers until they knurled and stiffened. She opened his shirt, and reached around to caress his bare back.

207

The fall afternoon seemed to blur. They pulled back the covers of the old four-poster bed and then, naked, scrambled between the sheets. He kissed her forehead, her closed eyelids, her mouth, her breasts. She kissed his narrow muscular chest, his flat stomach.

From behind the darkness of her closed eyes, she heard his breathing, soft and urgent and wanting. She lay on her side, with her back to him, and she felt her thighs parted from behind. He was panting harder and harder, as if he was running a race, or fighting against something, and she murmured: 'You're worked up. My God, but I love it.'

She felt him thrust inside her. She wasn't ready, and by his unusual dryness, nor was he. But he was so big and demanding that the pain was a pleasure, too, and even as she winced she was shaking with pleasure. He thrust and thrust and thrust, and she cried out, and all the fantasies she'd ever dreamed of burst in front of her closed eyes – fantasies of rape by brutal Vikings with steel armour and naked thighs, fantasies of being forced to show herself to prurient emperors in bizarre harems, fantasies of being assaulted by a glossy black stallion.

He was so fierce and virile that he overwhelmed her, and she seemed to lose herself in a collision of love and ecstasy. It took her whole minutes to recover, minutes that were measured out by a painted pine wall clock that ticked and ticked, slow as dust falling in an airless room.

She whispered: 'You were fantastic. I've never known you like that before. Marriage must definitely agree with you.'

There was no answer. She said: 'Peter?'

She turned, and he wasn't there. The bed was empty, apart from her. The sheet was rumpled, as if Peter had been lying there, but there was no sign of him.

She said, in a nervous voice: 'Peter? Where are you?'

There was silence, punctuated only by the clock.

She sat up. Her eyes were wide. She said, so softly that nobody could have heard: 'Peter? Are you there?'

She looked across the room, to the half-open door that led to the bathroom suite. Late sunlight fell across the floor. Outside, in the grounds, she could hear leaves shifting and the faint distant barking of a dog.

'Peter – if this is supposed to be some kind of a game—'

She got out of bed. She held her hand between her legs and her thighs were sticky with their lovemaking. She had never known him fill her with such a copious flow of semen. It was so much that it slid down the inside of her leg on to the rug. She lifted her hand, palm upwards, and frowned at it in bewilderment.

Peter wasn't in the bathroom. He wasn't under the bed, or hiding under the covers. He wasn't behind the drapes. She searched for him with a pained, baffled doggedness, even though she knew that he wasn't there. After ten minutes of searching, however, she had to stop. He had gone. Somehow, mysteriously, gone. She sat on the end of the bed and didn't know whether to giggle with frustration or scream with anger. He must have gone someplace. She hadn't heard the door open and close, and she hadn't heard his footsteps. So where was he?

She dressed again, and went to look for him. She searched every room on the upper landing, including the bureaux and the closets. She even pulled down the ladder from the attic and looked up there, but all Mrs Gaylord had stored away was old pictures and a broken-down baby carriage. Up there, with her head through the attic door, she could hear the leaves rustling for miles around. She called: 'Peter?' anxiously; but there was no reply, and so she climbed down the ladder again.

Eventually, she came to one of the sun rooms downstairs. Mrs Gaylord was sitting in a basketwork chair reading a newspaper and smoking a cigarette. The smoke fiddled and twisted in the dying light of the day. On the table beside her was a cup of coffee with a wrinkled skin forming on the top of it.

'Hallo,' said Mrs Gaylord, without looking around. 'You're down early. I didn't expect you till later.'

'Something's happened,' said Jenny. She suddenly found that she was trying very hard not to cry.

Mrs Gaylord turned around. 'I don't understand, my dear. Have you had an argument?'

'I don't know. But Peter's gone. He's just disappeared. I've looked all around the house and I can't find him anywhere.'

Mrs Gaylord lowered her eyes. 'I see. That's most unfortunate.'

'Unfortunate? It's terrible! I'm so worried! I don't know whether I should call the police or not.'

'The police? I hardly think that's necessary. He's probably gotten a case of cold feet, and he's gone out for a walk on his own. Men do feel like that sometimes, when they've just been wed. It's a common complaint.'

'But I didn't even hear him leave. One second we were — well, one second we were resting on the bed together, and the next thing I knew he wasn't there.'

Mrs Gaylord bit at her lips as if she was thinking.

'Are you sure you were on the bed?' she asked.

Jenny stared at her hotly, and blushed. 'We are married, you know. We were married today.'

'I didn't mean that,' said Mrs Gaylord, abstractedly.

'Then I don't know what you *did* mean.'

Mrs Gaylord looked up, and her momentary reverie was broken. She gave Jenny a reassuring smile, and reached out her hand.

'I'm sure it's nothing terrible,' she said. 'He must have decided to get himself a breath of fresh air, that's all. Nothing terrible at all.'

Jenny snapped: 'He didn't open the door, Mrs Gaylord! He just vanished!'

Mrs Gaylord frowned. 'There's no need to bark at me, my dear. If you're having a few complications with your new husband, then it's most certainly not my fault!'

Jenny was about to shout back at her, but she put her hand over her mouth and turned away. It was no good getting hysterical. If Peter had simply walked out and left her, then she had to know why; and if he had mysteriously vanished, then the only sensible thing to do was search the house carefully until she found him. She felt panic deep inside her, and a feeling which she hadn't felt for a very long time – loneliness. But she stayed still with her hand against her mouth until the sensation had passed, and then she said quietly to Mrs Gaylord, without turning around: 'I'm sorry. I was frightened, that's all. I can't think where he could have gone.'

'Do you want to look around the house?' asked Mrs Gaylord. 'You're very welcome.'

'I think I'd like to. That's if you don't mind.'

Mrs Gaylord stood up. 'I'll even help you, my dear. I'm sure you must be feeling most upset.'

They spent the next hour walking from room to room, opening and closing doors. But as darkness gathered over the grounds and the surrounding woods, and as the cold evening wind began to rise, they had to admit that wherever Peter was, he wasn't concealed or hiding in the house.

'Do you want to call the police?' asked Mrs Gaylord. They were standing in the gloomy living room now. The log fire in the antique hearth was nothing more than a heap of dusty white ashes. Outside, the wind whirled in the leaves, and rattled at the window frames.

'I think I'd better,' said Jenny. She felt empty, shocked, and hardly capable of saying anything sensible. 'I think I'd like to call some of my friends in New York, too, if that's okay.'

'Go ahead. I'll start preparing dinner.'

'I really don't want anything to eat. Not until I know about Peter.'

Mrs Gaylord, her face half-hidden in shadow, said softly: 'If he's really gone, you're going to have to get used to it, my dear; and the best time to start is now.'

Before Jenny could answer her, she had walked out of the living room door and along the corridor to the kitchen. Jenny saw an inlaid mahogany cigarette box on a side table, and for the first time in three years she took out a cigarette and lit it. It tasted flat and foul, but she took the smoke down, and held it, her eyes closed in anguish and isolation.

She called the police. They were courteous, helpful, and they promised to come out to see her in the morning if there was still no sign of Peter. They had to warn her, though, that he was an adult, and free to go where he chose, even if it meant leaving her on her wedding night.

She thought of calling her mother, but after dialling the number and listening to it ring, she set the phone down again. The humiliation of Peter having left her was too much to share with her family or her close friends right now. She knew that if she heard her mother's sympathetic voice, she would only burst into tears. She crushed out the cigarette and tried to think who else to call.

The wind blew an upstairs door shut, and she jumped in nervous shock.

Mrs Gaylord came back after a while with a tray. Jenny was sitting in front of the dying fire, smoking her second cigarette and trying to keep back the tears.

'I've made some Philadelphia pepper soup, and grilled a couple of New York steaks,' said Mrs Gaylord. 'Would you like to eat them in front of the hearth? I'll build it up for you.'

Throughout their impromptu dinner, Jenny was silent. She managed a little soup, but the steak caught in her throat, and she couldn't begin to swallow it. She wept for a few minutes, and Mrs Gaylord watched her carefully.

'I'm sorry,' said Jenny, wiping her eyes.

'Don't be. I understand what you're going through only too well. I lost my own husband, remember.'

Jenny nodded, dumbly.

211

'I think it would better if you moved to the small bedroom for tonight,' suggested Mrs Gaylord. 'You'll feel more comfortable there. It's a cosy little room, right at the back.'

'Thank you,' Jenny whispered. 'I think I'd prefer that.'

They sat in front of the fire until the fresh logs were burned down, and the long-case clock in the hallway began to strike two in the morning. Then Mrs Gaylord cleared away their plates, and they mounted the dark, creaking staircase to go to bed. They went into the bridal suite to collect Jenny's case, and for a moment she looked forlornly at Peter's case, and his clothes scattered where he had left them.

She suddenly said: '*His clothes.*'

'What's that, my dear?'

She flustered: 'I don't know why I didn't think about it before. If Peter's gone, then what's he wearing? His suitcase isn't open, and his clothes are lying right there where he left them. He was *naked*. He wouldn't go out on a cold night like this, naked. It's insane.'

Mrs Gaylord lowered her gaze. 'I'm sorry, my dear. We just don't know what's happened. We've looked all over the house, haven't we? Maybe he took a robe with him. There were some robes on the back of the door.'

'But Peter wouldn't—'

Mrs Gaylord put her arm around her. 'I'm afraid you can't say what Peter would or wouldn't do. He *has*. Whatever his motive, and wherever he's gone.'

Jenny said quietly: 'Yes. I suppose you're right.'

'You'd better go get some sleep,' said Mrs Gaylord. 'Tomorrow, you're going to need all the energy you can muster.'

Jenny picked up her case, paused for a moment, and then went sadly along the landing to the small back bedroom. Mrs Gaylord murmured: 'Goodnight. I hope you sleep.'

Jenny undressed, put on the frilly rose-patterned nightdress she had bought specially for the wedding night, and brushed her teeth at the small basin by the window. The bedroom was small, with a sloping ceiling, and there was a single bed with a colonial patchwork cover. On the pale flowery wallpaper was a framed sampler, reading, 'God Is With Us'.

She climbed into bed and lay there for a while, staring up at the cracked plaster. She didn't know what to think about Peter any more. She listened to the old house creaking in the darkness. Then she switched off her bedside lamp and tried to sleep.

Soon after she heard the long-case clock strike four, she

thought she detected the sound of someone crying. She sat up in bed and listened again, holding her breath. Outside her bedroom window the night was still utterly dark, and the leaves rattled like rain. She heard the crying noise again.

Carefully, she climbed out of bed and went to the door. She opened it a little way, and it groaned on its hinges. She paused, her ears straining for the crying sound, and it came again. It was like a cat yowling, or a child in pain. She stepped out of her room and tippy-toed halfway along the landing, until she reached the head of the stairs.

The old house was like a ship out at sea. The wind shook the doors and sighed between the shingles. The weathervane turned and grated on its mounting, with a sound like a knife being scraped on a plate. At every window, drapes stirred as if they were being touched by unseen hands.

Jenny stepped quietly along to the end of the landing. She heard the sound once more – a repressed mewling. There was no doubt in her mind now that it was coming from the bridal suite. She found she was biting at her tongue in nervous anxiety, and that her pulse rate was impossibly quick. She paused for just a moment to calm herself down, but she had to admit that she was afraid. The noise came again, clearer and louder this time.

She pressed her ear against the door of the bridal suite. She thought she could hear rustling sounds, but that may have been the wind and the leaves. She knelt down and peered through the keyhole, although the draught made her eyes water. It was so dark in the bridal suite that she couldn't see anything at all.

She stood up. Her mouth was parched. If there was someone in there – who was it? There was so much rustling and stirring that it sounded as if there were two people there. Maybe some unexpected guests had called by while she was asleep; although she was pretty sure that she hadn't slept at all. Maybe it was Mrs Gaylord. But if it was her, then what was she doing, making all those terrifying noises?

Jenny knew that she had to open the door. She had to do it for her own sake and for Peter's sake. It might be nothing at all. It might be a stray cat playing around in there, or an odd downdraught from the chimney. It might even be latecoming guests and, if it was, then she would wind up embarrassed. But being embarrassed had to be better than not knowing. There was no way she could go back to her small bedroom and sleep soundly without finding out what those noises were.

She put her hand on the brass doorknob. She closed her eyes tight, and took a breath. Then she turned the knob and jerkily opened the door.

The noise in the room was horrifying. It was like the howl of the wind, only there was no wind. It was like standing on the edge of a clifftop at night, with a yawning chasm below, invisible and bottomless. It was like a nightmare come true. The whole bridal suite seemed to be possessed by some moaning, ancient sound; some cold magnetic gale. It was the sound and the feel of fear.

Jenny, shaking, turned her eyes towards the bed. At first, behind the twisted pillars and drapes, she couldn't make out what was happening. There was a figure there, a naked woman's figure, and she was writhing and whimpering and letting out sighs of strained delight. Jenny peered harder through the darkness, and she saw that it was Mrs Gaylord, as thin and nude as a dancer. She was lying on her back, her claw-like hands digging into the sheets, her eyes closed in ecstasy.

Jenny stepped into the bridal suite, and the wind gently blew the door shut behind her. She crossed the rug to the end of the bed, her mind chilled with fright, and stood there, looking down at Mrs Gaylord with a fixed and mesmerized stare. All around her, the room whispered and moaned and murmured, an asylum of spectres and apparitions.

With complete horror, Jenny saw why Mrs Gaylord was crying out in such pleasure. *The bed itself, the very sheets and under-blankets and mattress, had taken on the shape of a man's body, in white linen relief, and up between Mrs Gaylord's narrow thighs thrust an erection of living fabric. The whole bed rippled and shook with hideous spasms, and the man's shape seemed to shift and alter as Mrs Gaylord twisted around it.*

Jenny screamed. She didn't even realize that she'd done it until Mrs Gaylord opened her eyes and stared at her with wild malevolence. The bed's heaving suddenly subsided and faded, and Mrs Gaylord sat up, making no attempt to cover her scrawny breasts.

'*You!*' said Mrs Gaylord, hoarsely. 'What are you doing here?'

Jenny opened her mouth but she couldn't speak.

'You came in here to spy, to pry on my private life, is that it?'

'I – I heard—'

Mrs Gaylord climbed off the bed, stooped, and picked up a

green silk wrap, which she loosely tied around herself. Her face was white and rigid with dislike.

'I suppose you think you're a clever girl,' she said. 'I suppose you think you've discovered something momentous.'

'I don't even know what—'

Mrs Gaylord tossed her hair back impatiently. She didn't seem to be able to keep still, but kept on pacing around the bridal suite, loaded with tension. Jenny, after all, had interrupted her lovemaking, however weird it had been, and she was still frustrated. She gave a sound like a snarl, and paced back around the room again.

'I want to know what's happened to Peter,' said Jenny. Her voice was shaky but for the first time since Peter's disappearance, her intention was firm.

'What do you think?' said Mrs Gaylord, in a caustic voice.

'I don't know what to think. That bed—'

'This bed has been here since this house was built. This bed is the whole reason this house was built. This bed is both a servant and a master. But more of a master.'

'I don't understand it,' said Jenny. 'Is it some kind of mechanism? Some kind of trick?'

Mrs Gaylord gave a sharp, mocking laugh. 'A trick?' she asked, fidgeting and pacing. 'You think what you saw just now was a trick?'

'I just don't see how—'

Mrs Gaylord's face was sour with contempt. 'I'll tell you how, you witless girl. This bed was owned by Dorman Pierce, who lived here in Sherman in the 1820s. He was an arrogant, dark, savage man, with tastes that were too strange for most people. He took a bride, an innocent girl called Faith Martin, and after they were married he led her up to his bridal suite and *this* bed.'

Jenny heard the wind moaning again. The cold, old wind that stirred no drapes nor aroused any dust.

'What Dorman Pierce did to his new bride on this bed that first night – well, God only knows. But he used her cruelly and broke her will, and made her a shell of the girl she once was. Unfortunately for Dorman, though, the girl's godmother got to hear of what had happened, and it was said that she had connections with one of the most ancient of Connecticut magic circles. She may even have been a member herself. She paid for a curse to be put upon Dorman Pierce, and it was the curse

215

of complete submission. In future, *he* would have to serve women, instead of women serving *him*.'

Mrs Gaylord turned towards the bed, and touched it. Its sheets seemed to shift and wrinkle by themselves.

'He lay in this bed one night and the bed absorbed him. His spirit is in the bed even now. His spirit, or his lust, or his virility, or whatever it is.'

Jenny frowned. 'The bed did what? *Absorbed* him?'

'He sank into it like a man sinking into quicksand. He was never seen again. Faith Martin stayed in this house until she was old, and every night, or whenever she wished it, the bed had to serve her.'

Mrs Gaylord pulled her wrap tighter. The bridal suite was growing very cold. 'What nobody knew, though, was that the enchantment remained on the bed, even after Faith's death. The next young couple who moved here slept on this bed on their wedding night, and the bed again claimed the husband. And so it went on, whenever a man slept on it. Each time, that man was absorbed. My own husband, Frederick was— Well, he's in there, too.'

Jenny could hardly stand to hear what Mrs Gaylord was going to say next.

She said: 'And *Peter*?'

Mrs Gaylord touched her own face, as if to reassure herself that she was real. She said, ignoring Jenny's question: 'The women who decided to stay in this house and sleep on this bed all made the same discovery. For each man who was absorbed, the bed's strength and virility grew that much greater. That's why I said that it's more of a master than a servant. Right now, with all the men that it has claimed, it is sexually powerful to an enormous degree.'

She stroked the bed again, and it shuddered. 'The more men it takes,' she whispered, 'the more demanding it becomes.'

Jenny whispered: 'Peter?'

Mrs Gaylord smiled vaguely, and nodded, her fingers still caressing the sheets.

Jenny said: 'You knew what was going to happen, and you actually let it? You actually *let* my Peter—'

She was too shocked to go on. She said: 'Oh, God. Oh, my God.'

Mrs Gaylord turned to her. 'You don't have to *lose* Peter, you know,' she said, cajolingly. 'We could both share this bed if you stayed here. We could share all of the men who have been taken by it. Dorman Pierce, Peter, Frederick, and all the dozens of others. Have you any idea what it's like to be taken by twenty men at once?'

Jenny, feeling nauseous, said: 'Yesterday afternoon, when we—'

Mrs Gaylord bent forward and kissed the sheets. They were snaking and folding with feverish activity, and to Jenny's horror, they were beginning to rise again into the form of a huge, powerful man. It was like watching a mummified being rise from the dead; a body lifting itself out of a starched white shroud. The sheets became legs, arms and a broad chest, and the pillow rose into the form of a heavy-jawed masculine face. It wasn't Peter, it wasn't any man; it was the sum of *all* the men who had been caught by the curse of the bridal suite, and dragged into the dark heart of the bed.

Mrs Gaylord pulled open her wrap, and let it slither to the floor. She looked at Jenny with glittering eyes, and said: 'He's here, your Peter. Peter and all his soulmates. Come and join him. Come and give yourself to him . . .'

Skinny and naked, Mrs Gaylord mounted the bed, and began to run her fingers over the white shape of the sheets. Jenny, with rising panic, crossed the room and tried the door handle, but the door seemed to be wedged firmly shut. The windless wind rose again, and an agonized moaning filled the room. Now Jenny knew what that moaning was. It was the cries of those men trapped for ever within the musty substance of the bridal bed, buried in its horsehair and its springs and its sheets, suffocatingly confined for the pleasure of a vengeful woman.

Mrs Gaylord seized the bed's rising member, and clutched it in her fist. 'See this?' she shrieked. 'See how strong it is? How proud it is? We could share it, you and I! Come share it!'

Jenny tugged and rattled at the door, but it still refused to open. In desperation she crossed the room again and tried to pull Mrs Gaylord off the bed.

'Get away!' screeched Mrs Gaylord. 'Get away, you sow!'

There was a tumultuous heaving on the bed, and Jenny found herself struck by something as heavy and powerful as a man's arm. She caught her foot on the bed's trailing sheets, and fell. The room was filled with ear-splitting howls and bays of fury, and the whole house was shuddering and shaking. She tried to climb to her feet, but she was struck again, and she knocked her head against the floor.

Now Mrs Gaylord had mounted the hideous white figure on

the bed, and was riding it furiously, screaming at the top of her voice. Jenny managed to pull herself up against a pine bureau, and seize an old glass kerosene lamp which was standing on top of it.

'*Peter!*' she shouted, and flung the lamp at Mrs Gaylord's naked back.

She never knew how the kerosene ignited. The whole of the bridal suite seemed to be charged with strange electricity, and maybe it was a spark or a discharge of supernatural power. Whatever it was, the lamp struck Mrs Gaylord on the side of the head and burst apart in a shower of fragments, and then there was a soft *woofff* sound, and both Mrs Gaylord and the white figure on the bed were smothered instantly in flames.

Mrs Gaylord screamed. She turned to Jenny with staring eyes and her hair was alight, frizzing into brownish fragments. Flames danced from her face and her shoulders and her breasts, shrivelling her skin like a burning magazine.

But it was the bed itself that was most horrifying. The blazing sheets struggled and twisted and churned, and out of the depths of the bed came an echoing agonized roar that was like a choir of demons. The roar was the voice of every man buried alive in the bed, as the fire consumed the material that had made their spirits into flesh. It was hideous, chaotic, unbearable and, most terrible of all, Jenny could distinguish Peter's voice, howling and groaning in pain.

The house burned throughout the rest of the night, and into the pale cold dawn. By mid-morning it was pretty much under control, and the local firemen trod through the charred timbers and wreckage, hosing down the smouldering furniture and collapsed staircases. Twenty or thirty people came to stare, and a CBS news crew made a short recording for television. One old Sherman citizen, with white hair and baggy pants, told the newsmen that he'd always believed the place was haunted, and it was better off burned down.

It wasn't until they moved the fallen ceiling of the main bedroom that they discovered the charred remains of seventeen men and one woman, all curled up as small as monkeys by the intense heat.

There had been another woman there, but at that moment she was sitting in the back of a taxi on the way to the railroad station, wrapped tightly in an overcoat, her salvaged suitcase resting on the seat beside her. Her eyes, as she watched the brown-and-yellow trees go past, were as dull as stones.

218

Dennis Etchison and Mark Johnson
The spot

*Dennis Etchison was born in California in 1943 and is getting
tired of being described as a young Californian writer. 'Do you
suppose that one of these days I'll pass an invisible peak and
suddenly become middle-aged without ever having gone
through my prime?' he wonders. I suspect that blurb writers
and such folk don't know how else to describe him, since so
many of his stories are uncompromisingly subtle and original.
They are collected as* Red Dreams *and* The Dark Country. *The
title story of the latter is the first work to have won both British
and World Fantasy Awards. He has also published a novel,*
Darkside.

*Mark Johnson is a cartoonist and illustrator, and a collector
of movie* memorabilia. *Their collaboration is more allegorical
than most of the tales in the book, but the allegory by no means
explains away the tale.*

The van crept up Elevado Way, its headlights stabbing like ice
picks at the encroaching darkness.

Martin kicked at the debris on the floorboard, but the cans
and paper bags were all empty; he tried to put the thought of
food out of his mind. He rolled down the window and peered
out at the old Spanish-style houses, at the sun as it disappeared
like a tired eye behind the tops of the palm trees that rimmed
the horizon of the city below.

'Better step on it, Rog,' he said. 'The Old Man doesn't like
it when we get in after seven, remember?'

'I guess he doesn't have much of a choice, does he?' said
Roger, bulldogging the wheels around a steep curve. 'He gave
us three buildings to do today – and overtime is overtime.
We're the best team he's got, aren't we? If he doesn't like it
we can always go back on unemployment, right, Jackie? Am I
right?'

219

Martin leaned his chin on his hand and watched the flickering tile roofs, which glowed now with a deep ochre stain from the setting sun, as he kept track of the house numbers with one half-closed eye.

He was thinking of the time he and Kathy had bought a map to the stars' homes, that first week in California. Now he felt that he might be following the endless bifurcations of one of those same winding streets with pretentious, foreign-sounding names. The only thing they had found that seemed alive that Sunday, however, was an old man with an Indian blanket over his legs, his wheelchair planted in the sun on the other side of an enormous lawn fronting a house that looked suspiciously like a misplaced Southern mansion. They hadn't got close enough to be sure, but he could not help wondering if there had been more to it than a false front, an old movie set installed around a modest house with a view, perhaps to improve the land value. They had waited there under a shade tree, eating their picnic lunch in the car, but the old man had never moved. For all they could tell, he might have been nothing more than a made-up skeleton set out as a prop on the too perfect grass.

Martin heard his stomach growl. He gave up. 'Hey,' he said, 'you don't have any more of that Kentucky Fried Chicken stashed in back, do you, Rog?'

Roger glanced reflexively at the equipment in the rear of the van. 'Aw, tighten your belt. We'll be able to cop something when we get inside – this neighbourhood's full of fat cats, I can tell. Anyway, I hear it's supposed to be good for people in our profession to stay a little bit hungry.'

Martin recalled the rotten stench from the refrigerator in the last place they had cleaned, and shuddered.

Our profession, he thought. And what profession is that, Roger? If you do that sort of thing you become that sort of animal, don't you, Rog?

He remembered to check the numbers. He blinked and turned his head, almost missing one.

'Hey, I think that was it,' he said, and then Roger was downshifting and swinging around a gravel circle and braking with a noisy ratcheting in front of the Carlton Arms.

It was another of those buildings taped and glued together back in the fifties around an indeterminate number of crackerbox apartments, somehow always more than you would guess from the outside. Martin thought of the architects for these quiet horrors, all right-angles of powdering stucco and rust from hidden drain pipes, as the ballpoint pen boys: they could be relied upon to make an infinite number of copies, but no originals.

The manager, a pale, nervous man who treated everyone as a potential process server, scrutinized the work order as they stood shifting their weight from foot to foot, as they studied their shoes and said nothing, and directed them at last to the elevator.

They passed an overweight housekeeper in a white uniform on her way out of the building. She picked her teeth and watched them suspiciously, as if they were in some strange way competitors. They ignored her and unloaded the wet-and-dry vac, the buckets and mops and cart full of cleansers and disinfectants from the van, clattered it all through the garage and up to the third floor, to what were undoubtedly still described in rental ads as penthouse apartments.

The tenant had probably moved out within the last couple of days, possibly within the last few hours; Martin noticed a half-loaf of not yet mouldy bread on top of an old copy of *Variety*, a can of crystallized honey and a plastic bag full of Blue Chip stamps. Martin pocketed the stamps as Roger screwed a 250 watt bulb into the kitchen ceiling, and they set to work to make the place habitable for the next occupant, whoever that might be.

Who knows what else got left behind? he wondered. In closets and back rooms, in cupboards and under sinks, on top shelves and in forgotten drawers, so much overlooked or perhaps simply and conveniently disremembered by those on the move, as though on purpose, as a way of shedding the collected burdens of a life gone on too long in one place. Like snake-skins, he thought, or the dead casings of gypsy moths. Still, when he thought of it at all, it always surprised him just how much they left behind, some of it inexplicably valuable.

There was a lingering smell about the room that Martin could not quite place. Another housekeeper or maid in a tight white uniform passed by outside. From time to time as they worked muffled sounds penetrated the paper-thin plaster, the echo of delicate movements as of mice busy under the linoleum or behind the peeling latex paint on the walls.

Martin had just begun cleaning the chipped metal grooves of the sliding windows with a toothbrush, when a door on the opposite landing swung slowly open. A beam of dingy light cut

221

through the twilight, tracing faint yellow streaks across the discoloured bottom of the empty swimming pool in the courtyard below.

'I think we're being watched,' he said, pausing between strokes.

The window frame had not been cleaned in years; a residue of soot and unidentifiable particles from the air had settled along with piles of sharp, corroded filings like insect droppings within the cracks. It was difficult to get rid of, even with the large wire brush and the chemical solvent.

'How much longer do you figure, Rog? We only have one unit to do in this building, don't we, and that's it?'

'Two more,' said Roger.

'You've got to be kidding.'

Martin swore under his breath, aware of the woman in the opposite doorway. Her features were lost in darkness, but he could see jagged points of hair sticking out from her head in the backlight like the spokes of a broken wheel.

'Get a load of that pose,' said Roger, mixing the rug shampoo. 'I wonder what she's waiting for.'

Martin made a quick mental note of the proportions, of the odd cant of the limbs. 'Do you remember *The Bride of Frankenstein*?' he said.

'I worked with Elsa Lanchester once,' said Roger. 'Did I ever tell you—?'

'You did.' Many times, he thought. 'Listen,' he said abruptly, dropping the brush. 'Will you tell me something? What in hell are we doing here?'

'About three-thirty an hour,' said Roger.

'Seriously.'

'Seriously,' said Roger, 'it's my latest role – it's called "paying the rent". Do you know that the average SAG member makes like seven hundred dollars a year?'

'But you didn't decide to be an actor for the bucks,' said Martin impatiently. 'You couldn't have. You'd have been a fool.'

Hell, he thought, the average guys I went to school with, the jocks, are all managing supermarkets or selling Porsches now. I could have had a piece of that. So why didn't I? Why did I turn my back on Kathy, a house, kids? There must be a reason. Or maybe I'm just a fool. Maybe that's all there is to it, after all.

Roger unwound the cord and tried to find an outlet. 'You

may not believe this, Jack,' he said, 'but there are times when I'm glad to be pushing a broom for a living. Like right now.' He groaned and stretched. Martin heard bones crack in the empty room. 'My mind's still my own, you know? I mean, when we leave here, we're through. And I'm my own man. Till my agent calls me for another reading. A commercial, anything, I'm not particular, so long as I have the chance to practise my craft.'

That's crap, thought Martin, but didn't say it. Because he didn't know why. But there was something basically wrong with the equation, though it had sounded reasonable enough for him to take this job himself until his next commission, until . . .

Roger was staring across the courtyard. The woman had left the doorway and was now making her way tenuously towards them, one hand on the railing for support.

'That one's about ready for the bone orchard, if you ask me,' said Roger. He backed up and fumbled with the cord reel, as if he recognized her, as if he did not want to. His hands were shaking. Why is he so upset? wondered Martin.

'Did I ever tell you about my next project, Jack? It's a real departure for me. I've been working on the treatment in my head.' He was talking too fast, rattling through the words as if they were beads. *The Adventures of Reggae Rat*. It's a children's story. Bet you didn't know I could write, too, did you? My agent's been after me for years to put together a property of my own. Naturally there'll be a part in it for me, so that when I sell the film rights – I'll need an illustrator for the book first, of course. Why don't you see what you can come up with? When you have the time. I know you're doing that other thing on spec right now, what's it called – *Pipe Dreams*? That's it, isn't it, Jackie? Am I right?'

Roger stopped talking as the woman arrived at their door. Martin stood to one side to let it happen, whatever it would be.

'How's it going, ma'am?' said Roger. 'Nice evening, isn't it?'

'Young man,' began the woman.

Martin stifled a laugh. How many more years can we get away with it? *Young men on the way up. Promising talents. Ageing enfants terribles*, he thought. Very rapidly ageing.

'You simply must help me. I have a terrible, terrible problem!'

Roger reached for the work order. 'Let me see here,' he said. 'What apartment was that now?'

'Number twenty-six,' she said. 'I'm only staying between engagements, you understand, until I can find more suitable quarters. But you must come at once.'

'I don't see it,' said Roger, scanning the clipboard. 'Are you sure—?'

'Oh, the coloured girls come in and clean around me once a week, or is it once a month? I've so much on my mind these days, you know. But you really must help me. Why, I've called and called to complain, but it never does any good!'

Roger exchanged glances with Martin. He seemed to be forcing himself to a decision.

'Now just you calm down, ma'am. We'll see what we can do, all right? I'll be over in a jiffy.'

The old lady wandered away, clutching her housecoat, muttering to herself.

'What . . . ?'

'It's good PR,' said Roger, grabbing a boxful of cleansers and sponges. 'See, we spend five minutes with Baby Jane here. She tells the manager, the manager tells the Old Man. The Old Man gets a lock on the building. She's satisfied – and we get a raise. That's called "priming the pump", my boy. "Greasing the pig".' He shouldered a broom and started out. 'Do what you can with this dump in the meantime, but don't knock yourself out. I'll be right back.'

Martin watched as Roger disappeared into the opposite apartment, ahead of the old lady, holding the screen door for her.

He shook his head. Great, he thought. Who knows when we'll get out of here now? He withdrew to a corner of the living room and leaned against the wall.

He looked around at the floor polisher, the scrub brushes, the plastic jugs of cleaning solution and germ killer and the packet of paper bands for the toilets that said SANITIZED in cheerful script.

He sighed.

He sank down so that he was sitting on the floor and took out his sketch pad and a Pilot Fineliner pen. He opened to a blank page. The sketches he had been working up for his *Red Dreams* concept were all grotesques; she would fit in nicely. Altogether they would form the core of a fantastic one-man show, if anybody in the La Cienega galleries were into that sort of thing yet.

He was trying to reproduce the lumpy outline of her coat

when a scream sounded from the other apartment.

He tapped the cap of his pen on his teeth. He squinted into the darkness and started to get up. At that instant the other door opened and Roger came running with his supplies, looking like a Fuller Brush man who has just been bitten by the family dog.

He stumbled in, out of breath. 'Jesus Christ,' he said with a wild look in his eyes. 'I feel more like I do now than when we got here!'

Martin put away his notebook. 'That bad, huh?' She had seemed like a candidate for the cackle factory, all right. 'What happened?'

'The usual. She wanted me to kill the rug.'

'What?'

'The lint, rather. On the rug. She says it's really bugs – cockroaches or something.'

'Is it?'

'Are Donny and Marie Osmond sisters?'

'I don't know.'

'My point exactly! I tell you, man, I had to get out of there. I thought I could handle her – I'm used to dealing with people. But I should have trusted my instincts. There's something about that old bird that gives me the creeps. Another minute and I wouldn't have known my own hole from an ass on the ground.'

Martin considered Roger's face. He was trying to make sense of his partner's overreaction, when the screen door slammed open across the way and the old woman staggered out, making unintelligible sounds in her throat.

'Here we go again,' said Roger. 'I can't do it, Jack. You try if you want to. Hey, maybe you can bring us back some eats. She's got something cooking in there, I could smell it. Just don't take too long, okay?'

Martin tried in vain to get a good look at her. Probably just an old Hollywood crank, he thought. There must be a lot of them around here. Maybe the whole building's full of them, who knows? Some sort of retirement set-up. There were no children visible, no pets, no tricycles. Now that he thought of it, the manager down below had had a certain thespian fussiness about him.

'I can pay you,' she said as she came up.

'Don't worry,' said Martin, stepping forward, feeling sorry for her in spite of himself. 'A regular service of the Sunshine

Cleaning Company. It's all free and it won't hurt a bit.'

He left Roger, walking behind her at a respectful distance. As he followed her into her apartment, he was finally able to see her bright orange hair and the eyes that bulged like poached eggs through flesh caked with accumulated make-up. There was something vaguely familiar about her, even under the wan light that filtered through the dusty tassels of the lamp, but he still could not place her.

She collapsed on to an overstuffed sofa, reupholstered in purple crushed velvet, as if the exertion had been more than she could bear. She was silent for a moment. Then her eyelids unfolded, twitching thickly as she caught him staring at her.

'It's there, by the table,' she said, pointing a long arm that would have been graceful if not for the arthritis.

He felt himself bow slightly.

Her hand retracted to cover her eyes, shielding them from the light that came through the burnt lampshade. Her chest began to rise and fall, as if she were sinking into a deep slumber.

He went to the table, realizing after a few steps that he was on tiptoe.

It was a fine old Chippendale with years of wax rubbed into the surface, but with an incongruous sample of frayed pink velvet thrown haphazardly over the top. There was a small open box of tarnished antique jewellery, a copy of *TV Guide*, and a framed photograph of what appeared to be a flying saucer.

His attention drifted automatically to other photographs and certificates on the wall, glossies gone sepia with age and news clippings and hand-lettered commendations. He recognized one of the faces, that of a young actor who had been killed tragically in a car crash when Martin himself was a teenager.

'It moves,' she said.

He turned, startled. 'I beg your pardon?'

'It goes away and then it comes back. I've told them to clean it, I've pleaded and begged, but they won't do anything about it. It always comes back. Small in the afternoons and then larger in the evenings, but it always comes back. I used to clean it twice a week with the carpet sweeper, but lately I've been so terribly, terribly tired, I don't know why . . .'

Her voice failed. Even now as Martin watched her, the last of her strength seemed to leave her body and seep into the cushions and pillows.

What was she talking about?

He heard the clinking of silver on dishes and low voices from the next room. He took another step and saw a doorway that led to the kitchen.

The old woman moaned and got to her feet. He felt her brush past him, trailing an aura of cheap perfume.

'Why, it's as plain as the nose on your face,' she said. With a crooked finger she directed his eyes to the floor, holding the door frame with her other hand. 'Will you help me? If you won't, I don't know what I'll do.'

'Of course I'll help you,' he said quickly. 'That's what I'm here for.'

That seemed to pacify her. She nodded shakily and went on into the kitchen.

Martin turned his attention to the carpet at his feet. It was a worn Oriental design with bone-white threads showing through. In the middle, extending outwards from the legs of the table, was a long, spider-like spot. It ended at a dark, oval outline in the shape of a stomach sac.

He knelt and suspended his hand above the pile of the carpet, as if trying to detect something from the feel of it, the texture.

The spot flowed over and covered his knuckles.

He drew back.

The spot returned to the carpet.

He stood up and stepped carefully around it. As he did so the spot enlarged, bleeding off the carpet and on to the floor.

Suddenly he let out a chuckle.

He looked at the lampshade, the curtained window behind it, the end of the sofa between the lamp and the table.

That was all there was to it, then.

The spot? It was only a shadow, growing as the sun went down, disappearing and then reappearing when the lamp was snapped on. A shadow. Nothing more.

He shook his head.

He walked around the room, strangely relieved, and again heard voices from the kitchen.

'None of the dead has been identified . . .'

It was a radio or television set, he realized.

He found himself back at the table. He noticed signed photographs on the wall of a man in a grey suit shaking hands with various minor celebrities. One of them was an old-time actor who had appeared in most of the cheapjack science fiction films of the fifties. Martin had seen them all, or most of them, either in theatres at the time or on the 'Late, Late Show' in the years since. One of the certificates was inscribed, 'To Albert Zugman From The Baron Frankenstein Society in recognition of his Contribution to the Genre'.

That was it: the man in the grey suit was none other than the late Albert Zugman, king of the 'B' Pictures. His movies had been Martin's absolute favourites as a boy. Perhaps they had even been the original source of his taste for the bizarre. How many times had he sneaked into the old Rialto Theatre on Saturday afternoons to see them over and over again?

He traced the edges of the publicity stills with genuine affection. *Robot Invaders, circa* 1953, if he remembered correctly. And *I Was a Teenage Dracula*, about 1958. Even *Hippie High School* from 1967. That one had been Zugman's last attempt at another kind of exploitation picture; it had failed. So, apparently, had Zugman. As nearly as Martin could recall, Zugman had died quietly in the early seventies, all but forgotten.

The flying saucer? That would be from *Mars vs Earth*. Of course.

And the old woman would be Mrs Zugman herself, the former model and actress. In person.

My God, he thought.

There must be something he could do for her, some way of repaying even a small part of the hours of pleasure he had received.

Then he remembered.

He lifted the end of the sofa and moved it twelve or fourteen inches and set it down so that there was no longer a direct line between it and the lamp. There. Now there will be no more shadows to bother her, he thought.

It seemed so little.

Well, wasn't there something more he could do before he left, some other detail, perhaps, further to ease her mind?

He waited, but she did not come out of the kitchen.

He circled the room, a patternless array of objects and *memorabilia*, a sad mixture of quality furnishings and the dreariest chintz. For the first time he noticed cardboard cartons along one wall, some of them containing odds and ends of statuary, vases, pictures. She – or someone – was in the process of moving her things in or out, he couldn't tell which.

He turned into the small hall.

It was a crackerbox apartment, all right, with two tiny

228

rooms, a kitchen and a bath. He flicked on the bathroom light.

The imitation-porcelain basin was coated with layers of spilled face powder, hardened into cement over the years.

He switched off the light.

In the bedroom was a transparent mask attached to an oxygen tank. Rays of light from a streetlamp outside slanted through the adjustable louvered panels of the window, casting sharp vertical shadows over her bed.

He heard a sound somewhere behind him. Feeling like a trespasser, he turned back to the living room.

She was standing by the table.

'Oh!' she cried. 'Oh, my dear! What have you done?'

'Excuse me,' he said hurriedly. 'I was just wondering if there was anything more I could . . .'

'You mustn't touch my things!' She pressed her hands to her face, her watery eyes fixed on the sofa. 'This is all I have left of the estate. I hear them coming in at all hours like thieves in the night, like ants. Oh, you're one of them, aren't you? You're just like the rest!'

She lunged unsteadily to the kitchen.

'Ma'am?' he called, following her. 'I was only trying to help, please believe me. Mrs Zugman?'

He saw another person with her in the kitchen, a woman in a white uniform.

'Don't make me hurt you,' one of them was saying. He couldn't tell which one.

He rapped on the door jamb. 'Ma'am, if you'll let me explain . . .'

She spotted him and hobbled out in a near-panic. He heard her closing the door to her bedroom and her bony fingers struggling with a lock that would not catch.

The other woman remained seated at the kitchen table. She leaned forward on her elbows, squeezing something in her fat hands. She might have been Mexican or middle-European, he could not be sure. A portable television set was propped across from her. Patiently her lidded eyes returned to it.

They must be cooks, he thought, all of them in their white dresses. That would explain why they're so well fed, their uniforms taut and bursting at the seams.

A huge kettle simmered on the stove. He smelled a familiar lingering odour and recognized it at last as a mixture of heavy spices about to boil, as if held in readiness for a long time. But why? The refrigerator stood open, the racks inside picked clean. It looked as if it had been empty for days, perhaps longer.

He took a tentative step forward, trying to think of something to say. There were questions taking shape in his mind, but he did not yet know how to frame them.

Her hands flexed almost imperceptibly in the white light, and he saw that she held nothing in them, after all. It had been only the fleshiness of her own hands, cupped expectantly around each other.

She glanced up at him, her jaws grinding in a steady, regular rhythm. Her lips fell open. There was nothing in her mouth, not yet.

And a sudden dread began to overtake him, creeping up the back of his neck and spreading across his scalp. It was like nothing he had ever felt before.

Her jaws clenched and unclenched, a trickle of colourless fluid starting already from the sides of her mouth, dripping from the corners of her faint but unmistakable moustache. She made no move to wipe it away.

'Was that trip really necessary?' Roger was saying. He had been muttering for several blocks, but this was the first of his quasi-observations to register. Martin let it go and tried to lose himself in the rush of foliage outside the van.

Can't you step on it? he thought.

Roger tore open a package of Mickey Banana Dreams with his teeth, devoured one and set the other on the dashboard. He pushed it towards Martin.

'Found 'em in one of the drawers,' Roger said. 'You know, it blows my mind sometimes, the stuff they leave behind when they go.' He tried to laugh but it didn't come out right. He licked his fingers and let the wrapper fly out the window. 'Anyway, I just hope the Old Man doesn't find out about those other two units, at least not till we get paid for the week. If the manager complains, we'll say one of us got sick and had to split. Which is true, right?' Roger eyed his partner in the semi-darkness. 'She really got to you, didn't she?'

'You recognized her before I did,' said Martin. Say it, he thought.

The van shook, turning downhill.

Roger took a long time to answer. 'She was Lylah Lord,' he said wonderingly. '*The* Lylah Lord. I wasn't sure at first.' He

230

adjusted the rearview mirror, his eyes glassy. 'But you saw her. That was what got to you, too, wasn't it?'

'I saw her,' Martin said. He saw her now, in fact, saw her no matter how hard he tried not to: the tattered robe, the spindly wrists, the veins and age spots on her legs. A tired, starved old woman, living with death and waiting helplessly for the end; it was her final, hysterical role, one in which she had awakened to find herself trapped and from which she could not escape. He tried, but he could not put her out of his mind.

'You want to get drunk?' said Roger.

'It's late.'

'That it is. And we have a big, new apartment complex over on the east side first thing tomorrow morning. I saw the order. But I just thought, when we get back to the valley, away from here—'

Unexpectedly Roger's voice, the trained instrument that it was, failed him.

'I know,' said Martin.

'I used to wonder what happens to old actors in this town. Now I wish I'd never found out. Did I ever tell you, Jackie, that I had quite a crush on her? She was the love of my life for years. I collected her pictures on trading cards. Even carried one around in my wallet. I wonder if it's still there? Lylah Lord! Jesus Christ.'

They approached the base of the foothills, where Elevado Way merged and become one with the plain of jewel-like streets and traffic signals and dimly lighted windows, each the tired eye of another private residence within which one more sad melodrama was playing itself out, alone, to the end. And among the lights, Martin knew, were the bright, cold flowers of theatre marquees and television screens where the faces of people long dead and forgotten spoke and gestured from another time and place, and where they would continue to do so, for ever perhaps, or until even the last remaining record of their lives would itself break and decompose into remnants to be carted away with the rest. Like the actors whose photographs were even now curling and disintegrating on the walls of her apartment. He reached for the pack of cigarettes on the seat.

'I didn't know you smoke, Jackie.'

'I don't.'

Martin lit up and sat watching the cigarette flare in the dark-

231

ness and then subside to an ember. He inhaled deeply but it did no good. Cars passed them on either side, taillights braking and then growing weak in the distance. Once a huge truck roared by, rattling the van from a great height, as if it meant to run them off the road, as if it did not even see them. The vibration knocked the ash from Martin's cigarette. He watched the burning continue the length of the cigarette, converting it all to ashes.

'Maybe we're in the wrong profession,' said Roger.

Martin looked over at him, trying to see his eyes.

'I don't just mean Sunshine Cleaning,' said Roger. 'I mean—' He cut the wheel sharply and they mounted an on-ramp. 'Look, the first thing I had to learn as an actor was to eat shit. Unsalted. You know? And it isn't much better in your field, am I right?'

Martin thought: Why is consensus so important to him?

'So what are we breaking our balls for? Can you tell me that? I mean, being an artist is fine if you get the breaks. But why should we waste our whole lives waiting for some kind of – I don't know—' Roger's hands trembled on the steering wheel, under the strobing of lights that passed above. 'I'm sure as hell not going to let myself end up like her. I know that now. The way I see it, we've just been fooling ourselves.'

What, then? wondered Martin.

'Let's get it together, Jackie. Who do you think hires those maids or whatever the hell they are, for example? Somebody, right? He must be raking in the dough, enough to make some kind of a life, you know? I bet he has guys who do nothing but haul them out in the morning, pick them up at the end of the day. You figure he needs more drivers? That's what we ought to be into, something with a future. What do you think?'

Martin was thinking about what he had seen at the Carlton Arms. Whether it was true or not in its particulars didn't really matter; the sense of it was the same. It was big fishes eating little fishes, consuming and being consumed, just as we feed and are fed upon in turn by the Old Man. And so on.

The feeling returned then. The feeling that had made him want to be out of there. I have to break the chain, he thought. And, feeling an even greater fear, he thought: *It stops here.*

They were nearing the end. The cigarette had burned down to the filter and was sputtering dangerously close to his fingers, but he was not aware of it. For some reason he was thinking of the young actor who had been killed in the car crash when he himself was only a boy. He felt pain; and his eyes filled with tears.

A shadow passed over them as an illuminated roadsign swept by overhead.

'I want out,' he heard himself say.

Roger smiled at him. 'I know. Believe me. I've got to get home and get something to eat myself. But, hey, I think there's a Bob's Big Boy coming up. If you don't want a drink, maybe we could grab a bite before we go back. Man, I sure wouldn't mind having one of those maids' jobs right now, let me tell you. I'll bet they sneak whatever they want right out from under those old birds' noses. Am I right, Jackie?'

'My name's Jack,' said Martin.

Roger drove on in silence. They left the freeway and headed along the main street, the restaurant logo becoming clearer until it dominated the night sky.

'You sure you don't want to stop?'

Martin did not answer.

'Well,' said Roger, 'you give the idea some thought, okay? This racket's for losers. Now, port-a-maid or whatever they call it, that's the kind of scam we should be into, I'm telling you. One thing about it – we'd never go home hungry. At least see if you can find out who they work for. You can do that, can't you?'

No, thought Martin. No, I can't. He was hungry, all right. But not that hungry.

Cherry Wilder

The gingerbread house

Cherry Wilder was born and educated in New Zealand but lived in New South Wales for many years. She now lives in Germany with her husband Horst Grimm and their two daughters Cathie and Louisa.

She began both reading and writing at six. The Auckland Herald bought a Santa Claus story from her when she was eleven. 'I was bound to get back to speculative fiction,' she says and, in 1974, after publishing 'literary and other short stories' (eh?) and reviews in Australia, she decided to follow up the success of her first sf story in a Ken Bulmer anthology. Since then she has appeared in anthologies edited by Terry Carr, Lee Harding, Virginia Kidd, Maxim Jakubowski and others, and there is a sequel to her novel The Luck of Brins Five.

'Germans do not think their country particularly haunted or haunting . . . they tend to believe that all the best ghosts live in England. On the other hand, as a newcomer, I see ghosts and ghost stories looming everywhere.' This is her first published ghost story, but will certainly not be her last.

Amanda stood in the road for a few minutes after the taxi had driven off. Then she walked back the way they had come, recrossed the rustic bridge and began to approach the cottage through the woods. It was early afternoon; the mist had begun to lift but under the tall canopy of beech trees there was a chill that reached through the layers of pale mohair that swathed Amanda and seeped in at the soles of her suede thigh boots.

She soon became aware that she had taken on too much; the pigskin bag was too heavy; the carpet of crisp leaves was uneven. She leaned against a tree; a woodpecker tapped, high up, against the golden roof of the forest. All around the leaves fell, with a light damp sound; at her feet she saw mushrooms of a

235

smooth pale lilac. The trees were widely spaced but even at a short distance the ranks of tall, green-scurfed trunks blurred and wavered. The profound stillness of the woods settled on Amanda; she drew the folds of her ridiculous model gear around her thin frame and walked on slowly.

She was not quite alone. A lady in a tailored gabardine raincoat and matching hat of Tyrolean shape walked her dog, a long-haired miniature dachshund. Amanda staggered on, past an inviting yellow bench, and saw the cottage.

It was small and greyish but not unbearably picturesque. The tilted roof dipped quaintly at the eaves; in the peak of the gable was an open window, with bedding set to air. The fence was of crumbling wooden slats and new wire; the garden was planted with potatoes, asters, chrysanthemums. Amanda stared; it really did not look like Douglas at all. She noticed with alarm a cream Volkswagen parked in the old, mossy garage on the far side of the house.

She was pressing on but suddenly the little dog, the dachshund, scuffed leaves at her feet; she saw its mistress hurrying towards her.

'Ein Moment, bitte!'

The woman had an inaccessibly ordinary, firm, plain face and sharp blue eyes. No trace of regional accent; not a scrap of make-up; gold studs in her ears. An Englishwoman of similar vintage . . . Amanda thought of her mother . . . would have worn tweeds, a pale lipstick, might have addressed Amanda as 'My dear . . .'

'Are you going to the cottage?' asked the woman in English.

'Yes,' said Amanda, 'my brother . . .'

It was out before she had time to think but the woman did not seem to notice her moment of panic. She stuck out her hand.

'Luisa Schneider.'

'Amanda King.' Amanda shook hands.

'An English lady rented this house,' said Frau Schneider. 'I was her friend.'

She turned her head and spoke to her dog, then turned back to Amanda with decision.

'Frau Winter was not happy about the house. There were things which . . . baffled her understanding . . .'

Frau Schneider said 'beffled' and Amanda caught it as an echo of the English lady's own voice. She realized what she was being told and what it must have cost the woman to speak up.

'We will be all right,' she said. 'I'm sure we will be all right.'

'I hope you will forgive me. Frau Winter would have wished me to speak to the next people . . .'

'Thank you, Frau Schneider.'

'Nickie!' Frau Schneider called her dog to heel.

'He would never enter the place,' she whispered suddenly, 'not even to eat meat!'

She snapped the lead on to Nickie who waved his golden plume of a tail and looked up at Amanda with melting eyes.

'He is a dear little dog!' she said.

'He is like a child,' said Frau Schneider wearily.

As she turned to go she established her kinship with Amanda's mother.

'You must help yourself to the garden vegetables,' she said. 'It is in the contract. You are too thin, Fräulein King . . . you must round yourself out. I have had daughters myself . . .'

Amanda felt her smile growing fixed; Frau Schneider let Nickie lead her away through the columns of beech trees. A well-worn path led Amanda to the side gate and she could not struggle round to the front of the house. She stared at a kitchen window with white net curtains and a box of geraniums on the sill. Her heart thumped; someone behind the curtains vanished.

She dragged her suitcase a little further down the path, the gate slammed shut behind her; she stood still and called:

'Douglas!'

The back door, half glass with white net covering the panels, swung open without a sound.

'Douglas . . . can you come?'

She looked at the garden beds on either side of the path; they were unweeded but still flourishing. A trowel and a single gardening glove lay by an old crock of parsley, half buried in the dark earth. She had been standing on the path for half a minute; Douglas was not coming out. She left her suitcase where it was, gripped the strap of her shoulder bag and stooped down unnecessarily to enter the doorway.

Douglas King slammed the door shut behind his sister and wiped his face with a checked tea towel.

'Christ,' he said, 'you take your time. Was someone watching you?'

'No,' said Amanda.

She backed into the kitchen to get a look at him; the sink was still full of warm suds. Douglas had been watching through the window and had ducked down out of sight when she appeared at the back gate.

Douglas was seven years older than Amanda and a few inches shorter; a muscular man, handsome, his hair black as a raven's wing. She had been taught to envy his hair and his long eyelashes . . . 'wasted on a man' her mother said. At this moment, in shirt sleeves, he looked paunchy; Amanda felt sure that his appetite was as large as ever.

The thought of eating overwhelmed her with desire and revulsion; must take something . . . it has been twelve hours, no, fourteen. She stumbled into the sitting room and folded into a chair.

'You idiot,' said her brother, 'you really shouldn't have . . .'

She bit her lip to stave off the wretched faintness and prepared to repel his kind inquiries. Even he could not refrain from urging his sister to eat.

'I'm all right,' she said. 'I'll have a brandy.'

Douglas was not making kind inquiries; she moved her head and saw him crouched down at the back door, lifting aside the white curtains.

'Idiot!' he said again. 'To leave that bloody great suitcase on the path.'

'Douglas, come and tell me what this is all about.'

Douglas came into the sitting room still clutching the tea towel and sat on the edge of a green velvet armchair. He looked like a hen-pecked husband.

'What did Helen tell you?' he demanded.

'Nothing,' lied Amanda. 'I haven't seen her. You know I've been at the clinic for weeks.'

'In Zurich?'

'Of course. Douglas, I want you to tell me. What is the matter?'

'Just the divorce.'

'*Tell* me . . .'

He shook his head; it was an admission that there was more to tell. It satisfied her for the moment. Douglas smiled at last.

'You do look all in . . .' he said.

He strode off into the kitchen and she heard the tinkle of glass; he would fetch her brandy. Amanda gazed slowly around the room taking in the narrow grate, the handsome old chairs and the dining table, the lamps. Surely it was unusual in this part of the world for a house to be let fully furnished. Douglas had not bothered with flowers and there were no ornaments except a pink and green shepherdess in Staffordshire pottery. It put Amanda in mind of the English lady.

The door to the kitchen and the back hallway closed slowly and she heard the click of the lock. The room was darker now but more evenly lit with a pale autumn light from the window. The door into the front hall moved six inches, remained ajar. Amanda extended long fingers into her handbag and brought out a packet of bitter Swiss chocolate. She ate two squares doggedly, then leaned back and closed her eyes; presently she must unzip the damned boots . . .

She fell into a light uncomfortable sleep, the kind of sleep she might have on a plane. Just beyond the boundaries of her sleep there was bustle and movement. She saw Douglas with a terrible expression on his face stumping past with her suitcase. She slept more deeply and began to dream.

She was on a picnic in the woods with a man, a man of her dreams, tall and warm, bearing only a superficial resemblance to her 'lost love', her old no-love-lost Roger Mallett. They ate raspberries, the taste was tart and clean and cured her of her disease. Between one tree and the next she lost him, she was lost, she wandered among the trees . . . fir trees . . . with a growing anxiety.

She knew in her dream that this was one of her usual anxiety dreams but suddenly it became much worse. The tang of the fir trees turned dank and sour like old water in a flower vase. She saw the cottage, shrunken and dark, in the distance, and a figure kneeling at the base of a tree, digging deeply into the thick leaf mould. The scene was flavoured with an old, aching fear, half out of mind. She nibbled on something from her pocket and it had an awful taste, stale, dead, peppery sweet.

Amanda woke up shuddering, her lips drawn back in a grimace. It was dark outside the room now and the lamps had been switched on. Her glass of brandy stood beside her chair on a little table, golden in the lamplight. She sipped it eagerly, savouring the relief of her escape from the dream. She called lazily:

'Douglas . . .'

There was a rattle of pots and pans from the kitchen. When she turned her head she could see her reflection in the glass front of a cupboard. She floated, incorporeal, the thin essence of Amanda. *I am transparent, I am made of spun glass, every-*

thing gross has been purged away. I will do what I want to do. I will have my way. She was thinking of Jane, thirty kilos, the fat nurse shrieking aloud and the scent of the fir trees in the grounds of the clinic. Jane would have her way.

There was a crash of glass from the kitchen. The sound went through her head like jagged lightning and Amanda cried out. The silence rolled back; she was not even sure that she had heard the crash at all. Her gaze returned to her own reflection; she altered her pose, rearranged a billowing sleeve.

The door of the cupboard swung open without a sound; Amanda's reflection became distorted and hideous. She felt cold, cold, the carpet under her feet was chill and damp as the forest floor. A whiff of foul air had entered the room.

Amanda felt for the cologne in her handbag but she was too late. The stench filled the room in a choking cloud. It was carrion, decay, a suppurating foulness. She rose up, gagging helplessly, and stumbled into the front hall. She tried to call her brother and could not. A light was switched on in the hall; she realized that Douglas had gone out, he was not there. She was, more or less, alone in the house.

She turned and raced up the stairs; Douglas had been careful to leave on some lights. She paused at the top landing. Two small bedrooms, a bathroom, a yard or so of corridor: the air sweet and clean, not a mouse stirring. She went to the window at the end of the corridor and looked down at the garage. Lights blinked through the trees; Douglas drove into the garage with a characteristic roar from the Volkswagen.

She went into the bedroom where her suitcase leaned drunkenly against the foot of the bed. The window was still wide open but the featherbed and the huge soft pillow had been taken in and set in place. Her tartan travelling rug trailed out of the straps on the pigskin bag; she picked it up and slung it around her shoulders. She closed the window. Down, far down in the reaches of the house, there was another rending crash of glass and crockery.

Amanda went quickly and quietly down as far as the first landing. The door into the sitting room was moving backwards and forwards; she heard little thumps and taps at the skirting board as if someone were sweeping behind the door. She knew, with deep resentment, that she was very much afraid. Steps sounded on the path, a key grated in the lock of the front door, and Douglas came in cheerfully with a plastic sack of groceries.

'Did you hear a noise?' Amanda heard her own voice shake.

Douglas stared at his sister and began to grin.

'*I heard the owl scream and the crickets cry,*' he intoned. '*Did you not speak?*'

Amanda drew the folds of the tartan rug about her and strode down the stairs.

'*Hark!*' she said. '*Who lies in the second chamber?*'

'*Donalbain!*' they cried in chorus.

Macbeth had cleared the air. They sat on the third step; there was just room for the pair of them.

'You're skin and bone,' said Douglas. 'Sorry I was strung up. Helen has been playing merry hell. I had to get away for a while.'

'The school . . .'

'I tossed it in at the end of last term,' he said with a touch of the old nonchalance. 'I've been doing some writing.'

'Why did you send for me?'

'Lonely,' he said, 'and I needed someone to improve the set-up. Helen could be having this place watched.'

'Douglas, this house . . .'

She drew back. The house was quiet and sweet smelling. A cuckoo clock chirred beside the coat rack. The cuckoo sprang out seven times but did not speak . . . it had been silenced. Don't speak, warned the silent cuckoo.

'Yes, this place is a marvellous find,' said Douglas defensively. 'Most flats don't have a stove, let alone all this furniture and crockery.'

'How did you find it?'

'Pure luck. Got talking to the agent in a train. They have trouble letting the place . . . something to do with a deceased estate.'

He helped her up and they strolled into the kitchen. Douglas began stowing food into the small, inadequate refrigerator. Amanda looked about for shards of glass and china knowing she would find none.

'Do most of the shopping in the evenings,' he said. 'I drive out to a huge supermarket . . . sells everything from bread to benzine.'

'Did you have trouble renting the car?'

'Of course not!'

He could not look her in the eye; she could not say any more. Douglas piled wrappers into the pedal bin.

'I had better have something to eat,' said Amanda.

'Good kid,' he said jovially. 'Did you finish that washing up or did I?'

241

They took their plates into the sitting room which was warm and wholesome in the lamplight.

'I've got the ordinary central heating going,' said Douglas, 'but in the winter I'll have an open fire as well.'

Amanda ate two tangerines, a cup of blueberry yoghourt, a slice of crispbread with cheese; she kept her eyes averted from her brother's laden plate. Douglas had rented an elegant, small colour television; they watched *Einsatz in Manhattan*. A policeman had his wife handcuffed to the bed because she was a heroin addict.

'Surely that's Lynn Redgrave,' said Douglas.

'She seems to have lost weight,' said Amanda.

'What's it called in English anyway?'

'*Kojak.*'

Amanda went up to bed and left her brother pottering about tidying up. She took two of her strongest capsules, curled up in the short wooden bed and fell into a deep, dreamless sleep.

In the darkness of early morning she half woke, then lay in a strange dreaming state. The feather quilt was hot and heavy; she was fat, her legs ached, her ankles were swollen. She was restless, she must get up and sweep the stairs, make them all clean, hide what must be hidden. Amanda woke up fully for a few seconds and dragged one skinny arm out from under the covers. *I am Amanda . . . like spun glass . . .* She flung off the clinging discomfort of the dream and slept again.

Next time she woke it was half-past nine; the mist outside was giving way to cool autumn sunshine. There were two tangerines on her bedside table. Amanda smelled coffee and remembered a time when she enjoyed the smell of coffee, even the smell of bacon frying. From the bathroom window she thought she saw Frau Schneider and Nickie, taking their walk.

She was adjusting the shawl collar of the pink sweater when she caught a look of panic on her own face in the glass. A regular sound of tapping . . . someone was sweeping the stairs. She peered through the bathroom door expecting to see nothing . . . the noise continuing and nothing else, no one. But what she saw was worse – a woman, a strange woman in a shapeless raincoat and headscarf, sweeping the stairs.

Amanda died of terror there on the spot, then rallied. The woman was solid as a tree trunk, not an apparition. She worked away, tap-tapping with her dustpan and brush, then raised her head to stare at the bathroom door with an expression of ferocious ill-will. And this was the worst of all. Amanda's stomach

tightened into a knot, she had to clutch at the door frame. She
went into all the old anti-fainting tricks, bit her lips, lowered
her head, held tight to the door frame. She gulped air and let it
out in a scream:

'*Douglas!*'

She flung open the bathroom door. Douglas was hanging up
the raincoat and scarf.

'What's the matter now?' he asked gruffly.

'You gave me a terrible fright!'

'What . . . this old coat? There was a shower . . .'

'You were wearing a headscarf . . .'

'No umbrella.'

Douglas picked up his dustpan and brush from the little
chest of drawers.

'Come and have some breakfast.'

He went into the kitchen. As she walked down into the coffee
smell he called:

'There is that wretched woman with the dog . . .' Amanda
went straight out of the front door and down the path.

'*Guten Morgen,* Frau Schneider!'

'*Guten Morgen!*'

Nickie sat down in the leaves and had to be dragged along on
his bottom towards the garden gate.

'How have you found the house?'

'Not very nice. There *are* things . . . What did your friend
. . . ?'

'Frau Winter was kind and friendly. Yet she changed, she
would not let me in . . . she spoke dreadful things, things I
would never have believed she could say . . . in German at any
rate.'

'Who lived here before she came?'

'I don't know, I could not ask,' said Frau Schneider. 'Some
poor woman. Frau Winter was found out of doors on a winter's
night, half-frozen. Mud and leaves were frozen to her fingers.
She never recovered.'

Amanda wiped her hands against her trousers.

'At first she loved the house,' said Frau Schneider. 'She said
it was from a fairytale . . . her *Lebkuchenhaus.*'

'Her gingerbread house,' said Amanda.

She remembered the dreadful taste in her dream . . . old and
stale and peppery sweet. Nickie was dragging Frau Schneider
off again. Amanda walked slowly back down the path, fumbling in her pocket for imaginary crumbs.

Gingerbread houses, the real ones, could be rather nasty because they were seldom eaten up. The beautiful frosted eaves and windows encrusted with jujubes were put away until next year. It was enough to make her shudder . . . it was her dream all over again, a dream that she might have had before. Old things, dead things, filthy dusty places that would never come clean. Sweetness gone stale, food left to moulder and rot, mad Miss Havisham's terrible 'bride cake', the haunt of mice and spiders. She looked up and saw Douglas at her bedroom window; she had to wait some time before he came downstairs and let her in.

When he did come down he was so much himself again that she put off any confrontation. Douglas settled down at the coffee table in the sitting room and typed with his maddening slowness. Amanda wandered about. Writing had been so much his thing at one time. She sat on the first landing of the stairs and looked up and down at the dimensions of the small house.

There was nothing to say how old it was, none of the bulging paintwork or uneven walls which suggested that a house was several hundred years old. She would guess that the place was built in about 1930, but perhaps the site was already old. Perhaps there had always been some sort of house here in the woods.

She put her head on her knees and thought of her friend Jane, who had looked a little like Snow White, and of the English lady. Really one could not escape a witch, if she were determined . . . either she came after you, snug in your cottage, armed with a poisoned apple, or she lured you inside her gingerbread house. Yet what else was here but an old cry of pain, the remains of some guilty ritual? She and Douglas were not children, left wandering in the woods.

Amanda laughed aloud. Because that was exactly what they were. She went down the stairs singing a little song and she did not recognize it until she came to the door of the sitting room.

Brother come and dance with me,
Both my hands I offer thee . . .

'Douglas,' she said, 'please take a break. I want to talk to you.'

'Fine,' said Douglas, 'but you must have something to eat.'

If he hoped to put her off it did not work. They went into the kitchen and Amanda selected a square of cheese, a tomato, a slice of *gelbwurst*.

'How is your friend Jane?' asked Douglas.

Amanda tightened her hold on the thin white plate.

'Jane had her way,' she said. 'She did what she wanted to do.'

She carried her plate into the sitting room; the cupboard door hung open a few inches.

'Jane was the most languid female I ever set eyes on,' chuckled Douglas, following with her glass of buttermilk. 'She never wanted to do anything except starve herself to death.'

He broke off, appalled.

'Yes,' said Amanda.

He sat on the couch and stared at his sister. She quickly bit into the tomato, nibbled a morsel of cheese, consumed a fragment of sausage. *Forgive me, Jane, I am not spun glass . . . I am skin and bone.*

Douglas stared until she was embarrassed. At last he said:

'You've got it too, I hope you admit that, Amanda. You've got this wretched thing, this *anorexia nervosa.*'

'I admit it,' said Amanda.

She choked on the tomato, felt the seeds crawl down her throat, sipped quickly at the buttermilk . . . tiny sips, a bird drinking. She wanted to eat as much as she could, get it down before he put her off her food.

'You've nearly killed Mummy with this starvation carry-on,' said Douglas. 'I hope you face up to the truth.'

'Mummy is tough,' said Amanda, finishing her cheese, 'but I admit that it must have been a bit of a strain.'

'You've ruined your life,' said Douglas. 'The modelling is too much for you; Roger didn't want to marry a skeleton. Helen thinks you're completely round the bend and doesn't want you to have anything to do with the children.'

'In case they don't eat their veggies?' asked Amanda.

She pushed away the plate and glass with a feeling of clearing the decks.

'I admit all this,' she said, 'and I'm trying to improve.'

'You take it far too calmly. I want you to face facts!'

'Douglas, will *you* face facts? You're five thousand pounds in debt.'

'Rubbish, I made some payments!'

'I didn't see Helen but she wrote to me in Switzerland. You worked a swindle over the car insurance. You were sacked from the school. But the worst thing of all, the thing you must go back for, is the hit and run . . . the boy in Hammersmith . . .'

'Do you believe this bullshit?' said Douglas in a trembling voice.

245

'Interpol believe it. They came to the clinic.'

'What did you tell them?'

'That I had no idea where you were. I said you had friends in Italy . . .'

'You probably led them right to this doorstep!'

'Now you're talking nonsense,' said Amanda. 'They are only an information bureau.'

'You left a trail a mile wide . . . staggering about like some bloody spectre . . .'

She could feel the room stirring into life; the cold came seeping up from the floor like mist. The hall door slammed and Douglas jumped. Something inexplicable was happening to the carpet, a heaving and wrinkling as if something crawled beneath it at the edges of the room. The cupboard door moved gently back and forth; the smell of corruption sidled out. Amanda felt a firm pressure on her shoulder; as she turned her head her glass bounced across the room and smashed. The butttermilk made a thick white pool among the jagged slivers of glass.

Douglas came up from the couch with his eyes blazing, his mouth pouting and twisted. He marched into the kitchen with an odd flat-footed walk and came back instantly with the dustpan and a cloth.

'Filthy . . .' he said thickly, 'a filthy liar . . .'

He wiped the fragments of glass into the pan and went back to the kitchen; she heard the clang of the pedal bin, the running tap. He came back with the rinsed cloth and wiped at the table with bent head. Douglas was muttering some words which she could not catch . . . or did not believe . . . and she saw that in his left hand he still held the base of the glass, broken off into long jagged teeth. The foul smell had become very strong; his hand began to come up in a long curve.

Amanda screamed and struggled to her feet. He made a long inaccurate swipe and Amanda felt the glass brush the hand she had flung up to shield her face. Then, heavy-footed, he was at the mantelpiece, wiping it down, wiping the wooden arms of the couch. He came to the cupboard and stood stock still, arms hanging by his sides; his whole body sagged. The hall door rattled briefly, the stairs creaked; the room still wavered, unsettled.

Douglas glared at her.

'Don't stand there gawping as if your throat was cut,' he said. 'What am I doing with this damned glass?'

246

Amanda's hand stung; she saw for the first time that it had been cut by the glass and was oozing fine beads of blood.

'Doug,' she said, 'is there anything in that cupboard?'

'No,' he said, 'no, it's empty. Mandy . . . what's wrong? You mustn't take any notice of the draughts in this place.'

He edged away from the cupboard and flung the broken glass into the fireplace among the crumpled newspaper and kindling wood. Amanda watched him and licked the blood from her hand. *Why does the taste of blood not revolt me?* Immediately it did revolt her, the whole room reeked of blood. She pressed a hand to her mouth and went to the casement window. Sunlight came in and a smell of roses; the house was a good creature again, quite docile. Douglas was sitting on the couch, his mouth still twisted; she thought: *He will be taken again; he will go so far away that I will never be able to get him back!*

'Doug . . . we must get out of this house . . .'

Horribly he began to cry. He covered his face with his hands and sobbed aloud.

'Doug, please . . .'

She knelt beside him while the room chirruped and rattled.

'Ran right under the wheels,' sobbed Douglas. 'Oh God, Mandy . . . it's in my head, I can't think of anything else. I killed the poor little beggar . . .'

'Douglas, listen to me . . .'

'Don't know what I'm doing half the time . . .'

'Douglas, the boy in Hammersmith is not dead . . . not even badly hurt!'

He took in great gulps of air and fumbled for his handkerchief.

'Is that a fact? I didn't kill . . .'

'Truly,' she said. 'You must go back. You must stop running away.'

'So must you,' he said, with a reassuring touch of the old self-righteousness.

'Yes,' she said, 'yes, I promise. I'll eat . . . I'll put on ten pounds, twelve. Only we must leave this house.'

'There is two weeks' rent paid.'

'Douglas, this is a rotten place. It plays tricks.'

His eyes swivelled nervously in the direction of the cupboard.

'You may be right,' he whispered.

'My things are still packed,' she said. 'Let me pack yours.'

'You mean now, at once?'

'I don't want to spend another night in this house.'

Douglas ran a hand through his black hair in what his mother had deplored as an artistic gesture.

'All right,' he said. 'I'll tidy up a bit down here.'

Amanda went up the stairs whistling. She stripped the beds and cleared the bathroom and packed. Douglas had been living neatly out of a suitcase: had he tried to leave the house? She paused, kneeling beside his bed and heard the distant roar of the vacuum cleaner. She felt for her watch, worn on a chain round her neck, and found that it was past midday.

Amanda, she asked herself quietly, *why do you wear your watch on a chain?* She felt the links of the chain run between her fingers; a chain of lies and evasions; the disease dominated her life. She could not wear a wristwatch, her wrist was a bird's bone, the bands slipped and chafed. Long sleeves and buttoned cuffs to hide her arms. No more dressing rooms, bedroom and bathroom doors always locked: no one must see Amanda stripped to the bone.

Years of lying about food; almost second nature now to say, 'I've just had something'; to pretend dietary quirks: 'I don't eat meat'; 'I can't digest eggs.' The silly strategems to make her eat. 'Finish this ice cream, pet, so that I can wash the bowl.' The Swedish *au pair*, who was really a nurse. She cracked much sooner than Mummy; seized Amanda bodily and forced custard into her mouth. Amanda leaned forward on to the folded featherbed and tenderly felt the spot where her rib had been broken.

A bitter childish hatred engulfed her; she was drowning in their care, it was like vile nourishing mush sliding down the back of her throat. She had endured force feeding more than once but at Zurich it was never permitted. But what was the secret? She knew, she must know somewhere inside herself, the reason for it. She was not Jane, she had her own reasons. She closed her eyes and tried to look for the secret. When she opened them again the darkness remained, the room had grown dark.

She sprang up awkwardly and thunder crashed overhead. As she closed the window huge drops of rain warm as blood fell on her hand; the black clouds had rolled up in an instant over the woods. Through the sparse raindrops she could see the misty fields, the ruined watchtower and the tall apartment blocks of the little town still in a shaft of sunlight. But the house was dark and wracked with thunder.

She called into the shadowy hall: 'Douglas.' There was no

answer. Amanda sagged against the banister and began to go
down one step at a time, her long legs trembling with fear.
Douglas had gone, had been taken again, but *she* could escape.
Fragile Amanda could snatch a coat from the rack and rush
off into the rainy garden. She called more loudly, 'Douglas,'
hearing her voice shake. It was oddly familiar, it sounded like
her mother's voice. And as she came to the foot of the stairs
pale lightning flashed and the thunder spoke and she regained
her courage. Amanda looked down some dusty corridor of
time and saw another self, a sturdy, yes, even a fat little girl –
a tomboy, enormously stubborn and strong willed. Strong
willed to the point of madness, to the point of death; no one,
nothing was a match for her.

She flung herself against the sitting-room door shouting her
brother's name. It came open then was slammed against her;
a voice, hoarse and unrecognizable, came out from under the
door. The German was thick and sibilant with a heavy Hessian
accent; she could not understand a word. Amanda ran into the
kitchen, seized a broom and let it fall, looked about for a
weapon to drive out evil. Cold iron, water, sunlight . . . then the
lightning flashed again and gave her the answer. She scrabbled
in the cupboard under the sink looking for paraffin or cleaning
fluid and found something better, a jerry-can of petrol. She
took the box of giant kitchen matches and went through the
narrow box of the kitchen into the back hallway. She burst
into the sitting room through its back door.

The room was pitch dark and the switch for the overhead
light did not work, but Amanda knew that she had not miscalculated. Douglas or that other was still crouched by the far
door. Amanda struck a match and saw the horror turning to
face her. Wrapped in the tartan rug, face pudgy, lined, transformed, the face of a madwoman, yet inexplicably her brother's
face.

'Let him go!' shouted Amanda.

The creature came for her, slow and clumsy, as if its feet
hurt, its joints were stiff from years of housecleaning. The
room was icy cold beyond the flame of the long match and it
stank of death and corruption. The cupboard opened with a
little scratching sound. Amanda moved towards the cupboard,
she deliberately flung the doors wide and looked inside. She
had been ready to cry out that the cupboard was empty, but it
was not. She made out the small folded limbs, the head like a
doll's head, waxy and putrescent, with a fluff of baby hair on

the peeling scalp; the little corpse seemed to give off its own light. The match burned Amanda's fingers and she flung it aside with a cry. Heavy steps came towards her in the darkness. The voice panted:

...'... *Muss graben* ... have to bury it ...'

Amanda blundered away towards the fireplace and struck another match. The madwoman ... Douglas ... leaned against the couch, arms outstretched, the hands crooked into claws for digging, for scratching. Some object came hurtling across the room from another direction right at Amanda's forehead and her anger was rekindled. She dropped the jerry-can and caught the china shepherdess in mid-air. She set it down carefully on the mantelpiece and unscrewed the cap of the jerry-can; she spilled petrol on the paper in the grate.

'Let him go!' she said again, hearing a furious malevolence in her own voice. '*Lass ihn los* ... let him go or I will burn this house!'

She threw the lighted match into the fireplace and the flames roared up.

This time, perhaps, she *had* miscalculated horribly. The jerry-can was half full of petrol, a spark would send it up like a Molotov cocktail. The firelight reflected in the dark window pane showed thin Amanda among flames, she could feel them in her hair, could feel the room grow into an inferno, with the crouching figure of Douglas burning like a Buddhist monk.

Suddenly the casement window burst open; wind and rain blew cleanly into the dark room. There was a long cry that sprang first from the contorted lips of Douglas then left him and echoed from the very walls of the house. The house was wracked with sobs and Amanda read them as an endless, an age-old sorrow, a female sorrow, that told of blood and filth and drudgery and hatred of one's own body and a useless grief for children dead. She ran to the window and flung the jerry-can far out into the wet garden. The rain struck at her face and mingled with her own tears.

'Please ...' she said aloud. 'Please ... I understand.'

Then she was talking to the empty air; the house was still, really still at last. The only sounds were heavy drops of rain on the sill or hissing down the chimney into the ashes of the fire. Douglas heaved himself up from the carpet and sat shivering on the couch with the tartan rug around his shoulders.

'The cupboard,' he said hoarsely. 'Did you see ... ?'

'There's nothing in the cupboard now,' said Amanda firmly.

She went and ran her hands over the empty shelves. She almost wished for some token . . . a scrap of cloth or paper that she could take out and bury. She wondered what might be found if the house were pulled down, if anyone took a spade to the forest floor.

'The packing is done,' she said. 'Douglas, I think we should . . .'

'Yes,' he said. 'Yes . . . as soon as possible. There's nothing to keep us here.'

The rain had stopped when they left but the sky was still overcast. As her brother got out the car Amanda walked through the trees to the bridge and met Frau Schneider.

'You think it best, Fräulein King?'

'I don't trust the place,' said Amanda, 'and Douglas has to go back to London.'

She reached into her bag and brought out the china shepherdess.

'Frau Schneider, I wish you would keep this. It will get broken if it stays in the house.'

Frau Schneider looked puzzled.

'It belongs to Frau Winter,' she said. 'All her things were packed up. This must have been left out.'

'Please keep it,' said Amanda, 'in memory of Frau Winter.'

Nickie began to bark at the base of an oak tree beyond the bridge and the two women saw a squirrel, two squirrels, whisking along the upper branches. The Volkswagen came roaring up and parked; Douglas and Frau Schneider exchanged a nod.

'But Fräulein King,' she said softly, 'the English lady is not dead. Frau Winter is not dead.'

'I thought . . .'

Frau Schneider reached out and patted Amanda's hand, holding the shepherdess, with her own gloved hand.

'You take it,' she said kindly. 'It is of no use if I bring it to the sanatorium. The poor woman would not know it.'

They turned together, as if at a command, and stared at the house, framed among the autumn trees.

'She has never recovered,' said Frau Schneider. 'She cannot even keep herself clean.'

Amanda could not speak. She stowed the pink and green figure in her handbag. Nickie began to give tongue even more loudly among the oak trees and Frau Schneider went to fetch him. Amanda walked briskly towards the car, her boot heels breaking through the crust of the fallen leaves as if the ground were already half frozen.

Russell Kirk
Watchers at the strait gate

*Russell Kirk was born in Michigan in 1918, and is one of the
few living masters of the ghostly tale; yet hardly a story of his
can be found in print in Britain, let alone a collection. A
selection from his superb book* The Surly Sullen Bell *is
included in his Arkham House collection* The Princess of all
Lands, *and his novels are* A Creature of the Twilight *(a
political fantasy) and* Old House of Fear. *He has received the
Ann Radcliffe Award for his Gothic fiction, and his story
'There's a long, long trail a-winding' won the World Fantasy
Award. He lives with his wife, Annette Yvonne Cecile
Courtemanche, and four daughters in a house which 'is
crowded with Vietnamese refugees [ten of them], reformed
hobos, university students, young mothers with babies, and a
congeries of fugitives from Progress'.*

*He is regarded as one of America's leading conservative
thinkers, as which he has published several influential books,
including* The Conservative Mind, The Roots of American
Eliot and his Age *(which was given the Christopher Award). In
his essay which concludes* The Surly Sullen Bell *he writes, 'I
venture to suggest that the more orthodox is a writer's theology,
the more convincing, as symbols and allegories, his uncanny
tales will be.' Here is a fine example of what he meant.*

'I am for the house with the narrow gate,
which I take to be too little for pomp to
enter. Some that humble themselves may,
but the many will be too chill and tender,
and they'll be for the flow'ry way that leads
to the broad gate and the great fire.'

            *— All's Well That
            Ends Well*

The rectory at St Enoch's, Albatross, was in poor repair. That did not much matter to Father Justin O'Malley, who felt in poor repair himself, and meant to leave the money-grubbing for a new rectory to the New Breed pastor who would succeed him here.

No doubt the New Breed types at the chancery would insist upon erecting a new church, as well as a new rectory, once Justin O'Malley was put out to pasture conveniently. They had succeeded in exiling him to the remotest parish in the diocese – to Albatross, away north among the pines and birches. The handsome simple old boulder church of St Enoch, built with their own hands by the early farmers of this infertile parish, could have stood with little repair for another two or three centuries; but the New Breed meant to pull it down 'to facilitate the new liturgy' once Justin O'Malley was disposed of. Meanwhile St Enoch's bell, at Father O'Malley's insistence, still was rung daily.

No, Justin O'Malley did not much heed the shutter that banged at his study window in this night's high wind, nor even the half-choked chimney that sent an occasional streamer of smoke towards his desk from the oak-limb fire flickering in the fireplace. He sat writing his sermon at three in the morning, or almost that, a decanter of whiskey on the corner of the desk, a handful of cigars beside it, and five battered volumes of Cardinal Newman stacked precariously before him. Now and again he hummed wryly when the shutter gave a particularly ferocious crack, mumbling the lyrics:

This old house once rang with laughter,
This old house knew many shouts;
Now it trembles in the darkness
When the lightning walks about . . .

He wasn't sure he had those lines quite right, but it was better to mangle lyrics than to mutilate dogmata. Sister Mary Ruth had called him a 'dogmatist' before she had shaken the dust of Albatross from her sandals – as if heterodoxy were ordained of God. Sister Mary Ruth had demanded that she be permitted to exhort from the pulpit of St Enoch's, and Father O'Malley had said her nay, dogmatically; so she had gone away to the world – and, he suspected, to the flesh and the devil. St Enoch's Elementary School had only two nuns left now, and he supposed that the next pastor would close it.

On Father O'Malley's study wall hung a Hogarth engraving,

'The Bathos', concerned with the end of all things. Father Time himself lay expiring in the foreground, amidst cracked bells and burst guns, and the word *Finis* was written upon the tobacco smoke that issued from Time's dying lips. A broken tower rather like the tower of St Enoch's hulked in the background. If only Hogarth had drawn also a torn-up missal and a roofless schoolhouse, the relevance to St Enoch's Parish would have been perfect. From the sublime to the ridiculous! So the Church, or at least this diocese, had descended in some fifteen years.

Father O'Malley sipped his whiskey and drew long on his thick cigar. He *must* stick to only one cigar an evening; otherwise the angina would come on worse than before. He had fought as best he could in this diocese, had been thrashed, and now lay eyeless in Gaza, otherwise Albatross. Defeat in the battle against innovation had left him a wreck – to mix metaphors – stranded on the barren shingle of the world. Perhaps, just conceivably, the Church might come to know better days; but he would not behold them. On he hummed:

> *Got no time to fix the shingles or to mend the windowpane;*
> *Ain't gonna need this house no longer . . .*

Oh, come now, Justin! You've got a sermon to finish; put the nonsense out of your head. Should he blast the New Breed one more time? *Come one, come all, this rock shall fly from its firm base as soon as I . . .* Yes: give them a dose of Newman, whom they never had read, actually.

He took up his copy of Newman's *Dream of Gerontius*. In Newman's spirit, very nearly, Vatican II had been conceived and convened; but that council had led, vulgarized, to much that Newman would have found anathema. Like Newman's Gerontius, the Reverend Justin O'Malley bent 'over the dizzy brink of some sheer infinite descent'. He asked now for little but to depart in peace.

Well, what should he call this comminatory sermon of his, here at the back of beyond, to his little congregation of ageing faithful? Should it be 'Prospect of the Abyss'? Would they be shocked, or would they notice at all – especially those among them who were in the habit of slipping out the church door right after the Sacrament? What would they think if he should quote certain chilling lines from *Gerontius*:

> *And, crueller still,*
> *A fierce and restless fright begins to fill*

The mansion of my soul. And, worse and worse,
Some bodily form of ill
Floats on the wind, with many a loathsome curse,
Tainting the hallowed air, and laughs, and flaps
Its hideous wings,
And makes me wild with horror and dismay.

Rather a strong dose for the old ladies who frequently confessed the great sin that their thoughts wandered at mass? Father O'Malley put the slim volume *Gerontius* aside and took up the fat *Development of Doctrine*. But the words blurred before his eyes. How he could use a cat nap! Nevertheless he persisted, covering half a page of paper with notes. He should have commenced this job earlier in the evening, and have abstained from even one whiskey. He ought to get outdoors more often, he knew, even in a winter so fierce as this, for the sake of his circulation. Why didn't he fetch those snowshoes out of the cellar? An hour or two of following a woods trail would put him in a better temper.

Once upon a time, he recollected, somebody had said that O'Malley was the one priest in the diocese who had a joke for every occasion. Had it been the bishop before this one? Well, why not laugh?

Life is a jest, and all things shew it;
I thought so once, but now I know it.

Should he put it in his will that they were to cut John Gay's epitaph on O'Malley's gravestone? But here, what was he scribbling on his sheet of sermon notes? 'O'Malley's a jest, and all things . . .' And he couldn't read half the sentences he had scrawled above that remark. Really, he must have a five-minute nap.

It required some force of will to remove the glass, the bottle, and the ash tray to a side table, sleepily, and to pile the books on the floor. Then Father O'Malley laid his face on his forearms, there on the old mahogany desk, and closed his eyes. High time it was for the nap, he reflected as consciousness drifted away: the pain in his chest had been swelling as he grew fatigued, but now it must ebb. The blessed dark . . .

Was it a really tremendous bang of the loose shutter that woke him? He could have slept only for a few minutes, but he felt rested. Then why was he uneasy? He glanced round his study;

the desk lamp showed him that nothing had changed. Getting up, he went to the window. Indeed that shutter was being torn loose altogether by the storm outside, the blizzard had increased, so that the snowflakes postively billowed against the panes. Why was he so uneasy? He had lived alone in this rectory for decades. Newman's line crept back into his mind: *Some bodily form of ill* . . . He crossed himself.

Then something rattled and fell in the little parlour, adjacent to the study, where usually he had parishioners wait if he was busy when they came to talk with him. In that parlour was an umbrella stand, and presumably some stick or umbrella had fallen. But what had made it fall, at this hour? Some strong draught?

With a certain reluctance, he opened the parlour door. The light from the desk lamp did not show him much. Was that a bulk in the further armchair?

'Father,' said a deep voice, 'I didn't mean to disturb you. I can just sit here till you're ready, Father. Ah, it's a blessing to be off that long, long trail and snug indoors this night. This chair of yours is like a throne, Father O'Malley . . .

'Up from Earth's Centre through the Seventh Gate
I rose, and on the Throne of Saturn sate,
   And many a Knot unravel'd by the Road,
But not the Master-knot of Human Fate.'

Justin O'Malley had sucked in his breath when the bulk in the tall chair stirred, but now he knew who it was: Frank Sarsfield, no other, with his quoting of the *Rubaiyat*. Frank had not come to him for more than a year. Now he would be wanting a bed, a meal, and a few dollars before he set out again. Oh, Frank was an old client, he was. Father O'Malley crossed himself again; this visitant could have been a different type. Only last month two priests had been hacked to death in their beds, at a house in Detroit.

'Frank,' he said, 'you gave me a turn. Come into my study and I'll see what I can do for you.'

'I think I was dozing off myself, Father, and my foot touched that umbrella stand, and something fell, I'm sorry. A little while ago I peeked in and saw you resting at your big desk, and I said to myself, "Nobody deserves his rest more than Father O'Malley," so I took the liberty of occupying that throne-chair of yours till you should wake. I'm not asking anything, Father, it's just that I came out of the blizzard, thinking we both might profit from a few words together. I know what I owe you already, Father Justin O'Malley, having kept track of it in my stupid head, year in, year out: it's a long-standing debt, most of it, coming altogether to the sum of four hundred and ninety-seven dollars and eleven cents. Is that the right sum, Father? Well, as the bums say when they're hauled before the bar of justice: *Jedge, I've had a run o' hard luck*. My ship didn't come in, Father, and none of my lottery tickets won big. But I know what I owe you, more than I owe anybody else in this world, and I've come here to square accounts, if that's all right with you, Father O'Malley.'

Perhaps Frank was careful with his diction when addressing the clergy; but his speech must be very good for a tramp, in any company. What damaged his polished address was the accent – and the intonation. There was a strong salt flavour of 'down east' – Sarsfield had been born on the Maine coast, O'Malley knew – blended with flop-house accents. ('Bird' became 'boid'.) The man had been a tramp since he was fifteen years or younger, Father O'Malley had found out, and he must be past sixty now. When not on the road during those weary decades, he had been in prisons chiefly. He must have slept here in the rectory nearly a dozen times, on his endless aimless peregrinations. Sarsfield professed to be a Catholic of sorts: if he should pilfer church poor-boxes, he preferred Catholic poor-boxes.

'Settle up?' Father O'Malley offered Sarsfield whiskey, as he always did; and as always Sarsfield declined the glass. 'Settle up, Frank? I'll believe that when you settle down, which you won't do until Judgment Day, I suppose. Have a cigar, then.'

'Get thee behind me,' Sarsfield answered, chuckling at his own wit. 'You know I never did smoke, Father, and only once I drank a bottle of wine – Million Bell it was – and it made me sick, as my mother said it would; so I'm not tempted, thank you.' At O'Malley's gesture, Sarsfield resumed his seat in the tall chair he had called a throne; apparently he did not intend to enter the pastor's study. It took a strong great chair to sustain Frank. For Sarsfield was a giant, almost, with a great Viking head, carrying more weight than was good for him. Yet he had a good colour now, Father O'Malley noticed, and seemed less elephantine in his movements than he had the last time he called at St Enoch's.

'Then you'll be wanting to raid the refrigerator, Frank? Mrs Syzmanski left some cold chicken there, I know. And you must be worn out, afoot on a night like this. There's a bed for you – the little room with the yellow wallpaper, if you're ready to turn in. How far did you come today – or yesterday, rather?'

'Far, Father, farther than ever – and found your door unlocked, as if you'd been expecting some tramp or other. Begging your pardon, Father Justin, I wouldn't leave the rectory open to all comers at night. Nowadays there's desperate characters on the move everywhere. You heard what was done to those two priests in Detroit, Father? And I could tell you about other cases . . . But I guess you're like that French bishop – *nisi Dominus custodierit domum, in vanum vigilant qui custodiunt eam.* What good are watchers, unless the Lord guards the house?'

Frank Sarsfield had succeeded several times in startling Father O'Malley with his scraps of learning and his faculty for quotation, which ran to whole long poems; yet this Latin, wretchedly pronounced though it was, staggered his host. He knew that this strange man, whose hair was perfectly white now, has been subjected to only four or five years of schooling; his knowledge of books came from public libraries in little towns, Christian Science reading rooms, prison libraries. 'Frank, I've told you before that you'd have made a good monk, but it's late for that.'

'Ah, Father, too late for that or for anything else, or nearly anything. Yet there's one thing, Father Justin O'Malley, that you've urged me to do, time and time again, and I've not done it, but I'll do it now, if you say it's not too late. If it pleases you, Father, it's one way of paying you back. It's this: will you hear my confession?'

What had come over this man? What had he done lately? During the several years of their intermittent acquaintance, Sarsfield had sat through masses at St Enoch's, but never had taken communion or gone to confession. 'At this hour, Frank? Right here?'

'As for the hour, Father, I know you're a night person; and I never sleep well, whatever the hour. As for the place – well, no, Father, I'd rather confess to you in that handsome old walnut confessional in the church. You'll know who I am – that can't be helped – but I won't see your face, nor you mine, and that'll make things easier, won't it? I hear that nowadays they call it "reconciliation", Father, and sometimes they just sit face to face with the priest, talking easy like this, but that's not what I want. I want you to hear everything I did and then

259

absolve me, if you can. What's the old word for it, out of King Arthur and such? You know – *shriven*, that's it. I want to be shriven.'

Father O'Malley never had expected this. He supposed that a psychiatrist might call Frank Sarsfield an 'autistic personality'; certainly Frank was a loner, an innocent of sorts, sometimes shrewd, sometimes very like a small boy, indolent, unmachined, guilt ridden, as weak of will as he was strong of body. Like Lady Macbeth, Sarsfield was forever washing himself, using up the rectory's rather scanty hot water, as if there were immaterial stains not to be washed away; he was every day clean shaven, his thick hair well-brushed, his clothes neat and clean. Sarsfield had been concentred all in self, turned in upon himself, his seeming joviality a mere protective coloration that helped him to beg his way through the world. He had been no solipsist, the priest judged, but had withdrawn ever since childhood within a shell – a mollusc of a man. *This* one was ready to confess to him at half-past three in the morning?

'It'll be cold in the church, Frank . . .'

'Why, this coat of mine is warm, Father – I bought it with my dish-washing pay, never fear – and you can put on your overcoat, if it's not too much trouble, and your gloves, and we needn't go outside, for there's that passage between the rectory here and the church that I scrubbed for you three years and seven months ago. You don't mind going into your own church, do you, Father, with a man who looks rougher than Jean Valjean, in the dead of night?'

Suddenly Father O'Malley did mind. There had come into his memory of this man a recollection of a certain evening – yes, about three years and seven months ago – when he had invited Frank Sarsfield to confess, and the man had declined, and he had given Frank a piece of advice. Some intuition then had told Father O'Malley that Frank, despite all his repressing of his impulses, despite his accustomed humbling of himself, despite his protestations of having been always 'non-violent' – well, that Frank Sarsfield potentially was a very dangerous man. A hint of madness, he had noticed then, lingered in Frank's light blue eyes that were forever furtively peeking out of their own corners. And that evening he had said bluntly to Sarsfield, 'Look out you don't turn berserker, Frank.'

Just what impelled this great hulking fellow to confess at last? What had he done – in Detroit, perhaps?

Some bodily form of ill floats on the wind . . .

260

It wasn't that Sarsfield seemed distraught; on the contrary, that strange giant seemed more easy in manner than ever O'Malley had known him before, more confident, all diffidence gone – as if a tension within him had been relaxed – or as if, perhaps, something within him had snapped at last.

Yet how could he refuse Sarsfield's request? Would it have been safe to refuse? Those Detroit priests – what face had they seen in the wee hours?

'Give me a moment to tidy my papers in the study, Frank, and then . . .'

'Now, Father, don't put me off.' That was said with a smile, but Father O'Malley watched Sarsfield narrowly, and did not smile back. 'Let your study tidy itself, and come along into the church with me, while the mood is on me. It was you that told me I ought to confess my sins, and told me ten times over. Here I am for you, Father O'Malley; come straight along, for Christ's sake.'

Frank at his heels, then, Father O'Malley went downstairs, willynilly, and opened the sticky door that gave entrance to the short passage between rectory and church. Why had Sarsfield prevented him from returning to the study? Had he guessed that there was a loaded revolver, never used, in one of the desk drawers?

He led the way along the chilly corridor to the yet colder Church of St Enoch. Something O'Malley had read in a book about the Mountain Men came into his mind: *Never walk the trail ahead of Hank Williams in starving time.* Frank Sarsfield, potential or actual berserker, was just behind him, silent except for the squeaking of one of his boots.

Father O'Malley reached for the light switch in the church, but Sarsfield said, 'We know the way, Father; the confessional's just over there; and we don't want any folks wondering what's up in the church at three in the morning.' So they made their way along the aisle of a musty church lighted only by some nocturnal candles in the choir, the wind flinging itself savagely against the tall painted windows, to the antique carved walnut confessional. There the two of them parted momentarily, the priest to his station, the penitent to his stool within the massive box; and then they sat invisible, facing each other, a black curtain between their faces.

'Forgive me, Father, for I have sinned,' said Frank Sarsfield. He was very rusty at this business. He was still for a moment; then, 'How shall I tell you, Father? Do I go through all my life since I was confirmed, or is there some other way?' The huge man was desperately embarrassed, Father O'Malley sensed.

'If you like,' the invisible confessor murmured, 'begin with the greatest sins, the biggest mortal sins, and then go on to the lesser, the venial ones.'

'All right, Father. I've thought about this many a time. Maybe the worst is this: one day or another, one year or another, I robbed seven churches.'

'That is sacrilege. How much money did you take?'

'Altogether, I reckon, three hundred and eighteen dollars and twenty-four cents, Father. And altogether I got fifteen years' imprisonment for it, and more the two times I tried to escape and was caught.'

'Why did you commit such sins?'

'Well, Father, most of those times I was up against it, in big towns where nobody would give me anything, and so I broke open the poor boxes.'

'What did you do with the money?'

'Oh, I spent it right off for meals and lodging and some better clothes, Father; and once I bought presents for two little kids with part of the loot.'

This was Sarsfield's greatest sin? He had paid for it ten times over, in prisons. He was an enormous boy, never grown up.

'After these robberies of churches, what was your next greatest sin, my son?'

There came a heavy pause. The deep voice at length murmured, 'Running away from home, I guess, when I was an ungrateful kid. I never saw Mother again, or Dad.'

'Why did you run away?'

'Well, Dad drank a lot – that's why Mother made me promise not to drink, and I never did, except for that one bottle of Mission Bell – and then he'd beat me up. One day he took to licking and kicking me out in the field. I couldn't take it, and I went down on my knees to beg Dad to stop, and I put my arms around his legs, begging, and that made him fall over, and he hurt himself on an old plough. Then I knew that when he got up he'd kill me – really beat me until I was dead, Father, beat me with anything handy, beat me over the head – so I ran for it. As Providence would have it, there was a rail line next to that field of ours, and there was a freight passing, and I got aboard before Dad could catch me, and I never went back, not while Dad was alive, not while Mother was alive. My Mother was a saint—'

Was the giant sobbing there in the dark?

The catalogue of mortal sins ran on; Father O'Malley was astonished at their triviality, though he kept his peace on that point. This man who had passed through some of the worst prisons in the land was almost untouched by such experiences. As if a little child, clearly he was guiltless of sexual offences. He fought only in self-defence – or for five or ten dollars, against professional pugs at county fairs, where he was beaten invariably. He never had destroyed property wantonly, or stolen without need. He had been arrested for mere vagrancy, on most occasions; and his long sentences had been imposed because he had tried to escape from serving his short sentences. Frank Sarsfield was a fool: a medieval fool, that is; one of Shakespeare's half-wise clowns; one of those fools who, the Moslems say, lie under God's particular protection.

They passed on to venial sins, there in the deathly cold of St Enoch's. Father O'Malley grew weary of the recital, but Sarsfield was so earnest! 'And is there anything fairly recent?' the confessor inquired at last, hoping that the ordeal was nearly over.

'Something that may have been recent, Father, though I'm not sure: it might have been last night, or it might have been sixty years ago. Let me tell you, Father, this was a scary thing, and I paid for it. I killed six men in one house.'

'*What was that you said?*'

'I killed six men in one house, Father – almost as good, I guess, as the Brave Little Tailor, "Seven at one blow!" ' Here the confessional shook, as if a heavy shudder had run through the man's great body. 'I kept yelling, "All heads off but mine!" and off they came. I used an axe that one of them had tried to use on me.'

Father O'Malley sat stupefied in the dark. Was Sarsfield a maniac? Had he really done this atrocity – and perhaps not in one house only? And having confessed this so fully, would Sarsfield spare the confessor? He managed to gasp, 'You classify this as a *venial* sin?' It sounded absurd – both the offence and the interrogation.

'Oh, the classifying's up to you, Father. I don't know if it was a sin at all. I hadn't much choice about it. Those were the worst men that had broken out of prison, killers and worse than killers, and they were after a young mother and her three

263

little daughters. After I butted in, it was either those six or yours truly. It turned out to be both, Father. It was the only time in my life I didn't behave like a coward, so you know better than I do whether I sinned. Maybe I took Heaven by storm.'

Father O'Malley, trying frantically to form some plan of action, played for time. 'You don't know whether you did this yesterday or sixty years ago?'

'No, Father, it's all mixed up in my head; and usually, as you know, my memory is good – the one thing I was proud of. Probably it's because so much has happened to me since that bloody fight, since I stood in that room like a slaughterhouse.'

The shudder came again.

'What do you mean, *something happened to you*?'

'Why, Father, being shot, and bleeding like a pig on the stairs and in the snow, and then the great long journey – all alone, except for the Watchers. But it turned out better than I deserved, Father. There's a poem by somebody named Blake, William Blake. I can't put into words most of what happened to me after I died, but these lines give you a notion of it:

> *I give you the end of a golden string,*
> *Only wind it into a ball,*
> *It will lead you in at Heaven's gate*
> *Built in Jerusalem's wall.'*

Justin O'Malley had been a voluble priest, sometimes jocular. But at what Sarsfield had just said, he was struck dumb. The silence grew so intense that Father O'Malley could hear his pocket watch, a good venerable quiet watch, ticking enormously in the empty church; but he dared not draw that watch to find out the time; perhaps this lunatic, this vast overwhelming lunatic Sarsfield, might think he was reaching for something else.

For his part, the madman sat silent also, as if awaiting the imposition of a salutary penance. Father O'Malley shook where he sat. Could Sarsfield detect his dread? Yes, yes, he was supposed to impose a penance now. What penance should a priest impose for the real or imaginary crimes of a homicidal maniac who thinks himself already dead? Father O'Malley could not collect himself. He began to babble hurriedly whatever came into his imperilled head:

'For your grave sins, say ten Hail Marys ...'

What trivial rubbish was he uttering? Ten Hail Marys for murdering a half-dozen men? Yet the brute on the other side of the curtain was murmuring, like a small boy, 'Yes, Father; I'll do that, Father . . .'

As if in a nightmare, Father O'Malley dashed from the insufficient penance to the implausible pardon. How much free will had this Frank ever been able to exercise, as boy or as man? Had he ever been perfectly sane? But put that aside, Justin: you've no time just now for casuistry.

'May the almighty and merciful Lord grant you pardon, absolution . . .' Had he gone mad himself? What impelled him to absolve so casually such a sinner as this? Yet Father O'Malley rushed through the old formula. Then Frank Sarsfield interrupted:

'Father, would you say the rest in Latin, please? They used it all the time when I was a boy. Maybe the words count for more if they're Latin, my mother, rest her, would have said so.'

'If you like,' O'Malley told his monstrous penitent – rather gratified, even in this dreadful moment, to encounter an Old Breed sinner. He hastened on:

'*Passio Domini nostri Iesu Christi, merita beatae Mariae Virginis, et omnium Sanctorum* . . . 'Father O'Malley stumbled a little; it had been long since he had run through the Latin for a penitent; but he finished: '. . . *et praemium vitae aeternae. Amen.*'

'Amen!' Sarsfield responded, his stentorian voice echoing through the high-vaulted church. 'Doesn't that mean *reward of everlasting life*? I heard those Latin words for years and years, Father, and never thought about them.'

O'Malley muttered some banality; he was more immediately concerned at this moment for his own aged mortal envelope, at the mercy of this night visitor. Sarsfield seemed to expect something more, here in the confessional. '*Pax vobiscum!*' Father O'Malley breathed.

'*Et cum spiritu tuo,*' Sarsfield responded, and then rose, bumping against the wooden wall of the confession box as he blundered his way out. Father O'Malley wished dearly that he might have remained in the confessional, for his part, until dawn should have come and this grim wanderer should have left St Enoch's. But that was not to be. He too groped his way to the aisle.

A baker's dozen of votive candles burned near the high altar, the only illumination of the church this fierce night; their flames wavered in the draught.

'Father,' the voice was saying right beside him, 'there's some prayer for somebody dying or dead. Could we go down on our knees and say that together?' He must mean the Recommendation for a Departing Soul.

'*Kyrie, eleison,*' Father O'Malley commenced, kneeling at the nearest bench. To his horror, Sarsfield knelt very close beside him, shoulder to shoulder, in this spreading empty church – as if there were happy contagion in sanctity.

'It will be all right to do this in English, Father,' Sarsfield muttered, 'begging your pardon, because I want to understand all of it.'

'Holy Abel, all ye choirs of the just, Holy Abraham . . .' Father O'Malley rattled through the calendar – John the Baptist, Joseph, patriarchs and prophets, Peter, Paul, Andrew, John, apostles and evangelists, innocents, Stephen, Lawrence, martyrs, Sylvester, Gregory, Augustine, bishops and confessors, Benedict, Francis, Camillus, John of God, monks and hermits, Mary Magdalen, Lucy, virgins and widows, saints. 'From Thy wrath, from the peril of death, from an evil death, from the pains of hell, from all evil, from the power of the devil, through Thy birth, through Thy cross and passion, through Thy death and burial, through Thy glorious resurrection . . .' Where was he? Where was he, indeed? 'In the day of judgment, we sinners beseech thee, hear us . . . O Lord, deliver him . . . *Libera eum, Domine.*'

'*Libera nos,*' Sarsfield put in, as if responding. 'Lord, have mercy, Christ, have mercy; Lord, have mercy.'

On and on Father O'Malley ran, the killer right against him in the dark, shifting from English to Latin, from Latin to English, as the spirit moved him, Sarsfield now and again responding irregularly or joining the priest in some passage that he seemed to recall. What a memory! Abruptly Sarsfield's voice drowned out O'Malley's:

'Mayest thou never know aught of the terror of darkness, the gnashing of teeth in the flames, the agonies of torment. May Satan most foul, with his wicked crew, give way before us; may he tremble at our coming with the Angels that attend us, and flee away into the vast chaos of eternal night. Let God arise, and let His enemies be scattered; and let them that hate Him flee from before His face. As smoke vanisheth, so let them vanish away; as wax melteth before the fire, so let the wicked perish at the presence of God; and let the just feast and rejoice before God. May, then, all the legions of hell be confounded

266

and put to shame, nor may the ministers of Satan dare to hinder our way.'

Then Father O'Malley was permitted to resume. The recommendation seemed to eat up hours, though really only minutes could be elapsing. At length he thought they had finished, and fell silent with a final 'Amen'. Would this killer make an end of him now? But Sarsfield said, 'I think, Father, there's a prayer to Our Lord Jesus Christ that a dying man says himself, if he can, and it won't do any harm for the pair of us to say that too.'

With fear and trembling, Father O'Malley began to utter that prayer, and Sarsfield joined him. Sarsfield's voice grew louder and louder as they approached the end:

'Do Thou, O Lord, by these Thy most holy pains, which we, though unworthy, now call to mind, and by Thy holy cross and death, deliver Thy servants praying here from the pains of hell, and vouchsafe to lead us whither Thou didst lead the good Thief who was crucified with Thee.' A few more words, and this second prayer was done.

Father O'Malley could not run away; for Sarsfield sat between him and the aisle, and the other end of their bench ended against the stone wall. To have tried to clamber over the bench-back in front of them would have been too conspicuous, perhaps inviting violence. Sarsfield remained upon his knees, as if sunk in a long silent prayer, but presently sat back on the bench.

'You must have read about those people that claim to have come back from death, Father,' Sarsfield told him, rather hesitantly. Father O'Malley scarcely could make out Sarsfield's face at all. 'You know – there's some woman doctor wrote a book about cases like that, and there's other books, too. Most of them tell about some long tunnel, and at the end of it everything's hunkydory.'

Justin O'Malley murmured acknowledgement. Did this fellow mean to experiment in that fashion with his confessor?

'Well, Father, it isn't like that – not like that at all.' Sarsfield bent to lift up the kneeler, giving more room down below for his big boots. 'Once a man's dead, Father O'Malley, he stays dead; he doesn't come back in the flesh and walk around, not unless Jesus Christ does for him what he did for Lazarus. Those tunnel people were *close* to death, that's all: they never went over the edge. Just being close isn't the same condition.

'It's my experience, Father, that when you cross over there's a hesitation and lingering, for a little while. Then you move on out, and that's scary, because you don't know where you're going; you've got no notion whatsoever. It's not that happy little tunnel with light at the end. Why, it's more like a *darkling plain*, Father. And you're all alone, or seem to be, except where those ignorant armies clash by night. On and on you go. And when you think or feel that at last you've arrived at the strait gate *which leadeth unto life* – well, then you meet the Watchers.'

The Sleepless Ones, the Watchers! Into Father O'Malley's awareness flashed some lines from *Gerontius*:

Like beasts of prey, who, caged within their bars,
In a deep hideous purring have their life,
And an incessant pacing to and fro.

'Understand, Father,' Sarsfield went on, 'I'm trying to put into words for you some experiences that words don't fit. Somebody said, didn't he, that all life is an allegory, and we can understand it only in parable? So when I tell you about the darkling plain, and about the Sleepless Ones, those Watchers, you're not supposed to take me literally, not all the way. I'm just giving you an approximation, in words, of what you feel at your core. That's the best I can do; I'm no philosophist and no poet.

'But sure as hell's a mantrap, it's no Tunnel of Love you find yourself in when you cross over, Father O'Malley. Even if the Watchers don't have claws literally, you sure know they're after you, and they sure know your weakness. I suppose I got past them, almost to the destination, because I'm a fool who took Heaven by storm.'

'But you tell me that you've come back amongst us living, Frank,' Father O'Malley ventured. Just conceivably he might be able to draw this mad Frank Sarsfield, this berserker, back towards some degree of right reason – if he were very cautious in the endeavour. Would that he could recollect his Thomistic syllogisms at this hour! 'So how can that be, Frank, when not long ago you told me that once a man's dead, so far as this world of flesh is concerned, he stays dead?'

From Sarsfield, almost invisible, there came something like a chuckle. 'Ah, I died right enough, Father; they shot me twice, and maybe three times. The thing is, I haven't returned to the land of the living. I've come just far enough back to meet you in shadow land.'

Had this thing returned seeking whom he might devour? But Father O'Malley said aloud, 'Why come back at all, Frank?'

'I give you the end of a golden string, Father. I'd gone down the narrow way, as they call it in those old books, until I'd almost forgotten about what I'd left undone. Then I thought of you.

'I can't ever pay you that four hundred and ninety-seven dollars and eleven cents, not now, Father O'Malley. But that doesn't much matter, not where rust doesn't tarnish nor moth corrupt. All the same, I might pay you back some of your friendship.

'Father Justin, I couldn't think of any friend but you, as I slowed down there on the narrow way. The Watchers had my scent, but I stood still and thought about you. Nobody else ever gave me a meal without being asked for it, or lent me over a hundred dollars without much chance of getting it back, or – that was best of all, Father – ever talked with me for hours as if I had a mind and was worth passing the time with. So there on the narrow way, when it seemed as if the end would be just around the corner, I turned back towards St Enoch's and you. I could do it because after I took up that axe in that lonely old house against those six men, I wasn't a coward any longer.

'I came back here, or maybe was sent back here, to lend you a hand on your journey, Father Justin. I know the way to the little gate, so to speak, fool though I am. It's fearsome, Father, groping that way when the Watchers are purring in the dark. But the two of us together . . .'

O'Malley's dread of this madman had diminished a little, though a little only. Sarsfield might mean to take his confessor with him down to dusty death, but his mood of the moment was not hostile. If he could persuade Frank to settle himself down in the bed in the guest room, the poor crazy giant might sleep off his present frantic delusion. Frank must have footed it through the blizzard all the way to Albatross, from God knew where; perhaps extreme weariness had snapped Frank's uncertain grip upon reality. Or if Frank Sarsfield actually had killed six men, only yesterday – why, Justin O'Malley could telephone the sheriff once Frank was abed, and check that out. The sheriff and his boys could take Frank sleeping, without harming him.

'Come back into the rectory, Frank,' Father O'Malley contrived to tell him, 'before I take the end of that golden string

of yours. Surely we've time enough to tidy my desk and have
a cold chicken sandwich apiece, before we start rolling string
into balls.'

'We may blow off like tumbleweeds any moment now,
Father,' Frank answered. They returned to the passage between church and rectory. 'Go on ahead, Frank,' his confessor
told him, dissimulating. 'You know the way.'

Sarsfield laughed. 'Don't you want me at your back, Father?
I always was non-violent, till the last. It's not Frank Sarsfield
you have to worry about: keep an eye peeled for the Watchers.
After you, Father.'

So it was Father O'Malley who led the way back to the rectory, and up the stairs to his study. Every step of the way he
had to nerve himself to keep from shuddering. Once, years
ago – it came to him now – he had told Frank Sarsfield that
some folk work out their Purgatory in this life, conceivably –
and that he, Frank, might be one such. On another occasion,
he had instructed Frank that for the Lord all time is eternally
present; and that, knowing the heart, the Lord might have
something especial in store for Frank Sarsfield, his failings
notwithstanding.

He might as well have preached in Mecca. Indeed the Lord
did seem to have reserved something for Frank Sarsfield,
heavy vessel for dishonour: the slaying of six men – and now perhaps
the murder of the pastor of St Enoch's. Why was this cup
thrust upon Justin O'Malley? This came of leaving doors open
to all comers. The Lord had dozed.

The two of them entered the study. Someone was sitting at
Father O'Malley's desk – or rather, had relaxed there with his
head resting upon his forearms.

Justin O'Malley started back, pale as a ghost. Frank Sarsfield caught him before he could fall.

'Ah, Father, it gave me such a twist myself, the first moment
of awareness. I was looking at myself all blood, head to foot . . .
Now don't be afraid of what's in that chair, Father. Look at it
for the last time. We shall be changed.'

Screwing his courage to the sticking place, Justin O'Malley
looked fixedly at that silent old husk. The body slumped there
had perished during sleep, without pain, the old heart ceasing
to pump. The face had been his own.

'We're off to the gate built in Jerusalem's wall,' Frank was
telling him. 'Few there be that find it, they say; but if we humble

ourselves, Father, we'll evade those pacing Sleepless Ones. I was sent to be your clown along the narrow way. Here, Father, take hold on yourself, we're going . . .'

The walls of the rectory fell away, and the winter landscape disintegrated, and for a moment Father O'Malley knew himself all fractured atoms.

Then the two of them were upon what seemed a darkling plain, and a path led through the marshes. It was all far more real than Albatross, and more perilous, and more promising. There was no pain at O'Malley's heart. Across the fens, drifting in the night breeze, corpse candles glimmered here and there. But the two of them could make out the high ground far beyond the bogs.

'Let's have no gnashing of teeth now, Father,' Frank was crying, with a wild sort of laugh. 'It's the faint-hearted that the Watchers catch.'

They strode forward as if they wore seven-league boots. At their backs, the sensual world which could be understood only in parable faded to the shadow of a shade.

Karl Edward Wagner

·220 Swift

*Karl Edward Wagner was born in 1945 in Knoxville,
Tennessee, and is a red-bearded giant who looks as if he should
be flinging his wench aside as Kirk Douglas calls the Vikings to
battle. In fact he was a psychiatrist before becoming a full-time
writer and publisher, and he and his wife are two of the reasons
(the others are the Wellmans and the Drakes) why you could
die of hospitality in Chapel Hill. His sword-and-sorcery novels
read like Robert E. Howard on LSD, though Wagner created
his character Kane ('an effort to go back to the hero-villain of
the Gothic novels') before he read Howard. His work has all
the energy and power of the best pulp fiction, but is more
intelligent than almost any of its predecessors.*

His books include Darkness Weaves *(originally altered by
the copy editor so that Kane would look like the cover!),* Death
Angel's Shadow, Bloodstone, Dark Crusade, Night Winds
and In the Wake of the Night. *He edits* The Year's Best
Horror Stories, *and his own horror tales are collected as* In a
Lonely Place. *Two of them, 'Sticks' and 'Neither Brute nor
Human' earned him the British Fantasy Award.*

*'"·220 Swift" has its beginnings in the summer I spent (1969)
living in an old log cabin in Haywood County, NC (on the NC
side of the Smokies, National Park that is, and not the fuzz).
According to my notes I started writing it in May 1973. Locales
are authentic, as are place names and the bits of data (legends,
place names, archaeological curiosa, etc.). I wanted to develop
the material into something more than the old dodge: Here's an
old legend – arrgh! it got me!'*

*I must say I began to wonder if I was ever going to see this
story, but it was worth the wait.*

I

Within, there was musty darkness and the sweet-stale smell of
damp earth.

Crouched at the opening, Dr Morris Kenlaw poked his head into the darkness and snuffled like a hound. His spade-like hands clawed industriously, flinging clods of dirt between his bent knees. Steadying himself with one hand, he wriggled closer to the hole in the ground and craned his neck inward.

He stuck out a muddy paw. 'Give me back the light, Brandon.' His usually overloud voice was muffled.

Brandon handed him the big flashlight and tried to look over Kenlaw's chunky shoulder. The archaeologist's blocky frame completely stoppered the opening as he hunched forward.

'Take hold of my legs!' came back his words, more muffled still.

Shrugging, Brandon knelt down and pinioned Kenlaw's stocky legs. He had made a fair sand-lot fullback not too many years past, and his bulk was sufficient to anchor the over-balanced archaeologist. Thus supported, Kenlaw crawled even farther into the tunnel. From the way his back jerked, Brandon sensed he was burrowing again, although no hunks of clay bounced forth.

Brandon pushed back his lank white hair with his forearm and looked up. His eyes were hidden behind mirror sunglasses, but his pale eyebrows made quizzical lines towards Dell Warner. Dell had eased his rangy denim-clad frame on to a limestone knob. Dan made a black-furred mound at his feet, tail thumping whenever his master looked down at him. The young farmer dug a crumpled pack of cigarettes out of his shirt pocket, watching in amused interest.

'Snake going to reach out, bite his nose off,' Dell ventured, proffering the cigarettes to Brandon, selecting one himself when the other man declined.

The cool mountain breeze whisked his lighter flame, whipped the high weeds that patchworked the sloping pasture. Yellow grass and weed – cropped closely here, there a verdant blotch to mark a resorbed cow-pie. Not far above them dark pines climbed to the crest of the ridge; a good way below, the slope levelled to a neat field of growing corn. Between stretched the steep bank of wild pasture, terraced with meandering cow-paths and scarred with grey juts of limestone. The early summer breeze had a cool, clean taste. It was not an afternoon to poke one's head into dank pits in the ground.

Kenlaw heaved convulsively, wriggling back out of the hole. He banged down the flashlight and swore; dirt hung on his black moustache. 'Goddamn hole's nothing but a goddamn groundhog burrow!' Behind his smudged glasses his bright-black eyes were accusing.

Dell's narrow shoulders lifted beneath his blue cotton work shirt. 'Groundhog may've dug it out, now – but I remember clear it was right here my daddy told me Granddad filled the hole in. Losing too much stock, stepping off into there.'

Kenlaw snorted and wiped his glasses with a big handker-chief. 'Probably just a hole leading into a limestone cave. This area's shot through with caves. Got a smoke? Mine fell out of my pocket.'

'Well, my dad said Granddad told him it was a tunnel mouth of some sort, only all caved in. Like an old mine shaft that's been abandoned years and years.'

Ill-humouredly snapping up his host's cigarette, Kenlaw scowled. 'The sort of story you'd tell to a kid. These hills are shot through with yarns about the mines of the ancients, too. God knows how many wild goose chases I've been after these last couple days.'

Dell's eyes narrowed. 'Now all I know is what I was told, and I was told this here was one of the mines of the ancients.'

Puffing at his cigarette, Kenlaw wisely forbore to comment.

'Let's walk back to my cabin,' Brandon suggested quickly. 'Dr Kenlaw, you'll want to wash up, and that'll give me time to set out some drinks.'

'Thanks, but I can't spare the time just now,' Dell grunted, sliding off the rock suddenly. The Plott hound scrambled to its feet. 'Oh, and Ginger says she's hoping you'll be down for supper this evening.'

'I'd like nothing better,' Brandon assured him, his mind forming a pleasant image of the farmer's copper-haired sister.

'See you at supper then, Eric. So long, Dr Kenlaw. Hope you find what you're after.'

The archaeologist muttered a goodbye as Warner and his dog loped off down the side of the pasture.

Brandon recovered his heavy Winchester Model 70 in ·220 Swift. He had been looking for woodchucks when he'd come upon Dell Warner and his visitor. From a flap pocket of his denim jacket he drew a lens cover for the bulky Leupold 3X9 telescopic sight.

'Did you say whether you cared for that drink?'

Kenlaw nodded. 'Jesus, that would be good. Been a long week up here, poking into every groundhog hole some hillbilly thinks is special.'

'That doesn't happen to be one there,' Brandon told him, hefting the rifle. 'I've scouted it several times for chucks – never anything come out.'

'You just missed seeing it – or else it's an old burrow,' Kenlaw judged.

'It's old,' Brandon agreed, 'or there'd be fresh dug earth scattered around. But there's no sign of digging, just this hole in the hillside. Looks more like it was dug out from below.'

II

The cabin that Eric Brandon rented stood atop a low bluff about half a mile up a dirt road from the Warner farmhouse. Dell had made a show of putting the century-old log structure into such state of repair that he might rent it out to an occasional venturesome tourist. The foot-thick poplar logs that made its rough-hewn walls were as solid as the day some *ante bellum* Warner had levered them into place. The grey walls showed rusty streaks where Dell had replaced the mud chinks with mortar, made from river sand hauled up from the Pigeon as it rushed past below the bluff. The massive river-rock fireplace displayed fresh mortar as well, and the roof was bright with new galvanized sheet metal. Inside was one large puncheon-floored room, with a low loft overhead making a second half-storey. There were no windows, but a back door opened on to a roofed porch overlooking the river below.

Dell had brought in a power line for lighting, stove and refrigerator. There was cold water from a line to the spring on the ridge above, and an outhouse farther down the slope. The cabin was solid, comfortable – but a bit too rustic for most tourists. Occasionally someone less interested in heated pools and colour tv found out about the place, and the chance rent helped supplement the farm's meagre income. Brandon, however, had found the cabin available each of the half-dozen times over the past couple of years when he had desired its use.

While the archaeologist splashed icy water into the sink at the cabin's kitchen end, Brandon removed a pair of fired cartridges from the pocket of his denim jacket. He inspected the finger-sized casings carefully for evidence of flowing, then dropped them into a box of fired brass destined for reloading.

Towelling off, Kenlaw watched him sourly. 'Ever worry about ricochets, shooting around all this rock like you do?'

'No danger,' Brandon returned, cracking an icetray briskly.

'Bullet's moving too fast – disintegrates on impact. One of the nice things about the ·220 Swift. Rum and coke OK?' He didn't care to lavish his special planter's punch on the older man.

Moving to the porch, Kenlaw took a big mouthful from the tall glass and dropped on to a ladderback chair. The Jamaican rum seemed to agree with him; his scowl eased into a contemplative frown.

'Guess I was a little short with Warner,' he volunteered.

When Brandon did not contradict him, he went on. 'Frustrating business, though, this trying to sort the thread of truth out of a snarl of superstition and hearsay. But I guess I'm not telling you anything new.'

The woven white oak splits of the chair bottom creaked as Kenlaw shifted his ponderous bulk. The Pigeon River, no more than a creek this far upstream, purled a cool, soothing rush below. Downstream the Canton papermills would transform its icy freshness into black and foaming poison.

Brandon considered his guest. The archaeologist had a sleek roundness to his frame that reminded Brandon of young Charles Laughton in *Island of Lost Souls*. There was muscle beneath the pudginess, judging by the energy with which he moved. His black hair was unnaturally sleek, like a cheap toupee, and his bristly moustache looked glued on. His face was round and innocent; his eyes, behind round glasses, round and wet. Without the glasses, Brandon thought they seemed tight and shrewd; perhaps this was a squint.

Dr Morris Kenlaw had announced himself the day before with a peremptory rap at Brandon's cabin door. He had started at Brandon's voice behind him – the other man had been watching from the ridge above as Kenlaw's dusty Plymouth drove up. His round eyes had grown rounder at the thick-barrelled rifle in Brandon's hands.

Dr Kenlaw, it seemed, was head of the Department of Anthropology at some southern college, and perhaps Brandon was familiar with his work. No? Well, they had told him in Waynesville that the young man staying at the Warners' cabin was studying folklore and Indian legends and such things. It seemed Mr Brandon might have had cause to read this or that article by Dr Kenlaw . . . No? Well, he'd have to send him a few reprints, then, that might be of interest.

The archaeologist had appropriated Brandon's favourite seat and drunk a pint of his rum, before he finally asked about the lost mines of the ancients. And Brandon, who had been given little chance before to interrupt his visitor's rambling discourse, abruptly found the other's flat stare fixed attentively on him.

Brandon dutifully named names, suggested suggestions; Kenlaw scribbled notes eagerly. Mission accomplished, the archaeologist pumped his hand and hustled off like a hound on a scent. Brandon had not expected to see the man again. But Dell Warner's name was among those in Kenlaw's notes, and today Brandon had run into them – Kenlaw, having introduced himself as a friend of Brandon, had persuaded Dell to show him his family's version of the lost mines. And that trail, it would seem, had grown cold again.

The chunky reddish-grey squirrel – they called them boomers – that had been scrabbling through the pine needle sod below them, suddenly streaked for the bushy shelter of a Virginia pine. Paying no attention, Dan romped around the corner of the cabin and bounded on to the porch. Brandon scratched the Plott hound's black head and listened. After a moment he could hear the whine and rattle as a pick-up lurched up the dirt road.

'That'll be Dell,' he told Kenlaw. 'Dan knew he was headed here and took the shortcut up the side of the ridge. Dog's one of the smartest I've seen.'

Kenlaw considered the panting black hound. 'He's a bear hound, isn't he?'

'A damn good one,' Brandon asserted.

'A bear killed young Warner's father, if I heard right,' Kenlaw suggested. 'Up near where we were just now. How dangerous are the bears they have up here?'

'A black bear doesn't seem like much compared to a grizzly,' Brandon said, 'but they're quite capable of tearing a man apart – as several of these stupid tourists find out every summer. Generally they won't cause trouble, although now and then you get a mean one. Trouble is, the bears over in the Smokies have no fear of man, and the park rangers tend to capture the known troublemakers and release them in the more remote sections of the mountains. So every now and then one of these renegades wanders out of the park. Unafraid of man and unaccustomed to foraging in the wild, they can turn into really nasty stock killers. Probably what killed Bard Warner that night. He'd been losing stock and had the bad sense to wait out with a bottle and his old 8 mm Mannlicher. Bolt on the Mannlicher is too damn slow for close work. From what I was told, Bard's first shot didn't do it, and he never got off his second.

278

Found what was left pulled under a rock ledge the next morning.'

Dell's long legs stuck out from the battered door of his old Chevy pick-up. He emerged from the cab balancing several huge tomatoes in his hands; a rolled newspaper was poked under one arm.

'These'll need to go into the refrigerator, Eric,' he advised. 'They're dead ripe. Get away, Dan!' The Plott hound was leaping about his legs.

Brandon thanked him and opened the refrigerator. Finger-combing his windblown sandy hair, Dell accepted his offer of a rum and coke. 'Brought you the Asheville paper,' he indicated. 'And you got a letter.'

'Probably my adviser wondering what progress I've made on my dissertation,' Brandon guessed, setting the letter with no return address carefully aside. He glanced over the newspaper while his friend uncapped an RC and mixed his own drink. Inflation, Africa, the Near East, a new scandal in Washington, and in New York a wave of gangland slayings following the sniping death of some syndicate kingpin. In this century-old cabin in the ancient hills, all this seemed distant and unreal.

'Supper'll be a little late,' Dell was saying. 'Faye and Ginger took off to Waynesville to get their hair done.' He added: 'We'd like to have you stay for supper too, Dr Kenlaw.'

The redhead's temper had cooled so that he remembered mountain etiquette. Since Kenlaw was still here, he was Brandon's guest, and a supper invitation to Brandon must include Brandon's company as well – or else Brandon would be in an awkward position. Had Kenlaw already left, there would have been no obligation. Brandon sensed that Dell had waited to see if the archaeologist would leave, before finally driving up.

'Thanks, I'd be glad to,' Kenlaw responded, showing some manners himself. Either he felt sheepish over his brusque behaviour earlier, or else he realized he'd better use some tact if he wanted any further help in his research here.

Brandon refilled his and Kenlaw's glasses before returning to the porch. Dell was standing uncertainly, talking with the archaeologist, so Brandon urged him to take the other porch chair. Taking hold with one hand of the yard-wide section of white oak log that served as a low table, he slid it over the rough planks to a corner post and sat down. He sipped the drink he had been carrying in his free hand and leaned back.

It was cool and shady on the porch, enough so that he would have removed his mirror sunglasses had he been alone. Brandon, a true albino, was self-conscious about his pink eyes.

As it was, Kenlaw was all but gawking at his host. The section of log that Brandon had negligently slewed across the uneven boards probably weighed a couple of hundred pounds. Dell, who had seen the albino free his pick-up from a ditch by the straightforward expedient of lifting the mired rear wheel, appeared not to notice.

'I was asking Dr Kenlaw what it was he was looking for in these mines,' Dell said.

'If mines they are,' Brandon pointed out.

'Oh, they're mines, sure enough,' the archaeologist asserted. 'You should be convinced of that, Brandon.' He waved a big hand for emphasis. Red clay made crescents beneath untrimmed nails.

'Who were the *ancients* who dug them?' Dell asked. 'Were they the same Indians who put up all those mounds you see around here and Tennessee?'

'No, the mound builders were a lot earlier,' Kenlaw explained. 'The mines of the ancients were dug by Spaniards – or more exactly, by the Indian slaves of the *conquistadores*. We know that de Soto came through here in 1540 looking for gold. The Cherokees had got word of what kind of thieves the Spaniards were, though, and while they showed the strangers polite hospitality, they took pains not to let them know they had anything worth stealing. De Soto put them down as not worth fooling with, and moved on. But before that he sank a few mine shafts to see what these hills were made of.'

'Did he find anything?' Dell wanted to know.

'Not around here. Farther south along these mountains a little ways, though, he did find some gold. In northern Georgia you can find vestiges of their mining shafts and camps. Don't know how much they found there, but there's evidence the Spaniards were still working that area as late as 1690.'

'Must not have found much gold, or else word would have spread. You can't keep gold a secret.'

'Hard to say. They must have found something to keep coming back over a century and a half. There was a lot of gold coming out of the New World, and not much of it ever reached Spain in the hands of those who discovered it. Plenty of reason to keep the discovery secret. And, of course, later on this area produced more gold than any place in the country before the

Western gold rush. But all those veins gave out long before the Civil War.'

'So you think the Spaniards were the ones that dug the mines of the ancients,' Dell said.

'No doubt about it,' stated Kenlaw, bobbing his head fiercely.

'Maybe that's been settled for northern Georgia,' Brandon interceded, 'although I'd had the impression this was only conjecture. But so far as I know, no one's ever proved the *conquistadores* mined this far north. For that matter, I don't believe anyone's ever made a serious study of the lost mines of the ancients in the North Carolina and Tennessee hills.'

'Exactly why I'm here,' Kenlaw told him impatiently. 'I'm hoping to prove the tie-in for my book on the mines of the ancients. Only, so far I've yet to find proof of their existence in this area.'

'Well, you may be looking for a tie-in that doesn't exist,' Brandon returned. 'I've studied this some, and my feeling is that the mines go back far beyond the days of the *conquistadores*. The Cherokees have legends that indicate the mines of the ancients were here already when the Cherokees migrated down from the north in the thirteenth century.'

'This is the first I've heard about it, then,' Kenlaw scoffed. 'Who do you figure drove these mines into the hills, if it wasn't the *conquistadores*? Don't tell me the Indians did it. I hardly think they would have been that interested in gold.'

'Didn't say it was the Indians,' Brandon argued.

'Who was it then?'

'The Indians weren't the first people here. When the Cherokees migrated into the Tellico region not far from here, they encountered a race of white giants – fought them and drove the survivors off, so their legends say.'

'You going to claim the Vikings were here?' Kenlaw snorted.

'The Vikings, the Welsh, the Phoenicians, the Jews – there's good evidence that on several occasions men from the Old World reached North America long before Columbus set out. Doubtless there were any number of pre-Columbian contacts of which we have no record, only legends.'

'If you'll forgive me, I'll stick to facts that are on record.'

'Then what about the Melungeons over in Tennessee? They're not Indians, though they were here before the first pioneers, and even today anthropologists aren't certain of their ancestry.'

Brandon pressed on. 'There are small pockets of people all

across the country – not just in these mountains – whose ethnic origins defy pinning down. And there are legends of others – the Shonokins, for example . . .'

'Now you're dealing with pure myth!' Kenlaw shut him off. 'That's the difference between us, Brandon. I'm interested in collecting historical fact, and you're a student of myths and legends. Science and superstition shouldn't be confused.'

'Sometimes the borderline is indistinct,' Brandon countered.

'My job is to make it less so.'

'But you'll have to concede there's often a factual basis for legend,' Brandon argued doggedly. 'And the Cherokees have a number of legends about the caves in these mountains, and about the creatures who live within. They tell about giant serpents, like the Uktena and the Uksuhi, that lair inside caves and haunt lonely ridges and streams, or the intelligent panthers that have townhouses in secret caves. Then there's the Nunnehi, an immortal race of invisible spirits that live beneath the mounds and take shape to fight the enemies of the Cherokee – these were supposedly seen as late as the Civil War. Or better still, there's the legend of the Yunwi Tsunsdi, the Little People who live deep inside the mountains.'

'I'm still looking for that *factual basis*,' Kenlaw said with sarcasm.

'Sometimes it's there to find. Ever read John Ashton's *Curious Creatures in Zoology*? In his chapter on pygmies he quotes from three sources that describe the discovery of entire burying grounds of diminutive stone sarcophagi containing human skeletons under two feet in length – adult skeletons, by their teeth. Several such burial grounds – ranging upwards to an acre and a half – were found in White County, Tennessee, in 1828, as well as an ancient townsite near one of the burials. General Milroy found similar graves in Smith County, Tennessee, in 1866, after a small creek had washed through the site and exposed them. Also, Weller in his *Romance of Natural History* makes reference to other such discoveries in Kentucky as well as Tennessee. Presumably a race of pygmies may have lived in this region before the Cherokees, who remember them only in legend as the Yunwi Tsunsdi. Odd, isn't it, that there are so many Indian legends of a pygmy race?'

'Spare me from Victorian amateur archaeology!' Kenlaw dismissed him impatiently. 'What possible bearing have these half-baked superstitions on the mines of the ancients? I'm talking about archaeological realities, like the pits in Mitchell

County, like the Sink Hole mine near Bakersville. That's a pit forty feet wide and forty feet deep, where the stone shows marks of metal tools and where stone tools were actually uncovered. General Thomas Clingman studied it right after the Civil War, and he counted three hundred rings on the trees he found growing on the mine workings. That clearly puts the mine back into the days of the *conquistadores*. There's record of one Tristan de Luna, who was searching for gold and silver south of there in 1560; the Sink Hole mine contained mica, and quite possibly he was responsible for digging it and the other mines of that area.'

'I've read about the Sink Hole mine in Creecy's *Grandfather's Tales*,' Brandon told him. 'And as I recall the early investigators there were puzzled by the series of passageways that connected the Sink Hole with other nearby pits – passageways that were only fourteen inches wide.'

The archaeologist sputtered in his drink. 'Well, Jesus Christ, man!' he exploded after a moment. 'That doesn't have anything to do with Indian legends! Don't you know anything about mining? They would have driven those connecting tunnels to try to cut across any veins of gold that might have lain between the pits.'

Brandon spread his big hands about fourteen inches apart. He said: 'Whoever dug the passageways would have had to have been rather small.'

III

Afternoon shadows were long when Dell drove the other two men down to the house in his pick-up. The farmhouse was a two-storey board structure with stone foundation, quite old but in neat repair. Its wide planks showed the up-and-down saw marks that indicated its construction predated the more modern circular sawmill blade. The front was partially faced with dark mountain stone, and the foundation wall extended to make a flagstone veranda, shaded and garlanded by bright-petalled clematis.

Another truck was parked beside Kenlaw's Plymouth – a battered green 1947 Ford pick-up that Brandon recognized as belonging to Dell's father-in-law, Olin Reynolds. Its owner greeted them from the porch as they walked up. He was a thin, faded man whose bony frame was almost lost in old-fashioned overalls. His face was deeply lined, his hair almost as white as

Brandon's. Once he had made the best moonshine whisky in the region, but his last stay in Atlanta had broken him. Now he lived alone on his old homestead bordering the Pisgah National Forest. He often turned up about dinner time, as did Brandon.

'Hello, Eric,' Olin called in his reedy voice. 'You been over to get that chuck that's been after my little girl's cabbages yet?'

'Hi, Olin,' Brandon grinned. 'Shot him yesterday morning from over across by that big white pine on the ridge.'

'That's near a quarter-mile,' the old man figured.

Brandon didn't say anything because Ginger Warner just then stepped out on to the porch. Dell's younger sister was recently back from finishing her junior year at Western Carolina in nearby Cullowhee. She was tall and willowy, green-eyed and quick to smile. Her copper hair was cut in a boyish shag instead of the unlovely *bouffant* most country women still clung to. Right now she had smudges of flour on her freckled face.

'Hi, Eric,' she grinned, brushing her hands on her jeans. 'Supper'll be along soon as the biscuits go in. You sure been keeping to yourself lately.'

'Putting together some of my notes for the thesis,' he apologized, thinking he'd eaten dinner here just three nights ago.

'Liar. You've been out running ridges with Dan.'

'That's relaxation after working late at night.'

Ginger gave him a sceptical look and returned to her biscuits.

With a ponderous grunt, Dr Kenlaw sank on to one of the wide-armed porch rockers. He swung his feet up on to the rail and gazed thoughtfully out across the valley. Mist was obscuring the hills beyond now, and the fields and pasture closer at hand filled with hazy shadow. Hidden by trees, the Pigeon River rushed its winding course midway through the small valley. Kenlaw did not seem at ease with what he saw. He glowered truculently at the potted flowers that lined the porch.

'What the hell!' Kenlaw suddenly lurched from his rocker. The other three men broke off their conversation and stared. Balancing on the rail, the archaeologist yanked down a hanging planter and dumped its contents into the yard.

'Where the hell did this come from!' he demanded, examining the rusted metal dish that an instant before had supported a trailing begonia.

Dell Warner bit off an angry retort.

284

'For God's sake, Kenlaw!' Brandon broke the stunned re-action.

'Yeah, for God's sake!' Kenlaw was too excited to be non-plussed. 'This is a Spanish *morion*! What's it doing hanging here full of petunias?'

Ginger stepped on to the porch to announce dinner. Her freckled face showed dismay. 'What on earth . . . ?'

Kenlaw was abashed. 'Sorry. I forgot myself when I saw this, Please excuse me – I'll replace your plant if it's ruined. But, where did you get this?'

'That old bowl? It's lain around the barn for years. I punched holes along the rim, and it made a great planter for my begonia.' She glanced over the rail and groaned.

'It's a *morion* – a *conquistador*'s helmet!' Kenlaw blurted in disbelief. Painstakingly he studied the high-crested bowl of rusted iron with its flared edges that peaked at either end. 'And genuine, too – or I'm no judge. Show me where this came from originally, and I'll buy you a pick-up full of begonias.'

Ginger wrinkled her forehead. 'I really don't know where it came from – I didn't even know it was anything. What's a Spanish helmet doing stuck back with all Dad's junk in our barn? There's an old iron pot with a hole busted in it where I found this. Want to look at it and tell me if it's Montezuma's bulletproof bathtub?'

Kenlaw snorted. 'Here, Brandon. You look at this and tell me I'm crazy.'

The albino examined the helmet. It was badly pitted, but solid. It could not have lain outside, or it would have rusted entirely away centuries ago. 'It's a *morion*, of course,' he agreed. 'Whether it dates to *conquistador* days or not, I'm not the one to tell. But it does seem equally unlikely that a careful reproduction would be lying around your barn.'

'Hell, I know where that come from,' Olin cut in, craning his long neck to see. 'I was with your-all's daddy time he found it.'

Kenlaw stared at the old mountainman – his eyes intent behind thick glasses. 'For God's sake – where?'

Olin worked his pointed chin in a thoughtful circle, eyeing Dell questioningly. The younger man shrugged.

Tanasee Bald in what's now Pisgah National Forest. There's a 'Place up on Old Field Mountain,' Olin told him, 'near sort of cave there, and I guess it won't do no harm now telling you a couple of old boys named Brennan used to make a little blockade from a still they'd built back inside. Me and Bard used to stop up there times and maybe carry wood and just set around. Well, one time Bard goes back inside a ways, and we worried some because he'd had a little – and after a while he comes back carrying that thing there and calling it an Indian pot cause he found it with a lot of bones way back in there. He liked to keep arrowheads and axeheads and such like when he found them, and so he carried that there back and put it with some other stuff, and I guess it's all just laid there and been scattered around the barn since.'

'You can find the place still?' Kenlaw pounced. 'Can you take me there tomorrow? Who else knows about this?'

'Why, don't guess there's nobody knows. The Brennans is all out of these parts now and gone – never did amount to much. Hardin Brennan got hisself shot one night arguing with a customer, and they said his brother Earl busted his head in a rock fall back there in the cave. Earl's wife had left him, and there was just his boy Buck and a daughter Laurie. She was half wild and not right in the head; young as she was, she had a baby boy they said must've been by her own kin, on account everybody else was half afraid of her. They all went up north somewheres – I heard to live with their mother. There's other Brennans still around that might be distant kin, but far as I know nobody's gone around that cave on Old Field Mountain since Buck and his sister left there better than twenty years back.'

Kenlaw swore in excitement. 'Nobody knows about it, then? Fantastic! What time tomorrow do you want to go? Better make it early. Seven?'

'Say about six instead,' Olin suggested. 'You'll need the whole day. How about coming up to the cabin – if that's all right with you, Eric? Shouldn't go back in there by yourself, and Lord knows my old bones are too brittle for scrambling around such places.'

'Sure, I'll go along,' Brandon agreed. 'Sounds interesting.'

'No need to,' Kenlaw told him. 'I've done my share of spelunking.'

'Then you know it's dangerous to go in alone. Besides, I'm intrigued by all this.'

'You all coming in to eat?' Faye Warner pushed open the screen. 'Ginger, I thought you'd gone to call them. Everything's ready.'

IV

There was chicken and ham, cornbread and gravy, tomatoes and branch lettuce, bowls of field peas, snap beans, corn and other garden vegetables. Kenlaw's scowl subsided as he loaded his plate a second time. Shortly after dinner the archaeologist excused himself. 'Been a long day, and we'll be up early enough tomorrow.'

Olin drove away not long after, and when Dell went off to see to some chores, Brandon had the porch to himself. He was half asleep when Ginger came out to join him.

'Did I startle you?' she apologized, sliding on to the porch swing beside him. 'You're jumpy as a cat. Is that what living in the city does to your nerves?'

'Keeps you alert, I guess,' Brandon said sheepishly.

Coppery hair tickled his shoulder. 'Then you ought to get out of New York after you finish your project or whatever it is. Sounds like you must spend most of your time travelling around from one place to another as it is.'

'That's known as field research.'

'Ha! Dell says you don't do anything but laze around the cabin, or go out hunting. No wonder you still don't have your doctorate. Must be nice to get a government grant to run around the country studying folklore.'

'Well, part of the time I'm organizing my notes, and part of the time I'm relaxing from the tension of writing.'

'I can see how lugging that cannon of a rifle around would be exercise. Why don't you use that little air pistol instead?'

'What air pistol?'

'You know. You use it sometimes, because once I saw you shoot a crow with it that was making a fuss in the apple tree in front of the cabin. I saw you point it, and there wasn't a sound except the crow gave a squawk, and then feathers everywhere. My cousin has an air pistol too, so I knew what happened.'

'Little spy.' His arm squeezed her shoulder with mock roughness.

'Wasn't spying,' Ginger protested, digging her chin into his shoulder. 'I was walking up to help Dell chop tobacco.'

When Brandon remained silent, she spoke to break the rhythmic rasp of the porch swing. 'What do you think of Dr Kenlaw?'

'A bit too pigheaded and pushy. They raise them that way up north.'

287

'That's one, coming from a New Yorker! Or are you from New York originally? You have less accent than Dr Kenlaw.'

'Hard to say. I grew up in a foster home; I've lived a lot of places since.'

'Well, folks around here like you well enough. They don't much like Dr Kenlaw.'

'I expect he's too aggressive. Some of these obsessive researchists are like that.'

Ginger lined her freckles in a frown. 'You're a researcher. Is Dr Kenlaw?'

Brandon went tense beneath her cheek. 'What do you mean?'

'I mean, have you ever heard of him? If you're both studying the same subjects pretty much . . . ?'

'I don't know his work, if that's what you mean.' Brandon's muscles remained steel tight. 'But then; he knows his subject well enough. Why?'

'He seems to be more interested in gold than in archaeology,' Ginger told him. 'At least, that's the way his questions strike most folks he talks to.'

Brandon laughed and seemed to relax again. 'Well, there's more acclaim in discovering a tomb filled with gold relics than in uncovering a burial of rotted bones and broken pot shards, regardless of the relative value to archaeological knowledge. That's why King Tutankhamen's tomb made headlines, while the discovery of a primitive man's jawbone gets squeezed in with the used car ads.'

'There was a curse on King Tut's tomb,' Ginger reminded him dourly.

'Even better, if you're fighting for a grant.'

'Grants!' Ginger sniffed. 'Do you really mean to get that degree, or do you just plan to make a career of living off grants?'

'There's worse ways to make a living,' Brandon assured her.

'Somehow I can't see you tied down to some university job. That's what you'll do when you get your doctorate, isn't it? Teach?'

'There's a lot of PhDs out there looking for jobs once the grants dry up,' Brandon shrugged. 'If there's an opening somewhere, I suppose so.'

'There might be an opening at Western Carolina,' Ginger hinted.

'There might.'

'And why not? You like it down here – or else you wouldn't

keep coming back. And people like you. You seem to fit right in – not like most of these loud New York types.'

'It does feel like coming home again when I get back here,' Brandon acknowledged. 'Guess I've never stayed in one place long enough to call it home. Would you like for me to set up shop in Cullowhee?'

'I just might.'

Brandon decided she had waited long enough for her kiss, and did something about it. Shadows crept together to form a misty darkness, and the cool mountain breeze carried the breath of entwined clematis and freshly turned earth. The creak of the porch swing measured time like an arthritic grandfather's clock, softened by the rustle of the river. A few cows still lowed, and somewhere a Chuck Will's Widow called to its mate. The quiet was dense enough so that they could hear Dan gnawing a bone in the yard below.

Ginger finally straightened, stretched cosily from her cramped position. 'Mmmm,' she purred; then: 'Lord, what is that dog chewing on so! We didn't have more than a plate of scraps for him after dinner.'

'Maybe Dan caught himself a rabbit. He's always hunting.'

'Oh! Go see! He killed a mother rabbit last week, and I know her babies all starved.'

'Dan probably saw that they didn't.' Brandon rose to go look. 'What you got there, boy?'

Ginger saw him stiffen abruptly. 'Oh, no! Not another mamma bunny!'

She darted past Brandon's arm before he could stop her.

Dan thumped his tail foolishly and returned her stare. Between his paws was a child's arm.

V

Olin Reynolds shifted his chaw reflectively. 'I don't wonder Ginger came to carry on such a fit,' he allowed. 'What did you figure it was?'

'Certainly not a child's arm,' Brandon said. 'Soon as you got it into good light you could see it was nothing human. It had to have been some type of monkey, and the resemblance gave me a cold chill at first glance, too. Pink skin with just a frost of dirty white fur, and just like a little kid's arm except it was all muscle and sinew instead of baby fat. And it was a sure enough hand, not a paw, though the fingers were too long and sinewy for any child's hand, and the nails were coarse and pointed like an animal's claws.'

'Wonder where old Dan come to catch him a monkey,' Olin put in.

'Somebody's pet. Tourists maybe – they carry everything they own in those damn campers. Thing got away; or more likely, died and they buried it, and Dan sniffed it out and dug it up. He'd been digging, from the look of him.'

'What did you finally do with it?'

'Dell weighted it down in an old gunny sack and threw it into a deep hole in the river there. Didn't want Dan dragging it back again to give the ladies another bad start.'

'Just as well,' Olin judged. 'It might have had somebody coming for to see what come of it. I suspect that'll be Dr Kenlaw coming up the hill now.'

Kenlaw's Plymouth struggled into view through the pines. Brandon glanced at his watch, noted it was past seven. He stretched himself out of Olin's ladderback chair and descended the porch steps to greet the archaeologist.

'Had a devil of a time finding the turn-off,' Kenlaw complained, squeezing out from behind the wheel. 'Everything set?'

'Throw your stuff in my pick-up, and we'll get going,' Olin told him. 'Where we're headed, ain't no kind of road any car can follow up.'

'Will that old bucket make it up a hill?' Kenlaw laughed, opening his trunk to take out a coil of rope and two powerful flashlights.

'This here old Ford's got a Marmon-Herrington all-wheel-drive conversion,' Olin said coldly. 'She can ride up the side of a bluff and pull out a cedar stump while your feet are hanging straight out the back window of the cab.'

Kenlaw laughed easily, shoving spare batteries and a geologist's pick into the ample pockets of the old paratrooper's jacket he wore. Brandon help him stow his gear into the back of the truck, then climbed into the cab beside Reynolds.

It was a tight squeeze in the cab after Dr Kenlaw clambered in, and once they reached the blacktop road the whine of the gears and fan made conversation like shouting above a gale. Olin drove along in moody silence, answering Kenlaw's occasional questions in few words. After a while they left the paved roads, and then it was a long kidney-bruising ride as the dual-sprung truck attacked rutted mountain paths that bore ever upwards through the shouldering pines. Kenlaw cursed and braced himself with both arms. Brandon caught a grin in Olin's faded eyes.

The road they followed led on past a tumbledown frame house, lost within a yard that had gone over to first growth pine and scrub. A few gnarled apple trees made a last stand, and farther beneath the encroaching forest, Brandon saw the hulking walls of a log barn – trees spearing upwards past where the roof had once spread. He shivered. The desolation of the place seemed to stir buried memories.

Beyond the abandoned farmhouse the road deteriorated into little more than a cowpath. It had never been more than a timber road, scraped out when the lumber barons dragged down the primeval forest from the heights half a century or more ago. Farm vehicles had kept it open once, and now an occasional hunter's truck broke down the young trees that would otherwise have choked it.

Olin's pick-up strained resolutely upwards, until at length they shuddered into an overgrown clearing. Reynolds cut the engine. 'Watch for snakes,' he warned, stepping down.

The clearing was littered beneath witch's broom and scrub with a scatter of rusted metal and indistinct trash. A framework of rotted lumber and a corroded padlock faced against the hillside. Several of the planks had fallen inwards upon the blackness within.

Olin Reynolds nodded. 'That's the place. Reckon the Brennans boarded it over before they moved on to keep stock from falling in. Opening used to just lie hidden beneath the brush.'

Dr Kenlaw prodded the eroded timbers. The padlock hasp hung rusted nails over the space where the board had rotted away. At a bolder shove, the entire framework tore loose and tumbled inwards.

Sunlight spilled in past the dust. The opening was squeezed between ledges of rock above and below, wide enough for a man to stoop and drop through. Beyond was a level floor, littered now with the debris of boards.

'Goes back like that a ways, then it narrows down to just a crack,' Olin told them.

Kenlaw grunted in a self-satisfied tone and headed back for the pick-up to get his equipment.

'Coming with us?' Brandon asked.

Olin shook his head firmly. 'I'll just wait here. These old bones are too eat up with arthuritis to go a-crawling through that snaky hole.'

291

'Wait with him, Eric, if you like,' Kenlaw suggested. 'I probably won't be long about this. No point you getting yourself all dirty messing around on what's likely to be just another wild goose chase.'

'I don't mind,' Brandon countered. 'If that *morion* came out of this cave, I'm curious to see what else lies hidden back there.'

'Odds are, one of those Brennans found it someplace else and just chucked it back in there. Looks like this place has been used as a dump.'

Kenlaw cautiously shined his light across the rubble beneath the ledge. Satisfied that no snakes were evident, the archaeologist gingerly squeezed his corpulent bulk past the opening and lowered himself to the floor of the cavern. Brandon dropped nimbly beside him.

Stale gloom filled a good-sized antechamber. Daylight trickled in from the opening, and a patch of blackness at the far end marked where the cavern narrowed and plunged deeper into the side of the mountain. Brandon took off his mirror sunglasses and glanced about the chamber – the albino's eyes were suited to the dank gloom.

The wreckage of what had once been a moonshine still cluttered the interior of the cavern. Copper coil and boiler had long ago been carried off, as had anything else of any value. Broken barrels, rotted mounds of sacks, jumbles of firewood, misshapen sculptures of galvanized metal. Broken bits of Mason jars and crockery shards crunched underfoot; dead ashes made a sodden raisin pudding. Kenlaw flung his light overhead and disclosed only sooty rock and somnolent bats.

'A goddamn dump,' he muttered petulantly. 'Maybe something farther back in.'

The archaeologist swung his light towards the rear of the chamber. A passage led farther into the mountain. Loose stones and more piled debris half blocked the opening. Pushing his way past this barricade, Kenlaw entered the narrow tunnel.

The passage was cramped. They ducked their heads, twisted about to avoid contact with the dank rock. Kenlaw carefully examined the walls of the cavern as they shuffled on. To Brandon's eye, there was nothing to indicate that man's tools had shaped the shaft. After a time, the sunlight from behind them disappeared, leaving them with their flashlights to guide them. The air grew stale with a sourness of animal decay, and as the passage seemed to lead downwards, Brandon wondered whether they might risk entering a layer of noxious gases.

'Hold on here!' Kenlaw warned, stopped abruptly.

Darkness met their probing flashlight beams several yards ahead of their feet, as the floor of the passage disappeared. Kenlaw wiped his pudgy face and caught his breath, as they shined their lights down into the sudden pit that confronted them.

'Must be thirty–forty feet to the bottom,' Kenlaw estimated. 'Cavern's big enough for a highschool gym. The ledge we're standing on creeps on down that fault line towards the bottom. We can make it if you'll just watch your step.'

'Is the air OK?' Brandon wondered.

'Smells fresh enough to me,' Kenlaw said. He dug a crumpled cigarette pack from his pocket, applied his lighter. The flame fanned outwards along the direction they had come. It fell softly through the blackness, showering sparks as it hit the floor.

'Still burning,' the archaeologist observed. 'I'm going on down.'

'Nice if that was natural gas down there,' Brandon muttered.

'This isn't a coal mine. Just another natural cavern, for my money.'

Clinging to the side of the rock for support, they cautiously felt their way down the steep incline. Although an agile climber could negotiate the descent without ropes, the footing was treacherous, and a missed step could easily mean a headlong plunge into the darkness.

They were halfway down, when Kenlaw paused to examine the rock wall. Switching hands with his flashlight, he drew his geologist's pick and tapped against the stone.

'Find something?' Brandon turned his light on to the object of the archaeologist's scrutiny, saw a band of lighter stone running along the ledge.

'Just a sample of stratum,' Kenlaw explained, hastily breaking free a specimen and shoving it into one of his voluminous pockets. 'I'll have to examine it back at my lab – study it for evidence of tool marks and so on.'

The floor of the pit appeared little different from the chamber through which they had entered the cavern, save that it lacked the accumulated litter of human usage. The air was cool and fresh enough to breathe, although each lungful carried the presence of a sunless place deep beneath the mountains.

'Wonder when the last time was anyone came down here?'

Brandon said, casting his light along the uneven floor. The bottom was strewn with broken rock and detritus, with a spongy paste of bat *guano* and dust. Footprints would be hard to trace after any length of time.

'Hard to say,' Kenlaw answered, scooping up a handful of gravel and examining it under his light. 'Sometimes the Confederates worked back into places like this after saltpetre. Maybe Bard Warner came down here, but I'm betting that *morion* was just something some dumb hillbilly found someplace else and got tossed on to the dump.'

'Are these bones human?' Brandon asked.

Kenlaw stuffed the gravel into a jacket pocket and scrambled over to where Brandon crouched. There was a fall of broken rock against the wall of the pit opposite their point of descent. Interspersed with the chunks of stone were fragments of mouldering bone. The archaeologist dug out a section of rib. It snapped easily in his hand, showing whiteness as it crumbled.

'Dead a long time,' Kenlaw muttered, pulling more of the rocks aside. 'Maybe Indian.'

'Then it's a human skeleton?'

'Stone burial cairn, at a guess. But it's been dug up and the bones scattered about. These long bones are all smashed apart.'

'Maybe he was killed in a rockslide.'

Kenlaw shook his head. 'Look how this femur is split apart. I'd say more likely something broke open the bones to eat the marrow.'

'An animal?'

'What else would it have been?'

Kenlaw suddenly bent forward, clawed at the detritus. His thick fingers locked on to what looked to be the edge of a flat rock. Grunting, he hauled back and wrenched forth a battered sheet of rusted iron.

'Part of a breastplate! Damned if this isn't the original skeleton in armour! Give me a hand with the rest of these rocks.'

Together they dragged away the cairn of rubble – Kenlaw puffing energetically as he flung aside the stones and fragments of bone. Brandon, caught up in the excitement of discovery himself, reflected with a twinge that this was hardly a careful piece of excavation. Nonetheless, Kenlaw's anxious scrabbling continued until they had cleared a patch of bare rock.

The archaeologist squatted on a stone and lit a cigarette. 'Doesn't tell me much,' he complained. 'Just broken bones and chunks of rust. Why was he here? Were there others with him?

Who were they? What were they seeking here?'

'Isn't it enough that you've found the burial of a *conquistador*?'

'Can't prove that until I've run some tests,'Kenlaw grumbled. 'Could have been a colonial – breastplates were still in use in European armies until this century. Or an Indian buried with some tribal heirlooms.'

'There's another passage back of here,' Brandon called out.

He had been shining his light along the fall of rock, searching for further relics from the cairn. Behind where they had cleared away some of the loose rocks, a passageway pierced the wall of the pit. Brandon rolled aside more of the stone, and the mouth of the passage took shape behind the crest of the rock pile.

Kenlaw knelt and peered within. 'Not much more than a crawl space,' he announced, 'but it runs straight on for maybe twenty or thirty feet, then appears to open on to another chamber.'

Brandon played his flashlight around the sides of the pit, then back to where they stood. 'I don't think this is just a rock slide. I think someone piled all these rocks here to wall up the tunnel mouth.'

'If they didn't want it found, then they must have found something worth hiding,' the archaeologist concluded. 'I'll take a look. You wait here in case I get stuck.'

Brandon started to point out that his was the slimmer frame, but already Kenlaw had plunged headfirst into the tunnel – his thick buttocks blocking Brandon's view as he squeezed his way through. Brandon thought of a fat old badger ducking down a burrow. He kept his light on the shaft. Wheezing and scuffling, the other man managed to force his bulk through the passage. He paused at the far end and called back something, but his words were too muffled for Brandon to catch.

A moment later Kenlaw's legs disappeared from view, and then his flushed face bobbed into Brandon's light. 'I'm in another chamber about like the one you're standing in,' he called back. 'I'll take a look around.'

Brandon sat down to wait impatiently. He glanced at his watch. To his surprise, they had been in the cavern some hours. The beam of his flashlight was yellowing; Brandon cut the switch to save the batteries, although he carried spares in his pockets. The blackness was as total as the inside of a grave, except for an occasional wan flash as Kenlaw shined his light past the tunnel mouth from the pit beyond. Brandon held his hand before his face, noted that he could dimly make out its outline. The albino had always known he could see better in the dark than others could, and it had seemed a sort of recompense for the fact that bright light tormented his pink eyes. He had read that hemeralopia did not necessarily coincide with increased night vision, and his use of infrared rifle scopes had caused him to wonder whether his eyes might not be unusually receptive to light from the infrared end of the spectrum.

Kenlaw seemed to be taking his time. At first Brandon had heard the sharp tapping of his geologist's pick from time to time. Now there was only silence. Brandon flipped his light back on, consulted his watch. It had been half an hour.

'Dr Kenlaw?' he called. He thrust his shoulders into the passage and called again, louder. There was no reply.

Less anxious than impatient, Brandon crawled into the tunnel and began to wriggle forward, pushing his light ahead of him. Brandon was stocky, and it was a tight enough squeeze. The crawl space couldn't be much more than two feet square at its widest point. Brandon reflected that it was fortunate that he was not one of those bothered by claustrophobia.

Halfway through the tunnel, Brandon suddenly halted to study its walls. No natural passage; those were tool marks upon the stone – not even Kenlaw could doubt now. The regularity of the passage had already made Brandon suspicious. Cramped as it was, it reminded him of a mine shaft, and he thought again about the mention in Creecy's *Grandfather's Tales* of the interconnecting tunnels found at the Sink Hole pits.

The tunnel opened into another chamber much like the one he had just quitted. It was a short drop to the floor, and Brandon lowered himself headfirst from the shaft. There was no sign of Kenlaw's light. He stood for a moment uneasily, swinging his flash about the cavern. Perhaps the archaeologist had fallen into a hidden pit, smashed his light.

'Dr Kenlaw?' Brandon called again. Only echoes answered.

No. There was another sound. Carried through the rock in the subterranean stillness. A sharp tapping. Kenlaw's geologist's pick.

Brandon killed his flash. A moment passed while his eyes adjusted to the blackness, then he discerned a faint haze of light – visible only because of the total darkness. Switching his own light back on, Brandon directed it towards the glimmer.

It came from the mouth of yet another passageway cut against the wall opposite.

He swung his light about the pit. Knowing what to look for now, Brandon thought he could see other such passages, piercing the rock face at all levels. It came to him that they began to run a real risk of losing their way if they were able to progress much farther within these caverns. Best to get Kenlaw and keep together after this, he decided.

The new shaft was a close copy of the previous one – albeit somewhat more cramped. Brandon scraped skin against its confines as he crawled towards the sound of Kenlaw's pick.

The archaeologist was so engrossed in what he was doing that he hadn't noticed Brandon's presence, until the other wriggled out on to the floor of the pit and hailed him. Spotlighted by Brandon's flash, Kenlaw glowered truculently. The rock face where he was hammering threw back a crystalline reflection.

'I was worried something had happened,' Brandon said, approaching.

'Sorry. I called to you that I was going on, but you must not have heard.' Kenlaw swept up handfuls of rock samples and stuffed them into the already bulging pockets of his paratrooper's jacket. 'We'd best be getting back before we get lost. Reynolds will be wondering about us.'

'What *is* this place? Don't tell me all of this is due to natural formation!' Brandon swept his light around. More diminutive tunnels pierced the sides of this pit also. He considered the broken rock that littered the floor.

'This is a mine of some sort, isn't it. Congratulations, Dr Kenlaw – you really have found one of the lost mines of the ancients! Christ, you'll need a team of spelunkers to explore these pits if they keep going on deeper into the mountain!'

Kenlaw laughed gruffly. 'Lost mines to the romantic imagination, I suppose – but not to the trained mind. This is a common enough formation – underground streams have forced their way through faults in the rock, hollowed out big chambers wherever they've encountered softer stone. Come on, we've wasted enough time on this one.'

'Soft rock?' Brandon pushed past him. 'Hell, this is quartz!'

He stared at the quartz dike where Kenlaw had been working. Under the flashlight beam, golden highlights shimmered from the chipped matrix.

'Oh my God,' Brandon managed to whisper.

These were good words for a final prayer, although Kenlaw probably had no such consideration in mind. The rush of motion from the darkness triggered some instinctive reflex. Brandon started to whirl about, and the pick of the geologist's hammer only tore a furrow across his scalp instead of plunging into his skull.

The glancing blow was enough. Brandon went down as if pole-axed. Crouching over him, Kenlaw raised the hammer for the *coup de grâce*.

When Brandon made no move, the murderous light in the other man's eyes subsided to cunning. Brandon was still breathing, although bare bone gleamed beneath the blood-matted hair. Kenlaw balanced the geologist's pick pensively.

'Got to make this look like an accident,' he muttered. 'Can't risk an investigation. Tell them you took a bad fall. Damn you, Brandon! You would have to butt in the one time I finally found what I was after! This goddamn mountain is made out of gold, and that's going to be my secret until I can lock up the mining rights.'

He hefted a rock – improvising quickly, for all that his attack had been born of the moment. 'Just as well the pick only grazed you. Going to have to look like you busted your head on the rocks. Can't have it happen in here though – this has to be kept hidden. Out there on the ledge where we first climbed down – that's where you fell. I'll block the tunnel entrance back up again. All they'll know is that we found some old bones in a cave, and you fell to your death climbing back up.'

He raised the rock over Brandon's head, then threw it aside. 'Hell, you may never wake up from that one there. Got to make this look natural as possible. If they don't suspect now, they might later on. Push you off the top of the ledge headfirst, and it'll just be a natural accident.'

Working quickly, Kenlaw tied a length of rope to Brandon's ankles. The man was breathing hoarsely, his pulse erratic. He had a concussion, maybe worse. Kenlaw debated again whether to kill him now, but considered it unlikely that he would regain consciousness before they reached the ledge. An astute coroner might know the difference between injuries suffered through a fatal fall and trauma inflicted upon a lifeless body – they always did on television.

Brandon was heavy, but Kenlaw was no weakling for all his

fat. Taking hold of the rope, he dragged the unconscious body across the cavern floor – any minor scrapes would be attributed to the fall. At the mouth of the tunnel he paused to pay out his coil of rope. Once on the other side, he could haul in Brandon's limp form like a fish on a line. It would only take minutes to finish the job.

The tunnel seemed far more cramped as he wriggled into it. The miners must have had small frames, but then people were smaller four centuries ago. Moreover, the Spaniards, who almost certainly would have used slave labour to drive these shafts, weren't men to let their slaves grow fat.

It *was* tighter, Kenlaw realized with growing alarm. For a moment he attempted to pass it off to claustrophobia, but as he reached a narrower section of the tunnel, the crushing pressure on his stout sides could not be denied. Panic whispered through his brain, and then suddenly he understood. He had crammed his baggy jacket pockets with rock samples and chunks of ore from the quartz dike; he was a good twenty pounds heavier and inches bulkier now than when he had crawled through before.

He could back out, but to do so would lose time. Brandon might revive; Reynolds might come looking for them. Gritting his teeth against the pressure on his ribs, Kenlaw pushed his light on ahead and forced his body onwards. This was the tightest point, and beyond that the way would be easier. He sucked in his breath and writhed forward another foot or more. His sides ached, but he managed yet another foot with all his strength.

No farther. He was stuck.

His chest aching, Kenlaw found scant breath to curse. No need to panic. Just back out and take off the jacket, push it in ahead of him and try again. He struggled to work his corpulent body backwards from the tunnel. The loose folds of his paratrooper's jacket rolled up as he wriggled backwards, bunching against the bulging pockets. Jammed even tighter against his flesh and against the rock walls, the laden coat bunched up into a wedge. Kenlaw pushed harder, setting his teeth against the pain, as rock samples gouged into his body.

He couldn't move an inch farther. Backwards or forwards.

He was stuck midway in the tunnel.

Still Kenlaw fought down his panic. It was going to cost him some bruises and some torn skin, no doubt, but he'd work his way free in good time. He must above all else remain calm, be patient. A fraction of an inch forwards, a fraction of an inch backwards. He would take his time, work his way loose bit by bit, tear free of the jacket or smooth out its bunched-up folds. At worst, Reynolds would find him, bring help. Brandon might be dead by then, or have no memory of the blow that felled him; he could claim he was only trying to drag his injured companion to safety.

Kenlaw noticed that the light from his flash was growing dim. He had meant to replace the batteries earlier; now the spares were part of the impedimenta that pinioned him here. No matter; he didn't need light for this – only to be *lighter*. Kenlaw laughed shakily at his own joke, then the chuckle died.

The flashlight was fast dwindling, but its yellowing beam was enough to pick out the pink reflections of the many pairs of eyes that watched him from the mouth of the tunnel –barely glimpsed shapes that grew bolder as the light they feared grew dim.

And then Kenlaw panicked.

VI

The throbbing ache in his skull was so intense that it was some time before Brandon became aware that he was conscious. By gradual increments, as one awakens from a deep dream, he came to realize that something was wrong, that there was a reason for the pain and clouded state of awareness. An elusive memory whispered of a treacherous attack, a blow from behind ...

Brandon groaned as he forced himself to sit up, goaded to action as memory returned. His legs refused to function, and after a moment of confusion, he realized that his ankles were tied together. He almost passed out again from the effort to lean forward and fumble with the knots, and more time dragged past as he clumsily worked to free his ankles.

His brain refused to function clearly. He knew that it was dark, that he could see only dimly, but he could not think where his flashlight might be, nor marvel that his albino eyes had so accommodated to give him preternatural vision in a lightless cavern. Remembering Kenlaw's attack, he began to wonder where the other man had gone; only disjointedly did he understand the reasons behind the archaeologist's actions and the probable consequences of his own plight.

The knots at last came loose. Brandon dully considered the rope – his thoughts groping with the fact that someone had tied it to his ankles. Tied him to what? Brandon pulled on the rope, drew coils of slack through the darkness, until there was tension from the other end. He tugged again. The rope was affixed to something beyond. With great effort, Brandon made it to his feet, staggered forward to lean against the rock face beneath which he had lain. The rope was tied to the wall. No, it entered the wall, into the tunnel. It was affixed to something within the narrow passage.

Brandon knelt forward and followed the rope into the crawl space. Dimly he remembered that this was the shaft by which he had entered – or so he hoped. He had hardly crawled forward for more than a body length, when his fingers clawed against boots. Brandon groped and encountered damp cloth and motionless legs – the rope pressing on beneath their weight.

'Kenlaw?' he called out in a voice he scarcely recognized. He shook the man's feet, but no response came. Bracing himself against the narrow passage, Brandon grasped the other man's ankles and hauled back. For a moment there was resistance, then the slack body slid backwards under his tugging. Backing out of the tunnel, Brandon dragged the archaeologist's motionless form behind him. The task was an easy one for him, despite that the pain in his skull left Brandon nauseated and weak.

Emerging from the shaft, he rested until the giddiness subsided. Kenlaw lay where he had released him, still not moving. Brandon could only see the man as a dim outline, but vague as that impression was, something seemed wrong about the silhouette. Brandon bent forward, ran his hands over the archaeologist's face, groping for a pulse.

His fingers encountered warm wetness across patches of slick hardness and sticky softness, before skidding into empty eye sockets. Most of the flesh of Kenlaw's face and upper body had been stripped from the bone.

Brandon slumped against the wall of the cavern, trying to comprehend. His brain struggled drunkenly to think, but the agony of his skull kept making his thoughts tumble apart again just as understanding seemed to be there. Kenlaw was dead. He, Brandon, was in a bad way. This much he could hold in his mind, and with that, the recognition that he had to get out of this place.

That meant crawling back through the narrow shaft where Kenlaw had met his death. Brandon's mind was too dazed to feel the full weight of horror. Once again he crawled into the tunnel and inched his way through the cramped darkness. The rock was damp, and now he knew with what wetness, but he forced himself to wriggle across it.

His hands encountered Kenlaw's flashlight. He snapped its switch without effect, then remembered the fresh batteries in his pockets. Crawling from the tunnel and on to the floor of the chamber beyond, he fumbled to open the flashlight, stuff in new batteries. He thumbed the switch, again without result. His fingers groped across the lens, gashed against broken glass. The bulb was smashed, the metal dented; tufts of hair and dried gore caked the battered end. Kenlaw had found service from the flashlight as a club, and it was good for little else now. Brandon threw it away from him with a curse.

The effort had taxed his strength, and Brandon passed from consciousness to unconsciousness and again to consciousness without really being aware of it. When he found himself capable of thought once again, he had to remember all over again how he had come to this state. He wondered how much time had passed, touched his watch, and found that the glare from the digital reading hurt his eyes.

Setting his teeth against the throbbing that jarred his skull, Brandon made it to his feet again, clutching at the wall of the pit for support. Olin, assuming he was getting anxious by now, might not find the passage that led from the first pit. To get help, Brandon would have to cross this cavern, crawl through the shaft back into the first pit, perhaps climb up along the ledge and into the passageway that led to the outer cavern. In his condition it wouldn't have been easy even if he had a light.

Brandon searched his pockets with no real hope. A non-smoker, he rarely carried matches, nor did he now. His eyes seemed to have accommodated as fully to the absence of light as their abnormal sensitivity would permit. It was sufficient to discern the shape of objects close at hand as shadowy forms distinct from the engulfing darkness – little enough, but preferable to total blindness. Brandon stood with his back to the shaft through which he had just crawled. The other tunnel had seemed to be approximately opposite, and if he walked in a straight line he ought to strike the rock face close enough to grope for the opening.

With cautious steps, Brandon began to cross the cavern. The floor was uneven, and loose stones were impossible for him to see. He tried to remember if his previous crossing had revealed any pitfalls within this chamber. A fall and a broken leg would leave him helpless here, and slowly through his confused brain was creeping the shrill warning that Kenlaw's death could hardly have been from natural causes. A bear? There were persistent rumours of mountain lions being sighted in these hills. Bobcats, which were not uncommon, could be dangerous under these circumstances. Brandon concentrated on walking in a straight line, much like a drunk trying to walk a highway line for a cop, and found that the effort demanded his entire attention.

The wall opposite loomed before him – Brandon was aware of its darker shape an instant before he blundered into it. He rested against its cool solidity for a moment, his knees rubbery, head swimming after the exertion. When he felt stronger once again, he began to inch his way along the rock face, fumbling for an opening in the wall of the pit.

There – a patch of darkness less intense opened out of the stone. He dared not even consider the possibility that this might not be the shaft that was hidden behind the cairn. Brandon fought back unconsciousness as it surged over him once more, forced his muscles to respond. Once through this passage, Olin would be able to find him. He stooped to crawl into the tunnel, and the rock was coated with a musty stickiness.

Brandon wriggled forward across the moist stone. The sensation was already too familiar, when his out-thrust fingers clawed against a man's boot. Kenlaw's boot. Kenlaw's body. In the shaft ahead of him.

Brandon was too stunned to feel terror. His tortured mind struggled to comprehend. Kenlaw's body lay in the farther chamber, beyond the other passage by which he had returned. And Brandon knew a dead man when he came upon one. Had he circled the cavern, gone back the way he had come? Or was he delirious, his injured brain tormented by a recurring nightmare?

He clutched the lifeless feet and started to haul them back, as he had done before, or thought he had done. The boots were abruptly dragged out of his grasp.

Brandon slumped forward on his face, pressing against the stone to hold back the waves of vertigo and growing fear. Kenlaw's body disappeared into the blackness of the tunnel. How serious was his head injury? Had he imagined that Kenlaw was dead? Or was it Kenlaw ahead of him now in this narrow passage?

Brandon smothered a cackling laugh. It must not be Kenlaw. Kenlaw was dead, after all. It was Olin Reynolds, or some-one else, come to search for him.

'Here I am!' Brandon managed to shout. 'In here!'

His lips tasted of blood, and Brandon remembered the wet-ness he had pressed his face against a moment gone. It was too late to call back his outcry.

New movement scurried in the tunnel, from either end. Then his night vision became no blessing, for enough consciousness remained for Brandon to know that the faces that peered at him from the shaft ahead were not human faces.

VII

Olin Reynolds was a patient man. Age and Atlanta had taught him that. When the sun was high, he opened a tin of Vienna sausages and a pack of Lance crackers, munched them slowly, then washed them down with a few swallows from a Mason jar of blockade. Sleepy after his lunch, he stretched out on the seat and dozed.

When he awoke, the sun was low, and his joints complained as he slid from the cab and stretched. Brandon and Kenlaw should have returned by now, he realized with growing unease. Being a patient man, he sat on the running board of his truck, smoked two cigarettes and had another pull from the jar of whisky. By then dusk was closing, and Reynolds decided it was time for him to do something.

There was a flashlight in the truck. Its batteries were none too fresh, but Reynolds dug it out and tramped towards the mouth of the cave. Stooping low, he called out several times, and, when there came no answer to his hail, he cautiously let himself down into the cavern.

The flashlight beam was weak, but enough to see that there was nothing here but the wreckage of the moonshine still that had been a going concern when he last set foot within the cavern. Reynolds didn't care to search farther with his uncer-tain light, but the chance that the others might have met with some accident and be unable to get back was too great for him to ignore. Still calling out their names, he nervously picked his way along the passage that led from the rear of the antecham-ber.

His batteries held out long enough for Reynolds to spot the sudden drop-off before he blundered across the edge and into space. Standing as close to the brink as he dared, Reynolds pointed his flashlight downwards into the pit. The yellow beam was sufficient to pick out a broken heap of a man on the rocks below the ledge. Reynolds had seen death often enough before, and he didn't expect an answer when he called out into the darkness of the pit.

As quickly as his failing light permitted, Reynolds retraced his steps out into the starry darkness of the clearing. Breathing a prayer that one of the men might have survived the fall, he sent his truck careening down the mountain road in search of help.

Remote as the area was, it was well into the night before rescue workers in four-wheel-drive vehicles were able to converge upon the clearing before the cavern. Men with lights and emergency equipment hurried into the cave and climbed down into the pit beyond. There they found the broken body of Dr Morris Kenlaw – strangely mutilated, as if set upon by rats after he fell to his death. They loaded his body on to a stretcher, and continued to search for his companion.

Eric Brandon they never found.

They searched the cavern and the passageway and the pit from corner to crevice. They found the wreckage of an old still and, within the pit, Kenlaw's body – and that was all. Later, when there were more lights, someone thought he saw evidence that a rock fall against the far wall of the pit might be a recent one; but after they had turned through this for a while, it was obvious that only bare rock lay underneath.

By morning, news of the mystery had spread. One man dead, one man vanished. Local reporters visited the scene, took photographs, interviewed people. Curiosity seekers joined the search. The day wore on, and still no sign of Brandon. By now the State Bureau of Investigation had sent men into the area in addition to the local sheriff's deputies – not that foul play was suspected so much, but a man had been killed and his companion had disappeared. And since it was evident that Brandon was not to be found inside the cavern, the mystery centred upon his disappearance – and why.

There were many conjectures. The men had been attacked by a bear, Brandon's body carried off. Brandon had been injured, had crawled out for help after Olin Reynolds had driven off; had subsequently collapsed, or become lost in the forest, or was out of his mind from a head injury. Some few suggested that Kenlaw's death had not been accidental, although no motive was put forward, and that Brandon had fled in panic while Reynolds was asleep. The mountainside was searched, and searched more thoroughly the next day. Dogs were brought in, but by now too many people had trampled over the site.

No trace of the missing man was discovered.

It became necessary that Brandon's family and associates be notified, and here the mystery continued. Brandon seemed to have no next of kin, but then, he had said once that he was an orphan. At his apartment in New York, he was almost unknown; the landlord could only note that he paid his rent promptly – and often by mail, since he evidently travelled a great deal. The university at which he had mentioned he was working on his doctorate (when asked once) had no student on record named Eric Brandon, and no one could remember if he had ever told them the name of the grant that was supporting his folklore research.

In their need to know *something* definite about the vanished man, investigators looked through the few possessions and personal effects in his cabin. They found no names or addresses with which Brandon might be connected – nothing beyond numerous reference works and copious notes that showed he had indeed been a serious student of regional folklore. There was his rifle, and a handgun – a Walther PPK in ·380 ACP – still nothing to excite comment (the Walther was of pre-war manufacture, its serial number without American listing), until someone forced the lock on his attaché case and discovered the Colt Woodsman. The fact that this ·22 calibre pistol incorporated a silencer interested the SBI and, after fingerprints had been sent through channels, was of even greater interest to the FBI.

'They were manufactured for the OSS,' the agent explained, indicating the Colt semi-automatic with its bulky silencer. 'A few of them are still in use, although the Hi-Standard HD is more common now. There's no way of knowing how this one ended up in Brandon's possession – it's illegal for a private citizen to own a silencer of any sort, of course. In the hands of a good marksman, it's a perfect assassination gun – about all the sound it makes is that of the action functioning, and a clip of ·22 hollow points placed right will finish about any job.'

'Eric wouldn't have killed anyone!' Ginger Warner protested angrily. The FBI agent reminded her of a too scrubbed bible salesman. She resented the high-handed way he and the others had appropriated Brandon's belongings.

'That's the thing about these sociopathic types; they seem perfectly normal human beings, but it's only a mask.' He went on: 'We'll run ballistics on this and see if it matches with anything on file. Probably not. This guy was good. Real good. What we have on him now is purely circumstantial, and if we turn him up, I'm not sure we can nail him on anything more serious than firearms violations. But putting together all the things we know and that won't stand up in court, your tenant is one of the top hitmen in the business.'

'Brandon – a hitman!' scoffed Dell Warner.

'Brandon's not his real name,' the agent went on, ticking off his information. 'He's set up other identities too, probably. We ran his prints; took some looking, but we finally identified him. His name was Ricky Brennan when he was turned over to a New York State foster home as a small child. Father unknown; mother one Laurie Brennan, deceased. Records say his mother was from around here originally, by the way – maybe that's why he came back. Got into a bit of trouble in his early teens; had a fight with some other boys in the home. One died from a broken neck as a result, but since the others had jumped Brennan, no charges were placed. But out of that, we did get his prints on record – thanks to an institutional blunder when they neglected to expunge his juvenile record. They moved him to another facility, where they could handle his type; shortly after that, Brennan ran away, and there the official record ends.'

'Then how can you say that Eric is a hired killer!' Ginger demanded. 'You haven't any proof! You've said so yourself.'

'No proof that'll stand up in court, I said,' the agent admitted. 'But we've known for some time of a high-priced hitman who likes to use a high-powered rifle. One like this.'

He hefted Brandon's rifle. 'This is a Winchester Model 70, chambered for the ·220 Swift. That's the fastest commercially loaded cartridge ever made. Factory load will move a forty-eight-grain bullet out at a velocity of over 4,100 feet per second on a trajectory flat as a stretched string. Our man has killed with headshots from distances that must have been near three hundred yards, in reconstructing some of his hits. The bullet virtually explodes on impact, so there's nothing left for ballistics to work on.

'But it's a rare gun for a hitman to use, and that's where Brandon begins to figure. It demands a top marksman, as well as a shooter who can handle this much gun. You see, the ·220 Swift has just too much power. It burned out the old nickel steel barrels when the cartridge was first introduced, and it's said that the bullet itself will disintegrate if it hits a patch of turbulent air. The 220 Swift may have fantastic velocity, but it also has a tendency to self-destruct.'

'Eric used that as a varmint rifle,' Dell argued. 'It's a popular cartridge for varmint shooters, along with a lot of other small calibre high-velocity cartridges. And as for that silenced Colt, Eric isn't the first person I've heard of who owned a gun that's considered illegal.'

'As I said, we don't have a case – yet. Just pieces of a puzzle, but more pieces start to fall into place once you make a start. There's more than just what I've told you, you can be sure. And we'll find out a lot more once we find Brandon. At a guess, he killed Kenlaw – who may have found out something about him – then panicked and fled.'

'Sounds pretty clumsy for a professional killer,' Dell commented.

The agent frowned, then was all official politeness once more. These hillbillies were never known for their cooperation with federal agents. 'We'll find out what happened when we find Brandon.'

'If you find him.'

VIII

Brandon seemed to be swirling through pain-fogged delirium – an endless vertigo in which he clutched at fragments of dream as a man caught in a maelstrom is flung against flotsam of his broken ship. In rare moments his consciousness surfaced enough for him to wonder whether portions of the dreams might be reality.

Most often, Brandon dreamed of limitless caverns beneath the mountains, caverns through which he was borne along by partially glimpsed dwarfish figures. Sometimes Kenlaw was with him in this maze of tunnels – crawling after him, his face a flayed mask of horror, a bloody geologist's pick brandished in one fleshless fist.

At other times Brandon sensed his dreams were visions of the past, visions that could only be born of his obsessive study of the folklore of this region. He looked upon the mountains of a primeval age, when the boundless forest was untouched

308

by the iron bite and poisoned breath of white civilization. Copper-hued savages hunted game along these ridges, to come upon a race of diminutive white-skinned folk who withdrew shyly into the shelter of hidden caverns. The Indians were in awe of these little people, whose origins were beyond the mysteries of their oldest legends, and so they created new legends to explain them.

With the successive migrations of Indians through these mountains, the little people remained in general at peace, for they were wise in certain arts beyond the comprehension of the red man – who deemed them spirit-folk – and their ways were those of secrecy and stealth.

Then came a new race of men: white skins made bronze by the sun, their faces bearded, their flesh encased in burnished steel. The *conquistadores* enslaved the little folk of the hills as they had enslaved the races of the south, tortured them to learn the secrets of their caves beneath the mountains, forced them to mine the gold from pits driven deep into the earth. Then followed a dream of mad carnage, when the little people arose from their tunnels in unexpected force, to entrap their masters within the pits, and to drive those who escaped howling in fear from that which they had called forth from beneath the mountains.

Then came the white settlers in a wave that never receded, driving before them the red man, and finally the game. Remembering the *conquistadores*, the little people retreated farther into their hidden caverns, hating the white man with his guns and his settlements. Seldom now did they venture into the world above, and then only by night. Deep within the mountains, they found sustenance from the subterranean rivers and the beds of fungoid growths they nourished, feeding as well upon other cave creatures and such prey as they might seek above on starless nights. With each generation, the race slipped farther back into primordial savagery, forgetting the ancient knowledge that had once been theirs. Their stature became dwarfish and apelike, their faces brutish as the regression of their souls; their flesh and hair assumed the dead pallor of creatures that live in eternal darkness, even as their vision and hearing adapted to their subterranean existence.

They remembered their hatred of the new race of men. Again and again Brandon's dreams were red with visions of stealthy ambush and lurid slaughter of those who trespassed upon their hidden domain, of those who walked mountain trails upon nights when the stars were swallowed in cloud. He saw children snatched from their blankets, women set upon in lonely places. For the most part, these were nightmares from previous centuries, although there was a recurrent dream in which a vapid-faced girl gave herself over willingly to their obscene lusts, until the coming of men with flashlights and shotguns drove them from her cackling embrace.

These were dreams that Brandon through his comatose delirium could grasp and understand. There were other visions that defied his comprehension.

Fantastic cities reeled and shattered as the earth tore itself apart, thrusting new mountains towards the blazing heavens, opening vast chasms that swallowed rivers and spat them forth as shrieking steam. Oceans of flame melted continents into leaden seas, wherein charred fragments of a world spun frenziedly upon chaotic tides and whirlpools, riven by enormous bolts of raw energy that coursed like fiery cobwebs from the cyclopean orb that filled the sky.

Deep within the earth, fortress cities were shaken and smashed by the hell that reigned miles above. From out of the ruins, survivors crept to attempt to salvage some of the wonders of the age that had died and left them exiles in a strange world. Darkness and savagery stole from them their ideals, even as monstrous dwellers from even greater depths of the earth drove them from their buried cities and upward through caverns that opened on to an alien surface. In the silent halls of vanished greatness, nightmarish shapes crawled like maggots, while the knowledge of that godlike age was a fading memory to the degenerate descendants of those who had fled.

How long the dreams endured, Brandon could not know. It was the easing of the pain in his skull that eventually convinced Brandon that he had passed from dream into reality, although it was into reality no less strange than that of delirium.

They made a circle about where he lay – so many of them that Brandon could not guess their number. Their bodies were stunted, but lacking the disproportion of torso to limbs of human dwarves. The thin white fur upon their naked pink flesh combined to give them something of the appearance of lemurs. Brandon thought of elves and of feral children, but their faces were those of demons. Broad nostrils and out-thrust tusked jaws stopped just short of being muzzles, and within overlarge red-pupilled eyes glinted the malign intelligence of a fallen angel.

310

They seemed in awe of him.

Brandon slowly raised himself on one arm, giddy from the effort. He saw that he lay upon a pallet of dried moss and crudely cured furs, that his naked body seemed thin from long fever. He touched the wound on his scalp and encountered old scab and new scar. Beside him, water and what might be broth or emollients filled bowls which might have been formed by human hands, or perhaps not.

Brandon stared back at the vast circle of eyes. It occurred to him to wonder that he could see them; his first thought was that there must be a source of dim light from somewhere. It then came to him to wonder that these creatures had spared him; his first thought was that as an albino they had mistakenly accepted him as one of their race. In the latter, he was closer to the truth than with the former.

Then slowly, as his awakening consciousness assimilated all that he now knew, Brandon understood the truth. And, in understanding at last, Brandon knew who he was, and why he was.

IX

There was only a sickle of moon that night, but Ginger Warner, feeling restless, threw on a wrap and slipped out of the house.

On some nights sleep just would not come, although such nights came farther apart now. Walking seemed to help, although she had forgone these nocturnal strolls for a time, after once when she realized someone was following her. As it turned out, her unwelcome escort was a federal agent – they thought she would lead them to where her lover was hiding – and Ginger's subsequent anger was worse than her momentary fear. But in time even the FBI decided that the trail was a cold one, and the investigation into the disappearance of a suspected hired killer was pushed into the background.

It was turning autumn, and the thin breeze made her shiver beneath her dark wrap. Ginger wished for the company of Dan, but her brother had taken the Plott hound off on a weekend bear hunt. The wind made a lonely sound as it moved through the trees, chattering the dead leaves so that even the company of her own footsteps was denied her.

Only the familiarity of the tone let her stifle a scream, when someone called her name from the darkness ahead.

Ginger squinted into the darkness, wishing now she'd brought a light. She whispered uncertainly: 'Eric?'

And then he stepped out from the shadow of the rock outcropping that overhung the path along the ridge, and Ginger was in his arms.

She spared only a moment for a kiss, before warning him in one breathless outburst: 'Eric, you've got to be careful! The police – the FBI – they've been looking for you all summer! They think you're some sort of criminal!'

In her next breath, she found time to look at him more closely. 'Eric, where have you been? What's happened to you?'

Only the warm pressure of his arms proved to her that Brandon was not a phantom of dream. The wind whipped through his long white hair and beard, and there was just enough moonlight for her to make out the streak of scar that creased his scalp. He was shirtless; his only attire a ragged pair of denim jeans and battered boots. Beneath his bare skin, muscles bunched in tight masses that were devoid of fleshy padding. About his neck he wore a peculiar amulet of gold, and upon his belt hung a *conquistador*'s sword.

'I've been walking up and down in the earth,' he said. 'Is summer over, then? It hadn't seemed so long. I wonder if time moves at a different pace down there.'

Both his words and his tone made her stare at him anew. 'Eric? God, Eric! What's happened to you?'

'I've found my own kind,' Brandon told her, with a laugh that gave her a chill. 'But I was lonely among them as well, and so I came back. I knew there must be an open passageway somewhere on your land here, and it didn't take me long to find it.'

'You've been hiding out in some caves?' Ginger wondered.

'Not hiding out. They recognized me for who I am, don't you understand! They've forgotten so much over the ages, but not all of the old wisdom has left them. They're not quite beasts yet!'

Ginger considered the scar on his head, and remembered that he must have been wandering in some undiscovered system of caverns for many weeks, alone in the darkness.

'Eric,' she said gently, 'I know you've been hurt, that you've been alone for a long time. Now I want you to come back with me to the house. You need to have a doctor look at your head where you hurt it.'

'It's certain to sound strange to you, I realize,' Brandon

312

smiled. 'I still sometimes wonder if it isn't all part of my dreams. There's gold down there – more gold than the *conquistadores* ever dreamed – and hoards of every precious stone these mountains hold. But there's far greater treasure than any of this. There's a lost civilization buried down below, its ruins guarded by entities that transcend any apocalyptic vision of hell's demons. It's been ages since any of my people have dared to enter the hidden strongholds – but I've dared to enter there, and I've returned.'

Ginger compressed her lips and tried to remember all she'd learned in her psychology course last year.

'Eric, you don't have to be worried about what I said about the police. They know you weren't to blame for Dr Kenlaw's death, and they admitted to us that they didn't have any sort of evidence against you on all that other nonsense.'

She hoped that was all still true. Far better to have Eric turn himself in and let a good lawyer take charge, than to allow him to wander off again in this condition. They had good doctors at the centre in Morganton who could help him recover.

'Come back?' Brandon's face seemed suddenly satanic. 'You'd have me come back to the world of men and be put in a cell? I think instead I'll rule in hell!'

Ginger did not share in his laughter at his allusion. There were soft rustlings among the leaves alongside the trail, and the wind was silent.

She cried out when she saw their faces, and instinctively pressed against Brandon for protection.

'Don't be afraid,' he soothed, gripping her tightly. 'These are my people. They've fallen far, but I can lead them back along the road to their ancient greatness.

'*Our* people,' Brandon corrected himself, 'Persephone.'

Ramsey Campbell
The fit

Ramsey Campbell – for a full biography, see page one. Most, if not all, fears begin in early life, and many are sexually based. Though this story isn't autobiographical, it felt as if it was.

I must have passed the end of the path a hundred times before I saw it. Walking into Keswick, I always gazed at the distant fells, mossed by fields and gorse and woods. On cloudy days shadows rode the fells; the figures tramping the ridges looked as though they could steady themselves with one hand on the clouds. On clear days I would marvel at the multitude of shades of green and yellow, a spectrum in themselves, and notice nothing else.

But this was a dull day. The landscape looked dusty, as though from the lorries that pulverized the roads. I might have stayed in the house, but my Aunt Naomi was fitting; the sight of people turning like inexperienced models before the full-length mirror made me feel out of place. I'd exhausted Keswick – games of Crazy Golf, boats on the lake or strolls round it, narrow streets clogged with cars and people scaffolded with rucksacks – and I didn't feel like toiling up the fells today, even for the vistas of the lakes.

If I hadn't been watching my feet trudging I would have missed the path. It led away from the road a mile or so outside Keswick, through a gap in the hedge and across a field overgrown with grass and wild flowers. Solitude appealed to me, and I squeezed through the gap, which was hardly large enough for a sheep.

As soon as I stepped on the path I felt the breeze. That raised my spirits; the lorries had half-deafened me, the grubby light and the clouds of dust had made me feel grimy. Though the grass was waist high I strode forward, determined to follow the path.

Grass blurred its meanderings, but I managed to trace it to the far side of the field, only to find that it gave out entirely. I peered about, blinded by smouldering green. Elusive grasshoppers chirred, regular as telephones. Eventually I made my way to the corner where the field met two others. Here the path sneaked through the hedge, almost invisibly. Had it been made difficult to follow?

Beyond the hedge it passed close to a pond, whose surface was green as the fields; I slithered on the brink. A dragonfly, its wings wafers of stained glass, skimmed the pond. The breeze coaxed me along the path, until I reached what I'd thought was the edge of the field, but which proved to be a trough in the ground, about fifteen feet deep.

It wasn't a valley, though its stony floor sloped towards a dark hole ragged with grass. Its banks were a mass of gorse and herbs; gorse obscured a dark green mound low down on the far bank. Except that the breeze was urging me, I wouldn't have gone close enough to realize that the mound was a cottage.

It was hardly larger than a room. Moss had blurred its outlines, so that it resembled the banks of the trough; it was impossible to tell where the roof ended and the walls began. Now I could see a window, and I was eager to look in. The breeze guided me forward, caressing and soothing, and I saw where the path led down to the cottage.

I had just climbed down below the edge when the breeze turned cold. Was it the damp, striking upwards from the crack in the earth? The crack was narrower than it had looked, which must be why I was all at once much closer to the cottage – close enough to realize that the cottage must be decaying, eaten away by moss; perhaps that was what I could smell. Inside the cottage a light crept towards the window, a light pale as marsh gas, pale as the face that loomed behind it.

Someone was in there, and I was trespassing. When I tried to struggle out of the trough, my feet slipped on the path; the breeze was a huge cushion, a softness that forced me backward. Clutching at gorse, I dragged myself over the edge. Nobody followed, and by the time I'd fled past the pond I couldn't distinguish the crack in the earth.

I didn't tell my aunt about the incident. Though she insisted I call her Naomi, and let me stay up at night far later than my parents did, I felt she might disapprove. I didn't want her to think that I was still a child. If I hadn't stopped myself brooding about it I might have realized that I felt guiltier than the incident warranted; after all, I had done nothing.

Before long she touched on the subject herself. One night we sat sipping more of the wine we'd had with dinner, something else my parents would have frowned upon if they'd known. Mellowed by wine, I said, 'That was a nice meal.' Without warning, to my dismay which I concealed with a laugh, my voice fell an octave.

'You're growing up.' As though that had reminded her, she said, 'See what you make of this.'

From a drawer she produced two small grey dresses, too smartly cut for school. One of her clients had brought them for alteration, her two small daughters clutching each other and giggling at me. Aunt Naomi handed me the dresses. 'Look at them closely,' she said.

Handling them made me uneasy. As they drooped emptily over my lap they looked unnervingly minute. Strands of a different grey were woven into the material. Somehow I didn't like to touch those strands.

'I know how you feel,' my aunt said. 'It's the material.'

'What about it?'

'The strands of lighter grey – I think they're hair.'

I handed back the dresses hastily, pinching them by one corner of the shoulders. 'Old Fanny Cave made them,' she said as though that explained everything.

'Who's Fanny Cave?'

'Maybe she's just an old woman who isn't quite right in the head. I wouldn't trust some of the tales I've heard about her. Mind you, I'd trust her even less.'

I must have looked intrigued, for she said: 'She's just an unpleasant old woman, Peter. Take my advice and stay away from her.'

'I can't stay away from her if I don't know where she lives,' I said slyly.

'In a hole in the ground near a pond, so they tell me. You can't even see it from the road, so don't bother trying.'

She took my sudden nervousness for assent. 'I wish Mrs Gibson hadn't accepted those dresses,' she mused. 'She couldn't bring herself to refuse, she said, when Fanny Cave had gone to so much trouble. Well, she said the children felt uncomfortable in them. I'm going to tell her the material isn't good for their skin.'

I should have liked more chance to decide whether I wanted

317

to confess to having gone near Fanny Cave's. Still, I felt too guilty to revive the subject or even to show too much interest in the old woman. Two days later I had the chance to see her for myself.

I was mooching about the house, trying to keep out of my aunt's way. There was nowhere downstairs I felt comfortable; her sewing machine chattered in the dining room, by the table spread with cut-out patterns; dress forms stood in the lounge, waiting for clothes or limbs. From my bedroom window I watched the rain stir the fields into mud, dissolve the fells into mounds of mist. I was glad when the doorbell rang; at least it gave me something to do.

As soon as I opened the door the old woman pushed in. I thought she was impatient for shelter; she wore only a grey dress. Parts of it glistened with rain – or were they patterns of a different grey, symbols of some kind? I found myself squinting at them, trying to make them out, before I looked up at her face.

She was over six feet tall. Her grey hair dangled to her waist. Presumably it smelled of earth; certainly she did. Her leathery face was too small for her body. As it stooped, peering through grey strands at me as though I was merchandise, I thought of a rodent peering from its lair.

She strode into the dining room. 'You've been saying things about me. You've been telling them not to wear my clothes.'

'I'm sure nobody told you that,' my aunt said.

'Nobody had to.' Her voice sounded stiff and rusty, as if she wasn't used to talking to people. 'I know when anyone meddles in my affairs.'

How could she fit into that dwarfish cottage? I stood in the hall, wondering if my aunt needed help and if I would have the courage to provide it. But now the old woman sounded less threatening than peevish. 'I'm getting old. I need someone to look after me sometimes. I've no children of my own.'

'But giving them clothes won't make them your children.'

Through the doorway I saw the old woman glaring as though she had been found out. 'Don't you meddle in my affairs or I'll meddle in yours,' she said, and stalked away. It must have been the draught of her movements that made the dress patterns fly off the table, some of them into the fire.

For the rest of the day I felt uneasy, almost glad to be going home tomorrow. Clouds oozed down the fells; swaying curtains of rain enclosed the house, beneath the looming sky. The grey had seeped into the house. Together with the lingering smell of earth it made me feel buried alive.

I roamed the house as though it was a cage. Once, as I wandered into the lounge, I thought two figures were waiting in the dimness, arms outstretched to grab me. They were dress forms, and the arms of their dresses hung limp at their sides; I couldn't see how I had made the mistake.

My aunt did most of the chatting at dinner. I kept imagining Fanny Cave in her cottage, her long limbs folded up like a spider's in hiding. The cottage must be larger than it looked, but she certainly lived in a lair in the earth – in the mud, on a day like this.

After dinner we played cards. When I began to nod sleepily my aunt continued playing, though she knew I had a long coach journey in the morning; perhaps she wanted company. By the time I went to bed the rain had stopped; a cheesy moon hung in a rainbow. As I undressed I heard her pegging clothes on the line below my window.

When I'd packed my case I parted the curtains for a last drowsy look at the view. The fells were a moonlit patchwork, black and white. Why was my aunt taking so long to hang out the clothes? I peered down more sharply. There was no sign of her. The clothes were moving by themselves, dancing and swaying in the moonlight, inching along the line towards the house.

When I raised the sash of the window the night seemed perfectly still, no sign of a breeze. Nothing moved on the lawn except the shadows of the clothes, advancing a little and retreating, almost ritualistically. Hovering dresses waved holes where hands should be, nodded the sockets of their necks.

Were they really moving towards the house? Before I could tell, the line gave way, dropping them into the mud of the lawn. When I heard my aunt's vexed cry I slipped the window shut and retreated into bed; somehow I didn't want to admit what I'd seen, whatever it was. Sleep came so quickly that next day I could believe I'd been dreaming.

I didn't tell my parents; I'd learned to suppress details that they might find worrying. They were uneasy with my aunt – she was too careless of propriety, the time she had taken them tramping the fells she'd mocked them for dressing as though they were going out for dinner. I think the only reason they let me stay with her was to get me out of the polluted Birmingham air.

By the time I was due for my next visit I was more than ready. My voice had broken, my body had grown unfamiliar; I felt clumsy, ungainly, neither a man nor myself. My parents didn't help. They'd turned wistful as soon as my voice began to change; my mother treated visitors to photographs of me as a baby. She and my father kept telling me to concentrate on my studies and examining my school books as if pornography might lurk behind the covers. They seemed relieved that I attended a boys' school, until my father started wondering nervously if I was 'particularly fond' of any of the boys. After nine months of this sort of thing I was glad to get away at Easter.

As soon as the coach moved off I felt better. In half an hour it left behind the Midlands hills, reefs built of red brick terraces. Lancashire seemed so flat that the glimpses of distant hills might have been mirages. After a couple of hours the fells began, great deceptively gentle monsters that slept at the edges of lakes blue as ice, two sorts of stillness. At least I would be free for a week.

But I was not, for I'd brought my new feelings with me. I knew that as soon as I saw my aunt walking upstairs. She had always seemed much younger than my mother, though there was only two years between them, and I'd been vaguely aware that she often wore tight jeans; now I saw how round her bottom was. I felt breathless with guilt in case she guessed what I was thinking, yet I couldn't look away.

At dinner, whenever she touched me I felt a shock of excitement, too strange and uncontrollable to be pleasant. Her skirts were considerably shorter than my mother's. My feelings crept up on me like the wine, which seemed to be urging them on. Half my conversation seemed fraught with double meanings. At last I found what I thought was a neutral subject. 'Have you seen Fanny Cave again?' I said.

'Only once.' My aunt seemed reluctant to talk about her. 'She'd given away some more dresses, and Mrs Gibson referred the mother to me. They were nastier than the others – I'm sure she would have thrown them away even if I hadn't said anything. But old Fanny came storming up here, just a few weeks ago. When I wouldn't let her in she stood out there in the pouring rain, threatening all sorts of things.'

'What sorts of things?'

'Oh, just unpleasant things. In the old days they would have burned her at the stake, if that's what they used to do. Anyway,' she said with a frown to close the subject, 'she's gone now.'

'Dead, you mean?' I was impatient with euphemisms.

'Nobody knows for sure. Most people think she's in the pond. To tell you the truth, I don't think anyone's anxious to look.'

Of course I was. I lay in bed and imagined probing the pond that nobody else dared search, a dream that seemed preferable to the thoughts that had been tormenting me recently as I tried to sleep. Next day, as I walked to the path, I peeled myself a fallen branch.

Bypassing the pond, I went first to the cottage. I could hear what sounded like a multitude of flies down in the trough. Was the cottage more overgrown than when I'd last seen it? Was that why it looked shrunken by decay, near to collapse? The single dusty window made me think of a dulling eye, half-engulfed by moss; the façade might have been a dead face that was falling inwards. Surely the flies were attracted by wild flowers – but I didn't want to go down into the crack; I hurried back to the pond.

Flies swarmed there too, bumbling above the scum. As I approached they turned on me. They made the air in front of my face seem dark, oppressive, infected. Nevertheless I poked my stick through the green skin and tried to sound the pond while keeping back from the slippery edge.

The depths felt muddy, soft and clinging. I poked for a while, until I began to imagine what I sought to touch. All at once I was afraid that something might grab the branch, overbalance me, drag me into the opaque depths. Was it a rush of sweat that made my clothes feel heavy and obstructive? As I shoved myself back, a breeze clutched them, hindering my retreat. I fled, skidding on mud, and saw the branch sink lethargically. A moment after it vanished the slime was unbroken.

That night I told Aunt Naomi where I'd been. I didn't think she would mind; after all, Fanny Cave was supposed to be out of the way. But she bent lower over her sewing, as if she didn't want to hear. 'Please don't go there again,' she said. 'Now let's talk about something else.'

'Why?' At that age I had no tact at all.

'Oh, for heaven's sake. Because I think she probably died on her way home from coming here. That's the last time anyone saw her. She must have been in such a rage that she slipped at the edge of the pond – I told you it was pouring with rain. Well, how was I to know what had happened?'

Perhaps her resentment concealed a need for reassurance, but I was unable to help, for I was struggling with the idea that she had been partly responsible for someone's death. Was nothing in my life to be trusted? I was so deep in brooding that I was hardly able to look at her when she cried out.

Presumably her needle had slipped on the thimble; she'd driven the point beneath one of her nails. Yet as she hurried out, furiously sucking her finger, I found that my gaze was drawn to the dress she had been sewing. As she'd cried out – of course it must have been then, not before – the dress had seemed to twist in her hands, jerking the needle.

When I went to bed I couldn't sleep. The room smelled faintly of earth; was that something to do with spring? The wardrobe door kept opening, though it had never behaved like that before, and displaying my clothes suspended bat-like in the dark. Each time I got up to close the door their shapes looked less familiar, more unpleasant. Eventually I managed to sleep, only to dream that dresses were waddling limblessly through the doorway of my room, towards the bed.

The next day, Sunday, my aunt suggested a walk on the fells. I would have settled for Skiddaw, the easiest of them, but it was already swarming with walkers like fleas. 'Let's go somewhere we'll be alone,' Aunt Naomi said, which excited me in ways I'd begun to enjoy but preferred not to define, in case that scared the excitement away.

We climbed Grisedale Pike. Most of it was gentle, until just below the summit we reached an almost vertical scramble up a narrow spiky ridge. I clung there with all my limbs, trapped thousands of feet above the countryside, afraid to go up or down. I was almost hysterical with self-disgust; I'd let my half-admitted fantasies lure me up here, when all my aunt had wanted was to enjoy the walk without being crowded by tourists. Eventually I managed to clamber to the summit, my face blazing.

As we descended, it began to rain. By the time we reached home we were soaked. I felt suffocated by the smell of wet earth, the water flooding down my face, the dangling locks of sodden hair that wouldn't go away. I hurried upstairs to change.

I had just about finished – undressing had felt like peeling wallpaper, except that I was the wall – when my aunt called out. Though she was in the next room, her voice sounded muffled. Before I could go to her she called again, nearer to panic. I hurried across the landing, into her room.

The walls were streaming with shadows. The air was dark as mud, in which she was struggling wildly. A shapeless thing was swallowing her head and arms. When I switched on the light I saw it was nothing; she'd become entangled in the jumper she was trying to remove, that was all.

'Help me,' she cried. She sounded as if she was choking, yet I didn't like to touch her; apart from a bra, her torso was naked. What was wrong with her, for God's sake? Couldn't she take off her jumper by herself? Eventually I helped her as best I could without touching her. It seemed glued to her, by the rain, I assumed. At last she emerged, red faced and panting.

Neither of us said much at dinner. I thought her unease was directed at me, at the way I'd let her struggle. Or was she growing aware of my new feelings? That night, as I drifted into sleep, I thought I heard a jangling of hangers in the wardrobe. Perhaps it was just the start of a dream.

The morning was dull. Clouds swallowed the tops of the fells. My aunt lit fires in the downstairs rooms. I loitered about the house for a while, hoping for a glimpse of customers undressing, until the dimness made me claustrophobic. Firelight set the shadows of dress forms dancing spastically on the walls; when I stood with my back to the forms their shadows seemed to raise their arms.

I caught a bus to Keswick, for want of something to do. The bus had passed Fanny Cave's path before I thought of looking. I glanced back sharply, but a bend in the road intervened. Had I glimpsed a scarecrow by the pond, its sleeves fluttering? But it had seemed to rear up: it must have been a bird.

In Keswick I followed leggy girls up the narrow hilly streets, dawdled nervously outside pubs and wondered if I looked old enough to risk buying a drink. When I found myself in the library, leafing desultorily through broken paperbacks, I went home. There was nothing by the pond that I could see, though closer to Aunt Naomi's house something grey was flapping in the grass – litter, I supposed.

The house seemed more oppressive than ever. Though my aunt tended to use whichever room she was in for sewing, she was generally tidy; now the house was crowded with half-finished clothes, lolling on chairs, their necks yawning. When I tried to chat at dinner my voice sounded muffled by the presence of so much cloth.

My aunt drank more than usual, and seemed not to care if I did too. My drinking made the light seem yellowish, suffocated.

Soon I felt very sleepy. 'Stay down a little longer,' my aunt mumbled, jerking herself awake, when I made to go to bed. I couldn't understand why she didn't go herself. I chatted mechanically, about anything except what might be wrong. Firelight brought clothes nodding forward to listen.

At last she muttered, 'Let's go to bed.' Of course she meant that unambiguously, yet it made me nervous. As I undressed hastily I heard her below me in the kitchen, opening the window a notch for air. A moment later the patch of light from the kitchen went out. I wished it had stayed lit for just another moment, for I'd glimpsed something lying beneath the empty clothesline.

Was it a nightdress? But I'd never seen my aunt hang out a nightdress, nor pyjamas either. It occurred to me that she must sleep naked. That disturbed me so much that I crawled into bed and tried to sleep at once, without thinking.

I dreamed I was buried, unable to breathe, and when I awoke I was. Blankets, which felt heavy as collapsed earth, had settled over my face. I heaved them off me and lay trying to calm myself, so that I would sink back into sleep – but by the time my breathing slowed I realized I was listening.

The room felt padded with silence. Dimness draped the chair and dressing table, blurring their shapes; perhaps the wardrobe door was ajar, for I thought I saw vague forms hanging ominously still. Now I was struggling to fall asleep before I could realize what was keeping me awake. I drew long slow breaths to lull myself, but it was no use. In the silence between them I heard something sodden creeping upstairs.

I lay determined not to hear. Perhaps it was the wind or the creaking of the house, not the sound of a wet thing slopping stealthily upstairs at all. Perhaps if I didn't move, didn't make a noise, I would hear what it really was – but in any case I was incapable of moving, for I'd heard the wet thing flop on the landing outside my door.

For an interminable pause there was silence, thicker than ever, then I heard my aunt's door open next to mine. I braced myself for her scream. If she screamed I would go to her, I would have to. But the scream never came; there was only the sound of her pulling something sodden off the floor. Soon I heard her padding downstairs barefoot, and the click of a lock.

Everything was all right now. Whatever it had been, she'd dealt with it. Perhaps wallpaper had fallen on the stairs, and she'd gone down to throw it out. Now I could sleep – so why couldn't I? Several minutes passed before I was conscious of wondering why she hadn't come back upstairs.

I forced myself to move. There was nothing to fear, nothing now outside my door – but I got dressed to delay going out on the landing. The landing proved to be empty, and so did the house. Beyond the open front door the prints of Aunt Naomi's bare feet led over the moist lawn towards the road.

The moon was doused by clouds. Once I reached the road I couldn't see my aunt's tracks, but I knew instinctively which way she'd gone. I ran wildly towards Fanny Cave's path. Hedges, mounds of congealed night, boxed me in. The only sound I could hear was the ringing of my heels on the asphalt.

I had just reached the gap in the hedge when the moon swam free. A woman was following the path towards the pond, but was it my aunt? Even with the field between us I recognized the grey dress she wore. It was Fanny Cave's.

I was terrified to set foot on the path until the figure turned a bend and I saw my aunt's profile. I plunged across the field, tearing my way through the grass. It might have been quicker to follow the path, for by the time I reached the gap into the second field she was nearly at the pond.

In the moonlight the surface of the pond looked milky, fungoid. The scum was broken only by a rock, plastered with strands of grass, close to the edge towards which my aunt was walking. I threw myself forward, grass slashing my legs.

When I came abreast of her I saw her eyes, empty except for two shrunken reflections of the moon. I knew not to wake a sleepwalker, and so I caught her gently by the shoulders, though my hands wanted to shake, and tried to turn her away from the pond.

She wouldn't turn. She was pulling towards the scummy water, or Fanny Cave's dress was, for the drowned material seemed to writhe beneath my hands. It was pulling towards the rock whose eyes glared just above the scum, through glistening strands which were not grass but hair.

It seemed there was only one thing to do. I grabbed the neck of the dress and tore it down. The material was rotten, and tore easily. I dragged it from my aunt's body and flung it towards the pond. Did it land near the edge then slither into the water? All I knew was that when I dared to look the scum was unbroken.

My aunt stood there naked and unaware until I draped my anorak around her. That seemed to rouse her. She stared about for a moment, then down at herself. 'It's all right, Naomi,' I said awkwardly.

She sobbed only once before she controlled herself, but I could see that the effort was cruel. 'Come on, quickly,' she said in a voice older and harsher than I'd ever heard her use, and strode home without looking at me.

Next day we didn't refer to the events of the night; in fact, we hardly spoke. No doubt she had lain awake all night as I had, as uncomfortably aware of me as I was of her. After breakfast she said that she wanted to be left alone, and asked me to go home early. I never visited her again; she always found a reason why I couldn't stay. I suspect the reasons served only to prevent my parents from questioning me.

Before I went home I found a long branch and went to the pond. It didn't take much probing for me to find something solid but repulsively soft. I drove the branch into it again and again, until I felt things break. My disgust was so violent it was beyond defining. Perhaps I already knew deep in myself that since the night I undressed my aunt I would never be able to touch a woman.

Christopher Priest

The miraculous cairn

*Christopher Priest is a lanky figure much in evidence at science
fiction conventions, discussing the mystique of creativity and
cursing publishers for putting rocket ships on his psychological
novels. He was born in 1943. He became a full-time writer in
1968, encouraged by a commission to expand two of his short
stories into his first novel,* Indoctrinaire. *His other novels
include* Fugue for a Darkening Island, Inverted World *(winner
of the British Science Fiction Association Award),* The Space
Machine *(which won the Ditmar Award) and* A Dream of
Wessex.*

*Chris is another of the science fiction writers I wanted to coax
into this anthology, and both of us were pleased when I
succeeded: he'd been suffering a writer's block (virtually the
worst thing that can befall a writer, an absolute inability to
write) and brooding over the Situations Vacant columns. Since
then he has written his two most disturbing novels,* The
Glamour *and* The Affirmation, *which bears a unique
relationship to the story you are about to read.*

I

The island of Seevl lies like a dark shadow over my memories
of childhood. It was always physically there, sprawling across
the horizon opposite Jethra Harbour, blurring sometimes into
the low clouds of storms, standing out at other times as a black,
rugged outline against the southern sky. Its landscape was not
unlike that of the mountains around Jethra, but there was a
saying amongst us that the rocks and soil our ancestors had no
use for had been thrown out to sea to make Seevl.

327

The closeness of Seevl to Jethra had created an inevitable bond – family ties, trading agreements, old alliances – but although to the Jethrans it was just an off-shore island, politically it was a part of the Dream Archipelago. Journeys between mainland and island were forbidden, except with official permission from the Seigniory, but a ferry still ran every day in defiance of the ban, openly and commercially. Officialdom turned a blind eye, because trade was important to Jethra, and crucial to Seevl. I myself travelled to Seevl many times, three or four times a year, for several years of my childhood.

II

It was twenty years since I had visited Seevl, and sixteen years since leaving Jethra. The last time I saw the city was when I left to go to university in Old Haydl, and I had never returned. Twenty years of mixed fortune, with most of the success on the surface, misleadingly. I had a passable education, an interesting career. I had avoided war-service so far, and was now probably too old to be caught up in it, except incidentally. Many friends of my own age (I was thirty-four) had volunteered, but it was not for me. As a teacher I was officially exempted, and if I searched my conscience I knew that the work I was doing was more useful than any war-work might have been. I had done well in teaching, or well enough to have self-esteem and the respect of my colleagues.

Internally, though, those twenty years had been less successful, and it was returning to Jethra, with Seevl looming on the horizon, that brought it to mind.

Jethra was the old capital of our country, but because of the war and the need for decentralized government, there had been an exodus to the newer, less exposed cities inland. There was still a token government presence in Jethra, but the Seignior's Palace was unoccupied, and the Senate House had been bombed at the outbreak of war. Now there was just the fishing, and a certain amount of light industry, and Jethra had become a large, desolate ghost of a city.

A return to the place of childhood is a gathering of reminders. For me, Jethra was life with my parents, schooling, old friends with whom I had lost contact . . . and Seevl. Not an uncommon grouping of memories, perhaps, but between them they had the effect of reminding me of what I had become.

This became clear as I sat on the train going to Jethra, thinking of the past. I had not actually chosen to make this journey, because there was family business I had to resolve, but neither did I make it unwillingly. I was curious to see Jethra again, and nervous of travelling to Seevl, but I felt it was time, after twenty years, to confront the past.

III

When I was a child, the closeness of Seevl had a foreboding quality for everyone, and certainly for the other children at school. 'Send you to Seevl', was the ultimate childish threat, with unstated connotations of eternal damnation and terror. In our alternate world of invented myth, Seevl was populated by bogeymen and creeping horrors, and the actual landscape of the island was thought to be a nightmare terrain of crevasses and volcanic pools, steaming craters and shifting rocks. This vision was as true for me, in an imaginative sense, as it was for all Jethra children, but with a child's unconscious ability to see the world from a number of different viewpoints, I also knew Seevl for what it really was.

It was no less horrifying to me in reality, but its horrors were acutely personal.

I was an only child. My parents, both Jethrans, had had another child before me, but she had died a year before I was born. I came into a world where my life was guarded for reasons I could not begin to understand until I had almost grown up. In some ways I can now sympathize with the protective way my parents brought me up, but it meant that when I was more than just a child – in my early and middle teens – I was still being treated as some precious object that had to be guarded against all the possible dangers and threats of life. While youngsters of my own age were hanging around in gangs, and getting into scrapes, and learning about sex, I was expected to be at home and sharing my parents' friends and interests. These were numerous, and although some were not uninteresting, they were hardly the normal activities of a teenager. Other filial duties, though, I entered into with a sense of duty and numb acceptance, suppressing the urge to evade them. The most unwelcome of these was to go with my parents on their regular visits to see my father's brother on Seevl.

My Uncle Torm was a few years younger than my father,

329

but had married at about the same time: there was a photo-graph in our living room of the two young men with their brides, and although I recognized the youthful versions of my father, mother and uncle easily enough, it took me years to realize that the pretty young woman holding Torm's arm in the photograph was my Aunt Alvie.

In the picture she was smiling, and I had never seen Alvie smile. She was wearing a gay, flowery dress, and I had never seen Aunt Alvie in anything except an old nightgown and a patched cardigan. Her hair was short and wavy, cut attractively about her face, and Aunt Alvie's hair was long and greasy and grey. And the girl in the picture was standing beside her new husband, raising one leg to show her knee coquettishly to the camera, and my Aunt Alvie was a bedridden cripple.

Torm and Alvie had moved to Seevl soon after their mar-riage, just before the war started. He had taken a clerical job at a catholic seminary in the remotest part of the Seevl moun-tains; his reasons for this I do not understand to this day, but I do know that it caused a bitter, if short-lived, row between him and my father.

They were there with their new baby on Seevl when war broke out, and were unable to return to Jethra. By the time the war had settled into its interminable routine of attritional skir-mishes, under which circumstances a certain amount of move-ment between Seevl and Jethra was possible, Aunt Alvie had been taken ill and was not to be moved.

It was in this climate that my parents made their occasional weekend visits to Seevl, to see Torm and Alvie, and to take me with them. For me they were weekends of unrelieved dreari-ness and depression: a voyage to a bleak, windswept island, to a cramped and dark house on the edge of a moor, and a house at that where a sickbed was the centre of attention, and where the conversations at best were about other adult relatives and at worst about sickness and pain and false hopes of a miracu-lous recovery. The only distraction from all this, and the ostensible reason for my being there, was Torm and Alvie's daughter, my cousin Seri. She was a few months older than me, and plump and rather stupid, and we were the worst kind of companions to each other. The prospect of her company did nothing to relieve those long days of dread before a visit, and afterwards the memory of it did nothing to help me recover from the profound moods of depression that always followed.

As I left the station, a young woman in Seigniorial uniform
opened a car door and walked across to me.

'Are you Lenden Cros?' she said to me.

'Yes.'

'I am Serjeant Reeth. I am your escort.'

We went to the car, and I placed my bag on the back seat.
She held the door open for me, like a chauffeuse, but before I
was properly seated she walked around to her own side. She
started the engine.

'Where are we going?' I said.

'The ferry does not sail until the morning. We will stay overnight at the Grand Shore Hotel.'

She drove out of the station square, and turned into a main
road leading towards the centre. I watched the buildings of the
city through the window. We had lived in the suburbs, and I
knew the centre only superficially. I recognized buildings,
names of streets, and some had vague but poignant associations
for me. As a child, I had known Jethra's centre as the place
where my father worked, where my mother sometimes went
shopping, and the street names were landmarks from their territory. The city now looked disused and unloved: there were
office blocks, shops, civic buildings, but many of them were
boarded up and litter blew across the steps. There was not much
traffic in the streets: several cars in various stages of decay, a
few trucks, a surprising number of horse-drawn vehicles.

We were held up for a few seconds at a large intersection.

I said: 'Are you from Jethra?'

'No.'

'You seem to know where you are going.'

'I arrived this morning. I've had time to explore.'

The traffic moved on, and the conversation ended.

I had never stayed at the Grand Shore Hotel, had never even
been through its doors. It was the largest, most expensive hotel
in town. In my childhood it had been the scene of society wed-
dings, business conferences and many glittering civic occasions. We drew up in the car park outside the main entrance,
with its imposing and solid façade of smoke-dirtied red brick.

Serjeant Reeth stood back as I registered for my room. The
clerk pushed across two pieces of white card for my signature.
One was for a room in my own name, the other, an adjacent
number, was for Serjeant Reeth.

A porter took my bag, and led us up the wide, curving stair-case to the next floor. There were mirrors and chandeliers, a plush carpet on the stairs, gold paint on the plaster ceiling-mouldings . . . but the mirrors were unpolished, the carpet was worn and the paint was peeling. The hotel's grandeur was in-herited from the days before the war. The muted sounds of our climbing seemed like memories of those famous parties of the past.

The porter opened the door to my room, and went in ahead of me. Serjeant Reeth went to her own door and inserted the key. For a moment she glanced back at me, and something in her expression took me by surprise: I detected a curiosity, a quick interest?

I tipped the porter, and he left. He had placed my bag on a low table by the door, so I took out my clothes and hung them in the wardrobe. I went to the basin, washed off the grime from the train journey, and put on clean clothes. Then I sat on the edge of the bed and looked around at the dingy room.

It was an unexpected position from which to contemplate my past; I had imagined that we would have gone straight across to Seevl, and had not realized that we were, of course, depen-dent on the ferry. How were we to spend the evening? I sup-posed the policewoman would have arranged that too.

I recalled the look that Serjeant Reeth had given me, as we went into our rooms. She reminded me of someone I had once known, a girl of about the same age, with similar build and colouring. She was one of many lovers I had had at one time, when a succession of young women had passed through my life. Perhaps if I had met Serjeant Reeth then, she would have been one of them, but I was older now. I knew that such affaires almost always ended in emotional disaster; I had made no casual pick-ups for years, preferring the less intense discontents of sexlessness.

Serjeant Reeth was the same sort of reminder of the past as Jethra itself had become, and she induced in me much the same quality of depression.

I was thirsty, so I left my room and went towards the stair-case, thinking I would visit the bar. When I reached the head of the stairs I thought I should, out of politeness, see if the policewoman would join me.

She answered my knock on her door after only a moment's delay, as if she had been standing by the door, waiting for me.

'I'm going downstairs for a drink,' I said. 'Will you join me?'

'That would be nice. Thank you.'

We went downstairs and found the bar. It was locked, and there were no lights on inside. We went into the lounge, rang a bell, and in a moment an elderly waiter came to serve us.

When he had taken our order and left the lounge, I said, making conversation: 'Have you worked as an escort before, Serjeant Reeth?'

'No . . . this is the first time.'

'Does the work come up very often?'

'I'm not sure. I have only been in the Seigniory for a year.'

Just then the waiter returned with our drinks.

'Will you be dining in this evening?' he said to me.

'Yes.'

When he had gone I looked around the lounge; we were the only people there. I liked the airy, gracious feeling in the room, with the big windows and long velvet drapes, the high Consort-ship lightshades, and the broadbacked wicker chairs grouped about the low tables. There were dozens of potted plants, great spreading ferns and tall parlour-palms, lending a feeling of sedate livingness to an otherwise decaying hotel. All the plants were green and alive, so someone must still be looking after them, dusting them and watering them.

We sat in silence for several minutes, and I had plenty of opportunity to try to assess my companion of the next day or two. I placed her age at about twenty-four or five. She was no longer wearing her cap, but the uniform – stiff, sexless and unflattering – effectively neutered her. She wore no make-up, and her hair was drawn back into a bun. She seemed shy and uncommunicative, and unaware of my regard.

At last, it was she who broke the silence.

'Have you been across to Seevl before?'

'I was taken there several times as a child,' I said. 'What about you?'

'No.'

'Do you know what it's like there?'

'I'm told it's bleak. Is that how you remember it?'

'More or less. It's twenty years since I was there. It won't have changed much.' I tried my drink, swallowing much of it, hoping it would ease the conversation. 'I used to hate going across there. I always dreaded it.'

'Why?'

'Oh . . . the mood of the place, the scenery,' I said vaguely, avoiding specific memories. The seminary, Alvie, the open moors and the dead towers. 'I can't describe it. You feel it as soon as you land.'

'You sound like my brother. He says he can always tell if a house is haunted.'

'I didn't say the place was haunted,' I said, quick to the defence. 'It's a question of the landscape. And the wind . . . you can always hear the wind.'

Jethra itself was built in the shadow of the Murinan Hills, but beyond these, to the west, was a wide, straight valley that led northwards into the foothills of the northern range. For all but a few short weeks at the height of summer, a polar wind came down the valley and escaped out to sea, whining across Seevl's treeless fells and moors. Only on the eastern side of the island, nearest to Jethra, were there villages of any size, and the only port, Seevl Town, was there. One of my clearest childhood memories of Seevl was seeing it in the springtime. I could look out to the south from my bedroom window, and see the blossom shining pink and white and bright red on the trees along the boulevards in Jethra, and beyond, out in the blue Midway Sea, there would be Seevl, still with its wintertime crust of snow.

Serjeant Reeth's mention of a brother had given me, for the first time, a little information about her background. I asked her about him. He was also in the Seigniory, she told me, serving with the Border Police. He was hoping for promotion, because his unit was soon to be shipped across to the southern continent. The war was still confused and confusing: neither side would admit to being the first to send an expeditionary force to the south – claims and counter-claims came from both sides – but almost every week there was news of more troops being sent out. That very morning, before setting out from home to catch the train, I had heard news of government claims that the enemy was building a transit-camp on one of the islands in the Dream Archipelago. If this was true it marked a new stage in the war, because the political status of the islands was controlled by a Covenant of Neutrality.

It was the precarious state of the neutrality that had involved me with the Seigniory: the request from the Father Confessor that I should visit my uncle's house to sort out his belongings had been channelled through the Seigniorial Visa Department If it had come direct to me, if the priests at the seminary had

334

had my address, I could have slipped across unofficially. But that was not to be. Thus my need to be escorted, thus Serjeant Reeth.

I was telling her the reason for my trip – the need to sign papers, to permit furniture to be burnt or given away – when the waiter returned. He was carrying two menu-folders, so discreetly implying that the dining-room staff were ready for us. While we perused the menu the waiter drew the curtains, then led us down the corridor to the dining room.

V

My last visit to Seevl. I was fourteen.

There were examinations at school and I was trying to concentrate on them, but I knew that at the end of the week we were going to see my uncle and aunt and cousin. It was summer, and Jethra was dusty and windless. Sitting by my bedroom window, distracted from my revision, I looked frequently out to sea. Seevl was green then, a dark, tough green; a coloured lie, a deceit of lushness. Day followed day, and I thought about feigning illness: a migraine attack, a sudden bout of gastroenteritis, but at last the day arrived and there was no avoiding it. We were out of the house soon after dawn – in the cool, lovely light of summer, when no one else is about – and hurried down to the tram-stop to catch the first of the day.

What were these visits for? Unless my parents spoke in some adult code I have never been able to decipher, they went out of a combination of habit, guilt and family obligation. I never heard anything of interest discussed, in the way I now know educated adults can discuss matters (and both my parents were educated, and so was my uncle, although I cannot be sure about Alvie); there was news to impart, but it was stale news, trivial events in the family, not even interesting when fresh. Everything that passed between the four adults was familial or familiar: an aunt or cousin who had moved house or changed jobs, a nephew who married, a great-uncle who had died. Sometimes, photographs were passed around Alvie's sickbed: Cousin Jayn's new house (hasn't he done well?), or this is us on holiday, or isn't she a lovely baby? Family banality it was; it seemed so when I was a child and it seems so now. It was as if they had no ideas they could externalize, no sense of the abstract, or if they had it was deemed dangerous, not to be spoken

335

of. News of the family and old conversations revisited were a levelling device: it was almost as if they were instilling a sense of mediocrity into Alvie, to bring her to their level, to make her, that is, no longer ill. Mediocrity as medicine.

And where were their recollections? Did they have no past together, that they could reminisce about? My only hint of this forgotten past was the photograph taken before I was born, the one that sat in our living room. I was genuinely fascinated by it. When was it taken, and where? What were they doing that day? Who took the photograph? Was it a happy day, as seemed from the picture, or did something occur later to mar it? Why did none of them ever mention it?

It was probably Alvie's sickness. It suffused everything in past and present: her pain, her discomfort, her doctor and her pills. Death surrounded Alvie's sickbed, and occupied it. The disease was creeping through her. Every time we visited her she was a little worse. First her legs lost all sensation; then she became incontinent; then she could not take solid food. But if her decline was steady, it was also slow. News of further deterioration came by letters, so that whenever I saw her I did so with the prospect of seeing her arms withering, or her face decaying away, or her teeth falling out; the ghoulish imagination of childhood was never satisfied, disappointed even, once I had resigned myself to having to visit her again. There was always an inverse surprise: how well she looked! Only later, as the depressing news was exchanged, would we hear of new horrors, new agonies. Yet the years dragged by and Alvie was still there in her bed, propped up by eight or nine pillows, her hair in a lank skein over one shoulder. She grew fatter, and paler, more grotesque, but these would come to anyone who never got exercise, who never went outside. Her spirit was unfailing: her voice was always pitched on one note, sounding sad and dull and dreary, but the things she said were self-consciously normal. She reported her pain and setbacks, she did not complain about them. She knew the disease was killing her, but she talked of the future, even if it was a future of the narrowest vision (what would I like for my next birthday, what was I going to do when I left school?). She was an example to us all.

Whenever we made our visits, one of the priests would come in to see Alvie. I always suspected that no one ever came from the seminary unless there was someone there from the outside world to witness it. Alvie had 'courage'; she had 'fortitude'; she 'bore her cross'. I hated the priests in their black clothes, waving their white hands sanctimoniously over the bed, blessing not only Alvie but my family too. I sometimes thought it was the priests who were killing her; they were praying not for a cure but a lingering death, and they were doing it to make a theological point to their students. My uncle was godless, his job was just a job. There was Hope in religion, and to prove it to him the priests were killing Alvie: no one works in the service of the Lord as one toils in the vineyards. We shall save.

The last visit:

The boat was late; the man in the harbour office told us the engine was being repaired, and for a joyous moment I thought the trip would have to be cancelled . . . but then the ferry appeared in the harbour, coming slowly to the quay to collect us, and the handful of other passengers who stood with us.

It seemed, as soon as the boat was outside the harbour, that we were almost upon Seevl: the grey, limestone cliffs were dead ahead . . . but it was an hour's voyage to Seevl Town, the boat swinging far out to sea to avoid the shoals beneath Stromb Head, then turning in again to take the sheltered passage beneath the cliffs. I stood apart from my parents, staring up at the cliffs, watching for the occasional glimpses of the high fells beyond, and feeling the onset of the real, stomach-turning dread I always felt as we arrived. It was cold at sea, and though the sun was rising quickly the wind came curling down on to the passage from the cliffs above. My parents were in the bar with the other passengers, and I shared the deck with crates of livestock, packing-cases, newspapers, cases of drink, two tractors.

The houses of Seevl Town, built up in terraces on the hills around the harbour, were constructed from the grey rock of the island, the roofs whitened around the chimney-stacks with bird droppings. An orange lichen clung to the walls and roofs, souring the houses, making them seem not warm, but crumbling. On the highest hill, dominating the town, stood the derelict remains of a rock-built tower. I never looked directly at this, fearing it.

As the boat glided in on the still water my parents came out of the saloon and stood beside me, one to each side, like an escort, preventing flight.

There was a car to be hired in Seevl Town; an expensive

luxury in Jethra, but a necessity for the wild interior of the island. My father had booked it a week before, but it was not ready and we had to wait an hour or more in a cold office overlooking the harbour. My parents were silent, trying to ignore me as I fidgeted and made fitful attempts to read the book I had brought.

Around Seevl Town were the few farms on the island, rearing their scrawny animals and growing their hybrid cereals on the barren soil of the eastern side. The road climbed up through these smallholdings, following the perimeters of the fields, and turning through sharp angles and steep climbing corners. The surface had been metalled once but now it was decaying, and the car lurched uncomfortably in the potholes and the wheels often spun on the gravelly sides. My father, driving, stayed silent, trying to master not only the dangerous road but also the controls of the unfamiliar vehicle; my mother sat beside him with the map, ready to direct him, but we always got lost on Seevl. I sat in the back, ignored by them both, except when my mother would turn to see what I was doing; I always did nothing, staring out of my window in mute suspension of thought.

It took nearly an hour to reach the first summit of the fells, by which time the last farm, the last hedge, the last tree, were miles behind us. There was a last glimpse of Seevl Town as the road went over the crest, and a wide view of the gun-metal sea, flecked with islets, and the indistinct shape of the mainland coast.

On the moors the road rose and fell with the whim of the country, winding through the scrub-covered land. Sometimes, the car would come out from a high pass, where on each side great crags of limestone loomed over the scree-slopes, and the blast of wind from the north would kick the car to the side. My father drove slowly, trying to avoid the loose rocks on the road, and the potholes; the map lay unconsulted on my mother's knee, because Father knew the way. Yet he always made mistakes, took the wrong turn or followed the wrong fork, and then Mother would sit quietly at his side until he realized. The map would be taken from her, the car would be reversed, and we would go back the way we had come to the place where we went wrong.

I left all this to them, although, like Mother, I usually knew when we went wrong. My interest was not with the road, but the landscape it passed through. I never failed to be appalled by the gigantic emptiness of Seevl, and Father's wrong turnings had for me the double advantage of not only delaying our eventual arrival at the seminary, but also of opening up more of the island to my eyes. The road often passed the dead towers of Seevl. I knew the islanders never went near these, but I did not know why; whenever the car passed one I could scarcely look towards it for fear, but my parents never even noticed. If we passed slowly, I would cower in my seat in anticipation of some ghoul of legend making a rush for the car.

Later in the journey the road itself deteriorated into a rough track, consisting of two gravel paths divided by a strip of long, coarse grass that scraped against the floor of the car.

Another hour passed, and then the road went down into a shallow valley where four of the dead towers stood like sentinels along the ridge. The valley was treeless, but there were many sprawling thorn-bushes, and in the lowest part, beside a wide stream, was a tiny hamlet with a view of the sea and the mainland. A part of Jethra could be seen: a black spread against the side of the Murinan Hills, and it seemed so close and foreign. Outside the village we climbed the high fells again, and I looked forward to one of the scenic surprises of the journey: the island was narrow for a distance, and crossing the moors the road touched on the southern side. For a few minutes we had a view of the Midway Sea beyond Seevl, with island after island spreading across it as far as the horizon. I never really considered Seevl to be a part of the Dream Archipelago. That was a different place: a lush, tropical maze of islands, hot and tranquil, forested or barren . . . but always dozing in the equatorial sun, and peopled by a strange race with customs and language as bizarre as their food, clothes and homes. But this fleeting glimpse, from the window of a car lurching along an unmade road on a cold grey island, was as close as I would ever be. The rest was dream.

Another valley; another hamlet. I knew we were approaching the seminary, and in spite of myself I was staring ahead, looking for the first sight of it.

VI

After dinner, Serjeant Reeth and I returned to our rooms, she because she said she wanted a bath and to wash her hair, and I because I could think of nowhere else to go. I sat for a while on the edge of my bed, staring at the carpet, then went to my suitcase and found the letter from the Father Confessor at the seminary. It was strange to read his ponderous, circumlocutory sentences, full of a stiff intent not only to engage my sympathies but also to intimidate me, and try to reconcile this with my adolescent bitterness about him and his priests. I remembered one occasion of many: I had been walking on a lawn at the seminary, innocently close to one of the flowerbeds, and a priest had appeared and reprimanded me severely. They could never leave it at that, because they had insights into the universe and I did not, and so I was warned of hell and my imminent and inevitable destiny. That priest was possibly now this reverend father, and the same implied threat was there: you must attend to your uncle's affairs, or we will fix the fates for you.

I lay back on the bed, thinking about Seevl, and wondering what it would be like to return. Would it depress me, as Jethra had done in the afternoon? Or would it scare me, as it had done in childhood? The priests and their heavenly machinations held no terror for me; Alvie was dead, and now so was Torm, both joining my parents, and a generation was gone. The island itself – as scenery, as a place – interested me, because I had only ever seen it with child's eyes, but I did not look forward to its emptiness. The dead towers . . . they were another matter, one I put aside. I had never come to terms with those, could only shun them as the islanders did. The difference, though, the factor that wrenched me into adult perspective, was the presence of Serjeant Reeth.

Her name was Bella; this she told me during dinner, and I, with wine inside me, had been unable to stop myself smiling. I had not known that policewomen had names like Bella, but there it was. She had an innocent quality to her, a certain wide-eyed ingenuousness; I liked it, but it made me feel my age. It seemed during the meal that our roles were reversing, that I, being older, was becoming her guardian for the journey. It had been too easy to forget that she was a member of the Seigniory, that if I spoke too freely or took her into my confidence, what I said might go into her report, might find its way on to a file.

Now I was alone again, it became a matter of personal reassurance. However much I might rationalize my fears, I did feel considerable trepidation about visiting Seevl again. If my Seigniory escort had been someone else – a man, perhaps, or someone older than myself – I might have sought psychological dependence on their presence . . . but because Bella was who she was, I felt differently. It would be I who took her to Seevl, not the other way around.

It was still too early to go to bed, so I found a book in my case, and lay on the bed to read it. Some time later, I was subconsciously aware that Bella must have returned to her room, because I heard her moving around.

Then, making me start a little, there was a tap on my door.

'Yes?' I called.

'Are you asleep, Lenden?'

'No . . . come in.'

The door opened, and she put her head around. She had a towel wrapped about her hair.

'I'm sorry to be a nuisance, but I'm trying to dry my hair. The plug on my drier is the wrong one. You haven't got an adaptor, have you, or a screwdriver so I can change the plug?'

She came into the room, closing the door behind her. I stared at her in surprise. She had changed out of her uniform, and was wearing a loose, silken wrap. Her face was pink, and where her robe was open at the neck I could see her skin had that glowing cleanliness that follows a hot bath. The wrap was thin and white, and I could not help but see that she was full-breasted, dark-nippled. Damp ringlets of hair fell from under the towel.

'I've got a penknife,' I said, trying not to reveal my reaction. 'We can take a plug off something in here.'

She stood by the door, holding her electric drier as I looked around for some appliance I could plunder. There was an electric radiator by the wall, but it had no independent plug. Then I saw the bedside lamp.

'Turn on the central light,' I said. 'I'll use this.'

'I know it sounds stupid,' she said, and gave me a little embarrassed smile. 'I have to dry my hair like this, otherwise it goes frizzy.'

I found my penknife, and started to unscrew the plug. She made me feel capable.

'Sit down, Bella. It'll only take a couple of minutes.'

She sat on the edge of the bed, folding one knee over the other, while I knelt on the floor, picking at the screws of the plug with the knife-blade. I did not look up at her; I was suddenly too conscious of her presence, her young body, her casually revealing wrap.

At last I got the plug off.

'Give me the drier,' I said, looking up at her. The towel had loosened, and more hair was falling free. I wanted to reach up and stroke it. She put a hand to the towel, rubbed it gently against her head with an up-and-down motion.

She said: 'Do you think we're the only people staying in the hotel?'

'It's very quiet. I haven't seen any other guests.'

The closed bar, the silent lounge. We had been alone at dinner, with the lights on around our table, but the rest of the room had been darkened. The attentive waiters, standing by the serving-door, responsive to every move we made, every request. Yet the menu had been a full one; the food had been freshly cooked, and was attractively served.

'I looked in the register this morning,' Bella said. 'No one else has booked in for more than a week.'

I looked up at her, but quickly bent my head over the plug. She was still towelling her hair; as she raised her arm she stretched the thin fabric of the robe across her body. The garment was working loose.

'It's the quiet season,' I said.

'I tried room-service just now, to see about the plug. No one answered.'

I screwed the back on the plug, and passed the drier up to her.

'That's fixed it,' I said.

'Do you mind if I dry my hair here? It won't take long, and I'd like company.'

I sat opposite her, in the one easy-chair in the room. She leaned down to connect the drier, then unwound the towel and played the warm stream of air over her. She swung her head, loosening the hair, then combed it through, playing the heat across it.

She was awakening things in me that had been dormant too long; I wished she had not come, yet I could not resist the feelings in me. With her hair loose she looked so young! As she dried her hair she was looking directly at me, with her head cocked on one side. She combed out several strands, holding them away from her head in the hot current, and as the hair dried it fell in a light cascade about her shoulders.

'Why don't you have your hair like that during the day? It's much more attractive.'

'Regulations. The collar must be seen.'

'Isn't it a strange job for a girl to have?'

'Why?' she said. 'The pay's good, and it's a secure job. I get a lot of travel, and meet people.'

'It just seems unfeminine.'

She was fingering the vee of her wrap, where the fabric crossed loosely above her breasts. 'Do I seem unfeminine?'

I shook my head, knowing that I had not meant it that way.

Her hair was dry. She bent down to unplug the drier, and for an instant, as her wrap fell forward, I caught a glimpse of her breast.

'Would you like me to stay?' She was sitting erect on the bed, looking at me.

I turned away, not knowing what to say. She got up from the bed, gathering the robe around her, and walked across to me. She gripped my arm lightly, just above the elbow. Her face was close to mine, and she was breathing quickly. I wanted to stroke her breasts, wanted to kiss her.

Still not meeting her gaze, I said: 'I'd like you to, but—'

I willed her to interrupt me before I had to invent an excuse, but she stayed silent.

'Do you find me attractive?' she said.

'Of course I do.'

She released my arm and picked up the drier, coiling the flex around it. She walked slowly towards the door.

'Please don't go!' I said.

'I thought you wanted me to.'

'Not yet . . . I want to explain. It's not your fault, and please don't be hurt.'

'I made a mistake,' said Bella.

'No . . . I'm not ready, that's all. I can't say why.'

She paused, with her head down, then turned and came back to me. For a moment her fingers twined themselves around my arm, and she kissed me quickly on the cheek. Before I could put my arm around her she stepped back.

'Goodnight, Lenden.'

She went quickly from the room, closing the door quietly behind her. I stood where I was, my eyes closed, deeply ashamed of myself. I could hear Bella in her room: a drawer opening and closing, water running, then silence. At last, when I could bear to, I went to the mirror and stood looking at myself for a long time, stretching the skin around my eyes, smoothing the tiredness.

I undressed and went to bed. I woke at periods through the night, straining to hear some sound of Bella, urging her mentally to come back to my room . . . for that, at least, would have resolved an uncertainty. Through it all, the nearness of her, the little glimpses of her young body, I had been attracted to her as I had not been attracted for a long time. Even so, deep down, I was terrified she would return. This struggle between attraction and repulsion had dogged my life. Ever since Seevl.

VII

The ticking clock by Alvie's bed, and the gusting wind rattling the window in its loose frame; these were the only sounds in the pauses between conversation. I sat by the draughty window, looking down into the gardens outside and watching a black-robed priest tending one of the flowerbeds with a rake. The lawns and beds of the seminary's grounds were brightly incongruous on Seevl, an island within an island, constantly watered and fertilized and prodded. When we went in the winter months only the lawns survived, but today there were clusters of tough-looking flowers, gripping the paltry earth with shallow roots. If I craned my neck I could see the huge vegetable garden where the students were made to work, and on the other side of the grounds, invisible from Alvie's room, was a small livestock farm. The seminary tried to keep itself, but I knew that food was brought in from outside, because that was part of my uncle's job to organize. Why had the priests lied about this, when I was shown around the seminary once? They must have known my uncle ordered food and fuel-oil from Seevl Town, so what was the point of maintaining the fiction that they were entirely independent of the world?

The priest at the flowerbed had glanced up when I first sat by the window, but since then he had ignored me. How long before he, or one of the others, came to see Alvie?

I looked across to the rising ground beyond the seminary walls. The skyline was a long, straight crag, with sloping scree beneath it, and below that the rank wild grass of the moors. There was one of the dead towers out there, a short way from the seminary, but it was one of the less conspicuous ones on Seevl, standing not against the sky, but against the duller background of the crag.

344

My parents had started to discuss me: Lenden was taking examinations, Lenden had not been studying properly, Lenden was not doing well. I sometimes wished I had the sort of parents who boasted about their child, but their method, at least with relatives, was to try to embarrass me into making greater efforts. I loathed them for it: the embarrassment I felt was the sort that made me resentful, even less willing to apply myself. I looked over at Seri, who was sitting by herself at a table in the corner of the room, apparently reading a book. She was listening, of course, while pretending not to, and when she saw me turn in her direction she looked back with a blank stare. No support there.

'Come here, Lenden,' said Aunt Alvie; it was the sort of moment I always dreaded.

'Go to your aunt, Lenden,' said my father.

Reluctantly I left my seat by the window, and went to stand beside the head of the bed. She stretched out a palsied hand, and took mine.

'You must work harder,' she said. 'For the sake of your future. For me. You want me to get well, don't you?'

'Yes,' I said, although I did not see the connection. I was acutely aware of my parents watching me, of Seri's feigned indifference, and the embarrassment intensified.

'When I was your age,' Aunt Alvie said, 'I won every prize at school. It wasn't as much fun as being lazy, but in the end I was glad. You do understand, don't you?' She wanted my future to be like her present; she wanted to inflict her illness on me. I shrank away from her, as if her disease were contagious, but the pressure on my hand increased. 'Now kiss me.'

I was always having to kiss Alvie: when we arrived, before and after every meal, as we departed. It was part of the dread. I leaned forward, presenting my cheek to her cyanotic lips, but my reluctance held me back and she pulled my hand towards her. As her lips touched coldly against my skin I felt her pressing my hand against her breast; her coarse cardigan, the thin nightdress, the flaccid flesh. In turn, I kissed her cold white cheek, then tried to move away, but my hand was still clasped against her chest.

'Promise me you'll try harder from now on,' Alvie said.

'I promise.'

I tugged my hand away, and, so released, I stumbled back from the bed and returned to my chair. My face was hot with the indignity of the interview, and I saw a satisfied look on my father's face. We had endless rows at home about the marks I got at school, and now he had recruited an ally. Sitting by the window, staring sightlessly out across the lawns, I waited for them to find another topic to discuss. But they would not leave me.

'Why don't you go out for a walk, Lenden?'

I said nothing.

'Seri, take Lenden to see your den.'

'I'm reading,' Seri said, in a voice that tried to convey preoccupation.

'Seri!' said Uncle Torm. 'Take your cousin for a walk. You'd like to see Seri's den, wouldn't you, Lenden?'

'Yes,' I said. We were being dispatched; something adult and perhaps interesting was going to be discussed. Medical treatment, no doubt, details of bedpans and suppositories. I should not have minded hearing about those.

Seri and I looked at each other with mutual resignation, and she closed her book. She led me out of the room, down the gloomy and must-smelling corridor and out of the house. We crossed the garden, and came out through a gate in a brick wall into the main grounds of the seminary. Here Seri hesitated.

'What do you want to do?'

'Have you got a den?'

'That's what *they* call it. It's my hide-out.'

'Can I see it?' I sometimes climbed a tree in the garden at home, to be by myself, but I had never had a proper hide-out. 'Is it secret?'

'Not really. But I don't let anyone in I don't want there.'

'Will you let me in?'

'I suppose so.'

We walked along a gravel drive edging one of the lawns. From one of the open windows there came the sound of voices chanting a psalm. I walked with my feet scuffing up the gravel, to drown the sound, because it reminded me of school.

We came at last to one of the long wings of the seminary building. Seri led me towards some railings beside the base of the main wall, beyond which were some narrow stone steps leading down to a basement. A priest, hoeing a flowerbed, paused in his work to watch us.

Seri ignored him, and went down the steps. At the bottom she got down on her hands and knees and crawled through a low, dark hatchway. When she was inside she turned around and stuck out her head to look at me. I was still waiting at the top of the steps.

'Come on, Lenden. I'll show you something.'

The priest was working again, but glancing back over his shoulder to look at me. I went quickly down the steps, and crawled in through the hatchway.

Seri's hide-out had once been some kind of store or cellar, because there were no windows, and the hatch was the only way in or out. The ceiling was high enough for us to stand erect. It was dark and cool, and Seri was lighting three or four candles placed high on a shelf. The tiny cell smelled of match phosphor and candlewax, and soot. There were two up-ended boxes to sit on, and from somewhere Seri had found an old mat for the floor.

'What do you do in here?' I said enviously, thinking at once of all the fantasies I could live out if it were my own.

'That's what I'm going to show you.'

The candles cast a weak yellow light, although now my eyes had adjusted from the bright daylight it seemed perfectly adequate. I sat down on a box.

I had been expecting Seri to sit on the other box, but she came and stood in front of me.

She said: 'Do you want to know a secret, Lenden?'

'What sort of secret?'

'The special sort.'

'All right,' I said, without much interest, still very much under the cloud of Aunt Alvie and the others, and so assuming it was going to be something to do with that.

'How old are you, Lenden?'

'Fourteen.'

'I'm fifteen. Have you got any hair yet?'

'Hair?' Of course I had hair; it was constantly falling in my eyes, and I was always being told to cut it.

'This is a dead secret. Just between you and me.'

Before I realized what she was talking about, Seri quickly raised the front of her skirt, and with her other hand pulled down the front of her pants. I saw a tangly black bush of hair, at the junction of her legs.

I was so surprised that I almost fell off the box. Seri let go, and the elastic in her pants snapped them back into place, but she did not release the skirt. She held this high against her

347

chest, looking down at herself. Her pants were dark-coloured and woollen, and the elastic bit into the plump flesh of her stomach.

I was acutely embarrassed – my own pubic hair had started growing some months before, and it was a matter of mystery, astonishment and shame, all mixed up together – but I was also compulsively interested.

'Let me see again,' I said.

She stepped back, almost as if she was uncertain, but then came forward again.

'You pull it down,' she said, thrusting her abdomen towards me.

Nervously, I reached forward, took the top of her pants in my fingers, and pulled the cloth down until I could just see the first growth of hair.

'Further!' she said, knocking my hand out of the way. She pulled the pants down, front and back, so that they clung around her thighs. Her triangle of hair, curling and black, stood unambiguously before me. I could not stop staring at her, feeling hot and prickly, and with a sudden and quite unmistakable stirring of arousal. I said nothing.

'Do you want a feel?' Seri said.

'No . . .'

'Touch me. I want you to feel.'

'I'm not sure I should.'

'Then let me have a look at you.'

That, by presenting an awful alternative, resolved my doubts. I was too shy to let anyone see me. I reached out and put my fingers on her hair. It was coarse and wiry, and I recoiled in surprise, mentally but not physically. Seri moved her body against my fingertips.

'Lower down, Lenden. Feel lower down.'

I turned my hand, so that it was palm up, and reached for the junction of her legs. It felt different there: less hair, a fold of skin. I snatched my hand away.

'What's the matter?'

'I don't know,' I said, looking away. But I looked back, and Seri had moved much closer.

'Touch me again. Go right inside.'

'I . . . can't.'

'Then I'll touch you.'

'No!' The thought of anyone, anyone at all, exploring my

348

body; it was unimaginable. I was still growing, there was too much unexplained. I was ashamed of my body, of growing up.

'You can put your finger right inside, if you want to,' Seri said. 'I don't mind.'

She seized my wrist and brought my hand up against her. Her body was warm, and the hairs curled against my palm. She pressed herself on my hand, encouraging my fingers to explore the cleft beyond. I felt the soft damp flaps of skin, and my fingertip played on the warm recess behind. I was in a heat of excitement, eager to do anything. I wanted to slip into her, sink my fingers, my hand into her. But then, just as I was going in to her, she stepped back and let the skirt fall.

'Seri—'

'Ssh!' She crouched by the square of daylight that was the hatch, and listened. Then she straightened, and hoisted up her pants with a sinuous movement of her hips.

'What are you doing?' I was distressed by her sudden withdrawal.

'Keep quiet,' she said, softly. 'I think there's someone outside.'

'You're just teasing me, making an excuse!'

'No . . . really. I heard something fall. Did you hear a clattering noise?'

'No. Let me touch you again.'

'Not now. I'm frightened.'

'Then when?'

'In a minute. We'll have to go somewhere else. Do you still want to?'

'Of course I do! Let's go now!' I was excited beyond anything in my previous experience. And this was Seri! My stupid cousin!

'I know somewhere safe. Outside the seminary . . . a short walk.'

'And then I can . . . ?'

'Anything you like, Lenden.'

She made me crawl first through the hatch, and she blew out the candles as I did so. I stood up at the bottom of the steps, then jumped with surprise. The priest we had seen earlier was standing at the top of the steps, leaning down with one hand on the railings, as if listening. He backed away as I looked up. I went up the steps, and saw him hurry across to where he had dropped his hoe on the path. By the time Seri had joined me at the top he was back at work, hoeing the soil with quick, sharp movements.

He did not look up as Seri and I walked hurriedly along the gravel path, but as we passed through the gate I looked back. He was standing with the hoe in his hand, staring towards us.

'Seri, that priest was watching us.'

She said nothing, but took my hand and led me running through the long wild grass outside the seminary grounds.

VIII

A hired car was waiting for us in Seevl Town, with a Seigniory pass attached to the windscreen. I sat in the front seat beside Serjeant Reeth as she drove slowly up the narrow streets towards the hills.

I was in a complex state of emotions, and this revealed itself by a forced exterior calm and an unwillingness to talk. She needed me to direct her, so I sat, as once my mother had sat, with the map on my knee, wondering if we should need it.

Last night had not been mentioned. Bella had appeared at breakfast, crisp in her uniform, once more the policewoman. Her straightforward proposition, my embarrassed refusal; I could hardly bear to think of them, yet how I wanted to speak of them! I did not want Bella to think she had made a mistake, but still I was incapable of explaining. I wanted some formula by which we could bring the incident forward into today, in an acceptable form, but by her silence and mine we were simply pretending nothing had happened.

She had, however, awakened my awareness of her sexuality, and that could not be pretended away, either by silence or by her starchy uniform. Waiting on Jethra dockside for the ferry, sitting together in the saloon of the boat, walking through Seevl Town to collect the car; I could not ignore her physical presence, could not forget that young body in the loose silk wrap.

Now we drove, and sometimes, as she shifted gear in the antiquated car, her hand or her sleeve would brush lightly against my knee; to see if it was as accidental as it seemed I moved my leg away, unobtrusively, and it did not happen again. Later, I let my leg move back, for the touch excited me.

Once, at a junction on the higher slopes of the moors, we went to the map for guidance. Her head bent down beside mine: another moment of physical nearness, but it ended as soon as we found the correct turning.

Watching the sombre green of Seevl's fells, my thoughts moved imperceptibly away from that intrigue to the other, the larger: the island and the seminary. My recollection of the road was unreliable, but the mood induced by the scenery was a familiar companion, twenty years absent. To someone seeing it for the first time, as Bella was seeing it, Seevl would seem wild, barren, grossly empty. There was the roundness of line that betrayed the millennia of harsh winters and unrelenting gales; where the rock was exposed, no plantlife clung to it except in the most sheltered corners, and then was only the hardiest of mosses, or the lowliest of lichens. There was a violent splendour to it, a scenic ruggedness unknown in our country. Yet to me, who had been along this route before, actual and mental, the scenery was merely the context. We passed through it as a hand reaching through luxuriant grass passes into a snake's nest. The moors were neutral, but contained a menace, and for me they were always coloured by it.

As Bella drove unsteadily along the narrow road I was already imagining ahead, seeing that valley at the other end of the island, with the cluster of grim buildings, the lawns and the incongruous flowerbeds.

Seevl was an island made for night. Although on this day the sky was clouded, the sun broke through from time to time, casting for brief periods a bright, unnatural radiance on the barren, grossly empty. There was the roundness of line that a damp stillness, chill and sad, filming the windscreen of the car. We had the windows closed and the heater on, yet the cold reached us. I shivered every now and then, shaking my shoulders, pretending to be more cold than I really was, because it was the island chilling me and I did not want Bella to know.

She drove slowly, steering more cautiously over the rutted track than ever my father had done. The car was in low gear for much of the time, the engine's note changing continually, making me irrationally irritable. Still we said nothing to each other, beyond intermittent consultations of the map. I watched for familiar landmarks – a cluster of standing stones, a fall of water, the dead towers – and sometimes I could direct her without referring to the map. My memory of the landscape was partial: there were long sections of the road that seemed new to me, and I was sure we had lost our way, then something I remembered would appear, surprising me.

351

We stopped for lunch at a house in one of the little hamlets, and here some preparation was revealed: we were expected, a meal was ready. I saw Bella sign a document, a form that would recompense the woman for her service.

When we reached the narrow part of the island, and travelled along the road above the southern cliffs, Bella pulled the car on to the side and stopped the engine. We were shielded from the wind by a high, rocky bank, and the sun warmed us.

We stood outside the car, looking across the glistering seascape, the view that as a child I had only been able to glimpse from my parents' moving car.

'Do you know any of the islands' names?' I said.

Bella had removed her cap, left it on the driver's seat in the car, and wisps of hair blew lightly around her face.

'A few. Torquin is the biggest; we have a base there now. My brother will probably pass through Torquin. And one of them must be Derril, where the Covenant was made. I'm not sure which one that is, though.'

'Have you ever been in the Archipelago?'

'Only here.'

Only Seevl, the offshore island.

The islands we could see were different shades of green, some dark, some light. It was said that of the ten thousand inhabited islands not one was like any other, that a true islander, if planted blind in a foreign island, would know its name by smell and sound alone. All I, a mainlander, knew was that the islands we could see from here were a part of the Dream Archipelago known as the Torqui Group, that they were primarily dependent on dairy-farming and fishing, and that the people spoke the same language as my own. This was school-knowledge, half-remembered, all but useless.

'Did you ever want to run away to the islands?' Bella said.

'When I was a kid. Did you?'

'I still do, sometimes.'

'At least you have come to Seevl.'

'At least.'

Talking about something outside ourselves had eased the tension between us; it was as if we had slipped unconsciously into another language. It came naturally to speak in the same tongue, so I said: 'Bella, about last night—'

'Lenden, I'm sorry about that.'

'That's what *I* was going to say.'

352

'But it is I who should say it. I shouldn't have gone to your room. I made a stupid mistake.'

I found her hand, and squeezed it quickly. 'No, not a mistake. I wanted you ... but I just wasn't ready.'

'Can we forget it?'

'That's what I want.'

Yes, to forget the misunderstanding, and the shame that followed ... but not to forget what still might be. I thought about that for a while, as we leaned together against the side of the car, watching the sea.

I said: 'We'll have to stay at the seminary tonight. You know we can't get back to Seevl Town?'

'Yes, I know.'

'They'll probably give us rooms in the college.'

'That's all right. I went to a convent.'

She went around to the driver's door, and opened it. We drove on. I knew it would take at least another hour from there, and the afternoon was drawing on. Bella said nothing, concentrating on the difficult drive, and I surrendered to my memories and the oppressive mood of the island.

IX

Seri held my hand, and we leaped and ran across the rough ground, the coarse grasses whipping against our legs. It was the first time I had ever left the seminary grounds, and never until then had I recognized how the stout walls became a symbolic defence against the rest of the island. Out here the wind seemed stiffer and colder, and we were more exposed.

'Where are we going?' I said, gasping because I was out of breath.

'Somewhere I know.' She released my hand, and went on ahead.

'Let's do it here.' Some of the tension that had built up inside her hide-out had been dissipated by our sudden escape, and I wanted to go on before she changed her mind.

'Out in the open?' she said, rounding on me. 'I told you this was a secret!'

'There's long grass,' I said lamely.

'Do you still want to do it?'

'Yes!' I said, sure of that if nothing else.

'Then come on.'

353

She set off again, leaping down a shallow slope towards a stream. I held back for a moment, staring guiltily towards the seminary. There was someone there, outside the walls, walking in our direction. I knew at once that it was the priest with the hoe, although he was too far away for me to be sure.

I ran after Seri, and jumped across the narrow stream to join her.

'There's someone following us. That priest.'

'He won't find us!'

It was now quite obvious where Seri was taking me. The ground sloped up steeply from the stream, rising towards the high crag in the distance. A short way from us, built with the limestone rock of the island, was the dead tower.

I looked back, and saw we were out of sight of the priest if he was still following us. Seri marched on, a long way ahead of me, scrambling up the hillside through the windswept grass.

The tower was not noticeably different from any other of its sort I had seen on Seevl: it was about as tall as a four-storey house, with window-frames higher up which once had contained glass, but which now were broken. There was a door in the base, hanging open on its hinges, and all around in the grass were pieces of broken brick and tile. The tower was not wide: perhaps fifteen feet in diameter, and hexagonal. There had once been a roof, built in candle-snuffer shape, but now it was all fallen, and only two or three beams stood out to reveal its former design.

Seri was waiting for me by the open door.

'Hurry, Lenden!'

'I'm coming,' I said, stepping over a heap of masonry, and looking up at the tower as it loomed over me. 'We're not going inside, are we?'

'Why not? It's been here for years . . . it's quite safe.'

All I knew about the towers of Seevl was that no one went near them; yet Seri stood by the door as if it were just another hide-out. I was torn between my dread of the tower, and what Seri would offer me inside.

'I thought these towers were . . . dangerous,' I said.

'It's just an old ruin. Something to do with the college, when it was a monastery. Years ago.'

'But they're all over the island!'

Seri shrugged dismissively, and went through the door. I hesitated a few seconds longer, then followed her. She closed the door behind us.

Daylight came in through two windows set high under the ceiling, which was a bare skeleton: dusty joists and broken planking. A fallen beam lay at an angle across the room, propped up against the wall. The floor was littered with glass, plaster and pieces of rock.

'See . . . there's nothing to worry about.' Seri kicked a few pieces of rock out of the way, to clear a space on the wooden floor. 'It's just an old dump.'

'Are you still going to let me touch you?' I said.

'If you want to.'

'I do . . . but that priest was following us. You said it was secret.'

Seri started to say something, but changed her mind and turned away. She opened the door, and peered out; I stood behind her, looking over her shoulder. We both saw the priest. He had reached the stream and was walking along the bank, trying to find somewhere to cross.

Seri closed the door again. 'He won't come here. Not to the tower.'

'But he's coming!' It was obvious that he was following us.

'Lenden, none of the priests will come here. They say the tower is evil. They're terrified of the place . . . that's why it's safe for us.'

I glanced around nervously. 'What's evil about it?'

'Nothing . . . it's just their superstition. They say something wicked happened. A long time ago.'

'But he's still coming,' I said.

'You wait and see what he does.'

I went to the door and opened it a fraction of an inch. I peered through the slit, looking down the hill for the priest. He was some way away, standing still, looking up towards me. I closed the door, and told Seri this.

'You see?' she said.

'But he'll wait until we come out. What then?'

'It's none of his business,' she said. 'He won't know what we're doing. I know him . . . it's Father Grewe. He's always poking around, wondering what I'm up to. I'm used to it. Shall we start?'

'If you want to.' The mood had left me.

'Get undressed then.'

'Me? I thought you—'

'We both undress.'

'I don't want to.' I looked at the rubble-strewn floor, shyly. 'Not yet, anyway. You do it first.'

355

'All right. I don't mind.'

She reached up under her skirt, and pulled her pants down her legs. She tossed them on the floor.

'Now you take something off,' she said. I hesitated, then complied by taking off my pullover.

Seri undid two buttons on the side of her skirt, and it slid down her legs. She turned away from me to drape the garment over the beam, and for a moment I saw the pinkness of her buttocks, slightly dimpled. 'Now you.'

'Let me feel you first. I've never done . . .'

Some compassion softened her determination to make me undress at the same rate as her. She smiled, quickly, then sat down on the floor, keeping her knees together and reaching forward to clasp her ankles. I could see none of her secrets, just the pale curve of her thighs, rounding towards her buttocks. Her sweater finished at her waist.

'All right. But be very gentle. You were jabbing me before.'

She sat back, resting her elbows on the floor behind her, and then she parted her legs. I saw the black thatch of hair, the whorl of pink skin, revealed but mysterious. Staring at her I moved forward, crouching down. I was suddenly as excited as I had been before; it switched on like a motor, compelling me towards her almost against my will. I felt a tightness in my throat, a sweatiness in my palms. That passive, lipped organ, lying between her thighs like an upright mouth, waited for my touch. I reached forward, ran fingertips across the lips, felt the warmth of them, the moistness behind. Seri sucked in her breath, tensing herself.

Something small and hard whacked against the door, startling us both. Seri swung away from me, turning to one side; my hand brushed against the top of her thigh, then she was away from me.

'What was that!' I said.

'Don't move.' She went to the door, eased it open and peered out.

I heard, distantly: 'Seri, come out of that place. You know it is forbidden.'

She closed the door. 'He's still out there.'

She sounded surprised, as if she had forgotten him. I had not, and I looked around for my pullover. 'Is he coming in?'

'I told you . . . he won't come near us. I'll have to go and talk to him.' She picked up her skirt and stepped into it, buttoning

356

it again at the waist. 'Wait here, and don't let him see you.'

'But he knows I'm here. I'll come with you. We ought to be going back to the house anyway.'

'No!' she said, and I saw the quickness of her temper. 'There's more to do, more than just touching. That's only the beginning.' Her hand was on the door. 'Stay here . . . keep out of sight, and I'll be back in a few moments.'

The door slammed behind her. I peeped through the crack, saw her running down through the long grass to where the priest waited. He seemed angry, but she was uncowed, standing near to him and kicking idly at the grasses while he spoke.

There was a faint, musky fragrance on my fingertips, where I had touched her. I drew back from the door, and looked around at the filthy interior of the tower. Without Seri I felt ill at ease in the old ruin. The ceiling was sagging; what if it fell on me? The constant wind of Seevl blustered around the tower, and a piece of broken wood, hanging by the window-frame, knocked to and fro.

Minutes passed, and as the aroused excitement faded for the second time, I began to wonder guiltily about the possible consequences of being caught here. Suppose the priest told Torm and Alvie that we had been up to something, or that we were gone long enough for them to guess anyway? If they knew the truth, or even a part of it, there would be a terrible scene.

I heard the voice of the priest, in a freak silence of the wind; he was saying something sharply, but Seri's response was laughter. I returned to the door, put my eye to the crack and looked out at them. The priest was holding Seri by the hand, tugging her, but she was pulling back from him. To my surprise, I realized that I was not witnessing a conflict, but what seemed to be a game. Their hands slipped apart . . . but it was an accident, because they joined again immediately and the playful pulling went on.

I stepped back, very puzzled.

X

We were in a part of the seminary I had never seen before: an office just behind the main entrance. We had been greeted by a Father Henner, thin, bespectacled, and younger than I had expected; condolences on the death of my uncle, a tragic loss, a servant of God. He handed over the key to the house, and we went for a meal in the refectory. Father Henner did not eat with us; Bella and I sat alone at a table in one corner of the room. Night was falling beyond the stained-glass windows.

I could hear the wind, made louder, it seemed, by the airy space above us, the high, buttressed roof.

'What are you thinking, Lenden?' Bella said, over the sounds of the students clattering their dishes at the other end of the hall.

'I'm wishing we didn't have to stay. I don't like this place.'

Afterwards, Father Henner took us across to the house, leading the way through the grounds with a battery flashlight; our feet crunched on the gravel pathway, the trees moved blackly against the night sky and the vague shape of the moors beyond. I unlocked the door and Father Henner turned on a light in the corridor. A dim, low-wattage bulb shed yellow light on the shabby floor and wallpaper. I smelt damp rot and mould.

'You'll find that much of the furniture has already been removed,' said Father Henner. 'Your uncle bequeathed the more valuable pieces to the college, and some of the effects belonged to us already. As you know, we have been unable to trace the daughter, so with your permission the rest may be destroyed.'

The daughter . . . ah, Seri. Where are you now, Seri? She left the island soon after Alvie died, but no one knew where she went. My parents would never mention her, and I never asked. Today she would be somewhere in the Archipelago.

'What about my uncle's papers?' I said.

'They're still here. We can arrange for them to be incinerated, if you will separate the valuable ones.'

I opened a door into a room off the corridor. It had been my uncle's office, but now it was empty, with pale squares on the walls where pictures had been; a dark patch of damp spread up from the stone floor.

'Most of the rooms have been cleared. There's just your dear aunt's room. And the kitchen. There are utensils there.'

Bella was standing by the door to my aunt's room. Father Henner nodded to her, and she turned the handle. I experienced a sudden compulsion to back away, fearing that Alvie would still be there, waiting for me.

Father Henner went back to the main door. 'Well, I'll leave you to your work. If there's anything you need, I shall be in my office during the day.'

I said: 'We need somewhere to stay.'

Father Henner opened the door, and his black habit blew in the sudden wind from outside. 'You may use the house, of course.'

'We were expecting you to give us rooms,' Bella said.

'In the college?' he said to her. 'I'm afraid that would not be possible. We have no facilities for women.'

Bella looked at me questioningly; I, stricken with a dread of spending a night in the house, shook my head.

'Are there proper beds here?' Bella said, pushing open the door and peering into the room, but my aunt's folding screen was there, making its temporary corridor into the room and blocking the view of the rest.

Father Henner was outside. 'You'll have to make do. It's only for one night, after all. God be with you.'

He went, and the door slammed behind him. Quietness fell; the thick walls effectively muted the wind, at least here in the centre of the house, away from the windows.

'What are we going to do, Lenden? Sleep on the floor?'

'Let's see what's in there.'

Aunt Alvie's room; my dear aunt.

Pretending to Bella that it was just an ordinary room, pretending to myself, I went past her and walked in. The central light was beyond the folding screen, so the way was shadowed. At the end, facing us, someone from the seminary had stacked two huge piles of old documents; tomorrow I should have to go through them. Dust lay in a gritty film on the top sheets. Bella was behind me; I looked beyond the screen to see the rest of the room. The double bed, Alvie's bed, was still there, dominating everything. Tea-chests had been brought in to the room, two extra chairs were crammed against the wall, books lay in uneven piles on the table beneath the window, picture-frames rested on the mantelpiece . . . but the bed, piled high with pillows, was the focus of the room, as ever. By its head was the bedside table: dusty old pill-bottles, a notebook, a folded lace handkerchief, a telephone, lavender water. These I remembered.

Alvie still lay in the bed. Only her body was missing.

I could smell her, see her, hear her. Above the bed, on the wall behind the top rail of the brass head-fitting, were two dark marks on the wallpaper. I remembered then: Alvie had had a characteristic gesture, reaching up behind her to grip the rail with both hands, perhaps to brace herself against pain. Her hands, years of her hands gripping like that, had left the stains.

The windows were black squares of night; Bella drew the curtains, and dust cascaded down. I could hear the wind again, and thought: Alvie must have known this wind, every night, every day.

'Are you all right, Lenden?'

'Of course.'

'Well, there's a bed, at least.'

'You have it,' I said. 'I'll sleep on the floor.'

'There'll be another bed somewhere. In one of the other rooms.'

'Father Henner said they had been cleared.'

'Then . . . will you share? Or I could go on the floor.'

We stood there in awful indecision, each for our own reasons. At last we came to silent agreement, changing the subject, pretending to look for enough space on the floor for me to lie down, but it was inevitable we would share. We were both tired, and chilled by the cold house. I let Bella take charge, and she tidied the bed, shaking out the old sheets to air them a little, turning them over. Spare pillows went on the floor, extra covers were found. I busied myself, trying to help, distracting myself from the thought: Alvie's bed, Alvie's bed.

At last the bed was ready, and Bella and I took it in turn to use the bathroom upstairs. I went first, and when Bella went after me I sat on the edge of Alvie's bed, listening to the sounds of her footsteps on the bare boards above. Here, in this room, my fears were conjoined: the shadow of my past and how it barred me from Bella, the memories of Alvie, and the winds and darknesses of Seevl that surrounded the house. I heard Bella above me, walking across the room, and she started down the wooden staircase. I made a sudden decision, stripping off my outer clothes and sliding in between the sheets.

Bella switched off the central light as she came in. She saw that I was in the bed, but her expression remained neutral. I watched, and did not watch, as she undressed in the glow from the table-lamp. The blouse and skirt of her uniform; suspender-belt and stockings; black pants and a sensible bra. She stood naked, looking away from me, finding a tissue to blow her nose on.

As she lay down beside me I felt her skin cold against mine, and realized she was shaking.

'I'm freezing,' she said, and turned off the light. 'Will you hold me?'

My arm went easily around her; she was slim and her body shaped itself naturally against mine. I could feel the plump weight of her breast on my arm, the prickle of her hair against my thigh. I was getting excited, but did not move, hoping to conceal it.

She ran a hand lightly over my stomach, then up to my breasts. 'You've still got clothes on.'

'I thought—'

'Don't be frightened, Lenden.'

She slipped her hand inside my bra, caressed my nipple, kissed me on the neck. Pressing herself to me she unhooked the bra and slid it down my arms. Her head ducked down, and with her hand cupping me she took a nipple in her mouth, sucking and pulling on it. Her hand crept down, went beneath the fabric of my pants and her fingers slipped expertly between my legs. I stiffened; excited and terrified.

Later, Bella sat astride me, her hair falling loose and touching my face. I caressed her beautiful breasts, playing with the small firm nipples, licking and kissing them. She guided my hand to her sex, but as soon as my fingers felt the bristle of hair, I snatched away. Again I was guided there, again I pulled back.

'Touch me, Lenden, oh, touch me . . .'

Bella was kissing my face, my neck, my shoulders, but I could not touch her. I shrank from her as once before I had shrunk from Seri, but Bella took my wrist in her hand, thrust my clenched fingers between her legs, clamped down on me, thrusting herself against my knuckles in repeated spasms. Afterwards, she sprawled across me, her sweat dripping down from her temples and into my open mouth.

I left her in the bed and stood, shivering, by the window. I leaned against the wall by the frame, staring out into the gusty night. The dark was impenetrable. There were no lights, not even the subdued glow of a cloudy night, and I could not see the bulk of the moors.

Bella turned on the table light, and after she had lit a cigarette I turned to look back at her. She was lying with the cigarette between her lips, her hands gripping the brass rail of the bed above her head. Her hair fell down across her shoulder, partially covering one breast.

'You do prefer men, don't you?' she said.

I simply shook my head, and waited by the window until she had finished her cigarette and turned out the light. In the darkness I returned to the bed. Bella did not stir, and I curled up against her, resting my head on her shoulder. I started to drift towards sleep, and I laid my hand gently on her breast. The bed smelled of bodies.

XI

While Seri was outside the dead tower with the priest something happened to me, and I cannot explain it. There was no warning of it, and I had no premonition of fear.

My main preoccupations were intense sexual frustration, and curiosity about what Seri was doing with the priest. She had suddenly and unexpectedly illuminated an area of my life I had always kept in the shade. I wanted the knowledge of her that she was offering, and I wanted the consequent knowledge of myself.

But she had told me to wait, to stay out of sight . . . and I was prepared to do both, but not for long. I had expected her to get rid of the priest somehow, but instead she was out there apparently playing with him.

So preoccupied, I barely noticed a low, snuffling sound that came to me over the noise of the wind. I was picking up my pullover, retrieving Seri's pants. I was going out to join Seri, because I wanted to know what she was doing.

I was stuffing her pants into the pocket of my skirt when I heard the noise again. It surprised me: because I had heard it the first time without really thinking about it I had subconsciously ignored it, but when it came again it was both strange and half-familiar. It was like nothing I had ever heard before. It was animalistic, but there was a human quality to it too, as if some beast had managed to form half a word before reverting to its usual grunt. Still I felt no fear, but a sense of curiosity. I suspected that Seri had returned, and was playing a joke on me. I called her name, but there was no answer.

Something about the animal quality of the noise had made me hesitate. I stood in the centre of the crumbling tower, looking around, thinking for the first time that perhaps some predatory beast was in the vicinity. I listened, trying to filter out the persistent noise of the wind, trying to distinguish the sound again. But there was no more of it.

A beam of Seevl's bright cool sunlight was striking in through one of the high windows and illuminating the wall beside the door. This, like the rest of the tower, was decaying away, and a short distance from the doorpost the plaster and brickwork had fallen away, leaving a jagged hole about the size of a man's head. Beyond, the cavity of the wall was revealed, with the great, grey bricks of the main structure dimly visible behind. It was one of several holes in the wall, but it caught my attention because some instinct told me that this was the source of the noise. I stepped towards it, still suspecting Seri of some complicity; perhaps having got rid of the priest she had returned quietly to the tower, and was fooling around outside the door.

Something moved inside the cavity, and although I was staring straight at the place I saw only a dark, quick movement. The sun went in, as one of the low clouds covered it, and it seemed suddenly much colder. Moments later the sun came out again, but the chill remained; I knew then that it was in me.

I placed my hand on the brickwork, leaning slightly towards the hole, trying to see down into it. I did not want to go too close, yet I was convinced someone, or something, was in there, and I wanted to know what it was. There were no more movements, no more noise, but an almost tangible sense of presence remained.

I was no longer alone in the tower.

'Is that you, Seri?' I said, and the sound of my voice seemed too loud and too feeble, simultaneously. I cleared my throat, noisily, giving Seri a chance to declare herself . . . but there was no response.

I moved my hand further into the hole, until I touched the bricks on the far side of the cavity. There was something warm in there, because I could feel a gentle heat, as of a living body. I reached down, into the dark.

There was a violent noise, a movement that I felt without seeing, and something grabbed my hand.

It pulled, dragging my arm down into the hole until my shoulder scraped painfully against the bricks. I screamed in surprise, gasping in terror. I tried to pull back, but whatever it was that had taken hold had sharp claws or teeth and they were biting into my skin. My face was jammed sideways against the wall, the skin of my bare upper arm was grazing against the rough bricks.

'Let go!' I shouted, helplessly, trying to tug my arm away.

As the thing had grabbed me I had instinctively balled my

hand into a fist, and I could feel it contained in something wet and very warm, hard on one side, soft on the other. I pulled again, and the grip of the teeth tightened. Whatever it was in there was no longer dragging me down, but was holding me. Whenever I pulled back, the sharp teeth tightened around me. They were backwards-pointing, so that to pull against them was only to drag my flesh against their edge.

I unballed my fingers slowly, painfully aware that to loosen them was to expose them. The tips pressed against something soft, and I clenched my fist reflexively again. I shuddered, wanting to scream again, yet lacking the breath.

It was a mouth that had seized me. I knew that from the moment it had taken hold, yet it was too horrible to believe. Some animal, crouching in the wall, some huge, rank animal had taken my arm in its mouth, and was holding me. My knuckles were jammed against the hard roof of the mouth, my tightly balled fingers were against the coarse surface of the tongue. The teeth, the fangs, had closed about my arm, just above the wrist.

I tried turning my arm, attempting to twist it free, but the instant I moved the teeth closed more tightly on me. I shouted in pain, knowing that the flesh must have been torn in many places, and that I was surely bleeding into the animal's mouth.

I shifted my feet, trying to balance, thinking that if I could stand firmly I could pull harder, but as the animal had dragged me down it had pulled me over. Most of my weight was on the shoulder jammed against the bricks. I moved a foot, shifted some of my weight on to it. The fangs tightened on me again, as if the animal sensed what I was doing.

The pain was indescribable. The strength that held my fingers closed was draining away, and I could feel my fist loosening. Again my fingertips touched the hot, quivering surface of the tongue, and drooped down towards the throat. Miraculously, I still had the sensation of touch, and I could feel the hard gums, the slick sides to the tongue. It was the most disgusting thing I had ever felt in my life: wild, feral, bestial.

The animal, having firm hold of me, was trembling with some kind of incomprehensible excitement. I could feel the head shivering, and the breath rasped in and out over my arm, cold against the wounds as it inhaled, wet and hot as it exhaled. I could smell its stench now: sweet with the saliva of gross animalism, rancid and fetid with the smell of carrion.

I tugged once more, in desperate, disgusted terror, but the agony of the biting teeth redoubled. It felt as if it had almost bitten through me; I had a ghastly, flashing image of withdrawing my arm at last, and seeing it severed through, the sinews dangling from the stump, the blood pumping away. I closed my eyes, gasping again with horror and revulsion.

The tongue started moving, working around my wrist, stroking my palm. I felt as if I were going to faint. Only the pain, the intense, searing agony of torn muscle and crushed bone, kept me conscious to suffer longer.

Through the veils of pain I remembered Seri was outside. I shouted for help, but I was weakened and my voice came out as a hoarse whisper. The door was only a few inches from me. I reached over with my free hand and pushed at it. It swung outwards, and I could see down the slope, across the long grass. The brilliant cold sky, the dark rising moors . . . but no sign of Seri. I was alone.

Staring through tear-filled eyes, unable to focus, I stayed helpless, leaning against the rough brickwork as the monster in the wall slowly ate my arm. Outside, the wind made light-coloured patterns on the thick, waving grass.

The animal began to make a noise, a reprise of the first sound it had made. It growled deep inside its throat, and beneath my helpless fingers the tongue was quivering. It sucked in breath and the head tensed, and then there came a second growl. Somehow, the sound made my fevered imagining of the animal more detailed: I saw a wolf's head, a long snout, flecks of foam. The pain intensified, and I sensed the animal's increased excitement. The throat-noises were coming regularly now, in a fast rhythm, faster and faster as its hold on my arm tightened. The agony was so acute that I was sure it must almost have bitten through, and I tried once more to pull away, quite ready to lose my hand for the sake of release. The animal held on, chewing more viciously, snarling at me from its hidden den below. My head was swimming; unconsciousness could not have been far away.

The animal noises were now coming so quickly that they seemed to join into one continuous howl; the pain was intolerable. But then, unaccountably, the jaw sagged open and I was released.

I slumped weakly against the wall, my arm still dangling inside the cavity. The pain, which surged with every heartbeat, began to diminish. I was crying with relief and agony, and with terror of the animal which was still there below. I dared not move my arm, thinking that one twitch of a muscle would provoke another attack, yet I knew my chance had come to snatch away what was left of my arm.

My tears stopped, because I was afraid. I listened carefully: was the animal breathing, was it still there? I did not know if my arm had lost all sensation, but I could not feel the animal's foul breath moving across me. The pain was almost indiscernable; my arm must be numb. I imagined, rather than felt, the fingers hanging uselessly from the mangled wrist, blood pulsing down into the animal's open snout below.

A deep revulsion stirred me at last, and, not caring if the animal should attack me again, I stood away from the wall, withdrawing my shattered arm from the cavity. I staggered away, and rested my good hand against the low-lying beam. I looked at the damage done to me.

The arm was whole, the hand was undamaged.

I held it before me, disbelieving what I saw. The sleeve of my blouse had been torn as I was dragged through the brick-work, but there were no marks on the skin, no lacerations, no teeth-marks, no blood. I flexed my fingers, bracing myself against the anticipated pain, but they moved normally. I turned my hand over, looking at it from all sides. Not a mark, not even a trace of the saliva I had felt running across me. The palm was moist, but I was sweating all over. I touched the arm gingerly, feeling for the wounds, but as I pressed down on the sore areas the only sensation I could feel was of fingertips squeezing against good flesh. There was not even a ghost of the pain I had suffered.

There was a faint, unpleasant odour on my hand, but as I sniffed at the backs of my fingers, at my palm, it faded away.

The door was open. I snatched at my pullover, which lay on the floor, and lurched outside. I was holding my wounded, un-damaged arm across my chest, as if I was in pain, but it was just a subconscious reflex.

The long grass swept around me in the wind, and I remem-bered Seri. I needed her then: to explain, to soothe, to calm me. I wanted another human being to see me, and give me the re-assurance I could not give myself. But Seri had vanished, and I was alone.

At the bottom of the slope, near the stream, a good distance from the tower: a figure in black stood up. His habit was caught in the band at his waist, and as he turned he was pulling at it, making it hang normally. I ran towards him, rushing through the grass.

He turned his back on me as soon as he saw me, and strode quickly away. As I dashed towards him he reached the brook, leaped over it and hurried up the slope beyond.

'Wait, Father!' I shouted. 'Please wait!'

I came to a place where the grass was flattened, and in its centre lay Seri. She was on her back, with her skirt rolled up above her waist. Her sweater had been pushed up to her neck, revealing plump little breasts, pink-tipped. Her eyes were closed, and her arms lay on the ground above her head. Her knees were raised, and her legs were wide open.

'Seri!'

She opened her eyes and saw me.

'Do you still want to touch me, Lenden?' she said, and giggled.

I looked at the place; a pale, creamy fluid trickled from the reddened lips.

A wave of nausea came over me, and I backed away from her, unable to look at her. She was still laughing, and as she saw my reaction her laughter became shrill and hysterical. She rolled around in the flattened grass, writhing as she must have writhed before.

I kept a distance between us, waiting for her to sober. I remembered that I had her pants in the pocket of my skirt, and I found them and threw them at her. They landed on her naked belly.

'You're . . .' I tried to find a word forceful enough to convey the revulsion in me, but failed. 'You're *filthy*!'

Her crazy laughing stopped, and she lay on her side to look at me. Then, deliberately, she opened her legs in tacit invitation.

I turned from her and ran away, towards the seminary, towards the house. I sobbed as I ran, and the torn sleeve of my blouse flapped around my arm. I stumbled as I crossed the stream, drenching my clothes; I tripped many times, cutting my knee, tearing the hem of my skirt. Bloodied, hysterical, bruised and soaked through, I ran into the house and burst into my aunt's sickroom.

My uncle and my father were supporting Alvie above a

chamber-pot. Her white, withered legs dangled like bleached ropes; drops of orange liquid trickled from her. Her eyes were closed, and her head lolled.

I heard my uncle shouting. My mother appeared, and a hand was slapped over my eyes. I was dragged, screaming, into the corridor.

All I could say, again and again, was Seri's name. Everyone seemed to be shouting at me.

Later, Uncle Torm went out on to the moors to find Seri, but before they returned we had got back into our car and were driving, through the evening and night, towards Seevl Town.

It was the last time I went to Seevl. I was fourteen. I never saw Seri again.

XII

We burned my uncle's papers in the yard behind the house: black charred ashes floated up, then were whisked away by the wind. There were also some clothes, and some chairs and a table the priests did not want. They burned slowly, and I stood by the fire, watching the flames reflectively.

Bella, standing by the doorway, said: 'Why do you keep staring at the moors?'

'I didn't know that I was.'

'There's something out there. What is it?'

'I was watching the blaze,' I said.

'Have you ever been out on the moors?'

'No.' I kicked a chair leg that had rolled from the fire, and sparks flew. Something in the fire spat, and a cinder shot across the yard.

Bella came towards me, took my arm tenderly.

'It doesn't matter, about last night.'

I said nothing because I knew she was right, but also that it did matter.

'Was that your first time?' she said.

'Of course not.'

'I meant, with someone like me?'

'No.'

What was she like, that was so different? She meant perhaps: was she my first female lover? I smiled sadly, thinking of the men I had loved, the women too. More women than men, over the years, because I only went to men in desperation. I, always the passive lover: excited and slightly appalled by their relish in caressing my body, envying them their lack of inhibition, and determined with each new partner that *this* one would be different, *this* one would find me active. No, in that sense, Bella was no different. I had not changed. I had thought a few years' abstention, a gaining in maturity, would cure me of the irrational fear. I should not have put it to the test; I had been weak, thinking that the return to Seevl would, in itself, be some kind of exorcism. I had fallen for Bella's youth, her hesitancy, her pretty body; these had drawn me, once again, to failure. I had not known that I had dried up, become a husk.

'I'm only trying to understand,' Bella said.

'So am I.'

'We're alone.' Bella, speaking softly. 'Be frank with me.'

'I am, I think.'

'Will we see each other again? After this?'

'Yes,' I said, postponing.

'I can travel freely. Let me visit your home.'

'All right. If you'd like to.'

It seemed to satisfy her, but she stood with her hand on my arm as we watched the fire.

I wondered what it was she saw in me; surely she had other friends? I was several years older than her, and she made me feel it, with her economical body, her youthful mannerisms. I had my first grey hairs, my breasts had started to sag, my waist was full, my thighs were thick. I was the older woman, more mature and presumably more experienced, yet it was she who pursued. I found it very affecting and flattering.

If it had been anywhere else: not Seevl, not Alvie's room and Alvie's bed. Would it have been any different?

The inevitable failure . . . but also the inevitable seeking for an excuse.

The real excuse, if there was any at all, lay out there under the crag of Seevl's moors.

That morning I had risen before Bella, and climbed from Alvie's bed to go to the window. From there I had been sure I would be able to see the tower where it all had happened, but I looked and I had not been able to see. The seminary gardens were just as I recalled them – although less well tended than I had thought – and so was the view across to the high, limestone crag. But there was no sign of the tower.

Bella was right: all that morning, as I worked through my uncle's papers, I had looked frequently towards the moors, wondering where the tower had gone.

There must have been a rational explanation: it had become unsafe, it had been demolished.

Or the other sort of rational explanation: that it was not there, that it had never been there. I shied away from that, unable to face the consequences.

Bella was still holding my arm, resting her cheek lightly against my shoulder.

She said: 'I've a confession, Lenden.'

I was lost in my own thoughts, and barely heard her.

'Is it important?' I said.

'I don't know. It might be. There's a file on you, in the Seigniory. Does that surprise you?'

'No, not really.' There were files on everybody, we were at war.

'I read your file. I know a lot about you.'

'What sort of thing?' A tremor of concern.

'Nothing political.'

No surprise; my isolation was almost total. 'What then?'

'About your private life. I suppose that's worse really.' I had drawn away from her, to face her. 'The file told me the sort of person you are . . . the fact that you have had women lovers. There was a picture of you.'

'When did you see this?'

'When the assignment was posted. I volunteered for this, I wanted to meet you. I thought . . . it's hard to say. I've been very lonely.'

'And it's hard to meet the right people,' I said. 'I've been through all that too.'

'You don't mind?'

'I object to it being on file. But I don't mind what you did.'

The fire was almost out. There was an old broom in the yard, and I used it to sweep the charred wood and ashes into a small neat pile. A few flames flickered, but they would not burn much longer.

There was nothing left for us to do at the house, and we had a long drive to catch the evening ferry. I took the key back to Father Henner's office, while Bella carried our stuff to the car. Walking back through the grounds, alone, I knew that this was my last chance to find the tower. I left the path and walked through the gardens until I came to the wall. I found a gate, went through, and stood looking across the rough ground.

I could not see the tower, could not even see where it might have been. I was standing there looking for it, when Bella found me.

She slipped her hand into mine.

'Something happened here once, didn't it?'

I nodded, and held her hand tightly.

'A long time ago?'

'Twenty years ago. I'm not sure what it was. I think I must have imagined it. It all seems different now.'

'I was just a child, twenty years ago,' Bella said.

'So was I.'

But thinking, as we drove back through the fells, it seemed different again. I was sure the tower was there, that it was simply that I had not seen it.

Bella talked, in the car, on the ferry, and we made our plans for future meetings . . . but we parted on the quay in Jethra, and I have not heard from her since.

John Brunner

The man whose
eyes beheld the glory

*John Brunner was born in Oxfordshire in 1934 and sold his
first novel under a mysterious pseudonym when he was
seventeen. He left Cheltenham College that same year, because
its syllabus interfered with his education (according to* Who's
Who in Science Fiction). *Soon he was a full-time writer, and by
now he has published over seventy books. He is best known
for his science fiction, which includes* Stand on Zanzibar *(which
won the Hugo and the Prix Apollo),* The Sheep Look Up, The
Jagged Orbit *and* The Whole Man, *but he has also written
fantasies (*The Traveller in Black*), and his Max Curfew stories
– thrillers from the viewpoint of a black detective – are feats of
imagination of a different order. His short stories are gathered
in* From This Day Forward, Not Before Time, Now Then, No
Future In It, *and other collections. His work is analysed by
various critics in* The Happening Worlds of John Brunner.*

*He founded and administers the Martin Luther King
Memorial Prize, and since 1958 he has toured many countries
to promote the Campaign for Nuclear Disarmament. He lives
in Somerset with his wife Marjorie, and appears suavely at
many science fiction conventions. Like most of his stories, this
one has a point to make.*

'So you went to Psylaria for your holidays this year,' Mr
Secrett said reproachfully. 'You should have let me know. I
could have given you some introductions.'

I almost dropped my plate of cottage pie. It was not because
– or at any rate not wholly because – he had taken me by surprise; this crowded pub into which, being hungry and thirsty,
I had turned at random was literally around the corner from
the Royal Society for Applied Linguistics where he is the
Librarian . . . although, come to think of it, I had always pictured him as taking lunch at his post, off some exiguous but
nourishing dainty like chopped-date sandwiches.

Nor was it solely because I had no least idea how he could have heard about my trip to that almost-unknown island, for I hadn't intended to go there, or anywhere in particular, when I obeyed my doctor's order to 'take a month's rest, for heaven's sake!' Besides, I had returned so recently that I was still having qualms of conscience over the number of my close friends I hadn't told yet. And Mr Secrett is not even, strictly speaking, a friend of mine. My visits to the gloomy aisles of his library are now few and far between. I keep finding excuses to look elsewhere for the information I need.

No, mostly it was because the mere mention of Psylaria conjured up visions of agonizing vividness: Psylaria, that uncompromising statement of rock thrust by a volcano out of the jewel-blue Aegean, bypassed by the ferries to and from Piraeus, inaccessible unless you rent or own a boat or hitch a ride with a fisherman (which was what I'd done); Psylaria, the place among all the many places I had visited in Greece and its islands where I had most clearly sensed what it means to *be Greek*, to have inherited the tradition of the Iliad and the Odyssey and the quest for the Golden Fleece. I had imagined that nowhere could outdo Delphi in that regard. I had been wrong. On Psylaria I had seen past the romantic veils of later ages and gained insight into an existence beset by so many random perils, it was small wonder gods had to be invented to account for nature's cruelty. I had met a proud but harsh people, whose manners made me understand how famous ancient leaders – Cleomenes, Themistocles, Alcibiades – could have turned on their kinfolk and taken service with those who had previously been their enemies. Choosing one fisherman rather than another out of six or seven who had brought their catch to sell in the port of Lemnos had been enough to ensure that during my stay half Psylaria would not give me a civil answer to a civil question. Though fascinating, my visit had not been wholly enjoyable. That largely accounted for my not yet having rung up all my friends to boast about discovering an unspoiled island.

Its mere name, nonetheless, filled my nostrils with the scent of wild thyme.

'It's some while since I was there,' murmured Mr Secrett, 'but judging from your reaction I take it Psylaria can't have changed very much. Come and sit down and tell me all about it.'

*

Tall though he is – a fact generally disguised by his stoop, which is of the kind excused as 'scholarly' – Mr Secrett is not a very impressive figure, with his straggly grey moustache, his heavy spectacles, his old-fashioned three-piece suit which is visibly shiny at the elbows. All his suits are shiny at the elbows, although he rotates them at biweekly intervals.

Nonetheless, approximately half a minute later, he and I were ensconced on a padded bench next to a table where there was plenty of room to set out our food and drink. A pair of eager young executives leaning on the bar had had their eyes peeled for any sign of a seat coming vacant; now they were blinking in amazement, wondering how this old stick could have been too quick for them.

Mr Secrett paid them no attention. Wiping his moustache clean of beer foam, he said, 'I've been hoping to bump into you, Scrivener old chap, ever since I heard you'd found your way to Psylaria.'

'And how *did* you hear?' I demanded.

He gave an airy wave. 'One tries to keep up old friendships. But how did the place strike you?'

For the next five minutes, taking advantage of an opportunity I feared might never recur – the presence of someone who had been there and might understand why Psylaria had so deeply affected me – I left my mash and mince to congeal on the plate while I struggled to define what was on my mind.

I recalled the narrow harbour and the little slanting town of whitewashed houses, too cramped by steep hills ever to grow larger. It's the only town on the island; a few more people, at most a hundred, live in outlying hamlets. And what I found I needed to describe was the return of the fishing boats at dawn, their lamps showing in the mist like luminous puffballs, the flowers of some unwholesome prehistoric plant whose fruit might be the fish that squirmed and writhed on the bottom boards, fin beating tentacle in a final empty struggle against death. Meantime the men shouted standardized insults at one another, always sexual, always gross, always forgiven under cover of the anonymity lent by the mist. By daylight and on shore it was a very different matter.

Likewise there is only one road on Psylaria, more of a track for most of its length, passable on foot or with a donkey but not recommended for cars; the few land-owners rich enough go about on tractors. And what I found I needed to describe was the way it wound from no particular place to nowhere else, if you gauged it by a map; the hamlets and farmsteads were served by short connecting spurs in even worse condition.

On the spot, however, I had at once realized that from the church of St Theodoula, a name which means something like 'godslave', it ran as straight as the rocky going permitted to a shrine on the west cape, of the usual Greek design – a waist-high whitewashed pillar with a niche at the top containing a lamp and an icon – and then to an abandoned chapel on the slope of the island's highest peak, the much-weathered stump of the dormant volcano. Earth tremors, presumably, had filled one end with rubble. An inscription declared it had been sacred to St Porphyrios, but nobody could or would tell me anything about him. And from there the track led to a shrine on the east cape, and thence back to the church. It was laid out as though since time immemorial the inhabitants of Psylaria had felt a road more important for making the round of their holy places than for trade or recreation.

Which made me think of the old blind priest, daily led clear around the island by one of several prematurely-aged widows identically clad in unrelieved black, who perhaps derived from the chore some credible assurance of grace but obviously no pleasure, for he was foul-tempered and foul-mouthed and sometimes struck his companion, especially when returning from the abandoned chapel.

'Dear me!' said Mr Secrett, blinking. 'I had no idea old Costas had been reduced to that condition!'

All during my recital he had been demolishing a pile of beef sandwiches with evident enjoyment. I now suddenly realized that unless I ate my own lunch it would be too unappetizing. I seized my fork.

'Why not?' I said with maximum irony. 'You do after all seem to keep up with the news from Psylaria.'

'Well, yes, I suppose I do. But, you see, Costas – his full name is Constantinos Eleftherides, by the way – he's one person I'd have given you an introduction to. I've known him over thirty years, and he sends me an annual letter.'

'Letter?' I said out of an over-full mouth, at the risk of spraying Mr Secrett with gravy.

'Oh, yes. He dictates to his niece. Whose handwriting, I may say, is atrocious, and getting worse as she grows older. One of the things he invariably informs me about is visits by English people to the island. He assumes I know them all . . . If you didn't actually meet him, that surprises me.'

'Not me. He was probably one of the majority prepared to hate me on principle because I arrived in the wrong boat.' I tried to keep bitterness out of my voice, and failed.

'That does him an injustice,' Mr Secrett said with a heavy sigh. 'Reading between the lines of his latest communication, I would hazard a guess that he was prevented from seeking you out because nobody told him you were there until you'd left. He's very much a minority of one; indeed, I often think that if it weren't for his Cloth nobody would talk to him at all. I know his family are at odds with him – not a question of wife and children, you understand; he did at one stage plan to marry, since celibacy is not obligatory in the Orthodox tradition. But after what happened . . . I don't suppose anybody told you why he's blind?'

'It never occurred to me to ask,' I said, staring. 'In any case I doubt whether my Greek would have been up to following the answer – if they'd deigned to give me one! Was it an unusual case?'

'That,' Mr Secrett said, 'is putting it mildly.'

I wound up on Psylaria in the late 1940s (he explained), completely unintentionally. While I was in Alexandria with the Intelligence Corps I'd discovered an interest in archæology, and among the theories I became enamoured of was the suggestion that Plato's Atlantis might have been a volcanic island, considerably closer to Greece than its traditional location beyond the Pillars of Hercules. I mentioned this to a friend who had as it were taken me under his wing, and we decided to inspect some suitable candidates. We had too little time and not nearly enough money to evaluate them all at leisure, so we made an arbitrary list and tossed a coin to decide which of us should go where. He drew the plum, and could have been the first person to report on Thera – Santorini – as the most probable Atlantis.

However, he was – I suppose the word has to be seduced – from his original intention, and I was left to hang around on Psylaria until the next time a fisherman made a catch large enough for the trip to Lemnos to be worth his while. It had taken me only a glance at the island to rule it out as a candidate for the Atlantis role.

However, it did have some very curious attributes. For one thing, although it's larger than some of its neighbours, it is bar none the least hospitable island in its chain. If I'd been a Psylarian, I remember thinking at the time, I'd have swum to Lemnos rather than go on living here!

But conceivably that was owing to the post-war mood. I'd realized as soon as I went ashore that the Psylarians were disinclined to be polite to foreigners, but I took it for granted that that was because they had been invaded and occupied by the Germans. I was still labouring under the burden of misinformation derived from endless Army indoctrination lectures.

I was therefore distinctly puzzled when my cries of '*Eimai Anglós!*' were greeted by frosty scowls.

It is perhaps a measure of the desperation this cold-shouldering generated in me that despite my then-militant atheism I welcomed the attentions of a priest. It was a shared interest in archæology that brought – more exactly, drove – us together. I did my best to excuse his profession of Orders by invoking the background of superstition and ignorance he had grown up against.

One afternoon when I had laid out almost all the money remaining to me in bribes along the quay in the hope of getting passage to a port nearer civilization, I wandered up the side of the steep hill which, I take it, gave Psylaria its name, inasmuch as *pseelos* means high or upreared, and investigated the chapel of St Porphyrios. I'd been there before, but I could read German as the result of a crash course I'd been put through in the Army, and there was a red-lettered notice in German and Greek to warn people that they risked being clobbered by falling rock. I translate freely, you understand.

No rock having fallen, so far as I could tell, since my previous visit, I ventured into the interior this time, and realized that the chapel was built against a natural cave. Plainly it had long been abandoned; equally plainly, it had once been the centre of an intensive cult, for walls and floor alike were dense with testimonial inscriptions. I had read half a dozen of them – those on the floor engraved, those on the walls painted – before I realized that they were couched in an antique form of the language, probably pre-Ottoman. Moreover several were dedicated not to St Porphyrios directly but to his adorer St Theodoula, whose name I was already familiar with from the church in the town, but whose story I had so far not persuaded anybody to recount.

These were the most recent and easiest to read. As I worked my way along the wall, finding the paint more and more faded, I realized I was crunching chunks of plaster underfoot. Somebody was stripping away a later covering from these inscriptions. The ones I was coming to gave me tantalizing hints of meaning, but many lines were still half concealed and the vocabulary was growing ever more archaic – either that, or (as I suspect is frequently the case) the scribe was himself barely literate.

'Hands up!' a voice barked behind me. In Greek. It wasn't a phrase I'd run across before, but the intonation made its meaning perfectly plain. I turned round slowly, arms in the air, and discovered Costas looking at me. He was shorter than me, plumper, with a vacuous moon-face on which a few whiskers traced a summary of the *papas*'s customary beard; he wore a very dusty black robe and held a shotgun. It turned out he had been taking a siesta in the coolest part of the cave, and when he heard noises was afraid someone had come to spoil the inscriptions. As he later explained, there were factions among the island's families who felt that instead of merely being plastered over these messages from the past should have been ground to powder. But they were known by the rest of the population as 'foreigners', for they had only been here a century, and anyway they were forever quarrelling among themselves, so that even though they outnumbered the aboriginal inhabitants their opinion did not always count.

He himself was descended from both groups, and both were ostracizing him.

When he realized I was seriously interested in the wall-inscriptions, he put away the gun and shook my hand, and accepted a swig from the wine bottle I had with me. Then he enthusiastically set about expounding what he had learned from his investigations. My knowledge of Greek was shaky in the extreme, but luckily he had acquired a smattering of French, albeit at two removes while in his seminary. Once I'd tuned my ear to his accent we made rapid progress.

The first thing he took pains to impress on me was his devotion to St Theodoula, which was a trifle off-putting. At least, though, she seemed to be more deserving of admiration than the majority of the saints in the calendar. She was a widow, living at the time of the Turkish conquest, who was forced by greedy relatives to leave her husband's old home. Some of this information was to be read on the walls of the chapel, by the way, for it was here that she had taken refuge.

But even if it was the only place she could find shelter, it was an unlucky choice. Although by that time it was in ruins, there had been a pagan temple on the site. Occasionally sulphurous fumes leaked into the cave from the pit of the volcano; I immediately suspected the shrine of an oracle. As a result, Theodoula was automatically accused of heresy, witchcraft and the like. Now and then she was stoned by passing children, whom she would curse in the name of St Porphyrios. This was well described in one of the few wholly intact wall-inscriptions.

Who was St Porphyrios? Well, this was my new friend's great discovery, he claimed. He was none other than the celebrated Neoplatonist, the biographer and editor of Plotinus, who towards the end of his life had come under the influence of Christianity and retired here to live out his days as a pious eremite, working such miracles on behalf of the Psylarians as creating a brilliant light at midnight during an unexpected storm so that the fishing boats might return safely. Of course he was not officially entitled to sainthood, but given that the chief grounds for Theodoula's elevation to the status of the island's patron saint consisted in her devotion to Porphyrios, he was sure it was only a matter of time.

Already, he hinted, he himself had had certain experiences in the cave which indicated something supernatural at work. For instance, he had twice or three times been so overwhelmed by unaccountable joy, he had burst out laughing and continued until his belly ached. Myself, I wondered sceptically whether nitrous oxide could be spontaneously generated by a volcano . . .

Since the inscriptions were by a mile the most interesting things I had run across here, I steered the talk back to them, and learned the rest of Theodoula's story.

A few people did not share the general view, and took to bringing her occasional gifts: a jar of oil or some fish or a loaf. They were not bold enough to hand these over personally; they left them at night where she was bound to find them in the morning. When she did so, she would invariably cry aloud to Porphyrios, invoking his blessing on her benefactors.

'But the oddest thing,' Costas said, peering at a much-faded inscription which he had just begun to release from its plaster incarceration, 'was this.' He beckoned me over, and with a little help from him on the translation I learned it had been reported by a number of those who stole up by night with presents that there was a bright light in Theodoula's cave, as though a colossal fire were raging, yet there was never any smell of burning – or indeed any fuel she could have used. Nor could this possibly have to do with the volcano, because from time immemorial the islanders had known the signs of an impending eruption and were resigned to having to evacuate Psylaria at short notice. Even in his own childhood, Costas said, he had once spent a chilly night in a boat with his mother, brother and sister while a column of smoke shot through with sparks rose a hundred metres into the night sky.

There had not, though, been a major eruption in modern times. I'd checked on that before coming to Psylaria.

After Theodoula had lived in her cave for ten years or so she had quite a flourishing little farm. People had given her kids, chicks and seed corn as well as food, and she had patiently scrabbled out the grey-green weeds from every patch of soil on the hillside and planted little gardens. Even her late husband's family, who had started all the trouble, were beginning to wonder whether they ought to beg her pardon. She had decided to attend church on Sundays again, and while no one would sit next to her, no one any longer attempted to drive her out.

There was a new priest at the time. Possibly that had something to do with it. His predecessor had been married to Theodoula's husband's aunt.

This brings us, by the by, to about the middle of the fifteenth century.

Listening to Costas, it occurred to me that the situation on Psylaria had changed very little in five hundred years . . .

The significance of the date is that the Turks were in the process of conquering the rest of Greece, with a few minor exceptions. Indeed they had been masters of most of the mainland since 1400. Some islands had held out, and a great many more had been beneath their notice, but they were now energetically gathering up these odds and ends. And since of course they were Moslems, and since they had all too frequently been known to disregard the injunction of Mohammed to 'cry unto the Christians and the Jews that their God and my God are one', despite being People of a Book – which was supposed to ensure them equal treatment before the law under Moslem domination – the Psylarians were justifiably apprehensive.

No, that's phrasing it too kindly. They went half-mad with terror. One woman, clutching a new born baby to her breast, leapt into the sea from the west cape. One suspects post-partum depression, of course, rather than alarm at the oncoming Turks, but the pair of them got mixed up in the Theodoula story anyway, because it was the woman's husband who first proposed that they call on Theodoula for aid. His argument was an entirely practical one; he said, 'She owes us plenty by this time!'

It is by no means certain whether the Psylarians expected Theodoula to help by prayer or by witchcraft; however, they rushed up to her cave one sundown, when the Turkish fleet was practically in sight, and begged on their knees for a miracle.

Which she undertook to provide. What she actually said, as recorded on the walls of the ruined chapel, was: 'I have made a compact with the angel of this place, the mighty Porphyrios. I shall put out the eyes of the Turks on condition that you strip and bind and scourge those who drove me out of my marriage-home.'

By this time, one deduces, her in-laws' grasping ways had made them unpopular with other people, too, for this order was quickly carried out, no one stopping to think that a merciful God would scarcely impose such a proviso. However, I suppose like most Christians they found the vengeful aspect more to their taste.

Also a good few bribes were brought to Theodoula, like silk robes and gold and silver rings. She turned these down, saying, 'I have managed very well without riches for ten years. Perhaps I ought to let the Turks come, because then you would have to learn to do the same.'

By this stage Costas was no longer relying on the wall-inscriptions. He had produced a large, quite handsomely bound though not very skilfully illuminated manuscript volume which had been preserved in the church and which, he confessed sheepishly, he ought not to have brought up here. But the correspondence between the version of the legend of St Theodoula which it contained, and the graffiti he was painstakingly uncovering, was virtually exact.

And one right-hand page displayed a large drawing of the promised miracle. It took place the following dawn. Theodoula had ordered everyone to cover his or her eyes, and babies to be hidden indoors, while it was happening. Only her greedy relatives were unable to comply; they had their hands tied behind their backs, as the drawing clearly showed.

When a great light shone out from the topmost point of the island, which dazzled the Turkish sailors and caused them to sail straight past, those who had done Theodoula out of her husband's house were all struck blind.

Thinking themselves safe, the Psylarians rashly promised to build a chapel before Theodoula's cave, to honour her as a saint, and to celebrate this day – 4 April, I think it was, but there's been a calendar adjustment since then – as a feast-day for ever and ever, amen.

Unfortunately they'd just about got the roof on the chapel when, two years later, the Turks realized they'd missed one not particularly useful island and, for the principle of the thing, occupied it. What happened to Theodoula went unrecorded. The Ottoman Empire discouraged the ability to read and write among its subjects; literacy bred disaffection. There were slanderous traditions that she married a Turkish sea-commander and accepted the Moslem faith, but Costas furiously rebutted such calumnies. With the eel-like ingenuity beloved of your von Dänikens and your Pauwels and Bergiers, he slipped from the mode of 'is it not more likely that—?' to the mode of 'inasmuch as we have shown that—'. He wound up depicting her dying a martyr's death before the mouth of her cave, commending her soul to the Lord and her people to the care of St Porphyrios. All this, from the shred of evidence afforded by the fact that when the Ottoman period came to an end, the local people piously rebuilt the chapel and covered it with these inscriptions, reflecting the story as it had passed down from generation to generation. In many cases, as I already mentioned, the form of the story had become fixed in an ancient form of the language, one reinforcing the other, and there were a number of baffling passages which had obviously been phonetically transcribed by someone who didn't understand about one word in three, but was doing his best.

Oh, I'm maligning Costas. He did have one other fact to support his argument. Records of the original dedication of the church in Psylaria town had been lost, but as soon as the Turks left it was reconsecrated to St Theodoula and the hillside chapel to St Porphyrios. At least, that was the way he worked it out.

By now, however, I myself was satisfied that a pagan shrine on the side of a volcano must have been of considerable significance, and without the least qualm that I would be poaching from Costas I set about exploring the cave, using a little lamp he had brought with him. He returned to his job of removing plaster, and between chisel-blows he explained how the inscriptions came to be covered up.

The island, it seemed, had been virtually depopulated during the Ottoman period; this was, as the phrase goes, a stiff-necked and unruly people. Quite a lot of the young men escaped and joined the overseas resistance movement of which Byron was such a keen supporter. After the establishment of the modern monarchy in the 1840s, some of their heirs came back, bringing their foreign wives and their families, to reclaim their ancestral lands . . . such as they were. The people who had stayed put despised them for, as they saw it, running away to live in luxury in Italy or France or Britain or Malta, while the returnees were appalled by what they found: a barbaric, ignorant, dirty, illiterate community of near-savages. Within a few years these 'foreigners' clearly outnumbered the rest, as well as being richer and healthier, and they closed down the chapel of St Porphyrios and covered over its inscriptions, permitting only certain excerpts to be copied – hence the manuscript book Costas had showed me – for the edification of future generations. Since Theodoula had performed her miracle to defend the island from the Turks, it would have been impolitic to erase her from the main church; however, the cult which had grown up around her was actively discouraged, because the Orthodox establishment doesn't approve, any more than the Vatican does, of people canonizing saints off their own bat. The case of Porphyrios was peculiarly galling, incidentally, for it seemed not to have occurred to anybody at the time – any more than it had to Costas in the 1940s – that there could have been a lot of people called Porphyrios.

With the arrogance of youth I had concluded that this priest, whose name as yet I did not know, was unequipped for the task he had taken on. Thinking more of the possibility of getting my own back on my friend, who was enjoying himself on a much pleasanter island, than of helping with Costas's investigation, I advanced further into the cave, whose sloping walls and low roof were blackened with ancient grease and soot. Nonetheless I examined them carefully, thinking that some item of genuine archæological interest might be found here.

My guess was right. Detectable under the grime were traces

of yet other inscriptions, this time incised – barely more than scratched.

I could not suppress a cry of excitement, which brought Costas running. His comment when he glanced at my discovery quite deflated me; he said, 'Oh, yes – I know about that. But I'm afraid of damaging it if I tackle it with the means available.'

Much annoyed, determined to justify myself somehow, I thought of producing a piece of paper from my pocket and pressing it against the wall so I could lightly run a pencil across the back in a crude approximation of the technique of brass-rubbing. To my vast relief, it not only worked, but made a tremendous impression on Costas. It was a trick he was un-familiar with. He literally gasped as legible words emerged to view.

A sheet from a notebook, though, was obviously useless, as was the only pencil I had with me, for exploring the full extent of the inscription. It was a good five feet high and the lines were anything up to six feet long according to the shape of the cave-wall. We would have to obtain wrapping-paper and some-thing like charcoal or crayons.

I explained this to Costas, who promised to locate suitable materials by tomorrow morning. Now he was obliged to return to town to conduct an evening service, in which he was going to include a prayer of thanks to St Theodoula for sending me to help him. He begged me to attend, and hypocritically enough I consented to do so, thinking it would at least be more amus-ing than the way I usually spent my evenings: sitting on a rock by myself and tossing pebbles into the sea.

Perhaps, seeing me at church, someone might even decide to talk to me . . .

And someone did, though what he said was not the least like what I was hoping for.

Emerging after the service, which had been attended by two old men and six widows of whom one, doubtless having lost her husband in the war, was young and pretty – and made me wonder what St Theodoula had looked like – I was accosted by a stout middle-aged man with a game leg which obliged him to walk with a stick. I had seen him now and then but never been introduced.

Now he presented himself as *Kyrios* Forticos, and I realized he must be descended from one of the 'foreigner' families, some of which Costas had referred to by name. Speaking low and earnestly in halting French, he warned me that even though Costas might tell me what he was doing was of God, it was of Satan and should be left alone. By way of evidence, he recounted the story of an ancestor of his a century ago, a rationalist and sceptic, who had pooh-poohed stories told about the cave and resolved to spend the night there. This was when the chapel was only partly completed. In the morning he was found to be quite blind and half insane.

I was pretty much in a pooh-poohing mood myself, but I judged it unwise to give offence. I contented myself with saying mildly that I hoped to leave Psylaria as soon as I could, and if he got word of a fisherman planning to visit Lemnos I'd be glad to hear, but that in the meantime I felt the cave might usefully be studied by someone with a grounding in archæology. Grudgingly he accepted my point, but insisted that I be careful, for its secrets were not of the kind to be learned from books.

I immediately tracked down Costas and asked why he hadn't mentioned the stories Forticos described, and, much embarrassed, he said they were fairy-tales used to frighten naughty children, not worthy of serious attention. In vain I argued for the value of the Grimm Brothers' work; he stuck to his guns, and eventually I went off to bed in a bad temper.

We had arranged to meet at the chapel next morning, and when he turned up – his arms full of what dictionaries and lexicons he had been able to obtain, as well as rolls of brown paper – Costas was full of apologies. He had had a sleepless night, and had resolved to make up for his rudeness by telling me frankly what he believed to be the secret of Theodoula's miracle.

Sitting down on a handy boulder, he leaned conspiratorially close.

'Are you familiar with the term *schechinah*?' he inquired.

Now it so happens I was brought up in rather a strict Methodist family, and early became acquainted with the Old Testament, so it took me only a moment to recognize the word, in spite of his unfamiliar pronunciation, as what I'd been used to hearing called *shekinah*, with a long 'i'. It's generally defined as the visible presence of God.

I could easily, though, have been at a loss to see the connection but for a couple of lucky accidents, due to my disloyal friend. He had introduced me to Greek mythology, so I had read stories about Zeus appearing in his full majesty in response to mortals' urging, invariably with disastrous consequences; and I had also read the one-volume abridgement of *The Golden Bough*, which for all its inaccuracies and generalizations had sufficed to inform me of concepts like *mana* and *tabu*.

Instantly I was very excited. Even before Costas had declared his solemn belief that thanks to her extraordinary devotion Theodoula must have persuaded God in person to appear to the Turks, my mind was racing ahead. I had visions of publishing a scholarly paper describing the discovery of a hitherto unknown classical or even pre-classical cult, and documenting the folkloric remnants which survived as fairy-tales and superstitions. Most of the friends I had made since leaving the Army were in academia or some branch of the arts, and I was determined to follow their example, or at least enter one of the professions.

Seizing a sheet of paper, I at once resumed copying the mysterious incisions.

Unfortunately, try as we might, we kept running across infuriating lacunae, but the broad sense was plain within a few hours. Costas was awed as he struggled with the dense, archaic terminology. In a near-whisper he asserted, 'Why, it's the order of devotion the saint devised for herself when she was forbidden access to a church!'

On the basis of the passages he was able to translate for me, I was not so sure. It was certainly a set of instructions, or more likely memoranda, but the ceremony it concerned struck me as most unlike a Christian office. However, I held my tongue. Without Costas's cooperation scarcely one in ten of these words would have been comprehensible to me.

When we were obliged to return to the town, he was babbling happily about the possibility of founding an order of monks whose Rule would be that imposed by St Theodoula on herself. We had unravelled a list of rather ghoulish penances some of which, for purely physical reasons, were not applicable to monks anyway, but Costas was so hurt when I jokingly alluded to the fact, I desisted.

He wanted me to attend church again, but I declined, being hungry, and went to Psylaria's only apology for a restaurant, which fronted on the square. There Manos Typhis, a bent old man, assisted by his grandsons of ten and twelve, sold grilled fish, coarse bread, and *souvlakia* on ancient rusty skewers. At least it was cheap. I was at the limit of my resources.

While I was wiping up the last trace of oil with my last crust,

I heard a familiar tapping, and looked up to find Mr Forticos approaching.

'If you really want to leave Psylaria,' he said, 'now's your chance. My cousin intends to take tonight's catch straight to Lemnos. Go with his boat. You'll arrive at dawn.'

For a long moment I was tempted, in spite of all, to stay and go on working with Costas. But it was impossible. I was broke, on the one hand, and on the other I'd assured Forticos of my eagerness to depart; if I went back on my word, that would add someone else to the long list of Psylarians disliking me.

I said, 'How soon does he sail?'

'As soon as you arrive,' was the answer. 'If he is to go to Lemnos, he must start work early to ensure a good catch.'

'Please tell him I'm on my way,' I said, and rapped on my wine glass for the bill.

Packing took me twenty minutes at most; then I wasted as long again in trying to find Costas, but nobody had seen him since evening service, and I realized he must have gone back to the chapel. I left a note of explanation with my landlady, promising to get in touch, and arrived on the quay to find Forticos's cousin about to leave without me.

Immediately I reached home I contacted all those friends of friends who had anything to do with Greek archæology and/or medieval history, and some eight or ten weeks later I received an invitation from a man at the British School of Archæology in Athens to visit Psylaria in a hired caïque. I borrowed more money than I could afford to pay back in a hurry, suffered through a train-ride even less comfortable than my trip to Lemnos, and scarcely a week after receiving the invitation I was again entering Psylaria port. It was a harsh hot summer day without a trace of wind.

News of a strange boat had brought a crowd out to the quay. Among them was Forticos. Pushing his way to the front, ignoring my companions, he took my arm without a word and led me towards the town square.

And thereby, I suspect, saved me from being lynched, or at least thrown in the harbour. For although nobody spoke above a mutter, everyone's eyes were on me, and on every face I could read that here were people ready not simply to dislike but to hate me.

I was sweating with fear by the end of our short trip.

Suddenly Forticos stopped, and so did I. On a bench in the

shade cast by the church was the unmistakable figure of Costas, his black robe now so soiled it had become a kind of Joseph's coat. I was about to hurry over and greet him when Forticos said softly, 'Look again.'

I did.

And this time I made out, covering the upper part of his face like an extension of his black hat, a cloth that hid his eyes.

'He is blind now,' Forticos said as quietly as before.

'How?' I demanded, clenching my fists.

'It happened about two weeks after you left, on the Feast of St Theodoula. He went on with the work you began together, and became so wrapped up in it he neglected his duties at the church. When we called him to account he boasted of his great discovery that would make Psylaria famous all over the world. But we do not want to be famous at the price of trafficking with Satan. We told him, many of us, that he was about the devil's business, and he laughed at us, and finally he said he was going to spend all night at the old chapel and if we tried to stop him he would curse us in the name of St Porphyrios. Some of us, even some of us "foreigners", knew what that would mean. So' – with a shrug – 'we let him go. We watched from a distance, and we saw a great light shine forth, and we knew it was the end. We went into the church and prayed together until dawn.

'An hour or so later he came down the hill, walking like a man in a daze. He came to old Manos's restaurant where the boys had left out some *souvlakia* skewers on a dirty plate. He picked them up, and before we could prevent him he had thrust them deep into his eyes.

'After that we brought some explosive which the Germans left behind and put it in the cave and blew it up.'

I had been standing there petrified. Suddenly I could bear it no longer. I rushed across the square and fell on one knee at Costas's side, babbling my name and demanding why he had done such a terrible thing. He gave me a beaming smile and said something that chilled my blood.

'Why, my friend, after what I saw in that light it would not have been fitting to look on the world again.'

Mr Secrett sipped delicately at his beer, and abruptly I was brought back to the rush and bustle of the pub.

'As well as blinding himself, of course,' Mr Secrett added, 'he had performed a sort of crude leucotomy on his forebrain.

389

He was lucky, or perhaps I should say unlucky, that he didn't contract a fatal infection as well. He was left in a childlike condition, rather lethargic, devoid of initiative, quite rational and indeed pleasant apart from occasional bouts of unaccountable rage. He could no longer discharge his religious duties, but "once a priest always a priest", so he was to be allowed to retain clerical garb and help with petty routine matters. He accepted his fate without complaining. He is firmly convinced that he saw the *schechinah*, and I think he's vaguely pleased that owing to the explosion which brought the cave down, and incidentally destroyed the notes and tracings he and I had made, he will be the last Psylarian to do so.

'Naturally the man from the British School of Archæology was furious, and I was a bit upset too, for it meant there was no way of establishing whether the theory I'd evolved was sound or not. My goodness, is that the time? I should have been back at work ages ago!'

He drained his glass and rose.

'Nice to have run across you again, Scrivener old chap! Do drop in whenever you're passing. You know you're always welcome.'

'I certainly shall,' I said mendaciously. 'But just a moment! What theory?'

'Oh, that the name Porphyrios was a corruption.'

'Corruption of what?'

Mr Secrett shrugged. 'Presumably Pyrophoros, the firebringer. Prometheus. Or, translating into Latin, Lucifer. Which leads to the interesting possibility that Theodoula, far from being a Christian saint, may have been the last in a line of priestesses stretching back to prehistoric times. You see, I find it hard to believe that she devised such an efficacious ritual all by herself. At any rate I've been quite unable to duplicate her work. But now, of course, we shall never know . . . I *must* dash!'

Halfway to the door he spun around and strode back.

'One more point before I go,' he said in an anxious tone. 'You do realize – don't you? – that I've never mentioned my idea in any of my letters to Costas. I'm not sure he'd be able to follow it anyway, not in his present state, but if he could it would be cruel. So I've never told him.'

I rather wish he hadn't told me either.

Robert Bloch

The rubber room

*Robert Bloch was born in 1917, and for much of the time is the
most charming and pleasant man you could imagine. Some
say it is his Mr Hyde who writes his horror stories, but it seems
to me that the opposite is true: when he feels compassion for
his audience he writes his horror stories, when he's feeling
evil he makes some of the most atrocious puns imaginable.
Luckily he's kept busy writing short stories (collected in* Cold
Chills, Yours Truly Jack the Ripper, Dragons and Nightmares,
Pleasant Dreams *and nearly a dozen more books), novels
(including* The Scarf, Firebug, *the Lovecraftian* Strange Eons,
and Psycho, *which was filmed by someone or other), and film
and television scripts. His short story 'That Hellbound Train'
won a Hugo, and at the first World Fantasy Convention he was
given a Life Achievement Award. Psychological horror is his
particular skill, and it has never been darker inside one of his
characters than here.*

Emery kept telling them he wasn't crazy, but they put him in
the rubber room anyway.

Sorry, fella, they said. Only temporary, we got a space problem here, overcrowded, move you to another cell in a couple
hours, they said. It's better than being in the tank with all them
drunks, they said. Okay, so you had your call to the lawyer but
just take it easy until he gets here, they said.

And the door went clang.

So there he was, stuck way down at the end of the cell-block
in this little room all by himself. They'd taken his watch and his
wallet, his keys and his belt, even his shoelaces, so there was
no way he could harm himself unless he bit his own wrists. But
that would be crazy, and Emery wasn't crazy.

Now all he could do was wait. There wasn't anything else,
no choice, no options, no way, once you were here in the rubber room.

To begin with, it was small – six paces long and six paces wide. A reasonably active man could cover the distance between the walls in one jump but he'd need a running start. Not that there was any point in trying, because he'd just bounce harmlessly off the thick padding.

The windowless walls were padded everywhere from floor to ceiling and so was the door. The padding was seamless so it couldn't be torn or pried away. Even the floor was padded, except for a ten-inch square at the left far corner which was supposed to serve as a toilet facility.

Above him a tiny light bulb burned dimly behind its meshed enclosure, safely beyond reach from the floor below. The ceiling around it was padded too, probably to deaden sound.

Restraint room, that's what they said it was, but it used to be called a padded cell. Rubber room was just popular slang. And maybe the slang wouldn't be so popular if more people were exposed to the reality.

Before he knew what he was doing, Emery found himself pacing back and forth. Six paces forward, six paces back, over and over again, like an animal in a cage.

That's what this was, actually – not a room, just a cage. And if you stayed in a cage long enough you turned into an animal. Ripping and clawing and smashing your head against the walls, howling for release.

If you weren't crazy when you came in you'd go crazy before you got out. The trick, of course, was not to stay here too long.

But how long was too long? How long would it be before the lawyer arrived?

Six paces forward, six paces back. Grey spongy padding muffled his footsteps on the floor and absorbed the light from above, leaving the walls in shadow. Shadows could drive you crazy too. So could the silence, and being alone. Alone in shadows and silence, like he'd been when they found him there in the room – the other room, the one in the house.

It was like a bad dream. Maybe that's the way it feels when you're crazy, and if so he must have been crazy when it happened.

But Emery wasn't crazy now. He was perfectly sane, completely under control. And there was nothing here that could harm him. Silence can't harm you. What was the old saying? Violence is golden. No, not *violence*. Where had that come from? Freudian slip. To hell with Freud, what did he know?

Nobody knew. And if he kept silent nobody ever would. Even though they'd found him they couldn't prove anything. Not if he kept silent, let his lawyer do the talking. Silence was his friend. And the shadows were his friends too. Shadows hid everything. There had been shadows in the other room and no one could have seen clearly when they found him. You just *thought* you saw it, he'd tell them.

No, he'd forgotten — he mustn't tell them, just let the lawyer talk. What was the matter with him, *was* he going crazy here after all?

Six paces forward, six paces back. Keep walking, keep silent. Keep away from those shadows in the corners. They were getting darker now. Darker and thicker. Something seemed to be moving there in the far corner to the right.

Emery felt the muscles tightening in his throat and he couldn't control them; he knew that in a moment he was going to scream.

Then the door opened behind him and in the light from the corridor the shadow disappeared.

It was a good thing he hadn't screamed. They would have been sure he was crazy then, and that would spoil everything.

But now that the shadow was gone Emery relaxed. By the time they took him down the hall and into the visitor's room he was quite calm again.

His lawyer waited for him there, sitting on the other side of the grille barrier, and nobody was listening.

That's what the lawyer said. Nobody's listening, you can tell me all about it.

Emery shook his head and smiled because he knew better. Violence is golden and even the walls have ears. He wanted to warn his lawyer that they were spying on him but that would sound crazy. The sane thing to do was not to mention it, just be careful and say the right things instead.

He told the lawyer what everybody knew about himself. He was a decent man, he had a steady job, paid his bills, didn't smoke or drink or get out of line. Hardworking, dependable, neat, clean, no police record, not a troublemaker. Mother was always proud of her boy and she'd be proud of him today if she were still alive. He'd always looked after her and when she died he still looked after the house, kept it up, kept himself up, just the way she'd taught him to. So what was all this fuss about?

393

Suppose you tell me, the lawyer said.

That was the hard part, making him understand, but Emery knew everything depended on it. So he talked very slowly, choosing his words carefully, sticking to the facts.

World War II had happened before he'd been born, but that was a fact.

Emery knew a lot of facts about World War II because he used to read library books when Mother was alive. Improve your mind, she said. Reading is better than watching all that violence on the television, she said.

So at night when he couldn't sleep he read for hours sitting up in bed in his room. People he worked with down at the shop called him a bookworm but he didn't care. There was no such thing as a bookworm, he knew that. There were worms that ate microorganisms in the soil and birds that ate worms and animals that ate birds and people who ate animals and microorganisms that ate people – like the ones that ate Mother until they killed her.

Everything – germs, plants, animals, people – kills other things to stay alive. This is a fact, a cruel fact. He could still remember the way Mother screamed.

After she died he read more. That's when he really got into history. The Greeks killed the Persians and the Romans killed the Greeks and the barbarians killed the Romans and the Christians killed the barbarians and the Moslems killed the Christians and the Hindus killed the Moslems. Blacks killed whites, whites killed Indians, Indians killed other Indians, orientals killed other orientals, Protestants killed Catholics, Catholics killed Jews, Jews killed Our Saviour on the Cross.

Love one another, Jesus said, and they killed him for it. If Our Saviour had lived, the gospel would have spread around the world and there'd be no violence. But the Jews killed Our Lord.

That's what Emery told the lawyer, but it didn't go down. Get to the point, the lawyer said.

Emery was used to that kind of reaction. He'd heard it before when he tried to explain things to girls he met after Mother died. Mother hadn't approved of him going with girls and he used to resent it. After she was gone the fellows at work told him it would do him good. Get out of your shell, they said. So he let them set up some double-dates and that's when he found out that Mother was right. The girls just laughed at him when he talked facts.

It was better to stay in his shell, like a snail. Snails know how to protect themselves in a world where everyone kills to live, and the Jews killed Our Saviour.

Facts, the lawyer said. Give me some facts.

So Emery told him about World War II. That's when the real killing began. Jewish international bankers financed the Napoleonic wars and World War I, but these were nothing compared to World War II. Hitler knew what the Jews were planning and he tried to prevent it – that's why he invaded those other countries, to get rid of the Jews, just as he did in Germany. They were plotting a war to destroy the world, so they could take over. But no one understood and in the end the Jew-financed armies won the war. The Jews killed Hitler just like they killed Our Saviour. History repeats itself, and that's a fact too.

Emery explained all this very quietly, using nothing except facts, but from the way his lawyer looked at him he could see it was no use.

So Emery went back into his shell. But this time he took his lawyer with him.

He told him what it was like, living alone in his house, which was really a big shell that protected him. Too big at first, and too empty, until Emery began to fill it up with books. Books about World War II, because of the facts. Only the more he read the more he realized that most of them didn't contain facts. The victors write the histories and now that the Jews had won they wrote lies. They lied about Hitler, they lied about the Nazi Party and its ideals.

Emery was one of the few people who could read between the lies and see the truth. Reminders of the truth could be found outside of books, so now he turned to them and started to collect them. The trappings and the banners, the iron helmets and the iron medals. Iron crosses were reminders too – the Jews had destroyed Our Saviour on a cross and now they were trying to destroy the crosses themselves.

That's when he began to realize what was happening, when he went to the antique shops where such things were sold.

There would be other people in these shops and they stared at him. Nobody said a word but they were watching. Sometimes he thought he could hear them whispering behind his back and he knew for a fact that they were taking notes.

It wasn't just his imagination because pretty soon some of the people down at work started asking him questions about his collection – the pictures of the party leaders and the swastika emblems and badges and the photographs of the little girls presenting flowers to the Führer at rallies and parades. Hard to believe these little girls were now fifty-year-old women. Sometimes he thought if he met one of those women he could settle down with her and be happy; at least she'd understand because she knew the facts. Once he almost decided to run an ad in the classified section, trying to locate such a woman, but then he realized it might be dangerous. Suppose the Jews were out to get her? They'd get him too. That was a fact.

Emery's lawyer shook his head. His face, behind the grille, was taking on an expression which Emery didn't like. It was the expression people wear when they're at the zoo, peering through the bars or the wire screens at the animals.

That's when Emery decided he'd have to tell his lawyer the rest. It was a risk, but if he wanted to be believed his lawyer must know all the facts.

So he told him about the conspiracy.

All these hijackings and kidnappings going on today were part of it. And these terrorists running around with ski-masks over their faces were part of the plan too.

In today's world, terror wears a ski-mask.

Sometimes they called themselves Arabs, but that was just to confuse people. They were the ones behind the bombings in Northern Ireland and the assassinations in South America. The international Jewish conspiracy was in back of it all and behind every ski-mask was a Jewish face.

They spread throughout the world, stirring up fear and confusion. And they were here too, plotting and scheming and spying on their enemies. Mother knew.

When he was just a little boy and did something naughty Mother used to tell him to behave. Behave yourself or the Jew-man will get you, Mother said. He used to think she was just trying to frighten him but now he realized Mother was telling the truth. Like the time she caught him playing with himself and locked him in the closet. The Jew-man will get you, she said. And he was all alone in the dark and he could see the Jew-man coming through the walls and he screamed and she let him out just in time. Otherwise the Jew-man *would* have taken him. He knew now that this was the way they got their recruits – they took other peoples' children and brainwashed them, brought them up to be political terrorists in countries all over the world – Italy, Ireland, Indonesia, the Middle East – so that no one would suspect the real facts. The real facts, that the Jews were responsible, getting ready for another war. And when the other nations had destroyed themselves, Israel would take over the world.

Emery was talking louder now but he didn't realize it until the lawyer told him to hold it down. What makes you think these terrorists are after you, he asked. Did you ever see one?

No, Emery told him, they're too clever for that. But they have their spies, their agents are everywhere.

The lawyer's face was getting red and Emery noticed it. He told him why it was getting so hot here in the visitor's room – their agents were at work again.

Those people who saw Emery buying the flags and swastikas and iron crosses had been planted in the stores to spy on him. And the ones down at work who teased him about his collection, they were spies too, and they knew he'd found out the truth.

The terrorists had been after him for months now, planning to kill him. They tried to run him down with their cars when he crossed the street but he got away. Two weeks ago when he turned on the television there was an explosion. It seemed like a short-circuit but he knew better; they wanted to electrocute him only it didn't work. He was too smart to call a repairman because that's what they wanted – they'd send one of their assassins instead. The only people who still make house-calls today are the murderers.

So for two weeks he'd managed without electricity. That's when they must have put the machines in the walls. The terrorists had machines to make things heat up and at night he could hear a humming sound in the dark. He'd searched around, tapping the walls, and he couldn't find anything, but he knew the machines were there. Sometimes it got so hot he was soaked with sweat, but he didn't try to turn down the furnace. He'd show them he could take it. And he wasn't about to go out of the house because he knew that's what they wanted. That was their plan, to force him out so they could get at him and kill him.

Emery was too smart for that. He had enough canned goods and stuff to get by and it was safer to stay put. When the phone rang he didn't answer; probably someone at the shop was calling to ask him why he didn't come to work. That's all he needed – come back to work so they could murder him on the way.

It was better to hole up right there in his bedroom with the iron crosses and the swastikas on the walls. The swastika is a very ancient symbol, a sacred symbol, and it protected him. So did the big picture of the Führer. Just knowing it was there was protection enough, even in the dark. Emery couldn't sleep any more because of the sounds in the walls – at first it had been humming, but gradually he could make out voices. He didn't understand Hebrew, and it was only gradually that he knew what they were saying. Come on out you dirty Aryan, come out and be killed.

Every night they came, like vampires, wearing ski-masks to hide their faces. They came and they whispered, *come out, come out, wherever you are.* But he didn't come out.

Some history books said Hitler was crazy, and maybe that part was true. If so, Emery knew why. It was because he must have heard the voices too and known they were after him. No wonder he kept talking about the answer to the Jewish question. They were polluting the human race and he had to stop them. But they burned him in a bunker instead. They killed Our Saviour. Can't you understand that?

The lawyer said he couldn't understand and maybe Emery should talk to a doctor instead. But Emery didn't want to talk to a doctor. Those Jew doctors were part of the conspiracy. What he had to say now was in the strictest confidence.

Then for Christ's sake tell me, the lawyer said.

And Emery said yes, he'd tell him. For Christ's sake, for the sake of Our Lord.

Two days ago he'd run out of canned goods. He was hungry, very hungry, and if he didn't eat he'd die. The terrorists wanted to starve him to death but he was too smart for that.

So he decided to go to the store.

He peeked through all the windows first but he couldn't see anyone in a ski-mask. That didn't mean it was safe, of course, because they used ordinary people too. The only thing he could do was take a chance. And before he left he put one of the iron crosses around his neck on a chain. That would help protect him.

Then, at twilight, he went to the supermarket down the street. No sense trying to drive, because the terrorists might have planted a bomb in his car, so he walked all the way.

It felt strange being outside again and though Emery saw

nothing suspicious he was shaking all over by the time he got to the store.

The supermarket had those big fluorescent lights and there were no shadows. He didn't see any of their spies or agents around either, but of course they'd be too clever to show themselves. Emery just hoped he could get back home before they made their move.

The customers in the store looked like ordinary people; the thing is, you can never be sure nowadays. Emery picked out his canned goods as fast as possible and he was glad to get through the line at the checkout counter without any trouble. The clerk gave him a funny look but maybe it was just because he hadn't shaved or changed clothes for so long. Anyway he managed, even though his head was starting to hurt.

It was dark when he came out of the store with his bag of groceries, and there was nobody on the street. That's another thing the Jew terrorists have done – made us afraid to walk on the street alone. See what it's come to? Everyone's scared just being out at night!

That's what the little girl told him.

She was standing there on the corner of the block when he saw her – cute little thing, maybe five years old, with big brown eyes and curly hair. And she was crying, scared to death.

I'm lost, she said. I'm lost, I want my Mommy.

Emery could understand that. Everybody's lost nowadays, wants someone to protect them. Only there's no protection any more, not with those terrorists around waiting for their chance, lurking in the shadows.

And there were shadows on the street, shadows outside his house. He wanted to help but he couldn't risk standing out here talking.

So he just went on, up the porch steps, and it wasn't until he opened the front door that he realized she had followed him. Little girl crying, saying please Mister, take me to my Mommy.

He wanted to go in and shut the door but he knew he had to do something.

How did you get lost, he asked.

She said she was waiting in the car outside the market while Mommy shopped but when Mommy didn't come back she got out to look for her in the store and she was gone. Then she thought she saw her down the street and she ran after her only it turned out to be another lady. Now she didn't know where she was and would he please take her home?

Emery knew he couldn't do that, but she was crying again, crying loud. If they were anywhere around they'd hear her, so he told her to come in.

The house smelled funny from not being aired out and it was very hot inside. Dark too with all the electricity turned off on account of the terrorists. He tried to explain but she only cried louder because the dark frightened her.

Don't be scared, Emery said. Tell me your Mommy's name and I'll phone her to come and get you.

So she told him the name – Mrs Rubelsky, Sylvia Rubelsky – but she didn't know the address.

It was hard to hear because of the humming in the walls. He got hold of the flashlight he kept in the kitchen for emergencies and then he went into the hall to look up the name in the phone book.

There weren't any Rubelskys listed. He tried other spellings – Rubelski, Roubelsky, Rebelsky, Rabelsky – but there was nothing in the book. Are you sure, he asked.

Then she said they didn't have a phone.

That was funny; everybody has a phone. She said it didn't matter because if he just took her over to Sixth Street she could point out the house to him.

Emery wasn't about to go anywhere, let alone Sixth Street. That was a Jewish neighbourhood. Come to think of it, Rubelsky was a Jewish name.

Are you Jewish, he asked her.

She stopped crying and stared at him and those big brown eyes got wider and wider. The way she stared made his head hurt more.

What are you looking at, he said.

That thing around your neck, she told him. That iron cross. It's like Nazis wear.

What do you know about Nazis, he asked.

They killed my Grandpa, she said. They killed him at Belsen. Mommy told me. Nazis are bad.

All at once it came to Emery in a flash, a flash that made his whole head throb.

She was one of *them*. They'd planted her on the street, knowing he'd let her into the house here. What did they want?

Why do you wear bad things, she said. Take it off.

Now she was reaching out towards the chain around his neck, the chain with the iron cross.

It was like that old movie he saw once long ago, the movie about the Golem. This big stone monster got loose in the Jewish ghetto, wearing the Star of David on its chest. A little girl pulled the star off and the Golem fell down dead.

That's why they sent her here, to pull off the iron cross and kill him.

No way, he said. And he slapped her, not hard, but she started to scream and he couldn't have that, so he put his hands around her neck just to stop the screaming and there was a kind of cracking sound and then—

What happened then, the lawyer asked.

I don't want to talk about it, Emery said.

But he couldn't stop, he *was* talking about it. At first, when he didn't find a pulse, he thought he'd killed her. But he hadn't squeezed that hard, so it must have happened when she touched the iron cross. That meant he'd guessed right, she was one of *them.*

But he couldn't tell anyone, he knew people would never believe that the terrorists had sent a little Jew-girl here to murder him. And he couldn't let her be found like this. What to do, that was the question. The Jewish question.

Then he remembered. Hitler had the answer. He knew what to do.

It was hot here and even hotter downstairs. That's where he carried her, downstairs, where the furnace was going. The gas furnace.

Oh my God, said the lawyer. Oh my God.

And then the lawyer stood up fast and went over to the door on the other side of the grille and called the guard.

Come back here, Emery said.

But he didn't listen, he kept whispering to the guard, and then other guards came up behind Emery on his side of the grille and grabbed his arms.

He yelled at them to let him go, not to listen to that Jew lawyer, didn't they understand he must be one of *them*?

Instead of paying attention they just marched him back down the hall to the rubber room and shoved him inside.

You promised you'd put me in another cell, Emery said. I don't want to stay here. I'm not crazy.

One of the guards said easy does it, the doctor is coming to give you something so you can sleep.

And the door went clang.

*

Emery was back in the rubber room, but this time he didn't pace and he didn't call out. It wouldn't do any good. Now he knew how Our Saviour had felt, betrayed and waiting for the crucifixion.

Emery had been betrayed too, betrayed by the Jew lawyer, and now all he could do was wait for the Jew doctor to come. Put him to sleep, the guard had said. That was how the conspiracy worked – they'd put him to sleep for ever. Only he wouldn't let them, he'd stay awake, demand a fair trial.

But that was impossible. The police would tell about hearing the little girl scream and breaking into the house and finding him. They'd say he was a child-molester and a murderer. And the judge would sentence him to death. He'd believe the Jews just like Pontius Pilate did, just like the Allies did when they killed Our Führer.

Emery wasn't dead yet but there was no way out. No way out of the trial, no way out of the rubber room.

Or was there?

The answer came to him just like that.

He'd plead insanity.

Emery knew he wasn't crazy but he could fool them into believing it. That was no disgrace – some people thought Jesus and the Führer were crazy too. All he had to do was pretend.

Yes, that was the answer. And just thinking about it made him feel better. Even if they shut him up in a rubber room like this he'd still be alive. He could walk and talk and eat and sleep and think. Think about how he'd tricked them, all those Jew terrorists who were out to get him.

Emery didn't have to be careful now. He didn't have to lie, the way he'd lied to the lawyer. He could admit the real truth.

Killing that little Jew-girl wasn't an accident, he knew what he was going to do the minute he got his hands around her throat. He squeezed just as hard as he could because that's what he'd always really wanted. To squeeze the necks of those girls who laughed at him, squeeze the guys at work who wouldn't listen when he told them about his collection and yes, say it, he wanted to squeeze Mother too because she'd always squeezed him, smothered him, strangled away his life. But most of all he squeezed the Jews, the dirty kike terrorists who were out to destroy him, destroy the world.

And that's what he had done. He hadn't cracked the little girl's neck, she wasn't dead when he carried her downstairs and opened the furnace door.

What he had really done was solve the Jewish question.

He'd solved it and they couldn't touch him. He was safe now, safe from all the terrorists and evil spirits out for revenge, safe for ever here in the rubber room.

The only thing he didn't like was the shadows. He remembered how they'd been before, how the one in the far corner seemed to get darker and thicker.

And now it was happening again.

Don't look at it, he told himself. You're imagining things. Only crazy people see shadows moving. Moving and coiling like a cloud, a cloud of smoke from a gas furnace.

But he had to look because it was changing now, taking on a shape. Emery could see it standing in the corner, the figure of a man. A man in a black suit, with a black face.

And it was moving forward.

Emery backed away as the figure glided towards him softly and silently across the padded floor, and he opened his mouth to scream.

But the scream wouldn't come, nothing was coming except the figure looming up before Emery as he pressed against the wall of the rubber room. He could see the black face quite clearly now – only it wasn't a face.

It was a ski-mask.

The figure's arms rose and the hands splayed out and he saw little black droplets oozing from the smoky wrists as the fingers curled around his throat. Emery struck out at the ski-mask, thrusting his fingers through the eye-holes, stabbing at the eyes behind them. But there was nothing under the mask, nothing at all.

It was then that Emery really went mad.

When they opened the door of the rubber room the shadow was gone. All they found was Emery and he was dead.

Apoplexy, they said. Heart failure. Better write up a medical report fast and close the case. Close the rubber room too while they were at it.

Just a coincidence of course, but people might get funny ideas if they found out. Two deaths in the same cell – Emery, and that other nut last week who bit open his own wrists, the crazy terrorist guy in the ski-mask.

Giles Gordon

Drama in five acts

*Giles Gordon says it all as tersely as I could, so let him do so.
'GG was born in Edinburgh in 1940 and lived there until 1962
when he came to London to work in publishing. He resigned
from Victor Gollancz Ltd in 1972 where for five years he'd
been editorial director (before which he'd been an editor with
Penguin Books) to be able to devote more time to his own
writing. He now works as a literary agent with Anthony Shiel
Associates where he represents, among other authors, Michael
Moorcock, and writes his own books. He's published five novels
(*The Umbrella Man, About a marriage, Girl with red hair,
100 Scenes from married life *and* Enemies *and has just
completed a novel,* Ambrose's Vision*) and three collections of
short stories (*Pictures from an exhibition, Farewell, Fond
Dreams *and* The Illusionist*). He has edited a number of
anthologies including* Prevailing Spirits: *a book of Scottish
Ghost Stories,* A Book of Contemporary Nightmares *and (with
Fred Urquhart)* Modern Scottish Short Stories. *He lives in
London with his wife Margaret Gordon, the children's book
illustrator, and their three children, Callum, Gareth and
Harriet. He is a member of the Writers' Guild, Writers'
Action Group and the Society of Authors.' The one point he
fails to make is that much of his career has been devoted to
extending the boundaries of fiction and experimenting with its
form, but this story makes the point for him.*

On the beach.

A beach. By the shore. Sand, sea, sky. The combination.
Tone and texture.

More sand on the beach than in the house though the house
built partly of sand, sand in the stone and in the cement.

What stone? What cement?

And who in their right mind, their upright mind, would want

405

to pour sand on to a white carpet, the carpet in the living room? White, or dyed red, the carpet. Or, for that matter, another matter, any carpet?

A white carpet. Or a red carpet.

The texture of the carpet.

A horizontal surface on which to stand, kneel, lie, sleep, cohabit, relate.

I will not dye my carpet red. If it is red to start with, when purchased and laid, why then it is red. If I have chosen it that colour, I and she who is to me, why then it is red, the colour of red, the colour of blood and wine, of bandages and the be-smirched linen battle flag, why then it is red, that colour, and lies on my floor, underneath my feet. And I wear a white suit of fine material on a hot day and grey soft leather shoes with high heels and stand on the red carpet. And the sun is pinned high in the sky, blue sky, dazzling sun, and the sun doesn't move and the Earth doesn't move.

Listen.

On the beach, or through the window of my summer house, the walls of the window being glass (there is sand in glass, too), the walls entirely glass, a glass house, I stare at the horizon, hoping that the sight will transform my eyes, my vision, hoping that my eyes and insights will be transformed.

Stand, looking.

Stare is too strong, too positive a word. I stand, happen to be standing. Look, happen to be looking.

The horizon is painted on, a line, blue against blue. Back-cloth. Act One.

On the beach, a man dressed in ... different clothes, strange to me because not mine, clothes that are not mine, pours liquid from an immaculate glass on to the sand, into the sand. The sand accepts. It is not in the habit of rejecting such offerings.

If you listen you may hear it, if your ear is cocked, tilted. The glass is turned, angled. The liquid descends, plunges in a line, a column, like a thin silver waterfall, a cascade. A dark patch appears on the sand, spreads, grows, then ceases to seep outwards.

My glass house is on the beach, on the sand. The end away from the sea.

A dark patch appears on my carpet.

You cannot *hear* the liquid falling. It is not sound that causes

it to fall, persuades it to fall. It is the hand that tilts the glass.
The stain spreads and I remember it in my dreams, will remember it spreading, day and night, from generation to generation, really. What the mind can encompass compared to the body!

What colour was the liquid in the glass?

Ah . . .

You smile at the question.

You did not think to ask about the texture, did not ask about the texture.

I look through the window. There is no glass there, between me and what I see. I see: the beach, the sea, the horizon, the sky. There are no holidaymakers on the beach with boiled bodies and bathing suits, no summer families playing ball games or lazing or feeling the water. It is not that kind of beach. A cluster of dark birds circle, circle the sky, their colour or tone (dark against light) not changing against sand, sea or sky. The sky rolls back, a domed head, extravagant, preposterous halo. What a physique. What a capacity. Cubic capacity, the world's skull.

On the beach, a man has been hacked at by another. Act Two. A man? A person.

Cruelly, though cruelty didn't enter into it. There hasn't been a war for years, decades, not on this shore, this coastline. Wars take place in the newspapers, or on television, in black and white or in colour.

A torso, live, wriggling, the body descending to the sea through a smudge of movement, life out of focus. It shunts, shuffles towards the water, the salt in the sea, to bathe what it imagines to be its wounds, but doesn't reach it, whether because of the slowness of its movement or because the tide retreats and retreats I cannot tell.

It is severed below the shoulders, a clean, ivory cut. Or was born that way. The blood has dripped. *Has* dripped. Years ago, years ago. Generations before. You cannot imagine, remember the cut. You turn away, in your memory, not daring to witness it.

You concentrate on the sword slashing. Shake your head, slowly, shake your head, shake your head, faster. You cannot imagine. No!

Your head doesn't move.

(My head doesn't move.)

Your body is static. Do you reject the choice of movement or is it that you cannot move your head from side to side?

On the beach, there is sand. Take away the sand and are you left with the beach? The beach is sand. The beach slopes towards the sea, touches the sea, the sea touches the sand.

The sand holds secrets, without telling, without speculating. The sand is, it goes without saying, so it does, inarticulate, silent. If it snores or snarls, cries or laughs, purrs or sings, the sound is not for your ears to hear, the conch of night. It churns over and over, over and over. And you are standing there, watching or not, standing there.

In your house.

Looking down the beach. And you stand on a marble floor, your feet encased in grey soft leather shoes, Italian with high heels, no more defined, no more precise than that, the heels high, too high for your age and the year of grace. And the house has gone, the glass has gone. Act Three. Or the house is being built. Built around you. Rebuilt. And there is no glass (who can see through glass?), you peer inside from outside, see nothing, you see through nothing, no house, landscape, seascape, the world, look.

What?

Look. And the inside of your head, your mind has moved. The body in your eye, your brain. Your flesh and blood.

On the beach, a red figure moving and squirming like a seething tin of worms or snakes, living shrimps in melting butter but red, carved from solid gore but gleaming none the less, bleeding but no blood spilling, staining the sand. And another person makes for the foreshore but the tide pushes up, surges, a sudden swell of water, no creeping prettily a few inches hour by hour as the Moon pushes or pulls, devious menstrual whore.

I stand looking.

Isolated.

In my own body.

It is possible, more usual than not, to be isolated in the body of another?

I nod to myself. Yes.

What, am I weary?

In the isolation of another body, the body of another, we forget our own. I try to forget my own, the loaned, lent body, the hair I've sprouted which assists at disguising the truth.

The what?

*

The figure steals away, she gives thanks for the morrow, shivers at the arm, born that way. And I do not know, cannot tell. There are explanations behind these events though my life is clear enough to me.

She is not mine, nor I hers. So the glimpse, the glance, suggested to me.

The form sinks to the ground.

I stand there. I tell you, I'm steadfast.

I am out of myself, the mind – mine or another's – is around the ceiling, above my body, watching, listening, involved too, taking a responsible part in the proceedings, God yes. And there is no roof on the house. No walls or roof but a marble floor. Black marble. (There is sand in marble, too.) No one needs to polish it, either on their knees or upright with a mop.

And I stand there in underpants and singlet and socks, no suspenders necessary. And my bellow, my roar grows and grows and I am disgusted, verily. That is: I am frightened, afraid. My world trembles.

Down the beach, the thing, the action. Act Four.

And I will not, and I cannot, and I will not.

It is wondrous to behold. It is, too. A human wonder become more than humanity or human imagination can accommodate. It splits, one comes out of the other and there is breathing, living. No destruction, only growth. One comes out of the other and each is whole. And I see the legs, and the froth and foam between the legs, the spread angle of one, and it doesn't necessarily come from there but I think it does. And there are two, wondrous to behold, from one, the shadow and the shadow woman, and the sunlight blinds the eyes from the marble and it is all red.

You close your eyes.

Your eyes scream.

It is all red.

Or whatever colour you think it is.

Expect it to be.

On the beach.

In the house, serenity, security. The white of the sheets, no more blood than is traditional, normal. The walls keep the wolves at bay as the cats are fed their bones and milk and they throb in their throats with pleasure.

The wolves watch, the walls are glass. The animals are outside. Their paws, when they try to enter, skid on the marble, they can get no nearer. Their feet are trapped in the sand.

There are no walls. There is no glass.

I stand on the beach.

Or the desert.

Not the desert, no, there is sea. And no palm trees, no camels or horses charging towards me.

I stand in the depths of the ocean. Touch down deep enough and there is sand. One step, and another: I can walk again. What joy!

I walk through the waters, I blur towards her, towards. No breasts.

Face to

face

but I don't see her, cannot, cannot cannot understand the features, their meaning, the nostrils in the kneecap, the hair in the eye, the stomach in the back, the mouth in the armpit, the chest in the foot, the arm in the thigh, the eyes in the arse, the ears in the navel. Orifices galore. The body is confused. Confusing.

Sand. Water. Sun.

Then suddenly, darkness.

I walked through the water. There was red, and glass, and a knife, the sand and the ivory, ebony cut.

Oh I saw so well, such things, and my mind blew, and my mind . . .

You stand, in a white suit, on the beach.

Act Five.

And there is me and only me and I saw them split, separate, the one come from the other, two where there had been one, and why and how and why and how

And on the beach, solemnly, silently, no nonsense,

no scream, no illness, certainly no illness, no great yob of vomit streaking, trailing down into a basin

and in the morning.

In the morning.

In the morning.

410

Jack Sullivan
The initiation

*Jack Sullivan lives in New York, where he teaches English and
humanities at New York and Columbia Universities. He wrote*
Elegant Nightmares, *a mongraph on the English ghost story,
and edited and annotated* Lost Souls, *by far the most useful
recent anthology of such tales. He writes concert programmes
for Carnegie Hall and the Brooklyn Academy of Music, and
edited the* Penguin Encyclopaedia of Horror and the
Supernatural. *I suspect he would say that New York is
sometimes even more dismaying that it appears in his story.*

As the IRT lurched forwards, he felt an instant distance from
the other passengers. He had heard New Yorkers were like
this, inattentive out of long habit to the ugliness around them,
especially the subway. But he hadn't expected people to be
quite this oblivious, not only to him, but to the train. He felt a
kinship with the train, as if they were both being ignored. No
one seemed to care that he had been in New York only a few
weeks, that this was all new to him: he was in the city for what
had turned out to be a successful job interview, and he was
still struggling over whether to accept.

People stared at newspapers, floors, blank faces. Conversation hung in the thick air and tried to synchronize with moving
lips, only to be cut off by the roar of the train. How could
people hear each other, or not care if they couldn't?

To his left, two young women clutched and jabbed, mime-
like, as they talked, their gestures cancelling each other out.
Across from him, a middle-aged man muttered back at his
Daily News. To his right, a drunk sprawled serenely beside his
shopping bag, the noise lulling him further into sleep.

None of these paid the slightest attention to the old woman with the tin cup, the accordion, and the empty eye sockets, who staggered past. He wondered whether they even heard the accordion vibrato quivering through the greater noise. Suddenly he realized that after only a few weeks he too was unmoved, in danger of becoming like the others. Like them, he had given the woman no money. Why hadn't he? Guilt made a quick stab at him, retreated at the next grate of the train, and flooded back as resentment. If the others could ignore her, why couldn't he? At least he had noticed her, more than he could say for them. He had seen her fall momentarily against the man across, who had only sunk further into his *Daily News*, burying his head beneath a typically tasteless *News* headline about the 'flap' over recent missing persons reported in Manhattan. The man didn't direct his mutterings at the old woman; he didn't seem angry, even annoyed. He didn't seem anything really. Why should he? The woman was gone now. And so was the guilt.

An awareness of the train began to fill in the space. The distance he felt from the others had returned, granting him the freedom to look, even stare about. Though an express, the train moved in a manic pattern of hesitancy and speed. It seemed unsure of itself, as if it might jump the rail. His head was a chamber of white noise, shrieking upward when the train grated on curves. The floor surged under his feet. Graffiti danced in front of his eyes. Miss Subway, the Salem girl, and Smokey the Bear grinned down from above. Speeding through a tunnel of its own, his mind decided to leave what it saw behind for a while.

That is probably why he was able to visualize this new thing, something very particular, for some time before he knew what it was. In looking up at the ads, his left eye had been teased to the side by a flickering outside the window where nothing had existed a moment before but blackness streaked with lights. He turned full around to take it in better. In the darkness another train had materialized, its windows parallel to his own so he could look into them. It was a local his express had overtaken and would soon pass by. Several feet away, its windows as greasy as those he was looking through, it didn't reveal much. The dimness gave him time to realize that the train had not caught his eye so much as something inside it, as if the train had been an excuse to turn around. What he actually saw, now

412

that he could no longer put it off, were backs of heads in windows, like a moving string of beads. All except one window, where the head was turned around. Was that what he was so anxious about facing directly? It was only a passenger on the other train, doing the same thing he was doing, peering through a dirty window. Maybe it was because the man was looking directly at him. And there was something disturbing about the face, even though he couldn't see much of it, perhaps because he couldn't. Also because something was picking at his mind: he'd seen the face before – and in the subway. Hadn't he?

No way really to know because through the distance and dinginess only the eyes, the mouth and the outline of a crumpled hat were visible. It was hard to see the nose and cheeks because the man had flattened his face, almost painfully it seemed, against the window, as if the face were trying to smash through the glass to reveal more of itself. The window mashed the mouth into what might have been an attempted smile, but the eyes had the usual dazed look of the subway rider.

It was not until after the face had passed back out of sight that he began to wonder why it had been staring at him. Even now he had no time, for a new sight captured him. A strange station was rushing by, one that shouldn't be there. The last local station he'd seen go by was 86th Street. He remembered going over the labyrinthian subway map, determined not to get lost. He was sure the next stop was listed as 96th Street. Where was he then? Dim lights glowed between unnumbered supports mazed with graffiti. No people on the platform, only graffiti swarming over the supports and walls.

As the deserted station vanished, he turned back around to sort out what he'd seen, only to feel his impressions pitched sideways with his body as the train ground abruptly to a stop. People pushing their way out of the train collided with people pushing their way in. Some cursed or frowned on the rebound, but only a few seemed to mean it.

He thought of robots and was struggling for a more damning image when he remembered he had to change trains himself. Feeling benign and superior, he stood up and waited by the door for the passengers on the platform to get in. Only when all the others were in did he make his move to get out. He was directly between the doors when they slammed on him, reverberating from his shoulders, jolting him out on the platform where he dumbly watched the express pulling away.

A local jerked to a stop on the other side, vomiting out a stream of passengers, sucking others in. This time he pushed, elbowed and muttered with the best of them. He was finally getting into the spirit of things. Somehow an old lady managed to muscle her way in front of him. The surprisingly intense satisfaction of jabbing her in the kidney was ruined by something he saw flooding out of the local.

He quickly calculated that this was the same local he'd seen in the tunnel. The man who had peered at him was getting out with the others, looking back as he moved. He was stung by resentment: he hated to be stared at, and there was no question that the man was staring at him, singling him out. A fucking drunk – but why should a drunk stare at him that way, twice in a row? And where had he seen him before?

It must have been on the subway. On the street he'd seen winos weaving and pleading for money; on the upper West Side he'd seen crazy people jerking and gibbering like chickens. They'd stared at him, sometimes lunged at him. But their eyes were full of pain, not menace. At least not calculated menace. The subway was different from the street. This man had no pain or pleading in his bloodshot eyes – only a kind of leering familiarity.

Hurrying towards the exit, the other passengers were reduced to backs of heads, as they had been on the train. Only the staring man with the greasy hat faced him, exactly as he had from the window. The only newly visible detail was the sootiness of the face, which made it impossible to tell his race or whether he was as old as his bulging eyes suggested. The rest of the figure was blotted out by other moving bodies, but the logistics were still puzzling: either the man's head was turned completely around on his shoulders or the weird bastard was walking backwards. He started to laugh at the grotesqueness of it all, just to release his silly, uncalled-for tension. The man's expression, just shy of a grin, almost encouraged him to, but he felt paralysed, strangely humiliated.

As the old lady returned his punch in the kidney with an elbow in the stomach, the clear flash of pain was almost a relief. He decided to resolve things with a well-aimed blow to the back of the head, but the lady had already moved briskly on to the train, well ahead now, shoving aside a man armed with a briefcase.

He was on the train too before it occurred to him to look out the window for the moving figure, but it had disappeared. Funny how much anxiety he was feeling from seeing a strange leering old man. He wondered for the first time how women must feel, how they could stand living in the city at all.

In front of him a pale, balding man choked and gasped on smoke and obscenities blown and shouted triumphantly in his face by a black teenager who refused to put out his cigarette. With a quick movement that probably surprised himself, the victim slapped the cigarette from the sneering teenager's mouth and fled the train. The teenager, wielding a bottle as club, bolted out after him. Of course no one took the slightest interest in any of this. It undoubtedly happened all the time, with much worse things going unnoticed, just as the movies and news stories said it did. No one seemed to see the strange figure outside either, no one but him. It only seemed strange to him after all.

He made a determination that if he stayed in the city he would resist the subway. He wouldn't become like the others, those blank lobotomized clichés from B movies who called themselves New Yorkers.

As the doors closed, he noticed the old lady standing next to one of them, looking dazed, and realized that he hadn't been in the spirit of things when he slugged her at all. He'd done it out of outrage, but she'd punched at him out of a purely mechanical reflex: no emotion behind it at all. She reminded him of the staring figure's expression, if anything one of deadening indifference. The spirit of the subway. But something else too, that he was at a loss to figure out.

He might have had a chance to had he not got drunk that night, visiting acquaintances uptown who had recently moved to New York for reasons he found increasingly hard to fathom, even though he would probably do it too.

'How can you stand it?' he asked, but the encircling beer cans, doubling as ashtrays, smoked and mocked his question. 'The same way I stand suburbia, I suppose,' he admitted, popping open another can.

He described the face on the train, but no one was impressed.

'Just another drunk.'

'Yeah, the same greasy hat, the same spacey eyes, the same smirk. Just a bum like a hundred other bums.'

'He's right. The horrible thing about New York is that there's nothing really weird about it. No mystery. You'll get used to it.'

'You'll just have to adjust whether you like it or not if you're going to live here. And it's getting worse. People seem a little stranger in the subway than they used to – a little more out of it, a little less civilized. But you'll get used to it.'

'But I don't want to get used to it,' he said. 'That's the point.'

'What point?'

The floor boomed beneath them as a train rumbled under the street. Outside a tyre screeched, several horns blared. The conversation floated, suddenly disconnected from the talkers. Disco music leaped into the open window, pummelled their ears, and slunk away up the street.

'You're lucky your apparition doesn't have a goddamn portable radio.'

At three a.m., waiting for the downtown train, he was more sleepy than drunk, but still fighting his mind. Focusing on the 168th Street station as a diversion, he stared up the stone arc and the elevated platform leading down from both ends into the dungeon-like space where he sat. A tremor shook his bench, and he walked to the edge of the platform to watch the train come in. Staring into the tunnel, past the other heads bobbing over the edge, he saw blackness, then a yellow glare which snarled as it came closer. He committed suicide by leaping on to the track, watching the train grow larger, waiting for a spectacular doom. He forgot the fantasy as the train pulled in as an oversized centipede with fat yellow appendages. Between its joints were cylinders held high by shadowy organisms. More cylinders were loaded on by other figures who had suddenly materialized on the platform, and the insect crawled back into darkness. Some kind of garbage train, he theorized, no longer sure how drunk he was. Down here, being high on drugs or booze was superfluous. This thought persisted as he saw the uptown train pull in ahead, tattooed all over with graffiti. 'Death' was inscribed on one of the cars in massive purple letters with black borders. As it moved away, he felt himself coming down from his high. He collapsed on the bench, wishing it were a bed.

Or at least a train taking him to a bed. Closing his eyes, he heard the rumble of 'death', still moving away, still audible, and thrust his mind ahead to meet it. Lumps of consciousness remained on the bench, too heavy to move, but the rest soared through the darkness, terrified of falling on the moving train. He glided briefly alongside one of the cars and swept through a window on to a seat. Much of the graffiti had blurred or vanished. From his corner seat on the train, he saw the 'death' letters in a reverse purple image. Others like himself seeped into windows: alert, casually dressed, but civilized people who talked amiably and helped each other find seats. Suddenly one of them, a young man, got up and walked into the next car. A long scream came from the car, a scream that modulated from outrage to horror to pain. Interspersed with it was a hissing or panting sound, and a banging and scuffling on the floor. The man processed back in stiffly, corpselike. Signs of a struggle were evident in his trousers, whch were torn, exposing his buttocks, but the most noticeable change was in his downcast eyes, which looked defeated, hardened, and somehow older. The moment the man sat back down, staring mutely while the others continued to talk, a woman got up, walked into the next car, and screamed and fought as the man had. When she wandered back to her seat, apathetically, another got up. He watched this in mounting panic, realizing his turn would come. Whenever anyone sat back down, graffitied dates separated by a dash seemed to materialize above heads on the wall. The second date was the current year. He stood up, shaking and beginning to weep, trying to decide which way to run as a formerly thin woman came back from the other car, pregnant. Before she could sit down, something black and oily plopped to the floor and scurried out from under her long skirt. It looked like a filthy baby, but it crawled into someone's shopping bag before he could be sure. From the window on the door to the other car, he saw the face from the deserted station peering in at him, sliding his pants down with its eyes, gnashing its yellow teeth in impatience, beckoning that it was his turn.

He screamed and woke up, banging his head against the stone wall.

Now he was looking at another train from his bench at 168th Street. The doors were open, waiting. Still shaking off his nightmare, he hurried in before the doors shut. It wasn't easy to banish. He had dreamed of death before, but the dreams had rarely attacked with such a peculiar combination of recent memories and images that seemed to come from nowhere. And all that sordid sexual stuff. God, if he moved to New York he'd soon be needing a shrink, just like everybody else here.

He grasped the nearest handrail, determined not to sit down and fall asleep again. The dream died briefly, then was called to life again by the gathering noise and velocity of the train. He fought it back down by taking a walk, passing from car to car through blasting passages of darkness. He reached the front car without seeing another passenger distinctly, although he glimpsed them from the corners of his eyes. He wanted to keep moving, to stay ahead of the dream, but he found himself stalled at the front of the train, pressing against metal and glass. Once again he found himself looking through a murky window. Out of the blackness, lights and columns rushed at his face, like comets in 3D movies he'd seen as a kid, as a station appeared and vanished. Just before he realized it shouldn't be, another station rushed by. Jesus, he must have been dozing again. He turned around to the other passengers, hoping to see signs of surprise or confusion. They *should* be pissed: it was going to be inconvenient for all of them. Approaching a man in a fading tweed jacket, he shouted loud enough so that several people could hear.

'Excuse me, isn't this a local? Why doesn't the train stop? Why is it going through these stations?'

He knew the bastard wouldn't answer; he was getting to where he could tell. Something about people's expressions, a listlessness mixed with hostility. He was getting to know who could most likely be approached for directions in the subway and there weren't any of them on this car. No one looked up at him. As another station went by, he felt powerless, then angry, as he turned on a young woman to his left and shouted the question in her ear. No acknowledgement. Trembling a little, he put the question differently:

'Are you deaf? Stupid? What the hell is the matter with you?'

He grabbed for images to cripple his anxiety. One was of men working on the tracks, the most probable explanation, but it faded ominously as he realized that someone should have made an announcement. Another was of some stations somehow closing down for the night, but the absurdity of that theory only made him aware of his desperation. Another station went by.

Turning on the passenger to his right, he felt an unexpected exhilaration. He wasn't alone. One of the doors separating his car from the next was open. Through the window of the other, he could barely see a woman near the door, her arms and mouth flapping at other passengers in a gesture that must be panic.

He was so intent on reaching her and hearing another normal, nervous human voice that his body, twisting to the right, failed to pick up the creaking signals of the train. As the train

418

stopped dead, violently, it flung him to the floor.

The doors banged open. He felt little pain, only numbness, spaciness, as he listened to the train wheeze and hiss at the darkness outside. Pulling himself back to his senses, he saw that it was very dark, almost black. A feeble glow, like a fading gas light, illuminated the graffiti-blackened posts that he saw through the open doors as he fell into the seat behind him. He was almost overpowered with the urge to flee through those doors, but he knew there was nothing out there but filth and empty benches. He thought he saw something shadowy rise from one of the benches with a crackling noise, like crumpled paper, but when he focused his eyes, it had gone. Must have been static from the train. The station was not really so mysterious. He had been through it before.

He was struggling to understand why the doors were opening at the empty stop when, like an admission of error, they suddenly closed and the train started again. No one had got out. Of course they hadn't. The train had only stopped to test its doors — maybe fix them. It had stopped so fast that there must have been something wrong with the brakes too. That's why it hadn't stopped at the other stations.

Then 86th Street went by and his fear returned.

As he struggled to smother it by telling himself he was on an express after all, he remembered the woman and decided to look for her in the next car. It felt good to move again, and passing the other passengers he felt more relief at realizing how many of them were asleep, or near it. No wonder they didn't care whether the doors opened — or care about anything: these were the people he'd heard about, the ones who lived on the subway. A fat woman in a dingy flannel shirt, barely awake, stared at his feet as he hurried by. A humped-over man in a wrinkled business suit, his tie lolling like a noose, did the same. A distorted picture of the man settled uneasily in his mind while he pushed open the doors to the next car. The woman fit. She was destitute, pathetic, obviously poor. But why would a business man not care where the train stopped, and why did he look so much like the woman, as if he'd been down here a long time?

The puzzle scattered as he opened the door into a near-empty car. The woman was gone.

Most of the other passengers were gone too. They couldn't have got off. They must have moved down to the next car. He was about to move to it himself when he saw a derelict sprawled directly in front of the door. His head was partially buried in a large shopping bag, his right hand groping for something inside. Probably food, for the derelict was surrounded by scattered chicken bones. He would have either to step on the man or ask him to move, but he didn't like the thought of either option. Besides the few strands of hair on the pinkish forehead and the usual oily clothes, there was a repulsive eagerness, and also a strange redundancy, about the way the man was rooting around in the shopping bag, stuffing fist-sized hunks of meat into an invisible mouth.

He was at the centre of the car, trying to decide what to do, when a sliding of metal and rush of air made him turn around. The fat woman, the man with the loose tie, and three others came through the door, walking stiffly. They stood by the door, shaking with the train, staring at the floor. They looked ravaged.

A thought pierced his brain from behind as a woman's scream of pain seemed to arc over the white noise from somewhere near the back of the train. He had just begun to understand that the doors of the train had opened not to let anyone out but to let someone on. The scream changed that. Not someone. At least two of them.

He didn't need to turn back around. The nausea seeping into his stomach told him that the man crouching by the other door had sprung up. Even above the blast of the train he thought he heard the man kick aside the shopping bag and begin advancing towards him. His panic spun him around anyway, to meet the dead staring eyes he had met before. Beneath the soot on its face and grease on its hands, wrinkles sprouted, bones protruded. But if he creaked and staggered a little, he also moved forward, steadily. He had, after all, just eaten. His body was now impelled forward by a different kind of hunger.

Suddenly the derelict halted a moment to look at something on the floor. A few bones, a partially eaten sausage, a wine bottle in a crumpled hat, a small jar that had rolled out of the shopping bag, its open mouth revealing a clear jelly-like substance. The derelict's eyes hesitated at the jar, trying to reach a decision. Then as he showed his yellow teeth to his victim, advancing again with new excitement, taking in the lower body before moving back to the eyes, he did something he had never quite managed before. He smiled.

John Burke
Lucille would have known

John Burke was born in 1922 and brought up in Liverpool (a good start for a macabre writer, believe me: other Merseysiders who have written in the genre include Rosalie Muspratt, May Sinclair, G. G. Pendarves of Weird Tales *fame and Lady Eleanor Smith). He has written over a hundred books, including* Swift Summer *(his first novel, which won an Atlantic Award in Literature), several novels based on Hammer and Amicus horror films, and a trilogy about a nineteenth-century psychic investigator* (The Devil's Footsteps, The Black Charade, *and* Ladygrove). *He also wrote the original screenplay for Michael Reeves' film* The Sorcerers, *which gave Boris Karloff and Catherine Lacey the chance for unforgettable performances.*

In the context of this book his tale may seem a reassuringly traditional ghost story – but there is one detail which may look reassuring but which, in retrospect, grows worse and worse.

There was one vacant seat in the mini-bus. It was the nearside rear seat which Lucille had always chosen to occupy so that she could address a running commentary at the backs of the others' heads and, as she laughed on each occasion they went out, 'Keep an eye on the lot of you, make sure you don't pick your noses or drop off to sleep.' This time perhaps they could have found somebody else to make up the numbers; but it wouldn't have seemed right, not yet, not so soon. It would take time to get used to the idea of Lucille not being with them any more and organizing everything for them.

Mrs Armstrong had suggested that this trip ought to be cancelled. But Madge Wright had insisted they must go ahead. It was not just a matter of their having paid in advance, though that in itself had been quite an expense: Lucille had never believed in cutting costs by amalgamating with other groups, in a larger coach on a vulgar package tour. Eleven was enough. Eleven, plus a driver, was manageable.

Now there were ten.

'Lucille,' declared Madge, 'would have wanted us to make the trip.'

Two women and one of the men – Madge's own husband, actually – remained dubious. But Madge had always been so close to Lucille, had been with her just before she died, and was so obviously Lucille's natural successor, that they allowed themselves to be persuaded. And so on this Friday afternoon, ten days after the funeral, they were setting out on their annual Getaway Weekend Study Tour.

Over the last few years they had, between a Friday lunchtime and a Monday evening, taken in Country Houses of Derbyshire, Gardens of Lincolnshire, and Yorkshire's Victorian Heritage. This year Lucille had opted for Romantic Castles of the North-East. 'The military history will appeal to the men,' she had said. Lucille had always made a point of appealing to the men.

'Well.' Madge took charge. 'Let's sort ourselves out, shall we?' She would sit where she had always sat, beside the driver. Only this time it would not be merely to relay Lucille's instructions. This time things would be different. And there were other things to be altered. As she stood by the door, letting the other four women and five men squeeze past, she saw her husband on his way to the back. 'Harold, come up here and sit behind me. Or behind the driver.'

He settled himself on the offside back seat, across the aisle from Lucille's empty place.

'I'll sit where I've always sat.'

'Harold, we don't have to make a religious rite of it.'

'I'm used to it here.'

Yes, thought the driver. Although they had all from time to time been shifted about to suit the late Mrs Bellamy's whims, this last few years Mr Wright had always sat level with her. Right at the back. He remembered them joking together and leaning towards each other, laughing, and sometimes tossing crazy remarks forward along the aisle.

She had been a right merry widow, had Mrs Lucille Bellamy.

It had been one of her ideas to space husbands and wives out of phase up the two sides of the bus. With Madge seated beside the driver, and Madge's husband on the opposite side at

422

the back, other husbands were placed opposite women other than their wives.

'You can sit next to your own spouse any day of the week.' Fred, the driver, remembered Lucille shrilling that the very first time he had been hired to drive them. 'Come on, now – much more interesting conversation if we're all mixed up. Lean across the aisle and make up to somebody new. Keep you awake!'

And each time she would reshuffle the order. Save for having Madge's husband always at her own side.

Her voice would ring down the aisle. 'Madge, tell the driver to turn left at the next junction. I'm sure it's a more interesting route.' Or: 'Madge, do tell the driver to go more slowly, this is beautiful countryside, it's a shame to race through it. We're not doing a safari rally, or whatever they call it.'

It had been suggested that Lucille herself should sit beside the driver, but she wouldn't have that. 'No, got to keep an eye on you all. Can't be craning over my shoulder the whole time to see what your'e up to.

They would laugh with her and at her. Sometimes ruefully. But nobody could take over the reins from Lucille. For one thing, the rest of them just didn't have that much spare time. Since her husband died, Lucille had had money and time to spend. If she didn't arrange things for the group, they might never get arranged.

Now somebody else would have to take over.

Fred changed down and began a long climb out of the valley, up above the town and on towards the shadowy ridges of Northumbria. Behind him there was not the usual babble of conversation. A glum lot. It would take them time to recover, he supposed. They were all conscious of that unoccupied seat.

'Sad about Mrs Bellamy,' he ventured quietly.

'Yes.' Madge looked steadily at the road ahead.

That was another thing he remembered. All the others, however often they might see one another at whatever fêtes and functions or bridge parties they shared, were Mrs This and Mr That and Mrs So-and-so. But the woman beside him and the one who used to sit far back were always Madge and Lucille, not only to each other but to everyone else in the party. Equals, almost; though not quite. Rivals, sort of, he supposed.

He said: 'What exactly was it she died of?'

'Most unusual.' Madge spoke in a clipped voice, apparently

anxious to keep it all as brief and unemotional as possible and be done with it. 'A rare form of osmotic oedema which didn't respond to the usual drugs.'

He had forgotten that she was something in the medical world. 'I'm afraid I haven't got much idea about—'

'Accumulation of surplus fluid in the body tissues. A variety of what used to be called dropsy.'

'Oh. Yes, I see.'

It sounded nasty and damp and sagging. Fred was squeamish about such things, and sorry he had raised the question.

'Poor Lucille didn't respond to the diuretics we used to draw out the salt, and the water along with it. We had to fall back on the old-fashioned method of drawing fluid off by tubes. As with poor old George the Fourth, you know.'

'Er . . . yes.'

'With *him*, the doctors tapped the fluid from his feet. Excruciatingly painful,' said Madge with a strangely mellow smile. 'With Lucille, something went wrong with the timing. The rate of extraction must have been wrong. Terrible shock to the system. I found her dead.'

'*You* found her?'

'I was on duty that night. But I'd had to attend to another patient, and when I got back to Lucille it was too late. In effect,' explained Madge with brisk finality, 'you might say she drowned in her own body fluids.'

They drove on towards their first stop at Raby castle.

Mrs Armstrong, striding out at the head of the party, came to a halt by the notice board. 'But it says here it's not open on a Friday.'

Flustered, Madge consulted the brochure she had bought from the Tourist Board. 'No. Oh, dear. Saturday and Sunday would be all right. But Friday . . . no, I don't know how I came to . . .'

There was one barely subdued comment. 'Lucille would have known.'

They climbed back aboard, disgruntled.

As he closed the door, Fred had a fleeting sensation of someone else edging past him at the last minute. He slewed round to count his passengers. Ten, just as before. Five married couples, as ever; and an empty seat where there had once been the domineering, know-it-all widow.

He drove on again.

424

Dark cloud shadows rolled in a sombre muddy tide down the slopes ahead, thickening into the pool of a dark plantation. On the crest he saw the road begin to curve and guessed that on the other side there would be a tight swing to the left. He slowed, and glanced in his mirror.

There was somebody in Lucille's old seat.

The slant of his mirror was such that it showed the road behind and a few heads in the coach, but cut out several on the nearside. Including the rear seat. Yet somehow he was sure somebody had moved into it – perhaps slid across from one of the other seats. When he had negotiated the awkward bend and was tilting downhill again, he cautiously twisted the mirror to get a glimpse of that corner.

Of course there was nobody there.

It was simply that on previous excursions he had been so conscious of her, calling out her instructions or jokes every five minutes. You were never allowed to forget she was there, in charge. And the rest of them felt the same, he could tell it: not chattering, hardly exchanging even the most casual remark on the scenery.

Madge said: 'Can't we go any faster? We'll never get there in time for dinner at this rate.'

Her irritable tone jarred in a way Lucille's long-drawn-out sigh had never done – the sigh when there was some minor hitch or people had failed to respond as she wanted them to, as if she were on the verge of washing her hands of all of them and then loftily relenting.

'Fancies herself in Lucille's shoes already.' The whisper drifted along the bus.

On their right was a heavy drystone sheepfold, but there were no sheep in sight. To their left the gaunt obelisk of an old lead-mine chimney stuck up against the tumultuous sky: a mine long since abandoned. The landscape grew bleaker, as flushed and mottled and dark and unpredictable as the sky: flushed but cold, growing colder.

Lucille would surely have known better than to specify this unrewarding route.

Their stop for the night was at a hotel above a gentle loop of the river Wear. When they booked in, the plump girl at the desk looked at the voucher Madge handed over and reached behind her for a set of keys.

'That's right. Four doubles and two singles.'

'No,' said Madge. 'Five doubles. And of course a single for our driver.'

'That's not what you confirmed, madam. It was going to be five doubles and one single when you first booked, but then you cancelled the single—'

'One of our members,' said Madge, 'has unfortunately passed on.'

'I'm right sorry to hear that.'

'But in any case it ought to have been five doubles and two singles. And then I wrote to cancel just one.'

'That's not the way I've got it down here.' The girl was patient but unyielding. 'Now let's see how we can help.'

It finished with Madge and her husband agreeing to take a single room each, since there were no other doubles available. The driver was allocated a hot little room at the back of the building, uncomfortably close to the kitchen extractor.

There was further confusion when Madge admitted she had not in her letter confirmed a dinner booking for the party, assuming that this would be taken for granted. 'But you see,' said the girl, her voice hardening, 'we've got a big formal party in tonight, and we have to fit everyone else round them. If you'd let us know in time . . .'

Fred was glad to retreat to the comfort of the public bar and have chicken in the basket and three pints of bitter for his supper.

The side window of the bar commanded a view along the terraced gardens of the hotel. One isolated lamp, an electric bulb in a converted old gas lamp standard, cast a faint glow like an illuminated float bobbing up and down in the rippling water below.

Between the lamp and the spray of light from the dining room, a woman walked slowly along a flagged path towards the wrought iron gate which led to the car park. She paused once and looked at the windows as if seeking some friend at one of the tables inside. Yet although the light fell full upon her face, there was no definition to her features. They were a badly blurred snapshot of someone Fred felt vaguely he ought to know. He put down his pint glass and rubbed the palm of his right hand across the pane to wipe away condensation. But there was no condensation. The garden was nice and bright, the terraces sharp-edged. Only the sauntering woman appeared hazy as she resumed her progress towards the curlicued gate.

It was only after she had walked through and vanished round a corner of the car park that Fred realized – was sure, in spite of the third pint of bitter – that she had not even paused to open the gate.

Next morning there was a groundswell of complaint as the five couples trudged out to the bus. The meal last night had been indifferently served and half cold. Breakfast this morning had been greasy. Madge had not made nearly as much fuss as Lucille would have done in such circumstances. And Mr Brearley had stumbled off an ill-lit step in a grubby corridor and now was limping badly. Fred hurried to relieve him of his overnight case and brought up the rear, behind Mrs Brearley and Mrs Catchpole.

'But of course,' Mrs Brearley was insinuating, 'Lucille and the Wrights were always in one another's pockets. I did sometimes wonder . . .'

'About Lucille and Madge's husband?'

'Oh, I've never said anything to a soul.'

'I mean,' said Mrs Catchpole, 'with Madge often away on duty all night at the hospital, and them so close . . .'

'I've never been one to hint at any such thing,' said Mrs Brearley.

There was no laughter in it. Not like the sly laughter the time they were visiting country houses, and there had been these jokes about Lucille and Madge's husband in that maze for so long. And all that chucking under the chin and the rest of it at the medieval banquet.

They climbed aboard and travelled on.

First to Durham, and then to Hylton castle ruins, where Madge read out the story about the Stars-and-Stripes emblem in the family crest, and they all muttered indifferently, 'Yes, you can see it, can't you?' and then on to Newcastle and Tynemouth and, late in the afternoon, to the massive peel tower of Langley. Madge recited from memory all she had learnt about peel towers; and got most of it wrong.

That night they stayed at a hotel almost on Hadrian's Wall. In the morning Madge appeared in blustery, decisive mood.

'Well, now. Let's have a bit of a shake-up, shall we? Change places. Let's see if we get more talk if the husbands and wives sit side by side, eh?'

'But we've never done it that way.'

'High time to try it.'

But they glared at her and got into the bus and settled themselves in the same order as the day before.

Fred headed for the river Coquet and Warkworth castle.

They had gone less than two miles when Mrs Brearley, sitting immediately behind Madge, announced that she wanted to be sick. Fred pulled into the side. Mrs Brearley scrambled out, with Madge leaning well away to allow her plenty of room. She stooped over a gap in the ragged brown stone wall, and vomited into brown and mauve scrub on the other side.

'I thought the bacon was even greasier than yesterday's,' commented Mrs Armstrong.

But when Mrs Brearley returned she said: 'It's sitting over that wheel that did it. Makes me feel funny.'

'Then we must change some places.' Madge was pleased by the thought of getting her own way after all.

The others looked at her with growing disapproval.

Mrs Brearley palely said: 'No, I wouldn't want anyone else to suffer.' Then she nodded, as if someone had prompted her with a brilliant suggestion. 'Yes, that'll do nicely.'

She made her way to the back of the bus and to the seat which had always been Lucille's.

There was silence save for the faint whine of the breeze along the shallow hillside. A shocked, tremulous silence; until Fred revved his engine more noisily than was necessary, and began to grind uphill fiercely in low gear. At the top of the hill he glanced automatically in his mirror.

It did not quite cover the seat which Mrs Brearley had vacated. But it showed enough to convince him that someone – one of the women, he was sure – had moved forward into the place behind Madge.

Madge put up one hand to dab at the side of her neck, as if a fly or strand of hair were tickling it; or someone were whispering in her ear.

They visited Warkworth, and then Alnwick.

'And this was one of the Percy castles,' announced Madge.

'Surely,' said Mrs Armstrong, 'it belonged to the Nevilles.'

'I'm sure I read somewhere . . .'

Madge flipped through the pages of her brochure.

It did not need to be spoken aloud: *Lucille would have known.*

On the way to Dunstanburgh no word was exchanged in the bus. Glimpsing his passengers' expressions from time to time in his mirror, Fred had a disturbing sensation that they were all retreating from him. There wasn't really anyone at all in the bus. They were thinning, growing weaker, incapable of talking or of doing anything for themselves. Even Madge had ceased to dab at her neck and was staring hypnotically ahead, waiting for some unuttered command.

In the seat behind her, the someone or something was growing stronger.

Fred twisted his mirror abruptly.

This time there was no doubt. Growing in substance every second, Lucille sat smiling at the back of Madge's head.

The bus veered, its wheels slithering along the narrow grassy verge and narrowly escaping a scrape against the stone wall. Fred gulped; straightened up, slowed; and concentrated on the road ahead.

The others couldn't have seen her, or they'd have said something. He wasn't going to mention it. He didn't want them reporting him back to the company for being drunk and putting the wind up them. Really, they were the ones who had put the notion of her into his head, because that was all they could think about today. Should never have come.

At Dunstanburgh he stayed well back when they began to clamber silently over the castle ruins. He had no head for heights. Even looking up as Madge appeared in a gaping embrasure made him dizzy.

She was saying something. They seemed to be crowding in on her and forcing her back. One more step and she would be out and down. He wanted to shout a warning but dared not risk it.

There was another figure in the shelter of a turret, watching. Waiting – in no hurry.

When Madge came down she was in tears. The others were remote, as if dismissing her and waiting for more competent guidance.

'I'm doing my best,' she cried.

They stared in blank accusation.

Only her husband blinked and shook himself in an effort to wake up. But all he could manage was: 'Madge, could you have saved Lucille?'

'No one could have saved her.'

'You didn't actually *help* her?'

'I did all I was supposed to do.'

'I mean, you didn't help her on her way?'

'Charles, you can't mean . . . you're not accusing me . . .'

'I thought you might have got the wrong idea. About that one time, you know, when Lucille was at our place and you came back early off night duty.'

'Just that one time?' she said with sudden cold fury. 'And was it such a wrong idea?'

'Then you did know. I mean, suspect. Madge . . .'

She walked on. Fred was sure nobody else had heard. Not that Harold Wright had lowered his voice: just that none of them was capable of registering anything at all. So there was a right turn-up. If Madge *had* done it because her husband was up to fun and games with Lucille . . .

The truth of it was something none of them would ever know now.

Lucille would have known.

They were on the road towards Bamburgh when Madge, jerking as if prompted by someone close to her, said: 'Let's have a look at Hawkby on the way.'

'Don't think I know that one, Mrs Wright.'

'The next turning but three to the right. Not as impressive as Bamburgh, but we ought to take it in while we're in the neighbourhood.'

Sure enough there was a faded little signpost pointing towards Hawkby. The road ran gently downhill and ended in a small village overshadowed by castle ruins like the teeth of some stranded monster tossed up by an ancient tide. The sea had eaten away much of the cliff, and the shore was a mixture of sand, rocks, and splintered stones.

Fred was thirsty. The pubs weren't open, but the post office by the village green advertised ice cream and cold drinks. He paused in the doorway and watched the party take the path round the castle to the beach – all eleven of them. Then he turned away into the dark interior of the post office.

When he had finished, he realized the afternoon was wearing on. If they were to complete their itinerary, it was time they moved. He strolled towards the castle, feeling inexplicably tired and out of touch with reality. No fit condition to be driving a bus, even a small one.

From the low cliff he could look down on the shore.

There they were, larking about like a crowd of kids. Four of the men were digging with their hands and throwing up a mound of sand. But there was no laughing and joking: unless it was lost under the rustle of the tide beginning to splash in across green-slimed rocks.

They seemed to be playing a silly game, burying one of their number in the sand, like he had done when he was a kid. Or maybe not one of them, but a rounded rock they had picked up somewhere – rounded and unusually smooth, quite distinct from the heavier whalebacked rocks.

Fred called. They all stood up and looked at him. He waved, beckoned. Obediently they began to return, following him to the bus. All ten of them. He counted as they got in: eight, nine, ten.

'Everybody aboard?'

Harold Wright settled into the seat beside him. 'All present and correct.'

Fred drove back the way they had come. The silence was almost solid within the bus: as solid as the woman sitting complacent and contented behind Mr Wright.

Until he heard that odd little, half exasperated sigh he remembered so well. And she was asking: 'Could we stop at the next garage with a café?' And at once there was a murmur of agreement.

A mile along the main road, and Fred pulled in. As he opened the door, she moved past him and he heard it again, the sigh: winging away into infinity, a last whisper and a last laugh.

Mocking them; and releasing them.

Mrs Brearley blinked across the aisle at Mr Armstrong.

'That's odd. I could have sworn . . .'

'Where did she *go*?'

And Mr Wright was looking round, puzzled, as they got out of the bus and leaned over, rubbing their knees and bending their legs against the pain of returning circulation. They were all stiff and weary, and all suddenly aware of it.

Mr Wright said: 'Where's Madge?'

'Funny. I don't remember her getting on the coach.'

'And I don't remember her *not* getting on.'

They stared accusingly at the driver. Surely he ought to have been responsible enough to ensure that everybody was aboard before driving off? Responsible enough to have known how many there ought to be. Lucille would have known.

Fred said: 'Look, there's ten of you . . .'

They all turned towards one another and counted.

Without Fred, there were nine.

'*She* got out.'

'But where's Madge got to?'

Gradually, incredulously, they began to remember. They all saw in their mind's eye, miles behind them, the picture of that little rounded ball like a head above the sand, packed in, imprisoned by their impressive sandy fortifications.

Fred was the first back into the bus. They bundled in after him, and he swung the wheel and twisted the bus round and began to race back the way they had come. But when he looked at his dashboard clock he realized how little point there was in hurrying.

By now the tide would be in.

Rosalind Ashe

Teething troubles

*Rosalind Ashe tells me what the jacket of one of her books says
about her: that she was born and brought up in Jamaica,
educated in Canada and England, and lives in London. Her
novels are* Moths, Hurricane Wake, Starcrossed, Takeover
and Dark Runner.

*Many ghost stories begin with people telling stories after
dinner – Peter Straub's* Ghost Story *makes the wittiest use of
this – but few end up as grisly as the following.*

Dessert, an elaborate ritual, and one of the glories of the College, was rounding to a close. At ten o'clock precisely, the Provost drained his port glass, dabbed his pale rosebud mouth with his napkin, pushed back his chair and made his adieux.

There was a general air of relaxation: a stretching of legs, a refilling of glasses, a loosening of ties and of tongues.

'You must not leave yet,' said my host. 'Once the Beak has gone, things begin to perk up—'

'Excuse me—'

The man sitting on his other side leaned forward. He was someone else's guest, and had sat almost silently, in saturnine, bearded mystery, throughout the evening. It was impossible to determine – as I had attempted to do once or twice – whether any emotion might be observed on such a countenance. Sometimes the splendid growth of facial hair rippled, and I anticipated laughter, or perhaps a smile; but if some spring of humour had indeed risen behind that granite front, it had trickled away and been lost in the sedges. Maybe, I thought – observing such a tremor as he sat listening to one of the Dean's lugubrious tales over dinner at High Table – maybe this motion was more closely comparable to that of the hair on a dog's back, signalling alarm, antagonism, even fear.

But now the pelt parted and gave tongue; the black eyes fixed us irresistibly.

433

'Excuse me,' he said in a low, pleasant voice, 'but I have not heard that expression since prep school. Do you know its derivation?'

'I assume it stems from "percolator",' said my host: 'an American term for—'

'Ah no – I meant "beak". Applied both to judges and to schoolmasters, and a good old word, no doubt; hearing you use it put me in mind of a particularly unpleasant nightmare . . . I'm sorry: I should introduce myself. Kahn, Marius Kahn, geologist – guest of Professor Dawlish. I hail from the Other University – the one that finds itself, as the French say, in the South Midlands.'

His playfulness was a little heavy – what my host, Milo Effingham, would call neo-classic arch; and I caught his eye for a moment.

'I'm Effingham,' he said; 'and this is Harry Sterne, real-life lawyer from London.'

I nodded. I said:

'We used to call them Beaks even at my public school, actually. I don't know why; unless it's to do with the vulturelike effect of cap and gown—'

Our overtures were interrupted by a general exodus; many left, and those that did not gathered their gowns and set off up a winding turret stair. College servants who had been hovering as long as a semblance of the ritual lasted, now moved in purposefully; and we moved out.

By comparison with the Aladdin's cave of the Queen's Chamber where Dessert was held, the Tower Room in which we now found ourselves was small and bare. After the long table, the silver dishes piled high with fruit and sweetmeats, the crystal decanters glinting by the light of a dozen branching candlesticks, the white napery and attendant minions, this was a hermitage. Nevertheless it was furnished with essentials: a sideboard of assorted whisky bottles, a siphon, some soft drinks, a barrel of biscuits, a humidor and a good coal fire. Dark brown portraits and similar leather chairs completed the picture; and the remaining half-dozen of us that made up the hard core of the evening's entertainment moved in like a hand into a well-worn glove.

While Effingham was dealing with the whisky, I turned to the saturnine stranger again. It seemed a pity, having found that he could speak, to let him fall into disuse again.

'You spoke of a nightmare,' I said. 'Are you one of those fortunate beings who can remember dreams?'

'Oh no,' he said. 'I am not given to fantasy.'

The tone was dismissive, and so, at that stage of the evening, a challenge. I took my glass and followed him over to the hearth.

'Except, presumably, in your subconscious,' I said. 'You did speak of it.'

'I fear I may have misled you, my dear fellow,' he said. 'I used the word "nightmare" loosely to describe a very alarming occurrence, a real-life situation, as they say, which your host's observations brought back to me, and which I have been trying hard to forget. A situation of some peculiarity; verging, I must admit, on the fantastic. No, not a dream, alas.'

Sensing a narrative in the offing, the hard core gathered round. Dawlish, who had, moments before, been consulting his watch, now settled himself in the best of the leather chairs and gestured his guest into the second best.

'A cigar, why not, Kahn? Effie, mend the fire, there's a good chap . . . And may we explore this peculiar situation, I wonder? Pin down? Define? And so, perhaps, render harmless? Must I plead the worthy cause of catharsis?'

Marius Kahn was very absorbed in lighting his cigar.

'Might we even anticipate that this peculiar happening came to pass in the other ancient seat of learning we sometimes hear murmur of – do you think?' Boiledieu chirped in his high nervous voice, bobbing his head as he did when he was excited. 'In such a light – indirect and flickering, if you please, dear sir – even that barbaric establishment might appear congenial.' Boiledieu's was gothic arch. Pointed.

All eyes were on the visitor from that alternative world. He inspected the glowing tip of his Havana, seemed satisfied; tossed the spill into the grate and turned to us.

'It is not a *nice* story,' he said. 'But it may have a certain novelty. You see, it's really a rather novel sort of ghost story – in that it took place in a brand new college – Yes: St Austin's, no less. And now, sadly, no more.'

'So it really is to be sold? Lock, stock and cellar—?'

'To an American religious cult—?'

'I understood that negotiations were still—'

'Surely one needs an Act of Parliament—'

He quelled us with one raised hand – the more effective for

its black silk glove. I had noticed it at dinner; noticed he wore only one.

'I can tell you, in confidence,' he said, 'what will soon be public knowledge: the new American owners complete on the first of September.'

'But was it bankrupt?' asked Effingham.

'The opposite, dear sir.'

'How very curious . . .' said Boiledieu.

'Just so.'

'There has been so little in the press . . .' I ventured.

'A closely guarded business,' said Kahn.

Dawlish said: 'I had no idea you were in on this, my dear Kahn. I should have—'

'You shouldn't have, professor: I was only in on it by the merest chance.'

'Will you tell us?' Young Gilpin had not spoken until now. He was leaning against the bookcase. His dress was both over-elaborate and untidy; he held a cane, and sipped at a lemon squash. But he spoke for all of us.

'I will – if you care to hear. It would, however, be improbable that you should know nothing of this affair: there were troubles and rumours of troubles even before the building was completed; so you must bear with me if I cover some familiar ground before breaking new.'

He sat down, savoured his whisky and drew on his cigar.

'John Milton Austin – a good old Oxford name; his father was a rag-and-bone man with a taste for epic poetry – John Milton Austin was of course a very rich man, and therefore a tax exile abroad during most of these troubles. I say "was", not because he is dead, nor because he is no longer rich; but his general circumstances have altered considerably in the last two years.'

Sensing a question, he raised the black-gloved hand again.

'We will come to that. Meanwhile, as you may recall, his decision to immortalize (and indeed canonize) himself by founding a new Oxford college was considerably facilitated by his possession of a sizeable tract of land within the City limits: Westwyke Farm.

'It borders a branch of the Isis, an area of some fifty acres; so low-lying and subject to seasonal floods that it was deemed over the years – over the centuries – unprofitable as anything other than dry-weather grazing; fulfilling no function save as a

436

pleasant prospect. J. M. Austin was left this by his father, while his elder brother inherited the flourishing scrapyard in Kidlington.

'That was 1963, which ended in one of the hardest winters in living memory; J.M. woke up one day and found himself gazing out over fifty acres of frozen marsh. The story goes that he was out there on the first morning of the Big Freeze, building a small booth by the gate on to the main road; and by three o'clock, when the children came out of school, he was charging one shilling for adults and sixpence for under-tens to skate and slide over his farm – as they had been doing *gratis* since time immemorial. The next day he put a strong-man on the gate and went round mending fences and putting up notices against trespassing. The third day, he produced a rubber date stamp to be used on the backs of hands, and sent his henchman out among the skaters to run spot-checks for non-paying customers.

'I relate this early history solely to illustrate John Milton Austin's talent for breeding money; also to show that the methods he employed were less than endearing – for that perhaps is the moral of my story.

'Now I shall move more swiftly – as, even on that first morning, looking out on to a solid, six-inch (and therefore safe) proposition, he was, I feel sure, already planning with a wider view. He added a hot-dog stall, and a slot machine that dispensed coffee and tea. Prices were high, but there was no competition within comfortable walking distance; and he made enough profit that winter to drain forty acres and build a high fence along the road. Behind this, and with the help of a substantial loan, he started intensive farming.

'Transport – sale – distribution was never a problem: local consumers bought fresh trout, poultry, eggs and pork from the farm shop by the gate. Soon a small car park brought in customers from farther afield; and the rest of the produce was absorbed by the covered market in the City Centre. Full production coincided with the start of the freezer boom, and J. M. Austin was able to stock his own and raise his prices in the lean season. In '66 he married a motor-millionairess some fifteen years his senior and moved to the South of France. His kingdom increased geometrically, involving not only her string of garages, but taking over an established freezer business, a fleet of container trucks and a hamburger-cum-soda-fountain chain with an All-American name and an all-Pakistani staff.

'It was during the period of Labour rule that he read the signs and portents which, he felt, might ultimately – at least in the event of a second term – threaten Westwyke Farm. Public ownership, compulsory purchase within City limits – it was all in the air. More sinister were reports telexed to him in the Bahamas – where his companies were now registered – that Westwyke Farm had been named in an *Ecologist* article on intensive farming methods, and a letter to *The Times* had complained not only of noisome smells suffered by residents along the Kenningdon Road but of their implications for "life as we know it"; while students had written slogans in spray paint on his curtain wall: WHAT GOES ON IN HERE? and NO SMOKE WITHOUT FIRE – REMEMBER BELSEN.

'It was about this time that J. M. Austin decided to found a college; and his mind was probably made up for him when a fire burned down most of the farm one night. A spark from a tractor was blamed: these things happen so quickly. He had the land; he had the insurance money, and more besides.

'He employed the best: Briggs and Brill, international builders of repute; Sixten Aardvik, the mighty Swede, as architect ... But you know all this. Austin had to mastermind it from Guernsey where he had established himself for just this purpose. His own plane ferried his business manager, planners, accountants and advisors to and from conferences; and each week he received a detailed cine-film of work in progress. But when everything started going wrong, it was in small and subtle ways that did not show up on film; and the grumbles of the hod-carriers and plasterers never got through to the top. The business manager chose not to worry the great man himself with desertion figures.

'Not until the buildings were complete and the interior well advanced did the top administrators get any inkling all was not well.

'Now, Sixten Aardvik, as you will all know from his work at Turin—? Atlanta, Georgia? Madingley, then – as well as from articles in the Sunday supplements – designs everything from the first girder down to the last doorknob and ashtray. It was at the point when an exhibition module and a medium-sized lounge on the ground floor were nearly complete and ready for inspection, and a small party had been arranged, that the great Swede summoned his assistant designer down from London to replace the curtains.

438

' "They smell – they *stink*!" he said. "You must get on to Courtaulds *and* the interior decorators to decide who is responsible. Remove all the curtains and replace them by Friday."

'He put the room out of bounds and mentioned the unfortunate business to no one else.

'Friday was warm. Austin landed at Abingdon airport and turned up unexpectedly early to look round before the party. The foreman took him to one side and apologized for the lack of manpower: six good men had left in the last fortnight, he said, and word seemed to be getting around that the site was jinxed. Then the business manager caught up with Austin and bore him off, apologizing in his turn for allowing such minor concerns to come to the Founder's attention. Yes, they had had problems with labour, but not insuperable, thanks to the generous wage-rise. The deadline would be met, and the men they had, working overtime, would see them through.

'They started towards the reception area up the main steps, a broad shallow flight of pale gold handmade bricks, and bordered by brushed silver handrails. As he ascended, J. M. caressed the silver; every two metres there was a row of hallmarks as big as pennies. But today his hand recoiled. The rail was tacky; he pulled out a handkerchief and wiped his fingers.

' "They haven't put polish on the banister, surely?" He grimaced. "It doesn't smell like polish. Is it some sort of seal?"

' "I'm sorry, Mr Austin," said the business manager. "It seems it hasn't been properly cleaned. Dear me – let me show you to the cloakroom: completed, now, and fully operational."

' "What the hell *is* this stuff?" The Founder was scrubbing his hands under the soap dispenser. "It's the devil's own business shifting it."

' "I don't really know, sir . . . Yes, it's been noticed before . . ."

' "Then get it bloody well sorted out," said Austin. "I want it cleaned up *now* – can't have my guests finding that sort of thing."

' "It was all cleaned just this morning, Mr Austin. Seems to come back."

' "Well, get it cleaned again! Now, where's this party?"

'The windows and doors of the exhibition lounge were open; but Sixten Aardvik looked as if nothing could cool him. The new curtains were no better, it seemed. After a night hanging in position, they smelt as terrible as the first consignment. However it was too late now: toasts were being drunk. Said J. M., lowering his glass:

439

' "Blow me – if it isn't that foul smell again!"

'There was no denying it. Something in the heating system – new paint – problems with the ventilation shafts – all were put forward; all had the hollow ring of having been put forward before. "It will wear off," they said.

' "Well," said the Founder menacingly when he had heard them out, "just you work on it. And it *better* 'wear off', whatever it is. Meantime we'll say nothing more about it: the first Fellows move in three weeks from now, and then there's the official opening with the Chancellor. It's taken the best part of a decade to get this thing off the ground, and I've no intention of putting off the launching while you lot iron out the bugs, is that quite clear? Just see you buy some air-freshener. In bulk. On discount."

'Getting a college working is an operation of infinite complexity. Austin left it to the experts; he returned for the opening, an occasion far too solemn and high-minded for any consideration of details like cooking smells or sticky banisters. The Founder received honours and heard speeches; there were compliments on his generosity, his farsightedness, his streamlined new building and newest wife (decorative, pliant, nineteen); while, behind the scenes, the caterers moaned about conditions in the ultra-modern kitchens. There was grease on every surface, they said; rusty spots appeared on their white napery, and they were sickened by a persistent smell of frying.

'Most of the staff and dons were now installed; and a third of the full complement of undergraduates arrived at the beginning of October. The student modules, the library, the labs, the gymnasium, the common rooms, the stores, cellars, boiler rooms and garages were all performing their correct functions; routines were established, life was lived, learning was advanced. Carpenters and decorators were still working on the sixty or so student rooms not yet in use; and a gang of cleaners arrived at seven each morning to prepare St Austin's College for its working day.

'These last were paid over the odds to cope with the irregularities they encountered; there would be a generous bonus at Christmas on condition no suggestion of gossip had come to the Bursar's ears in the interval. "Teething troubles" was the blanket explanation used by the administrators to muffle any criticism; and when the cleaners formed a deputation to complain that they could not get the reek out of their clothes, they

440

were all issued with a complete outfit, including stockings, shoes and protective headgear, to be kept, worn and laundered within the College.

'Everyone else was too busy, polite, hopeful or insecure to be disturbed by the minor discomforts of the new complex. They noticed them, of course. One of the Science Fellows, enjoying an after-dinner cigar by the floodlit water garden – an austere, rather Japanese, arrangement of pools, gravel and boulders – pointed out to a colleague that there was oil floating on the surface.

' "It seems to be everywhere," the other replied; "makes a terrible ring round the bath, don't you find? I use Perrier water for all minor ablutions now. I expect the Bursar is seeing to it."

'But when the Classics Professor accused the same Science Fellow, a chemist, of "creating a diabolical pong in that lab of yours"; and went on to say that no doubt the "fall-out" from such a brew would explain the nasty condensation on the coffee lounge windows, the scientist was piqued into proving his innocence. After a few discreet inquiries, he began to keep a diary of St Austin's "nuisances".'

'Just a moment,' said Effingham, topping up the storyteller's glass with malt whisky. 'Amidst all this discretion and rumour-scotching, how did you, on the outside, come to hear of it? Did you, for example, see this diary?'

'Indeed I did,' Kahn replied. 'The diarist was a close friend of mine. He had been at my own college until he was tempted away to Austin's by the promise of a higher salary and greater freedom for research. We continued to meet every week in my rooms to play sonatas – my instrument is the harpsichord; his, the flute. I observed he was preoccupied; I questioned him, and gradually, over the weeks – and very reluctantly on his part – the story unfolded. I can only assume that new loyalties, the touchy pride of a young Foundation, caved in to curiosity and the need to confide.

'He had started running laboratory tests on the slimy deposit that persisted on so many of the brand new fittings around the College; it seemed to be animal fat – very high in protein – often mingled with traces of the detergent-based coating that had been liberally applied to many surfaces in a desperate attempt at halting the greasy tide. This analysis lifted any possible blame from the scientific department. "But," he said, "I don't feel inclined to tell Professor Lauder, our chief accuser, until I find some reasonable explanation for it."

'I suggested it might be simply that the kitchen vents were badly designed; leaking, say into a ventilation shaft.

' "I thought of that," he said. "And made inquiries. One of the carpenters told me it was first noticed long before the kitchen or the heating system were in operation. He said that his brother, who was in at the start of the building work, complained of the bricks 'oozing' – new, handmade bricks as well as the common industrial ones used for cellars and inner walls. Apparently his wife made him leave after a few months because she couldn't get the marks out of his overalls – like bloodstains, they were. It seemed a minor inconvenience for the sort of wages they were taking home, by all accounts; I said as much. 'Ah!' said the carpenter: 'and my sister-in-law liked the money too. But she started having terrible nightmares about the dirty overalls coming alive and stifling her.' These persisted, life had become impossible, the brother handed in his cards. And apparently he was by no means the only one: they had a lot of labour troubles – never about pay: always about working conditions." '

'But this carpenter didn't seem to mind?' said Gilpin.

'The carpenter was happy with the money; he was unmarried, and determined to finish the job and collect the so-called holiday bonus: an extra month's wages, in cash. I gather he was, moreover, not a little fascinated by the very phenomena that had been driving others away. There was a wealth of fine imported timber in the common rooms and dining hall – I'm sure you will have seen the photographs. Well, the polyurethane seal refused to dry on it. He stripped it all back and tried epoxy resin – with no better results. It seemed even detergents could not break down the greasy film. "Now," my friend told me, "it has to be washed down with a soda solution every few days and polished lightly with wax. We have twice the normal complement of cleaners, I've found: and all this in a spanking new building expressly designed, so Aardvik claimed, to save on labour. Very rum indeed."

'I asked him if he had passed on his observations to the Bursar.

' "Yes, and I was told to mind my own business. Quite politely, of course. He's ex-naval, you know: a rear-admiral at heart – very hot on schedules, discipline and morale, and holystoning the deck. 'We are well aware things are not running

perfectly,' he said. 'Any new ship has its quirks and jinxes, as
you would know if you'd had a quarter of my experience, my
good chap. Teething troubles. We're dealing with it. And don't
go spreading alarm and despondency, please: it's a new ship
but it's a happy ship. Let's keep it that way." '

'I was looking through his diary.

' "What's this?" I asked. "I can't read it."

' "Muesli," he said. "Sorry: my writing. A sort of cereal we
have. Enlightened food, you know: roughage and honey ex-
tract and all that. In keeping with the young, clean, forward-
looking Austin image—"

' "But: 'a beak in the muesli'? That's what it says."

' "Yes – that was only last week, wasn't it." He muttered
something about "coming to the crunch", the "nitty-gritty";
and apologized. The point was, he said, he had felt it was the
final straw.

' "But I don't understand," I said. "A *beak*?"

' "Yes," he said. "One of the undergraduates found a chick-
en's beak – quite clearly that, albeit unattached to a chicken:
little nostrils, you know; yellowish, hard; the two halves still
joined by a thread of ligament. In a mouthful of muesli. It was
very upsetting for him. He vomited quite dramatically, I'm
told." And my friend went on to point out, with the diary's
backing, that the nuisances were on the increase. Only the
previous morning there had been quantities of bedraggled
feathers sprinkled round the corridors, and in the Senior Common Room.

' "A pillow fight?" I suggested.

'No: apparently all the pillows and duvets and cushions were
filled with pure nylon throughout the college. "And I've heard
of drawers full of 'clean' cutlery," he went on, "found gummed
together with a sticky dark substance – all cleaned up before I
got a chance to examine it; and the stained green baize had
been burnt. Wine that had been opened, as well as several
decanters of sherry and whisky and port, became quite un-
drinkable; a sort of burnt musty flavour. Overnight. Always
overnight. And when, at the end of an unusually warm October – on which many of the smells had been blamed, incidentally – the weather changed, the few superbly designed open
fireplaces were christened; but we were driven out of doors by
fumes and black smoke – for all the world as though a chip
pan were on fire. A week later the hearths were boarded over

and electric fires fitted in front. "It will be more convenient to trace the trouble during vacation," said the Bursar. "And anyway, electric heating is far cleaner when all is said and done."

'There was to be a big Christmas feast, attended by the Founder and important guests from many walks of life. The dons could ask their friends, and I was invited by my fellow scientist.

'I must say I did not notice anything untoward on my arrival. It was the first time I had dined; the first time, indeed, I had seen St Austin's properly since its completion – as my friend always came to me, a harpsichord being so much less portable than a flute. Now, ascending the main steps, I gazed round admiringly at Sixten Aardvik's brainchild, floodlit under a starry sky. It was handsome, original and impressively well made, only the very best wherever one turned; it was like the Ark of the Lord, but up-dated to the twenty-first century: spare in line and rich in texture – a spaciousness and quality that suggested cubits rather than metres, and the wealth of a new Solomon.

'Several old trees dating back to the days of Westwyke Farm had clearly been incorporated into the grand design, and now formed an elegant tracery of bare branches against the pale grey-gold bricks. I remarked on this.

' "They have spent the last two weeks washing down the most visible walls," my host confided. "The rear-admiral now claims it is a salt deposit in the clay, combined with the damp, rather smoky atmosphere of a largely industrial town, that is causing the 'weeping' effect." He broke off to point out the Founder, a tall broad man some way ahead of us. "I notice he is not using the handrail," he said. Curious, I put out my hand and grasped it. "It has just been cleaned up," he told me. So it may have been, but I felt an unpleasant suction as I released it. He watched me as I surreptitiously wiped my hand, and nodded.

' "That's nothing," he said. "This morning the counters in the breakfast cafeteria were bedewed with the stuff; and there was a positive snowdrift of feathers on the terrace this morning, up against the main door. My scout saw them and told me they were disgusting: 'all crumpled and bloody,' she said. 'Smelt like, well – carrion, really. The cleaners were sluicing it down with Jeyes fluid and stuff – quite put them off their tea-break, I can tell you . . .' She's never been so outspoken before.

444

Things are coming to a pretty pass . . . Ah, Lord Austin: I'd like to present Marius Kahn—" etcetera etcetera.

'He was a big heavy man, more florid of face than I had expected from the news pictures. "Like what you see, Kahn?" he asked loudly and went on without waiting for a reply: "I can remember when all this was poor grazing land, y'know – almost wet enough for snipe-shooting . . . Hope we're going to be fed well this evening, what? The best our streamlined kitchens can provide?"

' "Actually," said my host, "the kitchens are closed down. The staff wouldn't—"

'The Bursar cut him out smoothly.

' "We decided to use caterers this evening, Lord Austin, and give the staff a treat too. I am certain you will find the festive board leaves nothing to be desired – a London firm of some distinction—"

' "Haven't been going through labour troubles with the kitchen staff as well, have you?" The Founder's tone was no longer jolly, and he fixed the rear-admiral with a bulging glare.

' "Just the usual teething problems, Lord Austin. All will be worked out by the New Year." '

Our storyteller stood up and stretched.

'I think I might help myself to a soft drink,' he said, stepping out of the circle. 'Well, as you are probably aware, that New Year saw the closure of St Austin's – after just one term; and as a direct result of the events of that night: the night of the Feast, the culmination of all the troubles that had gone before. Oh, I know there were official explanations – too many and all contradictory; failure of funds, staff problems, unsuitability of position: unhealthily low-lying, they said. Even ground subsidence was mentioned, though that version was quickly suppressed when the American buyers became interested.

'No, my friends – I hope I may call you friends? And that my confidences will remain safe with you – No: the truth is always simple; and the truth is that St Austin's College was closed because it was haunted. Haunted by a very unusual ghost: a multiple ghost, a multitude of revenants, one might say, that had occupied that space – and still did, through some fearful freak in Time.

'I actually witnessed the denouement; saw the Founder, John Milton Austin, go down before a veritable wave of vengeful creatures on whose blood money, I suppose, the

Foundation stood. Hard to believe, I grant; but harder still to explain away – though of course they tried. The Press was told Lord Austin had suffered a massive coronary; and he is now reported to be an invalid – not up to interviews or even correspondence. Insane and shut away would be nearer the mark . . . But I anticipate.'

He was standing by the fireplace now, gazing into his glass of orange and selza. His voice was very quiet.

'It was a successful Feast, I believe; certainly judged a good evening by those who left early. The food was excellent – though not the traditional Christmas fare: Austin never touched turkey. The wines were superlative; uncorked perhaps a mite too lately for the more critical palates – but that was deliberate, according to my host's asides. For me, alert to every small irregularity, it was almost as if there were some threat in the air around us, some vapour, some cloud, as it were, of malign spores that might turn our victuals to carrion, our wine to bitter blood, our bread to a heap of mites, if we should linger too long.

'The magnificent High Table, a single thirty-foot plank cut from a Lebanon cedar, was furnished with space age silver, made in Sweden: not just cutlery, but bowls and platters and candelabra, all elegantly attenuated, asymmetrical – the vessels of the kings of Alpha Centauri, heaped with the Terran delights of fruit, flowers, sweetmeats. The table napkins, folded into tall cones, had that unnatural, luminous whiteness of road signs; and two enormous chandeliers, hanging high above us between the soaring buttresses of a polished aluminium ceiling, hovered like mother ships coming in to land. They seemed to be constructed from a million crystal snowflakes – pierced and galleried – floating palaces of ice.

'But as the meal went on, their light dimmed and grew murky, almost rusty. Pudding spoons were furtively polished below table level, and the cedar board acquired dark smears and streaks and puddles along its surface. I thought it was spilt wine, and absently licked my finger. It was rank cooking fat. Even the black fibreglass chairs seemed to sweat; and through the appetizing fragrances of salmon and *fillet en croute* there filtered a smell of singed hair and pork crackling; while the *Bombe Surprise* – for all its brandy and black cherries – actually tasted of it.

'No one mentioned these things, naturally. Conversation

flowed; there were speeches – but only short ones. We moved – gratefully – into the Senior Common Room for coffee. "Looks as if it might be snowing," said a fellow guest, admiring the floodlit terrace and water garden beyond the plate-glass wall. Then the Warden ordered that the curtains be drawn. Cups were handed round.

' "I propose we go up to my rooms," said my host. "We can't just yet, but things tend to be fairly informal here: the Warden will probably bear our Founder away for a quiet whisky and a tour of the new reading rooms. We'll just finish our coffee – I couldn't face another cup, I fear . . ."

'It was amazingly nasty coffee. I filled mine with sugar in an attempt to convince myself it was some exotic Arab brew, but still that brackish bitterness came through. In his pleasant and spacious study, my friend opened a new bottle of Glenlivet and we washed the taste away. It was an odd business, I said; and I asked if it bothered him even up here – this noisome poltergeist. He showed me stains on the walls, mostly concealed by large paintings.

' "I know the bad patches now," he said. "It's making quite a collector of me. The bathroom fittings were not very nice to touch; but I fitted those towelling gloves over the taps. And now they've issued everyone with brown towels and dark coloured sheets, one doesn't notice the spots on them."

'He did not seem to want to talk any more of it; and we settled down to play some of his records. For an hour or so I forgot the poltergeists and nuisances. We heard other guests making their departures; and my host lifted his blind and looked out. He remarked that the Founder's Rolls was still there. No, he was not staying at the College, but had booked in at the Randolph.

' "I see the feathers are back," he said. "By the way, did you notice that scratching noise when the Warden was proposing the Loyal Toast?"

'I said I had thought it was just the college cat trying to get in.

' "There is no college cat," he said. "And the sound came, I thought, from behind the fireplace." The Adagio movement started, and we fell silent again.

'When the quartet was over, I got to my feet; but he urged me to stay: he had been hoping for some chess, he said.

' "Gladly," I replied. "It's only that I've run out of cigarettes, and I think I must have left my pipe in the Common Room. Set up the board while I retrieve it." He started getting out the pieces, and I made my way back towards the main staircase.

'An ultra-modern institution, so bright and purposeful by daylight, is curiously dispiriting in the small hours. It was about one-thirty; and single inset bulbs at wide intervals made small pools of light in the long faceless corridors. I caught myself hurrying, and glancing back over my shoulder at imaginary fears. The walls, which were finished in a "pearlized" acrylic surface, gleamed pallidly like the forehead of a fever victim – a fanciful notion, perhaps, but one that the droplets and runnels of moisture on them did little to dispel. Moreover they seemed to taper inwards, to lean on me; and a faint dry pulse (the ticking of concealed radiators, I told myself: probably cooling, at this hour) was all at once as menacing as a time bomb amidst that deadly hush.

'I was glad to reach the stairs: the halls below were more generously lit, and somewhere towards the back of the great complex I could now hear the sounds of distant voices, and the clatter of crockery: the caterers were packing up.

'In the Senior Common Room, two Fellows were still drinking their port in a corner under the lamp like an aluminium praying-mantis. I picked up my pipe and lingered for a moment; I heard myself addressing them with the slightly desperate camaraderie of the traveller in foreign lands catching sight of a GB plate.

' "A superb evening," I said. "The Founder must be well content."

' "He certainly seemed to enjoy himself," said ᵥne of them. "He hasn't left yet, I gather."

'As I went back through the lobby, I felt a desire to see the great dining hall again. No: I was not "irresistibly drawn"; nothing so interesting, I assure you. Just curious. Ambiguous word . . . I walked over to the big double doors that led to it. As I did, the Warden and Lord Austin came down the main staircase.

' "I'll just get someone to call for your car," the Warden was saying. "Sure you won't have a night-cap before you . . . ? No? Well – if you'll wait just a moment . . ."

'Lord Austin saw me opening the door of the dining hall and came over.

448

' "Fine little room, this," he said, passing in ahead of me.

'By the dim illumination of a single sideboard lamp, it was like walking in through the jaws of a dead whale. Above us the steel ribs of the huge vaulted ceiling shone with a pale phosphorescence. The chairs had been set back against the wall and the space looked larger and barer, the long table in the midst of it a raw, dark slab streaked with moisture. On the floor, scattered and crumpled but shining with a surreal whiteness, lay dozens of discarded napkins, dropped by the diners or swept to the ground by the caterers as they cleared.

'We stood in silence, gazing round; and heard the scrabbling again; and I saw a couple of the table napkins twitch, and move. I shut my eyes, blaming the Glenlivet; but when I opened them and looked again, the whole flock of crumpled linen bundles seemed to be lurching across the floor, flopping about, taking off, streaming towards us: a cluster, a drift, a tornado of tarnished snow in the half-dark; rustling as double-damask would rustle, but also as feathers might – stiff, chopped feathers, perhaps, unaccustomed to flight – a rasping breath growing louder and harsher, the musty reek of the long-dead – a waft of caries from very Hellmouth.

'They filled the air; they converged on the Founder, brought him down, submerged him. I ran into the midst of them. I heard myself shouting "Shoo! Shoo!" as I tried to beat them off him. There was no time to think of poltergeists, to reason that this could not be happening. I can say now, of course, that far weightier objects than table napkins have been seen to move with a life of their own. But these things seemed to have eyes. Now they were so close I could see they had eyes – and small noseless faces with gaping mouths, misshapen holes that fastened on our faces and hands; and there were ragged stumps of claws . . . Scrabbling, crying, fluttering horribly, they fumbled and mumbled at us. Where they found a hold they hung on: I remember seeing two that clung like parasites to the Founder's neck – flailed from side to side as he tried to shake them off; his hands over his face were red. And the pain of those malformed beaks and talons was violent, was real. I tasted blood and gagged on feathers. Then I passed out.

'When they opened the doors of the dining hall, they found us both bloody and unconscious, lying amidst a pile of dirty table linen. Lord Austin was far more seriously cut about than myself; and he suffered a heart attack on the way to the nursing home. As for me, my worst wounds were on my face; and on this hand, which became badly infected and is still horribly scarred. I believe straight pecking and scratching might have done less harm: there had been a cruel desperation behind those broken weapons. The beard and the glove date from that time.

'But you can see why it is hardly a story to be given much exposure – the danger being not so much scandal as pure improbability. Fortunately for my own sanity, the Warden, the porter he had called to summon the Rolls, and the two dons in the Senior Common Room along the hall, all heard a noise like a barnyard fight coming from the great dining room. But when they burst in, the double-damask napkins were double-damask napkins once more . . . They kept the police out of it; they decided to say that cats had caused the scratches, and the cats had been put down. The private nursing home to which we were taken accepted the explanation; they were far more occupied with Lord Austin's coronary. My chemist friend took a napkin for analysis. He identified human blood and the usual animal grease deposit that they all knew so well. The rest of the linen was put in the incinerator.

'Perhaps it was over-dramatic to close down the College: things might have got better after that. I understand they have: perhaps the flock of battery ghosts was satisfied. My friend suggested that the insurance for that fire at Westwyke Farm was the root of it – though, as I pointed out, it would not be the first time bad money had been used in a good cause.'

Effingham finished his whisky and stood up.

'But the first time, maybe, that a cause of any sort has been destroyed by such a bizarre revenge,' he observed. 'Certainly those battery hens had plenty of time to brood on it.'

R. A. Lafferty
The funny face murders

R. A. Lafferty is quite inexplicable, but here are a few facts. He was born in 1914 and worked most of his life in the electrical wholesale business. 'The most interesting part of my life was the four and a half years in the US Army in WW II, mostly in the South Pacific. I began to write in 1959, at the age of forty-five, a time when most writers are about finished. I quit work except writing in 1970. I have never written very hard and I loaf a lot. I am a Catholic, a political Independent, a fiscal conservative. My hobbies are history, geology, languages, writing and travel.'

Never written very hard? Why, besides perhaps two hundred stories (by no means all collected), he has written at least twelve novels, including The Reefs of Earth, Okla Hannali, Fourth Mansions, Arrive at Easterwine, *and* The Three Armageddons of Enniscorthy Sweeny. *But then he suggests in an interview that stories choose their authors rather than anything resembling the reverse.*

Perhaps 'The Funny Face Murders' is comic relief, or perhaps not. It reminds me (very slightly!) of one of Chesterton's nightmares, say The Man Who Was Thursday, *without the theological reassurance. Beyond that, you're on your own.*

1

Judy Kingfixit filled a large paper sack with bundles of paper money and went down to Broken Bench Lane on the outskirts of T Town. She had a need to see whatever new face the Lane presented this morning.

'What we do on Broken Bench is look at the world and reality out of new faces,' Judy's husband Harry often said, 'and that's another name for the Science of Invention. And we

451

who invent, we see the world as wearing a new face every morning.'

'I will have to find Harry,' Judy told herself. 'He cannot get along without me, and he will *have* to be on Broken Bench Lane. That's the only place he knows to go. He isn't much fun, but he's habit-forming and I live by habits now. I wasn't paying attention when he said what he was on to this time, but he's got to be down here. Now there's an idea! I'll try it.'

There was a sign on a booth there that read *Trouble-Dissolver Ten Cents a Large Glass.* Judy got a large glass of it and drank it off quickly.

Two adventurous boys were coming to the Lane at that same early morning moment. They were coming at it from the woods to take it unaware, to ambush it and to be ambushed by it. To be an adventurous boy in the very early morning is even better than to be Judy Kingfixit with a large sack full of money. It was very much as though the boys came on a raft from those flowing woods. It was really a *Big Star Weed Rider* that they came on. But it is Judy on scene yet.

'This leaves me at loose ends,' Judy said when she had drunk off the Trouble-Dissolver. 'I hadn't expected it to work so quickly. My troubles are all dissolved and I become a balloon without ballast.'

'It takes a little time,' said the proprietor of the place with a happy leer. 'But now that I am used of it this way, I wouldn't go back to having troubles again for anything.'

Judy hadn't a whole lot of respect for Broken Bench Lane.

'I have an uncle just like this alley,' she said out loud. 'Disreputable, that's what they both are.'

She really hadn't a whole lot of money that she could afford to waste here; but there was an attraction (besides trying to find her husband Harry Kingfixit who was usually somewhere on the Lane), there was a seeking and a shabby interest that got hold of her sometimes and drew her down to the Lane. Sometimes? It drew her down there just about every morning, just as soon as the morning began.

At just this time there was a terrific crash involving that least dependable of all aircraft, The *Big Star Weed Rider*, and two boys, Roy Mega and Austro. The fact that they were travelling very low, about six inches above grass-top, probably saved their lives and got them off with nothing more than grass burns. But the crash was damaging to their reputations as aircraft designers. You can't have something go wrong with the design of your ailerons and still keep a sound reputation on Broken Bench Lane.

Broken Bench Lane, that bright ribbon in a sea of green, was particularly verdant because of the great quantities of Great Heart Discovery grass that grew so thickly in the whole region that the Lane traversed. The grass was the discovery of Great Heart Harkte who had been an inventive Indian man of several generations earlier. He had invented a sod buster plough superior to every other one. He had invented a poke-weed harvester and a coon skinner. He had grown the first puffed wheat and the first Golden Day sand plums. And he invented Great Heart Discovery grass that did not thrive well until after Great Heart Harkte himself was dead and buried. Then it grew richly, with every primordial root of it coming out of Harkte's buried heart, and it covered a region of several miles. Wherever it grew, there was inventiveness supreme; and Broken Bench Lane had the lushest Discovery grass of the whole region.

Where else but on the Lane was there such a merry, early morning chirping going on at every hour of the day and night? The barkers and cardinals and meadow larks all seemed to sing together:

'Lookie, lookie, lookie! Invent now! Be a millionaire by noon!'

Broken Bench Lane was the gaudiest-appearing of all those little streets and ways that tumbled and twisted down the green slopes all the way from Standpipe Hill to the south edge of town till they disappeared in the verdant haze beyond which, in the misty distance, rose Beautiful Downtown Broken Arrow. There were not streets and arteries like these everywhere, not like this bunch: Jenks Road, Clown Alley, Harrow Street, Five Shill Road, Lollywaggers' Left-Hand Lane, Speckled Fish Road, Leptophlebo Street, Trotting Snake Road, Broken Bench Lane! And the brightest jewel of them all was Broken Bench.

(Yes, Judy Kingfixit will be all right for a while. What can possibly go wrong with anyone who has had all her troubles dissolved and who is wandering around with a large sack full of large bundles of money?)

These streets are not necessarily located in the order here

given. There are many other streets, better kept and broader, that intrude between these. Half of these arteries are not even proper streets in the sense of accepting vehicular traffic; they are mere pedestrian walks or paths or alleys. (Broken Bench was in between the categories in that it accepted vehicles, but for only one hour a day.)

Quentan Whitebird, in his monumental work *Forgotten Lanes and Byways of Tulsa*, refers to this cluster of little streets (plus four others, and with Lollywaggers' unaccountably left out) as 'dream streets'. Well, there *is* a green haze over all of them that is very like a summer afternoon sleep. Even in the brightness and hustle of some of them, there is always this noddiness or nappiness. And there is the frightening snapping-out of it also, and the raffish terror at realizing that one hasn't quite snapped out of the spell after all.

There was a graffito on a wall that read 'Who is False Face Flaherty?' That was the beginning of a doubt.

'Oh, what is there so weird about Harry disappearing this time?' Judy Kingfixit moaned, 'and what is there so weird about me myself? And how has False Face Flaherty come into the thing these last several days?' The Trouble-Dissolver would really dissolve all troubles, but if new and different troubles should arise, it would require another glass of the stuff to get rid of them.

Broken Bench was the brightest and most hustling of all those little roads. What factories and shops there were there! What venture-houses! What money coining enterprises! What dreams that had taken flesh in solid crab-orchard stone with tomorrow-glass façades! There were bustling manufactories and tall financial empires and inventories (well, what *do* you call the studios where inventors work?). There was all the flowing lifeblood of newness. The Lane was so crammed with newness that those who visited it only once a day were always dumbfounded by the changes in it. Here were the waves of the future sold by the gallon or barrel or oceanful.

'Be on time,' read another graffito on another wall. 'The murders take place this morning at nine o'clock in Madame Gussaud's Wax Museum.'

And here was something new! The Lane never disappointed. Judy Kingfixit was at a Mokka-Chokka stand where she was both attracted and repelled by the hot odour of something new.

'You look like a lady I know,' Edith Thornbush said, and she was a bit puzzled. 'You have ankles and wrists kind of like hers. Her name is Judy Kingfixit.'

'And my name is Judy Kingfixit,' Judy said, 'and it's no more than eight hours since we were together last. What's the matter with you anyhow, Edith?'

'If you *are* Judy,' Edith said, 'and even if you aren't, it doesn't come well from you to ask *anybody* what's the matter with them. Just what *has* happened to you? Where did you get that face?'

'You *are* Judy Kingfixit, aren't you?' Ophelia Izobret asked in a pained way. 'Didn't you happen to look in the mirror this morning?'

'No, the mirrors kept breaking,' Judy said. 'I never did get a good look at me.'

'Well, sit down with us,' Ophelia said. 'None of us is perfect this time of day, but you miss it farther than anyone I ever saw.'

'Thank you, Ophelia,' Judy said and she sat down with them all in a booth in the Mokka-Chokka stand. Cornelia Falselove was there also. 'You have to be Judy,' this Cornelia said. 'No one else would ever imitate Judy Kingfixit. Who'd *want* to?'

'Thank you, Cornelia,' Judy said. She bought and began to drink a cup of hot Mokka-Chokka, the first time in her life she had ever drunk it or heard of it.

There was a new graffito on the wall: 'False Face Flaherty is a Corporation Man.'

Oh the drink was horrible! But, *oh*, it was sociable! Really, is there anything in the world so pleasant as to sit and drink hot Mokka-Chokka with friends?

'Oh yes, isn't it horrible!' Ophelia Izobret asked. 'The inventor said that he worked for seven years to find something bad enough to be this good. But he had precedent to go by. When first introduced to the western world six hundred years ago, coffee was almost as horrible, so ancient writers have indicated. It was instantly terrible and it was an instant success. And it came with its own furniture, which we still have with us, up until this morning at least. With the coming of coffee, there was born in one blinding flash the coffee houses or cafés, the eating-out places of ever since then. There hadn't been any regular eating-out places before that, except in the Asian regions that already had coffee. Kitchens were changed, or real kitchens were born. They are all coffee kitchens now, or were up till this morning.

'Now there is Mokka-Chokka the totally new beverage, and

it predicates totally new and different sorts of eating-out places and kitchens for the whole world. It is by such giant leaps or mutations that the world and its institutions change, but the changes are usually ascribed to lesser things.'

'Mokka-Chokka franchises and distributorships are going to sixteen figures,' Cornelia Falselove said, 'and that's a lot of Mokka. I hope that my – what's his name anyhow? – George is able to get in on it. He's here somewhere on the Lane, if I can find him. I'd like to get in on it myself, but I could hardly raise an eight figure ante. And George, he couldn't even raise a one figure ante, but sometimes he thinks of something. Oh, there is so much that is new here this morning! Whenever I am about to give up I come here and find out just how stimulating things are. Say, are you *sure* that you're Judy Kingfixit? You are very funny-looking this morning, even for Judy.'

On the wall, a writing finger wrote 'Cornelia Falselove is a Corporation Woman', and, having writ, passed on. But there is nothing like Mokka-Chokka to get the morning juices to surging through one.

'Invest in Broken Bench Lane!' a fuzzy-faced boy was calling. 'Ten cents a front foot!'

They all had dimes out to make deals with him when they heard that. Land on Broken Bench Lane usually sold somewhere between two dollars and a thousand dollars a front foot: ten cents a front foot was fantastic.

'I want eight front feet,' Edith Thornbush cried out. 'I'll set up my own little booth in the Lane, just eight feet wide.'

But the fuzzy-faced boy hadn't mentioned front feet of land. They were front feet of rabbits that he was selling for a dime each.

'Aw, Austro, that's cheating,' Judy Kingfixit said (the fuzzy-faced boy was Austro, that youthful genius of the Australopithecus race), 'Give me two more though. Where do you get them?'

'I get them from the Sooner State Rabbit Fattery out on the Sand Springs Road,' Austro said. 'They butcher a million fat rabbits a week there. They've always disposed of the left hind feet to *Luck Charms Limited*. And there is a very peculiar industrial application for the right hind feet only (I cannot tell you any more about that: I am besworn). But the front feet of the rabbits were always thrown away until I thought of this grift. Ahoy there, folks! Invest in Broken Bench Lane! Ten cents a front foot!'

Austro made several other sales to people who came into the Mokka-Chokka stand. This was extra income that would be needed to carry the *Big Star Detective Agency* over a slack period. Austro and his partner Roy Mega, a youthful genius of the Milesian race, had just moved their *Big Star Detective Agency* to Broken Bench Lane that morning. Barnaby Sheen had made the two young geniuses move their agency out of his electronics laboratory; but the new Broken Bench location was only a hundred feet from that hole-in-the-woods where the laboratory stood.

A hundred feet, but a million miles distant in spirit. For the magic of enterprise and invention was everywhere in the Lane.

'Where are all the funny-looking people coming from?' Ophelia Izobret asked them all. 'Some of them look even funnier than Judy does today.'

'They get their faces at *Funny Faces Incorporated*, that little pill-pushing emporium over there,' Austro told the ladies. 'It's one of the hottest enterprises thus far this morning.'

'Oh, do they glue the faces on to them?' Ophelia asked. 'They look so natural for not, ah, looking natural at all. They fit so well that they must be glued on.'

'No, it's a lot more scientific than that,' Austro said. 'Everything is very scientific now, especially on the Lane. That's why Roy and I have taken chambers here for contacts with our clients. The funny faces, they grow them on people with fast-acting pills. You pick out the face that you want to wear for a while, and False Face Flaherty who runs the pillory over there will engineer the pills to give you that face quick. He bought up all the assets and secrets of *Instant Physiognomists* and also those of the *Pow Nose-Shrinker* people. He has absorbed companies and he has absorbed people. He's put it together now with a line of the fastest-acting psychosomatic pills in the world. You pop them down, and your face begins to change within seconds. You will notice several people running around with faces like mine. They picked mine for a funny face apparently, I don't know why. But I can always tell the difference. I have a mark on me that none of them know about, and they haven't engineered a pill for it yet.'

'Is all that the truth, Austro?' Edith Thornbush asked.

'What is truth?' Austro inquired, and he used his owl face when he asked it.

'But how do they get rid of the funny faces when they're tired of them?' Ophelia Izobret wanted to know. 'How do they ungrow them?'

457

'False Face Flaherty asks the customer how long he wants to wear a face, an hour, a day, a week,' Austro said. 'Then he adjusts the pill (he says) to give that time effect. After that time, your own face will come back (he says), or an improved model if you wish. And there are no after-effects to the changes (he says). He lies though (everybody on the Lane lies till he gets a truth really rolling for him): none of the pills really has a time coefficient or a reversal effect. False Face doesn't know how long a funny face will remain. He never tried this line of pills before this morning, except on his wife accidentally last night, and the results aren't in yet.'

'Poor wife!' said Judy Kingfixit. 'I don't believe that I quite like that False Face Flaherty. And I don't believe that I can quite stay away from him. That is the ambivalence of my life.'

'I think that I will get myself a false face to cheer me up,' Edith Thornbush said, 'and I really don't care how long it sticks to me.' Edith left the Mokka-Chokka stand to go over to *Funny Faces Incorporated.*

'The implications of this are tremendous,' said Ophelia Izobret. 'Consider only the criminal aspect of the funny face movement.'

'You are always *so* good at considering the criminal aspects, Ophelia,' Judy said.

Really, funny faces were big. Oh the inventiveness of the people on Broken Bench Lane!

'Good persons, here are business cards of our main business,' Austro said, and he passed the cards out to all the good persons who would accept them.

'*Big Star Detective Agency,*' the cards were printed. 'Mega and Austro, scientists and artists in detection and improvisation. Interesting murders solicited. Tedious murders solved grudgingly. Skip tracing done. We locate anybody or anything. Husbands found cheap.'

'How cheap?' Judy Kingfixit asked Austro. 'I wonder if you could find my husband. I wouldn't want him for more than four or five dollars worth, but I'd go that much.'

'Find mine too,' Ophelia Izobret said. 'Complications, Austro? Oh, I'll pay for the complications also.'

'Find mine also,' said a funny-faced woman who just arrived there and who sounded like Edith Thornbush. 'Oh, that was fast! How do I look? Yes, find mine, Austro.'

458

'Yes, I guess so. Me too,' said Cornelia Falselove.

'Remember also,' said Austro, 'that the *Big Star Detective Agency* is not concerned entirely with crime detection. We also detect patterns and tendencies and unborn facts in the ethical and sociological and scientific fields. Folks, we're good.'

'But is your information and discoveries correct?' Judy asked.

'What is correct?' Austro asked, looking like an owl.

Three other Broken Bench widows, Hedwiga Pompey, Seraph Wideditch, and Lavinia Firstlight, gave Austro earnest money of one dollar each to find their husbands. The additional sums of three dollars and ninety-five cents each would be given on the actual uncovering or delivery of the husbands. This low price was extended to all of them except Ophelia Izobret. Ophelia had to pay one thousand dollars earnest money and gosh knows how much on final delivery (because of some complications in her case), but she paid the first payment cheerfully.

'Seven cases, carrock!' cried Austro with boyish satisfaction. 'That's good. But they are all little husband-missing cases. Not an interesting murder among them. Not even a tedious murder so far. That's bad.'

'That's bad, yes, Austro,' said a half-familiar voice encased in a new funny face (apparently a man voice and a man funny face), 'but you are wrong about there being no murder in the package. There *will* be a murder or several, and perhaps there has already been one. Whether it is an interesting murder or a tedious one will depend a little bit on the detective of record.'

'There will be a murder,' said Austro sombrely. 'I will have to watch for that, and at the same time I will have to figure out where we went wrong with our ailerons this morning.' (The *Big Star Weed Rider*, that most esoteric of aircraft, had crashed that morning with Austro and Roy, due to faulty ailerons. Fortunately for them, the elevation was only six inches when they crashed.)

'Are you my husband?' Ophelia Izobret asked the mysterious funny-faced man who had spoken of murders.

'Madam, that is confidential information,' said the person, and he moved away and merged with other funny faces in the hustle of Broken Bench Lane.

'He looks a little bit like my husband with that not-quite-right face of his,' Ophelia said. 'It's going to be hard to tell now. My husband always had a not-quite-right face too. What do you think of the ethics of wearing such a face, Austro?'

'What is right?' asked Austro looking like an owl. 'What is not-quite-right? What, on the face of it, is a face?'

But this isn't getting us into the early-morning wonders of Broken Bench Lane. Listen, travellers and natives alike, no other street anywhere has such sheer inventiveness as Broken Bench.

Clay-Eaters Enterprises! Could there be a company of such a name on your own street? This business had opened just this morning, and it had never been known before.

'Clay-Eating raised to an Art and a Science,' a banner on Clay-Eaters' Building proclaimed. 'Gourmets' clay from Georgia, Florida, Louisiana, and our own Oklahoma,' a sign announced. You know what? Some of the clay smells from that place were authoritative and they were nosy. Judy King-fixit went and bought a hundred dollars worth of stock in *Clay-Eaters*.

'Get in on the ground floor of this, on the clay-dirt ground floor of it,' another sign said. Judy got a hank (a long handful) of good, yellow, country clay. It didn't taste very good but it had possibilities. There must be a lot of clay in the world, millions of tons of it. This looked like a famine-proof industry. How could one go wrong for only a hundred dollars on one of the most basic foods of them all? Clay is even mentioned in Scripture, earlier than any other food that you can think of. It is the real staff of life. 'Clay makes the Man,' another sign there said. And it was easy to believe that this superior clay contained any number of rare earths.

Judy Kingfixit left them and went over to *Funny Faces Incorporated*. And False Face Flaherty who was the proprietor over there made more passes at her than a Vegas diceman.

'I love your face,' False Face said, and he kissed her. 'Is it your own?'

'I'm not sure,' Judy said. 'I thought you might know. I hadn't even known that I was wearing a funny face till my friends started to make remarks about it. I think now that my husband spiked my headache tonic last night before he skipped out. Are you my husband? He's an ambivalent man. Is your name as well as your face false?'

'Yes. But what did your husband spike your headache potion with? Is it possible that someone else knows my secret of physiognomenical freebooting?' False Face Flaherty asked. 'No matter. He cannot be my equal. He surely does not have my unique talents. Oh my dear, I must have your funny face. It is a masterpiece. Is it a masterpiece that I did in a dream and then forgot about, or is it the work of a different master? It is primordial, it is prodigious! I will make copies of it for the rest of my life.'

'Your voice reminds me of someone I know, but I can't remember who,' Judy said. 'And your hands remind me of someone I know. Oh yes, I'll buy a hundred dollars worth of your stock. Make it two hundred. Oh, False Face, you do something to me! But I have ramblings to ramble and people to find on the Lane.'

'My stock boy can handle things here at *Funny Faces Incorporated* for a while,' Flaherty said. 'He's already wearing a Flaherty Special False Face, so he looks like me anyhow. We will ramble together, my dear.'

Hand in hand, Judy Kingfixit and False Face Flaherty rambled the Lane together. They were both buffs of these hasty businesses which required so much daring to launch and which, when once launched, were so much more likely to sink than to survive. They visited the *Hot Sauerkraut Sandwich Drive-In*. Hot sauerkraut sandwiches were something whose time had just arrived, and where should such a timely thing more likely show its head than on Broken Bench Lane?

They visited the *Dog Dirt Gasoline Company* with its compelling motto: 'Our product alone contains volatile matter from high octane Great Danes.' Dog Dirt Gasoline would fill a need and remove a nuisance.

They visited the *Old Original Flea Market*, a hold-over from the day before when it had been named the *New Original Flea Market*. Judy Kingfixit bought one male flea and eight female fleas. She got the papers on them too.

'Hereafter they will have to give me the flea-breeders' discount on everything I buy there,' Judy told False Face, 'regardless of whether it is related to flea-breeding. That is part of the Flea Marketers' Franchise Agreements, but they won't give it to you unless you insist on it.'

They went to *Madame Gussaud's Wax Museum*, still going hand-in-hand; but each of them seemed to be carrying some-

461

thing in the free hand now. The Wax Museum was a very contemporary place. Funny faces, appearing on human persons by the pillatory magic of False Face Flaherty no more than fifteen minutes before were now displayed on wax figures at Gussaud's, by the magic of scientific reproduction and copying and the use of the new telestencils.

Gussaud's was rather a fun place. Everyone who came in there received free a Dirky Dave Rubber Dagger. It was a souvenir of the museum, for Dirky Dave was one of the most popular of the wax pieces. All the pieces were very lifelike.

One of them moaned horribly now as if it were death stricken. The figure that moaned was wearing one of the new Hamlet Izobret funny faces, the face that was a little wrong for the real Hamlet face. How did they make the figure moan so lifelike (or so deathlike) as that?

Edith Thornbush was in Gussaud's. So was Ophelia Izobret and many other persons.

On display were the wax figures of all the T Town notables, past, present, and future, in living wax; but one had to look at their name plaques to be sure who they were. False faces were popping out on more and more of them, by the magic and science of Madame Gussaud perhaps, or by the magic and science of False Face Flaherty who had great influence on his surroundings this morning.

'Who *is* False Face Flaherty?' a wax raven croaked.

Oh, the same or another wax figure moaned horribly again, a death-struck moan!

There were the waxen images of all the great Evangelists of T Town, all the great Western Swing Kings, all the great Inventors. There were absolutely authentic reproductions of—

—but here there was a disturbance and interruption. There was another moan like a death râle from one of the wax figures, one of them with the not-quite-right Hamlet Izobret funny face. Then, moaning unnervingly once more, the figure fell heavily with that peculiar squashing thud that is given off only by a column of wax, or by a column of human flesh, when it falls.

'He is stabbed to death!' Judy Kingfixit cried in a sharp liquid voice. 'There is a Dirky Dave dagger in him.'

'But it's only a rubber dagger, Judy,' False Face Flaherty laughed. 'See the words on the handle of it as on all the rest of them "Dirky Dave Rubber Dagger, Souvenir of Madame

Gussaud's Wax Works". It must be some sort of joke about him being dead, if they use a rubber dagger.'

'The rubber is steel-hard now,' Judy said, 'and steel-sharp' (and various persons were beginning to cry out 'Murder, Murder!') 'as a result, probably, of the all-pervading science of Broken Bench Lane. Who could have transmuted it so?'

'Oh, it was no great trick,' Flaherty said. 'There's a hundred different inventors of us on the Lane who could have done that at a minute's notice, without props yet.'

'And the blood! Look at all the blood, Flaherty! Did you ever see so much blood come out of a wax man? Do you think that's wax blood or rubber blood, F.F.?'

('Help! Help! Murder! Murder!' other people were calling.)

'No, it's real,' Flaherty said. 'Get the police, get an ambulance, get a doctor!'

'Get Austro. He's a detective now,' Judy said.

2

All those people were there quickly, the police, the ambulance people, the doctors, different laboratory crews, the detectives Roy Mega and Austro, a police detective named Otis Hardtack, honest citizens, and funny-faced rogues. They all milled around there, and they never did solve that murder.

'It's the funny faces that cloud the water,' said that police detective Otis Hardtack when he finally got his brains stretched around the fact that most of the people there were wearing false faces and that they were living and flesh faces that wouldn't come off easily. 'This dead man looks like Hamlet Izobret the con-man and inventor whom we have up often. He looks a lot like him, but not quite enough like. Hamlet is a pest that we all know down at headquarters, for the crime-solving inventions that he brings in as well as the quasi-crimes and frauds that he commits. Being an almost-Hamlet, this dead person is *not* Hamlet Izobret. Hamlet already had the original Hamlet funny face, and it was as good and authentic as any original could be. The one this dead man is wearing is not very accurate. It just isn't good enough to be the original, so the dead man can be anyone except Hamlet. What's behind this funny false face caper anyhow?'

'What is "funny"? ' asked Austro in his owlish way. 'What is "false"?'

'What we do on Broken Bench Lane is look at the world and at reality out of new faces,' False Face Flaherty was saying with the air of one who had often said it before. 'And looking out of new faces is another name for the science of invention. And we who invent, we see the world as wearing a new face every morning.'

'This man here, the dead man, told me that there would be a murder or murders,' Austro said. 'I wondered then how he knew about it.'

'Are you sure it is the same man?' Otis Hardtack asked.

'What is "sure"?' Austro asked. 'It was either this man, or one of those wax figures that were on each side of him when he fell. They have the same faces as he has, and they look as if they were ready to fall also. Why couldn't the man have told me who would do the killing and that it would be done to himself? He was thoughtless.'

'The one who did it took a little thought,' Otis said. 'This rubber-turned-into-steel of the dagger won't take prints. I always hate trouble anywhere in this Lane. There are always freakish elements to it.'

There was a horrible wail as of a demented siren.

'The murderer is identified,' Austro said. 'That is a new machine that my partner Roy Mega has perfected within the last five minutes. It will sniff out a recent murderer by the aura that he exudes, and it will not be silenced till he is apprehended.'

There was a second and a third siren wail that joined the first. And then a twelfth and thirteenth wail.

'The new machine is multi-voiced,' Austro said. 'That is for just such contingencies as this. The murderer *did not work alone*. He was part of a conspiracy. I hope that your men are apprehending the murderers as the machine directs them, detective Hardtack.'

'More likely they're trying to shut off that damned noise machine,' Hardtack growled. 'Oh, how could anyone ever come up with noises like that?'

And now there were about twenty separate wails coming from the machine as it identified target after target.

'My partner, Roy Mega, set out to discover the most irritating noise in the world,' Austro said, 'the noise that nobody could possibly ignore. We call it the murder-will-out noise, and that's it.'

'But, Austro, even you must realize that something has gone

464

wrong with it,' Hardtack said. 'It's howling for at least fifty separate targets now. There can't be that many people in on this murder. Even in Broken Bench Lane that isn't possible. Something's wrong!'

'Well, there *was* one slight thing he hadn't corrected yet. He decided, because of the immediacy of the murder, to go ahead and put the machine into action anyhow, is that not true, Roy? It seemed so unlikely that the case would arrive.'

'Uh, it's like the man who sold the horse to the other man,' said Roy Mega who had just returned to the wax museum after setting his machine into action. ' "I will acknowledge that the horse has one fault," the seller said. "He sits down on grapefruit. He cannot pass a grapefruit on the ground without sitting down on it, but otherwise he is an exemplary horse, and he is patient with children." '

'So the man bought the horse and started to ride him home,' Austro said. 'He went fine until the man rode him through a little creek, and the horse sat down in the middle of it and would not budge. Cudgels and calumnies would not move the beast, so the man walked back to the seller with his complaint.'

"Oh hell, I forgot to tell you," the seller said, "he sits down on fish too," ' Roy Mega finished it off.

'So???' police detective Otis Hardtack intoned, and everyone listened silently. Even the howling murder detector was quiet now, having been incapacitated by men with hammers and wrecking bars.

'It's the same with my new machine,' Roy Mega said. 'It howls when it comes on to a recent murder. It also howls (this is one of the quirks in it that I hadn't had time to take out yet) when it comes on anyone who had apple wine for breakfast. I didn't realize that there would be so many or even any of them.'

'It was likely those advertisements on the air last night,' detective Otis said. ' "Apple Wine, Apple Wine, Start Your Day with Apple Wine". A catchy tune and your loss. You have no idea what a sense of security you two boys give me. Police detectives sometimes are worried by their competition from outside the lines. That situation sure doesn't obtain here.'

There was a little slight-of-body business here. Laboratory men were working over that dead body in bunches, but the confusion could be channelled. The attention of all was called away several times. Hypnosis was used, and misdirection.

465

Austro and Roy somehow got the dead body over to their *Big Star Detective Agency*, and the police finally loaded an unscathed wax figure with a similar funny face on to their morgue wagon and took it down town with them.

Madame Gussaud was one of the few people who noticed that the switch had been made.

'But, in spite of it, I'm not short a wax figure,' she said. 'I'm two wax figures over! It's those damned false faces that have been popping out on them. How is anyone to keep them straight?'

Several of the folks gathered in the Gift Shop, the Wax Museum in the wake of the murder having attracted a number of persons of the grosser sort.

'Do you have the Gift of Second Sight for sale?' False Face Flaherty asked the Gift Shop proprietor.

'Oh certainly,' the man said. 'We have every sort of psychic and mental and personal gift for sale. We have the latest and most scientific things along the Lane. My own second sight tells me that you should have sought the gift of second sight yesterday and not today. My own uncanny-intuition gift tells me that you are in a jam. Sir, you are now in a room with only two doors leading out of it. The name of one of them is "Too Late" and the name of the other one of them is "Never", but either of them is better than staying where you are. For five thousand dollars I can give you the gift of second sight. Just put your head into this helmet, bite down on the bullet of your selection, and remember that pain has no memory.'

'It's cheap enough, I suppose,' False Face said. He paid the five thousand dollars and put his head in the helmet. For the next few minutes he went through numerous contortions as though he were in extreme pain. Austro and Roy Mega and a few others went next door to the *Air-Skate Rinkarama* so as to miss the sufferings of False Face Flaherty.

'Item,' said Austro, as he watched the air-skaters skim along two inches above the top of the grass of the rink, 'we have a dead man not yet identified by ourselves, though the police may have identified him by his prints. They don't tell us everything.'

'Item,' said Roy Mega, 'over in the Wax Museum there are two dead wax figures that are similar in face to the dead man and are similarly stabbed with rubber daggers turned to steel.

Those two are in addition to the unscathed wax figure that we substituted for the body. This business of *three* of the rubber daggers being transformed into steel is what puzzles me.'

'Oh, I've solved that part,' Austro said. 'One in six of the latest bunch of Dirky Dave Rubber Daggers (apparently manufactured during the night just past) was made of steel and honed to an edge. This is something that even Madame Gussaud doesn't know. But the junior underground along the Lane has been putting out the word all morning that *Dirky Dave Roulette* is the new In game in the neighbourhood. So it would be easy for three different persons to select the heavier steel daggers out of the souvenir dagger baskets and then plunge them into the intended victim, and mistakenly into the two adjacent wax figures that were funny-faced exactly like the victim.'

'*Dirky Dave Roulette* sounds like a childish game,' Roy Mega said, 'but I can see where it would be fun. "Stab your Bosom Buddy in the Bosom! One chance in six that you will kill him or wound him." Do you want to go by there and try it, Austro? We just reach in the basket blindly and take out the Dirky Dave Dagger that comes to our hand. And then we will have at it.'

'We will go by the Museum and maybe we will do it and maybe we won't,' said Austro.

And they didn't do it. They were diverted by crowds of scofflaws, hitsters, and hooded-crows. They were buffeted by these hurrying persons in the Lane, and they forgot all about playing dagger roulette.

The newcomers were visitors, from Kansas City and Memphis and Dallas, of the woolly sort. They had apparently come to town on the mid-morning planes, and they had headed for the Lane at once. News that a new wrinkle might be found on the Lane had travelled fast. The scoff-iaws wanted the funny faces that could be worn for either long or short times as ruddy and living flesh disguises. ('We get so damned tired of wearing those ski-masks when we make a hit,' one of them said.) They wanted whatever variety of funny-face pills might be had. They spotted False Face Flaherty instinctively as the Factor in Faces. They dragged him out of the helmet in the gift shop and began to shove money at him. So False Face went back to his base at *Funny Faces Incorporated* to attend to business.

'We really don't know who False Face Flaherty is,' Austro

remarked, 'even though he seems to have a leading role on the Lane. It seems to everyone that he has been here for ever, but he had never been on the Lane as late as yesterday. There's almost too much of him for one person, and there's a lot of things missing from him that even the poorest person should have.'

'Who is Cornelia Falselove?' a wax raven in Gussaud's Wax Museum was heard to croak.

'The mistake we are making is in dealing with surface or apparent persons rather than with psychological persons,' Roy Mega said. 'We might, for instance, inquire about the apparent person of False Face Flaherty: we would find, I suspect, that there is no such person at all. Ah, but let us examine the psychological persons that hover about this Flaherty, though not about him exclusively: the corporate *Substrate Lord*, the *Shadow*, the *Anima*, the *Animus*, the *Ego*, the *No*, the *Hemeis*; aye, and the *Id*. I believe that there is a corporate, but not a personal, personality behind those false faces of Flaherty.'

'I know a little bit about that corporate personality myself,' Austro said. 'I have just obtained a copy of the Articles of Corporation of *Funny Faces Incorporated*. The articles state that False Face Flaherty *is* a corporate personality that may be inhabited by Harry Kingfixit or Edgar Thornbush or by Hamlet Izobret; it states that all three of these have equal rights to this personality, especially the rights of entering it and leaving it.'

'Well, I wonder which one of them is inside Flaherty at the moment?'

'Oh, I'm sure that it is Harry Kingfixit,' Austro said. 'It could hardly be one of the others since Judy Kingfixit seems to have such a lively affection for it. It must be her husband Harry Kingfixit.'

'Hey boys,' said Cornelia Falselove as she came to them. 'Those two dead wax figures that were on each side of the dead man back at the wax works, well, it turns out that they aren't dead wax figures at all. They are dead live human people is what they are.'

'Who knows about this?' Roy Mega asked in his conspiratorial voice.

'I do,' Cornelia said. 'I have a sensitive nose and it says that they are people and that they are getting a little bit ripe already on this warm day.'

468

'Can you get the two figures for us without anyone catching on?' Roy said.

'Oh, I can buy them as wax figures I guess.'

'Do it. And bring them to the *Big Star Detective Agency* at its new location in its special *Two-Guys-in-a-Garage Invention Kit and Utility Building.*'

'All right,' said Cornelia Falselove who was an agreeable woman also. She went to buy the two figures who were actually dead human persons according to herself.

'Who *is* this Cornelia Falselove?' Roy Mega asked.

'What is "is"?' asked Austro looking like an owl.

Roy Mega and Austro went to their *Two-Guys-in-a Garage Invention Kit.* All that morning they had been fooling around with that kit that was both a building and a business, and they hadn't been able to put it together yet. This was strange, because they were the ones who had invented the *Invention Kit.* But it did take a lot of invention and genius to put one of those things together. Now, about those *Two-Guys-in-a-Garage Invention Kits*:

T Town Oklahoma had always been an inventive place beyond all others, and Broken Bench Lane had always been the heart of that inventiveness. The *Two-Guys-in-a-Garage* syndrome was the most common form of T Town inventive enterprises. It was the companies and factories started by *Two-Guys-in a-Garage* that had kept T Town afloat and thriving when big oil companies and big aircraft factories and mobile home factories moved away or closed down. You get a couple thousand of those *Two-Guys-in-a-Garage* going and you have burgeoning diversification. And pretty soon some of those companies will have grown to a thousand guys in a garage. But the accommodations of the *TGIAG* syndrome had been left to find their own blind ways – until just two days before this.

Then two boys, or under-aged young men, Roy Mega and Austro, had begun to market prefabricated module kits to house and equip *Two-Guys-in-a-Garage* set-ups.

They procured a quantity of odd-shaped and odd-length boards from the *Elite Lumber-Rippers and Board and Price Cutters Company* that was near by.

They procured a quantity of imperfect building blocks from the *Honest Goof Concrete and Select Seconds Building Stone Sales Company* that was also near by and was run by Honest Goof Gomez.

They procured small kegs of mixed nails, bolts, screws, turn-buckles, and odd angle iron fittings from Junky Joe's. They got mounds of old automobile accessories that one could spread around and make it look as though this had been a garage indeed.

They fixed up, in an imposing envelope, assembly instructions that read in full 'If you are real inventors, you will find a way to make a building and a business out of this kit. If you are not real inventors, then you shouldn't have bought an Invention Kit in the first place. It's lucky you find out now that you don't have what it takes.'

With each of their kits they included another envelope titled 'Three Red Hot Inventions Just Waiting to be Invented'.

Roy and Austro had sold two of the kits the first day and four of them the second day. All six pairs of purchasers had groused a little bit at the skimpy assembly instructions; but all of them, being real inventors, had gone ahead and built fine buildings out of the stuff, each of them different, each of them distinctive and effective.

So, on the morning of the third day, Austro and Roy tried it themselves with one of their own kits. They intended to build a home for that most inventive and begeniused of enterprises, the *Big Star Detective Agency*. And they sure had been having a lot of trouble making anything at all out of it.

Cornelia Falselove and several persons she had dragooned into helping her arrived with the two additional human bodies from the wax works and unloaded them at the *Big Star*. They stretched them out beside the first body that the boys had got by a slight-of-body trick that they played on the police.

'Wonderful, wonderful, wonderful,' Roy Mega said. 'We will just see what kind of flies these three bodies will draw here. And I will turn on my newly completed Confession Compulsion Machine and see who rises to the tainted bait.'

'That isn't the same thing as a Guilt Machine, is it?' Cornelia asked. 'I feel a little bit guilty buying human bodies for wax prices that way.'

'A guilt machine? Oh no, that would complicate it too much to have a Confession Machine and a Guilt Machine in the same unit,' Roy Mega said. 'I should scatter myself as someone else seems to have done. I have to activate my Confession Compulsion Machine, and at the same time I have to contemplate these three sets of remains here.'

'And at the same time figure out what went wrong with the ailerons of the *Big Star Weed Rider* this morning,' Austro said. 'What really crashed this morning was a part of our reputation. You turn on the machine, Roy, and I'll contemplate the remains, and we'll both think about the ailerons.'

The two boys set themselves to these three tasks. There came the ghostly humming as Roy Mega turned on the Confession Compulsion Machine. The ghostly humming had nothing to do with the *operation* of the machine. It was for effect. It was a good and impressive sound and the boys used it with all their machines when they put them into operation.

'Well, Austro?' Roy Mega said. He meant how was Austro doing with his assigned task.

'The most noteworthy thing about the remains is that they *are* remains,' Austro said as he looked at the three dead fellows with affection. 'That is to say, something, other than life, has been removed from them, and what remains of them is most incomplete. Something's lacking in these three. We come back to the same question: who is False Face Flaherty?'

'That man over there,' said Cornelia Falselove, 'the man with all the money and all the women.'

'But who is he really?' Austro asked.

'He really is the man with all the money and all the women,' Cornelia insisted.

But Flaherty lost one of his women just then. Judy Kingfixit left him and his group and came uncertainly towards the *Big Star Detective Agency.*

'The second thing about the remains is the now-you-see-it-now-you-don't syndrome,' Austro said. 'I keep taking blood out of these guys, and it keeps changing. Besides being too fluid for fellows who are dead almost an hour, it keeps flip-flopping. Sometimes it seems to be good *anthropino haima* or human blood. And then it tests as *kaoutsouk haima.*'

'And what is *kaoutsouk haima*, little fuzz-faced boy?' Cornelia asked.

'Rubber blood,' Austro said.

'Who is Cornelia Falselove?' croaked a wax raven that had somehow followed them out of the wax museum.

Judy Kingfixit, a bit dazed, arrived at the *Big Star Detective Agency.*

'I have this compulsion to confess that I killed Hamlet,' she said. 'Why ever would I have a compulsion to confess such nonsense as that?'

'Have you a feeling of guilt, Mrs Kingfixit?' Roy Mega asked.

'No, of course not,' she said. 'What a question!'

'The question, for you and for my machine,' Roy said, 'is how there can be a compulsion to confess without a feeling of guilt. My machine says they don't go together, and you say they don't.'

'The real question,' said Austro, 'is whether there is any criminality in crime.'

Somebody left them then like a cork plopping out of a bottle.

3

'Who was that?' Austro asked.

'It was that stringer from the International Universal World Press,' Roy Mega said. 'Nobody ever notices him when he's around with his pulsating ears; but he always makes that cork-out-of-the-bottle exit. I wonder what sort of story he got a lead on here that he's in such a hurry to spill it to the world?'

'I have this compulsion to confess that I stabbed Hamlet Izobret to death,' Judy Kingfixit rattled off with unseemly passion. 'Oh, I feel so much better for having confessed it!'

'But did you in fact kill Hamlet?' Austro asked.

'That is information I am unable to supply,' Judy said. 'The main thing is that I have confessed it. The confession becomes the act and the happening. It is like taking off from a dull rock and soaring into flight. The flight is what matters. The rock is an accident to be forgotten.'

'Why did you, in the context of the confession anyhow if in no other context, kill him, Mrs Kingfixit?' Roy Mega asked.

'Oh, he was trifing with my affections, I think. And he was after my husband to put more money into their things and not let me loot it all.'

'Ah, he was a threat to your paper-sack-full-of-money syndrome,' Austro mumbled. 'What do you call it?'

'I call it "Diversified Investment Procedure According to Educated Whim", and it works if I can really keep it diversified, a hundred here, a thousand there.'

'Can you say which of these three figures that are lying here is the Hamlet Izobret that you killed, Mrs Kingfixit?' Roy asked.

'No, they all look alike when they're spread out like that

with the same false faces on them all. They were already getting to look alike anyhow since they associated together so much.'

Several persons came in and gave Judy Kingfixit large sums of money for the investments that she had made in the various industries earlier that morning. When a person invests in enterprises along Broken Bench Lane, the harvest (before noon usually) will be thirty and seventy and even a hundredfold.

The *Plant Engineering Company* was right to the left of the *Big Star Detective Agency*, between it and the *Hasty-Wasty Planned Obsolescence Company*. They did some amazing things at *PE*. They engineered plants for every need and botany. They had a nutty tree or bush that grew nuts so fast that a prize was offered for anyone who could ever pick them all. The bush had a capacity of only twelve nuts, but it would regrow them faster than any two-handed person could pick them off. The bush would have solved the hunger problem of the world, if only the nuts had been edible.

But a half dozen other plants that *PE* had engineered *had* solved the world hunger problem. They had done this more than a week before, but the word hadn't got to remote areas yet.

And they had engineered, at *PE*, plants that would walk and talk – really – and these had been used (one use among very many for them) by Madame Gussaud at her wax works as scaffolds or armatures to build wax columns on. This accounted for the flexibility or liveliness of some of her creations.

Wait a minute! Someone else is coming into the *Big Star Detective Agency*.

Edith Thornbush burst into the Agency, and a rush of words burst from her as she came.

'I have this compulsion to confess that I stabbed Harry King-fixit to death!' she burst out. 'Say, confessing is fun, isn't it? Is it generally realized that confessing is one of the great creative acts? I believe, if I just let myself go, that I could confess to such a flood of things as would knock the ears off you.'

'Did you actually kill Harry Kingfixit, Mrs Thornbush?' Roy asked.

'Oh, there's no way of telling,' Edith said, liplessly as it were, and as if it were someone else using her voice. 'There is no sharp line between kill and not-kill. I banged a dagger into one

473

of those gawky look-alike people that were hiding among the wax figures in the wax museum. It might have been Harry I knifed (I hoped it was, I still hope it was), or it might have been one of the others, or nothing much at all.'

'Can you say which of these bodies is the figure that you banged the dagger into?'

'No I can't. They're all alike,' Edith said without moving her mouth. What was this business of her talking without seeming to talk?

The *Animal Engineering Company* was right across the Lane from the *Big Star Detective Agency*. The *AE* had formerly been named *Dog Designers Incorporated*. They did some amazing things at *AE*. They had branched out a long ways from their old *Dog Designer* days of the week before. Now they were into everything.

They had designed the Basic Ape that, with a bit of further creative tampering, could pass for any new-departure simian or bear or human. Madame Gussaud at the wax works had been using Basic Apes for two days now. She used them for her living wax figures as they were patient and would accept infusions and grafts. They would pose well. They would also work well and could do simple tasks like sweeping the floor or pouring wax; and they would (this was something that had been discovered within the last hour and a half) readily accept the new false face patterns that were so prevalent about the Lane this morning that they seemed to infest the very air.

AE had been using rubber blood in its Basic Apes for several hours, and this, blinking on and off, will simulate other bloods, animal or human or whatever, and will function well in many conditions.

'Oh, here they are,' False Face Flaherty cried and he strode into the *Big Star Detective Agency*, 'the three figures that were swiped from the wax works. Swiping, as some people don't seem to realize, is a form of theft. I'll just take them along back to my place as I have an agreement with the wax works.'

'I own them now,' Cornelia Falselove said, 'and you will keep your body-robbing hands off of them. I may be able to make something out of them, or use them for receptacles.'

Ophelia Izobret burst into the *Big Star Detective Agency*.

'I have this compulsion to confess that I stabbed Edgar Thornbush to death,' she burst out. Ophelia looked dazed and these words had come out of her mouth with very bad synchronization. It almost seemed as if Cornelia Falselove had been speaking the words for Ophelia.

'Well, that accounts for all three of the knifed figures,' Roy Mega said. 'And I'm not sure just what else it accounts for.'

The *Human Engineering Company* was just to the right of the *Big Star Detective Agency*, between it and the *Cat-Rat Fur Company*. They had been doing some amazing things at *HE*. One of the mottos at *HE* 'We can change the colour of your eyes in nine minutes' will give you a pale blue idea of what they were doing there. 'See us, and you will never been the same again' was another motto a bit on the chilling side.

HE was able to supply Basic Persons, coordinated humans with the personality and brains denatured. These went beyond the Basic Ape. They could not only perform simple tasks such as sweeping floors or pouring wax, but they were able to complain about them while doing them. Madame Gussaud used many of the Basic Persons at her wax works, and countless other firms along the Lane used the product.

'Are you trying to peddle these waxwork glories as our husbands, boys?' Judy Kingfixit asked of the three murdered figures on the floor that may or may not have been wax. Then Judy's face changed a bit and she said in words that were badly synchronized with her mouth 'Oh, I guess it will be all right then. I'll accept whichever one you say is mine if this is the state he happens to be in.' Then her face changed back to its first case and she spoke again in her regular voice 'Damnit, Cornelia, you are *not* spokeswoman for us. I, at least, will speak for myself. Get out of my mouth and get out of my voice.'

'Oh, I believe that it will be suitable for Cornelia Falselove to be spokeswoman for the three involved ladies, just as it is suitable for me to be spokesman for these three incapacitated or dead gentlemen,' False Face Flaherty said. 'Connie and I will settle whatever needs to be settled. And then we will inform the six of you of the settlement, or else we will *not* inform you of it.'

'Find out who False Face Flaherty really is,' one of the dead wax-or-flesh men said hollowly.

'How?' Roy Mega asked that length of stuff on the floor.

'Take him apart,' the figure said. So Roy Mega and Austro began to take False Face Flaherty apart.

'Find out who Cornelia Falselove really is,' Ophelia Izobret asked.

'How?' Austro asked her.

'Take her apart,' Ophelia said. So Roy and Austro began to dismantle Cornelia Falselove just as they were dismantling False Face Flaherty.

Ahhhh! Zombie Plant, Basic Ape, Basic Person with denatured brains and personalities, rubber blood, wax work (hexagon) structure modules, consensus figures and artificial figures! That's what False Face Flaherty who had all the girls and all the money was. That's what Cornelia Falselove was also.

Did False Face Flaherty really represent Harry Kingfixit and Edgar Thornbush and Hamlet Izobret as a corporate person?

Did Cornelia Falselove really represent Judy Kingfixit and Edith Thornbush and Ophelia Izobret as a corporate person?

What false process had put together such corporations?

'We leave it to you our clients whether you should pay us or we should refund to you,' Austro said. 'Have we located your husbands for you? I don't know. That's a question in semantics, and palaeonthropologists say (from the shape of our skulls) that we australopithecines were probably weak on semantics. What we have here are three boxes that your husbands have been in now and anon, and likely they are in them presently to a limited extent.'

'What if we insist on having all there is of them?' Edith Thornbush asked. 'We didn't contract for you to locate only pieces of our husbands. What if we insist that you produce them completely?'

'I suggest that the demand be lodged by all there is to you then,' Roy Mega said. 'You here present are only three boxes that three ladies have been in now and anon, and likely you are in them yet to a limited extent. But essential elements of you are missing or are hiding out somewhere.'

A harried little man came into the *Big Star Detective Agency*.

'Have you heard about the Murders of Speckled Fish Road?' he asked, speaking in a very apprehensive voice.

'Ah yes, interesting case,' Roy Megan said. 'Do you wish the investigation to be reopened? Ah, let's see, just when was it that the Speckled Fish Road Murders took place?'

'They are likely to take place this very afternoon or night unless I can get expert help in preventing them,' the nervous little man said.

'Ah yes, we will put you on hold for a while. Please be patient. We are winding up a triple-murder case now with our famous dispatch and efficiency.'

'See how busy we are,' Austro said. 'Let us now move to a consummation of the Wax Museum Murders. All we need is good faith from all parties, and we have not been getting that. There is hanky-panky somewhere in that you three ladies slew the figures of each other's husbands and not your own. This is related to what is known as the fooling-around syndrome. As to the stabbings or "murders" themselves, they really don't amount to very much.'

'It was slicker than going over an alley fence to a "little game" (in the old comic-strip context of that situation),' Roy Mega said. 'The three men slipped out of their skin and bones and left them behind. Every man needs a hiding-place, and the trail to it should be crossed by as many false clues as possible. The men delivered their empty skin-and-bone boxes over to a corporate person of their own creation, False Face Flaherty. That was the second stage of their evasive trail to their hide-out.'

'Why should they want to evade us when they love us so much?' the box that Edith Thornbush had been in now and anon asked.

'Why should *they* want to evade us when they love *us* so much?' the waxwork box in which Hamlet Izobret had lingered now and anon asked. 'But the dames have their hide-outs slicker than anything we could devise, and they spend a lot more time in them.'

'You are so tedious sometimes, that's why,' Judy Kingfixit said.

It was what is sometimes called a Mexican Stand-off. The boys of the *Big Star* had solved the disappearance of the husbands (and the technical murders of them or of the carcasses that they used now and anon), but they hadn't solved any of it very resoundingly. And the ladies might have made a case that nothing had been solved, 'but it would be like opening a can of crocodiles,' as Ophelia Izobret said. Nobody was very proud of the outcome.

There had been this very decadent influence (an unreal influence, really) along Broken Bench Lane for several days, and now the shattered fruit of that decadence had come to market. Simplicity had gone from the Lane.

It was decided that all should go to the *Hot Sauerkraut Sandwich Drive-In* for lunch and to discuss the financial aspects of the thing over hot sauerkraut sandwiches, try to resolve the who-owes-whom question.

And then the murderous malarkey-men of the media broke over them in wave after smelly wave!

'Which one is the illustrious Professor Austro who has made the "Quotation of the Season?"' a half dozen of those flash-pans bayed the question.

'*I* am the illustrious Professor Austro,' Austro said. 'Ah, which "Quotation of the Season" is it, boys? I get off a lot of good stuff.'

'The illuminating statement "The real question is whether there is any criminality in crime?", that is the quote that has rocked the country for the last six minutes,' said one of the media men there. 'Who else but the Great Professor Austro would have the temerity to phrase such a thing? The whole world must have skipped a second to hear an utterance so utter.'

'Everybody change watches one second to pick up the skip,' said Roy Mega ungallantly. 'I never remember whether we set them up a second or back a second.'

'Is there any particular childhood influence to which you might attribute your brilliance, Professor Austro?' a reporter-in-depth asked.

'What is "brilliance"?' Austro beamed like a beacon. 'Ah, we always ate a lot of rock soup when I was a kid on the Guna Slopes.' Austro liked the adulation.

'Would you care to tell us, Professor Austro, what brand of rock soup it was?'

'Ah, we're on live and nationwide, are we? It was *Rocky McCrocky Rock Soup*!'

'I will just take two hundred dollars worth of stock in this *Rocky McCrocky Rock Soup*,' Judy Kingfixit offered, and Austro had the money out of her hand before she finished.

'The news services are running five minutes behind in trying to supply data on you,' said another newsie. 'There hasn't been such a single-quotation stir since Tuesday.'

'Professor Austro,' a back-up analyst interposed. 'There are two disassembled bodies here on the floor—' (They were those of False Face Flaherty and Cornelia Falselove: the three stabbed figures had risen and were waiting to go to the *Hot*

478

Sauerkraut Sandwich Drive-In.) 'Are they some of the debris of your murder investigating trade?'

'Oh certainly, certainly,' Austro bubbled the words out. 'You can't have a murder investigation without breaking a few bodies. These last three murders we just solved, though, weren't our most successful ever. There's loose ends hanging out of them everywhere. We did solve them, and we contributed solutions to the nature of reality at the same time, but we didn't solve them with our usual verve and style.'

'Professor Austro, what would you say was your most towering characteristic?'

'My modesty.'

'Are you *sure* that this monkey-faced kid is the Great Professor Austro?' one of the reporters-in-breadth asked Roy Mega.

'He's the only Austro there is,' Roy said, 'so he has to be the Great Professor Austro. *The Great Professor Austro?* Oh, what a wet nose he's become now!'

'A wet nose, sir? What do you mean?'

'He's drinking the first of the four wine cups. It's enough to turn any kid's nose wet.'

'What is the first of the wine cups, sir?'

'The cup of adulation. It's sometimes called Monkey Wine. He's sure going to be hard to get along with from now on.'

'Do you solve any of the murders yourself, sir?'

'Only all of them.'

'And who are you yourself sir?' the newsie asked. 'Are you someone important?'

'Of course I'm important. I'm the Great Professor Mega.'

'Ah, cut it out, Roy,' Austro begged. 'You're poaching on my rock pile.'

'The Great Professor Mega!' another newsie gasped. 'You're, you're even newer than the Great Professor Austro!'

'Let me tell you about that—' Roy Mega began to unroll his tongue.

Marianne Leconte

Femme fatale
(translated by Mlle Alexis Kischkum and John Brunner)

Marianne Leconte was born in Nancy in 1944 but was on the move at the age of four, to the Congo and Mozambique, while her father searched for uranium. She married when she was eighteen, and has two daughters. From Paris she edits anthologies, including Méduse, Femmes au Futur, Les Enfants du Sturgeon, *and* Les Pièges de L'Espace. *She is the editor of a French publisher's science fiction list.*

'I am not a quick writer,' she says, 'and an idea must linger a long time in my mind before being written.' She brought 'Hyra La Rousse', one of her infrequent stories, to the Milford writers' conference in Britain. Everyone liked it, but where could she sell it? A chorus (Priest, Brunner and Rob Holdstock, I believe) cried 'Ramsey Campbell!' They were right, and I'm doubly grateful to Mlle Kischkum for rendering the story into English for Milford and to John Brunner for the energetic translation you are about to read.

> *Elle portait des culottes,*
> *des bottes de moto,*
> *un blouson de cuir noir*
> *avec un aigle sur le dos...*
> From Edith Piaf's song *L'Homme à la Moto*

In the fogbound streets beyond the old fortifications she roamed at random among the shadows of a moonless night. Her motorcycle throbbed and quivered under her like a mettlesome thoroughbred. For hours on end she devoured kilometres of asphalt, climbing narrow streets, rushing down the slopes of the hills encircling the decaying and tumbledown city of Paris.

And then suddenly she spotted, alone on a street corner, the girl-child. Now motorcycle and rider began their seductive

481

dance. The huntress passed and repassed the teenager, scanning her pale face which under the neon signs fragmented into streaks of orange, green, red, as though it had been lifted straight from a painting by Fernand Léger. It was a small face with immature features, new from the sculptor's touch, but on it might be read the hopes of hot young blood.

The dream, clearer and clearer, more and more detailed, harbingered awakening, rebirth, return to life.

It was time. It was her time. It was the hour when children of the war might emerge without fear of being recognized for what they were. The sleeper roused and stretched herself. Night was falling. Now, as at every dusk, red-headed Ira could go hunting.

> *She wore motorcycle gauntlets*
> *and boots and pants of black,*
> *and a big leather jacket*
> *with an eagle on the back ...*

Her motorcycle reared like a spirited horse before rushing away. Ira knew where she was heading. From the Montmartre cemetery with its gutted tombs which nobody had bothered to rebuild – those who lived on couldn't give a damn about the dead who were resting in peace – she went down towards the wasteland of the Place Clichy, turned left, sped past the countless sex-shops which like overripe and rotting fruit spewed forth clusters of men and girls ready to sell themselves for a mouthful of bread: a foul hangover from the days of Before. From the wreckage of the Moulin Rouge came a nauseating stench of broiled mushrooms and fried soybeans.

For a moment Ira, with her red hair, her wilful, almost emaciated face, her hollow cheeks and her pointed chin, was tempted to begin her search in these stews of debauchery for hayseeds. But her taste for a more challenging quarry gained the upper hand. In this district she would only find a few flabby tarts, overweight, half-cut, bloated with their unwholesome diet – livid-skinned creatures not at all to her liking.

So without hesitating she made a wide turn and entered Rue Fontaine. From there she continued to the ruins of Notre Dame de Lorette, then opposite the former Protestant church in the Place Kossuth took Rue Drouot straight towards the Palais Royal.

482

Behind her altuglass visor her feverish green eyes, dilated by fasting, watched the rutted roadway with hypnotic fixity. Inside her shining black helmet her temples throbbed. Her pressing natural need was making itself felt more and more keenly. Twisting the throttle wide open, she accelerated violently; her machine roared onward with a fusillade of farts that roused the whole of Rue de Richelieu. In the few apartment blocks which were still habitable despite the vast cracks across them, babies woke up howling, while their fathers once again cursed that fucking machine and their mothers crossed themselves in case it was the devil.

Now stabbing pains, as yet weak but nonetheless insistent, were shooting through her head. Desire was goading her on more and more, wearing out her patience – and the sickle was taking the brunt. Her wild and powerful steed seemed to be tuning itself to her suppressed complaints as it screamed along the road.

Suddenly Ira sighted a slender girl with an intersexual body: a barely sketched bust, a trim arse moulded by jeans so tight one could discern her pubic mount, a flat belly – a little pussycat pretending to be a liberated woman. Oh, her type was vulnerable, yes – once the hard veneer was flayed away.

Yet that kind would never quite give in. Right to the end they would clench their teeth and seal their lips. They would rather die than cry for mercy. They would never admit that the machine was going too fast, that its rider was frightening them.

It was very hard to make the children of Afterwards suffer.

Once more the motorcycle tore away at the behest of Ira's hand. Body welded to body, they flew as one on to the Carrousel Bridge. Tyres screamed as they made the sharp turn into Rue des Saints Pères. Already Ira could feel against her back a tense and supple body, pressing close, hanging on to her as to a life-buoy . . . But they never broke down. They were quite something, these end-of-the-twentieth-century teenagers. They never even gasped, let alone cried out . . . An extraordinary kind of courage, almost inhuman, a wild refusal to give in . . . As though, once having risked a lift on a motorbike, they must put up with the consequences at all costs, for the sake of bravado. Perhaps I'm picking them too young, the redhead thought for the first time in her life. Perhaps the generation left over from Before are not so brave? Shrieks, screams, fists

483

beating at her back while a frantic voice wails and howls . . . panic growing and growing, communicated from one body to the other along with the vibrations of the machine. Maybe I should try it at least once – a novel and different sensation.

Under the excited grip of its rider the motorcycle cavorted with joy.

The urge which had seized her would not go away; she wanted to hear someone shouting, moaning, begging, weeping. But whom to choose, and how? She must not be too old. A grimace of distaste twisted the red-haired Amazon's fleshy pink lips. Best would be a wealthy woman from an expensive district, in her thirties, with a firm, healthy body. But how to approach a woman like that, who would not be at all impressed by a motorbike, having seen too many in the old days?

The huntress crouched in her saddle to take the curve of Rue de Rennes. She sped on, disregarding the admiring whistles and lewd jeers of a small group of boys who every evening at this time turned out to await her split-second appearance – or rather, her motorcycle's, for it was one of only a few still on the road. No doubt they imagined that one night she would relent, stop long enough to pick one of them up and carry him away. But what did they think they were, these fashion-plates from well-to-do homes slumming on Boulevard St Germain? Their wealth kept these sons of the middle class from rotting away like other people; they had no need of the expedients she, Ira, was driven to.

You've got another think coming, chums! Me, I go for your naughty little sisters, the ones with the boyish looks who hang around Montparnasse. What sort of girl to choose tonight? Above all, how to make her get on behind? A woman in her thirties is not the daredevil type . . . unless . . .

An idea took hold of her little by little. With her tomboyish air, her short hair, a fringe over her eyes, her jacket and her motorbike, she was fully equipped to seduce that type of female. To hell with her usual habits. Tonight she was going to allow herself something different, a victim to frighten, to terrify – a real treat. With a connoisseur's tongue she licked her gilded lips, swollen with lust. Sheathed in supple chestnut-coloured kid, her thighs tightened on her broad black leather saddle. The machine's vibration coursed through her body, rising up her belly, quivering in her loins, massaging her breasts. Flat out, she drove her steed towards the stunted, warped penis

484

which was all that remained of the Montparnasse Tower. Only its concrete framework had endured. What had once been the boastful phallic symbol of a decadent society, a stiff, hard, black penis, was nothing but one more ruin. But Ira had never given a damn about it, even before the rain of fire and ashes. Men weren't her trip, nor were blacks, and pricks didn't turn her on . . .

She pulled up smoothly before the Nouveau Sélect, mounted the edge of the pavement and stopped a yard from the tables on the café's terrace. She closed the throttle. After jolting and snorting a bit, the machine quieted. Ira remained astride it, disregarding the lustful looks she was attracting. She, or the sickle? A black-clad silhouette with a scarlet eagle on her back: a disturbing, a demonic shadow.

Without moving, as though leafing through a book, she began to survey the customers sitting at rickety tables on this terrace littered with debris, chunks of broken wall, scraps of plaster which no one had bothered to cart away. This was the moment she loved most, and she didn't want to spoil it by being over hasty, despite the unsated desires which tormented her, made her belly churn and her head buzz. Unearthing a quarry always made her excited. She raised herself upright, her bust as square as if it were reinforced by plastic, her waist neat and tightly belted, her buttocks round and high, moulded by the leather garment that fused with the leather of the broad saddle.

On the pavement near by a tall crazy number was parading up and down. She had long skinny legs, such narrow hips that her shiny pants hung in creases around her thighs, a wide gold belt, a mauve lace blouse with a huge open collar falling on her unformed bosom, rings on every finger. Under the fascinated gaze of lustful males she simpered and gestured and showed off. She was there every night, turning the Nouveau Sélect into her personal theatre, spending her life on an imaginary stage, dedicated to offering the passers-by free entertainment. Her heart was in her *métier*. She came over as a genuine artist, who could enter honestly and entirely into her role.

Ira switched her attention back to the customers at the café. Glistening under the neon signs, her black blind helmet reinforced the mysterious aspect of the equally romantic character she was playing: the vamp, the *femme fatale*.

A brunette with slant eyes like an Oriental caught her interest: a little white Chinese shirt with a stand-up collar that set off her matt complexion, black hair cut page-boy style, dark eyes made softer by a stiff square fringe. It was a shame that too close to her sat a hail-fellow-well-met type with a beard, no doubt full of inhibitions, psychological hangups, sexual energy and the power to dominate . . .

Not for me, that kind of girl.

But they were all there, the midnight losers, those who in these artificial paradises among the company of friends sought refuge from visions of despair, boredom, depression. Survivors, almost healthy – healthy in body, if not in mind.

And then suddenly Ira snapped out of her brown study, snuffing the air like a hound. Among the three women in the second row . . . Smouldering under ashes, sharp remarks and bitter answers. The crestfallen air of the tense blonde with hair like an angel's; the cunning expression of her very young and very slender rival; the calmness of the butch one, well past forty, with her short hair, a cigarette in her mouth, cool, intelligent and oh-so-reasonable! Ira shivered. Over and over she had witnessed such a scene, and she knew how it would end. Diamonds, hearts and clubs, reproaches, sneers and sobs. The inevitable flight of the loser, while the new girl, pretending to be unaffected, moved in and over.

She would have her victim in a few minutes.

Her machine roared as it leapt back to life. People jumped. Startled boys shouted angry insults or propositioned her. But Ira was already on the far side of the street, taking station beside the other pavement. It was time to start stalking her prey. From a distance she kept watch on her quarry, her betraying movements, her gesture that grew more and more jerky, her bowed shoulders, her arms crossing on her chest as though to protect her against a violent blow.

At last the girl jumped up and ran into the road. Prepared for the event, Ira had already moved gently away. For once her accomplice the motorcycle made no noise. Together they closed on the blonde shadow crossing the street, heedless of what went on around her. At the last moment the machine bucked to avoid hitting the miserable girl, who uttered a cry. Ira caught her by the arm, held on to her, saved her from crumpling to the ground. Lifting her up, she supported her with one strong hand while with the other she raised her visor and revealed herself: smiling, beautiful, her red hair cut like a boy's, her green eyes shining firefly-bright against her pale skin: beautiful, calm, reassuring.

486

Neither spoke. Ira pressed the weeping girl against the warm, purring motor, then gently stroked her head as though to soothe a great sorrow. She rocked her thus for a few moments, brushing her fingers over her soft and satiny flesh; then she firmly ensconced this stray kitten on the long one-piece saddle. The girl complied like a helpless child. As soon as she was seated she huddled against her rescuer, drawing comfort from the warm contact between them.

The motorcycle seemed to be taking wing as it bore away the girl and her misery. Closing her eyes, she forgot the despair which had beset her when she saw her lover smile at her new partner. She forgot her rival's dark eyes, her teenage figure. Little by little she forgot all her troubles. They were borne off by the wind which tousled her hair and smacked it against her cheeks, salty with drying tears. She pressed even closer against the body of her new companion, to keep warm. She did not smile – not yet. But her memories of the evening grew fainter and fainter, drowned out by the throbbing purr of the engine, which had settled to a relaxed cruising speed.

She let herself be carried along, steered, directed, just as she had done all her life, relying on the strength of someone else, yielding up her life with no more resistance than a boat caught in a westerly gale and sinking before she has time to react. Intoxicated by their speed, dazzled by occasional lights, she felt herself drifting. With a very slight shift of her hips the rider brought her rounded bottom closer to her belly; she hollowed it to make a snugger fit. The thrumming of the machine surged back and forth in the very depths of her body. She began to regain normal physical awareness; she grew aware that the lips of her cunt were crushed against the black leather, that it was hot and moist under her slinky silk dress. She pressed her thighs tight on the slippery surface of the saddle, making them clasp its supple cover with a sigh of pleasure. The machine and its woman were carrying her away on a wild ride to nowhere. But she was not afraid.

Well, not really . . .

Really not? But she had a strange feeling. There was a prickling at her nape, shivers were running down her spine, her heart was in her mouth. Why had her belly suddenly tightened so, leaving a gap between her and the rider's back to be filled at once by a blast of icy air? Why this terrible giddiness? Suddenly she wanted everything to stop. She felt sick, as though she were riding one of the switchbacks of her childhood, before the war. She felt sick – sick – she wanted to throw up. Because of that dreadful parting – because of her misery, her anguish, all these curves, the way the machine leaned into the bends. But how could she warn the girl who was driving? It was useless to whisper in her ear, and just as useless to shout. Now the motorcycle was moving far too fast. Walls rushed by on either side, walls of light or of solid concrete, threatening walls, forming an alley that grew ever smoother and more featureless, with no way out.

Now she really began to be afraid, and with numb fingers tried to pinch, to bruise the strange woman to make her understand that everything was going wrong and she must stop. But there was no response; she was too well protected by her jacket to notice her passenger's frantic signals.

Accordingly she tried to take her hands from around the unknown's waist, but at this speed it was no longer possible. She clung on, panic-stricken. The motorbike seemed to have turned into a cannonball which nothing could stop, short of a wall of steel. She was terrified by the idea. That was what was bound to happen if this madwoman didn't slow down, if she did not at once get off this deadly projectile. But how? The driver seemed so intoxicated by the run that she might as well have forgotten she had company.

But she was wrong. True enough, Ira was relishing her onward rush, the speed, the power of her mount, but above all she relished the fear which little by little was invading every fibre of the young woman hugging her waist. She felt her body tauten with anguish, slacken with terror, yield to despair. She was aware of it all, because her passenger was flattening herself against her, against the machine, and all her feelings and all her agony were conveyed and amplified by the shaking and quivering of the motorcycle.

Lust seized her again, crescent in the hollow of her loins. But her victim was not yet ready. She accelerated faster still, pretending not to notice her terror which nonetheless came through to her in ever-increasing waves. Delight too mounted within her, mounted in precise proportion to the tightness with which the girl clung to her, mindlessly. The blood of her trophy was growing chill. By now she no longer knew how to attract the attention of her kidnapper.

The sickle tilted from side to side more and more often, whirling its two riders into a demonic maelstrom. It leaned over as though from now on there would be no more roads, as though they would turn and turn for ever, almost horizontally, on a wall of death. The girl had no idea where she was. She no longer saw, no longer felt anything save her anguish and the wind. Chilled to the bone, she endured in an unreal maze of dark and terrifying colours, the shades of cold and fear. Unable to endure her plight any longer, she sought in vain to utter a few words to comfort herself, to speak at least so she might hear her own voice and make herself believe she still existed. But the sounds would not pass the threshold of her lips.

Ira could guess that a scream was burgeoning in the chest which swelled to emit it – and suddenly it came, louder and louder and louder. Taken aback by its violence, shaken by the madness which was exploding in the misty brain of their passenger, rider and machine straightened up a little, but without slowing.

The girl kept on screaming for a long time, no longer capable of judging how much time was passing, nor how many kilometres they had covered. The dance went on. Pressed close, both tight against the motorcycle, one of them showed the face of a woman about to come, the other of a woman about to die in agony. One was tormented by overwhelming desire, the other by now was almost resigned to her pain and terror. Little by little the screaming became fainter, mingled with the noise of the motor, turned into a gentle moaning, much like the sound of a newborn child rocking itself to sleep by humming, always the same tune, always in the same key.

That wearied the red-haired Amazon, who was leading the dance. But once again lust rose within her, commandingly. It was more than simple desire which possessed her. It was a need.

The motorcycle slowed, sputtered, as though it too were tired. It seemed to gasp for breath as it used up its last reserve of fuel. Time to sound the mort. Ira too was worn out by the rush through the night, by the pleasure she had taken when she came, and by lack of food. Both of them needed a respite. Soon it would be time for the false dawn. They had travelled all night.

Letting go of the handlebars, Ira let the machine carry on by itself and drew off her black leather gauntlets. The girl behind noticed nothing. She was wiped out and could not react to this further recklessness. She was still lulling herself to the near-African beat of her rhythmical refrain.

A cruel smile turned up the lips of the red-haired she-wolf. Unfastening her jacket, she exposed her bosom; it was milky-pale, dotted with freckles, as though it had never seen the sun, had always been wrapped in leather. It was as pallid as the morning twilight, or as a corpse bled dry. It looked almost diseased.

Slowly she tucked her gloves in the hollow of her breasts, then eased free her companion's hands from their death-grip around her waist. She was obliged to pry them loose, first from each other, then from her belly.

With vast gentleness she took one soft white wrist, pearly, alive, silk-smooth, turned it palm up and bore its unprotected surface to her lips. Blue veins pulsed beneath the near-transparent skin. Deferentially Ira ran her moist mouth over the cool hand, up the length of the arm, down again. The young woman let herself be kissed without resisting. Ira inhaled the scent of this slender blonde. It filled her nostrils, it affected her like too deep a toke of grass. Her head spun. She could control herself no longer.

The sickle uttered a pitiable choking sound.

'There, there!' Ira murmured, speaking for the first time. She straightened from the hips, thus releasing herself from the other body still clinging at her back. Feeling her support suddenly removed, the girl desperately tried to regain contact, and warmth. She slithered close again across the saddle. Ira moved her hips further forward. The girl groaned, but followed her, matching the slightest of her movements. The motorbike, which had slowed down, nonetheless kept on rolling, level and dead steady, and without a sound.

Aroused, the girl stopped humming, fascinated by the lack of noise, by the perfect silence of the engine. Everything stood still; then there came a squeaking, and a sliding, and slowly, slowly, she felt a hard, cold, metallic object pressing against the lips of her bare cunt, parting them against her will, entering her carefully and gently, but irresistibly. This – what was it? – this piston, as it were, began to quiver, to vibrate, to make her moisten. Suddenly running wet, astonished by what she was feeling, she dared not move – dared not so much as think.

490

She was too shocked. Lust she did not comprehend arose in her, climaxing in a fireball of heartbreak which expanded and expanded until a final outburst made her entire body feel as though it was exploding, along with her consciousness, in a brief and brutal howl of orgasm.

Whereupon, like a river of rubies, the lovely nourishing liquid flowed down into the complex works of the motorcycle, pouring over every part and portion; then, once it had spread over every bit and bolt, the red blood seeped up towards the black leather saddle and was greedily absorbed by the body of Ira, the beautiful Amazon who was inseparable from her bike. They were two unnatural beings that made a monstrous whole: in fact, a machine invented because of and to meet the needs of the war.

Gorged with its fuel again, the sickle bucked under the vigorous grasp of the rider who was also its Siamese twin. The movement dislodged a limp puppet which flew through the air to land on the asphalt with its arms outstretched, making a cross.

Without even glancing at it, fiery-eyed, Ira – the vamp, Ira – leapt onward like a demon, bound for another of her night-time haunts.

Stephen King

Big wheels:
a tale of the laundry game

*Stephen King was born in Maine in 1946, and seems made to
be asked 'What's a nice guy like you doing writing stories like
these?' though I imagine he's growing tired of such questions
by now. (One answer may be that a writer of horror fiction
can be more honest about his subconscious than most people,
and perhaps suffer from it less.) He and Peter Straub are among
the small number of writers who prove that best-selling horror
fiction need not be junk. His novels deal with the dark side of
the familiar: of the Ugly Duckling romance (Carrie), the
American small-town epic (Salem's Lot), the alcoholic's last
chance (The Shining), the post-apocalyptic novel (The Stand).
His short stories are worthy of Richard Matheson, whom he
admires but equals rather than imitates; they are collected in*
Night Shift, *a collection so satisfying that I even forgive him
for using the title I planned to use myself, and* Skeleton Crew.
*He lives in Maine with his wife Tabitha and his children
Naomi, Joel, and Owen.*

This is his strangest story.

Rocky and Leo, both drunk as the last lords of creation,
cruised slowly through the streets of Crescent in Rocky's 1957
Chrysler. Between them, balanced with drunken carefulness
on the monstrous hump of the Chrysler's driveshaft, sat a case
of Kleinblatt's Beer. It was their second case of the evening,
which had begun at four o'clock; punch-out time.

'Crap in a jug,' Rocky said, stopping at the red blinking
light above the intersection of Mason Street and Highway 99.
He did not look for traffic either way, but did cast a sly glance
behind them. A half-full can of Kleinblatt's rested against his
crotch. He took a swig and turned left on to Highway 99. The
universal made a thick grunting as they started chuggingly off
in second gear. The Chrysler had lost first gear some two
months ago, back in August. 'What time is it?'

Leo held his watch up to his cigarette and puffed until he could read the dial. 'Almost eight.'

'Crap in a jug,' Rocky said. They passed a sign which said: HARTFORD 44.

'Nobody's going to inspect this,' Leo said. 'Nobody iniz right mind is going to inspect this.'

'Crap in a jug,' Rocky said. He reached third gear. The universal moaned to itself, and the Chrysler began to shudder deep in its guts. The spasm eventually passed, like the coughing spasm of a tubercular, and the speedometer needle climbed tiredly to forty and hung there precariously.

When they reached the intersection of Highway 99 and Devon Road (which ran next to Devon Stream, which formed the border between the townships of Crescent and Devon for some eight miles), Rocky turned on to the hot-top more or less at random. They had been driving more or less at random since they had left work. It was 31 October 1969, and the inspection sticker on the Chrysler ran out promptly at midnight, barring an act of God or the atomic bomb. Rocky was too drunk to imagine either, and Leo didn't care. It was not his car. Beyond that, he also was completely mummified beneath a cerebral shroud of Kleinblatt's.

Devon Road wound through the only heavily wooded patch of Crescent, and great bunches of elms and oaks crowded in on both sides, nude and skeletal in the decayed end of Connecticut autumn. The wooded patch was known as The Devon Woods. It had attained these capital letters after the torture-murder of a young girl and her boyfriend in 1958. The young girl and her boyfriend had been parking, and were found in the boyfriend's 1949 Mercury. The Mercury had real leather seats and a large chrome hood ornament. The occupants had been found in the glove compartment, in the front seat, in the back seat, and in the trunk. Mostly the trunk.

'This jughumper better not stall out here,' Rocky said. 'Ninety miles from noplace.'

'Bunk,' Leo said. This had risen lately to the top forty of his vocabulary. 'There's town.'

Rocky sighed and sipped his can of beer. Town was a faint glow on the near horizon from the new shopping centre. While peeking at it, Rocky drove the car over to the left side of the road, looped back, almost went down over the soft shoulder, and pulled it back on the road. 'Whoops.'

494

Leo burped and gurgled.

They had been working together at the New Adams Laundry since September, when Leo had been hired as Rocky's washroom helper. Leo was a small, rodent-featured fellow of twenty-two years who claimed he was saving twenty dollars a week from his pay to buy a used Indian motorcycle. He was going to go west to Arizona next winter, on the Indian. He had previously been through twelve jobs since he and the world of academics had parted company at the minimum age of sixteen. He liked the laundry fine. Rocky was teaching him to wash, a trade he was firmly convinced would come in handy once he got to Flagstaff.

Rocky, an older hand, had been at the laundry for fourteen years. His hands, ghostlike and bleached as he handled the steering wheel, proved it. He had spent jail time for carrying a concealed weapon in 1960. His wife, then puffily pregnant with their third child, announced 1) that it was not their child, but her child and the milkman's child; and 2) that she wanted a divorce on grounds of mental cruelty.

Two things about this situation had driven Rocky to carry a concealed weapon: 1) he had been cuckolded; and 2) he had been cuckolded by the for chrissake milkman, a pimply half-wit named Spider Milligan who wore his white cap cocked at a jaunty angle.

The milkman, for God's own sweet sake! The *milkman*! Even to Rocky, who had never progressed beyond reading the Fleer's Funnies that came wrapped around the bubble gum he chewed indefatigably at work, the situation had sonorous classical overtones.

As a result, he had duly informed his wife of two facts: 1) no divorce; and 2) he was going to blow a huge hole in the guts of Spider Milligan. He had a .32 calibre pistol, purchased shortly after the end of World War II, which he used to shoot at bottles, tin cans, and small yellow dogs. He left the house on that afternoon for Oak Street, where Spider Milligan denned in a rooming house for single gentlemen. He stopped on the way at the Four Corners Tavern to have eight or ten beers. In the interval, his wife had telephoned the bulls. They were waiting for him on the corner of Oak Street. Rocky was arrested for carrying a concealed weapon and spent seven months in county jail. During this period the divorce had gone through, just as slick as hog fat through a chicken, and his ex-wife was living with Spider Milligan on Dakin Street in an apartment house with a pink lawn flamingo in the front yard. They were possessed of a four-month-old son who looked every bit as vapid as his daddy, along with the two girls. They were also possessed of fifteen dollars a week alimony, which probably came in handy – a week after the marriage Spider lost his job with the Oak Hill Dairy Company and showed no signs of hurry in finding another.

'Son of a bitch,' Leo said. 'Can't we just pull over and drink?'

'I gotta get a sticker on my wheels,' Rocky said. 'A man's no good without his wheels.'

'Nobody in his right mind is gonna inspect this. It ain't got no flasher lights.'

'It's got 'em if I step on the brake at the same time.'

'The window on this side's cracked.'

'I'll roll it down.'

'Forty degrees and you're tooling around with an open window. Who's gonna believe it?'

'I'll roll it down any goddamn time I feel like it,' Rocky said coolly. He tossed his beer can out and got a refill. He popped the top. Beer splurted.

'Wish I had a woman,' Leo said, looking into the dark. He smiled strangely.

'If you had one you'd never get out west. Dint you tell me you wanted to go out west?'

'I'm going.'

'You'll never go,' Rocky said. 'Pretty soon you'll have a woman. Next you'll have alimony. Women always leads up to alimony. Cars are better.'

'Pretty hard to screw a car.'

Rocky giggled. 'You'd be surprised.'

The woods began to straggle away into new dwellings. Lights twinkled up on the left and Rocky suddenly slammed on the brakes. The brake lights, parking lights, and turn signals all went on at once; it was a home wiring job. Leo lurched forward, spilling beer on the seat. 'What? What?'

'Looky,' Rocky said. 'I know that fella.'

There was a tumorous, ramshackle garage and Citgo filling station on the left side of the road. The sign in front said:

BOB'S GAS & SERVICE
BOB DRISCOLL, PROP.
FRONT END ALIGNMENT OUR SPECIALITY

And at the bottom:

STATE INSPECTION STATION‡‡72

'Nobody in his right mind—' Leo began.

'Me an' Bobby Driscoll went to school together!' Rocky said. 'We got it knocked! Bet your fur!'

He pulled in unevenly, headlights illuminating the open bay door. He popped the clutch and roared towards it, and a stoop-shouldered man in a green coverall ran out, making frantic stopping gestures.

'Thass Bob!' Rocky cried. 'Hey, Bobby!'

A moment later they ran into the side of the garage. The Chrysler's carb went into a racking spasm of belches. A small yellow flame appeared from the end of the sagging tail-pipe, followed by a puff of blue smoke. The car stalled gratefully. Leo lurched forward, spilling more beer. Rocky keyed up the engine and backed off for another try.

Bob Driscoll ran over, profanity spewing from his mouth in verbal crepe banners: '—the hell you think you're doing, you goddamn sonofa—'

'Bobby!' Rocky yelled, his delight nearly orgasmic. 'Hey Stiff Socks! Whatcha say, buddy?'

Bob peered in through the window. He had a twisted, tired face that was hidden beneath the visor of a greasy ball cap. 'Who called me Stiff Socks?'

'Me!' Rocky fairly screamed. 'It's me, you ol' finger-diddler! It's your ol' buddy!'

'Who in hell—'

'Johnny Rockwell!'

Cautiously: 'Rocky?'

'Yeah, you sombitch!'

'Chrise Jesus.' Slow, unwilling pleasure seeped across Bob's face. 'I hain't seen you since . . . well, since the Catamounts game anyway—'

'Shoosh, wa'n't that some hot ticket?' Rocky slapped his thigh, spilling Kleinblatt's on to the seat. Leo burped.

'Sure it was. Only time we ever won our class. Say, you beat hell out of the side of my garage, Rocky. You—'

'Yuh, same ol' Stiff Socks. Same ol' guy. You ain't changed even a hair.' Rocky peeked belatedly at the ball cap to see if this was true. It appeared that, beneath the ledge of its visor, ol' Stiff Socks had gone almost completely bald. 'Jesus, ain't it somethin', runnin' into you. Did you finally marry ol' Marcy Drew?'

'Hell yeah. Back in '60. Where were you?'

'Jail. Lissen, can you inspect this muhfuh?'

Caution again: 'You mean your car?'

Rocky cackled. 'No, my hog. Sure, my car! Canya?'

Bob opened his mouth to say no.

'This here's a friend of mine. Leo Brooks. Leo, wantcha to meet the only basketball player from Crescent High who dint change his sweat socks for four years.'

'Pleesdameetcha,' Leo said.

Rocky cackled. 'Want a beer?' he asked ol' Stiff Socks.

Bob opened his mouth to say no.

'Here's the little crab-catcher!' Rocky said. He popped the top. The beer, crazied up by the headlong run into the side of Driscoll's garage, boiled over the top and down over Rocky's wrist. Rocky shoved it into Bob's hand, and he sipped quickly in self defence.

'Rocky, we close at—'

'Just a secon', lemme back up.'

Rocky popped the clutch in reverse, skinned a gas pump, and drove the Chrysler jerkily inside. He was out in a minute, shaking Bob's free hand. Bob looked dazed. Leo sat in the car, tipping a fresh beer. He was also farting. Beer made him fart heavily.

'Hey!' Rocky said, staggering around a pile of rusted wheel rims. 'You member Diana Rucklehouse?'

'Sure,' Bob said. An unwilling grin came to his mouth. 'She was the one with the—' he cupped his hands in front of his chest.

Rocky howled. 'Thass her! Thass the one! She still in town?'

'I think she moved to—'

'Figures,' Rocky said. 'Hey, you can put a sticker on this pig, cantcha?'

'Well, we close at—'

'Jesus, it'd sure help me out. I'd sure 'preciate it.'

Leo burped and looked closely at the Chrysler's horn ring.

'Yeah,' Bob said. 'I s'pose I could look it over.'

'Sure,' Rocky said, clapping him on the back. 'Same ol' Stiff Socks.'

'Yeah,' Bob said, sighing. He pulled on his beer. 'You beat hell out of your bumper, Rocky.'

'Gives it some class. Goddamn car needs some class. Hey,

wantcha to meet the guy I work with. Leo, this is—'

'You introduced us,' Bob said with a soft, despairing smile.

'Howdy doody,' Leo said. He fumbled for another can of Kleinblatt's. Silvery lines were beginning to trace their way across his field of vision.

'—Bob Driscoll. Only basketball player from Crescent High who never changed—'

'Want to show me your headlights, Rocky?' Bob asked.

'Sure. Great lights. They got real class. Pop 'em on, Leo.'

Leo turned on the windshield wipers.

'That's good,' Bob said patiently. He took a long swallow of beer. 'How about the lights?'

'He's been drinkin',' Rocky told Bob. 'On the left; Leo!'

Leo popped on the headlights.

'High beam?' Bob asked.

Leo fumbled for the dimmer switch with his foot. The lights came on high beam.

'Signals?' Bob asked.

Leo smiled slyly at Bob.

'Better let me do it,' Rocky said, bumping his head as he got in behind the wheel. 'The kid don't feel so good, I think.' He squeezed the brake and worked the turnblinker.

'Do they work without the brake?' Bob asked.

'Does it say anyplace that they *hafta*?' Rocky asked craftily.

Bob sighed. His wife had large, floppy breasts and blonde hair that was black at the roots. When she came to the garage on Thursday nights for her bingo money her hair was usually done up in large green rollers under a green chiffon scarf. This made her head look like a futuristic AM/FM radio. Once, near three in the morning, he had wakened and looked at her slack paper face in the soulless graveyard glare of the sodium streetlight outside of their bedroom window. He had thought how easy it could be – just drive a knee into her gut and screw both hands around her neck. How easy to whack her into bland and faceless prime cuts, and perhaps mail the pieces to someplace far away – Robert Driscoll, c/o General Delivery, Lima, Peru. It could be done. God knew, it had been done in the past.

'No,' he said, 'it doesn't say they have to.' The rest of the cold beer gurgled down his throat. It was warm in the garage and he had had no supper. He could feel the beer rising into his mind.

'Hey, Stiff Socks just came up empty!' Rocky said. 'Hand up a brew, Leo.'

'No, Rocky, I really . . .'

Leo, who was seeing none too well, finally happened on another beer and passed it to Rocky. Rocky handed it to Bob, whose demurrals petered out as he held the can's cold actuality. Rocky opened it. Leo farted homily to close the transaction.

All of them drank in silence for a moment.

'Horn work?' Stiff Socks asked apologetically.

'Sure,' Rocky reassured him. He bleeped the horn. It emitted a feeble squeak. 'Battery's a little low, though.'

They drank in silence.

'That goddamn rat was big as a cocker spaniel,' Leo said.

'Kid's carrying quite a load,' Rocky said to Bob.

Bob thought about it. 'Yuh,' he said.

This struck Rocky's funnybone and he cackled through a mouthful of beer. A little trickled out of his nose, and this made Bob laugh. It did Rocky good, because Bobby had sure looked like one sad bastard when they pulled in.

They drank in silence.

'Diana Rucklehouse,' Bob said meditatively.

Rocky sniggered.

Bob chuckled. He held his hands out from his chest.

Rocky laughed and held his hands out even further.

Bob guffawed. 'You member that picture of Rita Hayworth that Tinker Johnson pasted on ol' lady Freemantle's bulletin board?'

Rocky howled. 'An' he put those great big jahoobies—'

'She just about shit on the spot,' Bob said.

Leo farted. 'You two can laugh,'

Bob blinked at him. 'Huh?'

'Laugh,' Leo said. 'You two can *laugh*. You two ain't got holes in your backs.'

'Huh?'

'Don't lissen to 'im,' Rocky said, worried. 'Kid's got a skinful.'

'You got a hole in your back?' Bob asked Leo.

'The laundry,' Leo said, smiling. 'We got these big washers, see? Only we call 'em wheels. They're laundry wheels. That's why we call 'em wheels. I pull 'em, I load 'em. Put 'em in dirty, take 'em out clean, thass me.' He looked at Bob with insane confidence. 'Got a hole in my back.'

'Yeah?' Bob was looking at Leo with fascination. Rocky shifted uneasily.

'There's a hole in the roof,' Leo said. 'Right over the third wheel. They're round, so we call 'em wheels. When it rains, the water comes down. Drop drop drop. Hits me – whap – right in the back. Now I got a hole there. Like this.' He made a shallow curve with one hand. 'Wanna see?'

'He don't wanna *see!*' Rocky yelled. 'We're talkin' about old times and there ain't no hole in your effing back!'

'I wanna see it,' Bob said.

'They're round so we call it the laundry,' Leo said.

Rocky smiled and clapped Leo on the shoulder. 'Hand me a beer, kid.'

Leo handed up a beer.

The case was gone an hour later, and Rocky sent Leo stumbling up the road to Pauline's Superette for more. Leo's eyes were ferret-red by this time, and his shirt had come untucked. He was trying with myopic concentration to get his Camels out of his rolled-up shirt-sleeve. Bob was in the bathroom, urinating and singing the school song.

'Doan wanna walk up there,' Leo muttered. He walked in a drunken semi-circle, still trying to get his cigarettes out of his shirt-sleeve. 'Z dark. An' cold.'

'You wanna sticker on that car or not?' Rocky hissed at him. He had begun to see weird things in front of his eyes; a huge bug wrapped in spider-silk in the corner.

Leo looked at him with his scarlet, drunken eyes. 'Ain my car,' he said cunningly.

'You'll never ride in it either, if you doan go get that beer.' Rocky hiccupped and looked fearfully at the dead bug in the corner. 'By the Christ, you won't.'

'Okay,' Leo whined. 'Okay.'

He went after the beer, walking off the road twice on the way up to the corner and once on the way back. When he finally got to the warmth of the garage again, both Rocky and Bob were singing the school song. Bob had managed, by hook or crook, to get the Chrysler up on the lift. He was wandering around underneath it, peering at the rusty exhaust system.

'There's some holes in your stray pipe,' he said.

'Ain no stray pipes under there,' Rocky said. They both found this spit-sprayingly funny.

'Beer's here!' Leo announced, put the case down, sat on a wheel rim, and fell immediately into a half-doze. He had swallowed three himself on the way back to lighten the load.

Rocky handed Bob a beer and held one himself.

'Race?' he said. 'Jus like ol' times?'

'Sure,' Bob said. He smiled tightly. In his mind's eye he could see himself in the cockpit of a low-to-the-ground, streamlined Formula One racer, one hand resting cockily on the wheel as he waited for the green flag, one hand touching his lucky piece – the hood ornament from an old '49 Merc. He had forgotten Rocky's straight pipe, and he had forgotten his papery wife with her transistorized curlers.

They opened their beers and chugged them. It was a dead heat; both dropped their cans to the grease-darkened cement and raised their fingers at the same time. Their belches echoed off the walls like rifle shots.

'Jus like ol' times,' Bob said, sounding forlorn. 'Things sure do change, doan they?'

'Sure do,' Rocky said. He struggled for a deep, luminous thought and found it. 'We're getting older by the day, Stiffy.'

Ol' Stiff Socks sighed and belched again. Leo farted in the corner and began to hum *Get Off My Cloud*.

'Try again?' Rocky asked, handing Bob another beer.

'My as well,' Bob said; 'my jus' as well, Rocky m'boy.'

The case Leo had brought back was gone by midnight, and the new inspection sticker was affixed at a slightly crazy angle on the left side of Rocky's windshield. Rocky made out the pertinent information himself, working very carefully. He was seeing triple. Leo was snoozing in the corner with his mouth open. The silk-wrapped bug was still in the other corner. Rocky was morally certain that the bug was an hallucination, but he was taking no chances and keeping clear. Bob sat on the floor crosslegged, a half-empty can of Kleinblatt's in front of him, staring fixedly at nothing.

'Well, you sure saved my life, Bobby,' Rocky said. He kicked Leo in the ribs to wake him up. Leo grunted and whoofed. His eyes cracked partway open, closed, and opened wide when Rocky footed him again.

'We home yet?' he muttered.

'Take it easy, Bob,' Rocky cried cheerfully, carrying Leo around the Chrysler by one armpit and pushing him in. 'We'll stop back an' do it again sometime.'

'Those were the days,' Bob said, his eyes suddenly filling with tears. 'Everything jus gets worse 'n' worse since then.'

502

'That's right,' Rocky said. 'Take 'er easy, fella. Keep your thumb on it—'

'My wife gives me a crappy time in bed,' Bob said, but the words were blanketed by the coughing misfire of Rocky's engine. Bob got to his feet and watched the Chrysler back out, taking a little wood from the left side of the door.

Leo hung out the window, smiling like an idiot saint. 'Come by the laundry some time, skinner. I'll show you the hole in the back. I'll show you m'wheels. I'll—' Rocky's arm came out of the darkness like a vaudeville hook and pulled Leo into the dimness.

'Bye, fella!' Rocky yelled.

The Chrysler did a drunken slalom around the three gas pump islands and bucketed off into the night. Bob watched until the taillights were only fireflies and then walked carefully back inside. On his cluttered workbench there was a chrome hood ornament from some old car. He began to play with it, still crying cheap tears. Later, some time after three in the morning, he strangled his wife and then burned the house down to make it look like an accident.

'Jesus,' Rocky said to Leo as Bob's Garage shrunk to a white point of light behind them. 'How about that? Ol' Stiffy.' He was reaching the stage of drunkenness where every part of himself seemed gone except a tiny, glowing coal of sobriety somewhere in the middle of his mind.

Leo did not reply. In the pallid lights of the dashboard, he looked like the dormouse at Alice's mad tea-party.

'He was really bombarded,' Rocky said, driving on the left side of the road for a while. 'And you went an' told him. How many times do I have to tell you about that? Where am I gonna keep my rocks if you go around telling everybody?'

'It's my hole,' Leo said sulkily.

'They're my rocks. Found 'em all myself. So just—'

Leo stiffened. 'There's a truck behind us with no lights.'

Rocky looked in the rear view mirror. He saw a truck with no lights. A milk truck.

'It's Spider,' he whispered fearfully. 'Jesus, it's Spider Milligan.'

'Who?' Leo asked dully. He was still trying to remember if Rocky had ever told him before tonight that he was keeping rocks in the hole in Leo's back.

Rocky didn't answer. A tight, drunk grin spread over his

503

lower face. It did not touch his eyes, which were huge and red, like spirit lamps.

He suddenly floored the Chrysler, which belched blue oil smoke and reluctantly creaked its way up to sixty.

'Hey, you're too drunk,' Leo said. 'You're . . .' He paused vaguely, seeming to lose track of his message. The trees and houses raced by them, vague blurs in the graveyard of twelve-fifteen. They blew by a stop sign, flew over a large bump, leaving the road for a moment. When they came down, the low-hung muffler struck a spark on the asphalt.

'I was fooling!' Leo said wildly. 'There ain no truck!'

'It's him!' Rocky screamed. 'I saw his bug back in the garage! God *damn!*'

They roared up Southern Hill on the wrong side, and a station wagon coming the other was skidded crazily over the gravel shoulder getting out of their way. Leo looked behind them. The road was empty.

'*Rocky—*'

'Come and get me, Spider!' Rocky screamed. 'Come and get me!'

The Chrysler had reached eighty, its top speed. They came around the turn which leads on to the Johnson Flat Road, smoke spurting up from Rocky's bald tyres. The Chrysler screamed into the night like an affrighted ghost, lights searching the empty road ahead.

Behind them, lights flicked on at a side crossing, and an old '49 Mercury disguised as a milk truck pulled out at a sedate speed.

A mile ahead there was the sound of a huge, rending crash as the Chrysler left the road and sheared through a telephone pole. It crashed into a gully on its nose and exploded. Fire gouted up in a startled, roiling pyre.

'That's it,' Spider said. 'Let's go get his rocks before the cops get there.' But when he looked around, the seat was empty. Even the bug was gone.

Greg Bear
Richie by the sea

*Greg Bear was born in 1951, and saw the world with the US
Navy for his first fourteen years – Japan, the Philippines,
Kodiak in Alaska, and most of the United States. He sold his
first story in 1966, and his wife Tina supported him for a
number of years while he wrote and illustrated full-time (and
how many of us would never have made it as writers without the
same kind of support!). Now the risk has paid off: his
published novels include* Hegira, Beyond Heaven's River, *and*
Psychlone, *and his short stories are collected as* The Wind from
a Burning Woman. *'Richie by the Sea' is what used to be
described as science fantasy, and a quietly disturbing tale it is.*

The storm's final energy had been spent the night before. A
wild, scattering squall had toppled the Thompsons' shed and the
last spurt of high water had dropped dark drift across the rocks
and sand. In the last light of day the debris was beginning to
stink and gather flies and gulls. There were knots of seaweed,
floats made of glass and cork, odd bits of boat wood, foam
plastic shards and a whale. The whale was about forty feet
long. It had died during the night after its impact on the ragged
rocks of the cove. It looked like a giant garden slug, draped
across the still pool of water with head and tail hanging over.

Thomas Harker felt a tinge of sympathy for it, but a bit
more worry. His house was less than a quarter-mile south and
with the wind in his direction the smell would soon be bother-
some.

The sheriff's jeep roared over the bluff road between the
cove and the university grounds. Thomas waved and the sheriff
waved back. There would be a lot of cleaning-up to do.

Thomas left the cliff edge and returned to the path through
the trees. He'd left his drafting table an hour ago to stretch his
muscles and the walk had taken longer than he expected;

Karen would be home by now, waiting for him, tired from the class enrolment which had been scrambling the campus for a week.

The cabin was on a nice piece of property barely thirty yards from the tideline, with nothing but grass and sand and an old picket fence between it and the water. They had worried during the storm, but there had been no flooding. The beach elevated slightly to their property and they'd come through remarkably well.

He knocked sand from his shoes and hung them on two nails next to the back door. In the service porch he removed his socks and dangled them outside tentatively, then put them on the washer. Shoes and socks and feet had been wetted by an incautious run near the beach. Wriggling his toes, he stepped into the kitchen and sniffed. Karen had popped homemade chicken pies into the oven. Walks along the beach made him ravenous, especially after long days at the board.

He looked out the front window. Karen was at the gate, hair blowing in the evening breeze and knit sweater puffing out across her pink and white blouse. She turned, saw him in the window and waved, saying something he couldn't hear.

He shrugged expressively and went to open the door. He saw something small on the porch and jumped in surprise. Richie stood on the step, smiling up at him, eyes the colour of the sunlit sea, black hair unruly.

'Did I scare you, Mr Harker?' the boy asked.

'Not much. What are you doing here this late? You should be home for dinner.'

Karen kicked her shoes off on the porch. 'Richie! When did you get here?'

'Just now. I was walking up the sand hills and wanted to say hello.' He pointed north of the house with his long, unchildish fingers. 'Hello.' He looked at Karen in a way Thomas knew she was vulnerable to.

'No dinner at home tonight?' Karen asked. 'Maybe you can stay here.' Thomas winced and started to gesture.

'Can't,' Richie said. 'Everything's just late tonight. I've got to be home soon. Hey, did you see the whale?'

'Yeah,' Thomas said. 'Sheriff is going to have a fun time moving it.'

'Aw, next tide'll probably take it out,' Richie said. He looked between them, smiling broadly. They'd guessed his age at nine or ten but he already knew how to handle people.

506

'Tide won't be that high now,' Thomas said.

'Maybe not. But I've seen big things get washed back before. Think he'll leave it overnight?'

'Probably. It won't start stinking until tomorrow.'

Karen wrinkled her nose in disgust.

'Thanks for the invitation anyway, Mrs Harker.' He put his hands in his shorts' pockets and walked through the picket fence, turning just beyond the gate. 'You got any more old clothes I can have?'

'Not now,' Thomas said. 'You have all our cast-offs already.'

'I need more for the rag drive,' Richie said. 'Thanks anyway.'

'Where does he live?' Thomas asked inside.

'I don't think he wants us to know. Probably in town. Don't you like him?'

'Of course I like him. He's only a kid.'

'You don't seem to want him around.' She looked at him accusingly.

'Not all the time. He's not ours, his folks should take care of him.'

'They obviously don't care much.'

'He's well fed,' Thomas said. 'He looks healthy and he gets along fine.'

They sat down to dinner. Part of Karen's hair still had the shape of the wind. She didn't comb it until after the table was cleared and he was doing the dishes. His eyes traced endless circuit diagrams in the suds. 'Hey,' he shouted to the back bathroom. 'I've been working too much.'

'I know,' Karen answered. 'So have I. Isn't it terrible?'

'Let's get to bed early,' he said. She walked into the kitchen wrapped in a terry-cloth bathrobe, pulling a snarl out of her hair. 'You've been working too hard,' she said. 'Must get your sleep.'

He aimed a snapped towel at her retreating end but missed. Then he rubbed his eyes over the sink and looked at the suds again. No circuit diagrams this time, only a portrait of Richie. He pulled out the last plate and rinsed it.

The next morning Thomas awoke to the sound of hammering coming from down the beach. He sat up in bed to receive Karen's breezy kiss as she left for the University, then hunkered down again and rolled over to snooze a little longer. His eyes flew open a few minutes later and he cursed. The racket was too much. He rolled out of the warmth and padded into the bathroom, wincing at the cold tiles. He turned the shower on to warm, brought his mug out to shave and examined his face in the cracked mirror. The mirror had been broken six months ago when he'd slipped and jammed his hand against it after a full night poring over the circuit diagrams in his office. Karen had been furious with him and he hadn't worked that hard since. But there was a deadline from Peripheral Data on his freelance designs and he had to meet it if he wanted to keep up his reputation.

In a few more months, he might land an exclusive contract from Key Business Corporation, and then he'd be designing what he wanted to design – big computers, mighty beasts. Outstanding money.

The hammering continued and after dressing he looked out the bedroom window to see Thompson rebuilding his shed. The shed had gone unused for months after Thompson had lost his boat at the Del Mar trials, near San Diego. Still, Thompson was sawing and hammering and reconstructing the slope-roofed structure, possibly planning on another boat. Thomas didn't think much about it. He was already at work and he hadn't even reached his desk in his office. There was a whole series of TTL chips he could move to solve the interference he was sure would crop up in the design as he had it now.

By nine o'clock he was deeply absorbed. He had his drafting pencils and templates and mechanic's square spread across the paper in complete confusion. He wasn't interrupted until ten.

He answered the door only half-aware that somebody had knocked. Sheriff Varmanian was standing on the porch, sweating. The sun was out and the sky was clearing for a hot, humid day.

'Hi, Tom.'

'Al,' Thomas said, nodding. 'Something up?'

'I'm interrupting? Sorry . . .'

'Yeah, my computers won't be able to take over your job if you keep me here much longer. How's the whale?'

'That's the least of my troubles right now.' Varmanian wore round black-rimmed glasses and had frizzy hair; he looked more like an anarchist than a sheriff. 'The whale was taken out with the night tide, we didn't even have to bury it.' He pronounced 'bury' as if it was 'burry' and studiously maintained a midwestern twang.

'Something else, then. Come inside and cool off?'

'Sure. Thanks. We've lost another little kid – the Cooper's four-year-old, Kile. He disappeared last night around seven and no one's seen him since. Anybody see him here?'

'No. Only Richie was here. Listen, I didn't hear any tide big enough to sweep the whale out again. We'd need another storm to do that. Maybe something freak happened and the boy was caught in it . . . a freak tide?'

'There isn't any funnel in Placer Cove to cause that. Just a normal rise and the whale was buoyed up by gases, that's my guess. Cooper kid must have got lost on the bluff road and come down to one of the houses to ask for help – that's what the last people who saw him think. So we're checking the beach homes out. Thompson didn't see anything either. I'll keep heading north and check out the flats and tide pools again, but I'd say we have another disappearance. Don't quote me, though.'

'That's four?'

'Five now. Five in the last six months.'

'Pretty bad, Al, for a town like this.'

'Don't I know it. Coopers are all upset, already planning funeral arrangements. Damned fools. Funerals when there aren't any bodies. But the Goldbergs had one for their son two months ago, so I guess precedent has been set. It's morbid, you ask me.'

He stood by the couch, fingering his hat and looking at the rug. 'It's hard. Damned hard. How often does this kid, Richie, come down?'

'Three or four times a week. Karen's feeling motherly towards him, thinks his folks aren't paying him enough attention.'

'He'll be the next one, wait and see. Thanks for the time, and say hello to the wife for me.'

Thomas returned to the board but had difficulty concentrating. He wondered if animals in the field and bush mourned long over the loss of a child. Did gazelles grieve when lions struck? Karen knew more about such feelings than he did; she'd lost a husband before she met him. His own life had been reasonably linear, uneventful.

How would he take it if something happened, if Karen was killed? Like the Coopers, with a quick funeral and burial to make things certain, even when they weren't?

What were they burying?

Four years of dreams.

After lunch he took a walk along the beach and found his feet moving him north to see where the whale had been. The coastal rocks in this area were concentrated on the northern edge of the cove. They stretched out into the water for a mile or so before ending at the deep water shelf. At extreme low tide two or three hundred yards of rocks were exposed. Now, at normal ebb, about fifty feet was visible and he could clearly see where the whale had been. Even at high tide the circle of rock was visible. He hadn't walked here much lately, but he remembered first noticing it three years before. It was like a perfect sandy-bottomed wading pool.

Up and down the beach, the wrack remained, dark and smelly and flyblown. But the whale was gone. It was obvious there hadn't been much wave action. Still, it was the easy explanation and he had no other.

After the walk he returned to his office and opened all the windows before setting pencil to paper. By the time Karen was home, he'd finished a good portion of the rough diagram from his original sketches. When he turned it in, Peripheral Data would have little more to do than hand it to their drafting department for smoothing.

Richie didn't visit them that evening. He came in the morning instead. It was a Saturday and Karen was home, reading in the living room. She invited the boy in and offered him milk and cookies, then sat him before the television set to watch cartoons. Richie consumed TV with a hunger that was fascinating to watch. He would mimic the expressions of the people he saw in the commercials. Thomas thought he was memorizing a store of emotions. He left a few hours later.

'Think he's adopting us?' Thomas asked.

'I don't know. Maybe. Maybe he just needs a couple of friends like you and I. Human contacts, if his own folks don't pay attention to him.'

'Varmanian thinks he might be the next one to disappear.' Thomas regretted the statement the instant it was out, but Karen didn't react. She put out a lunch of beans and sausages and waited until they were eating to say something. 'When do you want to have a child?'

'Two weeks from now, over the three-day holiday,' Thomas said.

'No, I'm serious.'

'You've taken a shine to Richie and you think we should have one of our own?'

'Not until something breaks for you,' she said, looking away. 'If Key Business comes through, maybe I can take a sabbatical and study child-rearing. Directly. But one of us has to be free full time.'

Thomas nodded and sipped at a glass of iced tea. Behind her humour she was serious. There was a lot at stake in the next few months – more than just money. Perhaps their happiness together. It was a hard weight to carry. Being an adult was difficult at times. He almost wished he could be like Richie, free as a gull, uncommitted.

A line of dark clouds schemed over the ocean as afternoon turned to evening. 'Looks like another storm,' he called to Karen, who was typing in the back bedroom.

'So soon?' she asked by way of complaint.

He sat in the kitchen to watch the advancing front. The warm, fading light of sunset turned his face orange and cut an orange square in the living room behind him. The square had progressed above the level of the couch when the doorbell rang.

It was Gina Hammond and a little girl he didn't recognize. Hammond was about sixty with thinning black hair and a narrow, wizened face that always bore an irritated scowl. She was smoking a cigarette, as usual, and explained why she was there between nervous stammers which embarrassed Thomas far more than they did her.

'Mr Harker, this is my grand-daughter Julie.' The girl, seven or eight, looked up at him accusingly. 'Julie says she's lost four of her kittens. Th-th-that's because she gave them to your boy to play with and he-he never brought them back. You know anything about them?'

'My boy? We don't have any children, Mrs Hammond.'

'You've got a boy named Richie,' the woman said, looking at him as if he was a monster.

Karen came out of the hallway and leaned against the door jamb beside Thomas. 'Gina, we don't have any kids. Richie just wanders around our house a lot.'

'Julie says Richie lives here – he told h-h-her that – and his name is Richie Harker. What's this all about i-i-if he isn't your boy?'

'He took my kittens!' Julie said, a tear escaping to slide down her cheek.

'If that's what he told you – that we're his folks – he was fibbing,' Karen said. 'I don't know why he'd lie. He lives in town, closer to you than to us.'

'He brought the kittens to the beach!' Julie cried. 'I saw him.'

'He hasn't been here since this morning,' Thomas said. 'We haven't seen the kittens.'

'He stole 'em!' The girl began crying in earnest.

'I'll talk to him about them, next time I see him,' Thomas promised. 'But I don't know where he lives.'

'H-h-his last name?'

'Don't know that, either.'

'It's all strange, if you ask me,' Mrs Hammond said, looking unconvinced. 'I don't like the idea of little boys stealing things that don't belong to them.'

'I don't either, Mrs Hammond,' Karen said. 'We told you we'd talk to him when we see him.'

'Well,' Mrs Hammond said. She thanked them beneath her breath and left with the blubbering Julie close behind.

The storm hit after dinner. It was a heavy squall and the rain trounced over the roof as if the sky had feet. A leak started in the bathroom, fortunately right over the tub, and Thomas rummaged through his caulking gear, preparing for the storm's end when he could get up on the roof and search out the leak.

A small toolshed connected with the cabin through the garage. It had one bare light and a tiny four-paned window which stared at Thomas's chest-level into the streaming night. As he dug out his putty knife and caulking cans, the phone rang in the kitchen and Karen answered it. Her voice came across as a murmur under the barrage of rain on the garage roof. He was putting all his supplies into a cardboard box when she stuck her head through the garage door and told him she'd be going out.

'The Thompsons have lost their power,' she said. 'I'm going to take some candles to them on the beach road. I should be back in a few minutes, but they may want me to drive into town and buy some lanterns with them. If they do, I'll be back in an hour or so. Don't worry about me!'

Thomas came out of the shed clutching the box. 'I could go instead.'

'Don't be silly. Give you more time to work on the sketches. I'll be back soon. Tend the leaks.'

Then she was out the front door and gone. He looked through the living room window at her receding lights and felt a gnaw of worry. He'd forgotten one thing – a rag to wipe the putty knife. He switched the light back on and went through the garage to the shed.

Something scraped against the wall outside. He bent down and peered out the four-paned window, rubbing where his breath fogged the glass. Somebody was looking back at him — a small face. It was gone almost as soon as he saw it.

'Richie!' Thomas yelled. 'Damn it, come back here!'

Some of it seemed to fall in place as Thomas ran outside with his go-aheads and raincoat on. The boy didn't have a home to go to when he left their house. He slept someplace else, in the woods perhaps, and scavenged what he could. But now he was in the rain and soaked and in danger of becoming very ill unless Thomas caught up with him. A flash of lightning brought the beach into bright relief and he saw the boy running south across the sand. He ran faster than seemed possible for a boy his age. Thomas ran after with the rain slapping him in the face.

He was halfway towards the Thompson house when the lightning flashes stopped and he couldn't follow the boy's trail. It was pitch black but for the lights coming from their cabin. The Thompson house, of course, was dark. Thomas was soaked through now and the rain was running down his neck in a steady stream. Sand itched his feet and burrs from the grass were caught in his cuffs, irritating his ankles. Another flash brought out the Thompsons' shed and seemed to point to it.

That was it, that was where Richie stayed. He'd resorted to the woods only when the first storm had knocked the structure down.

He lurched through the wind-slanted strikes of water until he stood by the shed door. He fumbled at the catch and found a lock. He tugged at it and the whole thing slid free. The screws had been pried loose. 'Richie,' he said, opening the door. 'Come on. It's only Tom.'

The shed was dry and silent. 'You should come home with me, stay with us.' No answer. He opened the door wide and lightning showed him rags scattered everywhere, rising to a pile on one side, a pile that looked like a man lying on his back with a blank face pointed up at Thomas. He jumped but it was only a lump of rags. The boy didn't seem to be there. He started to close the door when he saw two pale points of light dance in the dark like fireflies. His heart froze and his back tingled. Again the lightning threw its dazzling blanket out and wrapped the inside of the shed in cold whiteness. Richie was standing at the back, staring at Thomas steadily with a slack expression.

513

The dark closed in again and the boy said, 'Tom, could you take me someplace warm?'

'Sure,' he said, relaxing. 'Come here.' He took the boy into his arms and bundled him under the raincoat. There was something lumpy on Richie's back, under his sopping T-shirt. Thomas's hand drew back by reflex. Richie shied away just as quickly and Thomas thought, he's got a hunch or scar, he's embarrassed about it.

As they lurched against each other on the way to the house, Thomas asked himself why he'd been scared by what he first saw in the shed. A pile of rags. 'My nerves are shot,' he told Richie. The boy said nothing.

In the house he let Richie give himself a warm shower and put an old mackinaw out for the boy to wear. There was a cot and sleeping bag in the garage and Thomas brought these into the living room. Richie put on the mackinaw and climbed into the down bag, falling asleep almost immediately.

Karen came home an hour later, tired and wet. Thomas pointed to the cot with his finger at his lips. She looked at it with her mouth open in surprise, then nodded.

In their bedroom, before fatigue and the rain sound ganged up on them, Karen told him the Thompsons were nice people. 'She's a little old and crotchety, but he's a bright old coot. He said something a little strange, though. Said when the shed fell down during the last storm he found a dummy inside it, wrapped in old blankets and dressed in cast-off clothing. Made out of straw and old sheets, he said.'

'Oh.' Thomas was too tired to worry.

Sunday morning, as they came awake, they heard Richie playing outside. 'You've got to ask him about the kittens,' Karen said. Thomas agreed reluctantly and put his clothes on.

The storm had passed in the night, leaving a clear sky for the morning. He found Richie talking to the sheriff and greeted Varmanian with a wave and yawned 'Hello.'

'Sheriff wants to know if we saw Mr Jones yesterday,' Richie said. Mr Jones – named after Davy Jones – was an old beachcomber frequently seen waving a metal detector around the cove. His bag was always filled with interesting junk.

'No, I haven't seen him,' Thomas said. 'Gone?'

'Not hard to guess, is it?' Varmanian said grimly. 'I'm starting to think we ought to have a police guard out here soon.'

'Might be an idea.' Thomas waited for the sheriff to leave

514

before asking the boy about the kittens. Richie became huffy, as if he were imitating some child in a television commercial. 'I gave them back to Julie,' he said. 'I didn't take them anywhere. She's got them now.'

'You're pinning a label on him without thinking how . . . without looking at how he can take care of himself, what he can do. But okay, I tell Varmanian about him and the boy gets picked up and returned to his parents—'

'What if he doesn't have any? He told Mrs Hammond we were his parents.'

'He's got to have parents somewhere, or legal guardians! Orphans just don't have the run of the town without somebody finding out. Say Varmanian turns him back to his parents – what kind of parents would make a small boy, as you call him, want to run away from them?'

Karen folded her arms and said nothing.

'Not very good to turn him back then, hm? What we should do is tell Varmanian to notify his parents, if any, if they haven't skipped town or something, that we're going to keep Richie here until they show up to claim him. I think Al would go along with that. If they don't show, we can contest their right to Richie and start proceedings to adopt him.'

'It's not that simple,' Karen said, but her eyes were sparkling. 'The laws aren't that cut and dried.'

'Okay, but that's the start of a plan, isn't it?'

'I suppose so.'

'Okay.' He pursed his lips and shook his head. 'That'd be a big responsibility. Could we take care of a boy like Richie now?'

Karen nodded and Thomas was suddenly aware how much she wanted a child. It stung him a little to see her eagerness and the moisture in her eyes. There was something to be said for ignoring economics and practicality in building a family.

'Okay. I'll go find him and tell him about it now.' He put on his shoes and started out through the fence, turning south to the Thompsons' shed. When he reached the wooden building he saw the door had been equipped with a new padlock and the latch screwed in tight. He was able to peek in through a chink in the wood – whatever could be said about Thompson as a boat-builder, he wasn't much of a carpenter – and scan the inside. The pile of rags was gone. Only a few loose pieces remained. Richie, as he expected, wasn't inside.

515

Karen called from the porch and he looked north. Richie was striding towards the rocks at the opposite end of the cove. 'I see him,' Thomas said as he passed the cabin. 'Be back in a few minutes.'

He walked briskly to the base of the rocks and looked for Richie. The boy was standing on a boulder, pretending to ignore him. Hesitant, not knowing exactly how to say it, Thomas told him what they were going to do. The boy looked down from the rock.

'You mean, you want to be my folks?' A smile, broad and toothy, slowly spread across his face. Everything was going to be okay.

'That's it, I think,' Thomas said. 'If your parents don't contest the matter.'

'Oh, I don't have any folks,' Richie said. Thomas looked at the sea-coloured eyes and felt sudden misgivings.

'Might be easier, then,' he said softly.

'Hey, Tom? I found something in the pools. Come look with me? Come on!' Richie was pure small-boy then, up from his seat and down the rock and vanishing from view like a bird taking wing.

'Richie!' Thomas cried. 'I haven't time right now. Wait!' He climbed up the rock with his hands and feet slipping on the slick surface. At the top he looked across the quarter-mile stretch of pools, irritated. 'Richie!'

The boy was running like a crayfish over the jagged terrain. He turned and shouted back, 'In the big pool! Come on!' Then he ran on.

Tom followed, eyes lowered to keep his footing. 'Slow down!' He looked up for a moment and saw a small flail of arms, a face turned towards him with the smile frozen in surprise, and the boy disappearing. There was a small cry and a splash. 'Richie!' Thomas shouted, his voice cracking. He'd fallen into the pool. the pool where the whale had been.

He gave up all thought of his own safety and ran across the rocks, slipping twice and cracking his knees against a sharp ridge of granite. Agony shot up his legs and made his vision fog. Cursing, throwing hair out of his eyes, he crawled to his feet and shakily hobbled over the loose pebbles and sand to the edge of the round pool.

With his hands on the smooth rock rim, he blinked and saw the boy floating in the middle of the pool, face down. Thomas groaned and shut his eyes, feeling dizzy. There was a rank odour in the air, anticipatory; he wanted to get up and run. This was not the way rescuers were supposed to feel. His stomach was twisting. There was no time to waste, however. He forced himself over the rim into the cold water, slipping and going head first. His brow touched the bottom. The sand was hard and compact, crusted. He stood with the water streaming off his head and torso. It was slick like oil and came up to his groin, deepening as he splashed to the middle. It would be up to his chest where Richie was floating. The boy had only seconds, if that.

Richie's shirt clung damply, outlining the odd hump on his back. We'll get that fixed, Thomas told himself. Oh, God, we'll get that fixed, let him be alive and it'll work out fine.

The water splashed across his chest. Some of it entered his mouth and he gagged at the fishy taste. He reached out for the boy's closest foot but couldn't quite reach it. The sand shifted beneath him and he ducked under the surface, swallowing more water. Bobbing up again, kicking to keep his mouth clear, he wiped his eyes with one hand and saw the boy's arms making small, sinuous motions, like the fins of a fish. He was swimming away from Thomas.

'Richie!' Thomas shouted. His wet tennis shoes, tapping tiptoe against the bottom, seemed to make it resound, as if it were hollow. Then he felt the bottom moving, lifting up slightly until his feet were flat on it, falling away until he was treading water, lifting again . . .

He looked down. The sand, distorted by ripples in the pool, was receding. Thomas struggled with his hands, trying to swim to the edge. Beneath him there was nothing but black water, like a pool of crude oil, and in it something long and white, insistent. His feet kicked to keep him from ducking under again, but the water was swirling. He shut his mouth after taking a deep breath. The water throbbed like a bell, drawing him deeper, still struggling. He looked up and saw the sky, grey-blue above the ripples. There was still a chance. He kicked his shoes off, watching them spiral away. Heavy shoes, wet, gone now, he could swim better. He was twirling with the water and the surface was darker. His lungs ached. He clenched his teeth to keep his mouth shut. There seemed to be progress for a moment. The surface seemed brighter. But three hazy-edged triangles converged and he could not fool himself any more, the surface was black and he had to let his breath out, hands straining up, touching nothing, spinning deeper.

The pool rippled for a few minutes, then was still. Richie let loose of the pool's side and climbed up the edge, out of the water. His skin was pale, eyes almost milky. The hunger had been bad for a few months. Now they were almost content. The meals were more frequent and larger – but who knew about the months to come? Best to take advantage of the good times. He pulled the limp dummy from its hiding place beneath the flat boulder and dragged it to the pool's edge, dumping it over and jumping in after. For a brief moment he smiled and hugged it; it was so much like himself, a final lure to make things more certain. Most of the time, it was all the human-shaped company he needed. He arranged its arms and legs in a natural position, spread out, and adjusted the drift of the mackinaw in the water. The dummy drifted to the centre of the pool and stayed there.

A fleshy ribbon thick as his arm waved in the water and he pulled up the back of his shirt to let it touch him on the hump and fasten. This was the best time. His limbs shrank and his face sunk inward. His skin became the colour of the rocks, ochre, and his eyes enlarged. Energy – food – pulsed into him and he felt a great love for this clever other part of him, so adaptable. It was mother and brother at once, and if there were times when Richie felt there might be a life beyond it, an existence like that of the people he imitated, it was only because the mimicry was so fine. He would never actually leave.

He couldn't. Eventually he would starve; he wasn't very good at digesting.

He wriggled until he was smooth against the rim, with only his head sticking out of the water. He waited.

'Tom!' a voice called, not very far away. It was Karen.

'Mrs Harker!' Richie screamed. 'Help!'

Margaret Dickson

Can you still see me?

Margaret Dickson comes to us courtesy of Stephen King, who read this story in his creative writing course at the University of Maine and sent it to me at once. 'He's been a good teacher, a meticulous reader of my work, full of encouragement,' she says. She had already written poetry for the Maine Review and the Maine Times, and a three-act play that won first prize in a University of Maine contest. As I write, she is working on a novel. She writes copy for a Massachusetts advertising agency. She and her husband have two children.

Her story, which says a great deal in a few words, can speak for itself.

Mason will tell you now that the dead do not rest no matter how flat you lay the marker to the ground, no matter how dust blows out of the cloud it makes in the air or how far you fling the cup that held the dust. A funeral is the acknowledgement of a physical fact, but the mourners don't believe it. They sit and listen and watch the coffin. How does he breathe, shut in there like that? A door opens or closes in the parlour and the relatives look up once, twice. Whom do they expect? The truth is, Mason will say, that a funeral does no good. When Merle Thompson died, Mason will say, he wasn't finished. No one is finished for ever.

Merle Thompson had a plaid jacket made of wool, black squares and green squares. The right front pocket had torn off the welt, snagged on a nail. His hat was blue with a visor and a grease stain around the bottom, softened with wood dust and grains of gypsum.

Once, home tough and fresh from college, Mason had gone straight to Merle, not to embrace him, but to take his hat off him and use a hatchet on it right in front of his eyes.

Merle had been dumbfounded. 'What you want to do that for? What you want to do that for?'

Mason, wiry with the energy and sparkle of this joke he'd

519

been planning for days, separated the hat into neat quarters and laid them out on a sawhorse. But then he looked up and saw the old man's face. It was grey. Mason reached into his back pocket.

'In order to give you this,' he said quickly, and handed Merle a new hat, identical to the old one.

Merle had taken the new hat and turned it around and looked inside it.

'I lost you there for a minute,' he said. 'But your heart's in the right place.' Merle did not smile, but he put on the hat and looked Mason over. 'Your heart's in the right place, after all. Ain't it.'

The old blue eyes, Mason still thought. Looking right through the joke at me.

And then Merle had turned and gone back to work.

He went through his whole life and his pants never fit him. They were baggy and patched at the knees. Doris, who was too fussy to allow the hat and jacket in her house – they stayed on a nail outside in the shop – worried over the pants and washed and mended them and his flannel shirt and the insulated underwear he wore from November to May. On Sundays she made sure Merle wore his respectable black suit. But even those pants rode low on his hips and bulged out around the ankles.

He had a scar at the base of his head from an operation that removed a blood clot. He'd lost one finger on his left hand. Two fingers of his right were permanently bent from what he called 'an argument' with a rip saw. He'd had a prostate operation. His skin rumpled down his stomach and when he lay for three months waiting, breathing with a sound like a gurgle under water, he developed bed sores. Mason, who often lifted Merle on to the commode for Doris, thought the sores looked more like bruises on a bottom as innocent-looking as a child's.

Dying, Merle choked. It took him ten minutes.

Doris would say later, 'He worked at it, didn't he? On and on.'

His choking frightened her so much she left him and ran to the back door and screamed for Mason.

'Mason! Mason! Help me! Help me!'

Mason saw her and climbed off his tractor and raced across his newly manured field. Then he'd stopped at the door long enough to take off his shoes. Also, he was scared. When he went to the bedroom, Merle was struggling, gasping, weeping.

Doris wept, too, and kept saying in a tight voice,

'Now, Merle. You're not going to cry. Don't cry. You're not going to cry.' Tears streamed down her face. She put one arm under Merle's shoulders. 'Help me, Mason!'

Mason went to the bed and lifted Merle.

'Sit him up! Sit him up!' Doris said. 'Sometimes it works...'

Together they held Merle up. But it didn't work. His body arched and flung them back. The eyes rolled up. The mouth pulled open over the teeth. Then he seemed to fall away from them.

'Now, Merle, Merle.' Doris wept and pulled back her hair and tried to lift him again. 'Come on now. You're all right.'

Mason felt sick. He leaned against the wall.

'I think he's gone,' he said.

Doris looked up. Her hair stood up around her head like grey fire. Her mouth stopped quivering. She touched the body lightly with one hand. 'There,' she said. 'Is he?'

'Yes,' said Mason, lowering his voice in case Merle should hear them and it would kill him, 'I think he is.'

Doris laid her hand on Merle's. She watched the body. It was still.

'Yes,' she said. 'Mason!'

He went to her then and she hung on to him. She seemed too small and old for this.

After a while, Mason patted her shoulder and said, as gently as he could, 'Should we cover him?'

Doris looked at Merle.

'We should,' she said. 'I can't! I can't! Let's call Lin. We'll call Lin.'

They left the body and helped each other to the living room. Doris sat in her chair, opposite Merle's chair. Mason went to the phone.

The relatives gathered. There was a funeral. It was a cold spring day and rained hard. Lin Howard, the undertaker, held two black umbrellas, one for the minister, one for himself and the coffin. The service was short; Doris did not believe in what she called 'a public display'. After everyone left, Lin Howard's assistant dug the hole. Just as if Merle was dead.

Lin Howard, heavy and florid, who sang deep true bass in the church choir, would have said that he buried Merle, or that his helper, Little Mick, had done it. It was Lin who snapped Merle's body into the plastic cover and rolled it out of the house on a stretcher. Then he came back and sorted through

Merle's clothes and found his respectable suit, a shirt, a tie. Doris went through the bureau drawers and sorted out some underwear. Lin agreed that he had to have that.

Would they come and view the body?

'No,' Doris said, 'I don't know if I could. It wasn't pretty, Lin. It was awful. Mason will tell you. It was awful.'

Lin looked at Mason. Mason nodded.

'This cosmetic business, Lin,' Doris said, 'we would know you had done it. It wouldn't really be Merle. Would it?'

Lin looked at the floor.

'Well, it's just as you like.' Quiet, his voice was still deep and melodic. 'But I'll fix his face up anyway. I always do. I don't charge for it. It's easier that way. You never know. I've been doing this a long time. Somebody has to. Sometimes people don't want to see the body again. Sometimes they do. Sometimes they change their mind between the death and the services. I always fix the faces up. It doesn't hurt. Sometimes I'm glad I did. You want to come see him, you call me. He'll be ready tomorrow.'

Lin Howard fixed up Merle's face and he was glad because the next afternoon Mason called him and made an appointment to come in with Doris and Mason's wife Nancy, Merle's daughter. They did come. Lin had fixed a peaceful look on the corpse's face. He left them there, but on the way out Doris came to find him.

'It's better, Lin,' she said. 'Thank you.'

The minister's wife, who got to the corpse even before Lin, had gone in to wash Merle, knowing that Doris would want him to go clean. But she looked Merle over and came out saying that Doris had kept Merle so beautifully there was nothing for her to do. On her way out of the house, she smiled and nodded to Lin who had just driven up. She was a practical, not a theological, woman. But she felt that death, which she saw often and did not fear except for herself, was an instance in which nothing could make something. Of course, if anyone asked her, she would say, in her practical way, 'It's over. He's in there with Lin. Doris kept him immaculate.' But she did not keep from smiling.

By the third day after the funeral, the relatives have been and sorted out all Merle's personal belongings. At Doris's request, they have taken them out of the house. When she has slept one night at Nancy's without a sedative, Doris moves back to her own home. It's important to her to do it alone.

The room where Merle was is now completely empty. To oblige her, the relatives have even removed the hospital bed and apparatus. Old bills, letters, records – all have been sorted. Clothes are gone.

'After all,' she says to herself, 'what need does he have of them?'

Alone in her house, she nerves herself and goes into the empty room. The tiny dishes are gone, the ones too large to hold what he would eat. She opens a closet door. Everything is empty, even the coffee cans that held his wool socks rolled with mothballs. The windows have been opened, there is no smell.

Perhaps, she thinks, I could do something in here. A guest room? No. Not yet. From the window she can see the door of the shop. But Merle's jacket and hat are not there. They took everything, she thinks. Was I right to tell them to? I'd like to see his jacket there. It would remind me that he's not out on a job . . .

Where is he? Where is he? Nowhere. She shuts the bedroom window. The slate, she tells herself, is clean.

She moves out of the room and closes the door. She is alone. Almost to prove it, she begins to hike up her dress on the way to the bathroom. Holding it with her elbows, she opens the bathroom door. She starts in, stops on the threshold, screams a little to herself although she knows it's silly to scream, comes out, shuts the bathroom door.

Later she tells Nancy, 'There's a snake. A big old black snake, coming out of the register. I know it's silly, but I saw it. Could you come?'

Mason and Nancy both go down with her and go all through the house. They find nothing. Mason closes the register. Nancy smiles a little on the way home.

But Mason is not immune either. At night, the snake bothers him. Merle bothers him. He waits for what he was told would happen, but it is too soon.

'Does it hurt you?' he'd asked.

'Yes,' she'd said. 'It hurts.'

'Then why do you have them?' He didn't know any better.

'You forget,' his mother said. 'By the time the baby smiles, you've forgotten.'

'But you yell when it hurts?'

'I yell like crazy. And when it's over I forget it. That's the way our minds work, Mason.'

But Merle is still there.

Sitting up at night, Mason thinks he is a little boy again, playing in Merle's living room. He would have liked to live there, if he could. He and Nancy line blocks up across the living room in a long, black train. Each block smells of the dark oil Merle has rubbed it with. The smell stays on the fingers. Merle stands outside the window and peeks in at them and grins. Mason and Nancy love it.

Then Mason thinks that he and Nancy are newlyweds and Merle has built them a house and knows where their bedroom is and forgets they're grown up. He comes across the lawn, leaving a wavy track in the dark grass. He thinks they are still children, sleepyheads late getting up. He comes to the bedroom window and stands outside it and grins and does not think and presses his nose to the glass and waves at them.

Nancy and Mason look up quickly from where they are lying, naked, on the bed. Nancy reaches for the covers and cries towards the old man,

'Go 'way! Go 'way!'

Merle looks horrified and is too ashamed to go near them for days afterwards. Eventually Mason and Nancy catch up with him and they all apologize.

'I should have thought,' Merle keeps saying. 'I should have thought.'

Nancy's voice comes to Mason now, as if he's hearing it through Merle's own ears and it hurts. A low-pitched, ragged sound. It coils in Mason, but he is helpless. What can straighten things out now?

The next day, Doris calls them again.

'Our friend is back,' she says to Mason.

'Oh?' He smiles, but something inside him plummets.

'I don't know how he gets in here,' Doris says. Her voice is shaky. 'This time I was getting up from my nap, and there he was, hanging from the ceiling fan. Could you come and look?'

Nancy and Mason both go. Mason cleans out the fan and closes it off. He checks the bathroom register. There is nothing. But Doris is trembling.

'It's getting so I don't dare move,' she says.

'Mother, come home with us. Please.' Nancy begs. 'You don't need to be alone.'

'No!' Doris says. 'This is my house! I am going to live in my house. I told Merle . . .' But the formula that worked does not work. 'A little old snake,' she says quietly. 'Haven't had a chance to be lonely yet. You go home.'

524

Mason sits in his living room and does not sleep. Nancy has gone to bed. He thinks he can hear her breathing. He watches the air. There is something about the spaces around the furniture. His eyes strain looking into them.

Merle Thompson is not dead. He appears. He has the face Lin gave him, smooth, younger. Merle's eyes are open. The forehead has slipped somewhat towards the chin, but the eyes are there and it is Merle. He is wearing his respectable black suit.

'Merle?' says Mason.

The fallen forehead nods.

'Is it you?' Mason cannot move.

'Are you afraid of me?' It is Merle's voice.

'Afraid of you! Merle, I . . .' Mason looks at him carefully. 'Merle? Have you begun to decay?'

Merle holds out his hands. They are black, round. The fists have begun to sink into the palms.

'It doesn't matter, Merle!' Mason says. 'It doesn't matter! You're here! You're alive! Don't you care about the hands, Merle! I don't care about them!'

Merle's hands come closer. The round black hole in the circle of the fingers is like the hole on a swan's beak. No. That is not it, Mason thinks. They're more like diamonds, black diamonds. He looks into the holes for a moment and then pulls himself back.

'Merle? Can you stay? I'd give anything if you could!' Tears sting Mason's eyes. 'Or as you were, Merle! I miss you! Trade hats with me, remember? And make faces! Come to any window you want, Merle, I don't care! You knew what I was. It wouldn't matter! Any window! Any window!'

Merle shakes his head. 'Can't do that, Mason.' It is not the air or the sound of breathing, but Merle's voice. 'Can't do that.'

Merle's blue eyes blink. Or do they have colour, so near the sides of his face? The arms move close to the body. Merle's knees buckle, he floats, sinks.

'Merle?' Mason cries, half-rising from his chair, 'wait!' But is there anything, a snake, anything, on the floor, in the fan, at the register, anywhere? 'Merle, where are you? Are you still there?'

Yes. It is Merle's voice that drifts to him from the spaces.

'Can you still see me?' Merle asks. 'Can you still see me?'

Dorothy K. Haynes

A song at the party

Dorothy K. Haynes' first collection Thou Shalt Not Suffer a
Witch *was illustrated by Mervyn Peake. Some of it is reprinted
in her recent collection* Peacocks and Pagodas. *She was born in
Lanark in 1918 and has never wanted to be anything but a
writer: her jobs have been 'temporary and stop-gaps' – library
assistant, English teacher at a Polish refugee school, flower
brusher in a hothouse, shop assistant, BBC audience
researcher. 'Why do other writers have such fascinating and
prestige jobs?' she says, though it seems to me she's had a more
varied career than many of us, and it shows in her work.*

*In 1947 she won the Tom-Gallon Award. The flavour of
much of her work is both Scottish and nightmarish. Here is an
example of the kind of tale that must have appealed to Peake.*

'Lisa – turn it down a bit.'

She pulled a face, and made a minimal adjustment to the
volume. It made no difference. Top of the Pops is noisy even
at a whisper.

The titles flashed past, weird names, weirder people. Soon,
I thought, they'll get past looking like Red Indians, and begin
to behave normally. I'd been hoping that for some time, but
each week they came up with some new gimmick; and each
week James and I, long suffering and old-fashioned, allowed
our daughter to wallow in the noise, the torturing lights and
the incomprehensible gabble of modern pop.

'Now, what's *that* one about?' I'd say, as yet another long-
haired moron postured at the microphone.

'Dunno . . .'.

It didn't seem to matter, so long as the sound was right. But
the sound was equally incomprehensible to me, harsh and
actively uncomfortable. I said this to Lisa.

'You don't have any tunes you can *sing* to yourself. It's just
noise.'

'There's Amazing Grace. You like that.'

'Until it was done to death.'

'Mull of Kintyre. That's a tune.'

Her father told her what he thought of Mull of Kintyre.

And so it went on, the usual Thursday argument, lit with flashing strobes and the epileptic frenzy of the dancers. And then Lisa gave a twitch, and huddled back into her chair.

'Listen to this, then, Mum. You'll really like this one. Serf Hale's new single.'

How had I missed it before? It was a straight song, unaccompanied, sung by a comparatively tidy young man with the obligatory microphone masking his mouth; a sad song, a weird song; and I didn't want to listen. I'd heard it before, though I hadn't been able to make out the words, because they were sung in Gaelic. Now I heard the refrain, something about

'On the field of blood,
On the cold grey field,
Oh my love . . .'

Lisa was quiet as the disc jockey began to yatter again and the dancers seethed and jerked. Her lip was quivering, her eyes full. 'Oh mum!' she whispered. 'Wasn't it great? Isn't it magic?'

She didn't know what she was saying.

'I'm going to buy the record. And I'm going to write to Serf Hale—'

'Don't be silly, Lisa. You should be past writing fan letters at your age.'

'But Mum, it's not really him. I just want to know where he got that song. It's supposed to be an old song—'

'You'll do no such thing,' I ordered, and God knows I had reasons for forbidding her; but like so many good reasons, they were not easy to explain. It went back to the time when I was at school (Lisa wouldn't believe that pop tunes sometimes go that far back) and I was invited to Jane Allison's for tea.

Jane's parents kept a baker's shop in a village a few miles away. By our family's standards, she was well off. Twice a week, after school, she went for music lessons, and just before teatime you would see her waiting for the bus home, with her black music case in her hand, and her schoolbag on her back. She was a dark, pinched looking child with bony knees, and once, when she played the piano at a school concert, an unappealing little tune called Valse Nasturtium, I remember feeling that her parents must be rich indeed to lavish piano lessons on one so obviously unmusical, and so unlikely to be a social success.

At weekends, after school, when she wasn't at music, Jane had to help with the family business. She cycled round the village on a black bicycle with the name 'J. ALLISON, BAKER' on a metal plate under the crossbar. In front of the handlebars was a large basket covered with a white cloth, and under the cloth, in rows, were scones, fern cakes, Empire biscuits, and every kind of pastry, warm and sickly, smelling of spice and jam. Jane had to knock at doors and deliver these goodies, and to me it seemed the most desirable and enviable job in the world. She pedalled the bicycle round first thing in the morning, too, with bread and rolls; and perhaps because of these out of school activities, she wasn't very bright at her lessons.

She wasn't all that popular, either. There was a reticence about her, a holding back, as if she had something to hide. Sometimes she came to school on her bicycle, and the advertising plate and the frame for the basket raised a certain amount of ridicule. It might have been better if she had quarrelled with her tormentors, but she acted as if she hadn't heard them. Me, I never scoffed at her. I rather envied the bike.

Surprisingly, in view of the way we all treated her, Jane arrived at school one day near Christmas with an invitation to the whole class to a birthday party in her house. I was intrigued and impressed. My mother let down my last year's party frock, gave me my bus fare, told me when to be back, and warned me to behave myself.

We had to be at the house by four o'clock. It had been raining, I remember, a miserable winter day, and the pavements were still damp, the village street empty, when I got off the bus right at the baker's shop. It was quite a large shop, with rows of little wooden stands in the window, decked with doilys and piled with different kinds of cakes, and at the sides were tartan tins arranged to show the picture on the lids, a Highlander pointing his sword at the inscription, 'Allison's Best Butter Shortbread'. On shelves above were rows of sweetie bottles, and everything looked rich and solid and prosperous.

The house entrance looked solid and prosperous too, with a big square bell pull, and an inner glass door with an amber handle. I could see a warm glow behind the glass, like an orange-shaded lamp, and when I rang the bell there was a squeal, and some giggles, and Jane opened the door with a crowd of girls behind her all keyed up with fun and excitement. The hall was warm and cosily carpeted, and I was rushed upstairs to take off my coat and tidy up in Jane's bedroom.

Why did Jane never look very happy? She had a room to herself, and furthermore, a room with a fire in it! The bedside light was on, and left on, for the benefit of the visitors, and some of them were changing into ankle-length dresses and dancing shoes, posing in front of the mirror and dabbing on powder. Jane, too, was in a long party frock, and her hair was curled, so as to make her look rather less waif-like. Her face was beginning to light up with excitement, and I realized that much of the time she must be lonely. It was a treat to her to be the centre of attention, to have the whole class in her power for an evening, and to know that, long after, even if they did not become friends, they would feel a sort of guilty gratitude towards her.

The excitement was beginning to affect me too. Shy, slightly out of it because I didn't have an ankle-length dress, I began to talk like the others, in a high, affected voice. We swept along the passage – what a lot of rooms there were! – past the stained-glass window on the stairs, and down to the dining room.

Mr Allison was obviously out of his element. A big beefy red-haired man, more like a butcher than a baker, he stood about awkwardly as we gaped at the laden table. The centre was taken up by an enormous cake, and all around it were dishes and dishes of Allison's best baking. It couldn't have been much of a treat for Jane, who was obviously sick of the sight of the stuff, but we thought it was wonderful.

The organizer of it all was Mrs Allison, a strong-faced, determined-looking woman with black hair parted in the middle, and a band of grey spreading gradually back from her forehead. Jane introduced us all, and her mother briskly pushed us into our places at the table. It wasn't till we were all seated, wondering whether or not someone was going to say Grace, that we noticed that there were two vacant seats; and then two elderly ladies came in, and were helped to the table.

'This is grannie,' said Jane, obviously schooled in what to say, 'and this is my great grannie.'

We all mumbled and fidgeted, and smiled at the two ladies; and by the way Mrs Allison treated them, considerate but bossy, I gathered that they belonged to her side of the family. The grannie's hair was grey, almost silver; the great grannie had what looked like a cap of flossed white wool. Both had Mrs Allison's strong features, but sagging a little, wrinkled out of shape; and though they were pleasant enough, and kind enough, their presence laid a blight on the party. They did not hear very well, and the older lady had trouble with her sight; her eyes were milky and vague.

Somehow we could not shriek and giggle as we had been doing, and we minced about with our food, afraid of seeming greedy. 'Come on, put out your hand,' Mr Allison urged us, passing round fruit slices and lilies of green marzipan filled with cream. We selected the dainties timidly, dithering between chocolate cups and tipsy cakes, while the old ladies were still nibbling at sandwiches and sipping tea from trembling cups. I began to see why Jane was a little old-fashioned, a little different from the rest of us. Did the bike and the big house and the music lessons make up for the continual company of the old, with all its restrictions? And why had Jane never told us about the old people? Of course, she had told us nothing because none of us had been close enough to tell.

The lights were switched off, the candles on the cake were lit and blown out. Everyone cheered, and the cake, too rich, was shared out in moist dark fingers. Soon after, the table was cleared, and Jane took us through to the sitting room, where we lolled about and groaned because we were too full, and were quite willing to sit idly and gossip in luxury.

But we were not to be allowed to relax. The party must be made to 'go'. Mrs Allison came through (we had an awful suspicion that Mr Allison was alone in the kitchen, washing dishes), and soon we were playing old-fashioned party games, spin the plate, hunt the thimble, blind man's buff, and enjoying them in spite of ourselves.

Then came the crunch. We all had to 'do' something. Betty Willis, who went to elocution, and was dying to perform, did her stock piece, 'Green Apples' with all the appropriate actions. Maisie Gillon did a tap dance, rather hampered by the carpet, and lack of music. Jane played 'The March of the Merry Mice' which sounded as if it came from the same book as Valse Nasturtium; and then, surprisingly, Jane's mother said that she would sing a song.

'Mummy, no!' said Jane.

We all stared at her in surprise. Her face was white, her

531

hands clenched. 'Daddy!' she screamed. 'She's—'

Her mother waved her quiet with one imperious hand. Jane sat down, trembling. When everyone was quiet, Mrs Allison started.

It was a sad song, a weird song, with a Gaelic refrain, and I think, though I'm not sure, that it was about men being lost in battle. I felt myself growing cold, and the skin at the back of my neck tightened. I wanted to cry. When it was all over, and we had clapped, everyone of us moved and bewildered, I heard myself saying, in a quavery voice, 'Wh-what song was that, Mrs Allison?' And yet I didn't want to know.

The strong face had melted a little, the black eyes were remote. 'Oh, it's a very old song,' she said. 'I don't know what made me sing it. My mother would know. Here.' She beckoned to me, and I got up shyly. 'Come here and she'll tell you. She's a good memory for the old things.'

I saw Jane put out a hand to stop me, but there was nothing I could do about it. Flattered, but a little nervous, I followed her mother to a smaller room to which the two old ladies had retired. Mrs Allison went up to her mother, leaned over, and spoke to her.

'This is Deborah. She wants to know about *that* song.'

'Eh? Oh, the song? Well, it's a long time ago . . .' She rambled on, as Mrs Allison slipped away back to her guests. 'I remember my mother taught it to me . . .' She hummed a few notes, sad, heartbreaking notes, and then broke off. 'She's the one to tell you. Go over and ask her, but make sure she sees you. She's got cataract, you know.'

I went over, wishing I'd never mentioned the song, and asked her about it. 'Mrs Allison sang it, and she said you'd tell me . . .'

Slowly, the notes creaking out, she went over it. 'Aye . . . it's a song you don't hear much nowadays. You forget. You forget. My mother would know . . '

Oh well, I thought, thank goodness that's the end of it. I'll never find out now. But the great grannie was struggling to get up, her lips working, her thin legs plunging to get purchase to lever herself upright. One hand on my shoulder, she propelled me towards the door and down the passage.

'That room there,' she told me. 'Ask her. Speak slowly, and she'll understand, if she's awake.'

'I don't want to disturb . . .'

'On you go.'

I didn't know what to do. I would have run back to the others, to the safety of the crowded room and the company of the young, but I wasn't sure of the way, and the old lady was leaning on her stick, watching me. Very timidly, I tapped at the door, and the old lady behind me said sharply, 'Well, go in. You can't expect her to get up to answer you.'

I went in.

Inside the room was a bed, with a candle burning beside it, and in the bed was – I can't go on talking about old ladies. This one was like a skeleton wrapped in skin, transparent like the skin on suet. She had no hair, no teeth, but she had seen me, and I couldn't back out. She lifted up an arm like a bone, and beckoned to me.

'The song,' I said, half crying. 'That old song. They said you'd know . . .'

I knew she would sing it. It was what I had been dreading. The sound came out of her like a hiss, an exhausted hiss, and then she moved her bones again and whimpered, 'Oh, I don't remember. My mother would know. Ask her.'

'But—'

'There. Over there.' The bone wavered towards the chest of drawers, and to humour her I went over, and looked back for instructions. The top small drawer was half open. The skull nodded, and I opened it further.

What was in was nothing but a trace of mist, a wisp of steam, a curl of smoke; and yet it had a shape, and a likeness, and it seemed to know. It could speak. It could even sing, a suggestion of sound, the *smirr* of a sigh. I cannot tell you how dreadful the song sounded, then. I can't tell you; and then it said, far, far away, 'I don't remember. Ask my mother . . .'

I ran away. I ran all the way home, in my party frock, without bothering about the bus. My mother wouldn't believe what I had told her, and said that first thing in the morning I would have to write a letter of apology to Jane's mother, whose kindness I didn't deserve.

So, after breakfast, with no school to go to, because the Christmas holidays had started, I settled down with pen and paper to write something which would please my mother and not offend Jane's; but while I was still struggling with it, Allison's van stopped at the door, and an envelope was handed in, addressed to my mother.

It was a letter from Mr Allison; an apology from *him*. I was never allowed to see what he had said, but later I heard bits read out and discussed with my father; something about 'unfortunate . . . not for a long time . . . never dreamed it would happen like that . . .'

Tantalizing as it was, I believe it was better that I *didn't* hear the explanation. Next term I went to another school. Jane was kept back a class, and later on we moved, and I lost touch with the Allisons altogether.

What worries me now is the fact that, if Lisa buys the record, she'll play it over and over, and I won't be able to bear it. I've a compulsion to listen, but I don't want to. Perhaps if I could trace the song right back to its origins it wouldn't bother me so much; but I wouldn't dare to delve again into the past, ghost after ghost diminishing into shades of nothing. But I'd like to *know*. Maybe Lisa will find out. She's young, and she's tougher than I was at her age. Yes, that's it. I'll get Lisa to ask.

Felice Picano

One way out

Felice Picano was born in 1944, and still lives in New York.
He graduated with honours from New York City University in
1964, and off he went to be (briefly) a teacher, a social worker,
a graphic arts magazine editor, a Rizzoli bookstore manager.
Most of the time, he says, he was a layabout and sixties hippie
type. In photographs he looks mournfully pensive and bearded.
He writes charmingly formal letters.

His novels include Smart as the Devil, Eyes *(which has*
nothing at all to do with the film Eyes of Laura Mars, *despite*
what the film poster would have you think), The Mesmerist,
and Lure. *There is also a book of poetry,* The Deformity
Lover. *It's an impressively varied bibliography, and one never*
knows what to expect from Picano, as you will see.

Bay threw down the apple core and stomped it into the soft
loam until only a little mound of dirt was left. The bells from
a distant steeple – the highest point of a tiny village nestled in
the New England hills – were just striking twelve. It was Sunday. That would mean even less traffic than usual, less chance
of truckers and easy pick-ups, especially as this wasn't a highway, only a double lane country tar road.

He tightened the straps of the knapsack over his shoulders
and loped off the ridge down on to the road. He tried to adjust
his mind and body for a long afternoon walk, trying to stay off
the frayed edge of the road and on the dirt as much as possible, to make the walking easier on his feet.

After ten minutes or so, he still hadn't seen a car. Everyone
must be at home, having dinner. The dark grey of the road
shot away from under his feet down a long incline, rising up
to another ridge half a mile away where it hid from sight, then
rose straight up to another ridge, rising and dipping, again and
again into the spine of hills – like a ribbon grabbed by the
wind.

Bay was just bracing his legs for the long incline when a rush of air and force slashed past him. Swop, swop it went, knocking him to the ground amid a flurry of dust and small pebbles.

Whatever it was, had been too fast for him to catch sight of it. He picked himself up, brushed off his denims, looked back in the direction he had come from, muttered a few curses, then started off again. Then he noticed something.

Ahead, like mechanical insects rapidly climbing down a wall, were two small, very fast vehicles, moving towards him down the ribbon of road. They fell out of sight for a second behind a ridge, and as they did so, two identical vehicles appeared at the top of the road, beginning the drop down.

They were going so fast that as he refocused from one pair to another, they seemed to change places. Then he saw the effect was caused by a third pair of identical vehicles which had now appeared at the top of the ridge.

They flashed so much in the noontime sun, that Bay could scarcely see them coming at him. He could make out that they were low, squarish and painted a metallic green. But what was so odd after seeing no cars at all, was that these seemed so regular – each one side by side, covering both lanes of the road, the second and third pairs exactly as far away from each other, as if in formation. Bay was reminded of a slot-car set he had once played with as a child.

Then the first pair were up to him. Then passing him. As they went, they made the same sound: swop, swop.

That left no doubts. An earlier pair must have knocked him down. This time he was braced; even so, he could barely stay on his feet in the dust and blast of their passing. He followed their squat retreating figures down the road, only a double blur now in all the dust they lifted, following them like little cyclones.

He couldn't help feeling there was something odd about the vehicles. He braced himself against an overhanging shelf of rock, and shaded his eyes, trying to catch a better look at the next pair as they passed. When they did, he was even more unnerved.

They were unlike any vehicles he had ever seen. Low flat boxes, angled towards some indefinite apex three-quarters of their length. No lights. No chromium decoration of any sort. And no glass – and therefore no way to see inside them, if they had an inside. He had thought they were painted a metallic green, and that was the closest he could come in describing their colour and material to himself, but it wasn't metal, and it wasn't green. It was both more and less than that. An unknown substance refracting light in a way he had never seen any material do, and a colour that seemed to absorb as much light as it reflected. Worst of all, as the vehicles had lifted over the ridge of road, they had lifted off the ground – going approximately 150 miles per hour any vehicle would have – and they had no wheels!

Bay was thinking whether he had noticed any military base in the area – on the filling station map he had carried with him. None. Could this be a testing ground for an automobile company? Might they be experimental cars of some sort?

The last pair finally shot past him, interrupting his thoughts, and making that dull, swop, swop sound again. He turned to see if any more were coming. None. Then he turned to watch the last pair speed off, and was amazed to see they were slowing down, and then almost stopping before quickly swerving off the road on to a pasture very close to the ridge where he had spent the night.

All the curiosity and vague discomfort he had felt came to a head. He had to see what these vehicles were. He turned around and ran after the last two.

It was only a few minutes back to the craggy ridge he had left so shortly before, overhanging the open meadows. But in the short while, the occupants of the vehicle had got out and had transformed the area.

What had been a dry grass pasture, now seemed to be a cleared area of some hundred feet in radius. Dark-clothed, helmeted figures moved about stiffly, but quickly, carrying strange tools. Two of them went into the open backs of the vehicles parked at the circle's edge.

Two other figures were setting up a hollow-looking platform exactly in the centre of the circle. From a long-snouted tool one of them held, a pressurized liquid shot out on to the ground and hardened into a concrete-like substance almost the instant it touched the dirt.

As they worked, the first pair edged a canister-like object out of the vehicle and on to the ground. Although Bay was concentrating on the object and the figures, he could see the insides of the vehicle were artificially lighted – half pink, half yellow.

The canister must have been extremely heavy or very fragile, as the figures carrying it moved very slowly, in exaggerated mechanically dainty steps. At length they got the canister into the centre of the cleared circle, and sunk it slowly into the cement material. Another shower from the spray instrument covered the canister completely.

The four figures retreated to beyond the edge of the circle, then one of them pulled a little hand-sized cartridge out of a deep pocket in his suit, adjusted one or two buttons on it, and the trod-down grass began springing up again in the clearing, so quickly and so completely that even from his bird's eye view, Bay could scarcely make out the exact location of the platform and the sunken canister.

Then the figures were inside the vehicles. The doors closed with two gurgling pneumatic slaps, the vehicles spun around as if on invisible axes, and were tearing down the main road in the wake of their companion vehicles as quickly as they had come.

The entire operation had taken perhaps ten minutes. All of it had been hidden from the road by the ridge of rock where Bay had watched them; even if there had been a traffic jam on the road to see it, no one would have noticed. And where the canister had been sunk, it now looked like nothing at all had happened.

That was when Bay started feeling a tingling along the back of his neck. He had had the feeling once or twice before in his life. Once when he was being followed down the dark, deserted streets of a Midwestern city, another time when he had heard prowling, heavy steps outside a tent he had pitched in the Rocky Mountains. Both times before it had meant danger, and now he knew it meant whatever was in that canister was about to go off, and go off big. Without stopping to ask why or how, Bay knew something momentous had been sunk in that meadow. He had to get away fast, now!

He almost stumbled running down the ridge on to the roadway when he remembered he had taken off his knapsack and left it on the rock. Leave it! Go! he thought. Then: No! I have to have it! I have to get away fast! In a car! That thing's going to go off any minute now. I need a car to get away from it. The knapsack will get me a ride.

He was still tying on the knapsack when he reached the road again. No cars. He started to walk as fast as he could, following the direction he had started towards earlier.

Why this way? This is where the vehicles came from. They might have laid a whole chain of these things. They might even be laying more at this moment, behind him. He had to go north. North.

There had to be a northern crossover ahead. He had to get to it. But first he needed a lift. Still no cars. Damn. He felt a little calmer now as he strode along the road, knowing he had a direction now, a way of escape. The thin hot trickle was still burning a network into the back of his neck and his shoulders, and he was beginning to feel a sharp little pain in his side from his exertion. He was sure the first was adrenalin rising, and the extrasensory fear of whatever was going to happen.

If it was? Just supposing it was what he thought it was, what could its radius be? Two miles? Five? What had been the radius of the last nuclear test? Five miles? Ten? Or was that only the radius of total destruction? And if so, what was the radius of the fire storms? Another five, another ten?

He turned to look behind him. No cars. As he turned back, one coming towards him passed by – but it sped on, and he scarcely had the chance to flag it down he was walking so hard, straining to keep up and yet stay in control, to keep himself from running ahead blindly, breaking out totally. No. He had to stay in control. To let go meant to invite the end. Survival lay only in holding on. Holding on.

And still the burning of his nerve ends. It seemed stronger the further he got away from the canister. And still no cars.

Then there was one, behind him. Dark and sleek, coming up to him. Bay almost fell, as he stumbled to a stop, and thrust his arm out dangerously over the edge of the road.

The driver made a great show of screeching to a halt, braking so fiercely that half the car was under Bay's outstretched hand when it came to a full stop.

He ducked down to open the door.

'Haven't asked you yet?' a voice said.

Bay stopped. Oh God, no! Not a joker! Not now!

'Sorry,' Bay said. 'C'n I have a lift?'

'Sure.'

Bay got in, closed the door. The man faced ahead. Nothing but profile.

'Where you headed?'

'North,' Bay said with a determination that surprised him.

'This way's west.'

'There's a crossover a few miles up. I'll get off there.'

'No need to. I'm going north there.'

Bay was still undoing his shoulder straps as the car took off. Finally the knapsack was loose and he swung it on to the floor and sat back, watching the v-shaped hood lap up the dark road.

'Nice car,' he said absently.

'It's all right.'

Thank God he's not in the mood for company, Bay thought. Imagine having a conversation about the weather now. Not now. It might slow him down. Just drive.

'You seemed to be in a big hurry there,' the driver said, 'almost as if you were running away from something.'

Did he know? Was he connected with the vehicles? Was he a scout, a clean-up man, to get rid of any possible witnesses?

Bay said nothing.

'Of course,' the driver went on, 'there's nothing there to run away from. Is there? Just a coupla nothing farms.' He laughed, and Bay looked at the driver. His own age. Good looking in a slick way, like the car. Heavy straight dark hair. Moustache, beard. Sultry lids over dark eyes. Tanned. Spoiled looking. But otherwise all right. Like a hundred others.

'Nothing farms and a coupla cows. Eh?' And he laughed again.

Even if he didn't know anything about the canister, he still might be a little off. Christ! Just what I need, a loony.

Before Bay knew it, they had come to the crossroad and the driver flicked the wheel and spun across the other lane right on to the crossroad.

'No!' Bay shouted. 'That's wrong! We're going south!' He almost jumped out of his seat.

'What?' the driver said, and cupped one hand to his ear, as if he were hard of hearing. Bay began frantically repeating that they were going the wrong way. But the car was already in a sharp U-turn, then across the crossroad of the east–west road.

'A little nervous?' the driver asked.

'Yeah,' Bay mumbled, collapsing into the bucket seat. But he felt no relief. This guy was a joker. And who knew, maybe insane too. And the burning fear from the knowledge that he was still within range of the canister was getting worse, pricking every nerve of his skin.

How in hell had he got into such a situation?

All he knew was that he was hitching east. Yesterday he had

got a ride out of Albany, and into Kingston. There, he had eaten a hamburger and malt shake at a roadside Friendly's, had been picked up by a sharp-faced woman and her two silent children, had driven through the Berkshires, been dropped off in a small town called South Egremont, had been picked up by a truckdriver, and finally had allowed himself to be dropped off where he had spent the night. And before yesterday he had travelled. Hitch-hiked. Through mountains, plains, cities, deserts – all of it blurred and vague now, unimportant, unreal.

He was certain it would go off soon. Why and who had done it were no longer questions. But he knew that being there and seeing it sunk into the ground had connected him to it, and that he carried the knowledge of it like a time bomb running out of time.

'How far do you think we are?' Bay asked.

'From where?' Suspicious.

'Oh, I don't know. From Boston? How about from where you picked me up?'

'About three hundred from Boston. Sixteen and a half from where I picked you up,' he tapped a dial sunken into the leather plush of the dashboard, 'according to the odometer here.'

'That's all?'

'That's pretty good time,' sounding offended. 'That's about sixty-five an hour.'

'Can't you go any faster?' Bay asked.

'I'm in no hurry.'

'The speedometer goes up to 140. Or is that just numbers?'

'It'll do that. These roads are lousy. You want me to rip the underside up, just so you can joyride?' Already the speedometer had tilted up to seventy mph.

'Car like this was probably built to cruise at 120,' Bay said, very wise-guy. Seventy-five now.

'I usually cruise around 100. On good roads.' The speedometer tilted 80 mph.

'I was told that if you don't open them up every once in a while, the oil lines clog up.' 85 mph now.

'Of course that could all be be talk, too,' Bay added.

90 mph. Then 95 mph. The car seemed to be slipping along the road. It was taking the dips so fast it was getting Bay queasy. The landscape was shooting by, trees going flick, flick, flick so fast they bunched and blurred. A stream alongside the road snapped and jerked past like kids shaking a dark rope along the ground playing snake.

541

100 mph.

And Bay's nerves were on fire. He could hardly keep still in his seat with the twitching. Soon. Soon. Any minute now. He had to get away. Out of the car. Soon. Soon. Throw himself clear. Or get the guy to stop and find cover. But where? Where?

There! In the stream. In the water. The water would protect him, keep him from being badly burned. Now. Now.

'Stop! Stop! I get off here. I get off here!'

'What?' The car sped on.

'Stop! Stop. Now!'

'You're crazy. There's nothing here!'

'Stop! Stop.' Bay rose in his seat, opening the window.

'Sit down! You'll get killed!'

The car swerved into a stop like a slingshot twanging.

Before it was stopped, Bay felt an agony all over his body. He threw the door open, ran to the side of the road and fell to his knees beside the stream. He thrust a hand into its brackish murk, up to his elbow. It would have to do.

Behind him, he heard the driver muttering and closing the car door.

Grabbing up two hollow onion-bulb stalks, he broke them off at both edges, and put one open end of each in his mouth. He breathed in one, out the other, then slid into the stream face sideways, hearing the rev of the car as it sped off.

The tubes worked. The minute he felt the cool sludge around him, he was calm. Then he twitched all over once, from head to toe, from every nerve and muscle and cell of his body, and was blinded by a whiteness of light that surpassed any white he had ever known, went into depths and subtleties of sheer white light, grasping at the edge of every inch of him and totally enveloping him. It grew, increased, and as it did the sludge around him grew tepid, then warm, then very warm. And still the white blared on, even whiter, like a thousand brass instruments, white and soundless. The sludge was receding from his head, and the reeds in his mouth were hot and useless, and he couldn't breathe the hot air through them anyway, so he dropped them, and turned over on to his face, filling his lungs with air from dark oxidizing pockets of dank around his face, while the universe went white white white.

Then orange, then red, then dark, then a vague, flickering colour.

But the twitching was over. And the pain. And the fear. His

hair no longer felt on fire. The sludge stopped bubbling around him. It was dried, encrusted on his head and hands and clothing.

Cautiously he rolled over. Cautiously he breathed a little. It was warm still. Acrid, with the smell of burning. But breathable. He took more breaths. They hurt his nasal cavities and throat, and he swallowed once or twice. Better. Then he sat up, and flicked the crusted dirt off his fingertips, then delicately picked the dried crust off his eyelids.

The sky was pink. Not quite: purple and orange and pink. All around him, the countryside was in sudden blackened desolation. Ahead, a grove of pines burned like a huge torch. In the distance, across flat charred fields, firs shot sparks from a ridge of hills. The air was still hot. But the worst was over.

Shakily, he reached his feet and got up, then fell weakly to his knees, and retched, vomiting chunks of his breakfast into the thick, cracked bed of what once had been a stream. He immediately felt lighter, and stronger. He wiped his mouth with the damp underside of his sleeve, then stood up again, and lumbered forward along the half-melted, disfigured road.

Everywhere the fires. Then the showers of ashes descending all around him. God knew from what. Like rain. But he was all right. He had got through it.

He walked on, just looking. Then, around a slight bend in the road, and through burnt trunks of trees, he saw the dull metal shine of a car. It was stopped dead in the middle of the road, as if its driver had just stopped a minute to go for a leak on the side of the road and would be back any time.

As he came closer to it, Bay saw there was no glass.

Even closer, most of the outside of the car – sheet metal, bumpers, fenders, roof – seemed intact, but as if heated and pounded in by a hundred thousand tiny hammers. Then he saw that it was the same car that had picked him up before, and he made out the back of the man's head, erect, sunk into the backrest.

And, if it weren't for the millions of gently trembling shards of glass splinters covering his head like a delicate lace helmet, and the red trickles staining their edges, the driver would have looked as if he were alive – just staring ahead, a little bit surprised.

Even the seats and floor and dashboard were rimed with glass shards. But the dashboard dials were still on, and the motor was still idling in neutral. The driver must have been suddenly blinded by the light, and by reflex stopped the car. And then the glass hit him and who knew, but probably the fire too that had seared all the leather inside the car and his skin and flesh too, until they were all the same mottled half brown, half bright pink.

Bay opened the car door, swept a drift of glass shreds off the metal with his foot, then gently pulled at the corpse's back, until the body fell over. Another push and it was out on the road. The burn smell was stronger now. Awful.

He swept off the front seat, reached into the glove compartment where he found a piece of chamois to wrap around the still hot, half-fused steering wheel. There were still a few remaining dangerous-looking pieces of glass left in the windshield and side vents. He knocked them out.

When he was ready, Bay sat in the driver's seat for a minute wondering that instinct was not telling him what to do next.

'I'll go north,' he said aloud. 'North.'

He switched into first gear. The car whined, then leapt forward.

An hour later, he ran out of gas.

He had been surprised and even a little alarmed that there were so few cars on the road. Where had everyone gone to? Were they all dead? In hiding? Or what? The further away he drove, the less there seemed to be any damage, even any signs of what had happened. But everything seemed abandoned. Everything meaning the few clapboard dinettes and gas stations he had passed. If he had only thought to stop and get some gas.

He left the car on the shoulder of the road, and began walking, again north — always north. Every once in a while, Bay would turn around and look behind him, seeing the sky still pink, with clouds of ashes falling in the distance, and one particular area to the southeast — could it be Boston? — bright red and orange, as if the air were consumed by flames.

He reached a large clapboard house off the side of the road, behind a wickerwork fence and gate. Several sedans and a pickup truck were parked on the grassy side lawn. There must be someone inside. They might have some gasoline. Or even be able to drive him to the next gas station.

Aside from blown-in windows, the house didn't seem at all

damaged. The front door was swinging open. Bay called 'hello'
and when he had got no response, walked in.

The place seemed deserted. The kitchen had been in use –
food was half cooked in pots on the big double stoves; two cups
of coffee were set out on the table. Bay called out again, still
got no answer, and half absently picked up one cup of coffee.

Was it all right to drink it? Would it be radioactive?

He went to the sink instead – an old-fashioned pump and
basin – and pumped out a glass of water. It was cool, slightly
minerally, but good. He had another glassful.

Was that a noise behind the door? Voices? Or one voice,
droning on and on?

'Hello,' he called out to whoever would be on the other side
of the door. 'Is anyone there. My car ran out of gas down the
road.'

No answer. But the droning seemed to go on.

Bay went to the door and tried it. Open. He carefully turned
the knob and half stepped aside, not knowing what to expect.

A steep, well-lighted stairway, leading up.

As he ascended, the hard, cracked old voice he'd first heard
became clearer. Bay thought he made out the words 'And
behold, there came up out of the river seven well favoured
kine,' followed by a pause, and what seemed to be the shuffling
of several pairs of shoes on bare wood.

At the top of the stairs he was in a long corridor with several
closed doors and on the floor, a worn, multi-coloured knitted
oval rug, looking like a faded rainbow.

One door was ajar. Behind it the old voice took up again.
Bay approached and slowly pushed the door open enough to
see in.

His first impression was a room filled with people: men,
women, children, old folks, all sitting or standing behind
chairs, leaning against the side and back walls, all of them
facing a corner of the room where because of the angle of the
wall, all Bay could make out was the shadowed figure of an
elderly man. Bay stepped into the room quietly. The old man
was still in obscurity, although now Bay could make out a dark
leather bound, frayed edge book, open on a lectern in front of
him, out in full view.

'So Pharaoh slept and dreamed a second time,' the old voice
repeated, tonelessly. Neither the reader nor anyone else in the
room turned to look at the doorway, at Bay.

545

The old man paused again, and there was a murmur from the group assembled. One little boy no longer able to hold back his curiosity, peeked out at Bay from behind a woman's shoulder. As Bay noticed him, the boy darted back into hiding, then timidly edged back into sight.

Half of the child's pale blond hair was gone, the remaining scalp a purple splotch with large brown blisters and smaller broken pus pink sores, as though he'd been raked from the crown of his head down over the closed congealed eye and reddened-black chin with an acetylene torch. It took Bay a great effort to look away from the boy, and to fix his sight on the worn natural grain of the wood floor.

'And behold, seven ears of corn came upon one stalk,' the old man read on, 'fat and good.'

Everyone murmured their approval. Bay looked up at the boy again. He was hidden again by the bulk of the woman, his mother?, who turned out of profile towards Bay. She too was burned and mispigmented, as though a swathe of intense fire had been whipped across her face and breast.

Bay backed up against the door, holding tightly to the dry wooden moulding behind him, spreading his feet apart for support, as he surveyed the others in the room.

Everyone else was blasted, discoloured, bleeding, suppurating.

'And behold, seven thin ears and blasted with the east wind sprung up after them,' the old man intoned, his voice as dry as the planking that Bay gripped so hard it was flaking into his fingernails.

A woman closest to Bay, her arms crossed over her cotton print housedress, turned to him as though first seeing him. Purple splotches mantled all but a tiny triangle of her face. Her lips were charred lines. Her teeth almost glowed green as she smiled. Only a few clumps of glossy auburn hair were still held in place by her blackened hairband.

Bay had to look down at the floor again, but he also couldn't stop himself from looking up again, now at one, then at another listener, all of them quietly, attentively listening to the old man's reading, monstrously ignoring what had happened to them.

'And the seven thin ears devoured the seven fat and full ones.'

The people were animated by these words, moving about,

gesturing, revealing new facets of their horror. One scabrous-faced man with only a projecting bone of nose leaned over to whisper into the blasted shell of what should have been another's ear.

Bay shut his eyes, then, held on to the door, the floor, for what seemed a long time, fighting down what was in front of him, declaring that he wouldn't open his eyes again.

He was out in the corridor again.

'And it came to pass in the morning, that Pharaoh's spirit was greatly troubled.'

Bay shut the door, held it shut, knowing that they would jump up from their chairs and smash it open on him. His skin felt like every pore was bursting with poisonous filth and infection.

When nothing happened, and the voice went on behind the door, Bay leapt down the stairs, stumbling over his own feet to get down, almost tearing the open stairway door off its hinges as he careened out, through the house on to the roadway, running.

When he stopped running, his body aching with the sudden exertion, he was far from the house. No one followed him. The house seemed deserted. Ahead, over slightly rolling country, he couldn't see another hamlet in sight. What was the difference, if the people there too would be as mutilated, as unconcerned as this group?

Then he came up to a local delivery bread van parked on the edge of the road. No driver, the key still in the ignition. Had the driver, too, been struck by the blinding glare, burned to the bones of his skull, and staggered off mutilated into the high grass, or even more likely back to that house?

When Bay turned the key on, the tank light on the dashboard showed half full. Ought he siphon it off? Or should he just take the van?

Before he could make up his mind, the ignition was on and he had thrown the clutch. All around him he smelled the fresh bread. He reached for a loaf of pumpernickel, tore the plastic wrapper off and ate three pieces, gulping them down. Then he threw the gear and took off.

He hadn't realized how hungry he had been. He ate the entire loaf, and part of another one, as he drove.

The van couldn't go anywhere near as fast as the car had gone, but it was taking him up north all the same. He couldn't help but think that there were going to be more bombs, more trouble, and that he'd be safe as far north as he could get.

He had reached the deep humps of the Green Mountains when he realized that the buzzing he'd been hearing since he'd got into the van came from the radio. The driver must have left it on when he stopped for a cup of coffee in the old geezer's house.

Bay tried tuning it. For a few minutes all he got was cracking and popping. Then he had a voice, distant and faint and high.

'. . . . to report to their local distrib . . . eleven oh seven two four . . . all battalions followed by code J, H, R and S . . .'

Then it was off.

He fumbled some more, leaning across the side of the high dashboard to tune it, until he got another station, this one more clearly.

'Minister and the Parliament declared full neutrality in the sudden, total conflict between the Government of the United Sta . . .' then it drifted. Bay tried tuning it again. ' . . . a participating member of the Geneva Convention, the Commonwealth of Canada has opened all borders to evacuees from the United States. Emergency centres, food, and shelter are offered to all evacuees. Repeat. Emergency centres . . .' it had drifted, and was gone.

So that was it. Nuclear attack. Full attack on a massive scale. Another world war. But Canada was neutral. There was food, shelter, safety there. He had been right to go north. Instinctively, Bay pressed down the gas pedal as far as it would go, then turned back to try to tune in the radio.

After fifteen minutes of nothing but hisses and words isolated in a radio drift, Bay pressed one of the buttons on the front of the set that said 'emergency'. For a long while there was nothing but more hisses and pops. He turned it down lower, but left it on in case it did catch radio signals. Then he drove on, thinking.

He had been lucky. Close. Too close. But lucky. If he had still been in Albany, been in any city, it would have been all over. That was certain. And he had been lucky to be so close to Canada. He could visualize evacuees from the cities trying to reach Canada over hundreds of miles of melted throughways. Horrible. It would be easier for him. Only another hour or so, and he'd cross the border. That was the value of hanging loose, travelling, being on your own. Nothing to hold you back. Always in the right spot when you needed it for survival. For survival.

He paused once on the top of a high ridge of mountains, and got out to look back, feeling like Lot in the Old Testament seeing the destruction of Sodom and Gomorrah. The skies south were still orange, fading to pink. The sun itself seemed contained within a flaming, new corona. A flock of birds were rushing northward over the mountains. They knew. They knew where it would be safe. He got back into the van and started off again.

Then there was static on the radio station. He raised the volume and tried catching the station. The static was unnerving, dizzying. Then there were voices. Calm voices. Men. Two men talking. He turned up the volume even more.

It didn't sound like emergency news – more like a private conversation overheard. Had he picked up a ham operator's conversation? And if so, why were they so calm? He turned the volume up full, and shut the van window, cutting off the wind current noise.

'So far the case exactly parallels our graph of reaction,' were the first words he made out. Then it was louder, clearer. 'Really quite extraordinary. Almost classic.' The voice was so calm it was annoying. Didn't they know what had happened?

'And you're certain the sudden communication will not be too much of a shock,' another voice said. 'I mean given the intensity of applied reality.' This man was less confident. What were they talking about?

'The shock is precisely what we want. By eliminating the possibilities to only two – one a total nightmare – the patient invariably will opt for the other. Voluntarily. Willingly even. The knowledge that there is a choice overrides any shock from the communication itself.'

There seemed to be a static storm over the radio and Bay fiddled with the dial. He was back on the channel again, but it was silent. He left it there, and continued driving, his thoughts divided now between the strange conversation he had somehow overheard, and the image of the country completely destroyed submitting to an invasion by . . . by who?

'Bay! Can you hear me?'

He almost jumped out of the seat. Then he realized the voice came from the radio. One of the two men who had been talking. He repeated his question.

549

'Bay, this is Dr Joralemon. Can you hear me?'

What the hell was going on?

'Dr Elbert is here with me too. You remember Dr Elbert, don't you? Bay, if you can hear us and understand us, then shake your head from left to right. Do you understand? From left to right. Slowly.'

Bay did as he was told.

'Very good. Now, Bay, do you remember who I am? Dr Joralemon. Again, Dr Joralemon. If you remember me, shake your head again.'

The name wasn't familiar. But the voice was. Or was it?

'Bay, did you hear what I just said?'

Bay nodded from left to right, thinking what the hell am I doing? where are these voices coming from? He opened the window and flipped the mirror all over the road, to see if someone was following him. Nothing. Nothing at all but forest: sparse, mountain forest.

'Now, Bay, do you remember Dr Elbert?'

'Bay?' the other voice came on. 'This is Jim Elbert. I'm your doctor. Or, at least I was. Do you hear me?'

Yes. Yes, Bay thought. 'Jim,' Bay said. 'How can I hear you through the radio?'

'Bay!' Elbert's voice interrupted his own. 'If you remember me, just shake your head. I see you're trying to talk, but we can't hear you.'

Bay nodded vigorously. What the hell was Elbert doing on the radio? Where was he? How had he located Bay?

'Do you remember me, Bay?' It was the other voice. The one that called himself Dr Joralemon. And now Bay did recall the voice. Not like Elbert's, pleasantly, like a friend, like growing up and playing stickball and going around driving together, but differently.

Dr Joralemon repeated his question, and Bay heard rooms in his voice. Rooms and doors. Far away rooms in pastel colours. Venetian blinds half-closed. The murmur of someone's muffled crying.

Bay nodded slowly.

'Good,' Joralemon said.

'Bay?' It was Jim Elbert again. 'Now that we've communicated, you must understand that what I'm going to tell you is fact. Do you understand that? Will you believe me? Do you have any reason not to?'

No, Bay thought. I don't. He nodded, then reversed the motion of his head.

'All right. Some twelve hours ago, you underwent a new approach in psychic surgery. It's only used in the most hopeful of . . . well, of extreme cases. Dr Joralemon invented the method. He calls it the dreamprobe.'

'And so far we've had 100 per cent effectiveness,' Joralemon interrupted to add in.

'What it does, Bay,' Elbert said, 'I mean, what it is is a combination of a drug that operates on the cerebral cortex, and a series of timed electrical shocks. What it does is to channel all of your fears and anxieties into one area, into one major fear and anxiety. Your unconsciousness then takes over, and makes that one fear and anxiety into a dream of a tremendous catastrophic experience.'

Bay didn't understand.

'You're asleep, Bay,' Dr Joralemon said. 'You may think you aren't, but you are. You're fast asleep.'

Bay gripped the wheel. What the hell! Sleeping? The trees were whizzing past the van window, clumps at a time. There were still no vehicles behind him, and he hadn't seen one coming his way at all.

'That's right, Bay,' Jim Elbert said. 'Sleeping. Dreaming. Everything that has happened to you has been a dream.'

'Not an ordinary dream,' Joralemon said. 'That's how the drug works, it doesn't approximate reality with symbols and foolish inaccuracies the way most dreams work. It has seemed very real to you. Intensely real.'

'You must realize that it was a desperation measure, Bay. I was against it at first, but your increasing catatonia, and Dr Joralemon's persuasion forced me to accept this way.'

'Do you understand this, Bay?'

Understand it? It was insane.

'Bay?' It was Elbert again. 'Can you still hear us?'

He nodded, yes.

'Can you understand what we're telling you?'

He half nodded.

'I know it's difficult to believe,' Joralemon said. 'Because it was all so concentrated, every aspect, every impression seemed completely accurate.'

'In effect,' Elbert said, 'it was another reality.'

'An alternative reality, really. Can you understand that?'

Bay couldn't. Whoever these jokers were, they must be off their rockers. He looked up to see if there was a helicopter or plane above him. He even looked out the window. Still nothing. How were they in contact? How were they tracking him? With radar? Sonar? Should he shut off the radio? Did that activate the beam on him?

'Fine,' Joralemon said. 'Everything is going to be all right now, Bay. You don't have to run any more. You've seen an alternative reality. You've faced up to the worst that you could ever have faced up to, and you've survived. That was the furthest you could could go in the direction you had been going in all these months. And now you're going to be all right and you're going to come back.'

'And we're going to help you come back,' Elbert said.

'Right. You see you don't really have much of a choice, do you, Bay? Because if you don't come back, then you'll have to continue living in a nightmare state. You're over the worst, but given that, what can you expect to follow: a catalogue of horrors, each one worse than the next – that's the logical extrapolation of the monumental trauma you've just experienced.'

'Now, Bay,' Elbert said hurriedly, 'in order to get out of your state, you must merely be able to move your right hand.'

Bay drove lefty. The right hand hung by his side.

'Move your right hand so it reaches over to your heart.'

Who were these guys? And why were they trying to stop him? Were they the enemy? The same people who had planted the bombs, killed so many people? Almost killed him?

Bay would string them along for a while. He must be getting close to the Canadian border soon. He moved his hand to where they had directed him.

'Now, you should be touching a pocket. Do you feel it?'

Of course, there was a pocket.

'Now, there's something very important in that pocket, Bay. We want you to reach in and take it out. Can you do that?'

What the hell could be in his pocket? Bay reached in, felt around, and touched something smooth and flat. He pulled it out – it was a plasticine packet. When did that get in there?

The road was beginning to dip now, out of the mountains. This must be the last stretch before the border.

'Open up the packet, Bay.'

He did. Inside were two small pellets. Like pink barrels.

'Good,' Elbert said. 'When you take those two pills, you will appear to fall asleep. But only to you. What really will happen, is that you will wake up. Do you understand that, Bay?'

Sure, sure, Bay thought, and black is white. Whatever these pellets were, how did they get in the pocket? He hadn't put them there. Had somebody? While he was sleeping? And what if they were what this guy who sounded like Elbert said they were? Where would he be then? Inside a hospital? An asylum, that's where. Probably tied down. No, sir.

'Can you understand us, Bay?'

He nodded.

'Fine. Just pop them into your mouth. All at once.'

Bay rolled them in his fingers.

'Is there anything wrong, Bay?'

'It will be all right, Bay.' Elbert again. 'If you aren't in a position to take them, if you're walking, or driving or something, just stop. Because you'll go to sleep with them.'

What if they were cyanide? Planted there as he slept?

'It will be all right, Bay. I assure you. In a few days you'll be fine. Fine enough to leave the hospital. The recovery programme is the finest around. You'll be proud of yourself. You won't be afraid any more. Not of anything.'

Afraid! The far away rooms. Hospital green and blue and canary yellow. The walls converging, tilting, falling in on him. The crying. No one ever coming. No one, except for a quick look and lying words and another syringe. Murmurs of soft crying all around, constant, interminable. His crying, his own crying, as if heard twenty rooms away. Through locked doors.

'Now, Bay, we have great faith in you,' Joralemon said, sternly. 'Great faith. That's why you were chosen for this dreamprobe over other patients. There were many who . . .'

'Is there a reason you can't take the pills, Bay?'

Bay nodded. Of course there was. He had to get to Canada. He'd be at the border any minute now. There might be other cars there already. He recalled that several major roads converged there. Others would be ahead of him, safer than he was. There might even be a wait. The road was going down more sharply now, he must be close.

'Whatever it is you're doing, you have to stop, Bay. These pellets are the antidote to the drug we gave you. Do you understand that?'

'Bay, no one will hurt you.'

553

Pastel rooms and medicine smells. Shadows squatting and burblings and murmurs and screams cutting through the walls. Shadows vomiting and screaming, colliding; and always the distant crying.

'Please, Bay. This is all a dream. A bad dream. It will be over just like that. Don't you want that?'

'You have to, Bay.'

'Bay! Bay!'

But Bay wasn't responding. Ahead, along the road, he could see the curve up, the converging of two other roads, and at their centre, the wooden log cabin building belonging to the Canadian Mounted Police.

'Never had to inject the antidote before, Elbert, never! We simply don't know where that will leave him.'

'You mean it won't bring him out!'

'We've never had anyone opt for the alternate before.'

'Inject it.'

'I'll need authorization.'

'I'll give you authorization. Inject it.'

No you don't, Bay thought. He lifted his foot off the accelerator as the van coasted down to the border, and kicked the radio hard, once, and then again. It crumbled and the voice jumbled, got mixed in with static, then died.

There were no cars down there, just a Mounted Policeman waving at Bay.

Bay waved back, laughed out loud. In his hand were the pink pellets. He threw them out the window, clear into the pine trees, and slowed down at the station.

'Welcome,' the Mountie said. He had no face. But Bay didn't mind. He would be safe in Canada.

M. John Harrison
The ice monkey

*M. John Harrison was born in 1945. He suffered from
education at Rugby, work in a fox-hunting stable, and
studentship at a teacher training college, before (presumably)
deciding he had suffered enough and moving to London and
writing. These days he lives in the Holme Valley, where he
writes and climbs. He can often be found at a typewriter in the
comics department of Bookchain in Manchester, making sure
that he doesn't lose touch with urban seediness.*

His books include The Committed Men, The Pastel City, A
Storm of Wings, In Viriconium, *and* The Stone Garden. *He is
probably the most underrated living British fantasy writer; he is
certainly among the most original. For seven years he was
literary editor of* New Worlds. *Reactionary science fiction fans
might call that a contradiction in terms, but in retrospect* New
Worlds *is one of the most distinguished magazines of
imaginative fiction. It published his superb story 'Running
Down' (also to be found in his collection* The Ice Monkey),
which was about the occult power of apathy. So is this.

When Jones turned up he was dressed to see his wife. Clothes
were meaningless to him. He had no taste, and needed none
until occasions became 'official'. This distinction, vestigial of
a middle class upbringing, caused him great pain. He drew the
line between official and unofficial himself, by some process I
have never understood; and on the far side of it, where the
habitual no longer offered its comfort and common sense no
alternative, lost his nerve and fell back on the usage of a red-
brick university youth – that is, he tried to make himself look
as much as possible like the ghost of some young Kingsley

Amis. It was a dim and propitiatory instinct and today it had also advised him to shave and have his hair cut, a process which, while it threw his harsh cheekbones into prominence and emphasized the aggressive boniness of his jaw, yet made him seem young and vulnerable and silly.

I knew what he wanted but I hadn't the heart to pretend to be out.

'Look, Spider,' he said. To hide his embarrassment he fiddled with the handkerchief he had wrapped round his knuckles. 'Could you do me a favour?'

'I'd like to, Jones,' I said, 'honestly—' Then I remembered that because of his performance that afternoon he couldn't very well ask Henry. And no one else he knew was in London, so I put on my coat and went with him to the tube station. 'It's my turn anyway, I think,' I said, trying to make light of it. He shrugged and stared at the platform. This was habitual too. 'I don't want another set-to,' I warned him as we got on a Metropolitan Line train: 'I'll have to leave if it's anything like last time.' But my voice was drowned by the hiss and thump of the doors closing behind us. At the other end the wind had dropped and a thick rain fell straight down on us, and on London E3, in rods.

'I quite liked Maureen, you know.'

They – by which I really mean Maureen and the child, since Jones rarely lived there even when she allowed him – had a small furnished flat on the second floor of a house somewhere between Bow and Mile End. For five years or more it had been scheduled for demolition, and now it stuck up with two or three others out of a contractors' waste land a mile across, the enormous floor-plan of a slum, full of lazy fires, silent bulldozers, and trees which seemed naked and doomed without the garden walls they had once overgrown. We forced a route through the rutted clay and piles of smouldering lath, and when we got there a plump West Indian girl put her head round the front door. She winked. 'He's here, Maureen love!' she called up the stairs. 'Don't you forget what I said!' She grinned defiantly at us, and stage thunder rolled over the Mile End Road, but I think the effect was wasted on Jones. It was more than a game to him and Maureen: neither of them had seen E3 until the age of thirty, and their failure to deal with it was ground into the stairwell walls along with all the other dirt.

'You aren't half going to catch it, Mr Jones,' the West Indian girl said to me.

Maureen was standing at the front window of the flat, nervously smoking a cigarette and staring out across the waste as if measuring it against some other landscape she'd once seen. Her shoulders were at once rounded and tense. At her feet the child was playing happily with an imaginary friend. 'About time,' she said distantly to Jones. She was thinner than the last time I'd seen her, a short, harassed blonde in paint-stained jeans and an unravelling Marks and Sparks sweater, the flesh carved off her originally heart-shaped face by anxiety and loneliness, her voice dull and aggressive. 'Oh my God,' she said, 'what *do* you look like?' She blew smoke fiercely down her nostrils and jabbed the cigarette into the bottom of a glass ashtray. 'Just look at yourself!' Instead Jones stood in the centre of the room like a marooned sailor and let his eyes roam helplessly over the open makeshift shelves stuffed with baby clothes, the brown carpet, the yellow plastic potty. He was already desperate and puzzled.

'Twenty years on,' Maureen told the fires and silent, shrouded bulldozers. 'Christ, it's still 1958 for you, isn't it?'

'*Up* the hill and *down* the hill,' chanted the child. It had rubbed chocolate into its hair and clothing.

Jones lifted his hands slightly. 'They're all I've got,' he said. 'Have you been decorating? It's nice.'

Maureen laughed. She compressed her lips. 'Sit down,' she told me, giving up the security of the window. 'Your turn this time was it? How's trade, Spider? How's Henry? It'll have to be tea. I can't afford coffee.' She went into the kitchen, scrupulously avoiding Jones still aground there in the middle of the room, and began knocking things about in the sink. 'Which of you decided to get his hair cut?' she called. She came back with a tray. 'It's not all that bad for 1958. Have a ginger nut, Spider. Where's my maintenance, Jones? You owe me three months and I can't get by without it any more.' She made her way quickly back to the window as she said this; and gazed out into the rain, measuring, measuring. Round her neck she was wearing a little silver monkey on a chain. The tiny hoop that attached its head to the middle link had broken, so she had wrapped the chain round its neck to hold it on. Jones cleared his throat and drank his tea. There was a silence. The child looked up at its mother. Suddenly it squatted down and made a loud farting noise. 'Up the hill and down the hill,' it said. A horrible smell filled the room. 'They knocked the pub down,' Maureen said, 'so I've got no job. This place goes next month and the council still haven't rehoused me. You've *got* to write to them about it this time.' She picked the child up and dropped it in Jones's lap. 'There's your daddy,' she told it. 'Ask him to change you.' It stared up at him for a second then set up a startlingly high-pitched whine. Jones stared back.

'Can't you see you're going to be in trouble with the maintenance? Tansy says they can easily make you pay—'

'Tansy!' yelled Jones suddenly into the child's face. 'Tansy?' he laughed wildly. 'Oh great! Who's bloody *Tansy*? That silly cow downstairs? Of course they can bloody make me, you've got your own brains to see that!'

'She's all I've got!' shouted Maureen, and burst into tears. 'Oh you rotten bastard, I've got nobody else to tell me—'

The child waved its arms and whined. Jones put it roughly on the floor and ran out of the flat calling 'Tansy says! Tansy says!' and laughing desperately. When he'd gone I took refuge in the kitchen, which was less smelly, and made some more tea. 'You don't have to stay, you know,' said Maureen. 'He'll be kicking about out there on his own.' She dabbed hopelessly at the child, found a clean nappy. ('Up the hill and down the hill,' it went, looking up over her shoulder at some invisible friend.) 'I don't know what happens when he comes here,' she said: 'I can't be any more reasonable.' And, 'Remember Swansea, Spider. It was all different then. I did Art. I loved his hands. Look at them now, they're all scabby.' She sipped her tea, staring past me out of the window, recalling perhaps the times when she'd been accustomed to wear a white two-piece and swim, while Jones made his name on the heroic Welsh sea-cliffs of a distant summer, and the water was the colour of a new blue nylon rope.

'His hands were pretty scabby then, Maureen,' I reminded her gently.

'Get stuffed, Spider. Fuck off.'

At the door I offered her a job serving in one of the shops. 'Get in touch if you need help with solicitors or anything,' I added.

She said: 'I'd believe you really wanted to help if you just made him come on his own for once.'

He was out among the smoky contractors' fires, his thin silhouette appearing and disappearing mysteriously as he moved from one to another in the rainy gloom, kicking at the embers and, I thought, trying to get up the nerve to go back inside again. It took me a while to attract his attention.

'They're the only good clothes I've got,' he kept saying as we sat miserably on opposite sides of the tube carriage. 'Why does she keep picking on them like that?'

It would have taken too long to explain it to him, so while the train roared and swayed its way back to the civilized areas west of Farringdon I let him stare dumbly at himself in its dark windows, touch curiously the sore shaved pink cheeks of his furry inaccurate reflection, and fuss (puzzled but on the edge of resentment and already taking advantage of the self-righteousness that would enable him to stay away for another month or two) with the mustard-yellow knitted tie, the tobacco-brown corduroy jacket and the white shirt with the thick chocolate-coloured stripes he'd had since the last proud birthday of his adolescence.

While I imagined Maureen, in E3 where all horizons are remembered ones, dwelling on vanished freedoms: how on Monday mornings in the summer term, after two nights toothbrushless in Llanberis, in a barn or cheap cotton tent, she would hurry down the long polished corridors of the teacher training college eating burnt toast, late for History of Art, still slightly crumpled and sleepy and hungover in one of Jones's unravelling Marks pullovers and pale blue jeans, focus of all interested, jealous eyes.

'I bought her that thing round her neck,' said Jones peevishly. 'I notice she's broken it.'

'Come on, Jones,' I said.

Preoccupation is easily mistaken for helplessness. This was how Jones survived in a world which didn't understand him, although I don't think he employed it often as a conscious device. His obsession with climbing was genuine, and had begun long before Swansea or Maureen. Five weeks after the maintenance fiasco, in the middle of the coldest February since 1964, I took him up to Scotland. I was going to see my parents who have retired to Bearsden, a comfortable suburb where they own a garage. The motorways were covered in black ice: there were extensive detours, and I ended up driving all through Friday night. Jones slept in the back, and then ate three fried eggs in a café straddling the road, watching with his head tilted intelligently to one side as the sparse traffic groaned away south and a kind of mucoid greyness crept into the place through its steamed-up windows. He talked of the time he had fallen off a famous limestone route in Derbyshire and broken his nose. His chalk bag had burst and his face had been daubed with blood and chalk. He had a photograph which someone had taken at the time. 'The worst bit was a feeling of not being able to breathe,' he said. 'I thought I was dying.' He repeated this two or three times with what seemed at the time a superstitious enjoyment.

He told me he wanted to do Point Five Gully on Ben Nevis that weekend, and asked me to go with him. 'Henry won't come,' he said. 'I suppose you know why.' He sat there pouring tomato sauce on his plate.

'I can't go, Jones,' I said. 'They're expecting me.' I hadn't been ice-climbing for years; neither of us had. After Bridge of Orchy I let him drive, hoping to get some sleep. He put us into a snowdrift in Glencoe; I watched the carnivorous bends of the A82 gape open all the way to Fort William. (Sitting on the back of his motorcycle ten years or more before, I had driven a tent pole straight through the rear window of a Mini as he tried to overtake it on one of those bends. I can't imagine why I had it under my arm, or how he persuaded me to carry it at all.) When I next woke up he had the van in a car park somewhere and cold air was spilling into it through the back doors. He had put on a pair of filthy stretch breeches and a Javelin jacket completely threadbare in the forearms from climbing on gritstone. An ancient Whillans harness flapped between his legs like some withered orange codpiece. He was talking to somebody I couldn't see.

'Excuse me,' he said. 'Would any of you have a cigarette?' Giggles answered him, and I went back to sleep.

We walked up to the climb early on Sunday morning. It was still dark, and the weather was appalling. 'Come on, Jones,' I said: 'Nobody bothers with it in conditions like this.' When you could see it, the Ben looked just like a mountain from a fifties film about Alpine guides: not pointed, true: but just as cardboardy, dioramic, painted on. Powder snow blew about like fog on a bitter east wind, cutting at our faces. We set out with some other people but got separated from them as we blundered about on Tower Ridge. For a few minutes we heard their voices thin and urgent sounding against the boom of the wind: then nothing.

Jones made me lead the first pitch.

With front-point crampons on your feet and one of the new

short axes – their acutely-angled picks like the beaks of ptero-dactyls – in each hand, even overhanging ice can be climbed. Waterfalls are the most fun: suspended up among the huge icicles which have grown together until they look like a sheaf of organ pipes, balancing on half an inch of steel two hundred feet up on a sunny morning, you can quite enjoy it all. *Chunk*! go the axes, as you drive them into the ice. I couldn't hear myself think on the Ben that day. Eddies of wind exploded continually into the gully. In places there was hardly enough ice to take an axe – it starred and flaked away under the pick; while elsewhere the route was choked with powder snow like a laundry chute full of Persil. After a bit I couldn't see Jones below me any more (or hear him singing), just a greyish space boiling with ice particles, the two nine-millimetre ropes vanishing into it. I could only go up – chopping, floundering, front-pointing delicately on black verglas while the wind first pushed me into the gully-bed then sucked me out again, forcing spindrift down my neck, under my helmet and into my eyes . . . Eventually bulges of good ice appeared. I got up on to one of them, smashed in a couple of ice screws for a belay, and gave Jones a tug on the rope to indicate he should climb.

By the time he joined me on my little melted ledge, conditions had improved. The wind had dropped; we could see each other, and hear each other talk. The next pitch turned out to be a fifty foot bulge, curving out above us fringed with short twisted icicles and showing up a greenish colour in the growing daylight. It looked like good firm ice. Jones lit a cigarette, rubbed his hands together and moved off up it at a terrific rate, showering me with chunks of ice. He quickly got up to the difficult overhanging section, beneath which he put in a tubular screw and had a rest. I could just see him if I craned my neck, a dark figure dangling from a bright orange sling, turning gently from side to side like a chrysalis in a hedge. The sound of singing drifted down. 'Come on, Jones, we haven't got all day.' 'Bugger off.' We had begun to enjoy ourselves. I flexed my fingers inside my Dachstein mitts; checked the belays; whistled. When my neck got stiff from looking up at him I rested it by peering out of the gully. No view. 'I'm moving off again,' called Jones. 'This is easy.' Rope ran out through my hands. He stuck both axes in the ice above the overhang, jabbed his front points in. The whole bulge exploded like a bomb and he tumbled backwards into space above me.

He'd been catapulted right out of the gully. His protection screw failed the moment his weight came on it and he hurtled down past me screaming. Thirty feet of rope slid through my hands before I braked his fall; even then the impact pulled my belays like rotten teeth. I fell a hundred feet, mostly through clear air, turning over and over. I was thinking 'Christ, Christ, Christ,' in a sort of mental monotone. Part the way down I landed feet first on something solid, tearing the ligaments in my legs. For an instant or two I was sliding down a slope: I tried to use the one axe remaining to me as a brake, rolling over and digging the pick into the ice: it ripped out. I fetched up at the bottom of the gully in a foetal position, gasping and groaning and choking on the powder snow which had saved me. My legs hurt so much I thought I'd broken both of them. I could see Jones a few feet away. He was kneeling there in a fog of spindrift making a queer coughing noise. I lay there thinking about being crippled. This gave me enough strength to get up and help him.

The ropes had wound themselves round him as he fell. One turn had gone round his neck and was supporting his whole weight. I couldn't get it off him. The rope was snagged on something further up. His tongue was still moving but he was black in the face and he was dead. He would have died anyway in the time it took me to crawl down the hill.

The funeral was awful. It was held a few days later in one of those places trapped between Manchester and the gritstone moors (Mottram, perhaps, or Stalybridge where nothing is clear cut and there is neither town nor country, just a grim industrial muddle of the two), in a huge bleak cemetery on the side of a hill. Jones's open coffin was displayed in the front room of the terrace in which his brother lived. When it was my turn to file past I couldn't look at him. His relatives sat dumbly drinking tea; each time one of them caught my eye, my legs hurt. We always blame the survivor, I suppose. The funeral cars took what seemed like hours to crawl through the grimy wet streets behind the town: and at the burial plot some old aunt of his teetered on the edge of the hole in the wind, so that I had to drop my stick and grab her upper arm to stop her falling in. Under my hand her bones felt as fragile as a bird's. We tried to talk to one another but the wind whipped the words away.

562

Afterwards there was a dismal meal in an assembly room above a baker's. It had wooden panelling, and the lukewarm roast lamb was served by local women wearing black dresses and white aprons. I was alone there. (Some of his other climbing friends had turned up earlier, but left after the ceremony in a group. In any case I didn't know any of them very well.) When they served him, Jones's brother jumped to his feet suddenly and said: 'No meat! I told them, no meat!' All the old women looked at him. He was much older than Jones, a tall thin man with lines of tension round his mouth that might have been vegetarianism or pain; he died himself a few months later, of cancer of the bowel, which just left the women. After they had persuaded him to sit down again he burst into tears. The place catered for functions of all sorts. Someone had left a crude little monkey, a tourist souvenir with limbs plaited from jute and a wooden head, hanging above the serving hatch; and there were faded Christmas decorations up in the ceiling.

I stayed the weekend in a hotel and before I left on the Sunday afternoon went over to the cemetery on my own. I don't know what I expected to find. The road outside it was littered with satin ribbons and florist's cellophane which had blown off the graves during the night. When I wound down the window of the van there was a smell of wet moorland, and I thought of how Jones had begun to climb here as a child, coming home ravenous and sore late at night from the outcrops near Sheffield. In the summer, as he inched out across the big steep gritstone faces, there would have been the sudden dry odour of chalk-dust; the warm rock under the fingertips; a laugh. The grave looked unfinished, and his brother was standing over it with his head bowed. He had heard me limping along the gravel path so I couldn't very well leave. I stood there and bowed my head too, feeling at once intrusive and intruded upon. After a few minutes he blew his nose loudly.

'She didn't come, then. The wife. You'd have thought she'd have made the effort.'

I pictured Maureen, staring out of the window at the ruins of east London, the falling rain.

'I think there was some sort of strain,' I said.

'Strain?'

'Between them.'

He obviously didn't understand me, and I didn't want to explain. I tried to change the subject. 'He'll be missed,' I said.

'He was one of the best rock climbers in the country.'

He looked at me.

'You'll all miss him, will you?' he asked bitterly. 'You should have had more sense than to encourage him.'

Maureen remained at the back of my mind but events kept me away from E3. The shops were doing well: in anticipation of a good summer season I went to New York and California on buying trips, coming away with a line of lightweight artificial fibre sleeping bags and the English agency for a new kind of climbing harness which I thought might compete with the Whillans. When I got back the weather in London was raw and damp, and it was late March. My legs ached intermittently, like a psychic signal. It was quite a sunny afternoon when I got off the eastbound train at Bow.

The mud of the contractors' battlefield had frozen into hard ruts, and only two houses were left standing, saved – if that is the word – by a temporary withdrawal of labour in the building trades. I couldn't remember which one it was. I chose the one without the corrugated iron nailed across its ground floor windows; I waited for someone to come and answer the door. Bulldozers lay all around me hull-down into the earth as if exhausted by a lengthy campaign, a hard winter. Grey smoke drifted between the little beleaguered aluminium huts which dotted the waste. Some attempts had been made to begin building. I could see trenches full of cement, piles of earthenware pipes, and here and there a course of new brick waist high above the ruts. They were fortifications already doomed: a kind of reversed archæological excavation was taking place here, revealing the floor plan of the slums to come. 'Oh, hello, Spider. It's a bit inconvenient just now,' said Maureen.

'I'd ask you in,' she said, 'but I'm waiting for someone.'

She'd had her hair cut short and was wearing clothes I'd never seen her in before. Her fingernails were varnished a curious plum colour, the varnish chipped where she had bitten them. She saw that I didn't quite know how to react. 'I'm a bit smarter than usual!' she said with a nervous laugh. 'Oh, come on up.' Upstairs she lit a cigarette. 'Coffee, Spider?' There was some new furniture in the kitchen – cupboards and a table with clean Formica surfaces, little stools with metal legs; while in the front room the makeshift shelves full of baby clothes had been replaced. In a bookcase with a smoked glass front were a few paperbacks and a dictionary. The flat was somehow unchanged by all this, resisting, like her fingernails, all her attempts to normalize her life. It still smelt of the child, which was squatting on its yellow potty looking vacantly up into the opposite corner of the room and whispering to itself. 'You must have finished now,' Maureen told it.

She looked at me anxiously. 'I would have come to the funeral but I just didn't have any money. They wouldn't give me social security that week.' She stubbed out the cigarette. 'I got a letter from his brother,' she said.

'You can always go up there later. I don't think they understood the situation, that's all.'

'I don't know when I'll have time now,' she said. 'I've got a job.'

It turned out she was the secretary of a local business man. I asked her how she managed with the child. 'It goes to a crèche,' she said vaguely. She was looking out of the window at a car making its way round the perimeter of the battlefield, a big European thing rolling on its suspension as its front wheels dipped into the holes left by the contractors' plant. As if the arrival of this thing, with its overtones of comfort and prosperity, were a signal, a reminder, she turned round suddenly and said: 'Spider, I expected that police car day and night for bloody years. They came in the middle of the night and they weren't sure which of you was dead. They got the names all wrong.' I tried to say something but she rushed on. 'I cried all night, what was left of it. For him, for you, for me, for all of us. What we were at Swansea. Oh, if only he'd just once earned some bloody money!' She started to cry and dab at her eyes. The car outside came to a halt under the window. A man in a leather coat got out and locked it carefully. He looked up, smiling and waving. Maureen went down to let him in.

His name was Bernard. He had a dark suit on, blue or brown, I forget; and neat, longish hair. He used some sort of after shave, and seemed ill at ease. He was decent enough but I gave him no help. 'How's the little chap, then?' he said, picking up the child. 'Oh Christ.' Maureen went to make him some coffee. 'Bernard's a computer programmer,' she called through, as if this might encourage us to talk. 'It's systems analysis, Maureen,' he corrected: 'systems analysis.' They held a whispered conversation in the kitchen and I thought I heard him say, 'But we were going to the *film* theatre. It's *The Exter-*

565

minating Angel. You said you'd love to see *The Exterminating Angel.*' When he came back it was to excuse himself and take the potty to empty in the lavatory. While he was out Maureen said defensively, 'We're getting married, Spider.'

After that we talked about Jones's climbing gear, which I had held on to in case she wanted it.

'I don't think it would be good for her to have all that brought back, do you, Spider?' Bernard appealed (certain perhaps that it never could be). He sipped his coffee which he took without milk. 'While she's still on her own, anyway.' He looked at his watch. 'Is it about time we were moving, Maureen love?' Maureen, though, sat forward and rummaged through the bag I'd brought the stuff in. 'There's a pair of double Alpine boots here,' she said: 'Quite new. Could you sell them in one of the shops, Spider?' Bernard looked irritated. 'I don't think we're that badly off, Maureen,' he said. He laughed. 'Could you, Spider?' Maureen said. I told her that I'd try. (I sent her the money for them a couple of months later, but it can't have been forwarded from Bow because I've never had an answer.) There was an awkward pause. They invited me to the wedding, which was to be in May. 'I don't think I can make that,' I said. 'I have to go to America on a buying trip. A range of sleeping bags I'm interested in.' The child crawled round the floor breathing heavily. 'Up the hill and *down* the hill.' As I got up to go it was trying to climb the side of the bookcase, its little feet slipping off the shiny new melamine.

Bernard saw me to the door of the flat. 'I hope I can make her happy,' he said, and thanked me for coming. Maureen, I realized, had already said goodbye.

It was getting dark as I went down the stairs. The landing windows showed a waste land; fires. Further down I met the West Indian girl Tansy. She was wearing Maureen's little silver monkey and chain. They glittered against her skin in the brownish gloom. She hadn't bothered to have the monkey repaired, and the chain was still twisted round its neck. Maureen must have given them to her, I suppose.

'Cheerio,' she said; and smiled.

andrew j. offutt
Symbiote

*Andrew J. Offutt has lived most of his life in a place called
Funny Farm in Kentucky. The first time I met andy (as he
likes to be printed) at the World Fantasy Convention in 1975,
he asked me to cut about 4,000 words from a 15,000 word
story, and it must say something for his charm that I agreed,
to the benefit of the story. (For much more about him, his
equally charming wife Jodie, and their daughter Scotty, not to
mention a splendid tale woven around them, see Harlan
Ellison's anthology* Again, Dangerous Visions.) *andy has
published over twenty novels that he admits to (including* The
Undying Wizard, Ardor on Aros, Conan the Mercenary, The
Iron Lords, Sword of the Gael), *dozens of short stories, and
erotica under a pseudonym which friendship prevents me from
revealing. He edits the* Swords Against Darkness *anthologies.*

*Nothing else in his career prepares one for the following
piece of unmitigated nastiness, but when I read it I received
another kind of shock: in several ways it was unnervingly
similar to 'The Depths', the story I had written for this book.
It wasn't the first time I'd experienced this kind of thing – once
I wrote, scene for scene, a Henry Kuttner story which I'd never
read – but I agonized for months over including 'The Depths',
until I wrote 'The Fit' (which appears in* New Terrors One)
*and my wife Jenny suggested that was an ideal story for this
anthology. Of course none of us knows where story ideas come
from, but 'Symbiote' has a dismaying suggestion to make.*

It had talent and power, the parasite Philip had named Joe.

The power, for one thing, to control him, totally. The power,
for another, to 'cloud men's minds' (for that was the way Philip,
remembering *The Shadow* of the old days of radio, thought of
it). The clouding of men's minds was handy and indeed necessary to Joe's purposes. It protected Philip from witnesses and
police and the like. It covered his tracks. Made him not in-

visible or invincible, but unlikely to be discovered. That he was neither discovered nor suspected was necessary to the lives of both Philip and the parasite living on him, with him. Directing him. The police would have taken Philip's life. That would have inconvenienced the parasite Joe, for he was now dependent, he told Philip, on Philip's life.

Thus, he explained, they lived in symbiosis.

Symbiosis. A biological name for a mutual-trade agreement. An interdependence. True exchange and true justice: tit for tat, value for value. For Joe could live only as a parasite. He had no arms, no legs, no eyes. (Or mouth, or voice either; he spoke in Philip's *mind*, where he lived.) Philip was necessary to his existence. And at little cost; at no cost, really, since Philip profited so greatly. (Unless you insist on being moralistic and thus incur the scorn of a vastly superior life-form, Joe.)

Joe lived on emotions. More specifically, mental emanations of a violent nature.

Humankind, Joe had explained to Philip after he had chosen him and set up housekeeping somewhere in the neighbourhood of his Central Control, had long ago discovered that the human brain was, in a manner of speaking, electrical. Its activities generated recordable electric 'current'. This was food to Joe. And Joe was a glutton. He preferred engorgement on the richest of foods to a steady but less exciting diet of mental hamburgers. He preferred the current, the emotions, the excitement generated in Philip's mind by criminal acts. Violence.

Just having Philip break laws, Joe explained, was lovely: mental steak. This was because engaging in prohibited activities excited humans, thus generating strong mental currents. (A lie detector indicates this, in another way, though it is by Joe's standards an incredibly crude device.)

After two robberies and an arson, Joe tried a (briefly) premeditated murder.

It was far nicer.

Philip was greatly excited, and Joe was dizzy with delight as they approached the house. Joe told Philip there'd be no outcries to betray them; he'd see to that. Should the intended victim be on the point of endangering Philip – and thus Joe – he'd see to that, too.

The man did not make an outcry. Nor did he endanger Philip/Joe's life.

Heart slamming, adrenal glands working at capacity, Philip

went silently through the little house and found his victim. He was right where Joe had said he'd be. (Joe had talent, and power.) The old man stared with enormous, terror-filled eyes. His mouth worked desperately and his Adam's apple bobbed like a fisherman's cork. No sound emerged, though, for Joe had hold of a nerve somewhere between the man's larynx and his brain.

Philip stabbed him thirteen times and staggered at the explosive reaction in his head. He returned to his apartment – with Joe clouding minds along the way – and slept for thirty hours. Joe was sated, and when Joe was sated he lay up and slept like a smug jungle cat with blood on its whiskers. And when Joe slept, Philip slept. Joe was sorry, but it was necessary. Once Joe had gone to sleep and aroused to find his host on the way to give himself up at the police station. Joe turned him around and directed his feet home and punished him by not letting him eat or drink for a day and a half.

After that Joe turned Philip off when he – Joe – slept.

You mustn't, you see, be too hard on Philip in your thinking. Once Joe had moved in, Philip really wasn't Philip any more.

After killing the old man and sleeping thirty hours, Philip awoke ravenous and he and Joe discussed the adventure, reliving it. Thus Joe fed again. He made it last three weeks.

During those three weeks Philip wrote nine short stories and retyped them for submission. (Joe helped, of course, or rather dictated; each story was his idea, as were the plot and the wording. Joe couldn't be bothered with Philip's having to spend a large part of each day working to earn money. So they wrote the stories.) Joe planned them to sell, and they did. (Joe had talent, and power.) Two sold to the highest-paying magazine in the nation and two more to the second highest. Each editor but one mentioned that she or he would look favourably upon more. submissions from Joe Philips.

After collecting the nine cheques, Philip gave up the post office box he had rented as Joe Philips. He banked the money so that he had collateral, and he and Joe bought a house, which was more convenient and private than an apartment. They also traded Philip's car on a station wagon and made some adjustments.

By that time Philip's recounting of the murder had become a tedious, repetitive hash, and Joe felt the need for more steak.

569

This time it was a woman, about thirty-five, who had been divorced exactly three weeks. (The murders were in the papers, of course, and investigated. But there is so much crime, so much murder in Los Angeles, that one more killing now and then was far from being a *cause célèbre*.) (Besides, Joe clouded men's minds, and there were no clues.)

After that second killing – Joe had Philip strangle her first, then stab her a few times, experimenting with various techniques – Philip and Joe exchanged observations, which is only normal and fair in symbiosis.

'I notice that murder is the source of your greatest excitement,' the symbiote Joe said. Or whispered, or thought.

'Of course,' Philip said. (He usually spoke, at first.)

'And this time you were more excited than before.'

'Yes.'

'Because this one was female.'

'Of course,' Philip said, remembering and thus giving Joe a nice lunch. (He had dessert when they read the papers, particularly one reporter's picturesque line, 'The young woman lay huddled on a carpet which appeared to have been painted with the same scarlet brush with which her nude body had been smeared.')

'Thus,' Joe said, 'the sensible, logical course is for us to forget other activities and concentrate on murder. Specifically, females.'

'Sensible,' Philip said, and the thoughts that rushed through his brain provided Joe with a nice snack. 'By the way, I think we'd be smart to leave some clues or something. I mean, if we're going to go on with this, some of the murders had better be solved.'

Joe explored Philip's mind and saw why this was true. 'Very clever, Philip! We'll do that. Now though, let's write. We need plenty of money. You have to keep your strength up.'

'Yes,' Philip said, 'and we really should buy insurance on the house.'

During the next three weeks Philip went through a great deal of paper and two all-black typewriter ribbons of the first quality. He also developed some trouble in his lower spine. Joe found it, and fixed it. The novel concerned a secret agent and government officials talking importantly and beautiful women and sex and of course one of the women was tortured to make her talk and the whole world was menaced; Joe wrote (or dictated) only material designed to sell, and sell well. Joe was pleased with Philip's delightful emotional response during the writing of the two torture scenes and the slow hanging of a government tax official. The symbiote snacked.

'Killing another human is the highest crime,' Joe observed. 'And humans like to kill. So killing is the most exciting and thus satisfying crime to me. Men are ruled by reproductive urges, and so killing a female is even more exciting and therefore more satisfying. Men like to torture, too. Mostly women. You know that, from Freud and Havelock Ellis and Krafft-Ebing. Those who make movies certainly know it, too.

'So – in future we will kill females, and slowly.'

Somewhere, way back in a dusty and dark corner of his mind, Philip was horrified. Joe noticed, but he wasn't disturbed. Joe was in control.

They were astonished when the novel returned from the editor – male, unusually – for the publisher they had chosen. He evinced unhappiness with what he called its 'sadism' but indicated he would be happy to publish it, with a few changes. Joe laughed in Philip's mind.

' "Disturbed at the book's sadism", is he? He means by what he calls sadism – but he doesn't know what that means. The innate cruelty of humans has nothing to do with the psychopathological term "sadism". He also doesn't know himself, like most humans. The scenes excited him, Philip, be sure of that. And that is exactly why he sent it back! He thinks it's wicked because he feels guilty at being sexually excited. You humans really are ludicrous lifeforms.'

'Shall we change it?' Philip asked.

'Of course not.'

They made a market study. They compiled a list of three publishers and mailed the novel to the first. She sent them a contract and later some money called an advance – to Joe Philips, Box 21372 – and assured them that royalties would be forthcoming. During the time thus consumed they wrote another story and an article and sold them to two magazines for several thousand dollars; Joe chose to write only for the best-paying publications. They also killed a twelve-year-old girl by stabbing and Joe did some other things so that her father would be accused. (He was, and convicted too, although that was much later.)

'The older female excited you more than the younger,' Joe

571

said grumpily. 'What if she had been much older?' Before Philip could reply, Joe had the answer from his mind. 'I see. Human reproductive urges again. Let's look at some magazines.' For Joe was not, after all, infallible. Philip remarked that, somewhere in a dusty and dark corner of his mind. Joe noticed, but he was not disturbed. Joe had talent, and power.

Joe found that the pictures in fashion magazines excited Philip very little, even when Joe prompted thoughts of torture and death. Old women too, and just-nubile or pre-nubile ones were quickly ruled out. They narrowed the researches. Joe considered it strange that Philip preferred pictures of women wearing some clothing, rather than totally nude ones. They refined the researches.

Joe learned that he would dine best when Philip's victim was a full-haired young woman, preferably with clearly defined hips and sitting and walking apparati. Also, he discovered with a puzzlement he admitted, the more pronounced the female's baby-feeding apparatus, the more delightful would be his repast.

They made some purchases and remodelled the house, particularly the basement. Philip found carpentry as easy as writing, with Joe's help. He had long ago been shown that he was capable of tremendous activity and exertion for long periods of time, although Joe was forced to let him sleep – totally relaxed, naturally, and very deeply – for long periods afterwards.

'The body is the temple of the mind,' Joe said once, 'and must be well looked after. Trust in me.'

Philip finished the remodelling job and bought the cameras and recording equipment Joe suggested. (Joe did not give orders. Joe suggested, pretty much on a 'Let's . . .' or 'Suppose we . . .' basis.)

The young woman was a dancer, if you're not particular about terminology. An ecdysiast, if you cherish a fondness for fancy-Greeky words. A stripper. Beautiful, of course. That is standard in LA, which leaves the tired ones and the homely ones to Chicago and Cincinnati and the rest of the country. Los Angeles teems with beautiful women and girls, most of them consummately shapely and possessing pronounced baby-feeding apparati (not that they'd dream of using them for that purpose). They flock in by the bus load, these beautiful girls and young women from all over the country, attracted by Movieland as butterflies are by flowers – or as lemmings are, by the sea. Naturally they are not all Discovered, and even that tiny fraction that does Make It must do something for rent – sometimes for months, oftener for years, frequently for keeps.

They model, dressed and undressed.

They do other things.

It was not unusual, then, that the stripper Joe and Philip found was a real winner. She danced. Danced and undressed. In that order. When first they saw her she wore an ankle-length dress of something black and shiny-slinky, with long side slits. A few minutes later it was gold lamé underwear – that was her *schtick*, the gold metallic cloth, and the mass of black hair rippling to her waist. Next it was sparkly gold pasties and an elastic string equipped with a couple of sparkly gold triangles.

Joe took note of Philip's excitement – merely an *hors d'oeuvre* – and noted that it heightened when the pasties departed their precarious perches. Joe asked, 'Will she do?'

'Perfectly,' Philip said. Something stirred in that dark and dusty corner of his mind, but neither he nor Joe took notice.

Not so strangely, if you know anything about most strippers and about Los Angeles, the young woman left alone when the place closed. (According to the papers a few days later, she probably had some studying to do. She was a Junior in University.) She did not study that night. The plan was to observe her habits, follow her, make a plan. Instead, a fine opportunity presented itself along the way and she became the first passenger, not counting Joe, in Philip's new station wagon. She became his – their – first houseguest.

Philip did not want her totally voiceless, so Joe obligingly paralysed the necessary nerve or nerves only partially, giving her what approximated a mild case of laryngitis. She could still plead. Quietly.

Philip found that there was more work involved than he'd expected in wrestling the unconscious guest to the basement and up against the wall where he had bolted the new leather straps. He held her sagging body with one arm while with the other he buckled her wrist. Then he secured her other wrist. She hung against the stone wall with her knees bent and her head hanging so that all that hair floated down like a rippling blue-black waterfall.

Philip shot some footage with the movie camera, then took several photographs from several angles.

'Would you like to begin,' Joe asked, 'or wait for her to become conscious?'

573

As Philip started to admit his impatience, the prisoner stirred and moaned a little. She moved her head and Philip went to her. She tried to scream, found that she could not, and whimpered. He had made artistic use of her hair in his pictures and she could barely see him, if at all, through the black curtain of it.

Erect, she stood shivering against the wall. The gooseflesh of fear and chill marked her skin, and Philip frowned angrily at the tiny eruptions. Gazing at her, he decided to fix two belts together and bolt a ring of some sort into the wall, high up. That way he'd be able to pull a guest's arms straight up and perhaps, were she short enough, force her to balance on tiptoe. It would display her to better advantage, be more interesting, and please his aesthetic sense.

Next time. Not this guest. The next one.

She pleaded. Pleaded and winced and tried to scream (in vain; Joe had both talent and power). She pled with him in the most piteous little voice Philip had ever heard. It gave him a tremendous, surging feeling of power. (Joe ingested it happily.) She pled and she bled.

He used a box cutter. It is a simple device, about the size of a pocket comb and only a little thicker. Stockboys in grocery stores insert a single-edged razor blade in one and use it quickly and usually skilfully to slice the tops of packing cases. It is extremely sharp, of course, this razor blade with a handle, and sometimes it slips and perhaps you find a slashed label or box on the shelf. Usually, though, the grocer saves the slashed package for the salesman representing the manufacturer of that product.

It opened human flesh, Philip found, with equal facility, leaving a slender little line that looked as if it had been etched with a pencil. A red pencil.

Joe supped with gusto.

It was an orgiastic meal he enjoyed, in an orgy of blood that lasted through the night and the next day and most of the following night. Then Joe, completely stuffed, fell into a sated sleep. Philip's sleep was that of exhaustion. Their guest's was that last long one.

Naturally they did that again, quite soon, with a few aesthtic refinements.

After several months and several young women Philip noticed that Joe's appetite was increasing.

574

'Perhaps we should move to another city,' Philip said, as they drove home after leaving most of the eleventh victim in a fruit truck whose driver had parked to take a nap. 'New York's bigger. That would be safer.'

'Why?' Joe asked, in that lazy, sated way. 'I'm not worried.'

So they stayed in Los Angeles, and wrote some more stories and drowned a nightclub hostess in the bathtub, slowly. Philip found her irresistible.

'That was interesting, Philip. Your reproductive methods are crude, but they certainly do excite you nicely! You should have done that with all of them.'

'How do you reproduce, Joe?' Philip asked, rather embarrassed.

'Impossible to describe so you can understand,' Joe said. 'But not so exciting. Parthenogenetic.'

A few days later, reading about the nightclub hostess in the paper, Philip asked, 'Joe: how can you say you're a symbiote, rather than a parasite? You – you force me to do these monstrous things, so you can . . . eat. But symbiosis means *mutual* benefit. In god's name – what's *my* benefit?'

'In god's name? Nonsense,' said the symbiote. 'In Man's name! For all that Man has achieved he has thanked god; for all the evil men have done they blame "human weakness". Unfortunately that leaves guilt. It is not truly satisfactory, the man-god relationship, since god is not visible and man cannot be sure that god accepts the blame. I don't force you, Philip. I *let* you. I am your excuse. I am here. You know it is my fault. I accept the blame and the guilt. You are free of it, human – while you do what you as a man truly want to do.'

'You are . . . god,' Philip said.

'Of course. Now think about the hostess again.'

A week later Joe was hungry again and Philip tried to dissuade him and Joe punished him by making Philip hit his thumb with a hammer. Thus Joe learned something new. It was a lovely banquet. And so simple! So little bother; no travelling, no witness minds to cloud. Joe dined at home, and thought about it. He put Philip to sleep and thought about it a great deal.

Then he woke Philip and made him cut off one of his fingers.

When the two medical examiners received the body, Robert groaned. Paul sighed. The creature the papers had dubbed the

575

LA Slicer had been at work again, and had branched out. And only two weeks after that hostess; the killings had become steadily more frequent. Now it was a man. This one was minus all his toes and fingers save the thumb and index finger of his right hand. His left leg had been sawed half through. He was a mess.

'Shock,' Robert said, bending over Philip's body. 'Or loss of blood. What think, Paul?'

Paul also bent. 'God. Looks that way, yes. It's up to us to—'

He jerked at a sudden sharp pain in his head. It was gone at once. He saw Robert jerk and clap a hand to his head.

'Hello, Paul,' a little brainvoice said. 'My name is Joe. I'm taking over.'

'Hello, Robert,' a little mindvoice said. 'My name is Joe Junior. I'm taking over.'

That was several years ago.

Be careful.

Charles L. Grant

Across the water to Skye

*Charles L. Grant was born in 1942. Before he made the leap
into full-time writing several years ago, he taught for nine years
in New Jersey public secondary schools. His photographs
generally show him gazing mournfully through thin-framed
spectacles. I met him first on a panel in Providence, at the
World Fantasy Convention in 1975, where I was afraid of him
because he was an officer of the Science Fiction Writers of
America and he (he admitted a year later when we were on a
panel in New York) was afraid of me, though I can't imagine
why: a gentler, more saintly person never walked the earth.
Presumably we stay in this business so that we can scare each
other.*

His books include collections (Tales from the Nightside,
Nightmare Seasons), *and novels:* The Soft Whisper of the
Dead, The Nestling, Night Songs. *He has won both World
Fantasy and Nebula Awards. Beyond the evocative titles you
will often find stories as poignant as they are chilling. Certainly
this is, and I believe it is his strangest story.*

Labor Day; and so it is quite literally for some. But for others it
marks the perennial end of a short-lived world, a frightening
one bordered by bungalows and beaches fast deserted by back-
pedalling lemmings; a Lazarus world of wood and plastic
fashioned into brightly tinted dreams from the stuffing of midnight nightmares. When the clown at the Fun House strangles
its old woman's laugh, the firefly machines whirr to a dying,
and life scuttles inland to lick at summer sun wounds.

For what it's worth, this is the substance of my mood as I
lean against the peeling metal railing that separates the boardwalk strollers from the short drop to the sand. Of course, I do

577

not deny I haven't felt regret myself when vacation ended. I hate being forced to return the sea/salt air to the nightwind, replacing it with the antiseptic shroud of the clinic. Not that I don't enjoy playing at healing, but I always feel somewhat older when I leave the lights behind.

And that regret is still there, but this time cloaked with a difference: I'm not going back. And, sadly, neither are the faces I see passing me by.

Which brings me to the beginning, to Danny sweet Danny and old man Ted; and also to a little-known riddle-rhyme my grandmother carried with her from the misted mountains she could see from the Isle of Skye.

> *Four old men sitting in a row*
> *Waiting for the black bird to take*
>   *them in tow . . .*

Though I've tried to train myself not to count, not to count on the past, it must have been six or seven years ago that I finally came back to this what they used to call honky-tonk seaside resort. I had been casting for a way to exorcise a double memory: of a wife who hiked with me through the Appalachians every summer, and one day awakening to the enervation of a withering carcinoma; and of a son without a name who slid unborn into a surgeon's bloody hands. Twice in eleven months I had been clubbed to my knees, and only my Highland stubbornness made me stand up again. For balm the mountains were useless, and I even moved my bed so I could not see them from the window. Thus, a return to the sea. I refuse even now, however, to consider facile symbolism; it was, simply, a place where my wife and son had not been.

I wandered the boardwalk, staring at the faces of the children who shrieked the rides faster. Munching on cotton candy, candy apples, apple cider somehow frozen on a stick. I was braced for bitterness and an insane jealousy of the men who escorted their families from stand to stand and lugged the huge stuffed toys and carried the squalling babies. But there was nothing, nothing at all, and I found myself intently studying the faces, the hands, the late night shuffling of little girls' feet. I didn't know what I was looking for, and so found nothing. Not that year, anyway.

Except, of course, for Danny and Ted.

There is a carousel – you know the kind – that hasn't been moved or altered since I was a kid carrying dripping ice cream and exercising fat lungs. All manner of animals, some down-right scarifying, others safe and lovely to hold. My favourite was, is, the llama: black, soft, whirling in the middle as if the rest of the universe did not exist. On the lion I got dizzy; on the llama I had dreams.

And beyond this spinning place that first time back, at the far end of the amusement area, was a freshly painted stand. Behind the counter an old man with an untrimmed black beard and battered yachtsman's cap sat on a stool and called hoarsely to the children to try out their luck. Flaccid and slick balloons were taped to a bewilderingly bright wall, and a hidden wheel spun lights across the playing area, turning concentration to frustrated tears. The darts were poorly balanced and dull, fraudulent and impotent, and everyone knew it and no one cared. The thrill was in beating the old man at his own game.

And if the wheezing challenge of the aged shill wasn't sufficient unto the suckers thereof, there was the young girl in the loose black shift with sunset red hair and forest green eyes. She laughed when the old man scowled, enticed when he cajoled, while the bank sack on the floor filled with sticky quarters.

I found them around eleven on Sunday. No one else was around and damned if my grin didn't turn to a self-conscious grimace when I allowed myself to part with a coin and throw a few misses. The girl laughed and handed me three more. I missed again. The old man lit a cigarette, leaned back and tapped the counter with a knobbed cane while I managed to pass four dollars, twelve quarters into his cloth strongbox.

'Hey, if I keep this stuff up,' I said finally, 'I won't have enough money to get me home.'

'When are you leaving,' she said.

'Tomorrow. Early. I like to pretend I can beat the Labor Day rush.'

'Next year,' she said, and with a quick look at the old man handed me a small doll from the far corner of the ledge holding the prizes. 'Start on your first night down, and maybe you'll make it by the time you leave.'

Annoyed because I felt a blush warming my collar, I ducked my head in a hasty farewell and fairly ran back to the car. It had been a long time since I'd felt so schoolboy foolish, and I remember trying to hide that doll until I was behind the wheel and could look at it in the green dashboard glow. She was no more than two hands long, with a plastic hula skirt and a drab lei painted over her breasts. Her hair was stiff and incongruously blonde, and her face – I squinted, raised it close to my eyes and turned on the dome light. Staring. Then shrugging. It was a kewpie doll like uncountable others, but it was several uncomfortable hours before I was able to shake off the feeling that I'd seen that look a hundred times before.

I doctored, then, from fall to August, but I never forgot that boardwalk night. For a while I kept my prize on the desk, thinking it would be a clever distraction for the children. Unfortunately, they hated it, and their parents told me in no uncertain terms that they thought it highly inappropriate considering the surorundings. So I surrendered and dropped it into a drawer, forgotten until one afternoon . . . I was examining yet another in an oddly endless parade of housewives who complained of chronic listlessness and an inability to latch on to outside interests.

'You need something to pep you up, Mrs Avaloni.'

'Yes, Doctor.'

'Why don't you get your mister to treat you to a steak dinner and a night on the town?'

'Yes, Doctor.'

I tried not to sigh.

'All right, Mrs Avaloni, let's have a look at those . . .'

I fumbled, pushing the examining stool back and hastily excused myself. In the corridor I grabbed one of my colleagues and got him to take over for me. Then I practically ran into the bathroom to hide.

Her eyes. Blank. The colour washed out as if soaked in salt water. Following my finger and the light well enough, but with all the animation of a still photograph.

I gripped the edge of the sink and stared at the reflection in the oval mirror, nodding even before I had thought the question: it was the same expression I'd seen on the kewpie doll, and the seaside faces.

Immediately, I launched into the tried and true pull-yourself-together-Simon routine. I dredged out coincidence. I blamed it all on a grief that continued to haunt me occasionally. I blamed it on stress, strain, the fantasies of the dart game girl that replaced the faces on my television screen.

And then I did some checking.

During the embryo days of the Cold War, tranquillizers became more than a fad – they were a national disease. Now, for a reason I wasn't quite yet ready to label, there was an abnormally high number of stimulant prescriptions, and in our clinic alone the youngest recipient was nine years old.

I did some asking and some listening.

'It's the Commies,' the drug salesman said as he took the order for our resident pharmacist. 'Stupid parents worried about the Bomb again, and the kids are worrying about schools and jobs, and the little kids are worrying about being big kids – have you ever seen the courses they make grammar school kids take nowadays? Hell, they might as well be in college. It ain't no fun being little any more, I guess. I'll say one thing, Simon, that doesn't make it too bad: it's sure been great for business.'

'Technology, you know?' my bartender confided as he pointed with a towel at the crowded lounge, the crowded tables. 'I mean, you got buttons for this and buttons for that, and what the hell kind of a life can you expect when you got nothing to do but push stupid buttons? Technology. Like television, for instance. Rots your brain. Take another drink, Doc, and take my advice: find yourself a dumb woman who don't ever read the papers and get yourself laid. It's the only thing you don't need a button for any more.'

I went to bed early every night because there was nothing to do.

> Four old men sitting on the croft
> Waiting for the raven to take them
> aloft . . .

The few years passed with parade-ground precision, and at least once a week in August I drove to the boardwalk and played with dull darts. I hadn't forgotten what I was looking for, but the urgency of those first few weeks somehow dulled into the background.

My mistake.

Generally, I couldn't stand the crowds that swallowed the public beaches. I spent most of my free summer days sitting on the porch of my ocean front cottage sleeping, reading, letting the breakers suck out the terrors of the city and the sick. I did meet a few women, I did wrinkle a few sheets a bit now and then, but it became more and more a mechanical thing and my middle-aged ego refused to settle all the blame

581

on me. So my nights, then, from sunset to twelve, passed as I crunched through a candy apple and shot down the hours with Ted.

Ted. The owner of two dozen amusement stands up and down the Jersey and Florida coasts. He drifted with the seasons, bagging the tourists and filling his bank account against the day, he said, when apples would once again be hawked on the corners. Danny, his niece, laughed at his preaching economics but she drifted with him, and I never found the nerve to provide her with an anchor.

Until today. Labor Day.

Just three afternoons ago a patient of mine died of heart failure: he was seventeen years old. Worse, a cousin in a tightly meshed clan. The night before, last night, I asked Danny for her company at the funeral.

'Why?'

'To tell you the truth, I don't want to be there alone. A Celtic funeral isn't what it used to be, and I'll need an excuse to leave early without offending anyone.'

To my surprise she accepted, and we arrived at the cemetery just before the first of the family.

It was grey, smelling of autumn, and a ground fog sneaked around the tombstones and climbed the dark trunks of the farthest trees. My cousins had kept close to the old ways, and as the coffin was lifted to rest on the straps that would eventually lower it into the ground, a piper began playing behind us. He was standing at the crest of a low hill, and when I turned I could only see his silhouette against the weaving clouds. A wind plucked at his kilt and dark tartan plaid, and carried over the words of the minister the mourning cry of 'The Flowers of the Forest'.

I looked to the others; I was the only one weeping. Danny pressed close to me and I put an arm around her shoulders. And still the piper called, and for a moment I could not remember who he was playing down.

As we drove back to the shore afterwards, Danny suddenly asked me why I'd never invited her out to dinner, to a picnic, for a drink at the orangeade stand. I was still hearing the music, still wondering who had died, but she insisted on an answer.

'Well, consider, m'dear,' I said finally. 'I, yours quite truly, am pushing so hard at forty-five that it's practically falling down. You, on the other hand, are not even thirty.' Looking thirty-five, but I kept my mouth shut.

'Is that all?' she said. 'I thought it was your wife.'

'No,' I said. 'No, Danny, the piper played her down a long time ago. It's over in some ways, many ways...'

'Then please take me out, Simon, before it's too late.'

I frowned. 'Too late? For what, for crying out loud? Are you moving someplace permanent for a change? Don't tell me your uncle is finally giving up his wicked worldly ways.' Unexpectedly, I was in a mild panic and babbled a bit more without giving her a chance to answer.

The traffic slowed, then, and I started the driver's litany of curses as we crawled behind the rubberneckers past the aftermath of a three-car collision. There was glittering glass on the highway, and standing by an ambulance were four small children. They were holding hands and listening intently to a patrolman kneeling in front of them.

'Look at that,' I said sadly as we picked up speed. 'They look like old men standing there.'

Danny snapped at me: 'Why did you say that?'

I was puzzled and risked a stare. Her face was pale, her hair disturbingly faded. 'I don't know,' I said. 'They just looked like that to me.'

In spite of my wit and wisdom, and my growing anger, she didn't say another word until I'd dropped her off at the boardwalk. Then she told me curtly to be at the stand after dark. I nodded and wrenched the car back on to the road, a defensive gesture to the sudden irritating mystery I thought she'd sprung on me. I hated things like that, and people who spoke in cryptic epigrams with supposedly meaningful glances only made me shed my patience. It all smacked of play-acting in an empty theatre and, especially on the heels of the funeral, an impotent way to jar me back to the land of the living.

Ten minutes later I was at my position on the porch, matching the retreating tide with the level of a pitcher filled with Southern Comfort laced with tea. Luckily this particular stretch of coastline was private, and I was spared the spectacle of sun oil gleaming off scorched bodies. Instead, I watched the waves pull away from me and wondered what the hell I'd said to make Danny draw off like that. I knew the piper had startled her, but it's a sadly beautiful thing to hear nevertheless and, coupled with what I'd been seeing lately, decidedly apropos.

I drank. Became maudlin. Dozed and dreamt: of little children with long grey hair dancing feebly beneath the image of a gigantic raven. Awoke and stared at the cloud scudding under the sun. Dozed, and the raven puffed its feathers until the entire scene hazed in shadow.

And the rhyme. That God damned rhyme!

Again I was awake, this time chilled in defiance of the sun, and gasping for air. The eyes of the raven had turned wine red, and swimming within were the faces of the world.

> *Along came the raven,*
> *Along came the bird . . .*

Simon, I thought, either you're drunk or in definite need of professional assistance.

I hurried inside, showered, dressed, decided to jog the two miles to the boardwalk. I used the wet skirt of sand as my track and spent the time recalling games I no longer saw: jumping over the snake-hiss foam, digging furiously for sandcrabs, taking imaginary potshots at wheeling gulls. The children were still there, but subdued. I also checked out a few bathing suits and the flesh they didn't cover to test my erotic stimulus level, and amazed myself by wondering why I was stalling in finding another mate.

Danny?

I refused to answer myself.

After a quick bite to eat at a pizza joint, I hurried to the dart stand. Ted saw me pushing through the crowd and lifted the counter flap to join me. Before I could pass a word to Danny, he took my arm and guided me away from the park to a bench that overlooked a slick brown jetty.

'Danny said the funeral was interesting.' He scratched at his beard, then lighted a cigar butt he'd had in his pocket. 'She also said something about an accident.'

'Hey, look, Ted, would you mind telling me if I've offended Danny?' I reviewed our conversation for him. 'And if I did hurt her somehow, why did I have to come tonight?'

He rubbed the side of his nose, crushed out the cigar with the tip of his cane. Small groups of people were passing us quickly as if they'd just realized the post-dinner sun wasn't going to do them any good. As one family huffed up the ramp not far from us, Ted pointed with his chin. 'Would you say those folks are typical?'

Trying not to stare at them, I noted the towels and the toys, the umbrella, sandals, the futile swiping at sand clinging like barnacles to ankles and calves. Books, magazines, a radio and battered tennis ball. I thought I was supposed to see through the trivial to the profound, but I saw nothing out of the ordinary, and said so.

Ted nodded. 'Precisely. Ordinary is the word. Right down to the premature bags under all their eyes.'

'So?'

'Simon, there's no sense my being as fancy as you can be. I've been watching for years now. Seen them here, seen them in Florida, and all up the West Coast. Simon, tell me if I'm wrong, but I think they're dying.'

I waited until he looked at me. 'Okay. Do you know those people or something?'

'Never saw those particular ones in my life.'

Another damned mystery. 'Sorry, Ted, but how can you say something like that if you don't even know who they are?'

'Oh, it's not just them, Simon. It's all of them,' and he covered the beach with a wave of his arm. He began lecturing even as I searched for labels from my premed psych courses, and damned if I didn't listen, caught myself nodding at figures he quoted. And as though I'd been struck in the face with a Catherine Wheel, my own half-hidden gropings meshed and blinded me.

And it was insane.

Of course it was.

In spite of the legends (and I don't even know how Ted had heard about them): stories in the Highlands of the earliest clans. Heroic men, fighting women, the prototypes for Rob Roy and the Black Douglas. And the First, with no name, known only as the Father Clan, the clan that had gone on too long, produced too many children and hunted and farmed for too many centuries. It's said that one night they vanished from the mainland, leaving behind only a hollow cairn in the keeping of a quartet of old men, all ex-chieftains. Speaking as one, reedy and faint in the Highland winter, they chanted the story of the Clan's greatest fear, and how it had sensed their longing and had come to relieve their burden, take them from the world.

Across the water to Skye. With the piper keening 'The Flowers of the Forest'.

And what do you think was the sound they heard?

'Simon, you're an educated man. You must have read or

585

heard about dozens of civilizations that tried to hang on to that one extra moment, that tried to see one more sunset. Didn't you ever wonder about the historians and the smoke screens they set up to answer the unanswerable? To cover their confusion over the Atlanteans—'

'Hold it, Ted.' I stood and backed away from him. 'You've been playing that dart game too long. You want my professional medical opinion? Okay. I think you've spent too many years behind that counter. You watch all those folks playing so hard at resting and you're bitter because you have to work to help them along. You like to think you're an observer of the passing scene and all that crap, but in your own way, Ted, you're just as jaded as Dorian Gray.'

'Is that your considered judgement, Doctor?' He didn't move, didn't look up. His shoulders lost their illusion of breadth, his arms suddenly became frail. And as the sun dripped shadows on to the low dunes, he sighed.

'Danny tried to warn you when she gave you that doll. She thought you'd understand and help try to stop it.'

'Danny can take care of herself,' I said angrily. 'She's certainly old enough.'

'Danny,' the old man said, 'is seventeen.'

I was like a man trapped in a hall of broken mirrors, believing I saw the truth every time I turned around.

Seventeen. Like my cold in the grave cousin.

I walked away quickly, afraid I would catch the plague of his soul, dodged through the last day of vacation crowds that had become moths teasing the bulbs of coloured lights. I saw the frantic looks in parents' faces, dragging children from attraction to attraction; one last spin, one last turn, one last wheel to gain a fortune. Feet scuffling, hands clapping, laughter rising and flirting with hysteria.

As if they knew something I did not.

But it just isn't possible, I thought, that a whole race, an entire planet, would want to be carried away from the reality it had created, the only life it had known.

I passed the darts and Danny waved. She was trying to call something over the carousel music, but I heard nothing. I kept on moving, looking back only once to see her staring after me, and as though I were peering through a telescope I saw her eyes . . . the kewpie doll's . . . Avaloni's . . . the funeral . . .

I ducked into the first bar I saw and began ordering beer.

There were dancers in cages, their gyrations less sexual than resigned, their costumes less provocative than functional. The music was loud, senseless, and soon enough I pushed off my stool and stumbled back to the boardwalk.

There were four children standing silently beside an over-turned stroller, and I almost screamed.

Perhaps I did, because several people turned to look at me.

I hurried away, hunched against the arrows of their stares, and began wandering ...

... and I wander even now. The boardwalk is deserted and my footsteps compete with the breakers to deafen me. I stand in front of the Fun House and watch the black in the giant clown's mouth twist into things that push me on; I wait at the window of the bar trying to see the ghosts of the dancers who could not now or ever arouse me; I reach out to caress the shuttered dart game stand, wincing at a splinter and in the pain evoking the talisman of Danny's smile. I don't even know when she and Ted left, but I do know they're running, speeding as fast as they can away from the sea. They wanted to help me, get me to play Paul Revere and warn the others. And God damn, but I failed them.

I may be old, Father William once said, but I'll be damned if I'm going to give in just when I'm starting to have fun.

I laugh at the notion that I can suddenly transform myself into a Lochinvar, subside to giggles when I realize the world will collapse like the slow motion fall of an empty circus tent unless I try ... something.

I must be wild, drunk, bordering on the psychotic ... but it stands there now, waiting to be my steed in the joust yet to be heralded.

The carousel. And the black llama.

I know nothing about the intricacies of machinery, but after pushing and pulling, jabbing and kicking, there is an explosion of light and the animals begin moving.

There are windows in houses looking out at the darkness, brittle with cold.

'Danny?'

There are sidewalks, deserted stages spawning echoes.

'Danny?'

Huddling people.

'Danny, goddamnit, look at me!'

I scramble on to the llama's saddle, using the worn leather

587

reins to whip its rippled wooden neck.

The music . . . calliope rhyme Scottish rhyme . . .

And then there is nothing but 'The Flowers of the Forest', and my bravado turns to tears as I swear in my shouting that I am not weary, clinging to the brass pole that pierces the llama's back.

And from out of the dark that envelops the ocean, over the gashes of white that push at the sand; sweeping across the trodden beach like the rhythmic slap of a sail in the wind, I can hear the truth of Ted's resigned madness, the answer to the riddle of the four old men.

The lights grow bright, the carousel spins, the clown starts to laugh, and the llama starts to buck; and relentlessly drowning the scale of my screams, the last things I hear are black wings

beating.

Kathleen Resch

The dark

*Kathleen Resch was born in 1955, and works as an
administrative assistant in a small California company. Her
poems and short stories have appeared in various little
magazines, her poem 'Revenant' sneaked into andy offutt's*
Swords Against Darkness III, *but this is her first anthologized
story.*

*Of the several first professional appearances in this
anthology, I believe I'm proudest to have set Kathleen Resch
on her road (which is certainly not meant to denigrate Laidlaw
and Rasnic and Sullivan and Dickson). Let me say at once
that it is about one of the oldest of all terrors. But I have never
seen the psychology of it explored so thoroughly, even by
Robert Aickman, and the talent, and imagination of
Kathleen Resch are all new.*

Dedicated to: andrew j. offutt, Barb Fister-Liltz, Bill Hunt,
Marcy Robin and Gerald Duet.

The figures below move, silvered by the moonlight. Each in its
own separate world, moving, pausing, ebb and flow, now shows
through the bars of the black iron grille. I kneel by it, resting
my head again the tangible hardness, an anchor in a shifting
world. Even the stars above me swim before my eyes.

Soon he will come to me. I wait, in a fierce and longing
patience. I do not want to wait on his whim; he has, after all,
the extent of eternity to move through, while I have but fleeting seconds in time. Fleeting, disconnected seconds, like beads
on a string now broken and scattered away, apart for ever. The
last that fell I called Charity Evans. The one I hold now I call
Charlene Armstrong. It is, perhaps, a rougher bead, of an irregular shape, but it serves, keeps its place, until the next should
come. If there need be another . . .

589

Live for ever, he has said. To live . . . yet is it really living? Or has he used that as a term, a euphemism, having no other description for his state? My head aches with such thoughts. Though he is not here, I feel that he watches and is aware of me through the distance that separates us.

It is very difficult to move. I lean against the railing and think, without emotion, of the empty apartment; of Malinda, now dead; of my father and the Reverend Wallace, gone also. Unimportant . . . these images, ghosts in my unsettled mind. Inconstant . . . I feel nothing. I grip the iron railing and try to pull myself to a more upright position, but my icy, nerveless hands do not have the strength to maintain my position and I slip again, head back, bathed in the moonlight.

Visions dance, cloud and clarify my sight. I look beyond the iron grille and watch the old houses, the massed trees, the narrow streets fade, shimmer, vanish, coalesce anew into the haunting and haunted faces of my life as past and present and future merge and blend and become as one. Time itself is broken . . .

. . . New Orleans. A name, a place, a lifestyle. The syllables evoke fragmented images of past glories and present vitality. Life flows here in surging, uncontained force. Perhaps if I had lived my life here it would just be home.

I walk the streets, smiling tourist smiles, remarking upon the colourful, commonplace sights. Malinda is at my side, drinking in the views of curio shops, outdoor art exhibits, counterculture posters, striptease bars. Magnolia scents mingle with those of hot dogs and fresh coffee. We explore the old French Quarter avidly, as if it would vanish tomorrow, as if we wouldn't have all the time in the world to do so. See? Here is the Haunted House where, if you listen carefully in the darkest hours of night, the screams of Madame LaLaurie's tortured slaves may be heard . . . if you believe. There is the old Ursuline Convent, primly white, neatly maintained. I can almost hear Vespers . . .

We flip through the pages of the guidebook, going from one street to the next, revelling in history – both the real and the fictionalized. The unfamiliarity is what does it, I imagine. I don't recall being very impressed with the old Spanish missions back in California. Given ten years here, I probably will not be able to see the incongruity of the last street car contrasted with the jet airplanes overhead.

590

The day ends too quickly. We return by taxi, a frivolous, marvellous expenditure, imagining ourselves to be rich. Father has the car today; we really need another. The house, colourless in the twilight, is quiet as we enter, muffled from the modern world by the barriers of its protective trees, its wrought-iron fence, the shield of its old neighbourhood. It bears with little animosity the decline of its fortunes in the world. Once a great family dwelt here, and perhaps business was conducted that changed the face of the world. Now it has been cut, divided into apartments rented by the descendants of its former servants. It awakens only slightly, not caring any more, at our laughing approach. Our voices are swallowed up by the old walls, repository of decades of dreams.

I reach the second floor first. Malinda has lost her struggle with the multitude of packages she's been carrying and has gone chasing one down the stairs. It's not the one containing that lovely Chinese statue, is it? With a laughing comment, I turn my attention to the door and fit my outsize key into the old-fashioned lock, all the while maintaining a precarious grip on my own packages. The door swings easily open. The electric lights snap to life under my touch, casting their alien glow on rooms never meant to receive it. My notions are romantic and foolish, of course. Practicality modifies all things.

A moment later we enter, scattering packages and brown paper over the heavy oaken table, admiring anew our recent purchases. Caricatures of both our faces, done by a street artist, are quickly and unceremoniously taped to the wall. A three-dimensional painting serves as a rest for a voodoo doll – a scrap of a thing made of corn husks and paint. Postcards and photo folders picturing the wax statues of historical figures and fictional monsters from the Musée Conti are sorted through. They only await addressing and mailing to envious friends who are, nevertheless, secure in their homeplaces, being well able to afford a wish or two to be elsewhere for a little while. Not for ever.

But it doesn't matter. What difference does it make, anyway? I was born in a city and this is a city. There are only surface differences, after all – more spice in the food, different flowers in the air. If either I or Malinda had had any real roots in California, we would never have come here with Father when he had been offered a position in the company of an old friend. Bookkeeping? My father knew all about that, from the years in his family drugstore, taking care of everything himself, knowing all his customers by name. But those customers had dwindled in the past few years, seduced by the cut-rate chain firms with their medicines secreted among the stacks of quickie records and vinyl-wrapped cheap pantyhose. Mother died years ago of breast cancer. I scarcely remember her.

It doesn't take long for life to assume a routine. A visit to an employment service, a few interviews, and I find a job typing reports for an insurance firm. As for Malinda, she marks products, does inventory and deals with rude people in a department store. Father's work occupies him greatly. We rarely see him – or each other, now that the novelty of being a family again has worn off. We were always apart, it seems – Malinda with her boyfriends, I with mine. And Father? His work, of course. But at least he enjoyed it then . . .

Malinda quickly finds herself a new boyfriend and this time, as always, she swears it is for ever. She never means it and we both know it, but she always had a liking for games.

She brings him to the apartment one time when I am there. A babble of voices ensues; introductions, acknowledgements, small talk, small smiles. His name is John Arnold, I am told. I am suspicious of people with two first names. John Arnold what? Just John Arnold, he assures me in a cornsilk voice. He is palefaced and pure-eyed; I distrust him unreasoningly for that. We make bad jokes about California freaks, life in Movieland, USA; a subtle dagger-tip conversation; only the first hint of animosity shown, purposelessly. I don't know why I distrust him. His blue eyes are perhaps too innocent, too intense. I feel it is a fraud – his pose as a country boy muddling into big city life, and wonder why I should trouble to concern myself. He is my sister's concern after all, not mine. Though he is hardly her type. She has had plenty of experience with men. I give John Arnold two weeks. She will drop him quickly enough when she meets someone more interesting, or to any whim of the moment.

She is smiling, effervescent. She offers us cheap whisky and water, which I drink and he refuses. A slight flush covers her face at his refusal; a confusion I haven't often seen in her. She puts the glass down, spilling it a little on the Formica counter, and refuses to drink her own. He protests, saying he does not mean to spoil our pleasure; it is simply a religious conviction he has.

But of course he meant to spoil our pleasure. I can see what he has in mind now. He will have difficulty in converting my sister. He needn't bother trying with me.

He is detailing those religious convictions now. His voice drones on and on as he speaks of the wonderful church he is a member of. The sound reminds me of flies blackening the air around meat.

What a bore, I think, shifting my position in the over-stuffed, worn chair. The ice clinks faintly in my glass, which is moist with condensation. I tilt it and drink it all, grimacing slightly at the bitter taste. I would not care to inquire too closely as to how this particular alcohol is made. At least it does not have a worm floating in it, like a type of Mexican tequila. The stuff is still powerful; effect is enhanced without good flavour. Already the room has acquired a faint haze, and I feel a slight lack of sensation in my hands and feet.

The air, so full of John Arnold's words, is an oppressive weight on me. I open a window, but it does not help. He and Malinda are huddled on a couch, discussing practical theology and department store blues. I leave, unnoticed. Doubtless they will turn to other subjects when I am gone.

The air outside is cool, crisp like iced apples. The faint encompassing alcohol haze dissipates readily. It is almost a disappointment to be totally sober again.

Restlessness overcomes me. Our car is parked in the rear; a small, older model, still carrying a dented fender as a relic of a minor accident I once had. I get in and drive through the streets from one pool of light to the next. The darkness of the night steadily gives way to the flash of neon, the splatter of tail-lights, turn signals, traffic lights. Scarlet splashes the pavement as a police car, its siren doppler-distorted, streaks through the traffic. I open my window all the way, letting the cool, scent-laden air drift in. Honeysuckle, jasmine and magnolia mix, redolent, weighing heavily on the air of the quiet residential district I have driven into, without purpose.

No excitement here. I U-turn the car in some rich man's driveway and return to the neon-choked business section. Before I know it, I am in the French Quarter.

The narrow streets make more cautious driving imperative, and I necessarily slow the car. A great eddy of human life flows on the sidewalks, changing from block to block. Middle American tourists, polyester-clad and camera-laden, throng the fringes, all choked with tasteless kitschy junk and hung about with strings of children. Farther on the scene changes. Black faces, white, brown, nearly all young, nearly all native, mingle with the hardier tourists, the ones in search of the night life. Clusters of hookers roam about; flashily clad pimps make arrangements; junkies, desperate sweat-covered faces ghastly in the streetlights, make contacts; pushers get rich. Homosexuals gather in front of a bar and disappear inside.

The sound of loud live music bursts from an opened bar door and is muffled just as abruptly as the door slams shut. Everywhere are advertisements for nude shows, strip shows, live action shows, XXX movie theatres.

What am I doing here?

I slow the car even more, preparing to turn. On a street corner just ahead of me, a lone figure breaks away from a surrounding cluster of whores. I catch the faintest glimpse of his pale face and intent eyes. Then he is gone, his black-clad form disappearing into an alley.

I immediately pull the car over to a kerb, stop it. The cement is painted red, but I don't care. The hookers stare at me with hostile eyes. Their black and white faces, heavy with paint, show harshly in the artificial light. I ignore them and go down the alley.

Why am I doing this?

Compulsion, irrational – can it still be the alcohol? Can I be drunk and not show it? I did not have that much. Garbage cans loom about me, stinking with last week's trash. I step into something soft and hastily step out again. Shapes and shadows move in the gloom, but fear still does not come to me. I move more rapidly now, and the only fear that impels me is that of loss, and with it a sense of something unattainable, long desired for, unbearably sweet . . .

A blank brick wall greets me. Dead end. I turn, feeling a severance in myself, a loss of something I once knew but can't define. Sadness touches my mind.

I turn back towards the street, but three shadows confront me, three men silhouetted against the distant light. It glints upon their drawn switchblades. My breath catches in my throat, escapes in a low moan of fear. I back away until there is nowhere at all to go, until the old bricks press into my back and fear shatters all my thoughts. They smile and step closer.

Then there is a man beside me, though there is no possible way he could be there. In a hurried, startled glance I see his pale face, his piercing eyes – as do my would-be attackers. They lower their knives, caught by the intensity of his gaze, the dreamy cruelty of his smile. The switchblades snap shut; they turn and stumble away.

I shift my gaze from them to him, seeing him clearly in the dimness of the light. Though I barely saw his face before, I know without doubt that this was the man I glimpsed on the street and followed to this place.

He looks at me appraisingly, dark eyes unreadable, and murmurs something about oddity and time. The smile has quite left his sensual mouth and without its modifying influence, I feel naked prey to his gaze. I am confused, afraid. He doesn't help matters with that anticipatory glow in his eyes, that look of speculation.

He says nothing to me. He turns and leaves the alley. For an instant, quite surprised, I stand there watching him retreat, then follow, wondering why I cannot do otherwise. Antiqued, transformed sensations, the intimation of visions struggle to enter my mind. I fight them down savagely. I do not want them; I do not want *him*.

A low strangled cry escapes me. He is amused. He laughs and tells me not to worry. Nothing will happen to me that I do not want. I should consider myself fortunate. He usually does not allow those he notices any choice in the matter.

I am not reassured. I want to go back to the threadbare familiarity of my apartment, to the comfortable world of family, co-workers, friends.

He is suddenly impatient. I sense an awful struggle for control, for suppression in his lean, black-clad form. He will not have any vacillation. Have I no gratitude? Or perhaps I am cursed with a short memory. He, rather, is cursed with a long one and there are things at this moment that it would profit him to forget. Go, he tells me, or come. He really doesn't care.

He walks away, his body illuminated in the flickering neon which leaves no shadows behind him. His face takes on the aspect of others on the street; he now appears no different than any of the other inhabitants of this sub-world. Have I passed him a thousand times on the streets and never even known?

Something tears in me – pain, loss, injustice; stranglehold stinging tendrils of despair. Half-running, I catch up with him. He smiles slightly, as if he had known all along that this is what I would do.

595

We walk rapidly through the changing of the streets, past bars and garbage and drunks on the ground. One poorly lit place is doing excellent business. We enter the smoke-clouded room. I look at the faces of the men at the tables and bar; impassive, lustful, all watching with narrowed eyes the extraordinarily well-built blonde on the spotlit stage. A tiny G-string is her only remaining hint of clothing. She groans, caressing her body, and the audience sighs with her.

My companion does not even appear to see her. A fat, balding man seated near a narrow staircase nods a greeting to him. He ignores him, sweeping up the staircase as if he were running downhill. I have to run up the steps to keep up with him.

I am getting tired. Suddenly rest seems very desirable.

He does not pause but enters a short corridor that runs to a dead end of paint-peeled wood and a blank door. Things scutter in the corners. He opens the door and we enter.

A bright jumble greets my eyes – paintings, statuary, tapestries, wall hangings, shelves upon shelves crammed to overflowing with objets d'art and books.

I turn and study him frankly. It is not so much that he is tall – for he is not – but something about him suggests height. Soft, thick black hair frames his face and spills down on to his collar. Thick eyebrows make a frame for his large, dark, unreadable eyes. He is pale, though not inordinately so. His mouth is mobile, capable of expressing a great variety of nuances of feeling. There is something peculiar about it that I cannot quite identify.

I glance around the room again. It is really very well organized, I realize as the images begin to sort themselves out in my mind. I wouldn't have believed so many things could be put in such a relatively small space. Everything is spotlessly clean. Paintings, displaying an eclectic taste, line the walls. I can see a Picasso, and a Van Gogh. Statuary, ranging from the abstract to the representational, occupies extraordinary places in the room. A large print by Salvador Dali dominates one wall; on another is a medieval tapestry. Vases and objects of antiquity are displayed in cases and on shelves. Books compete for space on the ample shelves; I notice titles on philosophy, a modern novel, the Kama Sutra. The furnishings are all of the best materials, and some seem barely used. The carpet is soft and muffles all sound as we walk through the room.

He touches a switch, altering the indirect, intense lighting of the room to a subtle glow that shows the paintings and tapestries to advantage. The air is faintly smoky, and there is a slight scent to it, like diffused incense. He touches another switch and music spills sweetly through the room. Something classic, I think, reminiscent of suffering tubercular musicians destroyed by their own passions, of light fairy-tale romances with happy endings. Music for old-fashioned dancing.

As if he knows my thoughts he suggests we dance and, almost as if he were grasping air, sweeps me lightly into his arms. We sway slowly about the room. I dance instinctively, knowing the motions before I make them. I have never danced like this before. Slowly I become aware of the cold pervading my body, the cold that emanates from him.

I shiver. He is concerned, mentions something about draughts. How could there be? There are no windows. We are as enclosed as if we were in an underground cave.

I look about the room again, marvelling at the incredible variety of objects it contains, thinking about the amount of money necessary to gather all this together.

When I turn back to him, there is something in his gaze that alarms me, something menacing, unreadable and oddly familiar in his eyes. I feel true fear for the first time and pull away from him, smiling inanely, heading towards the door. He grasps me by the arms and holds me as I would hold a struggling kitten, then winds one arm behind me as he pinions me, half lying on the couch. His cold lips brush my forehead, my mouth, my chin, then he bends his head down until his lips are just grazing the skin of my neck. I shiver from the frightening pleasure of it. I have forgotten to struggle. He remains as he is for an instant longer, then draws his head back slightly and strikes.

A tingling cold rushes through every part of my body. I gasp as my world darkens before my eyes and I become a part of his. Strange colours and unfamiliar lights flicker before my open eyes. I can hear a soft sighing and wonder if it is my own. Weakness grows in me almost overwhelmingly, as willingly I give, he takes, relentless, irresistible, intensely desirable. A shadow lies fully formed on my vision now and I do not will or wish it to leave.

He draws away from me, his eyes glittering into mine. Their power is the focal point of the universe. And then he asks me if I still do not know.

I don't quite understand what he is talking about. I think he refs to the bloodtaking, but when I say that, when I say the word vampire from imparted, previously unthinkable knowledge, he laughs bitterly and says it is unimportant, that perhaps he was wrong.

He stands and I can almost see the renewed life in him, the surge of briefly-consuming energy that must endlessly be replaced. I lie on the couch, half-fainting, and watch the room glimmer before my eyes.

He watches me speculatively and asks if I wish to stay.

Yes, I reply, always, for ever. I never want to leave.

He smiles, pleased, and says that we have made a beginning, but our wishes cannot be fulfilled in one night; I must return to my home. He will call me when he needs me. I must believe that.

He lifts me effortlessly from the couch and props me on my feet. I begin to walk somnambulantly, making all the proper motions. We go back down through the bar, through the streets to my car, left untouched though I had not locked it, unticketed although parked in an illegal zone. I enter and fall back against the seat. He frowns and directs me to move over into the passenger seat. I do this with great reluctance, not wishing to move, willing to stay on the worn imitation leather seat cover for ever. The gear shift is an Everest to overcome. Finally I manage, and slump down.

He gets in the car and takes my keys. The engine starts to life under his touch and we are off, speeding through the semi-deserted streets. I am surprised he knows how to drive. Bats, hearses, horsedriven carriages from a hundred bad films fill my mind with reinforcing images.

I mention this. He is frankly delighted. Why shouldn't he drive? An automobile is an amusing toy, and he has had plenty of time to learn anything he cares to.

The night air is cool and pleasant as it breathes in on my face, I succumb, mindless to it, allowing only sensations to penetrate my numbed mind, and those only distantly. Before I am half aware, we are back at my apartment. I hadn't told him where I live, I realize, and think on asking him about that, but it seems so unimportant.

He touches my hand briefly and then is out of the car. I get out myself, impelled by energy I didn't know I possess, for his leaving is far more important than my weakness. He walks away, fading in slow degrees to merge with the blackness.

598

The pain of severance is almost overwhelming. I struggle to keep my head up, to keep moving, like a drowning woman exhausted to the point of death. I see my own movements as if from a great distance. I take the key and let myself in. The carpet stretches before me, a brown narrow swatch lying neatly parallel across the wood floor. I direct my feet to move forward, one in front of the other. I walk, perfection, no swaying, nothing to alarm the uninitiated. They wouldn't think me anything but drunk, anyway. The stairs stretch up into a black cavernous hole. I almost pause before them, wondering if I have the strength to manage them.

But I do not want questions. I feel the banister faintly through the half-deadened flesh of my hands. One hand reaches and grasps it, then the other, and I haul myself up the staircase sideways, hoping no one will see.

Another key fitting into another lock, turning precisely with a faint click, and I am home. The room is dark. John Arnold must be gone. Perhaps he took Malinda with him. I can hear my father snoring from his room.

I find to my surprise that I do not need any lights. The furnishings are all etched clearly in the darkness. I make my way into my room with no difficulty, wondering all the while at the incredible richness and varieties of darkness, the many barely perceptible changes and shadings of grey and black, at the beauty of a restricted world.

I take my clothes off automatically, get into a nightgown and crawl into bed. Then I set to watching and cataloguing the shades of grey before they all merge together again in the cold light of day.

John Lennon's face stares at me from the poster on the wall. Close by, a smaller rectangle, two nude lovers merging in a beautiful shift of grey. In the daylight, I know, they shine in frenetic colour; colour I always thought reality. Could I have been wrong all along? Perhaps the colour is the lie, and this is the actuality. I feel as if I can see for the first time.

The last words he spoke to me fall lightly in my mind. I weigh their syllables, analyse, inspect, admire.

He told me his name.

Desmond Chabrol.

It echoes through my mind teasingly, evoking vague, candle-lit images, hazed as if seen through fine linen. There is someone beyond that veil, someone I know intimately, down to her

599

last thought. She sways through the corners of my mind, dancing with Desmond through perfumed halls, smiling, crying.

The images fade the more I try to grasp them, vanishing finally from my mind . . .

The smell of fried eggs wakes me up. I am still weak, but am determined to hide it, to conquer it. I know instinctively I must behave as if everything were the same as it always has been. I shower and dress, squeeze toothpaste from a curled tube, wash my face, apply make-up and perfume; performing properly all the morning rituals. I try to still the shaking of my hands; I grip the sink as I stare into the mirror. I look as solid as I always have; can any of this be real? My high-necked blouse hides the twin marks on my neck; they would be very obvious otherwise.

I go to the kitchen. Malinda is there, cooking breakfast. My father sits before a rapidly diminishing pile of buttered toast, engrossed with the morning disasters and Dear Abby in the paper. He greets me abstractedly, grinning at the comics. You should read Peanuts today, he says; don't know how they come up with them. And Dear Abby's got a good one today. Amazing all the nuts there are in the world.

I make all the proper responses, drink orange juice and refuse everything else. Even the smell of the food is nauseating. The sight of the grease-smeared eggs is revolting, and I control my stomach with difficulty, carefully not thinking about actually eating the matter.

Neither my father nor my sister notices. He has moved on to the editorials, and is making nasty comments about dishonest politicians. She is chattering about John Arnold and the church he belongs to. Something called the First United Church of Our Saviour. I have never heard of it but say nothing to her. It would take a great effort to cut in on her monologue anyway.

They are a wonderful people, she is saying; absolutely marvellous. John Arnold took her to a prayer meeting last night.

That is not quite how I had pictured them spending the evening, but no matter.

She continues in a rush of words: So refreshing, actually, and touching to find people who really believe in what they are saying and not just mouthing phrases and platitudes. Of course they are rather strict, but asceticism is a recognized religious force and should not be taken lightly. And they are not really narrow-minded; it only appears so to those who take just a cursory glance at their religion. If people could only see how well it is integrated into a whole.

So John Arnold has found a convert after all. I recall all the various movements Malinda had been briefly infatuated with in California. A brief flirtation with politics had given way to Zen and Eastern mysticism, which had given way to est and other fashionable psychological fads. Her active participation in any of these had rarely lasted beyond a month. That is how long I give her current interest in John Arnold and fundamental Christianity.

I listen to her words only vaguely, catching enough meaning to make intelligent replies. It all seems so unimportant, somehow. The weakness is still with me, but manageable. I am functional; I will be able to counterfeit my own life. I smile inwardly, thinking how so much can change in so short a time.

Malinda draws back the curtains. Sunlight bursts in with tidal wave force. I get up abruptly, complaining of a headache, and go back to my small room. I am due at work in half an hour. Somehow the day must be lived through. I go through dressers, boxes, until I find what I am looking for. The dark lenses of the sunglasses through which I saw so many California beaches will give the world a proper perspective. With them on, I gather my resources.

I exchange goodbye noises with my family. Malinda is in a rush now, having noted the passage of time. She is in a car-pool with other women from the department store who live in the neighbourhood. My father is also preparing to leave. I have the use of the car.

I make my way downstairs, fighting off a wave of dizziness. The world lies ordinary before me, properly segmented into large white houses, manicured green lawns, with children's toys – tiny booby traps – scattered about sidewalks and driveways. The sunglasses are not enough; everything still shines too brightly. The toys are dirty electric blues and reds; the pink terry robe of the woman retrieving the morning paper next door is far too brilliant. I long for the dark; I long for Desmond.

The car is waiting for me in its accustomed place. I slip inside and pause, thinking of how Desmond had sat in this very place last night. I grasp the wheel, seeking a sort of communion with him through the inanimate moulded plastic.

There is nothing there. I start the car and drive to work.

●

Sue Ellen tells me I don't look well. She is right, but I won't admit it. We sit, shuffling the papers that form our customers' lives, rarely looking beyond the dry facts. One 1969 Ford, single car collision on Interstate 71, minor injuries . . .

The typewriters click in ragged time. Sue Ellen frowns slightly as she concentrates, pink-painted fingernails beating in staccato, broken rhythm on the keyboard, her trim, polyester-clad form bending slightly as she types a neat row of figures. A wisp of straw blond hair has fallen forward into her face. She brushes it away abstractedly. I become aware I am not working; that I am frozen, a prisoner in the amber of my surroundings, watching my fellow creatures in their commonplace rituals.

I see everything with absolute clarity. The row of grey filing cabinets stands erect, lining the walls. The carpet is warm brown and contains a vague attempt at a pattern. The desks are fitted in wherever they will go. Mr Jenson's voice comes vaguely to me; he is in his private office, talking to a new customer.

Sue Ellen becomes aware that I am watching her. She is concerned at my lack of response, and again says that I don't look well. This time I agree, and rising carefully, I head for the bathroom.

The light snaps on, casting a garish, jaundiced penetrating glow through the institutional chamber. It is a pattern of ammonia-scented geometrics. I stand, having no inclination to move, and observe my reflection in the mirror. It stares back at me, hollow cheeked and pale. My brown hair hangs limply about my shoulders. I think that perhaps I should comb it, but the thought passes from my mind without protest when I take no action.

A while later – minutes? an hour? – someone knocks at the door. I can hear Sue Ellen's voice; I am not at all sure what she has just said. Sue repeats it, her string of foreign sounds catching on the air, dying. I don't answer, I don't understand. Then she comes in.

She suggests that it would be better if I went home, since I really am sick. I accept the suggestion, not having the strength to argue about it. She watches me worriedly. I assure her vaguely that I will be all right; that I must have some virus, one of those twenty-four-hour bugs. Nothing to be concerned with, really. She gives a lot of advice having to do with aspirins and bed rest, and runs through a catalogue of the symptoms she had the last time she had the flu. I agree with everything she says and drift out into the streets. She calls after me, something about driving me home, but I do not turn back and she does not follow.

I cannot go home, of course. The landlady might see me, might mention my early return to my father or sister. I do not want any questions at all, any concern, any words. I just want silence, and strangers. I walk a short distance, then sit on a bench at a bus stop. When the bus comes, I get on.

I ride aimlessly about for the better part of the afternoon, always in the rear where I can lean back, be far from people while being near. One driver, his face marked by early acne, watches me strangely; I ignore him and switch buses a quarter of an hour later.

Later, I walk. There is no point in going to the French Quarter; it is not yet dark. I do not feel his presence in my mind.

I barely feel the pavement beneath my feet, barely notice the aspect of the streets patterned with department stores, hurrying pedestrians, shrieking children.

I am glad to find the office closed when I return. No one there to ask why I left my car. No one to ask anything at all. The streets slide by me as I drive home.

My sister is already there, engrossed in a confession magazine. Something about a virgin who was raped by a Satanist. She is dipping into a sack of malt balls, chewing very slowly. She is frowning slightly as she reads. I sit on the couch and watch the shadows lengthen across the carpet. The light slants longer, reaching the linoleum of the kitchen. Malinda snaps the light on and drops the magazine with a sigh.

These stories are so dumb, she comments, heading towards the kitchen, adding that she doesn't understand why she reads them. She begins making some desultory culinary efforts. I turn the light off. It is spoiling the darkness.

Father comes in, looking exhausted. He switches on all the lights, wanting to know why I am sitting in the dark doing nothing. Tired, I say. Just tired.

He can understand that. He has had a hard day. He tosses down a newspaper and goes into the kitchen. Malinda is making spaghetti. The cooking odours waft out, unappetizing. I think I will be sick, and run to the bathroom.

Malinda shouts after me to come to dinner. I make excuses, saying Sue Ellen and I had pizza for lunch; that I'm still full. She tells me to suit myself, and they eat without me.

I become aware of an intense thirst, as if my body were dehydrated. I fill a glass with tap water, gulp it down, and then another. It is curiously unsatisfying. Through the bathroom door I can see my inviting bed, and I realize I can barely stand. I lie down, closing my eyes. Tomorrow, I think, I shall call in sick. Sue Ellen can handle it herself, for once. She's a great one for not showing up for work, anyway.

Sleep covers me like a wool blanket, suffocating, nightmarish. I wake with a start sometime later. The room is perceptibly changed. My vision has been subtly altered, and there is a faint, laughing presence in my mind.

I know the reason for the change.

The sun has gone down.

I go into the living room. Malinda is on the telephone, laughing, describing John Arnold to a friend. Father is watching a game show on TV, successfully ignoring Malinda's rapid-fire conversation. Someone has just won a car/trip to Hawaii/set of luggage and the audience is going wild. The light from the lamp picks out the grey in his hair but, repentant of its harshness, soften the lines etched into his careworn face.

I am going out, I tell them. To a movie. One of the insurance adjustors asked me.

Have a good time, comes the double reply.

I leave quickly, filled with new energy. I feel more alive now than I have all day. More alive, perhaps, than I've ever felt.

The drive to the bar in the French Quarter is shorter than it seemed before. Already familiarity lends ease. I do not hesitate about entering the half-empty building. The evening show has not yet begun, and the tables are, for the most part, deserted. A thin line of men and a few women occupy the barstools. Some are hunched over the counter, already half-dead from drinking. Some are watching the colour television. The electric light flickers over the figures, the array of liquor bottles behind the bar gleams; amber, clear, murky, red. I walk past them to the staircase.

The fat balding man who was there before is still here, behind the bar. His eyes follow me all the way, but he says nothing.

Desmond is standing at the foot of the stairs. I did not see him come down. A quick glance around shows me that no one else has noticed him.

He walks over to the bartender, and I follow. This is Brown, he tells me, then says to Brown that I am to have access to his apartment any time.

He turns, and I follow him upstairs. He closes the door behind us. His glassy, intent eyes stare through me, as if seeking out my soul – though that isn't what he wants, of course.

I brush the hair away from my neck, offering, but he shakes his head. Not now, he says. He has the choice of anyone at all. He goes from one to another, to another, and rarely drains any of his human toys. He is not yet sure if he will take me beyond my mortal life to his own existence.

I want to know when he will be sure. In twenty-four hours he has become the sole reason for my existence, and I cannot bear for him to deny it, to treat me otherwise. I ask him again. He shrugs, as if it were all some ludicrous and not very funny joke.

He goes to the far corner of the room. There is a door there. I had not noticed that before. I follow him through it, into a darkened hallway. Electric wall sconces cast pale, imitation light through its short length; candlelight would have gone as far as those weak beams. A few doorways open from it. He selects one and goes inside. I follow close behind.

The room is used for storage. It is filled with trunks and crates and dust. A stack of paintings leans against one wall. He goes through them purposefully, finally drawing one out. He hands this to me.

I hold it, perplexed and slightly dizzy from the faint rush of alien thoughts, impressions, emotions that surge and subside within me in an instant.

The Victorian lady smiles demurely out of the competent, uninspired work. Her eyes are a gentle, idealized blue and her hair wheatfield, impossible blond. Her hands are folded in her lap and her dress, on which the painter took the most care, is a complicated thing of satin and lace.

There is not one feature that matches my own. Why, then, do I feel this sense of self-identification?

He tells me to take it with me and not to return until I have fathomed its meaning. I will know it when it happens. If it never does, well, he has made a mistake, and I might not see him again. If I do understand, we shall work things out from there. He is not quite sure it will have any meaning at all. It has been a long time – a century, at least – and he does not view things as he did in life.

His smile is slightly askew. I take the portrait, wanting to do as he asks, wanting to please him, yet not understanding how.

He looks away from me, lost in thought, and I know I am to leave. He has cut himself off from me; if a wall were suddenly between us it would be no more effective. I feel alone and empty, like some dried-up thing cast up on a beach.

The lights dim at his touch. He is no longer in the room when I leave.

I go home again. Where else can I go? Father is there, though Malinda is not. He wants to talk. We speak of the portrait. It is a gift, I say, from Martin. Martin the myth, who took me to the movies this night; who doubtless is now bedding his girlfriend or watching the late show on TV. I can barely hear Father across the gulf that separates us. I nod, make all the proper noises. Nothing important, really . . . just an old man's hopes and dreams and the realization that, even though life has passed him by, it really doesn't matter. He lives on in his two daughters. I listen, not really caring, but when we part to our own separate rooms, tears have appeared on my face. Inconsequential . . . I brush them away. Where did they come from? What depth of human frailty, empathy produced them? And why doesn't it penetrate to my conscious mind? Or am I even that any more?

The portrait fits nicely in a corner of my room, dividing space, blissfully unaware of its diminished, unimportant position. At least it is visible here; there must have been three or four others stacked against it in Desmond's apartment.

I look at the portrait for a moment longer, then turn away from its disturbing, placid gaze. The painted woman has something to tell me, something I want desperately to understand, yet feel compelled to deny . . .

Intangible, impenetrable mists cloud my dreams . . . I am drowning in gossamer, in spider web. Thin, transparent filaments rain upon me, covering, smothering. I tear at them with my hands, struggle contortedly in their delicate, irresistible grasp. They stretch infinitely but do not tear, refuse to break, constricting, wrapping me in a grey cocoon. I scream, but the sound is lost as the stuff makes its insidious way into my mouth and reaches through me, dissolving my bones, drying my blood, until I stand, a petrified greying husk, watching the featureless world out of frozen eyes.

I awake with a sense of strangulation, to find my hand is clasping my throat, protecting the point where Desmond drew my blood.

It is very cold in my room. Winter means cold, but I never seemed to notice before. There are no extra blankets. I get a sweater, then a robe, and put them both on. Then I lie, huddling in my bed until the dawn. Sleep overcomes me then, deep and dreamless.

When I awake I call in sick. Sue Ellen is very understanding; she assures me there will be no problems.

The day passes. Hours blend and spill over into each other, and slowly the sun climbs the sky and sinks again. The dark comes, but I am still alone, and bereft.

Malinda comes in, looking quite cheerful in a new coat. You seem to be feeling better, she remarks; must be one of those twenty-four-hour things. She flits about the room, making notes in an address book, tossing down a magazine. Smiling dreamily, she adds that there will be a prayer meeting that night. Her tone goes light as she asks if I want to see the freaks, but something in her eyes tells me she does not mean that at all.

Why not? I have nothing better to do than contemplate my own emptiness. My mind cries out to Desmond over the distance, but there is no answer.

Sure, I say to Malinda; let's go see the freaks . . .

Anything will do to fill me . . . anything to keep me from thought, or its antithesis, its nullity. There is peace in motion.

John Arnold takes us, in an older model car that makes faint creaking noises during regular motion, and more alarming ones whenever he takes a corner. The upholstery is fraying, and bits of paper mingle with other, unidentifiable debris in the corners of the floor.

The church is not a church at all, but rather a large, remodelled house in a quiet residential district. The congregation occupies folding metal chairs. They nearly fill a large room that was once, perhaps, a ballroom in a more elegant past. In front, on a raised dais, is a plain wooden podium. Labouring men and women, dressed neatly in bargain basement clothing and well-used shoes exchange greetings and gossip. The lighting is from fluorescent tubes, revealing everything about everyone.

607

We take seats near the back. I am directly behind a large woman wearing an appallingly bright printed dress and a large helping of dimestore perfume.

John Arnold is greeting all the people around him. Introductions are made; everyone seems quite pleased to meet us, and we're invited several times to stay for coffee and cake after the service.

The voices in the room die to a whisper, then to nothing as a man steps up to the podium.

He is tall, with fiery, penetrating brown eyes. His dark hair is trimmed neatly, yet gives the impression of disorder, as if such things as grooming were unimportant. He is dressed in an inexpensive business suit, but I realize few would notice that detail under the dominance of his face, his eyes.

He greets us all and recites a short prayer. A thin, middle-aged woman pounds a tune on an old piano, and the congregation begins an enthusiastic, unmelodious rendition of 'Amazing Grace'. The service progresses.

He starts his sermon. There is much about evil, much about sin, about the Devil's work. We are strenuously warned about Satan's emissaries on earth, all seeking to corrupt the souls of the pure, of God's Chosen Ones. These agents can take human form; are, in fact, of no differing appearance from the rest of us. By means of their sweet and honeyed words they seek to lure souls into what appears to be harmless pastimes, but are in reality the first long step to debauchery, to dissolution, to Satan worship. These lures and temptations come in many guises and many pleasant, innocuous forms, and great care must be taken to distinguish the good from the evil.

He pounds on the podium, his voice powerful, inspired. His eyes are filled with a frenzy; I do not believe he even sees any of us any more. The congregation moans and cries, Amen! as he begs God for aid against the Enemy.

Demons! he screams, and the crowd shudders. He describes Hell in horrific detail, reveals the true form and appearance of Satan's emissaries and describes the punishments that await the damned.

He warns against any sort of traffic with the supernatural. Even the daily astrology columns are suspect, and any who read a book on the supernatural or consult a French Quarter witch has taken the first step on the road to damnation. Let all beware, lest they slip and the Devil catch their souls, for once

608

taken, they are beyond all hope, all redemption. Repentance now is the only way to Salvation. Believe in Jesus and follow his commandments, and the road to Heaven lies clear.

His voice dies to silence. I watch the rapt faces around me, wondering if it would have ever been possible for me to feel as they, respond as they did to his commanding voice as he drew out the tension, and then released it.

Pie in the sky. I watch as the collection plate is passed, is filled. Then another hymn is sung, and the service is over.

The preacher stands by the doorway, speaking to all as they leave. We are among the last to go, as John Arnold wants to introduce us.

The minister smiles, his eyes, calm now, meeting mine. He seems genuinely pleased to meet us. He is the Reverend Wallace, John had told us, but it's repeated again, by one or the other. I smile politely, taking my share of the literature he hands us. I glance through the stack of pamphlets, booklets and leaflets, noting some contain crudely drawn comic strips. I wonder if it is too early to begin looking for a trash can for them.

The Reverend Wallace hopes we will think very carefully about what we have heard tonight, and that we will read the literature. We are welcome back any time; the ladies are even now serving coffee and cake. We will stay, won't we?

Of course we do, and John Arnold introduces us to seemingly every member in the congregation. My face feels frozen from smiling; I give it up after awhile, sip at the coffee, nibble at the food. I am able to eat again, but hunger is distant, something sensed abstractedly, with nothing pressing or urgent about it.

The food wasn't enough for the rest; we stop at Jim Dandy's Fried Chicken on the way home. The others sit and crunch upon the quick-fried bird flesh; I cannot. John Arnold talks all the while, his face earnest as he speaks of his commitment to the Lord. Malinda hangs on to his every word. I would never have believed it of her. Perhaps she'll be happy.

She talks of it later that night, after we are back home. These people have roots, don't you see? Commitment, dedication, *faith*!

No, I do not see, but I do not say so. They are people, like anyone else, with failings, like everyone else.

But she isn't really interested in my answer; she is continuing to talk, I to watch her. She seems almost a stranger to me now; was this the girl I shared secrets with a month, a few years ago; is she the one I fought with over toys even before that? I feel cut off, enclosed – or is it everyone else who has been sealed from me?

She is giving me an odd glance. I smile, trying to look alert; she asks if anything is wrong.

Wrong? How can I tell her that the world is radically altered for me now; that I see everything in a new light? Where can I find the words?

I cannot. I yawn, not needing to pretend weariness. She is apologetic. I have been ill. She is keeping me up too late. We can talk about everything some other time.

She rises, her hair a golden swirl in the subdued lamplight. It casts upturned shadows on her face, emphasizing her blue eyes. She stares thoughtfully out the window, finally remarking on how she had thought she saw someone out there, but she hadn't really. It must have been a trick of the light. It is very odd.

No, it is not. He had been out there; his presence came to me, a brief passing in my mind. I feel vaguely comforted, though he has given me no sign of approval or disapproval. Whatever drew him here – curiosity, perhaps, or some other, more alien emotion – it meant he has not deserted me entirely. It certainly could not have been desire that had motivated him – I would have sensed that and gone to him, despite all obstacles.

Sleep is peaceful all night. My soul lies assured within me.

I feel much better the next day. Sue Ellen is glad to see me. Papers are stacked up halfway to the sky; letters to be answered, typing to be done. I do it all competently, an automaton, a letter typing machine. See how well I take orders, boss? You should order a hundred more like me. I do not think Sue Ellen suspects the change in me. The phone rings sharply, many times. I take messages, attend customers, get their signatures on dotted lines. All is as it was.

He told me not to return, but darkness finds me walking through the French Quarter. I do not seek him actively. It is enough to be in his chosen place, to be close by. He knows where I am, anyway. The faintest touch on my mind assures me of that.

I see him vaguely up the street, insubstantial, like smoke. He does not turn. He is talking to an older woman; one who I have seen before on the streets or in the bars. Her hair is greying but her face is still free from most indications of age. Her clothing is nondescript, a collage of conflicting styles blending into a unique, yet not outstanding whole. Her face is expressionless as she speaks, the motion like the faintest ripple in a placid lake. I have heard that she tells fortunes and sells charms. Someone once pointed her out to me, as we browsed through an occult store and told me she is called Anne-Marie.

The buildings show faintly through Desmond. How can she not see this? Or perhaps she does, but does not care.

I want to go to him but cannot cross the invisible barrier that separates us, like some unseen glass or hardened water. All is clear through it. I might not even know it was there. But I know I can move no closer to him.

He turns and walks away, but the woman does not follow.

I go over to her. She regards me calmly, with little interest, out of large brown eyes. I tell her that I saw who she was with.

She shrugs. It does not matter. Many here know Desmond, and he permits it, for they are all his creatures. No one who does not belong to him knows of him. Others see him only as a shadow, or dust, or nothing at all. Or perhaps they see a bum, a hippie, a businessman or a tourist. He presents the aspect they expect to see, and so they do not see him at all. It takes more than a casual glance to identify him. And who has the interest?

I ask her for help, though I don't know what she can do. She smiles slightly. I think she pities me, but I do not care. She motions for me to come with her.

Her place is a little shop, nestled in the old façade of buildings created before this century. A sign above gives it a name – 'Bell, Book and Candle'. For the tourists, she says.

Bells tinkle lightly as we enter. Thick incense clouds the air, conducting the faint glimmerlight of candles. A dried bat guards the door. Racks and tables hold incense, voodoo dolls, medallions, wax. Bookshelves line the walls, filled with books presenting their glossy or worn backs for inspection. A carved snake nestles around the cash register.

Anne-Marie leads me through beaded curtains and up a narrow staircase. We go through a door and enter a large room.

The place is a mess. Everything is askew, slanted. Books lie in precarious positions on end tables and oddments of furniture. Various jars, some labelled, some not, compete for space in corners, on the floor. Papers peer out of cubbyholes. Clothing is draped over everything. It is all lit by Tiffany lamps.

We sit on the bed and she takes my hand, turning it one way and then another. I must look to the past before I can look to the future, she says. I have a clouded destiny; she has rarely seen its like. But it need not be unpleasant. I must choose the path for myself.

I do not understand, I say. My mind is as hazed as the smoke from the incense.

She sighs faintly. I must awaken before I can understand, she says. It is all very well for the majority of humanity to dream for ever. They have nothing else.

She gathers up two jars, seemingly at random, and mixes their contents together. The herbs fall with a dry, rattling sound. She tells me to dissolve it in water and drink it, here, or at my home, it does not matter. She warns me to be careful, however. It is not a substance the law would approve of, though they would have some difficulty in identifying it.

Here, I say, and she nods and brings me water. I start to take it, then hesitate, mentioning money. She laughs. It is of no consequence. If I had not known of Desmond she would not have given it to me, or else would have charged many times its worth.

The leaves steep in the water, turning it a dusky brown. I drink it all at once. It tastes like dust, not unpleasant at all. I feel nothing.

I get up and wander around. There is a door in the back of the room; I had not noticed it before in all the jumble. Opening it, I step out on to a balcony. Wrought iron grilling encloses it neatly, encasing order. Below, the street is almost deserted.

Across the street, in the shadow of a doorway, a man leans. Even as I watch I see him slip and fall. There seems to be an aura of sorts around him, a haze of red which fades even as I watch.

I can see, even from this distance, that he is dying.

I feel exhilarated and do not know why. It must be the drug. Above me the stars glow faintly in their pyrrhic victory over the city's lights. They will abide till dawn, then one great star will make their light meaningless. I wonder why their light cannot affect Desmond, while that of the sun can. They are, after all, the same. It must be the distance. Their light is years away. The emptiness of space dissipates it. Perhaps it isn't even real. I heard once that if the nearest star should die, it would take four years before its light winked out of our skies. Perhaps all the stars are dead and we are alone. Perhaps . . .

How very odd. I am not given to such musings. I wonder what the drug is. I shall ask Anne-Marie, if I remember to.

I don't think I shall. Desmond is here with me. He appeared in the gap between one second and the next, whole and complete. I can no longer see anything through him. He has added substance with the night. I wonder whose blood he has drunk to effect this.

I wish it were mine.

He smiles. The streetlights gleam upon his white, pointed teeth. I still do not remember, he says.

I am sorry for that; I tell him so. I do not want to disappoint him.

But he isn't disappointed. It is not my failing if I could not meet a whim of his. He draws me to him. His hands are like ice; I relish his touch, welcoming the cold that penetrates into my bones.

He presses his lips to my neck. I cling to him to keep from falling. His grip tightens about me briefly, then he releases me. I sway towards him, unable to prevent my fall. He lifts me effortlessly and carries me inside, laying me down on Anne-Marie's bed.

His brilliant eyes become the focal point of my vision. He speaks, disconnected words and phrases. He does not need to be coherent; my mind supplies the rest.

He lies down on the bed beside me, his hand lightly over mine. I grasp it tightly. His hand is very light, almost as if the bones were hollow, as if it had no substance at all. I stare upward watching the broken square patterns of the ceiling. A spider is building a web in a corner. The light seems very dim.

I cease being Charlene. I become Charity.

War-ruined fields stretch before my gaze. The slave huts are empty now. There is nothing left for the vultures. Even the human ones have gone.

Beside me, my father surveys the destruction of his life; his face harsh and bitter in the unrelenting heat of the day. Something has broken inside him but he will never surrender. The Yankees have taken everything now, except me, and I don't think he even sees me any more. When they came, they caught hold of Mother, intending to rape her, but she broke away and ran, tripped and fell screaming down two flights of stairs. She broke her back. I had not been so lucky. I still remember their faces, their hands reaching for me. And that is all I knew until I awoke in one of the slave huts. My father had taken me there.

The soldiers were gone. The house lay in smouldering ruins.

We live in the overseer's house now, a tiny, mean dwelling, and work till exhaustion for food.

All my brothers are dead. The news had filtered in of their deaths, one by one. The last one, Charles, died in the final battle of the War Between the States. I had been fondest of him. When he was young, he had a favourite place to swim, in a little backwash of the river. I went there recently; the water still flows like it always did before. I can see Charles now, but his face is not the same. None of them are. They parade before my mind, haunted, wasted, agonized, like the soldier I found once in the woods. His leg had been blown off. He died but a few moments after I found him.

I think I shall never see the end of destruction.

I do not know what to do. I have been trained for nothing, am good at nothing. What purpose can French lessons and exercises to improve the posture do now? My back is strong though; it must be. I painfully learn the rudiments of keeping alive.

My father makes an idol of his hate. I hate, too, but it does not consume me like it does him. Perhaps it is only a numbness overlaying my feelings; something which has been stripped from him. He has found others like him and they have formed into a secret group, dedicated to keeping the past alive, to execute any hated Northerner who strays into their path. He comes to life slowly again, his eyes taking on a new gleam, rock-hard, like black diamonds.

He has found purpose again.

I do not even have that.

Then he returned, the man I had loved before the war started, the man I had thought to marry before this nightmare began and took him from me.

He stands on the road before me, his clothes hanging badly on his thin body. His eyes, once so clear and dark, are now lustreless, but at the sight of me, a faint light of hope comes to them.

I cannot speak at first; I thought him dead like all the rest and then, trembling, I go to his arms, and he can say nothing at all but my name.

His name is Desmond Chabrol and he was born and raised a Southerner though he had fought for the North. He had family there, and business interests and loyalties; he had not thought the South could win. Such pragmaticism does not endear him to my father, who knows what he has done and calls it betrayal, treason. Emotion-laden words, meaningless now. It would be treason only if we had won. I do not care. Desmond is no Yankee, no matter what father says and has said for four long years.

But if he finds him, he will kill him.

I hide him in one of the slave huts, the farthest one from the cottage. He is so very weak, so ill. When at last he can speak, he tells a tale of horror, of an entire company of soldiers lost in the woods in Georgia, falling prey to a mysterious illness. He himself had been a victim. I gently bathe the scabbed wounds on his neck as he continues to speak, saying he does not remember quite what happened. Two of his company had not sickened and they had cared for the rest. Some of the others had died and their bodies had been burned, as plague was feared.

They had scattered then, most back to the North, to recover their former lives, or at least make the attempt. But Desmond had no place to go. His family home had been destroyed by Yankees who didn't know or care that he was one of theirs. He had gone there first, before coming to me.

His pained, half-delirious words tell me what he never would have spoken of if he were in his right mind. The endless horrors he has seen, the dead children; the slaves who had thought all this was for them and learned the Yankees cared less for them than they did for the looting, the destruction. Starvation, fever, devastation, death. He mumbles words in his sleep. He has no place to go, no family to turn to. His business interests are destroyed, his father dead of apoplexy, his cousins uninterested if he lives or dies . . .

I am careful in how I tend Desmond. I must leave him alone most of the time, though it tears me to do so. I leave buckets of water and blankets, and bring him soup.

I thank God daily that father does not suspect. He is blind

to this secret so close to him. He courts his obsessions constantly, and I rarely see his face. He is with those men, planning revenge.

Desmond regains his strength slowly. The fever leaves his brain, and he does not speak now of what he said in his delirium. I rejoice to see the change in him, and for the first time in a long while dare to hope for a future.

We make plans together, whispered words against the outdoors backdrop of singing insects, warm days. The West is a magic promise. Perhaps there, or somewhere, we can find an unscarred land.

I have lost conventions with the War. What once seemed so important now fades into trivia. I do not tell him what happened to me. I do not want him to know. He has enough to torment him.

When his arms embrace me, gently removing my clothing, I respond fully. My dress is tossed aside; he is beginning to unclasp my petticoat when the sound at the door brings us around like marionettes.

My father stands full in the doorway. Behind him are the others. Outraged eyes take in every detail. The man behind him is smiling at me lewdly. He has not shaved his pockmarked face in a long time.

Then my father is by my side. He jerks me to my feet, his grip cruel on my arm. I gasp in pain. My arm feels out of place, as if something had given inside it. Tears come to my eyes.

The others come in the tiny cabin, five in all, dressed in old, patched clothing and vicious faces. They surround Desmond, drag him to his feet, hold him helpless. His face is pale, set; he has not yet recovered enough strength.

My father is screaming at him, calling him traitor, calling him nigger-lover, bastard, whoremonger. He includes me in his curses. I am low, a harlot, a fallen woman. He accuses me of giving myself willingly to my mother's murderers. I am no longer worthy to be called his daughter. He strikes me three, five times across my face. I try to bite back my cries of pain but cannot. Desmond tries in desperation to break away from his captors; is struck in the jaw, the stomach. He gasps out my name, cursing my father.

A savage light shines in my father's eyes. We will show these Yankee lovers what sort of men they truly are, he says. We shall make an example of this one. He orders the men to take him to the shed used to punish the slaves. The shackles are still there, and the whips. Desmond will die no longer a man. He will castrate him himself, my father says, smiling.

Desmond struggles in futile horror at those words. The others are laughing as they drag him from the hut out across the ruined field.

My father pulls me along by one arm. Pain blinds me. Stalks scrape the skin of my legs. My father is still speaking, saying that I shall witness it all. Then perhaps I will die after my turn-coat lover. Or perhaps he will lock me away for ever.

I beg him for mercy for Desmond, if not for me. I will do anything he wants if only he will let Desmond go.

He laughs shortly, a hard, mirthless sound. I shall do anything he says, and there are no conditions attached. He has the power. I am nothing, lower than the worms in the dirt. How dare I, a sink of corruption, ask him for one single thing? He disowns me, he denies me, he consigns me to Hell.

I scream at him in impotent fear and fury. He strikes me hard across the mouth. I fall heavily to the ground, tasting blood, seeing darkness. He drags me the short remaining distance.

The shed is before us. I search out the scene with dimmed vision. My father drags me inside and drops me to the dirt floor. He wants to attach the shackles himself.

I gather myself, trying to ignore the flashes of pain that rip through my body. My father has a gun. He is not watching me now. The others watch him avidly as he takes the shackle, reaches for Desmond's wrist.

I leap forward, grabbing the gun away from his belt. His hands jerk around mine in an iron, bonecrushing grip. I find a strength I never knew I had. The pain isn't even a consideration any more. I do not let go of the gun. He forces my arms up and around. I can see the cold smooth interior of the barrel now. Desmond's cry sounds in my ears, then is muffled by the explosion.

And everything goes black . . .

I am floating now, not in my memories, but his. At the struggle between me and my father, the men loosened their grip on him ever so slightly. At the report of the gun he breaks away. I see myself, eyes open wide in shock, mouth gaping in a ragged scream. Scarlet blood spouts out from my breast, staining the old white of my torn petticoat.

Desmond jerks the gun away from my father before he

quite understands what is happening. He raises the gun up, motioning them all back. He backs up slowly himself, running into the dense wood of the wall. The door is on the opposite end, a brighter rectangle in the half-lit room. Chinks and cracks allow in a small seepage of sunlight.

Father taunts him, saying there is only one bullet in the gun; that he cannot escape. Desmond looks down at my still body. My eyes are open, staring with dead horror at the empty ceiling. He looks back at the six men facing him, varied expressions of hate, contempt and alarm washing their faces. He lifts up the gun, puts it to his head and fires . . .

My eyes are still open, seeing the spider web, the cracks in the ceiling. I am lying in Anne-Marie's bed. The mattress is lumpy; the blankets smell of mothballs and sweat. Desmond lies beside me, his glittering eyes half closed. My hand feels numb. I try to move it and find that he is clasping it tightly. I do not attempt to move again.

He stirs presently, his gaze flickering over my form. His face is set in repose. I wonder how he can be so calm. My heart is beating rapidly in remembered terror. He smiles and sits up.

Was it the drug? I ask him. Yes, he says, the drug. It was in both of us.

But how? I ask him. He had waited, he explains, until the drug flowed into my blood, and then he took a little – a sip, as it were – that he might share it with me.

Then it wasn't real, I say. But it must be . . .

It is real, he tells me. That is how it all happened.

Then what do we do now? I ask him, still filled with emotions, with remembered and transformed love from a century past.

He shakes his head. He does not know. It is rather amusing, isn't it? It has been so long he has forgotten why he died. Some of the emotions he knew before are dead to him now. They did not die all at once but were dissolved slowly by time. He remembers the details in full clarity, but the motivations, the pain, are dulled or forgotten.

He stands up. If I want to, I can come with him.

I do want to. A slight dizziness touches me as I rise, but fades quickly. He was right; he took barely any blood. I tremble, nevertheless. There is a large mirror on the wall. It records my passing, but not his. I follow him from the room.

Anne-Marie is down in her shop, smoking a pipeful of

aromatic herbs. She acknowledges us by nodding slightly, though her vision is not focused on us but at some point beyond. She inhales deeply. The cloud of sweet smoke makes a canopy for her head.

We walk out into the night. Clouds have come up, obscuring the stars. The only lights are the dim quantities of street lamps, the purple flickering neon forming incomplete words on a striptease bar.

We walk silently through the streets. Before I half realize it, we have reached the place that is his home.

We do not go to either of the rooms I know. He has something to show me, he says, and leads me through the hall into another room.

Black velvet curtains shroud the entire room. The carpet, too, is black, as is the fur bedspread on the enormous bed. Light comes from banks of thick wax candles mounted on golden candlesticks, which makes the only trace of colour in the room. Their light, made steady by their number, reveals the woman in the bright red dress upon the bed.

She is a black woman, but the ebony of her skin is underlaid by pallor. Her lips are painted red; her mouth lies open, revealing pallid gums. Heavy make-up accentuates her deathlike stillness, making an abstraction, a mask of her broad, symmetrical features. There are two jagged, bloodless tears in her throat. She is still breathing, but I know it won't be for long.

Desmond confirms my thoughts. She will not live long, he says. Another quarter hour, perhaps a little more, and she will die, only to rise and join him beyond the barrier of death.

I feel a stab of jealousy at these words. Why should she join him and not I? But he continues; he does not want that. She means nothing to him. He does not have any need for others of his kind. She would doubtless look to him to be her mentor in her strange new world and he has no inclination to be so. There are very few people worth spending eternity with. The majority of humanity consists of unmitigated bores.

But the problem is so easily solved. He runs his hands lightly over her coppery throat, caressing the twin wounds. She stirs slightly at his touch but does not wake. Then, ever so gently, he cradles her throat in his hands and suddenly twists. I hear a sharp crack. She stops breathing without ever opening her eyes.

I should be horrified, I know, but I feel no more concern for her death than I would for that of an ant. Something has died in my soul already and I do not mourn its passing. How quickly the unthinkable becomes plausible.

He looks at me with approval. He has not forgotten everything but there is no turning back. If we are to share anything, that must be understood.

I have no doubts. He has become the sole purpose for my life. Nothing else is important.

Brown enters the room in response to Desmond's unspoken command. I had caught a faint trace of that summons when he made it and that fact pleases me. I am beginning to understand him already, beginning to change.

Desmond directs Brown to dispose of the body. Then we leave the room, following the corridor to its end. He opens the door and we step inside.

The windowless room is large and dominated by an ornate, heavily carved coffin. Mystic sigils cover the walls. They are, he explains to me, charms to keep out any unwelcome occult forces. There are many with power here, and some with reason to use it against him.

He caresses the wood of the coffin lovingly. He is not without vanity, he says. Am I surprised to discover a human emotion in him? Perhaps we can, after all, find a meeting place in our minds.

I am impatient. I want to be done with my former life, to join him in his. He rejects my pleas, saying haste is always an error. I shall learn a new perspective on time. Care must be taken in my re-creation. After it is done, I will not think the way I do now. I have already changed, but it is not enough. Perceptions shall be altered as well; reactions and actions changed. We must do this thing gradually if it is to be done at all.

I accept his judgement but doubt its wisdom. It is all very well for him to speak of gradual changes – but how long will that be? Does he even remember how swiftly the years can pass for one who must die like the rest of humanity?

I say nothing, but he senses the turmoil in my mind and takes it to prove he is right; that I am not yet ready.

We go out to walk in the night. He tries to explain to me some of what he sees. The blending of the dark, the formation of clouds that complete perfection, the intrusion of the moon reflecting painful light from the deadly sun. He speaks of shadow and substance, change, transition, death. I think I see something of what he does, but when I believe I have grasped it in its entirety it bursts apart and sparkles away.

Only a few pass us on the streets. They do not look at us. Sometimes, he tells me, they cannot even see us. I am under his aura and it is under his will.

I ask him, then, what made him as he is. I have seen the Dracula movies; I know how it is done. He laughs. He has seen them, too. They catch a corner of the truth and tear it away, letting the main body go. They are not wrong in everything, though.

He had been in Georgia just before the end of the war, along with the rest of his decimated troops. There were not many left – perhaps ten – and they had, by following an ambiguous order, become lost in the backwoods. Rain had been steadily coming down for an entire day, creating a soggy green mush for them to stumble through, searching for shelter. The trees strained the rain to them, adding torn off bits of twigs and leaves. The sky rumbled distantly, lit by shuddering sheets of electricity. They had pushed on, in search of refuge from the biting chill, the wet miserable drowning air, the coming darkness.

Desmond had not been the first to see the ramshackle house, but he had been as relieved as the others by its presence.

A young man, barely in his late teens, had tried the door. It swung open easily, and they had gone with relief inside.

The house was fairly small, containing only one main room, a cooking area and a sleeping room. One of the men, Thompson, had discovered the cellar and had volunteered to search it for the owners of the house, for food. While he was gone, the rest broke up what little remained of the rotting furniture and used it to build a fire in the ill-cleaned fireplace.

A while later Thompson had returned, not saying much, but the bottles of wine and the dried meat he had found spoke for him. Much later, the bottles near empty, the food completely gone, and what little money each had left exchanged again in games of poker, they had settled down to sleep.

While he had still lived, Desmond never recalled what happened next, but his change brought back his memory. From out of the dark figures had come, silent, unbreathing, an absence and counterpoint to life. He had been paralysed, unable to move or see, but aware intimately of their presence through the silence. He had been afraid, but that had passed.

One had fastened on to his neck, like an enormous leech. He remembered the draining, the weakness, and his willingness that this be done, his acceptance – even eagerness – for the final conclusion.

But it had not come. The creature left him as silently as it had come. He never saw its face but sensed its mind – a flashing, unreadable intimation of power, of the denial/acceptance/fulfilment/mockery of life . . .

He had fainted, but was able to reconstruct, after his memory had revived as he did, what had followed.

Of all the men in the house, only two had been left untouched by the creatures. Both Roman Catholic, each wore a small crucifix around his neck. When and how they discovered the truth, Desmond never knew, but the presence of the creature who had attacked him was gone from his mind the next day, and the old armoire in the sleeping room, the only piece of furniture left untouched in their search for firewood, had been broken into pieces. It had been made of a hardwood; quite suitable for forming stakes.

Two of the company died the next day. Their bodies had been burned.

Desmond ends his narrative abruptly. I watch him in fascination. His eyes shine like glass in an intent, rapt, distant gaze. I do not think he even sees the street any more. He murmurs something about a curiosity about his brothers in Georgia.

I ask if he has ever gone there to learn more.

He comes to himself suddenly, eyes changing as he looks at me. No, he says, he never has. Somehow he never found the interest.

I watch his face carefully. No curiosity? Is that possible? No, it cannot be . . . he has shown interest in other things . . . I just can't recall . . .

What they saw about the cross is true, then, I say, changing the subject. Vampires do fear holy objects.

He shakes his head. Not always, he says. Not all. Individuality persists, though in an altered way. Legend merges with truth and what one is ruled by, another ignores. He does not know why this is so.

Prove it, I say. I want to see Dracula dethroned. I want to see the movies made liars.

He smiles, a crooked, indulgent smile, faintly condescending.

What need does he have to prove anything? Nevertheless, it may prove amusing.

We walk for a long way through the tide of the streets, the changing of the buildings. The old church stands before us, its spire scraping the sky. It is Roman Catholic. The door is locked, but he does not care. He passes through the chinks in the wood like smoke sucked in. An instant later the door swings open. He stands in the darkened interior, beckoning.

I come in. The only light is from a bank of tiny candles flickering softly in their red glass holders. A blind saint watches above them, imperturbable plaster. Desmond dips his hand in the Holy Water and lets a few drops fall to the floor. He holds out his hand for my inspection. It is unchanged, the flesh neither melted nor burned away.

He walks about the church for my benefit, even going up to the altar, a dark priest. He touches the cross, smiling. Lightning doesn't strike. He does not collapse in a heap of ash.

It is just a place, he says, and we leave.

Why, then, did those other vampires fear the cross? I ask. I do not understand.

He thinks about it for a moment, then speaks in his low, compelling voice that flows like the currents of a deep river. He has heard of situations in which people believe they will die, and they do, though there is no apparent reason. Perhaps that is what happened in this case. Perhaps belief is enough.

But I still do not understand. What made him as he is.

He was tainted, he explains, and the taint was roused by his suicide. Suicides are cursed, he reminds me, and smiles, a flashing of white teeth.

Light faintly streaks the sky. The dawn is far distant, yet already he retreats into himself. He tells me to return home. I shall see him again soon.

I watch him walk down the street, shadow in shadow, until the street is empty and he is gone. And I want to cry but find I have no tears.

Father wants to know where I have been all night, but I do not tell him. A party, I lie, but he is not convinced. His eyes follow me with a look of disappointment. Malinda's face conveys a sense of disapproval. She has certainly changed. She would never have thought twice about it before. I suppose it is John Arnold's influence. I do not care.

I have been up for a long time and have lived two lifetimes

during it, but I am not tired. I cannot sit still, cannot rest, so I go out again and walk, and walk, until it is time for me to go to work. Sue Ellen comments on my new look, my new attitude. Stars in my eyes, she says. She wonders if I have found a new man.

Yes, I tell her, thinking that safe enough. I say I cannot talk about him, implying he is married. That is enough. She can accept a clandestine affair without troubling me with lectures.

I see Desmond several times over the next few weeks. At each meeting he takes a small amount of my blood. He wants me to become gradually accustomed to the dark, to see as he does, otherwise it will all be worthless; too much of a shock. A new vampire can be very foolish.

I accept this, sensing the gradual change in myself. The sun becomes exceedingly bright. It burns my skin now, even with very short exposures. I wear dark glasses all the time, and heavy coats, and I keep my hands buried in my pockets. It is winter, but very mild; Sue Ellen comments on it. I say my blood must be thin; the cold really bothers me. I am glad it is not summer; what would I do then? She mentions that I look pale, suggests I see a doctor. I murmur something vague, noncommittal.

Time seems to move more slowly, then more swiftly, or more in a dream, like a band stretched to its limit and snapped, again and again. It loses its accustomed rate. I lose track of dates, then days. Malinda has to wake me more than once to go to work on a day I thought was Saturday.

Malinda is seeing a great deal of John Arnold. He brings others with him to our apartment some nights and they sit around having theological discussions and rap sessions. Father is not interested at first, yet he cannot help but hear it and after a time begins to take part until he is as enthusiastic as Malinda. They divide leaflets among themselves and in their spare time go to distribute them to shoppers in supermarkets or theatre patrons waiting in line.

They try to draw me into their group. I decline politely. I am not interested.

They talk a great deal of being saved, of witnessing to others. Malinda's eyes carry a fresh glow. She does not wear as much make-up as she used to. Her vitality is not changed, only directed a different way. She wishes I could experience this too, and prays for me daily.

624

It is February. Time passes without transition. It is very difficult to move in the light now. I take to bringing my lunch to work in order to avoid going outside in the sun's powerful rays. I bring a fat book with me each time. I need to catch up on my reading, I explain to Sue Ellen, and dutifully open the book each noon and watch the black insects of words swarm before my hazing eyes. Sue Ellen goes to lunch then and does not notice. I turn the pages as I am supposed to, but it does not make any sense. The papers I must read at work burn my eyes; I cannot do any more.

This new order of things quickly becomes natural.

Malinda is concerned about me, I know, but I cannot find the energy to care. Once she sees the marks on my neck when my high-necked blouse slipped slightly and immediately wants to know what caused it. I berate my own clumsiness, speaking of a tight necklace that broke, cutting my neck. She speaks of tetanus, suggests a doctor. I am tired of hearing about doctors. I say I will take her suggestion. A day or so later I lie to her, saying I saw a doctor on my lunch hour; that I was given time off from work. I had to wait in the waiting room for a long time, I tell her. Something really ought to be done about that – it's just a matter of proper scheduling. I am really quite pleased about that comment; it sounds so natural, and it begins her telling of long waits for doctors who never arrived. I slip in that the doctor said I was all right; just needed vitamins. I buy several bottles and take them when I remember. She seems satisfied with that, but once or twice I catch a light frown furrowing her eyebrows when she looks at me, thinking I am not looking at her. I assume she is worrying about my soul.

The longing begins to fill me again, the impatience. Time seems to have slowed interminably, the band stretched to its farthest limits and beyond. I doubt if I shall ever truly be with Desmond.

It is dark again; I can breathe again. I stand by the window, glorying in the cool night air. Malinda has snapped off the TV; she is standing by my side. I can hear her speaking; I do not want to answer . . . Someone far more important is out there in the night . . . Surely he is calling me, needs me . . .

No one answers my call but Malinda. She takes my shoulders, forcing me to face her. Her face is stern, her eyes concerned. I do not care, do not answer when she asks what is wrong, when she asks who Desmond is. Her words are meaningless. She is meaningless. I must leave her; I must . . .

I know she is watching as I leave. Well, let her. I am filled with certainty that I shall never be back again, and it will not matter what she thinks or feels. Yes, after this night . . .

I enter the bar beneath Desmond's home. He stands smiling at the far end of the room. Two sloe-eyed hookers clasp his arms, their painted faces showing clearly through the smoke. His eyes meet mine across the distance and haze of the room instantly, penetrating through the swarm of people between us, knowing of my presence before I have even entered. I see the women he is with and feel an unreasoning pang of jealousy. Foolish, of course. I have never imagined I am his only source and yet, somehow, I wish I could be. It is an impossibility. I realize this, but why are my eyes suddenly moist, why is it so difficult to see anything through the smoke save his constant, unchanging eyes?

He beckons to me.

I move forward, drawn like a puppet on a string. He takes my arm and we go upstairs. The hookers watch in resentment but say nothing. They know better.

He is trembling slightly, something I have never known him to do. I can sense the overpowering blood lust in him, the terrible need as if it were my own. I have never sensed this aspect of it before and it both repels and attracts me. I long to satisfy his need, to fulfil his desire. Before, he always came to me sated, or nearly so.

Triumph surges in me. I need not wait any longer. He will be unable to resist his compulsion and I will never be able to survive his need. I may not even be enough.

He touches my throat. It is thrilling, electric. I draw in my breath in a sudden gasp of pleasure and move closer to him. He caresses my neck briefly, drawing my hair away. I am trembling too, in unison with him. Give/take/unite/please—

A voice cuts through the air, like scraping metal, like a siren screaming.

Malinda stands by the door of the room, her eyes wide in horror and shock. Evil, evil, she is saying; the Devil's own.

I cry to her to leave; she is spoiling it all.

She doesn't hear me. Desmond's eyes lock on hers. He moves forward to her. I scream, dragging at his arms, saying it is I he should take, not her. He shrugs me off like an insect. Malinda's eyes are wide with horror. She reaches suddenly into her purse, resisting the drag of his eyes, and brings out a small New Testament, which she holds at arm's length before her. He tears it easily from her grasp and is on her. She screams once and struggles wildly. I see him sink his teeth into her neck. Blood spurts out for an instant. He greedily drinks it, sucking deeper, draining her.

She stops struggling. Her eyes are open; I see the glassy fascination in them; watch with resentment as she slowly reaches up to embrace him.

He continues, his lips pressed to her neck. Her arms drop to her sides. His arms go around her, preventing her from falling, and still he drinks. Jealousy fills me as I watch.

Finally he releases her and she falls heavily to the floor. He seems disoriented for an instant, then becomes aware of the blood that has spattered on his face and clothing. He brushes at it abstractedly, then recalls her. He turns to complete the job and kill her, but it is too late. She is already dead.

I look at her. Her skin is white, like paper. Even her lips are colourless. Her eyes are still open, glassy and blank.

Desmond is irritated. She has already changed. He will do nothing to destroy her now.

She will need a coffin or some safe dark place. He lifts her easily; I follow as he carries her into the bedroom curtained with black velvet. It is a place to contemplate the dark, he says, as he deposits her on the bed. He does not draw the covers over her. There is no need.

I study her so familiar face, wondering how long it will be before she wakens, how long it will be before she takes the place that should be mine.

It sickens me; I turn and leave the room. Desmond is waiting in the living room. He has summoned Brown there.

Desmond is very angry. Why did Brown let the woman come up?

Brown cringes away, excuses tumbling from his mouth. There was a drunk fighting, smashing the furniture. He was trying to break it up. He did not see the woman.

Desmond takes Brown's arm. The bald man watches in horror, sweat glinting on his face, his skull. With great deliberation Desmond selects a finger, then snaps it as if he were breaking a match.

Brown's screams end on a sob. Desmond watches him, his face unreadable, as if he were observing something under a microscope.

627

I, too, am detached. The scene might be a movie for all the personal involvement I feel. A boring movie. Brown means nothing to me. I know Malinda ought to count for something but that, too, is lacking. I wonder if this state of mind is to be as he is. I wonder if I can care.

Brown retreats, nursing his hand, and stumbles out.

Desmond sits down on a tapestry-covered couch and picks up several books. I sit beside him, watching as he looks through them.

They are travel books, filled with pretty pictures and harsh, wildly beautiful landscapes from foreign countries. China takes fifteen minutes to cover. We dispose of Scotland in five. We see temples in Thailand and English pubs, Whitehall, the changing of the guard. He does not seem to read any of the text but makes observations on it later on. These are places he once wished to see, he says. Perhaps he will go to them all some day. He wishes humans would get their petty affairs straightened out; they cause him no end of inconvenience.

He lets the book we are holding close of its own accord. It does not take long, he says, to create a vampire, but one made as swiftly as this may be a threat to us. Or she may mean nothing at all.

We go back to the bedroom. Malinda lies still on the bed, her eyes open as we left them. She is not breathing, but her eyes are alive in a type of awareness, though there is no recognition but rather a small insanity.

She narrows her eyes, watching us, but makes no effort to move. Desmond picks up one of her small pale hands and lets it drop limply back to the bed. She is still changing, he says. The structure is not yet complete; the teeth not fully formed. There is a catlike glow behind the eyes, as if all the light in the room is being gathered up and reflected back by them. I have seen such eyes in the dark staring at me before their feline owner leaped lightly away. It is disconcerting to see this in my sister.

She will not move this night, Desmond says. It is almost dawn. She will be safe in this room. His coffin is a mere trapping, a sop to the legends, a whim of his own. Besides, he was buried; he had contact with the earth, however briefly. That instilled a longing, a need in him. Since she shall not be buried she will have no need to lie in the earth.

Her eyes follow us as we leave. We walk to the room where he keeps his coffin.

What shall I tell Father, I wonder, when Malinda does not come home?

What difference does it make? he asks. Tell him nothing.

No, I shall make up a story. I try to concoct a logical one in my mind. It is important to carry on the charade of normality a little while longer.

But what will Malinda mean to our plans? I ask.

Nothing. He gets into his coffin. Nothing, he repeats. He wishes to have nothing to do with her. She can find her own place tomorrow. Tonight is all the concession that he will give her. It is her own fault, anyway. Curiosity is a trait of fools.

And the lack of it the trait of dullness, I think, but I say nothing. He must know my thought, though. He grins at me like a wolf as he lowers the lid.

I go home. Father is there, furious, worried. He should be leaving for work. He will be late. I remind him of this. He doesn't pay any attention, barely lets me get the words out before he begins his tirade. Where have I been all night? And where, for God's sake, is Malinda?

God had nothing to do with it, I think, but of course I don't say this. I restrain an insane urge to giggle. She ran away, I say, composing my face into suitable lines of concern; ah, yes, the older sister, standing by, her heart breaking, while the foolish younger sister ruins her life. All this time she has been seeing another man – other than John Arnold, I mean. He is a sailor. He has taken her away. I spent the whole night trying to convince her of her folly. It was no use. She wouldn't listen to me. I did all I could. I am very tired now; I would like to go to bed.

But she cared for John Arnold, Father protests, his eyes reflecting hurt and disbelief and numbness. And her beliefs, her commitment to the Lord – these were *real*!

She lied, I said, as I go into my room. I lie upon the bed fully clothed. It is too much of an effort to attempt to undress. Father follows me into my room, still arguing, still protesting. He will call the police. A search must be made. She must be found and convinced to give up her sin. Her soul is in jeopardy; don't I see?

I think that he need not worry about Malinda's soul any longer. I don't think it is there any more. I close my eyes, hoping that if I fall asleep he'll leave me alone.

He sighs in frustration and leaves the room. I hear the door slam.

The shrill incessant ringing of the telephone brings me struggling through layers of consciousness. I do not want to wake up. I lie there and listen to it ring, taking pleasure in the thought of the frustration of the person on the other end. Serves them right. When I get up I will pull it out by its root and throw it out the window. There is no one I wish to talk to.

It finally stops. I slip back into sleep again. It is dusk when I awake, only because I am no longer capable of sleep while Desmond is active, aware.

Father has come home. John Arnold is with him. I go out into the living room and pass by them, ignoring them, taking a perverse delight in my tangled hair. I must look a mess. Let them be shocked. I go to the kitchen and drink a great deal of water. Father calls to me. I answer after a minute, reluctantly. He wants me to come out and talk to John Arnold. I drink another glass of water before I do.

John Arnold wants to hear the whole story so I must repeat it again. I am letter-perfect. I have not forgotten a single detail. No, I have not met the man, but Malinda told me he came from Mobile. He has seen the world. She wants to see the world, too.

John Arnold shakes his head. He looks as if the roof had collapsed on him. He reminds me of a puppy dog whose toy has been taken away. I sip water and stare out the window.

Sue Ellen called, Father says. She is very concerned – so concerned she called him at work. He explained that we are having family problems and that I was not feeling up to coming in. She hoped I would be better in the morning. He hoped I would be also. Am I?

Of course, I say. Never felt better. I wonder how I shall be able to work. I do not think I will go back. I cannot be conscious twenty-four hours a day, and I cannot sleep at night. Perhaps I will go to Anne-Marie, surely she has some herbs, some drug to keep me awake, to keep me going for a little while longer. I do not think it will be for very long.

The department store called also, Father says, about Malinda. He gave them the same explanation.

I shrug apathetically. Let him take my attitude for concern. Let him take it any way he pleases.

John Arnold and Father begin to commiserate with each other on Malinda's betrayal. They are incredibly boring. I wish they would go away. I would like to leave, to go to Des-

630

mond, to see what has befallen Malinda. I would like to see what I shall become. They would ask questions if I tried to leave, and I don't have any more answers. Not right now. I can't mention Martin the myth – he got married a while ago. Inconsiderate; he made such a good excuse; all those movies and parties we never went to together. I seem to have lost a good deal of contact with the people I once knew. They can't even serve as my excuses any more. I shall have to make up some new myths, some safer ones, ones who never existed.

Father has decided he is hungry. Life goes on after all. There's no dinner in the house. He will go out and get pizza.

I am not hungry. I cannot remember the last time that I ate. I go back into my bedroom. Charity Evans stares at me out of her imitation, canvas eyes. I ignore her. Let her stay at the back of my mind.

The reflection in the mirror catches my attention. I look terrible. Dark circles frame my eyes; my face is more hollow, more ethereal than it ever has been before. I see why it is so easy to convince people that I'm ill.

A faint strangled cry comes from the next room. If Father had returned with the pizza I would suspect John Arnold had choked on it; he's the sort. But Father left only a moment ago. I go into the living room.

Malinda is bent over John Arnold, her teeth fastened to his neck. She drinks his blood greedily.

How stupid, I say. Have you no sense?

Her eyes glitter whitely as she looks up from what she is doing. Her mouth is smeared with blood. She licks her lips daintily. John Arnold slumps down on the couch.

Father will be back soon, I say. What if he sees you?

She says that she will take care of him just as she did with John Arnold. She would do the same to me, but it isn't necessary. Her voice is low and slightly changed, as if the vocal cords had somehow altered. Her blond hair falls down, a tangled mess. She is still wearing the blue jeans and T-shirt she had on when she died. They are smudged and torn. She looks a sight.

A slight colour comes to enliven the pallor of her face. She has John Arnold to thank for that.

I am curious and slightly concerned. After all, she is my sister – or was. What difference does the technicality of death make? Blood is thicker than water. I laugh at that and repeat it out loud.

She has no sense of humour. Her face is like a stone statue. I wonder if it will come back to her.

I ask her what she will do now. She doesn't know. She has plenty of time to find out.

I wish her luck. Perhaps it is foolish to do so – a portion of my brain insists so, constantly pointing out the unreality, the absurdity, the diminishing horror of it – but that part of my mind recedes daily. It is an effort to recall what sort of person I was before I met Desmond. I can understand why it is so difficult for him to recall what he felt in life.

She thanks me for my kind wishes. We keep on with the odd masquerade of a conversation, like old friends separated for a long time and now reunited, but with the knowledge that one has a fatal disease. How odd, the barrier that is suddenly there . . .

Well, the other is dying also. I no longer resent the fact that Malinda made it to the other side before I did. In a short time I will follow, and then I'll forget all these petty concerns.

She disappears into the air. That looks like a good deal of fun. What couldn't a bank robber do with such an ability?

I look at John Arnold lying unconscious on the couch. It is disgusting. Now I shall have to take care of him. I hadn't bargained on that.

I wet some paper towels and wash his neck. Malinda was very messy. The blood is still flowing from the twin jagged wounds. It soaks through the paper towels unevenly. I take them and flush them down the toilet, then tear up a pillowcase and wind it around his neck. Blood seeps through it also. There is no help for it. I button his shirt, pulling it as high as it will go.

We used to have some whisky around here, I remember, before everyone got religion. I search through the kitchen for it. There it is, on the bottom shelf, behind the Drano. Medicinal use only, no doubt. I pour half the bottle down the sink, then take it and a glass back to John Arnold. I pour a little whisky in the glass, then smash it on the coffee table. It shatters very satisfactorily. The stench of the whisky is also quite appropriate. I put the bottle on the end table, within John Arnold's reach. Since he is already slumping, I point him in the direction of the broken glass. Then I realize my father will think it strange of me to take the trouble to bandage his neck and leave that mess untouched. The problem is very easily solved. I remove the bandage.

Blood is still flowing slightly from the wounds. That is good, I think; it will look natural. It glistens thickly in the lamp-light. I watch it in fascination, compulsion seizing me, sharp delicate brief twinges of longing, of desire. I know what will satisfy it. I lean forward and lick up the blood.

It tastes warm, salty, vaguely pleasant on my tongue. It is almost a disappointment – somehow I had hoped for more. Or perhaps I can't fully appreciate it yet.

John Arnold moans slightly. I straighten and leave the apartment. I will go to Desmond now.

He is outside in the streets, somewhere in the French Quarter. I know vaguely where he is, but don't make any effort to find him. He does not want my company now. He knows where I am and he will come sometime this night.

I go to Anne-Marie's. She answers my knocking after a few minutes. Her grey hair is dishevelled, her eyes are bright. She motions me in.

She is busy now, she says, but I can wait here if I like. She says I look tense. I shrug, say nothing. She hands me a hand-rolled cigarette saying, have something to relax you.

I accept it, watching as she goes back upstairs. A man's voice drifts down. I do not try to make sense of his words. The bed-springs begin a frantic squeaking. I draw on the cigarette, in-haling the sweet smoke.

It has little noticeable effect. I feel weak and tired, yet hyper-active. I could not rest if I tried. The dark is outside but it seeps into my bones, my nerves, combating the debilitation of the day. I get up and pace around the room. My hands are trembling; the lit end of the cigarette dances redly in the gloom. I can almost see the bones through my pallid skin. The sounds of moaning, of endearments come faintly to me. I sit down again and stare at the dried animals.

Anne-Marie and a man come out after a while. He is tall, black like ebony, handsome like a carved statue of a god. He directs a greeting at me. I respond in some way; I am not truly aware. The room seems to have faded away into some other reality. I sit passively, mute, like an empty vessel aching to be filled.

The man leaves. Anne-Marie exchanges some last-minute banter with him. The door closes, jingling like Christmas.

Anne-Marie lights a cigarette for herself, her old, wise face set in repose. She remarks that since she is known as a bruja, many men come to her for power. She obliges them, in her own way.

633

I don't know quite why, but I tell her of Malinda. She nods. Her cigarette makes small arcs as her hands move. She thinks there will be trouble. A new vampire is always a bad thing. They take to their powers too quickly, too carelessly.

We sit meditating in the dark.

Desmond is outside, as if waiting. I rise without a word and leave. I do not think Anne-Marie is surprised. I have seen the marks on her neck once or twice.

We walk down through the streets, through the twilight subterranean life that surrounds us. I tell him what Malinda did. He says it is her affair. She will not return to his apartment. He will not permit it. The light casts garish shadows on his pale, finely carved face. He looks less human than he usually does. I want to emulate him, but don't know how.

He kisses my throat briefly. I protest as he draws away; I want to be drained. It is not fair.

There is trouble, he says. We will wait a few days more. He wants to know what Malinda will do.

I want to know why, since he does not care what happens to her. He tells me I have yet to learn patience. I tell him I will never learn his definition of it as long as I am mortal. He smiles briefly at this, but says nothing.

It is barely midnight when I return. Father is there, waiting for me. A cold pizza sits on the table, its cheeses and tomato sauces, like blood, congealing. The glass and the whisky have been cleaned up. John Arnold is not there.

I remark on the pizza. He wants to know where I have been. Out, I say. I do not have to account for every minute. He is irritated with that, but he has other concerns. He tells me John Arnold had an accident. I express all the proper sympathy and ask what happened, as a matter of form. He tells me, watching me closely, that he cut his neck on a bottle.

How unfortunate, I say.

I lie awake in my room the rest of the night staring at the ceiling, which sometimes isn't there. I see the stars, the moon; I am filled with some atavistic emotion. The memory of the taste of blood is still in my mouth. It is good.

Dawn emerges over the horizon, its first painful tendrils inching their way up, like so many worms. I draw all the curtains. The light burns like fire. I lie again on my bed and fall deeply asleep. If I dream any more, I do not remember.

A day or so passes. I do not return to work. Sue Ellen calls, concerned. It is doubtless because she is having to do my work as well as her own. I tell her I'm not coming back. Father doesn't know yet. I try to keep up the pretence. I say I have been given a few days off; that work is slow; that I'm due for a vacation anyway. He doesn't really hear me. He's thinking about Malinda.

It is now almost a week since she disappeared. Mardi Gras is not far off. Long ago, in another world, I had looked forward to it. Another New Orleans trademark, like Creole cooking and magnolia trees.

The apartment is in an uproar. I wake up, disconcerted. It is not yet dusk. I get up anyway, to see what is going on. I doubt if curiosity will ever die.

People are swarming over every available inch of the living room. It's the prayer group; I thought they had stopped meeting here. John Arnold is with them, pale face desperate in the electric light. His mouth is white. I can see the whites in his eyes. He is sweating, though it is not warm. He is not restrained, though people hover near, constraint implicit in their postures. His eyes meet mine in a desperate plea to a kindred spirit. I look away.

A woman is talking. Her hysterical voice grates like nails on a chalkboard. She is John Arnold's sister; I recognize her. She is describing the face of the demon she saw, and all are listening, faces intent with horror, with fascination.

Blood, she said, her mouth dripped blood. That thing took the face of Malinda – ugly, evil thing! It was at his throat.

The Devil is here, someone says, and it's repeated again and again. The Devil is here!

Someone becomes aware of me, then they all turn and look. Father watches me, his eyes old and unreadable.

What's going on? I ask, though I know perfectly well. What a fool Malinda was.

They ask me what's going on. I shrug. It's useless to waste time with fools. The sun just set and Desmond fills my thoughts, the dark fills my mind. I long to be out in it, searching, hunting . . .

Father grabs me and pulls at the neck of my turtleneck sweater. I twist away, but it is too late. They see the marks and begin the mutter. I stare at them with hostility.

Reverend Wallace steps up to me, fanatically sober in black. He says he knows the truth. The Evil is loose on earth and John

Arnold and I are its pawns. It is not too late to save our souls, if we aid them.

I remain silent. I have no interest in my soul. He shakes me. I allow him to, not resisting. It sets my teeth clacking and is not at all pleasant. My head begins to hurt. I scream an obscenity at him.

He releases me. You see, he says sadly to Father, to the others. She may be beyond help, but there is still hope. If the creature can be found in time, both of us can be saved.

Father asks me how I could do this thing. How could I let myself be corrupted in this manner? He has tried to raise me properly but Lord knows it hasn't been easy since Mother died. He had higher hopes for me.

Yeah. Charlene Armstrong, the All-American Girl. I say that, giggling. He slaps me hard across the face. I become interested in the taste of blood in my mouth. The pain is a slight, distant inconvenience. I lick the blood from the corner of my cracked lip. He stares at me, repelled.

They are all watching me closely. What does it feel like, Charlene Armstrong, to be the centre of attention? Very well, thank you, but I don't know what act I shall perform. What about a striptease? They've already begun with my neck . . . What can I say now, dear father, dear Reverend? The expressions on your faces are amusing, but I am getting tired of this . . .

. . . It is almost dawn. They spent the night plaguing me and John Arnold with questions. The fools. Of course we said nothing. As the saying goes – even if we wanted to tell you . . .

They sit about the room, voices raised in prayer and murderous plans. Why was John Arnold so stupid? Why was Malinda? This is a great inconvenience to me . . . and, to be honest, I do not want to see her destroyed . . .

I get up. I want to go to the bathroom. Reverend Wallace is at my side instantly, his hand on my arm, demanding to know if the evil one has summoned me. I suggest he come witness me communing with him on the toilet. He is disgusted; he speaks of filth, blasphemy. Yes, a little of that right now might be interesting . . .

He does not follow me after all, but stands guard outside the door, faithful watchdog. I shall have to remember to get him a bone, pat his head, good boy. I'll take you to the kennel tomorrow and they can gas you to sleep . . .

The transition comes again, dark to dark. I come to myself on my bed. The sun is disappearing outside. I have missed an entire day now. That is good. It can't be much longer . . .

I get up and wander around. Besides my father and John Arnold, only Reverend Wallace and two other men are left. They are bristling with crosses and a heap of garlic. The room stinks. Sneezing, I hurry into the kitchen. Their interest caught, they follow me. I study their florid, overripe faces, their bodies full to bursting with sweet blood. I run my tongue over my lips.

One of the men, bored, drifts back into the living room. Almost immediately there is the cry – John Arnold is gone.

We are instantly into the other room. He isn't far away. I can hear his heavy tread down the stairs and wonder if their ears are sensitive enough to catch it. Yes, unfortunately. Reverend Wallace grabs my arm, half dragging me on, as we leave the room.

John Arnold is going down the back stairs, a hurrying, desperate figure. I want to scream at him in frustration. Doesn't he realize he is leading Malinda's destruction to her? He runs on, reckless, uncaring, but he is too drained to sustain it. He slows to an unseeing walk. Doesn't he know? Doesn't Malinda? She must indeed be a fool to summon her own death. Or perhaps she has not yet learned perfect rapport with her chosen ones.

My arm feels as if it is being torn from its socket. I drag back but Reverend Wallace pulls harder. We walk briskly along. Air streams in and out of my lungs. It is cold. I do not have a jacket. But I don't really need one, anyway.

John Arnold falters. I can hear his tortured gasps for breath through the distance that separates us. He stumbles on, almost lifeless, a puppet pulled on a string. Can't he hear us following? Or is he deaf to that as well, hearing only Malinda's call, feeling only her need?

Street changes into street. The trees above interlace, cutting off the light from the stars, separating, blending streetlights. John Arnold casts a long shadow, but it is an extremely dim one.

He enters a private home. Windows are shuttered by curtains. There is a 'Sold' sign on the immaculate lawn. It is very pretty. The door is not locked. Reverend Wallace, Father, and the other two men cling to their crosses. Then one opens the door and we enter.

The room is furnished in bourgeois modern. Pile carpet, mirrored walls, cabinet TV. By the bar, John Arnold is in Malinda's arms. Her teeth are fastened to his neck; her eyes are closed. Her face looks peaceful, ecstatic, as if she were experiencing a pleasant dream.

An instant later her peace is shattered. She opens her eyes and first astonishment, then anger and fear show there. She jerks her head away from John Arnold's neck. He reaches out to clasp her. She tears his arms away from her, eyes darting about, as the men surround her, brandishing Bibles and crosses. She cowers away, not facing them.

I scream at her to pay them no attention, to forget the myths and legends and save herself. She does not hear me, or if she does, she cannot understand.

Reverend Wallace and another pull her away from John Arnold. Her mouth is running with blood. They grab her arms and then they are all on her, forcing her to the floor. She struggles in their grip like a demon. Her gaze rakes me and she begins to scream my name.

I watch in fascinated horror as Reverend Wallace takes out a stake and hammer from a briefcase he has been carrying.

Malinda is screaming all the time, giving voice to the most amazing obscenities, calling for my help, begging Father to spare her. Once she calls for Desmond. Father is shaking uncontrollably, his eyes wide with shock. John Arnold is slumped to the floor, unconscious. I suddenly realize I am not being held and jump forward and grab Reverend Wallace's arm. He shouts an order, trying to shake me off. Father pulls me away. I stand, trembling, not having the strength to struggle. Reverend Wallace places the stake upon her breast above her heart. She twists wildly in their grasp. Wallace's arm makes an arc as he brings the mallet down.

Malinda's scream tears through my soul. I think I scream, too. Blood spurts out from her burst heart, staining her clothing, raining upon Reverend Wallace's hand which is still clasping the hammer. Malinda dies, choking on blood, her body giving a final shudder before it lies still, her face fixed in agony.

Reverend Wallace comes over to me. My sister's blood is staining his sleeves. I am now limp in Father's arms. He releases me a little at a time, like a machine with its batteries dying, making one final effort. I stand swaying, the room fading and brightening before my eyes.

They ask questions, questions, questions; the words tear my mind, torture my understanding, swarming in like locusts. Was Malinda the one? Did she victimize you? Was she the one? Was she was she was she—

And I scream – yes, it was her! It was always her! And I fall sobbing to the floor.

They consult among themselves, unmindful of the bloody horror a few feet away, unmindful of John Arnold, of me. They will burn the body, they say.

A haze has crept sickeningly across my vision. It is composed of blood and agony. I almost welcome it. Their voices recede along with my vision and I plunge into blackness . . . I awake, comfortable, in my own bed. How much time has passed? I try to rise but cannot. Light seeps in through the cracks between the curtains. It is day already. I fall back with a moan.

Father and Reverend Wallace come in. Father's face is haggard, drawn, his eyes on the knife edge of insanity. Reverend Wallace's face is tight, grim, unreadable.

They ask me how I feel. I wonder how to respond. Tired, I say. They accept this, then ask how much I remember. I shudder, then say it is a blur, a horror; I cannot face looking back on such memories. This seems to satisfy them.

Reverend Wallace examines my neck. My skin crawls at the touch of his hand; I bite my lip and remain silent as I look into his opaque eyes. I will mine to reflect their blankness.

He walks away and with one abrupt motion draws the curtains completely open. I moan and cringe away, unable to control my instinctive reaction to the fiery, painful touch of the light. I cower, trembling, my face averted. He pulls my head back to face the light. I squeeze my eyes shut, feeling nauseated. His voice pounds in on my ears, like the stake into Malinda's heart, repeating phrases, praying for my soul, for my life. He asks me if I want to live. Will I accept Christ as my Saviour? It is the only way I can be saved.

The light lances through me, fresh, unceasing agony, ripping my body with fire, drying the precious blood in my veins. I am scarcely aware of anything other than the pain. His voice tears at me, stern, the ultimate father figure, authoritative, terrible. Will I repent of my sins?

Yes! I scream. Yes, yes, I want to be saved. Oh, God, help me . . .

A Bible is thrust into my hands which close around it automatically. His voice comes again, telling me I must keep this by me always, that the creature which leeched off Malinda might attempt the same on me. He has heard of such cases, of whole families sickening and dying. He is determined not to let it happen here. If our prayers are strong enough they will create an impenetrable bulwark, and Satan's creature will look for easier prey. The Lord's work will be done, he says. They will hunt down this foul and loathsome thing and destroy it, burning it from God's earth like the excrescence it is.

I ask in a low dry voice if they can draw the curtain. I cannot sleep, I say, with the sun in my eyes. Reverend Wallace looks at me with suspicion, but he draws the curtains and they leave the room.

I awaken to find tears on my face. Images crowded a dream I had; the first I remember having in a long time. California beaches, Malinda and I laughing; the taste of salt on my tongue, sparkling on my skin as I leave the water; the gritty crunch of sand beneath bare feet. We sat around a campfire a hundred times or so, and our companions male and female had ever-changing faces. The beautiful young men I had admired face me again across the flames, thin wisps of smoke softening their faces, the flickering light glinting off their sun-lightened hair, throwing their sun-darkened bodies in splendid relief. I had loved one or two, gone to bed with them, almost married one. And I can no more remember their names than I can recall the feelings I had for them. There is nothing there any more except an exquisite poignancy, an empathy felt briefly for a stranger, or for an image on a movie screen. I try and recall Malinda, of shared secrets and jealousies, but she, too, fades as all the images go silvery blank and I sink back into the spun dreams . . .

I awake promptly at dusk. Father is in my room, sitting by my bed, watching me because he has been told to do so. His face is blanked out; all that is left is an infinite weariness. If I did not know him so well, I would not recognize the old stranger he has become.

Malinda's death haunts me. Is this the way it will end? For me? For . . . Desmond?

He is out there somewhere, moving through his beloved darkness. I can feel only the faintest abstract traces of his mind. I do not understand this – can the link that joins us be stretched somehow, drawn so very thin that going back to what we had before is impossible? Or has he dissolved it himself, recognizing danger instinctively, as an animal does? If this is what has happened, I feel no resentment – no, only loss – for I understand now something of what motivates him. He moves through his own world, trusting his responses to protect him, relying on finely defined instincts, atavistic, reactivated impulses that serve him far better than any sense known to humankind. I understand now because I have begun to share it, and if the connection between our minds has grown weaker, my own acclimatization to his world has grown stronger. This must be what he meant when he said he wanted me to become adjusted to the dark . . .

Father makes a brief attempt to speak to me, but the words falter and die before he has half uttered them, as if he has forgotten he started to speak. He is not even looking at me. His eyes are unfocused, seeing only the nightmare within. I feel pity for him, knowing he will see it for the rest of his days, even if he relinquishes his tenuous hold on sanity. Especially then.

Reverend Wallace comes into the room. He asks how I feel.

I am still so weak I can barely lift one hand, but I try to dissemble, to convince him that I am better than I actually am. He is not fooled. He sits by my bedside and opens his Bible. He reads me several passages from it, then asks my opinion. This surprises me. I had hoped to be passively read to. I had not been able to concentrate on the words. They had flitted through and blown apart in the corners of my mind. I cannot even remember what he is talking about. I say something clichéd, noncommittal. He continues to read.

He, or another of his followers, sits with me all night. I am irritated by this. Despite my weakness, I would like to leave. I am sure I could find the strength for that.

They bring me consommé to eat. I force a little of it down and feel ill immediately after. Even the way my body functions has begun to alter. It will no longer accept this gross matter as nourishment. I get up and go into the bathroom, staggering slightly, saying I need no assistance. I lean over the toilet and vomit what I have just eaten. With difficulty, I pull myself up. My image wavers past me in the mirror, inconstant. I frown, trying to keep the room from swaying, trying to focus my blurring vision on the silvered glass.

641

It is true, after all. My reflection is not all it should be. It is blurred, streaked in places, and I can almost see the wall through it.

They must not see this! I go back into my room, trying to stay as far from the mirror in there as possible. The dizziness, the weakness overcomes me and I fall, only to be caught up by strong arms. Reverend Wallace leans over me as he carries me to my bed. His neck is temptingly, frighteningly close. I can sense the blood pulsing close to the surface, feel the intricate delicate patterns of arteries, veins, capillaries. Fierce hunger overcomes me. I bring my head up slightly, wanting to taste his blood, but he deposits me on the bed before I have made more than a tentative move in that direction.

I look at them surreptitiously. Neither one appears to have noticed my lapse. I run my tongue over my eyeteeth. They are noticeably sharper and perhaps a little longer. I resolve to keep my mouth shut, to mumble in response to their questions.

After a time they leave, and another of Wallace's followers comes in. He is young, with a rough, lived-in face and the eyes of a fanatic. He sits with me for the rest of the night.

There is no help for it. If I am to escape, it must be during the day, when they would not expect it.

I doze after dawn, but it is a troubled sleep. I awake many times during the day, only to slip back into a deep, smothering sleep. Drifting back, I enter another period of wakefulness. It is almost five o'clock. I am quite alone in the room.

I rise and dress hurriedly, but it is a difficult task, my hands are trembling so. I cover as much of my body as possible to protect it from the sunlight. I get my sunglasses and start to leave. The portrait of Charity Evans catches my eye. Do I want to take that? No, I don't need it. I carry with me all that belonged to her. It isn't a very good likeness, anyway.

The apartment is deserted. Can Father be away, so soon after Malinda's death? Or, if not, where is he?

I do not question my good fortune. Taking the car keys, I leave the apartment quickly, thinking illogically that if I hurry I shall reach my destination before my strength has deserted me.

It is no good. I reach the bottom of the stairs and stand swaying. Outside, a car engine dies. Doors slam. I can hear every footstep, every breath, the sounds preternaturally augmented.

There is a closet beneath the staircase where the landlady keeps cleaning supplies. It is open. There is room for me among the straight stalks of mop handles, the tin buckets and petrified scrub brushes, the cutting smell of ammonia.

Voices drift through the hallway. No, not voices, just one. Reverend Wallace. There is someone else with him, unless he has taken to talking to himself. The footsteps are too many for one. Perhaps it is Father.

They climb the stairs. The sound of their passing creaks, like a miniature army, an experiment in retribution. I hardly breathe. They must have reached the apartment by now.

I run from my hiding place. Father begins to call my name.

The sunlight, still intense, strikes me like a blow as I run from the house. I stagger, reeling across the neat lawn. The car is an infinity away. The keys fit, jagged metal, in my hand. Dimly I hear them shouting at me. I slump into the car and fumble the key into the ignition. It comes to life and jerks forward. Drunkenly I guide it into the street, pulling down the sun visors, squinting against the agonizing, unrelenting glare, leaving them far behind. I catch a final glimpse of them in the rear view mirror, running impotently down the street after me. I swerve around several corners. They cannot possibly follow me.

I slow the car, my body trembling uncontrollably, and grip the steering wheel. Traffic passes by and around me, like scuttling insects, a giant antheap. Instinct takes me where I wish to go, for I have lost almost all conscious awareness. I respond to the stimuli of traffic signals and streetlights like Pavlov's dog, well trained.

I go to Anne-Marie, of course. Where else can I go? I am dimly aware that today is Mardi Gras. I must have passed by parades without knowing it – or perhaps I paused and watched. Yes, I must have; the sun is a good deal lower in the sky than it was when I left the house. There is a beaded plastic necklace wrapped around the car's antenna. I pull it off. It snaps, spilling the bright red beads on to the ground where they scurry and roll into patterns and ruts, each finding its appointed place. I go into the shop.

The incense she burns today is strawberry. Two tourists are inspecting some of her offerings. She is fantastically garbed as a gypsy. A wide skirt of a violent combination of yellow and violet swirls about her as she steps back to show them some merchandise. Metallic gold jewellery dangles on her wrists, her waist, her ears. She has made up her eyes with broad lines of black, emphasizing their slight slant, or perhaps creating it. She should look ridiculous, but emanates power instead.

The tourists leave without purchasing anything. She says something obscene, then comments on my pallor. I follow her upstairs. She busies herself in the kitchen for a moment, then brings me a glass of clear, greenish liquid. The faintest steam rises from it. I sip it gingerly. It burns my tongue but I do not half feel it. Whatever it is, it revives me somewhat.

The streets are alive with people. I look outside, catching glimpses of fantastic costumes, surreal in the twilight, then draw the curtains against the pervading, dying sun. I lie down on the bed.

I know the instant the sun sets. I rise, already filled with new energy. I go to the balcony and watch the people below, content. Desmond is beside me before another quarter of an hour passes. We go inside and he smiles fully, easily, revealing sharp glittering teeth.

Tonight, possibly, he says, biting my neck tenderly. He draws his head away after only a second. But not now, he says. He wants to see the festival. I should go out in it also. After all – it is my last night as a mortal. I should observe the rest of my kind on their frivolous, fascinating habits.

I almost do not hear all he says in the wonder of those casual words. My last night . . .

But I sense he is already replete. Jealousy fills me of the unknown person who satisfied him at dusk.

I shall have to vanquish that emotion, he tells me. What do I expect after I am as he is? There is no way we could feed off one another.

This startles me. It had not occurred to me. I find myself realizing how much I do not know, how much of an unknown journey this is.

But it does not frighten me. I do not draw back. I made my decision long ago.

We step out into the night and are caught up in the swirling crowd of revellers. I see pirates and cowboys and a Marie-Antoinette. Her head is intact. I ought to congratulate her, I think, laughing out loud, sharing the thought with Desmond. He smiles at me, watching everything around him with a kind of wide-eyed interest. We walk about for hours. I feel utterly fresh, full of strength, as if I had never known weakness in my life.

I realize he is now sustaining me with his life force through the bond that links us. I sense that I am, in a way, feeding off him as he has fed off me, and I am glad of this shared vampirism.

He says to me that the festival should go on for ever, the night should go on for ever, that the earth should never be cursed by light again.

A young man passes by. He is dressed as a vampire, in white pancake make-up and a cape copied from bad horror movies. Desmond grins. He will have some fun with this one. He moves off, almost floating through air, in the young man's direction.

I wander through the drunken, laughingly abandoned crowd. I can sense something from them, a strength that need not come from their blood, as if their very life was pouring from them and all I had to do was reach out and bathe myself in it. It is a heady, sustaining feeling. I walk through the hordes of life surrounding me, turning down a dozen propositions, losing myself in the glorious, oblivious, jubilant crowd.

A heavy hand descends on my shoulders. I turn, expecting another offer of a bed for the night, and freeze. Reverend Wallace's harsh eyes bore into mine. Father hovers just behind him.

Before I have a chance to move he has pushed my hair from my neck. I hear his sharp intake of breath as he sees the fresh marks. His eyes narrow and his mouth opens for an accusation. The crowd moves in against us for a second, loosening his grip ever so slightly. I break free and run.

Faces flash by me, flesh, bodies in nightmare costumes, in ostrich plumes, in panniered skirts and powdered wigs, leering, bored, startled, indifferent, rapt.

Breath catches painfully in my lungs. I do not have the strength for this. What Desmond gave me is fading.

I know where he is, of course, but will not go to him. I am not the fool John Arnold was. Nothing is more important than Desmond's existence.

I will go back to Anne-Marie. Surely she will know what to do.

She is having a party when I burst through the door. A half dozen startled, painted faces watch me as I clutch the edge of the counter, unable to speak, pointing desperately towards the door.

An instant later Reverend Wallace and Father burst in and stop abruptly. Before they can make any move to leave, to accuse, to attack, they are surrounded and restrained at Anne-Marie's direction. Reverend Wallace struggles furiously, hurling out the Lord's invective. Father does not resist at all.

I gasp out a little of my story, and theirs. I look at Anne-Marie; she nods slowly, guessing my thought, and says I may speak freely to all here. I tell them how these men have destroyed one vampire and want to destroy another. They listen in silence, their eyes hardening against the two men. They are all Desmond's creatures, or Anne-Marie's; they share the undercurrent of control he has spread through this city. Anne-Marie listens in silence, revealing little in the set of her smooth, aged features. I finish my story with a sob of exhaustion.

She looks at them for a moment, only a trace of regret on her features. They have given her no choice, she says. None at all. She knows of a Satanist group that is holding a Black Mass. They intend to sacrifice a goat. Perhaps they would accept a substitution . . .

She motions to the group. They come forward and take them away. Reverend Wallace screams at them as they drag him out the back way. Father walks with them willingly. He looks as if he has already died. I think I have killed him. He does not look back at me. Surely I must feel something now – a few tears, at least. He is my father. I raise my hand to my face to check for their presence. I found them there once before. But my face is dry.

Father disappears behind Anne-Marie's beaded curtains. She looks at me for an instant, then follows.

I go upstairs, to the balcony off her bedroom. Any further effort is impossible. I slide down, grasping the wrought iron grillwork, watching the revellers below through the bars of my imaginary prison. I wait for Desmond to come.

They call it the flashing before the eyes – the remembrance of one's life a dying person has. That is ridiculous. I have remembered everything and now it seems that I am awakening again. No, I am not dead yet. Just dying, alone.

I do not know how long I have looked down from the balcony. At times it seems that it isn't there and I'm falling through dizzying depths, experiencing the vertigo of my life. But they always return, these cold iron bars, and I am always alone in the dark.

I wonder if he will come for me after all. He said he would and yet promises mean as little to him as anything else. I hope he has not forgotten.

Light is faintly touching the horizon when he comes to me. The streets are nearly empty. Fat Tuesday was over long ago. He stands above me and I rise and face him. The one who masqueraded as a vampire, he tells me, now serves one.

There is a brilliant light in his eyes. I see the hunger, the insatiable lust there, and move to him willingly as he reaches for me. One last time, he says, and presses his mouth to my neck. I feel his teeth slide into my flesh, seeking out what little I have left to give him.

Cold envelops me, first my limbs, then my body, a swift progression of numbing. I feel my arms fall limply from him, but I do not fall; he holds me tightly. My vision is fading now. I look at him, his dark hair close to me, wanting him to be my last sight. It is as if I were being embraced by air, his strong hands are so soft around me. All light vanishes, though I still retain a slight awareness, of the fulfilment of death within me, the need to lie in earth, accepting.

The dark has now surrounded and entered my soul, eating at it like corrosive acid. It is only a fraction of what it was, almost gone now. I do not even miss it. Not really. Why should I have any regrets? This is what I want. Isn't it?

Then the little awareness I still retain shimmers and dies and the dark overwhelms me completely.

I feel as if I am floating, a union with the air. I open my eyes slowly, seeing the drawn curtains, the endless clutter of Anne-Marie's bedroom. I do not move. Everything has changed and yet remains the same. Something is missing, something is added. I lie quietly, seeking out the sensations in my altered body.

I am cold, in an intensity that I have never known before, yet it is not unpleasant. I realize this will now be the natural state of affairs. I flex one hand slightly, experimentally. It responds to my will as it always has. I lift it. It seems to float, hover in the air, translucent, insubstantial. I can see the light hollowed bones through the flesh and through them the room beyond.

I rise slowly. My mouth feels fuller. I touch my teeth, running a finger over their elegant, elongated curve. Metamorphosis is achieved.

Anne-Marie enters the room. With her is a young man. Her eyes meet mine briefly, then look away. She is afraid, I realize. She does not want to meet my eyes. I smile slightly at this first brief taste of power, beginning to sense the hypnotic intensity inherent in my gaze. I look at the young man.

He smiles at me, leering, slightly drunk. In the shadows of the room he cannot see the unnatural pallor of my skin, cannot see a quarter as clearly and distinctly as I.

I smile in return, my mouth shut, seeing the life pulsing in his veins, hungering for it with a lust incomparable to any hunger in life. I hear Anne-Marie say I am the best of her girls, and am amused at the various roles she can play.

She leaves the room and I move into his arms.

My longing is too fierce for subtlety. I sink my teeth into his neck. He starts, jerks back, then almost automatically reaches for me. I drink the warm, sweet blood, nectar and ambrosia, the food of the gods and demons, until thirst is satisfied, then release him. He staggers and falls back on to the bed. A trickle of blood flows thickly from the wounds, staining the sheets. I watch it, fascinated, then wipe my mouth. My hand comes away red. I stare at it for a moment. My hand falls to my side. Then I wipe it clean on a blanket.

I draw the curtains open. The moon is full and riding high in the sky. I dislike the light and jerk the curtains together again. They do not quite meet, falling open slightly, letting a thin sliver of light spill into the room.

The mirror catches my eye. The silvered glass reflects the bed, the man upon it, the furnishings and clutter of the room. Of me there is no trace. My image vanished with my soul.

The nothingness in the mirror angers me. I take it and smash it on the floor. It lies there, a thousand brilliant empty shards shimmering in the elongated rectangle of moonlight slanting in through the window.

Is it, I wonder, a portent of the emptiness that awaits me in a thousand thousand nights? How long will it be before it doesn't matter?

Desmond stands in the darker rectangle of the doorway. I see he is looking at the mirror. I go to him, unsure. I still have a feeling for him, but what is it?

Is humanity such a little thing I could have lost it all at once? Was it love that drew me here? And will that be what keeps me?

648

I do not want to be alone. I do not want to be with any other. I need a guide now, a helper, one who knows the passageway through the dark corridors I am on the verge of exploring.

Our hands meet and clasp, flesh of one flesh, alike in death, in this artificial, brilliant reflection of life.

He is right. It's very odd . . . It didn't fade all at once, but I really don't recall the transition. I'm not sure why I died.

I smile up at Desmond, a silent promise in my eyes. Tonight, yes, and perhaps tomorrow. And after that? What does a new-born child know of her choices? I'm going to have plenty of time . . .

The man on the bed lies there, forgotten. We walk downstairs together and step out into the dark.